THE DEAD
FOREST

THE DEAD
FOREST

THE FAITHWALKER SERIES BOOK THREE

DARRYL MARKOWITZ

FAITHWALKER PUBLISHING

The Faithwalker Series
Book III: The Dead Forest

Copyright © 2021 by Darryl Markowitz

Published by:

Faithwalker Publishing
An imprint of Darryl Markowitz

Cover and Interior Design: Creative Publishing Book Design
Cover Art: Bogdan Maksimovic

ISBN Paperback: 978-1-7374936-0-0
ISBN eBook: 978-1-7374936-1-7

Printed in the United States of America

Acknowledgments

To all those who know that the being part of the human is founded in conscious goodness and that conscious goodness is founded upon a Greater Conscious Goodness which can only be rightly called God and that this Goodness can only be understood as the very Essence of Reality to which it does not make sense to ask where it came from because then you would step outside of Being Real.

To all those who understand that the birth of Freedom is the First of Creation, the Same was in the beginning with God, the part of God that always beholds Him but Free to love Him perfectly so through whom we may have true being, if we choose to love God through the Same.

To all those who know that to perfect *our* love, it had to be done here on Earth by the Same, because there was no other way to make us a new heart and a new spirit that can overcome all evil.

The Faithwalker Series is dedicated to the Same and to all those who understand and seek more understanding and love of Being.

CHAPTER ONE

Parents

Princess Rana sat with her friends on the castle room's stone floor around the strange, dead branch while her daughter and her friends played kid games down the long hall. The oil lamps flickered as one of the adults urged, "Rana dear, is this not scary? Legend will have it that if we all chant 'round this sacred branch, we'll see visions. But you've always had abilities. Help us see if we all can influence people and things."

They chanted ... and chanted ... until the branch glowed gray....

Rana disappeared!

"Well, well, I've been expecting you!" The demon's hideous voice and nauseating stench intensified Princess Rana's sense of blindness and disorientation, yet raw instinct brought remembrance of how she made fire come from her hands. She began to raise her arms but the fiend immediately wrapped her in his coil.

Screams, laughter, hopelessness... while being sucked slowly and wholly into eternal torment, she screamed her daughter's name, "Alexandra!" Rana's uniqueness suddenly became clear in her understanding. With her last bit of free

1

will, she hurled her gift away lest it also be consumed, and so the bright light left her, disappearing from wherever she was.

Alexandra's head shot up and her friends' eyes opened wide as a bright glow descended upon her and disappeared into her. She knew. After slowly standing up, she left her girlfriends and came before the remaining adults.

Seeing the dead branch glowing gray on the floor, Alexandra's eyes narrowed and a new, instant natural reaction brought fire flaring from within them. She held out her hand and a burst of bright light shot out at that branch. After the brightness subsided, only a pile of dust remained. She turned her twelve-year-old eye upon the adults. "Mother is dead! She never understood nor appreciated her wonderful gifts and all of you only sought to use her. Get out! And never come back!" The adults fled in terror. "Lord Father, if it be possible, forgive thy poor servant's Mother her foolishness, for it hath slain her. Let me come to understand the reason for this great blessing."

Vaughn patted Spot's head as he crouched on the trail through the woods that paralleled a road heading south, back toward the Sacred Cave. It was a trail he was sure would lead to his death, but knew he had to follow it anyway. He recalled telling his loyal friend Waverly, who had kept watch by his hospital bedside, just why he planned to flee west to find Stephanie. "I choose to leave because the only place there's any chance of a real life for me is far, far away. It's far more meaningful for me to at least try, even if I die trying, than to submit myself for a single second longer to this abominable, meaningless death of an existence here!"

Powerful words. But what good would that power be to him or Stephanie now? It seemed that for every evil they defeated, a far greater evil took its place. Still, Vaughn banished the thought that this might all be a cruel game, a hoax played on the foolish... *No! I know what true Goodness, true Life, true Love is. This is too miserable to be a game... unless demons ... NO! Besides, even if I was some kind of pawn, well, then this game piece would* rebel!

Besides, he would be following this trail even if he didn't owe Stephanie his life. He vividly remembered her spirit, her hands from some other realm extended inside of him, healing him from his brutal beating. Even if they hadn't made passionate love all night in their shared dream where they also beat back the demon's spirit attempting to drive them both quite insane, he would be following this trail. The simple fact is, as much as evil had intensified its attack upon them, the growth of their love for Goodness and for each other even defied quantification.

Ever since Vaughn read that ancient letter King Mafferan had left for Stephanie, declaring her the rightful heir to the Appendaho's sacred treasure, and by God, the protector of the Seed to the Tree of Life, all he wanted to do was kneel on one knee before her and pledge his undying devotion to his Queen and to God. *True, this is a bit romanticized, but that's the way I feel!*

Everywhere, birds chattered and flitted through tall pine trees, looking for emerging insects and mates, while red squirrels rooted in the forest floor for old seeds and nuts. New light-green growth sprouted on the trees, and colorful spring flowers began to make their appearance. The vibrancy, the fresh living smells, the soft earth under his feet, and his own maturing strength all blended into a single exuberant feeling. *So much new life, just like Stephanie and me.* And he shook his head at the contrast because the more knowledge he gained then the more alive he felt, yet the knowledge he now possessed proved that neither he nor Stephanie would live much longer.

But I still have the Book, and I haven't looked inside, yet. Wisdom: From the Inside OUT. Even before he heard it existed, deep down inside he'd always wanted to possess the Book of Wisdom, but really, this was simply his desire to be that wise. He still couldn't get over the fact that Mafferan had placed that book in the painting especially for him, and that it waited there, undisturbed, for thousands of years.

Yet, how could any amount of wisdom get them out of all the troubles that threatened their lives? And even though Jargono's immediate threat to Stephanie demanded all of his current attention, he still couldn't keep all his other worries from also assaulting him. *What about my visions of the Blackness and the human-demons? Oh God, I haven't even saved the first little girl, yet, let alone thousands more. Does this mean I won't die until I do?* There was no answer, and then he finally hung his head. *Or does it mean that I've screwed up somehow, so badly that I've simply failed?* He shook his head, remembering, *Better to die fighting being what you are than lose the battle from within.* Rule one, *The Art of Fighting.*

Sensing Vaughn's troubled temper, his dog nuzzled into his master's hand, drawing a mood-breaking smile from him.

"Good Spot, you've kept the trail warm. Thank God for my dearly departed farmer friend. He taught and gave me *so* much. He gave me *you*, Spot," he rubbed his ears affectionately. "You're my best friend next to Stephanie. I think you're the only two who really understand me." Spot just stared up at his master, thoroughly enjoying the attention... but there really *did* seem to be a doggie look of understanding about him. "I think we could catch them tomorrow. I don't know why they're traveling by foot, sticking to these back roads and paths... They're taking their time. Why? It's still a good week's walk to the cave, so I guess we'll just keep following and figure out what to do. Eh, what *can* we do?"

Vaughn saw a small clearing just off to his left and he veered off the trail. Every now and then Spot kept turning around listening, but he didn't growl. Immediately dropping his pack off his back, Vaughn continued his discourse, "Well, let's make camp. I want to finally look at this Book of Wisdom. I think I need some. I was waiting to prepare myself special, before even touching it again, but now I need it to help Stephanie and me."

Spot stared at his master, listening to his voice. Vaughn had grown accustomed to discussing just about everything with his faithful companion. Well, sort of discussing.

Setting up the tent came automatically, without thought, and such a task actually refreshed his spirit, seeing he'd walked and brooded all day. Spot grabbed several tent pegs from the pile and dropped them at the tent corners, just as his master had trained him to do, then he sat patiently, waiting for the ear rub he knew would be his reward.

"Good boy. You're the best dog I ever had. Well, you're the only dog I ever had, but you'd still be the best, anyway."

Picking and choosing from the abundant dead branches strewn around, Vaughn built a low smoke fire, making sure there was plenty of air space between each piece of kindling. And when its fiery life became firmly established, his next mundane need became apparent as he discerned sounds other than the crackling blaze. A clear stream ran near to the trail and Vaughn went to wash as the wood burnt down to coals. Spot went out exploring.

Hearing the rush of water always seemed to generate a more peaceful mood in spite of other pervading factors. Its flowing sound sinks in and wears away unseen obstacles. Right now, though, washing away the dirt and smell of a long, hard day was satisfaction enough. After Vaughn finished bathing, he headed back to camp but the stream's gentle gurgling-burbling, which now trailed off from the distance, beckoned him to stay. He paused, turned, thought a moment, then retraced his steps, pulled off his shoes, sat on a boulder, and just let his tired feet dangle in the moving water. Yielding to the fact that he was in troubles way over his head, this acceptance produced a sort of letting go and, accordingly, his focus shifted to the yearning in his heart for... *What?* He began to perceive a calling that slowly but definitely grew in intensity, its profoundness grabbing his attention away from all his problems. In some sense of living connectedness, he suddenly became keenly aware of all his surroundings. The damp earth, decaying leaf litter, budding shrubs, skittering rodents, birds hopping through undergrowth, and even the air itself, all seemed to speak as one. He could swear he heard a single word whispered within the sounds of the stream, as if the very action of the stream itself was uttering an answer, *Purpose*. *"Purpose"*, he whispered to himself.

There is a communication common between all life, often expressed in nature's peaceful cohabitation. Obvious signs of it are also detected before impending disaster, when animals act with foreknowledge and even the trees seem to move a little differently. Some common feeling seems to pass between all life in some basic language. Humans often ignore many drifting feelings that pulse just below their narrow mental awareness. That common language of life's spirit must first be felt in the heart, before the mind may understand and hear. *But how does this help me? OK I'm somehow in the hands of something greater. But I still have to act. I still have to choose. I still need to* win!

He remembered the old farmer's wise words, *"Since almost the beginning of time, when evil entered into the world, living things have been giving up their lives for the sake of other lives. That kind of death is not the death of the dying, but a living sacrifice for the living."* A tear formed as he nodded his head in understanding. *Whatever I do, I must do it knowing I am part of this wonderful greater life. Yes. Purpose. I understand now. At least this gives me strength to do what's* right.

They both returned to camp about the same time. Vaughn pulled Jean's bread and roast beef from his pack, stuck a hunk of beef on a stick, and propped it above the coals to blacken the meat a bit. He broke the bread and threw Spot a piece. Most of his things were back at the store, so he could carry more food than usual. Having to go shopping would have slowed him down and he couldn't afford that, so he crammed all his camping needs into his pack. Spot watched the hunk of meat, and Vaughn watched Spot as he sat on a log warming himself by the flameless glowing bed of coals.

"Spot, that's for *both* of us." Spot's eyes flicked briefly toward his master.

As much as Vaughn was sure Spot loved him, he knew he was still a dog.

Suddenly jumping up, fur bristling, Spot began to growl, then stifled it before growling again. He repeated this odd behavior several more times while staring at a very wide spruce tree, whereupon a wiry young man casually eased himself out from behind it, zipping up his pants. He seemed diminutive, though actually taller than Vaughn by a good six inches. Keeping his head down most of the time and with tentative steps, he entered the camp and sat down by the fire between Spot and Vaughn. Silently, he stretched out his hands toward the glowing coals which sputtered flames every time the meat's fat dripped on them. Both Spot and Vaughn couldn't make up their minds as to the nature of this intruder. There was no greeting, no *may I*? Nothing! And there he sat, every now and then looking at the food.

Vaughn nodded, broke off a piece of bread and offered it. The lad with short, dirty, somewhat wavy brown hair took the bread without a word and hardly a smile but for some reason, Vaughn felt compelled to inform him, "The meat will be ready shortly."

With just a slight nod of acknowledgement, the young man rubbed his cheek, and took a bite. Spot sat down in peace.

Well, it's obvious he's not going to talk unless I get him to. I don't think I've ever seen anyone quite like this. Part of me wants to chase him away but I just gave him my precious food! "Hey, my name's Vaughn!"

It was very rare to give one's name, but frankly, Vaughn hated that custom, and he needed something to jolt or spark some kind of life into this character that seemed, well, fairly lifeless.

"Trevor! But you can call me Trev." Again his hand went up to cheek to rub something away.

"Well… Nice to meet you. Welcome to my camp. So what are you doing way out here?" For the first time their eyes met, and Vaughn's gut tightened, but he still didn't understand the empathy he felt toward this stranger.

"I could ask you the same thing but I figure you're following those two just up the way."

Vaughn's demeanor instantly darkened. *Should I kill him right now?* But Trevor hadn't taken his eyes away and now Vaughn saw a deep shrewdness in him.

Reading Vaughn's face, Trevor replied, "Don't worry. I'm not trying to meddle in your business!"

Not in my business? But you're in my food! In my camp! UNINVITED! "Well, since you know my business, what's yours then? And how come you're not in school? You've obviously been following me. Spot, here, has been keeping track of you." Spot shot his master a quick look full of embarrassment and certainly as puzzled as Vaughn's. But as soon as he asked the question, Vaughn realized that it applied to himself. Why wasn't *he* in school?

Trevor narrowed his eyes and Vaughn noticed sharpness in his heretofore apathetic manner. "This is my territory. I work it, see? School is lame. Just one more year after this one and I'm outta there, anyway. Besides, I already know far more math than I'll ever need. I learned it by eighth grade. I read on my own far better books than they require. And why do I need to know history or anything about the world anyway? The world is fucked and it's gonna get more fucked! The Government, their schools, they all lie about it anyway. Twist it all up to what they want, and as far as they know, I'm sick a lot. Besides, my work is important to a lot of them!" Again, Trevor brushed his cheek, but this time Vaughn obviously shifted focus on the gesture and Trevor made a conscious effort to ignore that attention.

Vaughn always despised that four-letter gutter kind of language and his irritation with Trevor's vulgarity manifested in his overt notice of the cheek compulsion. Yet, Trevor's nervous habit also brought to mind Vaughn's torment over his own many nervous tics and grueling contortions that he fortunately had defeated years ago. But even more than that, he remembered how almost everyone used to tease him about his odd behavior, yet, also, because he wouldn't use profanity. But now, Vaughn being so much stronger and clearly having superior qualities to all his former tormentors... Well, all that put together just soured Vaughn even more toward his *guest*, so now it was Vaughn's turn at shrewdness. "You *work* it." Vaughn knew he wasn't going to like the answer.

Trevor reached into one of several belt packs around his waist and pulled out a small bag and tossed it to Vaughn. "It's on me. For the food. I don't need to beg. I just don't carry money. I have it wired to my account. In a few years, I should be able to retire!"

Vaughn's countenance darkened considerably but when he touched the small brown bag laying on his lap, he found that even his hand instinctively revolted with an unexpected sense of impropriety. In a way, this was akin to that empathy for Trevor that Vaughn still didn't understand, except his hand seemed to know it touched the profane. Unrolling the bag's top, Vaughn glimpsed little round white balls inside, and sneered, "Drugs! But this doesn't look like anything I've seen or heard of." Vaughn crushed the bag and threw it into the embers which surprisingly erupted into a shower of sparks, at which point Spot growled more menacingly and Vaughn squinted his eyes at the gray smoke that billowed up. *Gray! Why gray?* And the smoke didn't exactly dissipate. It was more like it fled! Staring as it disappeared, Vaughn tried to resolve if he actually saw what he saw.

Trevor went back to his indifference and flat tone. "That was a waste. But probably better that way. It *is* different. You start taking this stuff and you won't be able to stop. And it lasts a lot longer and gives a much stronger high than Angel Seed." Trevor's hand began to rise toward his cheek but he stopped it by reaching out toward the fire instead.

Vaughn's indignation went way beyond any passive aggressive derision of Trevor. "WHY? Why would you do that to me after I've been so kind to you?" With part of Vaughn now primed to spring on Trevor, another part became more amazed at *still* being unable to attack. Something just didn't feel right, inside, though he couldn't quite tell what that might be.

11

Trevor simply shrugged, just not caring. "Hey. It's valuable. Your choice. You could have even sold it!"

Vaughn felt a deep blackness invade his eyes and it seemed that Trevor saw this shadow, given the way he focused on Vaughn, but it still didn't seem to really faze him at all. *Does Trevor know how close I am to killing him? The last time I let a drug dealer live, he cut off my escape and almost got me killed. I can't let anything interfere with me trying to rescue Stephanie, even if I am going to die when I fight for her!*

Suddenly, Vaughn remembered what he'd learned at the State Work Farm. "Wait a minute. You're saying this stuff is *addictive?* But even the Gov doesn't allow that stuff. Only non-addictive Angel Seed. That's all. They don't want a bunch of addicts they can't control, who'll kill their own mothers to get a fix."

Trevor just shrugged again. "Money talks. The admin at the schools are easily bought to keep their mouths shut. No one's gonna tell the Gov, and by the time they do find out, it'll be too late, and I'll be retiring then."

Vaughn stood up, fuming. "But doesn't it *bother you? At All?*"

He looked Vaughn straight in the eye. "No! Why should it? It's their choice. And my profit."

Something held Vaughn back, like a single word begging him, *Listen.*

"What about your parents? Your folks? You want your brothers or sisters addicted to this?"

That got a laugh and a sneer from Trevor, the first look of disgust from him, or any intense emotion at all. "My parents?"

he scoffed, "They don't give a flying fuck. And I already told my sis if she even touches this stuff, I'll kill her!"

Vaughn was shaking his head without even thinking about it. "They don't care what you're doing?"

"No. But it's not what you're thinking. I mean, they don't care, *period*, about *anything* I do, good or bad. They don't care about me or my sis at all. Whatever we do, we just do, as long as we don't get in their way. They don't care one way or the other. They leave us food, if they remember. Leave us some money for things, sometimes."

Vaughn couldn't seem to get his head or his heart around it. *I know I have rotten parents, but in their own sick way, they cared. I mean, they never understood me, and sure, they disowned me and let the Gov send me to the Farm and all, but at least they were angry and disappointed at me! Hmm, even though I didn't deserve it.* Vaughn found himself in a quandary as he contemplated his own parents' cruel treatment of him, yet actually considered there might be some merit to it! *Because at least they cared enough to have* some *feelings toward me. Even though they should have been proud of me, damn it!* And now he found himself strangely angry at his parents and at Trevor's parents. Perhaps even at all parents, though he quickly corrected himself, *There has to be good parents somewhere.* Suddenly, Vaughn felt deeply sorry for making an issue of Trevor's nervousness, but when he turned around and looked up from his deep thoughts, Trevor was gone!

I don't believe this! How can he be gone just like that? "Spot! Why didn't you say something?" His master's tone made Spot whine. *Oh God, he's gone, what if he tells the man I'm following him? I should track Trevor and kill him.* But instead, Vaughn found himself sitting back down at the fire shaking his head, attempting to collect his thoughts. Now remembering what he was about to do before being interrupted, he tried to put aside everything that just happened.

CHAPTER TWO

Wisdom Talks Back

Children from all corners of the castle gathered around her throne, eagerly anticipating her next story, while the guards, attendants, all and sundry did their best to hide their scowls. This was not queenly behavior, nor was it proper use of the throne room, but Queen Alexandra laughed to herself, knowing their thoughts.

She smiled at her audience, thinking, It may not be your custom, but it *is* mine. Besides, the throne adds ambiance to my lessons.

Lillian, one of the maidservant's daughters, who was all of seven years old, couldn't restrain herself any longer. "Last time you said yer gonna tell us 'bout yer histry... Ma'am, m'Lady." *All the other children nodded vigorously, their love fully apparent.*

She cleared her throat, affected a regal posture, and all the children did the same. "That's history, Lillian."

"That's what I said... Ma'am, m'Lady."

"That's what you meant." *She motioned Lillian onto her lap, as was her custom to sit a different young lady there at* each gathering. *"This evening I share with you what has been passed down to me for...."* she cocked her head as if deep in thought, *"well, I'm not sure how far back it goes. Because me Great-great-grandma was the first teller from this part of the world. And then, she was tellin' 'bout things way 'fore that!"*

The children whispered, *"This part of the world!"*

"Yes darlin's. I'm not from anywhere even close to here. Well, really, me Great-great-great grandma came from a land no one yet knows of, which lies across the great ice land far, far to the north. To get there, you would have to travel over the top of the world and then down again to the other side!"

Their eyes all widened, their mouths dropped open as they whispered as one, *"The other side!"*

"Yes darlin's. In life, no matter how it may seem, there is always a side you don't know until you travel there." She shot the adults a sharp glare and then turned back to face the children with a soft gaze. *"That's why I gather you all here, so that you may know that even though I'm your Queen, I am still a person just like you! This eve, my story shall take you there!"*

While sitting on a log by the camp fire, Vaughn reached into his pack and pulled out the special leather case he bought from Jean. Inside was the Book.

"Well, let's see. Spot! The cover is different!"

The cave pictures were gone and the cover now resonated with the deepest blackness but the title shined in brilliant gold lettering that seemed to float against its background – *Wisdom From the Inside Out*. The word 'Out' was no longer all capital letters. *Hmm, perhaps that means there's really no way out this*

16

time. Vaughn remembered how the word 'OUT' had been set right over the picture of the very place where the hidden exit in the cave had been.

"What is this? One blank page?" Vaughn's eyes popped and he couldn't believe what he saw next. "SPOT!" The dog had been lying down, but now he sat up.

"Did you see that?"

Spot ambled over to his master. "Did you see what just happened?" Spot watched him closely.

"I don't believe it! Words!"

Words had mysteriously appeared on the blank page, written in eloquent gold:

All wisdom starts with a question. Your first: "What is this, one blank page?"

Wisdom: What cannot truly be said in less than a page is not worth saying. Wisdom that can be uttered as such could have a whole book written about it and not be complete.

Vaughn set the Book down on his lap, because he felt his hands unworthy to hold such a thing. Already there was more than he had time to think about, but right now he needed to understand how to use the Book to help save Stephanie.

"Spot! Oh my God, do you see what this is?" Spot barked his assent. "Oh God, what should I ask next?"

The next words appeared: *Your second: "What should I ask next?" Wisdom: What does your heart desire most?*

"SPOT! It answered my question with a question!" Spot nudged Vaughn's arm with his head and whined as he sat watching the Book.

"OK, OK, I'll continue."

"Book… ahhh… wait a minute… I don't think I should address the Book. It's communicating from Wisdom, that part of Life. I've been asking my questions to that part of God all along! Yes, this isn't magic out of a fairy tale! This is real. Oh God, what my heart desires most right now is to save Stephanie from that evil man, but I don't know how to defeat him." Nothing happened on the page. "Hmm, that wasn't a question! How do I defeat the evil man holding Stephanie?"

Nothing appeared.

"Hmm. No answer. I wonder why?"

Third question: "Why was there no answer to previous question?" Wisdom: The question cannot be answered within the space of this page. Fundamental consideration of that specific question requires background Understanding, to which Wisdom may be applied.

Vaughn grumbled with disgust, "*Great.* So what I'm being told is that I'm too stupid to even begin to understand the answer."

But a hunch came to Vaughn concerning the way he had phrased that last question, and about how the Book had been answering. "Hmmm! Proper use of language is important to obtain true understanding. It seems the Book is trying to give me hints on the proper way to approach it. An answer that is less than a page, but that a whole book could be written about, must be an answer in which every word has tremendous meaning. In that short space, such an answer could be complete, yet take more than a book to expound its depth. I encountered this basic principle in the *Art of Fighting* series. Those books always apply general principles to specific types of problems. My question only concerned a single man and would technically require an answer with many specifics regarding his personal life, and that falls out of the scope of a page. It's really not wise to ask the question from that perspective, but from the more general principle first, as the Book hinted." Spot barked again and Vaughn nodded in agreement to his companion.

"Alright, how do I defeat an evil enemy that is more knowledgeable, stronger, older, and wiser than I am? You don't have to repeat my question!"

Question has been reserved in index!

"Index?" Thrilled, Vaughn flipped the single page over and found a list comprised of the questions he'd just asked! He turned the page back over to see if the Book would supply an answer this time and he found his hunch to be right.

Wisdom: To defeat great evil that is from outside, you must first purge yourself of evil from the inside.

That was what Jean had been telling him, but he knew he didn't have time, unless…

Vaughn inquired anxiously, "How do I do that?"

Wisdom: This question falls under the category of Understanding and Faith, and is not answered by Wisdom.

Vaughn sighed in frustration and tried another approach. "Why do I have to first purge myself?"

Wisdom: Great evil has two fronts of attack, from without and from within. If you win the battle without, you will lose the attack from within, if evil is within you.

He nodded understanding as Spot lay down with a sigh.

"If I do purge myself from evil within, then am I sure to win?"

"You may win the battle within if you hold true, but may lose the battle without and join your fathers who have passed on."

My fathers who have passed on? I don't have time to inquire into that now. God, I know why I'll lose, because I don't have time. This battle needs to be fought soon, or I have no chance of winning on the outside at all.

Stephanie's life, the little girl in his vision, Jean and Lana, the evil blackness, the evil heart monster, Glen, *What happened to Glen?* But most of all, Stephanie. All of them were shouting *NOW* in his mind, act *NOW,* and his heart suddenly verged on breaking. Vaughn slumped, as a wave of heat exploded inside of him, almost causing him to weep, but he fought it back, regretting his weakness and ignorance. He hung his head over the Book as tears welled up in his eyes, and while doing his best to keep from sobbing, he began to speak to the Book as if it was person: "I know that already, but that won't help Stephanie."

Sacred tears have touched the Book of Wisdom:

Advice: If winning cannot be accomplished at this stage, seek an alternative outcome. However, if the evil desires your destruction, it may not allow this. If the battle must be joined, knowing that you are not able to win, fight with the integrity of your whole being and meet death with bravery. Knowing you will do that, give yourself every opportunity for Life to bring an alternative that you have not known.

Vaughn bowed his head.

"Thank you, Lord, for the Wisdom."

Gratitude has been expressed: Insight: When facing a superior force, in every way possible, meet the battle on your terms as regards time and place.

Vaughn understood. "Spot."

Spot was still lying down, but he rolled his eyes up at Vaughn.

"We know where they're going. I think we should get there before them! You can stand guard and warn me in plenty of time before they get there." Then Vaughn realized the implications of this plan. "Oh God, but this means I'll have to leave Stephanie alone with him."

Vaughn put the Book back into its leather case and prayed, "Oh God, since You have brought us together, my life, *our* lives have been so full, so meaningful. I cannot even come close to thanking You for all You have done for us. Please, help us. Keep Stephanie from harm as she travels with this evil man. Neither of us understands, nor do we have even close to enough experience to deal with the trouble we're in." Then Vaughn heard a familiar voice in front of him.

"Vaughn!" King Mafferan stood in his traditional Appendaho garb consisting of a humble, dark brown, fringed tunic and pants.

"Sir...King." Vaughn was at a loss for words being so glad to see him.

"Please, Father would do nicely. I haven't been King for a very long time. But I will always be a father."

The contrariness Vaughn had sensed about him before had vanished. He was very much the man Queen Yinauqua held dearly in her eyes when she spoke of him.

"I wish you were my father."

The King began to answer, "Reality is…"

But Vaughn finished for him, "What it is."

"Yes, my boy, but I'm very proud of you, and if I could've had you as my child, I would've rejoiced greatly."

Vaughn stared, as the King's words carried him away because they came with such meaning that had never touched him before. But there was no time to explore it, so Vaughn pulled himself out of his ruminations. There simply was no time for him to indulge in such feelings now, no matter how important. Vaughn pleaded, "Sir, Father, why have you come? Are you here to help me?"

"I came for your prayer, and for the prayer of a little child!"

Shocked, Vaughn remembered Lana's prayer. *They even hear little ones. How beautiful.*

Mafferan continued, "I cannot fight for you. This battle is to be fought by the life on your side of life, the mortal side. But I can tell you what you're up against, and provide you with the background you need to know. I feel it's my duty, since it's *my* offspring that now endangers you, as well as my last surviving daughter."

"Your offspring?"

"Jargono is Appendaho, and the last remaining male."

Jargono! He was the bad man at the store! He must have wiped Jean's memory somehow. She definitely would have recognized him. I knew I had a bad feeling about him. The train owner was right. Vaughn's thoughts shifted, as he looked away from King Mafferan, "I read your letter to…"

But Mafferan reassured him, "I know. It was meant for you to do so, otherwise you couldn't have …"

"Seen the words."

The king smiled at the boy's quick understanding and nodded. "Yes." Then he waved his hand and a stump appeared beside Vaughn by the fire. Vaughn noted it but didn't want to be sidetracked. As the king sat down to begin teaching him, Vaughn twisted on his log to see his face.

Mafferan's words tasted bitter. "The man you go to fight has sold his soul to Darkness, but he believes he serves himself. He was born tainted by some means I do not know and has been taught directly from Darkness from his youth till now, *and* he has inherited all my gifts!"

Vaughn's eyes widened as he peered at the stump Mafferan had conjured.

Mafferan continued: "He doesn't know what was in the sacred box, no one does, seeing no one has opened it since I put the contents into it, except for Stephanie, of course. She is aware of all this, and now you know, too"

Vaughn interjected a question, "Sir, why does he want what was there when he doesn't even know what it is?"

King Mafferan nodded. "Jargono has a dream, and in this dream, he's the all-powerful ruler of the whole world, both here and beyond. He knows a great ancient mystery was placed in the box."

Vaughn jumped in before he realized his rudeness, "And any great ruler needs to control great mysteries. Oh, sorry."

But the king smiled and waved Vaughn's apology away. "Yes, but that's only part of it, because he knows the mystery came from me, and that the legends say I had powers, and as you just saw, concerning what I did with this stump, well, it's apparent I *still* do." Mafferan waited to see if Vaughn would fill in the next part.

"And he thinks you may have placed something powerful in the box?"

"I did, but not anything he could use."

"Because this Seed to the Tree of Life is only goodness."

Mafferan raised his eyebrows and waited.

So Vaughn continued, "I'm taking it on faith that the name of it is accurate. From the description in your letter, this Tree of Life, and of course its Seed, is somehow a manifestation of the actual Spirit of Life's presence through which God made all of us."

Mafferan couldn't hide his satisfaction with Vaughn, and being impressed with the lad, he decided to give him a history lesson. "You would be correct, my boy. In history, God gave special words to certain special people, other than the Appendaho, and sent special people to them to tell them more words of truth, but to the Appendaho, God sent meaning! The Tree of Life is manifestation of pure meaning!"

Vaughn's eyes widened with understanding. Meaning was always what he sought first, followed by the correct words that fit that meaning, and not the other way around like the government's meaningless religion. "I understand this!"

Mafferan's eyes began glowing in appreciation and he reflected on how he'd chased after Vaughn the day of the burial. "I see that you really do understand. The Seed of the Tree of Life is feeding you, calling to you. However, the Seed, or the Tree when it grows, is just…"

Vaughn finished for him with revelation, "This Tree of Life was supposed to be a focal point where all people could come to seek the meaning of God at its highest concentration?"

Mafferan nodded, but Vaughn began to frown and continued speaking, "But your people must have kept it to themselves. No one knew you had such a great thing, else, well, we all would have known." Vaughn's statement was more to pose the question, why, but also from somewhere deep within him, even a criticism! He couldn't help himself, something was forcing the words from him before he could assess their full impact.

Mafferan turned to stare into the fire and Vaughn felt a little embarrassed for speaking so boldly. The king's thoughtful words came softly. "What happened to you when you began speaking truth to the people in your home town?"

Vaughn leaned back with a scowl. "They hated me. They mocked me. They couldn't see it. I understand what you're saying. In the same way, neither would most people understand the Tree of Life. They would think it was some kind of magic, or something they could, oh my God, control. Jargono must think the same way about the contents of the box. It doesn't matter to him what it is, he would still feel he could subvert it."

Mafferan nodded deeply, but Vaughn continued to wonder. "But since he can't use it, is there really any worry if he does manage to acquire it somehow?"

Mafferan raised an eyebrow at Vaughn. "All of us are born with a piece of the Tree of Life inside of us. Does that stop evil from trying to conquer us?"

"No, but…"

"Remember, the Seed and the Tree that sprouts from it are focused manifestations of the actual Spirit Tree of Life. At best, Jargono could hide it where it could never be found, *but at worst*, perhaps he finds a way to put it into so much torment that …"

Vaughn finished again with grave concern, "That it would leave us?" He knew this, because he knew how the goodness often felt in him. Many times he sighed and wished to simply be done with it all, even now. But Vaughn was hoping to get help from the Tree of Life and he regretted the possibility of losing it. Now he began regretting all of *his* dejected sighs! *Hanging on is important.* He thought again of the little girl crying for help in his vision. *She and I are just alike! Somehow, I've got to hang on. For everyone.*

Mafferan leveled a stern gaze at Vaughn. "If it leaves us, then meaning leaves the world with it!" He paused, watching as the weight of this meaning fell upon the boy.

Dazed, Vaughn's eyes became teary and his heart skipped a beat. He shook his head to drive away the mental image of it. *Too much to bear. I can't even imagine it…* But if he really couldn't imagine it, then why did he react so strongly?

Mafferan continued, "God has chosen the Tree of Life as the focal point through which meaning is given to all the living and to all creation as we know it! There is an old saying, 'The highest does not stand without the lowest, and the greatest without the smallest.' A glacier is built out of single snowflakes, a beach out of single grains of sand. This pattern is repeated all through creation to portray Almighty God's nature."

Vaughn sat in stunned silence. *All meaning comes from that single Seed of the Tree of Life that's hanging around Stephanie's neck!* He felt small before, but now it was like he barely mattered at all. *If meaning completely left the world, the world would be turned into hell, it's not that far from it now!* "Oh my God," he whispered.

Mafferan continued, knowing the boy's thoughts, "When the Tree of Life is here, it reaches out to all, but when only its Seed is here," he felt overwhelmed, himself, at what he was saying, "it only reaches out to special people it chooses!"

How much more can I stand, Oh God? That means the rest …

But Mafferan couldn't help speaking further. He knew he had to leave soon because there was something important he had to do, but he wanted Vaughn to have this knowledge now. "Long, long ago, man was so *wicked* that there was only one family left in the whole world that had true meaning. To save the Tree of Life, God flooded the whole world and destroyed everybody and started over with that single family!"

Vaughn whispered, "My God, I didn't know."

Mafferan continued, "But people grew corrupt again and God once again found a true man and woman who lived in the meaning of the Tree of Life."

"And that was you and your Queen."

Mafferan shook his head. "No! That was the other special people I told you about. From that man and woman, God created the people to whom He gave the words of truth I told you of. At one point, those words spread all over the world!"

Vaughn's heart pounded, no, it shouted! *How could that*

be? All over the world? "My God, but I never heard such words. I *know* I haven't. I would recognize them if I did!"

"I am sure you will!" Mafferan said. "But about five generations before those two, God divided the Earth. It was, at that time, to those two special people's *ancestors* that I and my queen were born. God brought me and my queen about and our descendants to live from direct meaning, and five generations after, He brought about the other people to whom God gave the words. But when *we* were born, the Earth was divided, and the Tree of Life was on *our* side! The rest of the family, through whom the other special people came, were on the *other* side. They were destined to spread across the world carrying the words of God, while we were destined to live a life of solitude, protecting the Tree of Life."

Vaughn sat in awe at the wisdom of it all. *The Appendaho protected the actual source of meaning, where no one could bring it to torment, and the other people brought the words, which mankind would seek in the spirit of the Tree of Life if they wanted to get the true meaning. The two sides of the family, though separate, worked together.*

Mafferan looked deeply into Vaughn and read his thoughts again. "You now understand in words and true understanding what Stephanie understands through true feelings and actual experience with the Tree of Life."

The next question rolled from Vaughn's lips, "Was there ever a time when the two sides reunited?"

"Twice! Two generations after the two who gave birth to the people of true words, that third descendent took his whole family and went into a now departed ancient land and had many, many children. But the ruler there turned on them and enslaved them for hundreds of years."

Vaughn's mouth dropped open. "That's terrible."

"Indeed it was, but God visited the people, and saved them with terrible signs and wonders, and brought them out, and gave them many special words, and a splendid land on which to live. It was God's hope that a people who knew the horror of injustice would be better suited to protect the Holy Words He gave them. But during the time they were in bondage, my people were also going through dark times."

Vaughn's mind opened further as he began to get a greater feel for the interplay of good and evil.

Mafferan noted it and continued, "The leader of our people had actually become the richest man in the whole land where he dwelt. He was even sharing true meaning with many outsiders."

Vaughn interrupted, "So you didn't always seclude yourselves."

Mafferan sighed. "That had been the only time we did not. Anyway, The Dark Powers became enraged that light was *leaking* into their domain and in one day, they took away *all* his wealth and *all* his children."

Stunned, tears clouded Vaughn's eyes again, but he remained silent, not wanting to interrupt or delay the story.

"For almost a year, he suffered from the pain, the poverty, and the doubts against him from his now impoverished people. It was the only time the Appendaho were divided against themselves, until now."

Vaughn nodded that he understood the implication, and Mafferan understood that Vaughn wanted him to continue uninterrupted. There was something Mafferan noticed that Vaughn was concentrating deeply upon.

Mafferan resumed the account, "After almost a year, the Dark Powers came again to be very upset, because the man would not turn against the Tree of Life, in spite of all the torment they heaped upon him. They had tried many deceptions to either convince him to say he had been wrong in the way he was following meaning, or to plainly turn him against the Tree of Life."

Vaughn at first replied with confidence, "But it didn't work, did it?"

Mafferan saw how enraptured he was, and that brought back memories of how he had taught all his children. Giving Vaughn a deep, broad smile, Mafferan reassured him, "No, so the Dark Powers smote the man with terrible sickness until his flesh rotted on his bones, but yet he still lived!" Vaughn's hairs stood on end and now he really couldn't imagine it, or rather, he was sure he didn't want to. "Then evil turned his wife against him, because she was so grieved, and desperately desired to put an end to the pain her love caused her."

Vaughn's reaction was instantaneous, "NO...Oh no, she didn't."

Mafferan knew he was thinking of either himself or Stephanie failing. "Reality. But don't worry, it didn't last long."

"What did he do?"

"Told her the truth, that she spoke foolishly!"

Vaughn was shocked, yet, again, "And that was *it*? She believed him?"

Mafferan smiled. "Don't you think either you or your wife-to-be would listen to the other when telling the truth, no matter how difficult?"

Vaughn's eyes widened, as he felt in his heart what he hoped in his mind was true. All he could say was, "I see."

Mafferan gave a satisfied nod, and continued: "Then, since the leader, even in the face of all that evil, would still not turn against God, against the Tree of Life, or against the way he had lived, the Dark Powers tricked certain people, namely, his friends, to accuse him and argue with him. Of all he suffered, this was the worst for him!"

Vaughn nodded with understanding, which greatly surprised Mafferan, who fixed him with a questioning look.

So Vaughn explained, "Because, to a man like that, with that deep a love, the people were more important to him than himself! Their turning against him threatened all his efforts to make the truth meaningful to people, both to his own and those on the outside with whom he was sharing."

It was King Mafferan's turn to be stunned. "Yes, my boy, you are *absolutely* correct. Anyway, in answer to your question that started this part of the history lesson, when our leader began to suffer all those things, God led a particular young man from that enslaved but special people to escape. That young man traveled more than a year and showed up in the middle of the strongest attacks against our leader, attacks that came at the hands of his best friends."

Vaughn whispered, "Oh my God."

"Yes, indeed! The young man spoke powerfully, with true understanding and true words, and encouraged our leader to see the way out of the trap he'd fallen into, and because it has always been our way to listen to truth, regardless of the age of the person who speaks it, our leader deeply considered his words. This opened our leader's heart to receive what happened next!"

Mafferan mischievously paused, knowing what that pause would do to Vaughn.

Vaughn wanted to jump off his log and grab Mafferan to make him keep speaking, instead, he just twisted from side to side, ran his hand through his hair, and unintentionally raised his voice, "*What?*"

Mafferan's eyes glinted with mischievous glee. "God, Himself, appeared to our leader in a great whirlwind and spoke for quite a long time to him." Mafferan paused to bask in Vaughn's ultimate surprise. He could see him trying to imagine it. "After that, he was healed, blessed with much more wealth, more children, and the people came back to him. But we never again sought out the outside world until…"

The implications hit Vaughn like a sledgehammer, as he whispered and hung his head. "*Until now*, because to meet Stephanie as your letter indicated the Appendaho were supposed to do, you had to be in contact with the outside world again and the Dark Powers must have been very angry, again…" Vaughn's head and heart were swimming, as a much larger picture, too large for him to see, flooded in upon him, but he realized that, in part, the Appendaho's destruction was somehow a destined consequence from their providing aide to Stephanie. Amidst his grief, it made her seem even more precious to Vaughn. *But was it really destiny or just their choices?* Another metaphysical picture appeared in Vaughn's mind of the interplay between free-will and destiny, but then something even more important tugged at him, until… "*Wait, you said twice.*"

"Twice?" Mafferan acted as if he didn't understand the question.

"Yes! I asked if there was ever a time when the two sides of the family reunited and you said *twice*. When was the second time?"

Mafferan leveled his eyes with Vaughn's and gave a two word answer, "Not was!"

Vaughn shook his head, not understanding.

Mafferan held his deep gaze and gave a one word answer, "Now."

Vaughn just stared at him blankly, waiting…

With a look more serious than Vaughn had yet seen on him, Mafferan explained, "You and Stephanie are the second time, *now!*"

Vaughn felt that Mafferan believed he was telling Vaughn the truth, but Vaughn didn't see at all how it could be so. "Sir, I know *nothing* of such a special people, nor of special words."

Mafferan had a tear in his eye. "Ahhh, but you do, my boy. They have long ago been written upon your heart, passed down to you through the blessing of generations. Your ancient people used to call the Light, the Lord God."

"But my parents never told me of such a people. Ha! And they *certainly* are no special people. They…"

Mafferan cut him off with a retort, "Your parents and their parents and their parents' parents, all the way back to the beginning of them being a people, *are those special people!*"

Vaughn just looked on helplessly, not being able to argue with the king's tone of voice.

Mafferan explained, "The blessing has always been there in each generation, but they ignored it for a long, long time." He paused to look deeply into Vaughn's eyes in order to stress the next point. "Until *you* paid attention! But *who* you are is miniscule compared to *what* you are. The people are the who, but the virtue you may choose is the *what*."

Vaughn nodded with tears in his eyes, remembering similar meaning in Stephanie's letter. *The what is far more important than the who.* Feelings roared inside him, feelings that claimed the truth of Mafferan's words as their own truth. This was his heritage, even though he woefully lacked the ability to process or accept it all. All he could say was, "My God… Forgive me. I didn't know."

But Mafferan corrected him, "My dear boy, but you *did* know, and that is *precisely* why we are now able to have this conversation. There is nothing to forgive in this matter, because you … *you,* after so many dark generations, have paid attention to God's blessings. It's just that the only knowledge your parents had, and their parents, and theirs before them was that they came from a distinct people and were supposed to marry their own. They would have told you that much when you came of age in their eyes."

Totally overwhelmed, Vaughn knew, *The amount of meditation time needed to absorb all this is like an eternity!*

Mafferan told him one more thing concerning his birthright. "God has also blessed you with powers you have yet to learn or understand!"

Vaughn looked at him quizzically, wondering if he should ask, but somehow felt it wrong to do so.

Mafferan read his mind and addressed his thoughts, "Yes, you are correct. It's not for me to tell you of the blessings that are within you. You must..."

Vaughn knew. "Learn of them from the inside, not from the outside."

"Yes."

"Because that's the only true way."

"Yes."

Vaughn's eyes darkened to a deep black as his heart and mind united into one, with one purpose. Given all he had learned, one thing stood out above all else, and he swore to it, "I swear I will do all that I am able to protect the Seed of the Tree of Life and to keep its ways."

Mafferan understood, but he also knew Vaughn wasn't ready to fully keep such an oath. "Stephanie has already sworn that same oath in her prayers, but you must seek the mystery, as she has done, so that only the Tree of Life is in you."

Vaughn sighed, as a deep pain wracked his heart. He shook his head, while speaking, "I know, *I know*. It's just that right now..."

Mafferan comforted him, "I know that you don't have time right now. *Listen to me*, your future wife is very clever. You must have complete faith in her or there is *no* chance for either of you to win."

Vaughn was quick to give his oath. "I *do* have complete faith in her."

King Mafferan leaned forward and met Vaughn eye to eye. For Vaughn, it was like looking into the world beyond. "You must have complete faith beyond what your understanding is now."

That shook Vaughn, because he didn't believe in blind faith, since he knew true faith is always based on understanding. "I... I don't understand."

The king straightened back up, and said, "*Precisely*. I cannot tell you too much, because that would alter the true reaction you will have at a time when you will need it. To be effective, your knowledge must come from the inside-out, otherwise there will be no power to it. So I cannot tell you. But I *can* tell you that Jargono has innate powers as I do, *and* powers from the Darkness. He will use them against you from the inside, because when you confront him on the outside, he will not be able to defeat you easily. Before he risks a prolonged physical confrontation, he will attack from within."

Vaughn paused, because of all the feelings and understandings swirling through him, along with their implications. He dreaded to ask the question, because he felt the evil still lurking somewhere in him, but he had to. "Can I resist him?"

But the king also paused. *A strange reaction*, Vaughn thought.

Finally, Mafferan said, "You can resist him, but you'll not yet be able to prevent what he does to you on the inside. He'll be very surprised at what you *are* able to do as an outsider. He does *not* know of Stephanie's power or strength. She was wise to hide it from him."

With a tear in his eye and a choked voice, Vaughn asked the other question he dreaded to ask, "Can Stephanie beat him?"

The king paused again, and that made Vaughn's heart drop. "She can win the battle within to prevent being beaten herself."

Vaughn hung his head, understanding. *Better to die fighting, being what you are, than lose the battle from within.* And then he mumbled aloud, "But not win from without."

The king looked down, the first time Vaughn had seen him do such a thing, and it tore at him.

"No, my son, she cannot win against the battle from the outside. She has kept him from harming her by doing something to him that no one has done before."

Intrigued, Vaughn lifted his head. "What?"

"She has made him think about something truly important to him."

"What?"

"About having a mate that would truly appreciate him!"

A picture from Vaughn's heart began crystallizing itself into his mind, but he couldn't help resist it somewhat. "But … her stalling will only be short-lived." His mind had shifted to thinking about the Seed, and not Mafferan's words. He couldn't think about his words, not *those* words.

Mafferan sighed, seeing the boy wasn't facing reality, so he pressed the issue. "She'll be tempted beyond anything she's ever conceived in his attempt to persuade her. He's able to operate at spiritual levels she's not aware of. He's able to enter into hearts and minds where evil still exists, and into those where evil does not. He's able to draw their attention by operating on levels deeper than they know or understand."

Vaughn, overcome by it all, buried his head in his hands, and began to weep uncontrollably. The thought of losing Stephanie, of losing everything…. The knowledge Mafferan imparted to him about his life, his heritage, made him feel so much more alive, which made facing certain death that much more painful. That new knowledge joined in common plea with his whole being, "Oh Father…"

Mafferan put his hand on the boy's shoulder. He hadn't felt another's pain in a very long time, and it brought back memories of terrible battles fought long ago. He needed to give Vaughn something. "My *son*, look into my eyes."

Complying reluctantly, Vaughn lifted his head. Mafferan's eyes glowed, just like Stephanie's did, only they shined brighter. At first, Vaughn wanted to quickly look away, but being faced with an unknown tremulous future, he knew that to win, he needed to look into the unknown, so he allowed himself to sink deep into Mafferan's gaze. It was like looking into the king's whole life, like having already read a huge novel, but it was in Vaughn's heart, not his mind. Vaughn felt very small, and different tears slowly rolled from the corners of his eyes now. "You've been in this kind of torment."

Mafferan nodded. "Yes, and I had to watch my loved one endure many cruel things, abominable things, while I was powerless to stop them. Many times I desired to join in battle, to show how much I loved her, but it was really just so I would be killed! But I recognized that this was dishonesty in me, not true love, but the desire to avoid the severe pain that true love suffers."

Vaughn began weeping again with his heart pounding at the prospect of Stephanie having to endure such things, and him being powerless to help. He could feel all her tenderness, her sweetness, her goodness, being put into terrible torments. They were *his* torments. He wanted to know, so he lifted his head out of his hands. "What did you do?"

King Mafferan's posture straightened as he peered sharply into Vaughn's eyes, to transmit the severity of his ordeal. With a tightening voice, he answered, "I *waited,* not knowing if ever there would be victory on your side of life. Each day I waited seemed like a thousand years of pain."

Vaughn wagged his head, as a clear picture bloomed within his mind. He wanted to drive that picture away, but he wanted to look even more deeply into it, too. He whispered through his weeping, "Oh Father, I'm not able to ..."

With eyes peering like sabers disemboweling an enemy, Mafferan grabbed him tightly by the shoulders and shook him. Then, speaking clearly and slowly he asked, "*How real is your love?*"

This took Vaughn's breath away as he was being challenged, and he knew it. He was too overwhelmed to respond, but the king's words seemed to echo within him, cutting him up inside. Vaughn wanted to run, but how does one run from oneself? How does one run from their weakness, or the truth of their love?

Still holding his shoulders, Mafferan leaned even closer to draw his attention back, and Vaughn looked into this wonderful man and listened once again. "Your *only* chance to win is to use that part of you where you're strongest. When all else fails you, you may have enough strength in that part of you to keep from being destroyed."

Then Mafferan went back to his stump and they both sat in silence for a while, until Vaughn finally spoke, "Jean said that Stephanie said he had some kind of Black Oil that countered the power of your people."

Anger clearly darkened the king's countenance. It surprised Vaughn to see it in him, because Vaughn recognized that same deep feeling in himself!

Mafferan spat out the words, "The Dark Powers have interfered in this world, but cleverly, in such a way that we're not allowed to reciprocate. That Oil is not from your world!"

Vaughn wasn't surprised. "But… but that's not fair!"

The king looked at him wryly.

Vaughn grimaced. "Gee, that's a *stupid* thing to say, isn't it?"

"Yes."

Vaughn expounded in order to recover his dignity. "Since when is evil ever fair? But then, shouldn't the Light have some counter to that interference?"

Mafferan smiled. "That's a good question, Vaughn. But to whom are you directing it?"

Looking at him in amazement, Vaughn remembered, *How many times have I asked Stephanie that same question?* After hesitating again, Vaughn continued, "What can this Oil do?"

"Nullify good effects that have been applied to those too weak to hold onto them, and…" Then King Mafferan seemed to trail off.

But Vaughn needed to hear as much as possible. "Father, what else, *please?*"

Mafferan sighed deeply, then drew a long breath. "If the Oil is put upon you, it will plunge you into a place you have been before, a place from which you would have no escape."

Vaughn shivered with the memory of lingering at death's door. "Oh God!" But he had even graver feelings for Stephanie. "And if it's placed upon your daughter?

Pain clearly crossed the king's face now, and he didn't want to speak the words, but Vaughn's eyes drew them from him. "It will cause her pain that she has never known before, and may cause her existence here to fail." He left out the other part.

Spot had vanished for a good while, and so had the hunk of meat, but he returned in time to seemingly ask an important question, one common *arf* followed by two serious *Arfs*.

King Mafferan looked Spot over and rubbed his ears in their special place. "Spot, is it?"

"Yes, that's my dog's name."

"Well, Spot, if the Oil is placed on you, it has no effect, except to make your coat shine black. But whoever touches you before the Oil is washed away, they may suffer, or perhaps after a while, your animal life would simply denature it."

Vaughn distinctly noticed something he had wondered at before. "Wait a minute! You just answered as if Spot *really* asked you a question."

"Of course, why does that surprise you? You've been doing the same ever since you got him!"

Vaughn looked at him quizzically. "Yeah, but I was just kinda imagining that he was, you know."

Mafferan smiled with a twinkle in his eye. "Are you sure it was your imagination?"

41

In spite of everything, Vaughn smiled and even laughed, grateful for the change in mood, but his attentions quickly turned back to the problem at hand. "Is there anything else you can tell me, *please?*"

"Yes. Prophecy now begins with you and Stephanie."

"But … but what does that mean? Father? *He's gone!* I wish they'd stop doing that!"

Mafferan had left but the stump he created was still in the same spot. Shaking his head, Vaughn went over and rolled it back to the log where he had sat, then retrieved the Book from its case, and placed it upon the standing stump. He opened it and noticed that there was writing right in the center of the otherwise blank page. It was the answer to the question he just asked.

Wisdom: When a person's choices have the ability to determine a future that flows naturally, a future that has not been locked in by previous prophecy, that person is said to be the beginning of prophecy.

CHAPTER THREE
Courtship

As Lillian rushed to Queen Alexandra's bed-chamber, she remembered that special day so many years ago, when the Queen sat her on her lap and recited a love story that had been handed down from generation to generation. The Queen even thought it had been told for thousands of years. From that day forward, Lillian felt undying love for her, so she couldn't allow her to be murdered now. Bursting unannounced into the Queen's private room, she didn't even bother to curtsy. "Forgive me, m'Lady, but there's no time. You once told me you were a person just like me, well now I need you to look just like me, too, Madame." She held out some common garments. "We can leave this castle by the servants' entrance before the heathen are upon us. I've heard they won't kill us common folk, especially if we convert to their religion, Madame."

Queen Alexandra smiled warmly. "Thank you, dear Lillian, but the Muslims will be expecting to find me, and if they don't... I can't allow harm to come to others on my account. Please, take my daughter instead. From now on, she is no longer a princess." The Queen beckoned Princess Stephanie out from a corner, as if she had been waiting there already. Queen Alexandra handed the garments to her.

Lillian fell at the Queen's feet. "M'Lady, I shall never forget thee," but she knew the Queen was right. "From now on, your daughter is me sister, and I shall always be her best friend, as well.

The Queen looked somberly upon her only daughter. "From this day on, dear Stephanie, you must no longer tell of our ancient history. The people whom you will serve will be learned people, and they must not know whence we come, nor about the Tree of Life. There must be no written record at all."

Lillian's eyes widened. She had never heard this part of the story, about a Tree of Life. She took Stephanie's hand. "I'll protect you and your secrets with me life, me Lady."

But Queen Alexandra spoke for the last time. "You are sisters. Neither of you is more important than the other. You shall protect each other. Never forget the meaning of goodness, no matter what religions, practices, or beliefs that are foisted upon you. Now go before it is too late."

Stephanie studied him by the evening firelight as she sat upon a heavily cushioned chair he had created for her out of thin air. She made sure he noticed how comfortable she was, but she knew he didn't know how little she cared for any of it. *Press the advantage, press the advantage. Make what was little, bigger.* It was a sub-rule Vaughn had taught her from *The Art of Fighting.*

"Well, I'm curious. How will you attempt to win my heart? Honestly, I'm *not* easily impressed. And you want my honest, real reactions, which as you well know, because of the poor alternatives you've given me, are not exactly going to be glowing towards you!"

He smiled warmly at her, appreciating her candor, her utter nerve, as he sat in a twin chair next to hers. "By showing you what you haven't seen before, by giving you *my* honest reactions. Frankly, I'm truly worth loving! Take my hand and let your mind go free." He reached across to her chair, expecting her to reach out and take his hand.

Immediately on guard, Stephanie's inner sense rang like the warning bells at school. *I must be careful. How do I hide myself from him and do this? My feelings. He'll be able to detect them, but not understand them. But I must give him the perspective in which to view them.*

She took his hand. Immediately, he sensed something out of place, and raising his voice, declared, "YOU have…"

Stephanie responded quickly and sharply, cutting him off, "I was taught just like you. Did you think winning my heart would be easy? You're not a very strong man, are you?" But she kept her hand in his!

He let go of her, seeming the slightest bit dazed, the slightest bit hurt. He looked her in the eye. "Why have you enticed me?"

She looked back at him with impudence. "Isn't it obvious? You're threatening my life… but…" That hanging "but" did its job effectively.

He pounced. "But what?"

Stephanie baited him further with silence, and then she looked away. He sensed she was trying to resist telling him the truth.

"WHAT?" he pressed.

She told him the truth. "You know things I don't."

He refocused with intensity, as he saw a way into her heart. "HA! That interests you. Admit it."

She acknowledged him. "You can tell truth is important to me, so, I have to be truthful. Yes."

"Then we'll start there. Just as you have interested me, I have interested you."

She wrinkled her mouth into a frown, "We shall see."

He pressed her, yet, again, desiring to win this battle. "ADMIT IT. Be *truthful.*"

She squinted at him. "In the narrow meaning of interest, yes."

"You want to know about my power."

"Yes."

"Why?"

"I don't understand it."

"Why else?"

"I may want to defeat it!"

Jargono wasn't the least bit fazed by her remark, and waved it away with his hand. He urged her, saying, "Yes, yes, of course. What else?" Gaining information without reading another's mind was becoming exciting for him, but he kept probing her, subtly, trying to find a way in anyway.

She offered him more silence.

"Come on, be honest," he pressed.

She sighed. "Power is enticing. It *might* be nice to…" She stopped short.

"HA!" he pointed at her, "To be able to do what I can do. I'll show you." He grabbed her hand, and everything around them vanished. Disoriented and dizzy, Stephanie began to collapse, but Jargono, being the gentleman he is, capitalized on the opportunity by chivalrously wrapping his arm around her waist to steady her, and pressing her tightly against him.

Swooning, she moaned, "Ahha, where … where are we?"

They were standing in the middle of a dead forest, but it wasn't on Earth. There was no sun, nor even sky, and the light wasn't exactly light, but dimness all around, yet, she could see quite clearly, after everything stopped spinning. She had to admit, he *was* very handsome.

"We're standing in what I call the Forest of Reality. From here, I can see inside the hearts and minds of people. Each tree is the manifestation of a person and each can be quite easily interpreted." He turned her around by her waist. "Here is your tree!"

Stephanie had made up her mind that she would not allow anything he said to determine her perspective. In fact, for her it would be the other way around. *This much I have power to do, and naturally so, I'm a woman!* "Hmm, why does my tree … not look like the others?"

"All that erratic glowing is a misconception, which implies that you were taught by my *dead* relatives." He placed emphasis on the word 'dead.'

Stephanie scrunched up her face as she gazed at her tree, trying to understand its intricacies. She freed herself from his grasp, so she could walk around it. Then it occurred to her, *Idiot. It's YOU. Just look inside* yourself. *That tree is* you, *you're not* it! From that point on, whatever part of her tree she looked upon, feelings and senses inside her automatically connected to it, a good many of which she couldn't put into words, but then, the deeper she concentrated, it almost seemed as if the distinctions between herself and her tree … well … disappeared! She shook her head, not liking the outcome at all. Jargono, seeing her faltering, returned to her side with his comforting arm back around her skinny waist.

Jargono laughed at her silly faces as her eyebrows went up and down, rotating between squints and brow wrinkles. "You don't understand that glow, so there's hope for you. You have to forget all about it, in the *way* that you think about it. If you felt like you *really* understood it, you'd be lost, condemned to a boring, narrow-minded existence."

Stephanie realized Jargono was shrewder than she anticipated. Even if he couldn't read her mind, he could read her tree, and he wanted her to know that. *But should I believe that? He's already wrong about my feelings toward the Light. Oh God, goodness can see truly, both good and evil, but evil cannot see good. I understand this. But how do I make my tree appear as if I'm considering evil, without becoming truly evil? What would appear to him as darkness? Oh God, You created both day and night, neither of which are evil, so … what's the counterpart to what causes my tree to glow? What if I just imagined being evil, imagined feeling evil? Oh God, that's dangerous. Vaughn said the imagination is a doorway into another world that is ruled by the principle of that world. If I imagine evil too deeply, I would give it access to me. No, no, that's dangerous enough at any time, but now.... No, no.*

Stephanie turned away from her tree to Jargono. "What things are you talking about that make my tree glow?"

He squeezed her almost imperceptibly tighter, and with a bit softer voice, said, "All their conception of love and fairness and their conception of life, it's mush. Not true because there's no *power* in it. If you really want to love someone, you first have to have *power*, JOIN *TOGETHER* IN THAT POWER!"

Stephanie suddenly swooned again. "OH GOD ... what is this *feeling* in me? Yes! Oh YES! What is this I FEEL?" Stephanie became flooded with several different, overwhelming feelings, but only one she recognized, *Lust. I know what that is.*

Jargono made his move. He was getting tired of waiting. He found that he actually, truly desired to have her, and he didn't want her simply because he *could* have her, not even due to the fact that the memories of her nakedness, and the intense receptivity of her flesh, together with her scent, haunted him. But now, it was her reaction to his advance that really ignited him. "Mmm, you feel my power touching you. It *excites* you. Let's test it out, shall we?"

He ran his other hand over the top of her dress, across her belly, and she instantly burned inside with desire so powerful she could barely keep from grabbing him. She knew that if she reacted to his actions with even the slightest of responses, he would pounce and overpower her last shred of resistance. *This is like my narrow escape from the cave where I couldn't get good footing, where the smallest misstep down that narrow, rocky path....*

She knew she could use her power to drive it all away from her, but she was sure he would pick up on it, and that was something she couldn't afford him knowing. She could even pray it away, but that would anger him for sure. But this was even more intense than what he did to her at the store. *Oh God, no ... I still have to do this the hard way, just by myself, my own will power!* She felt her lust pushing her, shutting down parts of herself as if a heavy fog had descended on her being, giving her tunnel vision for one express purpose, that her body ached to be satisfied. She remembered those feelings with Gary, she remembered her horrible degrading dreams where a part of her reveled in unbounded lust, while another part watched from a distance in helpless, abject horror and disgrace.

Panting, she grabbed his hand and held it away, just before she would have given in. "Not ... so fast. You'll have to do better than a rush of lust to win me over. I'm *not* looking for anything temporary. I've been there before." Anger flashed in her eyes. It was the anger she had toward Gary and all those dreams, and everything associated with them.

No woman has ever been able to resist me like this! He burned to have her, but nodded knowingly. *She has been there before!* "So you have. If I look closely, I can still see the remaining scars on your tree. Join with me and that *wild* glow will disappear along with the scars. Your tree can become perfect, with no weakness.... Oh, very *good*. You're letting go of that *glow!* But learning to channel it is even better."

In her first reaction, Stephanie worried at his statement, but then realized, *What an* idiot *I am! I can't trust anything he says.* Feigning ignorance, she asked, "Am I?"

50

Pointing excitedly, he proclaimed as if for the whole world to hear, "YES. Look at your tree."

Shock! In place of some of the glow was a kind of blackness. Stephanie didn't understand it, but she remembered it was only a representation of what was inside of her. To understand it, she had to look within. *To control it, I have to understand from within.* She smiled at him for the first time. "Hmm, well, what d'ya know Jargono?"

He smiled hopefully. "There is hope for you, yet."

She told him the truth. "I'm glad. Life without hope is *miserable.*"

Stephanie embellished her swooning, as she thought deeply. His arm once again tightened around her waist and she noted it. One of the tremendous feelings he was pumping into her was a kind of power, but it felt quite different than hers. At first, it was an inundating rush of invincibility and seeming freedom to control everything and anything, the power of unquestioned domination over everything. This was mixed with the tremendous lust he excited in her. And there was another feeling she couldn't figure out right away, but now realized that this third feeling wasn't coming from him! It was coming from the natural reaction of the deep goodness in her!

Memories of her weeping just after she'd rebuilt her shelter in the woods flashed in her heart. She remembered placing that last raincoat piece in place and then breaking down into a miserable session of bawling. So many feelings tossed upon a tempest sea. And then she remembered crying, 'Oh God, I can feel again. I can feel again.' The drug induced haze was gone! What Jargono was doing to her now, suddenly seemed similar to what she'd freed herself from!

Stephanie examined more deeply Jargono's feelings. *These power-feelings, they're not unlike the feelings I experienced when I used to get high! They don't really evoke power. They're empty, and without meaning, selfish.* She remembered the monster that stung its victims into bliss while it ate them from the feet up. She remembered Tracy saying, 'I just want to feel like a person, again.' She remembered Vaughn's oratory: '*True love never dominates. The meaningful qualities of goodness only flourish in freedom.*' And that brought her to reflect: *And right now those qualities feel squished in me!* Stephanie darkened. *Damn it! I didn't quit drugs just to substitute something even worse!*

As her third feeling revealed itself ever more clearly, she understood. Just as she came to herself at her little shelter in the woods, seemingly oh so long ago, now her disorientation also faded away into, *This anger is* me, *not Jargono.* The parts of her mind and heart that Jargono had addled now re-owned their true nature of goodness. Understanding and owning this was like opening a door, flooding anger all through her, despising the vile touch of Jargono's invasion down to its very concept, to say nothing of its associated perverse feelings, but it left a residue of nausea in her heart.

Not owning Jargono's subversion gave it no place to root and, resultantly, her tree darkened deeply. *ANGER DARKENS MY TREE! RIGHTEOUS ANGER IS TO THE NIGHT AS LOVE IS TO THE DAY, BUT BOTH ARE GOOD. But to evil, unjustified anger and righteous anger look the same. Dark!*

Let's not overdo it for now. Make him work harder for me! The glow re-enveloped her tree.

"Oh no, darlin', you're slippin' back. Damn… I shouldn't have drawn your attention to it."

Stephanie hesitated, looking *very* tentative, but inside herself, for only her eye to see, she began to understand him in potentially useful ways. *The things he values most are the things he believes to be irresistible, and therefore would be most believable to him.* She appeared to be enticed but also brought forth some of her anger, darkening her tree again. She began to ask him, "Would I be able to…" And then she drew back and reestablished her stern face and put her anger away.

He saw the progress in her. He felt it, and so he pounced, yet, again. Like an animal on the hunt, his appetite began to rage, as he drew nearer to catching his prey, but he realized in amazing wonder that he didn't want to devour her. *This time, it's very different!* He paused. *She's done it again to me without even saying anything! She's made me think.* He asked eagerly, "Would you be able to what?"

Stephanie hesitated. It was extremely difficult to handle what she finessed inside herself, *Darkening my tree won't be enough. To be believable, I have to let what he's doing get very close inside me, so close it would be hard to distinguish the feelings he's pumping into me as his and not mine.* So Stephanie withdrew her resistance and at times her mind fuzzed for an instant and then only his feeling was there, but her mere memory kept her from believing it. She pulled back with sternness. "Never mind!" Inwardly, she groaned, *Oh God, that was close … too close.*

Instead of trying to read her mind again, which for some strange reason was often very difficult, he simply drew the obvious conclusions concerning her behavior. With elation, he stated the truth, "You're embarrassed to ask. Don't let that cursed light make you *glow* so uncontrollably. *Master it!*"

Stephanie looked away, slowly summoning a bit of anger, and then almost unwillingly, she turned to him, her eyes ever so slightly deferring to him, a first for her. "Would I be able to do to people what you did to my Mom?" Her tree flashed a deep black.

He couldn't help but notice the disappearance of so much glow and he smiled with the sense of victory because he knew what she now wanted. The same thing he did. He reassured her, "Of course you can."

But then, an unsettling feeling came into his mind. Something was warning him. *Hmmm, almost feels like a Dark Power is trying to invade my mind. Those tricks won't work on me. I do what I want to do for me. Still... her change was too easy. But she's an outsider, everyone is now ... still....*

He snuggled up to her, squeezing her, speaking softly into her ear. "If you weren't an outsider, you would've been *born* with that glow, and not simply *attained* some of it. You're fortunate."

The tone of his voice floated all around her like a satin blanket flush to her skin, lightly caressing, endearing her to him. This time she felt *his* lust pressing around her, pressing to engulf her. Now, it wasn't what he was manufacturing inside her that beckoned, but his own lust waiting inside him to be sated. This called to her in that very common language between man and woman. She remembered how often she had held Vaughn that way, but they had refrained. *Vaughn has dignity. Jargono doesn't.* Stephanie took a hard swallow, her chest rising and falling, and she quickly redirected him, "But *you're* not an outsider. You *were* born with that glow."

He eased himself off her, taking his arm from her waist as a deeper darkness invaded his eyes and bitterness escalated in his voice. "I was born with the *true* light. The light of *man.* Everything that old man taught you, even the bond you formed," he turned and checked Stephanie's tree, and then raged at her, "I HAVE ALL THOSE POWERS. BUT I HAVE THEM TRULY."

Stephanie saw him being swallowed by something very evil, even beyond Jargono. A very black arm shimmered over his head. *It's so black now, not gray. But I can't chase it away or he'll know.* She redirected him, yet, again.

"So… are you feeling alright? How do you work your power on people?"

He stilled himself, almost frozen for a moment. *No, I'm not feeling alright. Damn Dark Powers. I could chase them away, but I don't want her to see those powers, yet. It would scare her too much. She's the first woman to really care how I feel. I can tell she's worried about me.* He shook his head and pointed to a dead tree nearby.

"Watch. Here's a tree close by. Some person in a town near us." He raised his hand toward the dying tree.

Stephanie watched as the tree suddenly shook, as if wind had passed through it, but there was no wind in this place. She stepped back from it reflexively. And then….

"Ahhh … that branch *cracked!* What did you do?"

Jargono squared his shoulders and stood a little taller. "I focused my heart on that branch and simply told it, no, *showed* it reality. When it saw the truth, it conformed."

Stephanie tried in vain to translate that into something she could understand. Her heart sank inside her. "But what happened to the person?"

Jargono waved her question off as though he was shooing away a bothersome gnat. "He's weak, so he doesn't appreciate the power and insight I just gave him. I merely showed him how the Dark Powers and the *glow* had robbed, and *still* rob him of being himself. But he can't see beyond being robbed, so all he feels now is emptiness and deep despair. Seeing all this more clearly caused his branch to crack. I didn't do any harm to him. He did it to himself!"

Stephanie truly became his student as she pleaded for understanding, "But I saw no glow in his tree at all."

Jargono smiled, realizing the respect she had for him. "All the trees in the front, here, "he waved his hand out and about, "are still living people, which means there is hidden *glow* in their very fiber."

Truly confused, Stephanie complained, "Then why aren't they glowing? I don't understand *any* of this."

"Because the way this Forest of Reality is set up, the trees only glow when either the mind, heart, or general soul becomes aware of some aspect of the *glow* and begins to be led by it. That's what my *former* people did to you. They made you aware and tricked you into thinking it was you, that you should follow it instead of controlling it. But since you weren't born with it, as you've already demonstrated, you can get rid of it. But even better, I can show you how to control it, to be a *true* woman."

Stephanie began to consider the implications, *Hmm, he doesn't understand what goodness is, so he can't understand how the glow could be the real him. He doesn't understand that as soon as you try to control it, you're fighting against it, against your true self. He doesn't understand how to simply be. But he's saying he's his own man, not ruled by either glow or Dark Powers… that he even thinks he can control them both. So what could he possibly imagine exists between the essences of good and evil?*

As if in response to her question, a clearer picture of Jargono flashed across her mind's eye. *Oh my God, I think I know. He doesn't see good or evil as intrinsic to either the glow or Dark Powers. To him, they're merely just two different wills, and for that matter, his is also a different will! What matters to him is that he has his way, regardless of whether he does good or evil. Oh God … so he can access the power of good when he yields to it, or evil! Oh God… You let him use Your powers like that?* Stephanie listened to the silence a moment until she scolded herself, *Stupid question, I have the same capacity. I can walk for good or for evil or … Hmm, just for myself?*

Something didn't feel quite right concerning that last thought that entered her mind, which now became her orientation. Her heart was struck by a sudden pain, a feeling of being let-down, but that sense of Jargono's power, of power over all, quickly came to reassure her.

Having exposed the roots of her tree, Jargono studied them and watched much of the glare from their glow disappear.

Nodding approvingly, he encouraged her further, "That's right, control it. See how the glow still resides in the roots but it doesn't leak out all over the ground? Why waste it?" He smiled, motioning his hand across the ground and the soil responded to his command, covering over her roots again as if sealing their current state of affairs forever. Roots that now seemed to trap the light within them, offered only a yellowish tinge to their skin as the only sign at all that any *glow* remained.

Stephanie shook her head, trying to dislodge a feeling of pressure inside it. In some ways, she felt as if she had gone days without sleep, struggling just to maintain a meager perspective of the immediate situation. She pressed her temples, rubbing them, as if trying to massage more clarity back into her mind. *Telling me to control the glow has to be a trick, because walking just for myself, that doesn't allow me to escape from doing either good or evil.*

A sharp pain now shot like electricity through her head. *I know we're supposed to control ourselves … but … well … for instance, what about love? The very nature of love is just what it is … am I supposed to change* that? *Then it would no longer be love at all. What I think he really means by his word, "control" is to change the nature of … everything? It's true that wisdom and understanding* guide *my expression of love, but they don't change its fundamental nature. They guide the root where and how to grow, but it's* still *a root, still true love! My mind isn't really controlling that.*

Trying to control any of our good fundamental natures isn't really controlling them at all, but destroying them. He doesn't understand you have to end up belonging to either good or evil

*because that becomes the fundamental nature of your heart ...
his heart ... ahhh, my heart. Good and evil are more than just
concepts, they're actually completely different natures of consciousness with wills of their own, mutually exclusive from each other.
God, Himself, doesn't control being Love. He IS Love, though He
controls how He expresses it. Jargono's wrong about controlling the
glow. His idea of controlling it would be like putting a condition
on loving, I'll love you if you do what I want you to do, instead
of loving a person for what they truly are. His way turns his love
into selfishness. I wonder if I can show him that, prove it to him.
If I could, would he truly change? Is it possible for him? Oh God,
even for him?*

Again, Jargono kept looking back and forth between
Stephanie and her tree. Stephanie's little thought interlude
was a lot longer than any he had seen before from her, but
having witnessed so much progress in her, he declined to
disturb her now.

*According to what he's saying, everyone has glow, but most
don't appreciate it. That's why I couldn't see any glow in all those
trees. Hmm, but they benefit from it nonetheless. But when
Jargono invaded his mind, he perceived through Jargono's view
of him and despaired and then the branch cracked. So ... it's a
matter of perception and reaction, even for Jargon's powers, or at
least this particular power.*

*I wonder if it's possible to show people the truth by entering
their mind and then stepping back.* This time, a cold silence
invaded Stephanie's pause, until ... *Oh God, what am I saying?
Yeah, just force yourself into someone's mind* Stephanie, *for the
sake of goodness. God, this is so tricky. But I can understand*

Jargono's point of view. I CAN APPRECIATE IT! She paused again, but smiling this time. *Ha! But I don't have to* believe *in it! Now, how can I use all this to affect this tree of mine? I'm glad he covered my roots back up. Hmmm, how'd they get uncovered in the first place?*

Stephanie adjusted her internal workings, as she integrated her new understandings. She accessed Jargono's perspective, imagining going that selfish way. This mostly involved her mind, and was a lot less dangerous than allowing alien feelings too close into her heart. *I know I can undo my mental imagining anytime.*

Jargono had been studying her tree the whole time she'd been thinking. Even though he was getting used to her little thought interludes, it still troubled him that he couldn't read her, yet, but it also excited him. Her tree instantly sprouted several small, twisted, calloused branches.

He responded with joy. "Oh, very *good*, you're beginning to understand." Jargono began to walk around her tree, staring deeply into it. Stephanie immediately felt consumed by another strange, rushing feeling, and she thought she might pass out. Jargono, of course, expected this and caught her fall.

"OH! What feeling is *this?*"

Dangerous! She lost track of her inner workings. She couldn't resist falling into his arms which squeezed her tightly against his body. As one hand pressed into the small of her back, his other hand caressed her up and down. But his hold wasn't strong enough to keep her standing, though, so to avoid slipping down against him, she had to hold tightly to him, which unexpectedly increased her lust. And his desire began to pour over her once again, but added to that was the fact that she now returned his embrace, even if only out of necessity. Yet, for some reason, he withheld forcing lust inside her as before. He was trying to seduce her like any other normal man. With Stephanie feeling very much fatigued, all of her sensations overran her. Yet, he sensed she still withheld any extra contribution that would indicate a clear 'yes'. *I want a definite YES! I know it would be so very easy now to make her give in … but I know her. She'll look back on it later and hate me just like all the rest. She's too precious to treat that way. I know I can make her truly love me.*

He answered her question triumphantly. "What you feel is POWER! Let's find you a tree to practice on!"

As Stephanie's head began to clear, her alarm raised sharply. *I can't harm someone.* Then, as he held her against him, she gazed around his shoulder seeing a distant tree with glow through most of it, with many beautiful, green branches…. *Oh no, I know that wasn't there before! I would have noticed it, I'm sure.* She strained her eyes, *Oh God, is it … moving?*

Searching for the perfect practice tree, Jargono began to turn Stephanie away from the beautiful tree, which meant he was turning towards it. Stephanie's heart pounded, *No, no, no!* Quickly finding her own strength again, she pulled away and directed Jargono, "Let's look over here. I think I saw something interesting."

She led him away from the tree she knew to be Vaughn's tree. She didn't know how, but she knew. After a minute of walking through disfigured, half-living, half-dead trees, she glanced back in the direction she came from. There was no sight of glow in the distance. She stopped in front of a sickly tree that had one strong, healthy branch among many other broken or disease-ridden ones. Jargono beamed with satisfaction as he looked it over, sporting a sort of childlike glee with even a hint of mischief.

Not being near her tree anymore, put Stephanie a little more at ease. She realized, though, that she couldn't undo her deformed branches because he could check her tree at any time. *This isn't going to be as easy as I thought. Damn! What am I doing to myself?*

Jargono instructed her, "Very, very good! I placed power within you, so all you have to do is stretch out your hand toward this branch here and try. It's the only branch he has left where he ignorantly follows the nature of the *glow*. Focus on the truth of the power inside you belonging only to *you*, and let that power permeate the branch and guide it to its trunk. The very presence of your power will show this tree how useless its branch is because neither your power nor that branch belong to him. His branch belongs to the *glow* and your power will also make it evident that he can't control that *glow*."

Stephanie once again dropped into deep thought, *Oh God, I can't harm. What is he doing to me?* Stephanie's arm began to raise, her fingers stretched out towards the living branch. Frantically, she thought, *Why is my hand raising? I know I could stop him, but then he would know. Oh God, help me. I can't HARM SOMEONE.*

Stephanie decided to turn and fight him. She couldn't harm anyone. Anger swelled in her. She began gathering all her power to full strength, but just before she turned on him, a burst of energy released from her extended hand. The tree shook.

She was perched on the edge of attacking Jargono, but now she fought the momentum that had built up. At the same time, dread descended concerning the harm she'd done. *I'm too late!* The power had left her hand. The tree seemed to shake for an extended period of time while she shook from the tremendous guilt that seemed to drop her stomach down to her knees. Stephanie cried inside, *Oh God, what have I* done? *I waited too* long. *Oh GOD!*

The branch had instantly blighted, and the leaves began, one by one, to fall off. Stephanie wasn't sure which caused her to shiver more, her stopping her assault on Jargono, or her assault on the tree, but her heart definitely focused upon her guilt.

Jargono ecstatically danced around, laughing, "Very good! See what you just did? Look at what you've done. Look at what you've just done!"

Even as a faithwalker, Stephanie felt sick beyond words, and even sicker from the dreadful feelings Jargono was still stoking in her. As Jargono kept celebrating her 'victory', her anger began to burn tenfold more than before. She'd never known such rage, never knew she was capable of such ferocity. His continued laughter kept rubbing raw her guilt, her pain, her severe self-disappointment even further.

But just as movement catches one's peripheral vision, and reflex makes us look, one of Vaughn's sayings flashed in her memory. *NEVER make a battle decision in anger. NEVER go into battle without it!* So she paused to think. *Oh God, help me, what did I do? I didn't feel harm. I felt righteous anger against evil.* Then she heard herself speak aloud. "What ... what did I do?" Her voice trembled, but not because she wanted it to.

Jargono laughed again, "Oh poor girl, you're an outsider and you don't understand. You're not acquainted with feeling such power and now that you released it, and it's gone, you feel so small. I can see how small you feel! But I can train you, and after a while, you'll feel powerful again." He turned toward the tree to finish his lesson. "This person was on the road to truly understanding darkness. That branch was greed in action! You destroyed the branch."

Confusion riddled her. Her voice was that of a little girl, "But ... but it was a very *alive* branch and didn't look like greed at all."

Jargono's eyes seemed to take pity on her ignorant self. "That's because that branch first manifested all his physical vitality. The greedier he became, the surer he was of being physically well, and so he was. The more vitality he felt, the more insatiable he got, and the more strength he could feed his greed. He cultivated that branch very carefully, very cleverly, actually using the energy of the *glow* to achieve perfection of darkness! You have to look at the *whole* tree to understand this. See how the veins of all the dead branches course over the trunk and enwrap what used to be that green branch? And then they travel down to a corresponding black root, representing the epitome of covetousness. They were using, tapping all of that branch's energy for themselves." Jargono couldn't help another bout of jovial laughter, "Until you showed him reality!"

Stephanie thought, *Well, damn! What d' ya think of that? If that's the case, the bastard deserved it! That's the second time I almost screwed everything up. If I had tried attacking Jargono....* She didn't want to complete her thought, remembering when Jargono had found King Mafferan's letter to her and how she almost gave everything away for nothing. She shook her head, realizing, too, her guilt had vanished along with a terrible weight, and in its place, thankfulness radiated. She also realized she needed to understand more, "But why is that a good thing to you? And how did I really do that?"

Jargono waved his hand and created a cushion chair for the obviously troubled Stephanie who gladly sat down. He continued his instruction, "Don't you see? It's great because greed is a threat to others. Oh, I've withered many a branch like that to keep danger away from me." Once again he laughed with particular satisfaction, "Once destroyed, it causes them to sort of wander around aimlessly. Some even lose their minds when they find their greed suddenly ripped away from them. They just don't know what to do with their pathetic lives after that. They're so weak and ignorant. As to the question of how you did it, well, you just used, with my guidance of course, a deeper understanding of greed to make him feel totally inadequate with his own understanding, so he shriveled his own branch!

Of course, my understanding of greed goes much deeper than all these. You see, I have no problem understanding that the *glow* should serve me. But you also showed him that the *glow* was the power of that branch, not him, and he was severely disappointed, thinking he could no longer be sure to control it. Consequently, his whole cycle of vitality and greed instantly fell apart."

Stephanie's eyes opened wider with understanding, as her mind examined the technicalities. *I see … he thinks it was deeper greed that did this, but was it? His power was pumped into me, but at that instant my anger drove it away, I'm quite sure of that now.* Stephanie rechecked her memories one last time before coming to her conclusion, *No, my anger, righteous anger against evil blighted that branch! But, he still controlled me releasing it! He thought he was having me release his power, but instead he released mine! His power and my anger, he can't tell the difference! Hmm, now I know to be on guard against his tampering with me.*

Jargono had been watching her expression quite closely, relying on what normal men depend upon to understand women. "Ahhhh, very good, I see by your eyes you understand." Stephanie had another idea, so she asked with childlike curiosity, "Where's your tree?"

Jargono doubled over with laughter for a couple minutes. The way she asked the question tickled his funny bone. "I put it away where it can't be found so easily. You think I'm a fool? If there are any others out there with my kind of power, they would use my tree against me."

Transfixed, Stephanie continued to probe his knowledge. "You… *transplanted* your tree? How can you do that? You just dug it up?"

Jargono felt like bragging at just how powerful he really was, "Even the Dark Powers can't do that. They didn't realize when they taught me about this Forest, that I would eventually gain the power to move within it, even change it! Do you know that they actually think this is *their* Forest? Do you believe that? I mean, after all, these are *our* trees. When I'm done unifying the Earth, I'm coming here and taking *my* Forest back!"

Stephanie noted that he spoke with equal animosity toward both the Appendaho and the Dark Powers. That confirmed her earlier supposition, *Jargono is for no one but himself.* She looked up at him. "But how?"

He put his right index finger on her cheek, running it up and down its curve as he spoke, "What does every new child do?"

Stephanie could see in his expressions that he saw her as his protégée. She shrugged her shoulders in silence and Jargono gladly continued, "I simply explored my new world, my new perceptions, until I learned how to manipulate my world. THIS ALL is *my* world." He spread his arms out wide and spun around like a dancer. "Once I have the Earth secured, I will train people to be Forest tenders, and I will put defense around the Forest to keep the Dark Powers from meddling. If I catch them *here,* I will *destroy* them!"

She began to sense that in Jargono, too, there was a thread of the maniacal, but he usually kept it well under control. She sighed as she assessed the situation. *Oh God, he is so far beyond me. How am I ever...?*

But her thoughts were interrupted all of a sudden, as in a very authoritative tone, he dismissed class, "Enough lesson for today!"

But Stephanie decided to be a good student and impress her teacher, "But I don't want it to end yet." It was the truth.

"*GOOD*. But there are things you don't understand, requirements when you enter here, and *consequences* if you stay too long. You've already stayed way too long, but I can actually stay much longer."

"But I feel fine." Actually, she felt exhausted.

"Ha! Wait till you return! My power is keeping you from feeling the affect while we're here."

Stephanie suspected that his power would not be able to do anything like that for her, but that in fact it was hers that had been sustaining her. But that meant… *Oh NO!* He took her hand and the world vanished again and once again she was disoriented, but this time, "Oh God! I feel so weak, so cold."

Stephanie collapsed beside the camp fire, hardly able to move, hardly able to think, but she knew she was in serious trouble. By now, Jargono was seething with lust. He had never experienced it like this before, it having so much power over even him. He waved his hand and a large, exotic, circular tent appeared out of the dark night. "Here, I know how you feel. Let me comfort you."

Jargono scooped up Stephanie's limp body and carried her into the tent where there was a luxurious bed with elegant purple satin covers already turned down. Stephanie groaned as he gently laid her down, as she didn't even have strength to bring her flopping arms up, but she could hear her distant thoughts. *Oh God! He tricked me. No strength … to resist.* Jargono laid down beside her, placed his hand upon her cheek and rested his arm between her breasts. Her holy dress was all that separated him from her.

"You know, allowing me to try to win you, showing you *my* reality, has made me very, *very* desirous for you. Mmm, you feel so *good*."

He pressed himself tightly into the softness of her hip, and she could tell it was more forceful than he had wanted. Tears crept from the corners of her eyes. She thought of Vaughn and that thought, itself, somehow carried with it a grain of strength. She seized that spark, remembering another of Vaughn's admonitions, *Fight, fight, fight with your last iota of strength.* "Is this ... the way ... you want me? Before ... I choose to ... really give ... myself ... to you? I'll ... *hate* you ... *forever!*"

She had no strength even to whimper, but laid there with tears slowly running from her eyes, wetting the satin pillow on which he'd gently placed her head. Her flaming red hair, still in braids, rested above her head, exposing her neck. She could feel his panting on the side of her face, each breath echoing his consuming lust over her. No longer able to discern whether that was just his natural force or his powers, she became acutely aware that his scent and presence had that raw appeal to conquer ... well, probably any woman.

Jargono picked his head up so she could see his face. He knew she had spoken the truth. He was coming to understand her, to know her. *She's exceedingly stubborn and proud. She'd carry that grudge against me until either I killed her or somehow she...* He dismissed further thought.

He gazed at her helpless form for a while then traced a finger over her lips. Running it down her neck and stopping between her breasts, Jargono felt the Seed to the Tree of

Life nestled under her garment. His finger used it as a toy, making it roll back and forth from breast to breast while he contemplated his next move. His physical need urged him, his memories of her nakedness and receptivity embellished the moment. His heart pounded to have her but there was no hurry to answer her. She was his whenever he wanted. Of course, that had always been true.

"Hmm, there you go again, making me think about things I had never thought about before. I'm sure you would enjoy it now. Oh, I would see to it that it feels better than anything you ever felt. But still, I don't want you as a conquered object. I want you to *appreciate* me, to want me as much as I want you because you appreciate me. And I would be interfering with that if I took you now. *Not* taking you now, that should actually make you appreciate me. YES! Then I will have you forever, over and over again, with the same delight or more! Yes, I will listen to you on this!"

Stephanie mustered her last bit of ability to think. *Oh thank you, Lord of Light. Let me feel some righteous anger before I sleep.* Her heart used its last strength, and then she passed out. She could hear him saying in the distance …

"Oh, very good. Your glow fades. How do I know this? I've come to be able to read people without the help of the trees! Sleep well, my future wife."

And then, time disappeared into utter exhaustion, but within this timeless void, a strange world came to life in which Stephanie was as a mere puppet.

Ah… feeling much more than any sex I ever had! Her pelvis contracted again, so hard it almost felt like she cramped, but that cramp just fed into the next exhilarating wave, escalating.... *I can't believe it feels like this! ... What? Oh God! I'm dreaming. He's doing me in my dream! Bastard! BASTARD!*

In her dream, Jargono ravished her while she willingly gave in to every pleasure that seemed to continually multiply in intensity through the entire night. Consequently, in the morning, Stephanie awoke covered in sweat, feeling refreshed but quite *angry*, even if also satisfied. Remembering when she'd stormed into Arlupo's bedroom because of just such a dream, *Thank you Arlupo for helping me understand. I'll not let it harm me.*

If it wasn't for the nagging thought reminding her she still had to conceal her powers, she would have marched out of that tent to do everything possible to dismember Jargono one small piece at a time. Stephanie burst out of the tent flap. The sun had already risen a good hour but mist still lingered all around. She spat on the ground, remembering, trying to get that bitter taste out of her mouth.

Jargono spoke good-naturedly, "Did you sleep well, Stephanie?" His smile was telling, but so was her fury.

She picked up a thick stick and threw it at him as hard as she could. His power deflected it. She tried a rock ... then two more! "*You broke your word.*"

He vehemently protested, "*I did NOT!*" Then he became very docile. "Dreams are not reality... Did you enjoy it?" He raised his eyebrows, seemingly really concerned as to whether she had a good time, as if his manhood or something was on the line.

That query sent Stephanie over the edge. She grabbed another stout branch, banged it on the ground a couple times

71

to see how it would hold up, then she ran at him! His eyes got larger the nearer she drew but he seemed frozen in place. He knew he could stop her by any number of ways but couldn't seem to find one at that particular moment, but he somehow managed to find his feet. After the first blow connected to his shoulder, sending a spasm of pain through his neck, he remembered how to shield himself. From then on, the blows connected, but really just bounced off. He was reminded of an old saying, something about hell and a woman's fury, but the exact words didn't come to him.

Stephanie chased him around the fire, he lost count how many times, until she couldn't stand up any longer. As she began to collapse on the ground, he manifested a recliner to catch her. She was too spent to roll off it to lie in the dirt. As she gasped for breath, he repeated his question timidly, "But did you enjoy it?"

Stephanie glared at him, then couldn't believe the replies that came out of her mouth though she knew it was her saying them, and not the result of Jargono's influence. "YES! Very much!"

This delighted Jargono like a little child thrilled with rides at an amusement park. Eager to please her more, he asked, "Would you like to feel it again?"

Again, Stephanie hesitated. She was glad she had pre-established a pattern, a persona of how to treat him, because her tremendous anger prevented her from thinking. Her role automatically answered for her, "*Yes*, I would like to feel that again, but is that all you want, a woman of *mindless* passion?"

As he paused for a bit, Stephanie could tell she was once again making him think, and that he was getting used to her doing so. He knew that her mind wasn't in the dream and sensed her loathing. "No, I'd be bored. I've had plenty of women like that. They're not worth anything. You know, you're pretty smart for only fifteen years old."

She glared at him, again, *How did he know I just turned fifteen?* "Yea, well, our age is highly underrated. Besides, all you have to do is just *think!*"

Jargono opened his heart and confessed to her, "You remind me of me when I was your age!" That spurred Stephanie to deeply wonder. *Oh God, he is so far beyond my abilities. He could be playing me this whole time, knowing everything about me.*

As they stared into each other's eyes, trying to discern the other's thoughts and feelings, they suddenly found they were not alone! Someone had sat down at their fire with them! For Jargono, who had extra-perception akin to the best hunting animals, this was more than disconcerting. But before he could take action, the rude lad at the fire introduced himself, as he brushed something from his cheek, "Trevor."

That was it! Just his name in the flattest, most uninteresting tone one could imagine, then he turned away, stared into the fire, warmed his hands, and brushed his cheek again. Stephanie and Jargono stared at the intruder and then at each other. Both looked perplexed as they turned back to observe a young man whom in many ways didn't seem to be there.

And there was silence! Jargono could have probed the stranger's mind straight away but the young man's vibe was so unappealing, Jargono elected to simply scoff, "Excuse me, but I don't remember inviting you to my campsite."

Trevor noted Jargono's irritation but responded with nothing more than a nod and another rubbing of the cheek. Jargono got more aggravated by this idle gesture since he hated any lack of self-control, and Stephanie, understanding this, her eyebrows rose, desiring to interject … something, anything. She knew what Jargono was capable of, but somehow her heart had trouble maintaining concern. Jargono became even less tolerant of the young man's lack of respect, or ignorance, but he really couldn't tell which. "Excuse me," Jargono tried again, "Do you know…"

"Who you are? Of course, who doesn't?" His tone was slightly appeasing, not exactly uncaring, but more plainly unimpressed. "I was cold, but really I didn't want to miss the opportunity to introduce myself. I take care of things around here." Trevor's hand once again brushed his cheek but only just briefly.

Jargono debated again whether to enter the young, scrawny man's mind but again couldn't bring himself to even test it out, being repulsed by the young man's failed attempt at self-control. "Ok, I'll bite. What do you take care of?"

Trevor reached into one of his belt-packs and tossed a small brown paper bag at Jargono, who caught it by reflex. *What the hell am I doing? I should never have allowed myself to catch an unknown object! I should have at least used my powers to stop it in mid-air!* Jargono didn't like feeling unsettled, that uncomfortableness coming from Stephanie was one thing, but who was this insignificant bum to bring such disturbance his way? *I could simply destroy him right now. I should.* But there was that same dullness again, that same unappealing vibe that dissuaded him from even entering the lad's mind. Trevor just didn't seem worth the effort!

Jargono opened the little bag and immediately scowled at Trevor, "You've *got* to be kidding!" He tossed the bag to Stephanie, seeing how curious she was. As soon as Stephanie caught it, she couldn't place the strange feeling that arose in her hand, but when she looked inside, she immediately turned her scorn on Trevor, as well. She balled up the little bag and disgustedly tossed it into the fire.

As she did so, Trevor spoke to Jargono in a flat matter-of-fact tone, "Look. I know who you are. Go ahead, read my mind! Yeah, I even know 'bout some of your powers. I know you could kill me on the spot if you wanted, but what profit would that be to you?"

Jargono's attention was drawn by Trevor's words. He didn't notice the strange sparks or the gray smoke that whisked away in a far less random motion than would be expected. But Stephanie couldn't take her eyes off it.

Jargono began to laugh, and even though Trevor's tone had no concern in it at all for his own life, it did amount to a lot of nerve. "Well then, why aren't you afraid?"

"Hey, what can I do? I gotta play the hand I been dealt. I don't know any other way. If I die playin' it, I just die."

Any other answer would've probably got him killed before he finished, but this one got him another question. Jargono leveled his eyes into him. "Trevor ... what the hell are you doing messing with me? Taking up my time. What profit could you possibly be to me? Frankly," Jargono snickered, "you're just the most uninteresting person ever! And why aren't you afraid to push your drugs my way? They're not government certified. I could just turn you in."

In that same I-don't-care-about-myself-or-life tone, Trevor explained, "Well, since you asked, I can tell you don't give a damn about this government. You know they want to use you but you're too smart for that and too powerful. Soon, I figure, you'll be runnin' everything. This is my territory, and jus' like I knew 'bout you, I know and will know 'bout a lot of other stuff. All you gotta do is jus' read my mind and you know what I know. For you, knowledge is gold. And my drugs help give me the power to get that knowledge. I'm on the inside of a lotta stuff. Go ahead, read my mind."

Jargono studied him, and so did Stephanie. Both were thinking, *There's a lot more to him than meets the eye.* Jargono began to read his mind but withdrew. *No! He's too insistent. What? Does he think if I read his mind we'll become* friends? Jargono revolted at the very thought of it, but he did pull one other quite clear picture from Trevor. How completely uncaring his parents were towards him and his sister. *Well, that explains why he doesn't give a damn about anything.* Jargono shook his head at the irony of his life and Trevor's. *I couldn't stand my parents because all they dripped was that inordinate caring and that so called mush of love and light, but Trevor has had the opposite. Hmmm ... he should have learned to deal better with that, just like I did. No wonder I can't stand to be in his mind. I hate failures. They're worse than dull, but Trevor's also painfully uninteresting, no feeling at all. Ok, I'm ready to be done with this.* Jargono looked Stephanie's way, and it almost seemed as though Jargono was asking for her help.

Stephanie put her hand to her temple as if trying to pull out a thought that just wouldn't manifest. Her eyebrows strained with the effort! "Trevor … don't you care about your life … at all?"

He met her eyes straight on. There was nothing in his stare for her to grab on to! "Does that answer your question?" he spoke flatly.

A pain shot through Stephanie's heart and she had to remind herself to be careful how she acted in front of Jargono. *I've never in my life met anyone like this, nor have I ever had so much trouble feeling … anything for someone. Why?*

Trevor got up from the fire and did a little nod toward Jargono, "Look, I'll be around. Kill me anytime you like, or use me, or ignore me. All the power is in your hands. Bye!" And as he turned away, they could see his hand go to his cheek, rubbing vigorously.

Jargono used his power to hold him in place but Trevor didn't even show any sign at all of being bothered, or being afraid. He really didn't care. That fact made Jargono feel he was wasting his effort, and he released him. "Trevor, is there anything you know now that you think might be valuable to me?"

Trevor told him the truth, "Yeah. The drugs I'm selling!"

Jargono shook his head. "I despise that stuff! I value a clear mind…" But Jargono paused in his thoughts, realizing there was more depth to Trevor's answer. "Alright, is there anything related to your business that in your estimation might be valuable to me, in fact, *any* knowledge you have now?"

"The ones I work for only care about themselves."

Jargono shook his head again. Trevor's answers were about as useless as he appeared to be. Jargono just shooed his hand at him, sending him away, but Stephanie found herself getting to her feet and walking up to Trevor. Her back was to Jargono. *There has to be more to him than this. He's a human being. He's not twisted like my father, nor evilly inclined like Jargono… He's not like anyone. There has to be more to him.*

Stephanie took Trevor's arm, turning him around, and as soon as she did, he looked at her hand that held him. "Trevor," she tried looking deeply into his eyes, and for the first time in what seemed like ages, she felt like herself again, felt her eyes soften. Trevor felt the pull of her stare and couldn't help but meet it. "Trevor … be well!"

Trevor nodded, began to raise his hand to his cheek but it fizzled, then somewhat awkwardly, he turned away from her, but moments later he turned back, giving Stephanie a slight nod, and then off he went into the woods.

Jargono couldn't help but ask her, "What was all that about?"

Stephanie was honest, "You know, Jargono, I really don't know! I've never met anyone like him, so …"

"Worthless? Dull? So … I really don't know either! Part of me wanted to kill him, but mostly I just didn't want to waste any time on him at all."

"I know, me too! That's why I went up to him … to try to … spark some kind of life into him."

"Ha! Well, if you had, that *would* have got him killed!" Jargono laughed as if it was a joke but Stephanie took it for truth.

CHAPTER FOUR
Plans and More Plans

The Mullah eyed them both, "Those two." He beckoned with his hand and a guard grabbed them both, dragging them forward. "What are your heathen names?"

"I'm called Lillian, Sir, a humble maid, and this is ..."

"I'm Stephanie," the Princess interjected, but that wasn't the name Lillian was going to give her.

His dark eyes narrowed upon her. "You look like your mother, the deceased Queen."

"I cannot help me looks, me Lord, but there be many Stephanie's besides the sad Princess. I am Lillian's sister, of the house of servants."

The Mullah nodded as he walked around her, appraising her every detail. "You carry yourself quite finely to be a mere servant." He grabbed her hands, examining them, but was surprised to find calluses. Still not convinced, he propositioned her, "I will appoint you to be one of my wives!"

"Me Lord, I do not deserve such honor."

"Very well, I will appoint you to be my servant."

Me Lord, I am but a heathen. How could I serve you in yer noble house, and bring you disgrace?"

"Very well, you shall be a whore in the service of Allah for our armies."

"Even a heathen has some bit o' honor, me Lord. But pray tell me, what is the difference between one of yer wives, servants, or whores?"

He eyed her even more sharply now. "Such wit is not found amongst the common folk."

Lillian bowed before him. "Forgive me sister her intelligence. It runs in our family, me Lord. Tis better that you should avail yerself of our graces, rather than yer servants! And for the same requirement, tis better to be called a wife than a servant."

He nodded appreciatively. They were both quite fine, healthy stock. "Very well, you shall both be my wives ..." And then he paused in consideration, "Decide between you which of you shall be wife thirty-nine, and which shall be forty!"

Lillian lifted her eyes, "Gracious are you, me Lord, but pray tell, what be the difference?"

"Forty serves thirty-nine and so on and so forth. You seem quite accustomed to bowing."

"Me sister Lillian be older than I. It not be right for me to be wife before her, even in yer custom. I am forty." Stephanie bowed lower than Lillian had, first to Lillian, and then to the Mullah.

In the darkness of the night, Vaughn forgot about time, but occasionally interrupted his concentration only to tend the fire for light so he could further consult the Book. To stave off his hunger, he rummaged in his pack for some dried beef that every now and then he nibbled. Spot, with quite a full stomach, slept at his feet. Vaughn kept glancing over at him. *Well, nature is nature, he's still a dog. You can take a dog out of nature, but you can't take the nature out of a dog.* He leaned over and rubbed his head, but Spot was out cold. Vaughn's stomach growled as the aroma of the hunk of beef that he didn't get to eat still rose from the drippings in the campfire. But he didn't want to cook more because he figured he needed to conserve his food.

"Would I be able to fool that kind of person about the sacred object?" Vaughn thought that perhaps he could swap the Seed of the Tree of Life with something else.

Wisdom: That kind of evil man perceives in a spiritual plane. You cannot fool him with an object solely of the physical world.

"How do I obtain an object like that which would work?"

"You cannot."

Vaughn's tiredness and frustration mixed into a mess, as he leaned over the book on the stump the King left behind.

"Oh that's just *great*! What the hell am I supposed to do then?"

Wisdom: Hell is his domain and he knows it better than you know your domain!

Vaughn nodded to the truth, and there was nothing he could do about it.

"King Mafferan said he couldn't intervene on this side of life. Yet, he made the Earth quake and sealed the cave. Wasn't that intervention?"

Wisdom: That was in answer to prayer and sent by the Light. It also was not direct intervention upon the person of evil. You beat him with a combination!

Vaughn sat back. He had been at it for hours, but this answer was something new. "A combination?"

Wisdom: Justice and Wisdom combined.

As he considered this, he did see that it was Justice motivating him to maneuver Glen, and that Wisdom gave him the finesse to make it all work out. *I wonder where Glen is. But no time for that now.*

"What combination do I need to beat a person like Jargono?" *Wisdom: No combination from you can beat him at this time, because he exists on a deeper level than you live."*

"What combination do I need for Stephanie and I to escape from him?"

Wisdom: Love, Justice, Anger, Understanding, Faith, Life and Wisdom.

Vaughn sat back again, but this time he felt a presence of goodness surround him. This was the first answer that gave hope, even if it was extensive.

"Oh God ... but isn't understanding and wisdom the same?" *Wisdom: No. Understanding knows the true essence or nature of things, such as Love. Wisdom is the application of such knowledge to affect all things. It relates to the consequences and the way all parts fit into the whole.*

"Ah, but how does anger go with the others?

Insight: There are two types of anger. That which is used to destroy out of hatred, envy or jealousy and that which is felt because Life wants people to live and they refuse!

"Which type of anger is in the combination?"

Wisdom: The Righteous Anger. But to escape, you can only fight from one tree."

"One tree?"

Wisdom: Until you are purged, you have two trees. The Tree of Life and the tree of death. You cannot fight from both trees and escape.

"But … but since the tree of death is still in me, how can I only fight from the Tree of Life?"

Wisdom: With choice there are always possibilities. Ponder that. There can be no further Wisdom given you on this subject at this time!

Vaughn had distinctly detected that the book had a *personality* all its own, but this was not the time to let it be stubborn. He scolded it, forgetting that it was just a conduit for Wisdom to help him.

"WHAT? WHAT THE HECK IS THAT ABOUT?"

Wisdom: You are using the book to think for you instead of thinking for yourself! What the heck is that about?

❧

The High Councilor ScrabaGag's personal leave, as well as his return and the weeks that followed, had gone unnoticed. He needed a vacation, he had told the High Council then stormed off. No one knew his new special assistant was *his* first offspring. High Councilors were not allowed to have their own offspring as assistants in order to prevent old-style dynasties. But since he *is* a High Councilor, who would challenge him on it, and who would know? Besides, soon he would be the *only* High Councilor, but also, that prohibition was not written into the revised and codified law. He laughed to himself as he distinctly remembered leaving it out when as an underling, he had been assigned to draft the law's next edition.

Now that the Father's stamp of approval had gone onto the new edition, that old law was as if it never existed, but only ScrabaGag knew it. He snuck up and patted his tail on his offspring's back, startling Grinchback's orb concentration.

"Well Grinch, everything's going quite according to my plans."

Darker than any offspring ScrabaGag remembered ever being born, Grinchback was comprised of quite a few special souls and even parts of a couple Alphas that Scraback's former Master GrrraGagag had previously consumed. That was necessary to *glue* all those souls together, but of course, a precious component of Scraback himself was set to rule over the whole concoction. ScrabaGag didn't want any other Alpha's component to be his offspring's primary essence. What would be the sense of having any offspring at all if he did as so many other foolish Alphas who were unwilling to contribute their own essence to the future? For his part, Grinchback could feel them all twisting inside him from the very moment of his birth and onward. *Positively delightful,* he kept exclaiming, but Master ScrabaGag immediately charged him not to reveal his birthright, nor even his birthplace, to anyone. It was part of ScrabaGag's very long range plan.

Right before Grinchback's birth, High Councilor ScrabaGag had savored knowing that his former master had a particular spot by the Black River specially chosen for its extremely concentrated vapors of Black Essence and its utter secrecy. This concentration of the Black Essence made its joining with the other components all the more exciting and Grinchback's birth all the more violent. ScrabaGag could still feel the Black Essence hurtling inside him from all directions as his mind directed it to the prey he had selected within himself. The ecstasy of the moment imprinted itself upon ScrabaGag's bulbous mind and he immediately knew he would have to sire many more offspring.

And then there was the little matter of Grinchback's name. ScrabaGag knew how Earth-lore irked other Alpha, particularly GrrraGagag, so Grinchback's name became his own private little joke. Instantly proud of his creation, ScrabaGag realized the contradiction between his life and Grinchback's. *No one has ever been proud of me. They had always thought me a fool, a disgrace to be a demon, the tail of all jokes. That was their downfall. It will be the rest of the High Council's downfall, too.*

His underling brought him out of his deep thoughts. "High Councilor ScrabaGag, what about Jargono? He's not doing as you requested."

Now ScrabaGag's master plan could finally be put into full swing, commencing with educating his offspring. ScrabaGag laughed, "That doesn't mean he's not doing what I want him to do. Do the rules state that I must request of him what I want him to do?"

Grinchback momentarily stopped rippling. "Sir?"

"Most times it's better to get what you want by asking for something you don't!"

Grinchback's Great Eye held appreciation for his sire's lesson. "High Councilor, you are the kindest Master I have ever had."

ScrabaGag crossed his tail over his arm to relax. He had allowed his offspring to tour through several different Masters, including the other High Councilors. It was very important that each High Councilor thought Grinchback was the other's offspring and so neither of the two wanted such a permanent annoyance for themselves. That made Grinchback's natural placement with High Councilor ScrabaGag a given. Besides, the scheme that they'd make ScrabaGag suffer with babysitting underlings as they had done to GrrraGagag made them chuckle!

High Councilor ScrabaGag explained his kindness to his dear underling, "I have no need for rash displays against fellow Alpha. I need not brag. I am quite confident in my abilities. *My* former Masters were arrogant, overconfident, and weak so they did all those things. I have climbed quicker than any Alpha in history with the Father's blessing. Do you understand, Grinchback?"

"Yes, Master."

ScrabaGag's Eye twinkled, as he calmly went on, "I don't think you do. I know that given half the chance, you would eat me in an ethereal second. Let me forewarn you, I know the rules that protect you. And I know … let's just say I know how to avoid breaking the rules but satisfying my Eye at the same time. You see *I codified the Father's rules.*"

Grinchback stopped shimmering for an instant. "Yes, High Councilor ScrabaGag … Sir."

In that same, kind, calm tone, ScrabaGag continued, "Do you now understand my kindness?"

Grinchback gave the answer as if giving a salute, "YES, Master High Councilor ScrabaGag."

That lesson taken care of, the High Councilor got down to business. "We need to discover what the girl took out of the box. I made Jargono think I wanted her handed over because

I knew that would make him want her even more for himself. If he succeeds in converting her, he'll find out the treasure and we'll know. If he doesn't succeed, they'll fight and the girl will die taking the secret with her. It's my second preference.

"Another possibility is that Jargono may not discover the treasure himself but may cause us who watch to figure it all out. The longer we keep those two in co-habitable contact, the better our chances. It's increasingly more difficult to get any clear images of that girl, except when Jargono is tampering with her, but also there are long periods of time when the boy is out of focus, too. This can only mean that the *glow* is interfering. We have their trees in our Forest, but that does us little good. They have to be destroyed."

"Why is the content of the box so important?"

"The simple principle that what's crucial to our enemy should be important for us to possess. If there is anything at all on Earth with the possibility of preventing the Earth's transformation, it's likely the Appendaho's box contained it."

"Jargono keeps our Earth-offspring imprisoned. Will you free him?"

"*No.* That's all the *glow* would want. I'll give it no excuse to interfere. Besides, he'll figure out on his own how to break Jargono's hold. We have everything to gain by patience. In that regard, our Earth-offspring actually favors Jargono and the girl fighting. It may weaken Jargono enough to allow his escape. But there's another good reason to have the girl die. Together, she and Jargono might just have enough power to prevent the transformation. I know it's unlikely, but considering all possibilities is wise"

"You've talked with our earthly offspring?"

"Talked with him? Heaven Grinchback, I'm mentoring him!"

"But I thought...."

"We've been extending our arm into the Earth all along. Why should it matter that this time it extends to someone who welcomes it! Besides, I know the *glow* has sent their own to meddle with the humans."

"Then what, Master?" Grinchback hovered just lower than his Master's Great Eye.

"We will see ... it depends. In the meantime, it seems likely that he'll kill the girl and the boy. I bear no animosity against them as my former Master did but they must simply be done away with for the greater good. I will not be blinded by excessive rancor as my colleagues are, hating me because they're pompous and moribund. *I will eat them in time.*"

Grinchback shuddered, growing dim upon hearing his Master's threat against the other High Councilors. He begged his Master, "Master, *please*, do not tell me such things.

ScrabaGag smiled slyly, twisting his Eye in delight, "Why is that?"

"Because you know how they ... question us."

ScrabaGag laid his tail across Grinchback's neck and spoke softly, even affectionately. "I know ... and now you're caught in the middle, between me and them. You'll have to decide where you're safest. If you decide correctly, you'll help me bring an end to the old Alphas." ScrabaGag tapped his tail softly on Grinchback's neck.

"But... but ..."

High Councilor ScrabaGag was full of demon compassion. He did his best to comfort his underling, "Yes, I know, it's a very dangerous position for you. Would you simply like for me to arrange your demise now?"

Grinchback bowed his Eye, "Sir, *you* are in control."

ScrabaGag peered at him with a touch of coldness. "Don't try to flatter me, Grinchback. It makes me *uncomfortable* with you. I have a plan and I'm attempting to carry it out, that's all. If I was in control, I wouldn't need your help! *We* are in control … that is, if you decide to join me."

Grinchback floated in stunned appraisal. Although he hadn't been around that long, *I don't believe there's ever been an Alpha like my Master*, "Yes Master, *WE* are in control. Hmm, I like that." Grinchback began singing and bouncing, "We are in control, we are in control…" He was still a baby demon and given to playfulness, but the resemblance to his sire couldn't be missed because they both liked to sing and bounce.

ScrabaGag's eye smiled, "Let's not overdo it. It's a private song between you and me. The next time one of them questions you, try to rush off as quickly as possible. They, of course, will interpret this as a sign that I have forbid you to talk to them which will make them chase you all the more. They'll feel the need to threaten you with a greater threat than I've threatened you. Don't give in to them until it seems to you that in their Eye their threat against you is unbearable to you."

"Master? You're allowing me my own judgment in this?"

"Of course! You're not an *idiot*, you're my offspring. I'm sure you'll do just fine."

Grinchback truly bowed his Great Eye, "Master, what else would you desire I do?"

"First, remember I've told you not to tell anyone you're my offspring. That would endanger *you*, not me. Tell one of them that I've discovered one of the ancient Objects of Disgrace and have sworn you not to tell because I'll be collecting it in the Forest the next day."

Grinchback's Eye grew wide. "But Master, we're *forbidden* from actually entering that realm, except to reproduce."

"You've learned all your pre-Alpha lessons well. You're right, but that doesn't mean we can't do it. That Councilor whom you tell won't want me to have such an object and he *will* enter that realm."

Grinchback shook his bulbous head. "Master, he'll not enter that realm because he knows he'll be vulnerable to the orb."

ScrabaGag rippled with glee at the sharpness and quickness of his offspring, "Yes, of course, but only vulnerable if others know he's there. Since you and I are the only ones who know and he figures I'm in that realm already…"

Grinchback's Eye widened with initial understanding that the High Councilor would feel safe to go in, but then realized, "Then… that would mean … Sir, he'll perceive me as a threat and *eat me*!"

ScrabaGag's Great Eye smiled to the very limits of his big, bulbous head. His first born was already fearful of being eaten. That was good. "No, he can't do that because he'd break the rule of not eating underlings for no good reason but he'll take you with him!"

Grinchback's rippling steadily declined the deeper he descended into his sire's plans, "But Master, then *I'll* be vulnerable, *besides* breaking the rule of entering the Forest. And if I break *that* rule, then what's to stop him from just eating me for that?" Grinchback shrunk down in his coils, feeling his short Alpha life at an end.

But his Master intended to comfort him further, "There are certain rules you better not break, others where you can try at your own expense, and still others that are meant to be broken! Eating underlings is of the first class. As far as being vulnerable, I told you, you're already vulnerable to me no matter where you are. But I have no desire to eat a faithful servant, and an offspring whom I am proud of!"

"Proud? Master?"

High Councilor ScrabaGag bowed to his offspring! Grinchback floated away in fear, at first not at all understanding such a … a … humble gesture! Yet, it inspired Grinchback further, "But Master, he'll first look for *you* in the Forest to destroy *you*."

ScrabaGag noticed how his underling paid serious attention to his Master's welfare. It was an amazing sight. *I have changed demon relations, but I shall change much more!* "I won't be in the Forest. He'll not see me. I'll fix the orb with a vision that I've gone in but not returned. He'll figure I've hidden myself and that Jargono will bring me the object so he'll call to Jargono to get to him first."

Grinchback brought even more concerns, "But when Jargono tells him…"

ScrabaGag held up his arm to hush him. "It doesn't matter, because first of all, he won't believe Jargono, and second of all, I'll need no more time than that to eat him through the orb."

Grinchback never rippled so fervently, his shimmering was a black light display. "Master, *you* are a genius."

ScrabaGag narrowed his Eye at him and growled, "What did I tell you about flattery?" ScrabaGag began tapping his tail in his arm.

"Sorry, Master, what should I tell the other Councilor?"

"Tell him that the other Councilor has planned on retrieving the object. Simply tell him the other Councilor's plans."

"MASTER, he'll try to get there first … but then … he'll take me with him. And then … I won't be able to go with the other Councilor because he'll already have taken me with him!" Grinchback's bulbous head began to ache.

"Precisely, that's why you tell him the other's plans, except you move the time enough so you can be back for the second one."

Grinchback's Eye was near to popping, "But won't *he* check the orb?"

"I'll take care of what they all need to see in the orb, if you would be so faithful as to take care of your part. *We* are in control!"

"Oh my grayness, you're going to eat them both *in the same ethereal night!*"

"If all goes according to *our* plan." ScrabaGag stopped tapping his tail.

Grinchback began repeating, *"Our plan, our plan … we are in control, we…* as he headed out the ethereal door in song.

His Master called out to him, sharply, "*Grinchback,* that's our *private* song!"

"Oh yes… sorry, Master."

CHAPTER FIVE
Breaking the Rules by Making Your Own

"You must leave this place, Mara. The crusaders are coming." Mara could not hide her tears as she ran her fingers across the elegant mosaic wall of the Tree of Life. It was her favorite artwork, although she never could figure out why but her heart seemed to know. She turned to her servant, "You know, I remember seeing in an old trunk, when I was but a small girl, a very old dress that belonged to my great-great-grandma. I could put that on and …"

Her servant lightly took Mara's hand. "We can flee with the horsemen, north, back to our heartland."

Mara turned to her, "Your heartland."

"Yours, too! For the last four generations, you have been ours."

Mara seemed oblivious, "Strange how only daughters, only a single daughter is ever born to my line. I think I shall stay here … you can go. My husband, my family … they have already abandoned me. Truth be told, I, nor my ancestors have never been pure enough to fully be accepted here. Royal titles and all cannot change reality."

Her servant began to weep, "Mistress, I have only served you my whole life, please. The Christians are coming and they are not as refined as we have become. They rape, they pillage, they ransack, and they even do that to their own. You cannot stay here."

"And where should I go? All this war has enflamed hatred. Do you think they left me behind because they loved me? And they have taken my daughter, my only child with them. God only knows what shall become of her. I have no place to go, and one hell is no less appealing than another. Go, before it's too late. Save yourself."

Mara's servant kissed her cheek and then fled through the palace while Mara turned back to the Tree of Life, to running her fingers over its tiled branches. All alone, leaning against the Tree, she slowly slid down to the floor weeping ...

Traveling in the corridor between realms always tired Jargono, but there was so much to do, especially now that he spent so much time with Stephanie. It was already mid-morning and they should have been on their way, but now he needed a nap. He waved his hand and a hammock appeared strung between two trees.

Stephanie stood in the midst of their campsite, arms folded, studying him. She'd thought deeply about him during her bath and was sure he'd watched her somehow, but though she could feel it, she just didn't know how he spied on her.

He looked exhausted but she had no intention of letting him rest now. She pulled a chair over to the hammock he'd mounted and sat brushing her hair. She started questioning him. "Jargono, *what* is power to you?"

Jargono lazily turned his head to look at her, his eyes deepening as he watched her brush her lush, wavy, deep red hair. The care, the precision, the delicateness, yet the strength and determination of each stroke, almost transfixed him were it not for the lure of her question. In a tired voice, he summed up, "Very simple. It's control."

She squinted at him and with very distinct enunciation, "Control of what, to do what?"

He sighed, because he wanted to rest, but knew he was hooked by her insight and stimulation of his mind. "Control of others' minds and hearts to do whatever I desire."

She paused a bit, watching him intently. As his eyes began to close, Stephanie leaned forward and spoke with that same acuity, "Which comes first, your control or your desire?"

He rolled over to face her, shaking his head in serious amazement. "My, my, but how do you think of such questions? I suppose I would have to say my desire. Why?"

She watched as his hammock swayed from his movement and waited for their eyes to fully meet. With honest, unchallengeable confidence, because she knew the power in the knowledge she was about to transmit, she leveled her eyes into his to communicate a tremendous depth.

"Because you said control is power, but if your desire comes first, then it preempts your control. Desire has power over what you call power!"

Jargono saw for the first time that she truly offered her eyes to him and this was no small offering. He could feel her depths enwrapping him. Surprised by feeling her love pouring through him, his breathing stopped in self-reflection, *I've never experienced this!* He studied her then unwittingly yawned while asking, "What's your point?"

Her words didn't seem to faze him but Stephanie was about to change all that. Locking her gaze into his, she continued to lead him into knowledge, "There are many different desires. All sentient things have them, but you wouldn't say that because they desire, they have power."

"No, *of course not.*"

Totally blind to the direction of her inquiry, Jargono felt something else he'd never felt before, that of being held in place by another's mind. Placing all her hair behind her back, Stephanie leaned forward again, as her rich brown eyes began to take on a piercing quality. With even sharper pronunciation, she continued her quest, "What *particular* desires, then, constitute power for *you?*"

Jargono felt her connecting to him in a way he'd never felt before with *anyone.* She was engaging his mind and heart exactly where they were by meeting him, asking for his real response as to what he is. The very depth of it made him hunger for more but that unknown territory made him nervous … quite nervous. He didn't remember the last time he'd been this weak. He thought for a second to word his reply more carefully. "The desire to control all other life, to bend it to my will. This gives power to my power."

Stephanie understood this answer for more than just its worldly meaning. She understood its depths as a faith-walker, being able to have power over the very nature of physical reality and beyond. *Nevertheless, he's still bound by that literal meaning.* Jargono felt as if she was tunneling into an unknown place in him, as she specifically asked, "To do *what?*" Stephanie hit him in his blind spot.

He had nothing definite in mind beyond the short-term though rather extensive goal of total domination for domination's sake. He had only the same circular answer, "Whatever I desire ... Hmm." And as he heard himself, he began to realize the logical problem with his answers.

Jargono looked up to find her eyes widening in acknowledgement of his current feelings. Her deep rich brown eyes confirmed his new thoughts. Their mutual understanding brought their minds together and this was amazing to him. Besides the Dark Powers, he had never connected to another mind on anything, but this was qualitatively different because there was no imposition by her, only a sort of waiting, an embracing of his situation, and a warmth.

Stephanie knew he was now vulnerable to her next questions, so she softened her voice with compassion. She knew this could enter and touch his heart, but she also knew her words had the power to rip his mind apart. "Jargono, why is it power, particularly when you don't even know what you'll desire from moment to moment? If those desires aren't substantial nor understandable, then it seems to me that your power is powerless! What then would be the point of your rule?"

For a moment, it seemed as if everything went blank inside him, as if her words turned an off switch. *Oh God, he's vulnerable right NOW! If I used my powers right NOW, I think*

I could kill him! But Stephanie found herself similarly frozen, waiting to see which way he would turn.

Jargono wasn't prepared for her to be so loving and yet in the next instant, make him feel so very helpless, as if he was the biggest fool who ever existed. But then he realized the truth in what she was saying! "Amazing … You're right! But now I do know one thing I truly desire that's constant and substantial."

Stephanie raised an eyebrow, wondering, hoping … "What?"

Staring deeply at her with boundless longing, Jargono proclaimed, "*You!*"

But she countered his affections, yet still with compassion so leaving very much open the possibility for him to succeed. She even placed a yearning within her voice, "How can you win me, when you haven't even thought of the most basic of questions?" Stephanie knew the beginning of true knowledge started with honestly asking those questions. *If I can just get him to start …*

He smiled at her tenderly. "I'll let you think of them for me. Tell me *your* desire and I shall grant it."

She matched his congenial tone, also smiling warmly, "I desire to be free of you."

She continued to smile as Jargono laughed, "Oh my, that would defeat the purpose."

Stephanie's eyes sparkled, as she almost turned it into a tease, "Are you powerless to grant my desire?"

He propped up his head as if to gain alertness, not realizing where she was leading him next, "No, I just don't wish to grant it."

She leaned back, folded her hands together, and once again locked her eyes into his gaze so that he was powerless to turn away, "Yet, you want me to freely appreciate you!" Her whole expression made one more clear statement, TRUTH.

He shook his head at her, overwhelmed by her abilities to think, *and* her mere presence. Sitting all the way up in his hammock, now, his eyes were sparkling back, almost teasing. "Hmm, you *are clever*. If I let you go, there's no point to this experiment. Do you see the flaw in your logic *little girl*?"

Stephanie knew that he couldn't be set up any better than he was now. "Why do you think that control is power, if it cannot give you what you desire most?"

The truth stung him before he knew he was in the hornet's nest. His eyes widened and his head jerked back. He darkened and then reacted accordingly, by yelling, "ENOUGH OF THIS. I am *beginning* to understand why so many men *refuse* to marry; they don't want to be *nagged to death*!"

With all the power he seemed to have, it surprised her that he resorted to such a common line. He got out of his hammock and walked around looking very tired and *very* irritated. A darkness had descended over him.

She quizzed him again, without even looking at him as he paced, her tone still sweet and warm, "The black oil I saw you use, what is it?"

He thought to himself, *Yet another question,* but this time he answered irritably, "That's also power. It's the essence of reality."

She continued her kindness, ignoring his nastiness, "Where did you get it?"

He sighed and softened. All he really wanted to do was sleep. "One of the Powers showed me a river that runs through the Forest I showed you. It's a river of reality."

Stephanie couldn't believe it. Her reaction broke from her before she could call it back and she had to adjust in mid-sentence, hoping Jargono wouldn't decipher her mistake, "THERE'S A WHOLE river of it?" Stephanie wanted to kick herself *hard* for letting her true reaction begin to slip out. Then she remembered that he was perceiving everything about her only as he wanted to see it, and even possibly that, that was the *only* way he could see her.

He confirmed her fear, "Yes, a whole continuously running river. If I wanted, I could enlighten all mankind with it!"

Stephanie was glad they weren't looking at each other. Quickly wiping away escaped tears, her thoughts exploded with the impact of this new knowledge. *Oh God, this is much, much worse than I thought. This isn't just about me, or even the Tree of Life, anymore. Oh God, why am I the one to know these things? Oh God, why did I even ask?* But she inquired anyway, "How come we've never heard of this at all?"

He seemed to calm a bit more. "It was known in ancient times, until some stupid rules were drawn up. But the Powers broke their own rules," Jargono chuckled, "and I think they've now paid for that but it's too late because I have unlimited access to the Forest and its Sacred Oil. There's a legend that if we drink the Oil in a special way, we become immortal, *become* one of the Powers."

Stephanie's thoughts whirled. *Worse and worse ... getting*

worse and worse. He's already so powerful. She queried yet again in a doubting tone, "Do you believe that?"

He mocked at his own previous statement, "Considering the source, it could be true or false. I'm in no hurry to test it out on myself."

Stephanie walked up to him, taking his arm. He noted this first expression of freely given affection. She wanted to be looking him in the eye for her next question, "Jargono, everyone knows you've promised to stop people from blowing up. I witnessed a blow-up myself in the woods back East…" Her eyes finished asking the question.

But his tone suddenly became business-like, "I've answered many of your questions. I think you should answer just one of mine. Let's start with the Sacred Object you're going to give me. We'll be there tomorrow. Now, *woman,* I'm *very* tired. You've exhausted me with your *endless* questions. We'll camp here the rest of the day and night then tomorrow we shall see, won't we?"

He vanished out of her sight! Stephanie could feel him watching her though, but she gave no indication that she knew it. After a while, she knew he'd stopped and decided she needed a fuller bath. Stephanie wanted very badly to use her powers, even in some small way, through some special prayer, but she dared not. There was no sense using them until she'd collected every scrap of knowledge from Jargono that she could. *One of those scraps might be the one that saves my life, or Vaughn's, or even the whole world's.* She spent the rest of the day in silent prayer and meditation as she went out and about.

☙

The first High Councilor looked around suspiciously, anxiously, lustfully, "Jargono, where are you?"

Jargono's ethereal ear picked up the call but he was studying Stephanie by spying from the Ethereal Corridor that connected the Earth to the Dead Forest. That passage went somewhere else, too, but he hadn't explored it, yet, because it didn't feel as interesting. Not wanting to be bothered, Jargono sent a spiritual reply while he continued to watch Stephanie, "Why do you disturb me? I'm *busy*. Go away!"

"I taught you how to soar through the Forest and now you betray me?"

"I look out after my own interests, just as you do. I *want* the girl for *myself*." Becoming quickly bored with him, Jargono hummed for a while to block out the demon's ethereal voice. "Hmm, lah, deh, dah…"

"I am *not* speaking about…" First High Councilor screamed.

Jargono kept humming until he sardonically checked to see if the Power was gone. "Lah, deh, dah… oh *Great Power*, are you there? Good."

౷

The second High Councilor didn't want to waste time. Get in and get out was what he planned. "Jargono, *come to me!*"

There was *no way* in hell, well, anywhere, Jargono would even consider obeying a tone like that. Besides, now Stephanie was bathing in the stream, again, and Jargono was still busy scrutinizing her from the Ethereal Corridor. Stephanie did make him promise not to come anywhere near her while she bathed, but technically he wasn't near her at all, not physically.

Though if his concentration grew any stronger, he felt as if he would materialize right next to her. He watched her hands rubbing soap over her breasts and now noted her nipples had the larger areola that he loved. He studied how her flesh yielded to her touch and became intensely more vibrant. He swallowed and in his mind estimated that he was making progress. Soon, she would appreciate him for who he was. But the Dark Power's voice began to echo around the Corridor and it became increasingly distracting.

Finally, extremely irritated, Jargono sneered, "Why should I come to *you*? I don't take *orders* from *you*."

"I know you have the Sacred Oil! *It is forbidden*."

"If you think I'll return it then you're not as wise as I thought. Not only that, I will *take* whatever else I need!"

"I don't care about the Oil, but I want you to give *me*…"

Jargono distinctly heard the Second High Councilor cry out a hideous wail! *That's odd! What could possibly make a Dark Power scream? Something quite strange is going on. But why should it matter to me? I have what I want. Oh yes! And even more than I want the Sacred Object, I want Stephanie. All the same, though, I don't think I should be in this corridor right now.*

Whatever could make a Dark Power scream was beyond Jargono's understanding. So, knowing he was more vulnerable to them in the corridor, he exited, but not before taking one last, lingering gaze at Stephanie washing her backside.

☙

Grinchback beheld his sire, his beloved Master, his Highest Councilor.

"Master, you've done it! You … you are so BLACK!"

ScrabaGag's eye was now like no other in Alpha history, his blackness much deeper, his shimmering more intense, his rippling sublime. He spoke like in a daze and his voice possessed a power, "Yes, there has *never* been one like me in all our recorded history. The three have truly become one! I needed all their power to fulfill our great purpose. Now, we shall rest a while and watch things unfold. The time of the old demons is *dead*. The old ways are *dead*. The world has never seen the likes of me and I shall bring about a new race of Alpha, a united race based on mutual Alpha love and respect! You, Grinchback, are the first!" ScrabaGag waved his super-powerful looking arm and disappeared before his offspring's eyes.

I am the first! Grinchback went back to studying as much as he could through the dirty blue orb. He was proud of his Master, his sire, his Highest and only Councilor. *I am the first... the first...* He began to put it to tune....

❧

Vaughn and spot made their way back to the familiar, desolate, winding trail that led up to the cave but before they entered the cleverly hidden rocky gate, Vaughn told Spot to enter after him. Spot looked just a bit disappointed, which made Vaughn think he'd avoided another face washing and lump on his head.

Vaughn thought about how before they'd reached the gateway, he'd noticed that many of the fruit trees had sprouted new growth from where they'd survived the fire. It sickened him that there was no one left to tend them. It also sickened him that he never met the Appendaho, and in light of this,

Stephanie's preciousness as their last worthy remaining descendent came to the fore. *I just* have to *find a way to save her.* Tears burst unexpectedly upon him.

Any sign of the previous tracks left by Stephanie, her friend, or the man had long since vanished due to the forces of rodents, birds and weather. The trail appeared simply pristine, giving Vaughn even more a sense of walking into the unknown, of first encounter. It brought to mind that final sacred journey that elephants undertake when treading to their elephant graveyard to die, or perhaps the sacred climb that some of the ancient Appendaho performed in a quest for … Vaughn wasn't sure what. Walking back up that ancient rocky path brought into Vaughn's heart the full focus of what he would soon face, but his mind still couldn't comprehend it.

Vaughn's eyes grew black, but this time he became aware of how that change came upon him. Somehow, he was able to see the sequence of rapid thoughts and feelings that were all squeezed into that brief moment when this power descended, overwhelming him. All of the injustice he had suffered in his life had built up a gut wrenching prayer against such insult. When that prayer was triggered, the answer was immediate, and the power inundated him. Its goal narrowly focused into destroying evil. But this was different from his personal anger that used to yell and argue with his parents. The operating principle of this new power descended laden with meaning. That, in part, was what made it so hard to understand, but now Vaughn's capacity to understand Goodness had matured considerably. The source of that power came from Justice. Pure, unfiltered Justice.

Vaughn climbed up the path and brooded, considering Mafferan's words about fighting from his strongest ability. *I know what that is now! And I even know why ... but even that won't be enough. I just can't even imagine what I'm facing or what I should do. That's why I can't get my mind around it. Stephanie's life ... my life ... the world's future ... Oh God! Will it* really *all be determined so shortly?*

And before he knew it, he beheld the enormous stone blocking the Sacred Cave. It had fallen in answer to his prayer to seal him and Glen inside. Spot sat now before that boulder, watching his master intently.

Vaughn thought of how Glen killed the old farmer who gave him Spot. That gentle man who shared his most precious understanding and felt that in sharing it with Vaughn, he had fulfilled his purpose for hanging on to his old family-less life. *No one has ever regarded me so preciously.* Vaughn's eyes went pitch black as tears dripped from his chin. Spot backed away with a whine, feeling the tremendous rage gathering in him.

So much had been lost. So much had been missed. So much knowledge crucial to life had been hidden from him by people not loving Goodness. Vaughn looked inside himself and embraced the depths of the power's meaning. *Justice.* He looked up at the boulder blocking his way into the Sacred Cave. He was the one who'd asked for it to be there. *Now, I'll be the one to ask for it to be gone!*

He put his hands on that huge rock, crying out in all his anguish, in all his remorse, in all his fury, "*Lord God* of the special people I *never* knew, Who gave the words of *Truth* to the whole world that I *never* heard, help me move this boulder!" And as Vaughn leaned into that stone, there was nothing in him, now, except those plaintive words. These pounding thoughts, these consuming feelings … and all time stopped on those words, a continual echo, as his mind and his heart refused to go anywhere else besides right *there*, waiting with all his effort, all his strength and not accepting 'no' for an answer. When the boulder made no sign of movement and doubt tried to gain his attention, he cast it away from him by burying himself even deeper into his purpose until nothing was real to him except those words and all they entailed, *knowing* that the God to whom he spoke them is real, and that his request is Just…. And just as his very person seemed to vanish away in all his effort, a horrendous sound entered his reality. Before he even noticed anything else, the sound of something grinding in angry protest echoed around him. The huge rock began to move and then suddenly it flopped over with a roaring crash, fell off the cliff and crumbled into many small pieces.

Spot laid down putting his head on his paws and stared at Vaughn. There was a certain obeisance in the dog's demeanor. Catching his breath, Vaughn slowly stood up out of his crouch. Eventually standing up straight, he began to be cognizant for the first time of what really just happened. He carefully peered off the edge of the cliff to where the giant stone had fallen and smashed into pieces. After gazing, and then re-gazing several more times to confirm what he saw, he eased himself back to lean against the rock wall for support. He looked up to heaven, staring into the beyond, and then he bowed his head, holding his hands out away from his side.

Tears fell from his eyes, as he felt so small, lost in some great power. "Help me to understand, Lord God."

Even though he prayed it, even though he believed it… still… it was quite a shock! Though one thing Vaughn knew for sure then, he felt Meaning claim him, its full attention directed at him! *How real God is, and the world doesn't know it.* Then he knew that somewhere back in time, feats such as he had just accomplished had been done before! *Yes! … somehow, I just know it.* And not only that, a picture unfolded unto him of a whole history of God's pleading with mankind that seemed to say, 'I Am,' and within that 'I Am' he heard himself say, *I also have a special heritage.* By the Lord God answering his cry to move that boulder, God was showing him that indeed this knowledge was all true.

A new feeling came over him. A new kind of love detonated in his solar plexus and head with intense heat that radiated from them throughout his body. His fingertips tingled, the hairs all over him tickled, his feet felt out of place just standing on the Earth. *I have to know You. I mean,* really *know You.* And then love for his obligation came to the fore, the responsibility to find out his own ancient history, and what God had done for his people, *and what they have ignored for so long.*

But for now, *I have to keep my mind on the present.* "Lord God, if You preserve me, I'll find a way to learn of all the things you've done for my people, and I'll honor You." Spot gave a muffled *ruff.*

Vaughn resolutely turned to Spot, wondering at how Spot kept reinforcing all the good in him, so he asked his advice, "Well, we're here … now what?"

Spot got up and pressed against his master's side for comfort. and Vaughn was equally comforted by his dog, as he stared down upon the demolished village and beyond it, to where he had buried them all. The words of his oath to avenge them pounded through him, craving to be satisfied, absorbing his concentration, until Spot went into the cave, sitting and whining for his master to join him. Vaughn took his sparker, relit the torches, and then walked over to stare at the life-like painting of the royal couple. An automatic magnet for his attention, this mural also focused him on his own deeper feelings.

Standing still, shaking his head woefully, Vaughn barely uttered, "Spot, I'm so ignorant. If King Mafferan hadn't told me of my heritage, I wouldn't have known *anything*. God did something *very* special for my ancestors and I should know it, besides all the meaning I seek now." He addressed the king's picture, "Yes, meaning shall always be central and most important, but I also want to know the rest, about my side of the family, because there's also meaning there … even if it wasn't appreciated."

Then a fantastic thought came to Vaughn. Goose bumps prickled all over him at this realization, "My God, Spot, if Stephanie and I have children, it would marry her ancient people to mine, making them one. If what King Mafferan says is true, and I'm sure it is, that the blessing of my ancestors is passed down through the generations, making the words already somehow in me, well, that means that in our children both true meaning and true words would be married! *My God!*"

Vaughn stepped closer to the paintings and the king and queen's obvious feelings for each other brought before Vaughn his longing for Stephanie. He ran his fingers down their arms, down their hands, across their fingers, imagining their great love and suffering for each other. He tried to imagine the king beholding his wife in humiliating agony and his gut clenched, his mind recoiled, he pushed it away … he searched for hope.

He touched the image of the Book of Wisdom that had taken the place of the real book and he thought about the treasure Stephanie now carried between her breasts. He smiled, thinking aloud, "If only Stephanie and I can survive … all the gifts we've received weren't put here for us not to be married."

Spot lay down with his head on his front paws, as when he did when Lana prayed, and he whined at Vaughn, seemingly telling him something.

Vaughn understood. "Yes, pray and meditate. The only chance we have is for me to confront Jargono with all my heart and strength."

Vaughn pulled up a stool in front of the paintings and as he did so he realized how much they comforted him. He remembered how Mafferan had told him that Vaughn had powers that he didn't even know he had, but now Vaughn knew and understood at least one. *The power of Justice … I don't know what else to call it, but I think that's what I have. I wonder what else is in me, besides the power of Justice. And what exactly is that? It's not really my power at all.*

"Spot, licking me doesn't change reality. Let me pray." Vaughn bowed his head. "Oh Lord God, You're Light and Love and Life … Understanding, Wisdom and Justice. I know that for You to be God, You have to be all these things together, because Your Power comes from the whole of what You are, not from any one part alone, because if any one part were missing, the others would not be what they are ..." His mind halted upon the profundity of his prayer, suspended somewhere—he knew not where—but he knew he had to continue, "I'm just a boy. I know very little. I didn't even know that I'm from a people whom You made special. My feelings are small, but they're all I have. At least grant that I fight this fight with all that I *do* have. If You could add to me what I need for victory, please do so. Stephanie is risking her whole life to protect Your Tree's seed, so surely You will protect her. Grant us defense against all evil ..."

And so he continued his prayers, his meditations, all that day and into the night. He didn't remember when he laid down and curled up with Spot to sleep, but he awoke at first light, feeling whole and resigned.

Standing in the cave entrance, Vaughn and Spot stretched. The air had an unusual crispness that carried upon it the mingled scents of burnt wood, morning flowers, and dampness from an impending storm. Vaughn couldn't take his eyes off of the sky.

Heavy, low hanging, dark gray clouds stretched everywhere, in various swirls and shapes that seemed to be standing still ... waiting... as if Sky and Earth had stopped time for an important consultation. The very thickness of the air seemed to carry this unintelligible conversation. No sky-blue at all in the whole sky then just under the clouds at the horizon a ball of golden fire literally connected Heaven and Earth. But as Vaughn beheld transfixed, that diminishing connection vanished. An odd combination of peace and heavy foreboding hung like the clouds in the sky. Vaughn had never seen nor felt anything like it. Secret and so mysterious.

❦

Yinauqua appeared beside Mafferan, as he looked through the golden vision. "My dearest husband, word has come that the Darkness has broken the rules."

He laughed with a smile, "When do they not?"

"But this time, it is no *small* thing."

Mafferan looked at his wife and raised an eyebrow in question. It was more a question about her underlying purpose.

She continued, "The dark three are no longer three, but just one!"

Mafferan turned very dark. "And what has this *one* done, now that he is *one*?"

"Nothing! Absolutely nothing, yet."

"You know Yinauqua, there's really nothing we can do because it will always be up to souls to freely serve God. We can't tamper and evil knows this. The days of overt presence of them and us are gone and we *must* stay that way for mankind's sake. Man must look within and not at outward manifestations. To bring those days back would be backtracking. We've walked a *very* thin line with what we've *already* done." He hoped that reminder would be firm enough even though he merely stated facts.

Yinauqua grew stern and impassioned while pointing through the golden tree's split visions of Stephanie and Vaughn. "*Mafferan!* There are precious few left alive that hold the world together. Those two down there are the strongest of them all. Stephanie is our long lost daughter and Vaughn has come back to the Lord God. That's simply tremendous. Evil *knows* how important they are."

He leveled his eyes into his beloved. "My wife, my Queen, if we fight for ourselves, we fight for nothing and shall cause those two to lose! Just because we've been up here for so long does not mean we automatically do right no matter what we do. We have to remain within the Light and the ways of faith and Goodness. Do you *not* think that all these things are sent by the father of Darkness to also tempt us? He lets his demons do many things but he would sacrifice them all if he could just tempt us to fall because then, in consuming us, he would bring forth so much more evil. *Please*, Yinauqua, you *know* this." He put his arm around her waist.

For the first time, ever since he joined her up here, she had tears, then her tears turned to weeping. She knew, Mafferan didn't. The rest of the last prophecy. But she could see it clearly, feel it down to her spiritual marrow. She remembered how he had cut her off so long ago, when she had told him: *When the faithwalker dies, hope dies with her, for there is no one left for whom the seed will grow.*

◦⁀◦

Just before dawn, Stephanie exited the lavish tent and went down to the stream to bathe, no longer caring if Jargono watched her. The sting of the unusually crisp air made her skin fill with bumps. The cold, fresh water chilled her to the bone but she ignored it. The sound of the stream that normally brought her inspirational feeling was just another sound.

The soap she lathered, smelled of lavender, but brought no cheer. As she rubbed the suds over her breasts, her hands also caressed the seed to the Tree of Life, the treasure Jargono so hotly pursued, there in open sight. When she finally stepped out of the water, she didn't immediately rush to cover herself but laid the towel over a low hanging branch and sat on it for a long time while brushing her hair.

She was naked, but it wasn't to Jargono that she bared her weakness. She was telling God how she felt inside. Finally, she put her undergarments on and donned her holy dress that she had washed out yesterday after Jargono had disappeared. She braided her hair into the three traditional Appendaho braids-of-salvation, and retied her long lost foremother's ribbon in the middle of the central braid. *I wonder what happened to her. I don't even know her name. If I live, I think I would like to ask Queen Yinauqua for it.*

This was the morning. Stephanie knew this was the day her whole life would be placed on the line to protect the seed to Tree of Life that God had entrusted to her through her ancestors. *No matter what,* she had learned that from Vaughn.

It's strange to see myself as I am now, then to think what I was, and then again what I am now. I think everything that happened to me, all the evil, all the good, even Vaughn, well, I think it was to prepare me for this very point in time! And yet, I know I can't win. Maybe, it's not about how I can't win but about how I'll die.

She sighed with strange tears running down her cheeks. They weren't exactly of sadness or regret but they weren't exactly numb either. They were tears of hope for the future that she had accepted she wouldn't have. Feeling the vibrancy of life beating within her as never before but that life would go unfulfilled. They were goodbye tears. *I will always love you, Vaughn. I only wish I could see you in person so you could see me in person, what I am now … so I could make you proud of me.*

All she had learned was not enough to beat Jargono. This she knew. She didn't know how but she knew it. Before she would betray the Tree of Life's seed, she knew she would die. And before she would die, she would use her own power to destroy the Seed. *It cannot fall into his hands!*

Vaughn… This is bigger than you, bigger than me, bigger than even both of us together. No matter what, I have to take the course of action that will give the best chance of defeating Jargono, protecting the Seed and hopefully finding a way to prevent the Black Oil from entering this world anymore. She sighed deeply, accepting that this was all her burden, no longer crying why it had to be her. *Reality is what reality is. I am the* faithwalker *… and I have to die* being *that faithwalker … even if I can't accomplish what I desire.* Stephanie decided how to make her last attempt to affect Jargono, now regretting she hadn't killed him when she had that narrow window of opportunity while his mind and heart were briefly addled by her before.

Nothing seemed to surprise him about her anymore, or rather he was getting used to always being surprised. When Stephanie arrived back at camp, Jargono had made sure everything was gone except for her pack, which he had slung on his back. After silently twirling her finger, telling him to turn around so she could add her brush and soap, she approached his back.

When he turned back around, he stared deeply into her but still couldn't read her and she knew this. Yesterday, she had spent a good bit of time manipulating her internal feelings, actually laughing when she imagined Jargono watching her tree, trying to figure out what was going on.

They traveled in silence. At one point, he even took her hand without her objection and she squeezed it, pouring love for him through it, hoping to wake him up. She imagined the good he could come to be, him turning away from evil and then understanding goodness. After a while, he let her hand go. When they came into the Appendaho Valley from the East, Stephanie could see the panorama of the sky and began her last attempt to sway him.

"Jargono, look at the sky. What do you see?" It was the first time she had spoken to him that day and her voice was a relief to him.

He spun around, taking in the whole sky, trying hard to please her. He answered with more cheer than he had ever felt toward such a question, "I see heavy dark clouds and a bit of sun that will not be there in a moment or two … but I see you as the sun of my life always!"

Her eyes were warm and loving toward him, and she took hold of his arm with affection. She knew, now, she could use her powers to extend her feelings into him, even as he had done to her, but she decided not to risk it. *My natural power of my feelings will have to suffice.* "Is that all you see?"

He wasn't used to such a stare, such a full, loving tone of voice. He was captured by it, without knowing by what he was captured but instantly loving it, yet nervously not knowing how to feel. *She's already done it to me again! First words out of her mouth, and she's done it again!* He was beginning not to like feeling so unsure around her all of the time, yet he also knew that much of his unsureness was just plain ignorance. He hated that even more. Ignorance was weakness for which he had little toleration. But being so close to the cave, he decided it was time for *him* to be the teacher and *not* her student.

Jargono took an instructional tone with her, "What else is there to see? Much of this world is … well frankly… boring. What do you see?"

As they kept walking toward the cave, she leveled her eyes into his, as deeply as she could naturally reach, to share her understanding, "Jargono, we're made of the same matter as the Earth and the sky and sun. All reality is connected. But there's consciousness in us, and if we think about it, our design is for conscious purpose. This is evident by the fact that the body is for the sake of the person, not the other way around. That's why a person's bodily needs can all be satisfied, but when their mental and emotional needs aren't met, they'll be miserable. However, many times people have suffered physically, yet been happy through their suffering. The body is for the sake of the person. And since all reality is connected, so, too, must all physical matter be for the sake of the consciousness that is greater than that bodily matter!"

Awed by her power with words and understanding for an outsider, he merely reiterated it, "You do have a way with words, but you don't need so many to say the obvious. The Powers are spirits." But once again, he didn't see where she was leading him.

"But you've said those powers don't have control over the physical world. Therefore, they're not the original consciousness because they can't directly touch all aspects of reality. They couldn't have made us. Since we're part of the physical world. also, that means we're not for the sake of *those* powers. *We're not supposed to serve them!*"

Jargono became ecstatic, amazed that she figured it all out! He took her by the arms. "*Wonderful!* You're right. But I know that, too. I figured that out, also, by myself."

Stephanie was ready to make her point and raising her eyebrows for emphasis, she took hold of his arms to help rivet his attention. "Then who or what is the *original* consciousness?"

Jargono simply delighted in her, beaming almost an actual physical glow. He longed to share his discovery with someone who would understand. He burst out with conviction and joy, squeezing her arms even tighter, "OH, YOU *ARE* GREAT, BUT I HAVE THE ANSWER … most would not believe it!"

Stunned, Stephanie's heart began to race, *Could it be?* She, also, grabbed his arms more tightly, pulling on them, looking and sounding very much like a little girl in loving expectancy, and she begged, "Really? Tell me …"

Recognizing this as a profoundly special moment in his life, Jargono straightened proudly and declared, "WE ARE! We are the original consciousness!"

Stephanie's hope quickly turned to dismay that she frantically fought to hide, employing for that purpose a certain instant numbness that hit her with his answer but her grip on his arms still loosened. All she could say was, "Huh?" And it was clear her emotions had drastically shifted and there was no making up for it.

Jargono could see that she hadn't gotten as far in her metaphysics as he had in his, but that was O.K., because it was amazing to him that she'd even gotten this far. *I'll have to teach her the rest.* "Originally, I think *man* was *the* Power, but something happened, and he lost it. After all, you said it yourself, *we* connect the physical and the spiritual. *We* are able to influence both aspects of reality. But I was born with some of what had been lost." He looked, again, deeply into her, wondering if he could trust her with his heart. "Now, I will share with you my dream. I intend to regain the *whole* power!" His look was as honest as any could be.

Stephanie's heart sank into the pit of her stomach as she saw that he believed completely in what he was saying. It would be of no use to continue her attack. *He's spent years developing his philosophy. I simply can't undo it in an hour ... perhaps even never ... perhaps.* But she had to ask, "How will you do that ... become the *whole* power?"

Jargono gave her a coy look as he turned and led her into the village square, but then he stopped her there, gently turning her by her shoulders to face him. "We shall see. Patience is important for such a great goal." He stared into her rich brown eyes, the same color as his. "But let's climb up to the cave now ... only ... I have a request of you, first."

Stephanie felt drained. Her hopes having been quickly lifted up to the verge of becoming fulfilled, only to be dashed to the ground, shattered to dust. Her attention waned as she inquired, "What is it?"

Jargono looked away at first, then with difficulty showed her his heart. "Will you let me kiss you, and will you kiss me back? I find … that I have a feeling for you … that I don't really understand."

He asked her permission! She could see his genuine vulnerability but she also knew that his timidity could turn in a flash to brutality. She remembered her father, and that she was used to mad men … but perhaps there was still a way into Jargono, if not through his mind then perhaps through his heart. *Perhaps … But to kiss him like he desires would mean that I really have to… Oh no, I can't refuse him! Those feelings he has may be the key. I have to do what I can, oh God, with all that I have … no matter what.*

CHAPTER SIX

No Matter What

Rushing down the narrow, dark, centuries-worn, stone stairway into the damp, lantern-lit basement, Benjamin almost tripped on several uneven steps. Rabbi Hertzog smelled the clamoring middle-aged man's fear even more distinctly than the burning oil or mildew.

"Rabbi, the Muslims will be at the walls by this very evening. We must flee west, now!"

"What do you fear?" Came the aged Rabbi's calm reply.

"What do I fear? What do I fear?" Reiterated Benjamin.

"I'm old, but I'm neither deaf, nor daft and I don't need you to repeat the question, just give an answer!"

"First, those crazy, crusading Christians come to torture, rob and impoverish us. Now, the Muslims return to do the same thing and you ask what do I fear?" When his question met with the Rabbi's glaring eyes and silence, the younger man felt the need to answer, so throwing open his arms, he added, "I don't understand. The crazy Christians claim one God, the fiendish Muslims claim one God, and we claim one true God …" Benjamin shook his head then went further, "and just look at the shape we're in! What God then?!"

Rabbi Hertzog grabbed the man with his gnarled, bony hand, jerked him to just inches away, eye to eye. Then with some force unknown, the Rabbi hurled him against the cellar wall where the man thudded and shrunk to his knees in terror. With the Rabbi's bony finger now inches away from his face, the Rabbi spoke calmly, "Don't you ever, ever, judge God by what men do with His blessed name, or do with anything else that God has so graciously allowed us to use."

Spot began to growl even before they came into sight. It was that dog sense the old farmer warned Vaughn about, telling him it could save his life. But this growl was qualitatively different from any other. A growl of knowing, warning for sure, but, also, perhaps vengeance within that knowing?

Vaughn stood back from the cave entrance and peered past the village square to the valley's entryway. Now that the huge overhang was gone, he knew he could be seen if he wasn't careful. Vaughn espied Stephanie pointing to the sky, talking to Jargono. That sight brought to mind how Stephanie had done the same with him while back home on top of the hill while they sat under the oak tree, when she showed him her vision of the wholeness of Life and Creation. Now Vaughn saw Jargono spinning around then replying to her.

At seeing Stephanie, Vaughn's arms longed to hold her, he longed to run up to her. Vaughn had traveled almost two thousand miles and with every mile his desire had intensified. As soon as he saw her, it was as if a door opened in his heart and mind and he could feel everything about her as she loomed closer.

Vaughn watched her tightly grab Jargono's arms, sensed her deep affection for Jargono and a sick feeling began to edge its way into Vaughn. He felt her amity toward Jargono, there was no mistaking it. He observed Jargono's joy over her and Vaughn could feel the depths in which she communicated with him, depths he recognized and shared only with her. Vaughn looked away.

Spot, in between low growls, began to whine but Vaughn paid no attention to his dog. Finally, Vaughn picked his head back up to witness Jargono turn her by her shoulders to face him, and he noticed how Jargono held her so warmly. Vaughn felt Stephanie hesitate ... then ... he felt her ...

Vaughn began talking to Spot without realizing it, as if in a daze. "I see, Spot ... I see. And she's kissing him of her own choice." Vaughn's heart knew what it perceived, no doubt about it. She had come to love Jargono! Tears were streaming down Vaughn's cheeks. His gut had terrible pain, he even trembled.

Spot kept listening to his master, as Vaughn found he could only think if he talked out loud to his faithful pet, "But ... I know Stephanie ... I don't understand ... I could understand her trying to fake a kiss with him ... but ...that was the real thing.... I can *feel* it! Oh God, help me!"

Vaughn paused but distinguished no answer. "Faith. Mafferan said I had to have faith beyond my understanding ... but I've *always* been against such a lie. Besides, I *know* what I'm looking at, I can't call it anything different. *That* kind of faith doesn't make sense. All my prayers and meditations, Oh God, didn't prepare me for *this!* Is it possible that Stephanie has changed? How do I go on living? I can't fight alone … I just can't. Everything that's meaningful to me … just died!"

Vaughn hung his head weeping, leaning back against the cave, no longer caring. Everything seemed to be connected to his love for Stephanie, even the seed to the Tree of Life, but now everything just died.

Spot *ruffed* repeatedly but Vaughn ignored it so Spot bit him on the leg! Vaughn jerked up, looking into his doggy face. Something about his doggy expression caught Vaughn. It was urging, even challenging, expecting, waiting, depending. Vaughn narrowed his eyes at Spot then began to nod his head. It appeared to Vaughn that the dog actually had meaning and that Spot's doggy life brought him back to his senses.

"NO! I'm thinking wrongly. Both Stephanie and I decided we would *first* live for Love, so that we could love each other truly. If she's changed, I must *still* honor that which we had. I must keep my word because it was *true*…. Did she change? That kiss was a *real* kiss. Only love. I sensed no evil, no lust in that kiss. It was *not* a kiss like she might have given before she met me, but … neither was it like one such a wicked man would desire. But … he accepted it. Is she trying to change him? Did she? She couldn't … wouldn't abandon her love for me. But … she doesn't know I'm here. Oh God, *now* is not the time for me to be confused. They're coming."

Vaughn knew, as they disappeared out of sight, that in about a half-an-hour or less, they would be at the cave. A mere thirty minutes max to try to resolve something like this! It was impossible and he knew it. Shattered like the stone he had pushed off the cliff, he prayed, "*Lord God, help me, please. I must honor You always first,*" he begged, but no answer came.

☙

She was in tears, begging him to let her go, "Mafferan please, *please*, let me go to him!" But he held her with more than his spiritual arms. He held her with his power.

"My love, please don't make me restrain you. You cannot go. The Light is not sending us. There is a difference between even our love and that of the Light. We must wait. We cannot fight his battles for him."

"But you sealed the cave," she wept.

"The Spirit of Justice allowed it to be so. Which part of the Light now sends you to him?"

She fell against him, weeping hysterically. "Only my own love, my husband, just my *own* love."

Mafferan found that he, too, had tears. He had done something up here that he had never done in life down there, he had restrained another soul against their will and it was the soul he loved most. But he knew that ultimately, she would have wanted him to. She would have wanted his strength to take over where hers failed.

☙

Jargono sensed a presence in the cave and wondered how someone could find his way all the way up here. He spoke gleefully to his future wife, just before they entered the Sacred Cave, "Well, it seems that we have a squatter in our cave, my bride to be."

A terrible, sinking feeling overcame Stephanie as soon as she heard Jargono's words and as she entered, her eyes confirmed her dread. Such a possibility had come to her yesterday. Somehow, he *always* showed up when she needed him most. *But I don't want you here!* Too much went through her heart and mind and all at once, choking off her ability to focus but through her light headedness and immobility, she heard herself wail, "No!"

Her defenses now down, Jargono briefly read her mind and Vaughn's and continued with his joy. "This must be Vaughn." Jargono flashed an amiable smile.

As Vaughn continued to straddle a wooden chair, with his arms propped atop the back of it and the royal pictures just behind him, he matched Jargono's friendliness. "I see you've heard of me."

"Oh, Stephanie has an open mind!"

The levels of his meaning were not lost on Vaughn, sensing right away Jargono's utterly devious and perceptive nature.

Their eyes fully met. It was an eternal moment for them both. At that instant, they knew that in some strange way, they were familiar with each other's depths ... and stranger still, those depths sought a kind of bonding ... but both quickly rejected that propensity. Vaughn selected which level of Jargono's meaning he wanted to address, as he locked his eyes upon Jargono's. "And what did you see in that open mind?"

It tickled Jargono's fancy to see this outsider staring into his eyes, most instantaneously averted Jargono's stare after the briefest of contact. He played along, realizing Vaughn's ignorance and met Vaughn's gaze with polite explanation and confidence. "That you confused her, but I can tell that she's beginning to understand now."

Stephanie read Vaughn's face and saw that he believed Jargono. She couldn't believe he had lost faith in her! She uttered without realizing, "No!"

Jargono turned toward her, raising an eyebrow, "What is it my future bride? Are you turning me down?"

The trap snapped shut... and she couldn't even allow herself to wince with the pain of it. Stephanie's mind froze, her heart became a maelstrom, but her visage was as blank as she could make it when she whispered, "No."

Her answer ripped through Vaughn as final confirmation and Stephanie saw what she'd done to him.

Falling, falling... through the blackness... endlessly falling. Jargono read more of Vaughn's mind, picking what would be most fun for him, while still being affective. Jargono squared himself and deepened his voice with a more manly tone, "You see, *boy*... why don't you run along? I want to spare Stephanie more confusion and pain. If I killed you, well, she's not quite ready to accept that, not *yet*. But she *would* understand if you *forced* me to."

His words snapped Stephanie out of her stupor. Vaughn noted that Jargono somehow picked the phrasing that would be most personally irritating to him. He also recalled Jargono's previous words, *Open mind*, and all their implied levels of meaning seemed to rebound off each other in Vaughn's head. But regardless of Stephanie's mind, Vaughn knew what he had to do to stay true. The old farmer had taught him, *Dying doesn't matter. It's how you leave that's important.*

There was no longer any need to hold back. Now, images of the dead Appendaho danced in Vaughn's mind, dancing and chanting in an ancient tongue all together around a sacred fire. They beckoned him to avenge them, their blood still running from their bodies. Jean's account of what Stephanie had described of their slaughter filled his ears. Vaughn's eyes went pitch black. Spot whined and eased away ... but Vaughn remained silent.

Jargono noticed the boy's anger, felt it radiating toward him and he had to restrain himself from laughing. Vaughn looked toward his love.

Stephanie's mind implored but only she could hear her pleas, *Oh God, just go Vaughn*. Please, *just go. I'm begging you. LEAVE ME!* Then, as she looked into the depths of Vaughn's eyes, she realized why Vaughn had lost faith in her. She secretly gasped inside, but couldn't restrain herself from holding her stomach. *OH GOD, Vaughn saw me kiss him! I can see it in his eyes. Worse, he* felt *it! I* know *he did. That terrible pain in his eyes. I'm responsible for making him lose faith. Oh God, he doesn't want to live!*

Vaughn could see her guilt, that guilt being further confirmation that she had betrayed him. And now Stephanie could see that her reaction only deepened Vaughn's misjudgment.

Finally, Vaughn uttered his plea, his first words to Stephanie as he turned his palms out toward her, "Stephanie ... Stephie?" It was all he could say as he silently thought, *I can't believe I'm being rejected like* this. *He called me, 'Boy!' And she gave* no *indication against that insult. How could she abandon me like* this, *throw me back like everyone else has done.*

Stephanie felt Vaughn's thoughts and her heart pounded so hard she could hear it in her ears. She had to *think*. She had to save his life. She scolded herself bitterly, *DO SOMETHING*, remembering Arlupo's words, *Would you honor us more so if you failed? THINK Stephanie, THINK! OH GOD, I have to act.* Words came from her mouth and she listened to hear what she was saying, "I've … I'm sorry, Vaughn! You … *have to go!* I want you to understand. What we had *through our prayers* … is … what we had. They're just prayers, that's all. *Do you understand?*" She blurted out, unable to restrain her tears, and she hollered, *"JUST GO!"*

Vaughn stood motionless as he entered into another eternal moment. Jargono heard the words he wanted to hear and his heart sung with sweet victory. But Vaughn was in his moment, listening to her words over and over again. He grasped the way she said them, hearing not just the words but also the way she meant them. The Appendaho were people of direct meaning. He recollected their fight right after they learned Gary lived, how he ran away from her, the pain in her eyes at his leaving, and his confusion then. *We almost failed each other before, because we were so* painfully *sure each was leaving the other … but we were wrong*! He remembered how she earnestly prayed the last time they were really together, how she transported him into a reality of peace he had never known, how she called back to him with such certainty, *through our prayers,* as she walked away. *Through our prayers. Our secret so we could always trust our communications were true. Why use that phrase now? To assure me that what we* had *was real, but* not *now? She didn't say,* was, *but is what we had. To convince me that what we* really *had, we have no longer? But if it was real back then, because it is what we had, then …* Feeling the realness of what they had, he intently looked upon her, past her blank face. It could never really be blank to him. He saw that same virtue in her that he knew was her, *is* her. *Yes. That same virtue, even more so. True, they are* just *prayers, no more, but no* less. *They would never be less to Stephanie. Never!* Her oft repeated words flashed in his heart and mind: *Ever since your head popped in that window in answer to my prayers and you saved me that terrible night, I have found myself praying, always praying.*

This picture he now had of her conflicted with his picture of her betrayal. He seemed sure of both realities. *One of these pictures is a lie!*

Vaughn calmed himself and focused, understanding now what he had to do. He stood up from his chair, smiling at Jargono. In one way, Vaughn was relieved, but he didn't want that relief to take away from the power of his fighting. And he needed more time to regain his full strength. Jargono had no problem taking time to revel in his victory but Vaughn stalled even more by asking, "What did you do to her?"

Jargono tired of this game. He got what he wanted, and hated to waste further time on this *boy*. Still, if the goal was to have Stephanie appreciate him, there was yet advantage to gain from this. He told Vaughn the truth, "I allowed her to see me for what I am, that *I* am worth appreciating. And more than *you*."

Hearing such ironic pretentiousness out of Jargono's own mouth seemed amazing to Vaughn. Standing there, looking at Jargono, at this heinous man, Vaughn suddenly felt very foolish for ever doubting Stephanie ... then he felt utterly foolish, period. *I don't want to die anymore!* Vaughn straightened, remembering Mafferan's confession of dishonestly wanting to die, and Vaughn feeling convicted by that memory as well, he made an oath, *If I die, it will be honestly, bravely, and not to escape the pain of living, the pain of loving.*

The more Vaughn looked into that wretched fellow, the angrier he got in realizing to what extent Stephanie had to bend for him. He remembered Mafferan's letter and the new love it kindled in him as he read it. Not only did he love Stephanie as the person he knew, he also loved her now for that noble person who was thought about thousands of years ago and so much that she was entrusted with the fate of the world's most precious treasure. *She is truly someone to protect.* Since reading that letter, he had felt an urge to kneel at her feet and proclaim, *My Queen.*

A tear crept into the corner of Vaughn's eye. *To think Jargono almost tore us from each other … Unbelievable!* Vaughn again gazed deeply into his queen. *Fear! … Oh God, I see fear in her eyes!* Suddenly, her torment flooded him. *She would sacrifice herself to protect me, and she would die to protect…* He cut his thoughts off. *I can feel that bastard probing me somehow.*

The cry in Vaughn's depths had never been fuller, and the answer was immediate as blackness enshrouded him. He looked inside himself, embracing the depths of this power's meaning. Once gaining that fully, Vaughn spoke with deliberation as he rubbed his adolescent beard, never taking his ebony eyes off Jargono. "I see…appreciation … for you." Then Vaughn returned his gaze to her. "Stephanie, I understand … *Just* prayers. Reality is what reality *is.*"

From the way Vaughn replied, Stephanie discerned he might just have picked up on the true meaning of what she'd said.

A tear came to her eye, her heart aching for him to no longer believe she'd betrayed him, hoping he understood the terrible sacrifice she was about to make. She reinforced her meaning that she was so sorry they couldn't be together. "Yes, Vaughn. I'm *sorry*, but that will *always* be true." Stephanie used all of her strength to keep herself from collapsing, her answer finalizing her decision to give herself to Jargono. *I have to ... If I'm to have any chance at all to defeat him and all the other evils ... I have to.*

Vaughn's eyes radiated blackness as he answered his beloved, "I'm sorry, too, Stephanie, but I am afraid that I gave an oath and I *must* be true to it."

Stephanie's eyes widened. *This doesn't sound like he understands! He's supposed to GO!* Her voice became cautionary. "Vaughn, there are things you are way too young to understand. Jargono has showed me just a bit of things much greater than you or I could imagine. *You must go, NOW.*" Never before had she sounded demanding to him, but she was every bit demanding now.

Jargono began to feel left out so he interjected, "I'm afraid, my *boy*, that the Lady has asked you to go, so you better run along." Jargono gestured walking fingers and Stephanie secretly groaned inside.

Vaughn, not taking his eyes off Jargono, squared himself. "Like I said, I gave an oath. You are responsible for all those that died." He nodded toward the cave entrance.

When Stephanie heard his words, she was shocked. *How could he know?*

"I and her father, we did a beautiful piece of work." Jargono knew the boy was going to try to fight him and he knew

Vaughn was going to die. "You should have just sacrificed like you were supposed to do! Maybe none of it would have been necessary! You, alone, might have solved the problem and I wouldn't have had to kill all of them to get what my future wife is about to give me!" Jargono shook his head remorsefully, "Needless death! But the Black Essence must be contained. I just can't have all these people blowing up from the inside out, and besides, I promised a solution."

Vaughn's eyes went distant, remembering… *Sacrifice! That voice over my bed. I recognize it now. It was him!* A larger picture began to flood Vaughn as he recalled talking to the voice in the cloud … but he knew he didn't have time to be distracted now. He saw Stephanie's incredulous eyes widen even further.

Stephanie thought she had determined how events would unfold but now… *Black Essence! The people blowing up! Sacrifice? What's he talking about? They've never met… have they?*

Still staring at Jargono, the sub-rule of the twenty-first rule to the *Art of Fighting* now merged again with him: *If the cause is just, better to sacrifice oneself in battle than in surrender.* It was from the last book in that fighting series—the seventh, *Advanced Future*—the one he had yet to teach Stephanie. This was the rule that had determined him to fight the demon in Tracy.

Vaughn remembered that one word, *Sacrifice,* that was spoken to him out of nowhere right before Tracy's battle. Suddenly, he realized that, too, was Jargono's voice, so this scoundrel must have had something to do with Tracy's demonic possession. *He had wanted me to be possessed, not her!* Vaughn's anger even intensified. *Just pawns? That's all we are to you?* He recalled Jargono's words from the cloud over his bed: *True power can only come from true sacrifice.* The cloud had vanished right after!

"I *remember* your voice! Sacrifice? Only *true* love brings true sacrifice, just as only the *Lord God* can deal true *vengeance!* You know *nothing* of the first, but you *shall* know the second! There are things here greater than *you* understand, Jargono. Stephanie, now that I do understand, it's OK... Really... But, I gave my oath." Vaughn heard words pounding in his head: *Love, Justice, Anger, Understanding, Faith, Wisdom and Life.*

Stephanie's dread escalated. She could see and feel something terrible building in Vaughn that she never saw the likes of before in anyone. Still, she knew this could be no match for Jargono. Stephanie's thoughts raced, as her heart felt like it would come out of her chest. *I thought at first that he understood, but then why does he keep going on about some stupid oath? What oath? Oh God, NO!* She knew Vaughn was about to attack Jargono. She cried out to stop him, "Oh Vaughn, NO! PLEASE..."

Spot crept even further away. Vaughn's heart and mind were set into one purpose. Fulfill all goodness, fulfill his oath, fulfill his love, fulfill his anger, *embrace Justice.* He ran at Jargono. Stephanie, with hands on her cheeks and eyes never wider, moved quickly aside.

Jargono spoke, but at the same time reaching out with his mind, "Not so fast, *boy.* W*ha* ... *?*"

Vaughn tackled him! His impact hurled them both to the cave floor. Their physical collision was only matched by the bolt of surprise Jargono felt! Vaughn had leapt upon him, grabbing him by the throat! As they tumbled backwards, Vaughn could see the astonishment in Jargono's eyes but Vaughn also felt his mind being invaded from the start. Yet, he was singular in his purpose and he knew he had an advantage and had to press it for all it was worth.

Frozen in terror and also in shock, Stephanie shrieked, "VAUGHN!"

Vaughn knew he couldn't win a protracted battle. He tried to work his fingers in, to rip out the wind pipe but Jargono used his power to physically strengthen his neck. And, yet, severe pain stabbed him and then something Jargono hadn't met before bit him. *Fear!* He felt his attacker's choke hold breaking through his power!

"I *swore* to avenge their death!"

Jargono recovered from his shock of this outsider getting as far as he did. Fear had the ability to wake one to reality. Fighting back hard, Jargono twisted and rolled over to put Vaughn underneath.

Stephanie still couldn't believe it. *Oh God, could this be happening?*

"You're strong for a *runt! You* must have buried them."

Vaughn rolled back again on top, but couldn't clutch as he wanted and had to change tactics. "That I did, as I will bury *you!*" He punched hard at his opponent's face but Jargono saw it coming so the blow caught him on the side of his head instead.

As they tumbled across the cave floor with Stephanie still in stark terror but with hopes daring to grow, Jargono began to tire of this game. Vaughn managed to hit him hard in the jaw and Jargono's head snapped back against the cave floor, jarring him. Stephanie remembered the last time Vaughn had fought to save her life. *He's got so much more power now. Maybe ...*

Jargono tried again to invade Vaughn's mind and couldn't believe what was happening. "What *are* you? How can an outsider..."

Vaughn, still struggling to stay atop him, punched Jargono low in the gut. His blow emphasized his reply, *"Outsider? The Tree of Life does not belong to people, but people to it!"* Vaughn hit again with emphasis. "And I hold *tightly* to it." The words Vaughn remembered from his old farmer friend and the meaning he understood, now more than ever, quite clearly for himself.

Stephanie couldn't believe he knew and she loved him even more upon hearing those words. *How does he know such things? Oh God, should I use my powers to help him? But what would I do? Oh God, I can't yet risk revealing myself...*

Jargono had heard enough from this *boy* and yelled in anger, *"ENOUGH!"* From seemingly out of nowhere, the thing Stephanie dreaded most appeared. The small, open black bottle suddenly swung into his hand. Its thick black content streaked across the side of Vaughn's face. Its horrible smell was only matched by Vaughn's screams as he rolled off Jargono, writhing in agony.

Vaughn twisted across the floor with the contortions of a worm impaled upon a fish hook. Stephanie, with dashed hopes, now cringed with Vaughn's every scream. With his every painful twist, her gut wrenched. Her feet kept attempting to move for him, but they wouldn't. Weeping within, she silently begged for Vaughn's pardon. *Forgive me, Vaughn, but I can't help you! Oh God, our lives are nothing compared to what's at stake.* And as little by little Vaughn died, Stephanie died inside, as well. Her knees became weak as that awful word spat inside her thoughts, *Sacrifice!* She had a new hatred for that word, and yet a deeper love. She wanted to look away, but she couldn't. She wanted to die, but dared not. *I am the faithwalker. I must not put* anything *above the greatest good. Oh God! ... but why do I have to let him die? Why do I have to watch?*

Jargono sneered as he quickly rose with triumph and malice and he headed for Vaughn to settle the battle for good. *Almost doesn't count,* he laughed again to himself.

Stephanie steeled herself to accept Vaughn's death, or, at least, she tried. She had made up her mind what the best course of action *had* to be, and again she tried to look away but couldn't.

Jargono's sadistic laugh foreshadowed impending murder, impending victory. That unrestrained, boastful chortle penetrated Stephanie's every fiber while she repeatedly told herself, *Sacrifice is the best course of action, sacrifice is....* But that wicked, wretched laughter galled her and her heart's revulsion began breaking her mind's bonds, even as her mind tried clamping her emotions down, even as Vaughn's death began to hollow her out inside.

As Jargono reached for Vaughn's throat, at the threshold of his triumph, Stephanie couldn't help but look away. But neither could Stephanie's heart stand such violation any longer, her heart would have none of it *anymore.* Being too late this time was not an option. Fire burst in her eyes and all through her as flames seemed to leap from all over her body. She couldn't contain her power anymore. It overwhelmed her.

"VAUGHN!" Stephanie wailed as she threw her hand out toward Jargono and an invisible force hit, slung him through the air and crumpled him against the opposite cave wall, against the pictures yet to be explored.

Ꮹ

The glowing netting began to flicker. Demon Glen felt the pain of it almost disappear. He began to reach out to rip it open, but a voice called to him.

"Don't touch it, or he'll know." It was his teacher. "How am I to escape then?"

"Use the power I've said you have. You're part of the Earth, but part of the Ethereal. You may travel freely in both realms. Go now while the power of the netting is not strong enough to keep you in. *But remember to return as soon as I call you.*"

"Why should I return?"

"You are but a child to us, even smaller. It would do you well to respect your elders. If Jargono sees you've escaped at all, he'll search for everywhere you've been and destroy all your offspring before they have a chance. I told you, you must be patient. Keep secret what you do."

"But what good is it to return? He'll surely suspect I've traveled away when he finds me outside his prison."

"Don't let him suspect you've been out then. The netting's power is designed to keep you from leaving, not from entering! You'll be able to rematerialize back within your prison even though the netting is at full strength."

Demon Glen scowled. "You want me to submit myself to more humiliation and prison *again* after I get free?"

The voice spoke kindly, gently: "You are always free to do as you desire, as am I. You will not be the only Earth demon. And no one will object if I consume you off the Earth!"

"I don't think you have that capability!"

"The knowledge you possess from our primal essence is infantile, but if you wish to go it alone, so be it." Demon Glen became silent. The voice continued, "I will accept that your silence is wise. Go to the village I've told you of. Focus on the images I've transferred to your mind and you'll materialize there. They've been waiting for their god to come to them for a long time! You're it! I know you'll mate with as many as you're able but do so only with humans. For now, anything else is a waste and a risk, since animal nature is not a thinking nature. If animal hybrids are discovered, it will lead to your offspring's destruction. Mate only with humans who will wisely protect your children. But be back the *instant* I call to you, no matter what you are doing."

Demon Glen vanished.

೮౦

With grief squeezing Stephanie to breathlessness, she ran to where Vaughn was slowly ceasing to writhe because his consciousness was slipping into a place of doom. As she held her hands out just about to touch him, she withdrew them, then she approached again but withdrew again, not knowing what to do. She heard Vaughn whisper through his agony.

"No, no… so sorry." Vaughn's words trailed away.

And then Jargono spoke with an unusually super pleasant voice," Well, this day is *full* of surprises! You've been hiding from me!"

Stephanie glared towards him. He was smeared with the same black oil that he poured upon Vaughn. She cast her hand out at Jargono again, felt the invisible force leave her hand, cross the cave, and hit him full force. But he merely smiled. Her power had no affect at all.

Jargono felt betrayed. He couldn't begin to express his anger, and how *stupid* he felt… and he had never felt stupid in his whole life.

"I'm afraid you have a lot to learn but … ahh, no time to learn anymore."

❧

Way past hysterical, Queen Yinauqua struggled to break free from her husband's arms, fighting him hard. "We can help them! We can help them! *Why* won't you *help* them?" she cried.

Mafferan managed to speak while his heart was breaking for those down below, and for his wife here above. "Do you want to break the most fundamental of rules?"

"*Rules,*" she said in anger, "They have *already* broken them."

"But not like you want to do. You would open the Earth up to be a full battle zone between us and the Ethereal. But for us, the humans must still freely make the choice to serve. No human being's soul could survive such an open battle, being forced by ethereal powers they can't even begin to imagine. And it would be far more an open war than ever before … while mankind is still weaker than ever."

Yinauqua buried her head into his chest, weeping over and over. "She's our long lost daughter! … she's our daughter… After so long… after so long… then *she's going to die, too? And worse…* those taken by the oil of corruption can't come up because it prevents their choice! She'll be *lost* in that eternal torment… and so will Vaughn! *Lost!* Do you *hear* me? *LOST!*"

Yinauqua could still feel Stephanie from when they hugged. Her arms ached to hold her now. She could feel her daughter's suffering and there was little choice but to react as she did. Feeling for life, be it mortal or otherwise, is feeling for life.

Mafferan knew his wife was right about the Black Oil. He wasn't even sure of the value of their sacrifice because after their death the Earth was sure to fall completely to evil. One moment he was sure not to intervene but the next he wavered, until, finally, her weeping uncontrollably in his arms moved his heart to tip over his better judgment. He extended his hand toward the golden vision to give in to his wife before it was too late, but then he remembered how terribly hopeless he had felt when he was mortal, and yet, somehow, he had overcome. He called back his power just before he would have released it, lowering his arm and tightening his grip around Yinauqua. Weeping with her, he spoke his thoughts aloud, "I know… I know *Heaven is not like what people on Earth believe. We are all free up here. And we love their life down there, just as we love Life up here.*"

☙

"I'm afraid you have a lot to learn, but … ah, no time to learn anymore."

"No matter, you've been a *very good teacher*." Stephanie's eyes blazed with her full power and then some. Seeing this, Jargono wondered greatly at the girl. She pointed to the ground beneath him and it opened then swallowed him up! "*And* you underestimate the power of goodness." She turned back to her beloved, begging. "Vaughn, come back to me! Vaughn ..." But her frantic petitions were cut short with a scream.

Jargono grabbed Stephanie from behind by her main hair braid then yanked her up. He could have snapped her neck right there but he still wanted the Sacred Object. He dragged her by her hair to the wall with the royal paintings then slammed her face and body up against it. She could taste blood and feel it cover her face even as the impact dazed her. The pain had yet to set in but when he pressed into her tightly, her whole being revolted in agony. He couldn't believe this mere child played him for a *fool*. He promised she wouldn't live to tell anyone she had.

Whispering in her ear in a menacing tone, "Don't you know I'm at home under the ground? You *really* thought you could bury me alive? There's nothing you can do to me. *NOTHING!* And where do you get such *power?*" Then he eyed the painting of the Queen and focused back at her. "Could it be? Sister? Eh, it doesn't matter. *Give me what you took from the box.*"

Still gripping her hair, he ground her face hard into the wall but Stephanie no longer cared. Vaughn lay dying or perhaps dead already and she would just as soon join him. She thought about trying to use her powers again but she honestly just didn't know what to do. She could feel Jargono's power all around her, as if holding her own power in. He wasn't a demon so she figured the spiritual attack she used on them wouldn't work but she began to try anyway. She started to look away from all the danger.

Jargono pulled her back then smashed her against the wall again. "*Stop it!*" he ordered her. "Each time you begin to do that, I'll slam you until you won't even be able to think straight."

Amazed, Stephanie attempted to consider, *He knew what I was trying to do. He must have entered my mind when my guard was down... Oh God!* She threw her guard back up to block him from entering her mind any further,

"Damn, you realized. Give me what is *mine!*" He slammed her again.

Though her head throbbed in terrible pain now, Stephanie still managed to focus her will on keeping him from her secret. Somewhere, she could hear a girl's distant sobbing, she thought it might be herself as there could be no other girls around.

Stephanie's scalp seemed to burst as Jargono gripped her braid, using it like a rein to twist her head back and forth to grind her face repeatedly into the wall. She caught glimpses of her blood smeared across King Mafferan's picture as a strange weakness flooded through her. Realizing she would lose consciousness soon, Stephanie began to gather her will to destroy the Seed rather than risk Jargono discovering it. Unfortunately, he felt that power building in her and crashed her hard against the cave wall, yet, again. She passed out, probably just for seconds. Upon reviving, she immediately blocked her mind again and also deduced why she couldn't employ the same strategy against Jargono that she used to fight the demons, *They really weren't able to physically attack me in any meaningful way.* Physically speaking, it was far worse to be in Jargono's clutches than wrapped in even demon coils!

"Give me the Sacred Object and maybe I'll yet spare Vaughn."

She knew better. Through her agony, her head pounding, her whole body feeling death clawing at it, she thought, *There's no way he's going to let me live, and if he kills me, he* can't *let Vaughn live! And Vaughn's been the only one who's ever been able to challenge Jargono.* Stephanie didn't know how he even possibly did that. Suddenly, she felt so much pride in Vaughn. *It's time now… for me to die, too.*

With what little strength she had left, Stephanie scoffed at Jargono. "You want the Sacred Object? My mind is *open.* Why don't you *just go get it?!*"

How she had yelled at him in the store came to Jargono's mind. Her biting words now made him realize she'd never changed her feelings from the first time they met. Jargono leaned close to her ear again and pressed his whole weight against Stephanie's bruised body. "I thought you were really serious about my proposal. Do you have *any* idea how you have disappointed me?" *Just killing her isn't enough. First, I'll make her suffer, and then I'll take her body and soul into the Ethereal and give her to the Dark Powers so they can feast on her while she's yet alive… and I'll watch.*

Stephanie thought she knew just what to say to make him end all this for good but she had no clue about his plans for her. "Turn yourself to the Light and we can share the Sacred Object, and…"

She couldn't see what he was about to do to her because he still had her pinned against the cave wall. All Stephanie wanted now was to die, so her secret could die with her, but she never got to finish her sentence as Jargono took both her cheeks in his oily black hands. He kissed her mouth hard and deep, tasting her blood and relishing it. Jargono pressed his body hard against hers, holding Stephanie up against the wall as all her strength left. Smothering his mouth over hers so she couldn't scream nor breath, her nose having swelled from being smashed, Stephanie completely choked, both inside and out. When he finally let go, leaving black oily handprints across her face, she shrank to the cave floor in so much agony, mouth agape, but no sound came out, no breath was drawn.

Jargono spoke bitterly, "What's the matter, *my love*, can't deal with reality?"

Stephanie's every nerve fiber blazed in pain, every recess of her mind twisted in torment, every emotion became tortured by a searing emptiness. After a long, breathless pause, dear Stephanie inhaled reflexively with a gasp until her lungs could hold no more air and then she wailed a hideous cry which can only be described in myths and legends. She gasped again and repeated her cry with even more force! And then, again, but by then, her voice began to deteriorate. Jargono soaked up every bit of her suffering as pleasure. In fact, he became so engrossed in it that he thought of somehow prolonging it with his powers. *This is justice!*

Spot had been franticly hovering over Vaughn, licking his face, licking the vile Black Oil… until Vaughn heard Stephanie and came back to reality. Her screams pounded in his heart, igniting him with tremendous fire and rage. Deep red fire and pitch blackness both danced and swirled together in his eyes. As Jargono heard him coming from behind, he turned and caught a vicious left fist under the chin that hurled him over Stephanie. His back slammed into the picture of the King, and he fell to the ground with legs draped over Stephanie's writhing body.

As soon as Jargono hit the ground, a bottle slipped from under his right sleeve into his hand, and he threw its contents out toward Vaughn. But being perched for attack, Spot keyed to Jargono's motion and leapt at him, blocking the vile Black Oil from reaching his master. As the Oil streaked across his front white patch, Spot's mouth clamped down hard on Jargono's wrist. The dog landed on top of Jargono, viciously shaking the bitten arm. Jargono couldn't move away because of his awkward position atop Stephanie and could only curse Spot, "Aaahhh, damned *dog!*"

He wasn't accustomed to this much pain. He'd always been able to avoid it. Spot, growling like a lion, savaged the hand till the bottle flew out somewhere over and past Stephanie. Enraged, Jargono picked Spot off his lap and slammed this filthy dog over his shoulder into the cave wall. Spot let go of his wrist and fell down, reeling and yelping.

With rage intensified, yelling for his faithful dog, Vaughn kicked the vile bottle into the far corner of the cave. Now, without any ethereal tricks up Jargono's sleeve, it was just the two of them, with personal power against personal power, anger against anger, mind against mind, heart against heart. Vaughn reached across Stephanie, grabbed Jargono by his shirt and with one hand, pulled him over her then whirled, ducked and threw Jargono over his shoulder, slamming him onto his back.

Instinctively rolling away, dazed in spite of his power's protection, Jargono oddly realized he was fighting for more than just control, he was fighting for Stephanie, too! *This is all so very confusing!* Even though he didn't understand why, it made him hate Vaughn all the more. *And why can't I control his mind?* It was a question he knew he needed to answer. This kind of ignorance was dangerous.

Vaughn was stronger even though Jargono was a good five years older and taller. The boy was stocky, solid from all the hard labor he did. Jargono considered his best course of action, *Now is NOT the time to finish this war. There's much for me to learn from him … besides, this is kinda fun! I enjoy being challenged! Makes me feel even stronger!* He then projected into his adversary's mind the image of Stephanie's dying breaths.

Stunned by pain, Vaughn lost strength. Jargono leapt up with a left hook across the jaw and knocked Vaughn backwards. As Vaughn reeled from the blow, Jargono fled out the cave entrance hollering, "Tell that *bitch*, if she lives, I'll be waiting for her *sister* when she comes of age. You got lucky this time. Next time…"

Vaughn finished for him, "*I will fulfill my oath.*"

Spot knew the unconscious, red-haired girl was in bad trouble and that his master fought to protect her as she also did for him. He recognized her scent from the store and the trail. Spot crawled over to Stephanie while ignoring his own pain and began licking the Oil from her cheeks but… it was too late!

Her breathing stopped as Vaughn knelt beside her. There was nothing Vaughn could do but wait for Spot to clean off the Oil first. Clutching his stomach, retching from seeing and feeling his love, his life, his queen, dead on the cave floor from crushing evil, all Vaughn could do was repeat, "*No, no…no…*"

Gone. Just a bloodied, inanimate heap for a body. *Worse,* Vaughn had no sense of peace for her. And all that they had fought for, hoped for, prayed for … was *gone!*

When Spot finally finished licking, Vaughn tried to revive her. *Hasn't been that long,* he told himself. He breathed into her mouth, while he lifted her chin, tilted her head back, and held her nose. Her mouth was still warm, he could taste her blood. Her chest rose and fell with the two breaths he blew in. Then he straddled her and gave chest compressions just above the end of the breast bone, counting out loud—*One, two, three*—just as he had seen at the hospital. *It wasn't that long. It wasn't that long* … But he was dealing with more than stopped breathing, because there was internal trauma, too … and he knew she was gone and not coming back but he wouldn't admit it… couldn't admit it. Again—*one, two, three*—and again two more breaths, and again chest compressions—*one, two, three*—until he couldn't maintain the illusion any longer.

Finally… he stopped. There was a moment when Vaughn went dead calm … and then deep blackness enveloped him.… Roaring like a lion, with all his neck veins popping out, then wailing in unfathomable pain, he raised up his head, attempting to look into the beyond. "IS THIS JUSTICE? IS THIS WHAT SHE GETS FOR PROTECTING *THIS*?" In bitter rage, he tore open her holy dress to reveal the seed to the Tree of Life.

Vaughn continued his lament to God with arms outstretched, "What have we done to deserve this? How can

You let her die? How can You let her die for THIS, this SEED when this *seed* was supposed to be for OUR LIFE? What will it be NOW? There is no one to PLANT it now, except that *beast* who did this! I can never, EVER love anyone else… Take my life, too, then!"

Feeling betrayed, Vaughn went across the cave to find the Black Oil so he could drink it and die. He knew he had kicked it over into the corner somewhere but his weeping clouded his vision so he couldn't focus well, as he yelled, "*Where is it? WHERE…?*"

Spot, having cleaned all the cursed oil away, laid his head upon Stephanie's breast, whining softly. Vaughn sank to his knees, groped around the dark corner and finally felt the bottle at the foot of the demon's picture. He picked it up as he stared at the demon's visage. It seemed to be laughing at him! *Fine, then!* Vaughn raised the bottle to his mouth but images of King Mafferan's life and suffering suddenly came to his mind. They were what the King had transferred to him. *But Stephanie is* gone! *There's no more hope for me. The King at least had the hope to be with his wife.*

"I wouldn't do that if I were you!"

A voice! In the back of Vaughn's mind he knew that voice. Then footsteps close to him and a shadow pierced the torch light over him. Vaughn didn't want to be disturbed but couldn't help turning around, and then exclaiming in shock, "Trevor!"

The wiry lad stood above him, shaking his head in disgust. "You know, I had *just* been thinking I was *beginning* to respect you … and I want you to understand, I don't respect *anyone*

... never have." Trevor turned to look at Stephanie, and then back to Vaughn. Pointing at Stephanie he declared, "*Her* I respect! She died ... with meaning!" Trevor had never spoken such words, *ever*, and part of him even wondered from where they came, but he realized they really did come from somewhere inside himself. He began to reach for his cheek but the urge to rub it vanished.

Vaughn hoarsely answered this miserable wretch of a drug-dealer, "You have no right..."

But Trevor cut him off, "*I* have no right?" He scoffed at Vaughn, "*Look at yourself!* About to drink the devil's brew! *I'm the one who has no right? Who's worse, you or me?*"

Trevor turned away from Vaughn and went to Stephanie's side and Spot's eyes glanced up at him. Trevor's hand felt his arm where Stephanie had grabbed to pull him around and wish him well just before he'd left her and Jargono. He remembered the look in her eyes. *She cared! She really cared.* Trevor knelt down beside her, to get one last look at her face but her tangled, bloody hair was stuck there. Shaking his head, unfamiliar tears dropped from his eyes onto Stephanie's corpse. He reached out to the necklace she wore, and ran his finger lightly over something that Vaughn had called the Seed, not understanding its meaning. He turned back to Vaughn, still in that corner by the demon. "Go ahead! You're in the right corner! *Drink that damned stuff! Go ahead!* That's what she'd want you to do, right?" And Trevor got up to go but had to turn around just before exiting to murmur at Stephanie, "I wish to G— I wish I could have done something to help you ... I'm sorry!"

151

As Trevor made his way down the mountain trail, part of him cursed himself for following them up there, for watching, for not helping, and for even caring! *Why should I care?*

Trevor's words and his intrusion galled Vaughn but they made him think, *I don't want to die in this corner under this damned demon's picture,* so he went over and knelt beside Stephanie with the cursed bottle in his hand.

Vaughn bowed his head, speaking softly, "Stephanie, my only love, my Queen, I'm *sorry* I *failed* you. Please forgive me. I'm sorry I ever doubted you. I should be dead, not you." He raised the bottle to drink it and Spot howled, "HOOOOOO, HOOOOO, HOOOOO…"

Vaughn paused with guilt about leaving his dog, "I'm sorry Spot… I just can't. There are plenty of farms around here for you to go to."

Spot rested his head back upon Stephanie's breast with a long, mournful whine. Vaughn took one last look at the dead body but it didn't look like Stephanie. It is amazing how different a corpse looks from when there's life in the body. He also saw the Seed to the Tree of Life still around her neck, and thought, *How ironic this is!*

Then he bitterly cried aloud, "How *ironic!* Here you are, the Seed to the Tree of Life, *still* hanging around the neck of the DEAD girl who gave HER life to protect YOURS! … Is this Justice? How can you let her die?"

Vaughn wept, still holding the bottle. "None of this makes any sense. If there is to be no sense in this world, then there is no reason to live in it." Vaughn began to gather his will so he could drink the oil and die. *What's the use of an oath to protect a Seed that won't protect us?*

Yet, heeding his thoughts and prayers, the spirit of the Seed to the Tree of Life beseeched God to hear Vaughn's heart. King Mafferan and Queen Yinauqua lamented. Lana and Jean somehow knew Stephanie had died, as they felt a terrible hole in their hearts, and they wept. Spot mourned for Stephanie and for his master, too.

But there are many things that happen in life to good people of which we as mortals have no understanding. Some things may be obscure even to immortals. Only a true *faith-walker* is able to see the whole picture and explain how the Greater Good has been served. Yet, at times, we who are mortals, in the pure integrity God has granted us, may petition for a change in circumstance and the Greater Good is served by answering our prayer. Sometimes the answer is as great a mystery as was the precipitous event.

Suddenly, the cave began to glow. Light shined through Vaughn's closed eyes making him feel *very* small. Daring to open them, he beheld the whole cave radiating brighter and brighter. Placing a hand on his pounding chest, he glimpsed Stephanie with the Seed beginning to glow until it looked like a mystical burning star. Shaking all over, Vaughn set the vile bottle far behind him and raised his hand to shield his eyes from its brilliance... then Stephanie began to glow.

Vaughn fought for his life as he felt his chest would rip open. He tried to keep focus as his consciousness faded, but then she coughed, snapping him back to awareness! Vaughn lowered his hand to see the Seed crumble to ash, leaving an empty gold chain! And Stephanie knew what had been done and mournfully asked Vaughn, "No, oh no Vaughn! *What have you done?*"

Scared by her question, her stare, and the seed crumbling to ash, he shrunk inside. He could barely speak, "I... I... prayed. That's all... I prayed."

But the *faithwalker* enlightened him. "Vaughn, that Seed was worth a million of me. *What have you done?*"

And Stephanie's feelings consumed her in one total picture of reality without the Seed of the Tree of Life. Stephanie rolled on her side away from him, weeping bitterly, feeling the utter loss of the hope of the Tree of Life for all mankind, the loss of true meaning. "*No, no, no... What are we without you? What are we? No, no...*"

Her fight, everyone's trust in her, the Appendaho's sacrifice, her sacrifice... all had been in vain, betrayed by the one she loved more than anything except for the Tree of Life. Betrayed because he who loved her prayed with all his heart out of his grief despite knowing the meaning of the Seed. And Vaughn wanted to die, because he couldn't comfort her and could see the harm he'd done, harm that surely could not cut any deeper. Nor could he fathom the further harm to all life.

Vaughn laid down on his stomach a few feet away from Stephanie, weeping as well, wondering if it might be better to have drank that bottle than to live.

Spot crept between them with mournful howls, as if saying a prayer for the dead.

CHAPTER SEVEN
Reality Is What Reality Is

A neutral room of neither dark nor light accommodated both demon and Saint. One of the three High Councilors pointed at the document setting on the table that Mafferan had materialized. "Fine ... when your Christ has left the Earth, we shall no longer invade it. But those of us who have dwelt there since time immemorial..."

Mafferan held up his glowing hand against the angry voice. It hushed the demon. "We will find them and cast them out."

Clearly further angered by such injustice, the demon's voice grated, "Then there is no truce, what balance ..."

Once again the glowing hand. "The balance is this. After the appointed time, we do not add our direct presence permanently but via cursory appearances only."

The demon demanded, "We shall extend our arm into our Earth because mankind must feel us in order to choose us, unless you are afraid man knows we are better than you!"

"Fine! We shall also extend our Spirit shall they call. The demons you still have on Earth are free to remain ... if they can avoid being found and casted out."

"Your word is the bond for all heaven, if you break the balance, the Earth is rightfully ours. If even just one of you breaks this word, you are all rightfully ours for you speak as one."

"My word is only as good as all the people."

"So be it. So let it be done."

Mafferan smiled and pointed, "Have your underling draw up all the nuances and we shall study it for ratification."

Underling HrorrarrAggrang reached over, took the document, bowed to all, and disappeared.

Highest Councilor ScrabaGag slowly shook his bulbous head from side to side. He had wondered how the *glow* would to try to get around all his traps. If the girl died, the Cursed Object has no more protector and the *glow* loses. If the *glow* interfered, breaking the rules, the Alphas win because mankind would certainly fear Alphas more than it could muster any love for *glow*, especially during direct confrontation. *Well, really, we win even when it's not direct. And if someone in heaven interfered in a sort of 'gray' way … Well, gray belongs to us. But right now, there are no ethereal rooms for rent. Nonetheless, I could be very accommodating in remodeling their realm!*

Yes, the now Highest and Only Councilor had planned for every possible deviation. He was now so close, so very close to destroying so much more than those two mere children. He couldn't help ruminating over it all. Yesss, love is definitely their weakness. Not since the Vile One *came to Earth through the* glow's *chosen, (hmm, the glow still owes us for that one) no Alpha in history has ever devised a scheme successful enough to tempt even the Tree of Life until now. Who would have thought it would take this way out? Since it gave its Seed's life up to bring the girl back, no balance was upset, so no ethereal demon can blatantly run loose on the Earth, No lost ancient monsters or the like can be brought back, unless an Alpha willingly gave up his life to bring them back. Ha! Not likely … NO, IMPOSSIBLE! But now there can be no more Earthly Tree of Life! Tsk, tsk, tsk…. Perhaps I ought to send a message of condolence to my lost glowing brethren. I so love it that they adhere so strictly to all the rules. Like I've always said, live by the rules, die by the rules. Yesss, a simple, polite thank-you-note is certainly in order.*

"Well, Grinchback. Isn't that just something else! Amazing … simply amazing. I was overjoyed to learn what the cursed object was, and those *poor* Appendaho kept it secret for so long. Who would have thought the boy would give it away, although I *really* thought his outcome would've been different. The actual manifestation of the spiritual Tree of Life, no less. I see it made the plan work that much better … actually perfectly … but to see it crumble to ash, just to save a mere, lone girl…!" ScrabaGag laughed long and hard. "Well, that I had not anticipated. But now, I'm not sure what all this means. This is new to all history and *there's not supposed to be anything new under the sun.*"

"But Master, neither has there been one such as you, ever! I'm not flattering, Sir."

Highest Councilor ScrabaGag folded his now very long tail several times around his neck and began tapping the end of it in his hand, while he appreciated his offspring's observation, considering it more acutely. "Hmm, true."

❧

Climbing down the mountain, Trevor cursed at himself while rubbing his cheek vigorously. *You shouldn't have even gone up there, you weren't supposed to.* But then he wondered, *Why am I addressing myself as 'You' instead of 'I'?* That was an odd question to come to his mind. *Saying the word 'you'... am I the one speaking or the one being addressed? Saying 'you' is like someone else is speaking to someone else! Why wasn't my thought 'I', not 'you'? I shouldn't have gone up there.*

Trevor shook his head at himself. He didn't care, but then again... this was indeed bothersome... for some reason. He was really never supposed to have followed Stephanie in the first place. He had been having such strong feelings to head north, not south, but he just had to follow her anyway. And he wanted to know more about Jargon. *OK... OK, I'll head north now. Fine! I need to get more supply, anyway. And I have to check on my sister and make sure I don't have to break her neck for getting into things she has no right to be into.* And there it was again, another oddity... *Why am I even talking to myself this way, as if I'm arguing with...? This is ridiculous!* Trevor rubbed his cheek so hard it hurt.

But his problem wasn't in his cheek. Trevor took both hands and rubbed his scalp vigorously, as if trying to expel something troubling him that he couldn't identify clearly. *I hate such complexities ... two more years of this crap, and then I'm taking Alyssa away from all this ... this ...*

❧

They didn't know how long they laid there. They didn't know how long they wept. It felt as if all life had drained out of them. But a stir in some recess of feeling, some whispered thought, brought Vaughn's head around to look at Stephanie lying on her stomach. Her face was still in her hands and her long, blood-matted red braids splayed over her shoulders and the cave floor. Her anguish pricked his heart.

Spot moved away and Vaughn rolled himself over twice to her side. He tried to draw her into him with an arm around her shoulder but she rolled on her side with her back to him, curling up into a ball. Vaughn slid his arm under her head for a pillow and cradled her as he brought his legs up against hers, smoothing back some hair that had escaped her braids so he could see her tear-stained, bloodied face.

So thankful she was alive, in spite of everything else, he took time to feel every fiber of her precious presence, his only thought being, *Treasure her.* Holding her now brought into him such peace that could only be rivaled by the actual presence of Spirit of God.

But during that long time he had laid there on the cave floor, he began to also understand things as never before. He began to realize the truth of King Mafferan's warning about faith. *It's not that true faith isn't always based on understanding, but we may not always have the understanding we need at the time. He never said I had to have faith in Stephanie without understanding, but that at the time I did not yet have the under-standing I needed to support the extra faith I would need. Perhaps it is so, even now!*

Yes! The more Vaughn thought about it, the more his heart told him that what they were now facing had to be another one of those times, and once he conceded this, a door opened through which precious comprehension began to flow. Now, he needed to help Stephanie understand, so that her faith could be whole again because there is no more miserable a sight than a *faithwalker* robbed of her faith.

"My love... why did it happen?"

Her voice was empty, "What... which... all?"

"The thing that you grieve the most."

She replied with bitter sarcasm, deriding herself, "The loss of the Seed I was entrusted to *protect* with my *faith?*"

Vaughn leaned over her shoulder to see her face better. He stroked her cheek lightly with his fingers, seeing she was bloodied but healed, and spoke tenderly, "Why do you say it like that? Why are you scorning yourself?"

Tears began to roll down her cheeks again, as she realized how so very good it felt to be in his arms, comforting her ... but she didn't feel entitled to feel good at all. "Vaughn, I failed. I was supposed to protect it. It's *gone*. You wouldn't have had to pray that prayer if I hadn't failed." She felt the deadness reawaken and knew she deserved only to feel shame.

Vaughn pleaded with his heart breaking because he knew her feelings and thoughts, "Stephanie, you did *not* fail! Please listen to me. If there was something you held back, something you failed to perceive when you should have, then perhaps you could say you failed. There is a difference between failing and being overpowered."

She twisted her head around to catch his eye, expecting pain, and realized for the first time that not only had her life been restored, but she had been healed as well but she continued to debase herself. "What *difference?* The Seed is gone.

I'm supposed to be a *faithwalker*. *Nothing* is beyond my potential. *I failed*. He brushed me aside like my faith was *nothing*."
She turned her head away as she didn't want to be comforted.

He gripped her shoulder. "Stephie, please listen," he
begged, "you did protect the Seed with your faith. ALL of it."

"Then it wasn't much," she said dryly.

But he countered, "I'm sorry but you are *wrong*. You
protected it with faith that cannot be bettered!"

She turned her head around again, not believing he could
say something so foolish. "Vaughn, *please* don't patronize me.
At least *your* prayers were answered!"

Vaughn turned her whole body around towards him,
tenderly holding her face in front of his, her dried blood
reminding him of her bravery. He looked at her until she raised
her rich brown eyes. "I will *never* do that to you, and I am not
now being patronizing. I can prove it to you!"

She gave a perfunctory, "How?"

"You had ample opportunity to betray the Tree of Life.
You were tempted by spiritual darkness that moved in many
ways you didn't understand but despite all that, you remained
true. When it seemed to me that you may have given your
heart to him, you found a way to tell me you hadn't and that
you would always love me."

His words brought something back to life in her so with
eyes warming to him, she asked meekly, "You understood?"

"I did once you said our secret code, *through our prayers*.
Then you're saying our prayers were *just* prayers was your
telling me to just accept them for what they are, no more but
very much *no less*. I knew that we *know* we have true love and

hope forever through our prayers. Prayer is never *just* prayer to you, and you basically told me those prayers were *still* in affect by saying, '*is* what we had.' Also, I could tell you were the *same* Stephanie I loved and will always love. Even though I didn't understand what you were doing with Jargono, I knew you loved me."

"Oh Vaughn! From that first night we met, when you popped your head in that window in answer to my prayers, it has been so with me. I knew that's why you replied 'just prayers, reality is what reality is.'"

"Yes, my beloved Stephie, and that's why you said that will *always* be true."

She caressed his cheek with her hand and his heart with her eyes, "You understood ... I don't know how the words came, but I guess they were just right, weren't they?"

"Yes. Only we understood their true meaning, and *that* was by our faith. But I could *not* let you sacrifice yourself to him because it would have done no good. He wanted the Seed. And even if he wanted you more, you couldn't live like that, because there was no guarantee that at any time he would not demand from you the Seed of Tree of Life. I knew you could never give in. But he would've leveraged you more and more to prove your love for him by betraying yourself. And if you had a child together, it would destroy you! Besides, *we're* meant to have children together, *just* you and me!"

"Oh Vaughn," she reached behind his head, grabbing his thick hair to kiss him, but he continued.

"And... I'm sorry, but I swore a solemn oath to your ancestors that I would avenge their children's blood for the cruel injustice done to them. But Stephie, most of all, when you realized I was giving my whole life to fight him, you gave your whole life to protect the Seed. STEPHIE, you gave your life up rather than betray the Seed of Life to evil *because you had faith that it was more valuable than your whole life.* The first words out of your mouth when you came back to life were that the Seed was worth a million of you. Stephie... there is no faith greater than to give your life for the sake of greater goodness because of your faith in that goodness."

Vaughn's words entered the parched ground like a rain storm that turns cracked earth into soft mud. Her tears flowed again, not in bitterness but in recognition of the truth of his words and the life it brought back to her heart. Never had she wept more uncontrollably because never had she felt of having failed more miserably. *But maybe I didn't fail... not exactly.* Never had she been more grateful to see Vaughn's view. Yet even with the understanding that she had done all she could, emptiness still pressed upon her.

Between sobs, she managed to restate the obvious. "Still Vaughn, the Seed is *gone.* Whether I failed or was overpowered, the Seed is *still* gone. I'm sorry for scolding you when I came back to life ... but it was still *my* responsibility. So do you see my point that it would have been better to keep the Seed and just let me go?"

Within Stephanie's eyes Vaughn beheld the beauty of her sacrifice still living inside of her, inextricably now an eternal part of her character, a sacrifice she would make again without hesitation. He loved her for this beyond any possible expression, and cherished this incomparable treasure in his arms. But...

"Stephie, I'm not done proving the point to you."

She wrinkled her brow, "But… I see your point, now."

He slowly shook his head, while staring into her rich brown eyes, his expression telling her he had something more profound to say. "No, not yet, not the full point."

She thought to herself, *Oh how I've missed him.* His point-pressing brought back all her love and memories of him in one, all-encompassing reflection with also a sense of something even greater. Her face opened to him, eager for the full point. "What, Vaughn?"

"Why did God answer my prayer? Or, if not God, if the Tree's Seed chose for itself, then why?"

She knew Vaughn always found special questions and this was always humbling. "I don't know."

He did it to her again. He transported her to a place where she didn't know, and he hadn't even gotten his new will yet. But this time he did something strange, too. He gave the answer to his own question instead of prodding her to find it for herself.

"Because, my dear, *dearly beloved*, you were more important to either or both of them than the Seed!"

Her reaction was instantaneous, but no sooner than she did, she began to leave the possibility open simply because Vaughn is Vaughn. "NO…no, that can't be."

Opposing her denial, he fixed his gaze into her eyes while pronouncing his supposition as if it was an unchanging natural law, like gravity: "But Stephie, *it is!* Otherwise, God would not have exchanged the Seed's life for yours and the Seed would not have agreed to give it up. They held *your life* to be more important."

Her eyes grew large with the desire to weep, again but didn't know why. She didn't understand, "But ... but how?"

Sobs of unknown awe flowed like the rain, not only soaking the ground but even forming peaceful lakes for fish and fowl. The contrast, the shift in the power of the feelings between ultimate failure and ultimate worth was overwhelming. Vaughn held her for a long time, smoothing and re-smoothing her hair, just as he did that first night they met, her dried blood being truly a badge of honor to him.

When Stephanie calmed, Vaughn continued with a twinkle in his eye. "Let me prove your importance by the gift your forefather King Mafferan gave to me."

Learning that Vaughn knew of her ancient ancestry and had met her forefather totally amazed her but she didn't want to interrupt his train of thought.

Vaughn retrieved his pack from where he'd hidden it under a large piece of stone table. Sitting in front of Stephanie as she sat up, Vaughn smiled at the surprise on her face.

She couldn't restrain herself any longer. "Vaughn, you met ..."

Vaughn began answering casually, "Oh yes, both him and his queen. I'll tell you more later, as I'm sure you'll tell me of your encounters, but let me *first* show you this *wonderful* book."

Now it was Vaughn who couldn't restrain his excitement. "Stephie, *THIS is the book I asked you to find! The Book of Wisdom.* Created by King Mafferan! Watch! Why was the Seed's life given for Stephanie?"

Wisdom: Her life is more important than the Seed.

Stephanie gasped when not only did she see the golden words appear, but also what they said. Her hands went to her chest as her heart pounded. "VAUGHN! OH MY GOD! But… but without the Tree of Life? It was for all mankind!"

Stephanie knew the Tree, had touched it, held it, prayed with it. She knew it prayed with her. She'd traveled through it to save Vaughn, but most of all, it was the Tree's Spirit that gave her a new will as it would be for anyone who would seek it. She was intimate with its feelings and thoughts and her tears flowed at feeling the loss of it.

The Lady grieves truly:

Insight: You are the Tree of Life now!

Silence. Then Stephanie fell over in a faint.

Vaughn sat her back up, cradling her cheek until she revived, exclaiming, "No! But… how?"

Vaughn didn't expect this either. His eyes widened and kept looking from the book to Stephanie, and back again, and back to Stephanie.

Wisdom: The Tree of Life is within you.

"Oh my God!" was all they both could say as Stephanie bowed to the ground on her hands and knees, barely able to comprehend because she realized that the very life of the Tree of Life had not only brought her back but *is* her life! It was truly inside of her.

Vaughn, equally astounded, also bowed. He had not foreseen nor figured out what actually happened, only that she was more important in some way. His prayer had been based on some small understanding of her importance, that for the sake of Justice, given how she had died, that it would be right to bring her back. He'd also guessed that such particular Justice may have been even more important than the manifestation of the Tree here on Earth. But this? They bowed together in silence a long time, as the Spirit of God inundated them with appreciation, Love and blessing.

Stephanie finally spoke as the Tree of Life within her revealed itself and the answer she sought. "Vaughn, The Tree was given a choice! To stay as the spiritual seed on Earth that would possibly grow into another great Tree, or to give its life up to give me mine! When I asked why it chose to sacrifice, it replied, 'One true life is as valuable as all others, and if that value isn't held for one, then it isn't held for all!' It explained that it was placed here to bring sense to the world but my death would have taken that away!"

Vaughn rocked back on his heels while he couldn't keep from staring at her. But it wasn't Stephanie he was seeing but in his mind were his own last words right before he would have killed himself, '*None of this makes any sense. If there is to be no sense in the world, there is no reason to live in it.*'

"Stephanie, what the Tree did saved my life, too!"

She stared at him, wondering and making a mental note to clarify after she told him the rest. "Vaughn, it said since I gave my life up for it, it could do no less for me! *And* it said *you* would come to understand this more deeply when you learn of *your* people's history, that what was done in your history made the Tree much stronger! Vaughn, what is the Tree talking about? Your parents ..."

"Apparently, I've been *ignorant* of belonging to a long line of special people. The counterpart to yours! Yours were given the Tree of Life with direct meaning of the truth. Mine were given true words, which if they truly sought the meaning of, the Tree of Life would supply. King Mafferan noted that at one point those words even spread across the whole world!"

"Vaughn! You come from a special people! My God! What are they called?" Stephanie's excitement carried more emotion than Vaughn liked.

"I don't know. I wasn't told. Seems their name must have been on the government's restricted list." Vaughn looked away and Stephanie wondered why he seemed ashamed when he should be feeling wonderful. "Stephanie, I read the letter you got out of the box and part of it stressed the 'what' over the 'who'. King Mafferan also reiterated that knowledge to me that the *who* is miniscule to *what* a person is."

Stephanie gleefully nodded her understanding, "*Oh* you were able to read it! I'm *so* glad. I saved it, special for you, so you could read it. I almost screwed up really badly because of it but I'll tell you everything later."

"Stephanie, I'm sorry I read it without you but I needed to, so I could help you. Look … there's so much we need to know about each other. If we just start talking from any old point, it'll get really confusing. One of us should start and just tell everything that happened to them in the order it happened, and then the other."

Stephanie couldn't believe her happiness, when just a short time ago she was at her lowest. "I think that's very wise. I want to tell you *everything*. Hey, what happened to that *stuff* he put on my face?"

Vaughn smiled at her twisted expression. "Oh, the Black Oil? Ha! Spot seems to like the stuff. He licked it off you and me, and now he's cleaning off himself. There's a bottle of it just back there. I ..." Vaughn hung his head down with the memory, ashamed to speak it.

Seeing his feelings but not understanding, Stephanie prodded, "Vaughn ... What?"

He deeply sighed. When she heard that kind of heavy sigh, she took his hand. "Vaughn, what? Please tell me ... we share everything! We're one!"

Meekly he admitted, "I was about to drink it, right before you came back to life."

Her body shivered in terror as her voice shook, "Vaughn... why would you? Oh *God!*" Realization of how very close they both came to unfathomable disaster hit her like a board across the head. "Vaughn, if you had drunk that stuff, legend says you wouldn't have died, not exactly, you would have been changed into a demon! I learned about it from Jargono."

Vaughn entered another eternal moment as the puzzle came together. *"The bastard knew!"*

"Huh?"

"There are a few things I didn't tell you before we got separated because I didn't want you to worry and I didn't understand them. Jargono came to me like a spirit in a glowing cloud above my bed, and told me to help people by sacrificing myself by accepting the Blackness that transforms people. Now you tell me the Oil has something to do with such transformations. The Blackness and the Oil must be linked and Jargono knows how."

Stephanie clarified, "But he said it was just a legend … that he didn't know if the Oil worked."

"He lied. He's responsible for the Blackness blowing people up, I just know he is. Oh God, he's trying to create his own demon!" Memories of how Spot reacted when Glen vanished came flooding back. Knowledge poured over Vaughn making him tingle. The implications of Jargono's plan brought tears to his eyes. "He may have already done so. I'll explain everything in order, in a bit." But one thing pressed upon his heart now. "I … I'm sorry, Stephie! Forgive me. I didn't know. I felt all was lost … betrayed! I couldn't bear it. I was going to … kill myself." His shame was shrinking him and Stephanie saw this.

She fixed her eyes at him. "Vaughn, it's my turn to make a point and yours to listen! You've done more than could be imagined. My last thoughts before I died were that I was so *proud* of you." Her words so deeply touched him all he could do was surrender to her eyes and continue to listen. "How you were able to fight a man that has totally given himself to evil … I don't know. And I have a new will, Vaughn, given purely to me by God through the Tree of Life, but I couldn't beat him … *yet*. However, even with your old will, with evil still in you somewhere, somehow trying to destroy you, you were able to beat Jargono."

Vaughn shook his head, "I didn't beat him. He got away."

"Because he knew if he had stayed, you would have killed him. That's a clear victory. You also gave your whole life to fight evil, and you fought on *two* fronts at the same time, from within and without. I don't know how you did it. I'd never have that kind of strength."

Vaughn smiled and touched the dried blood on Stephanie's face. "I don't know ... it looks like you were doing more than playing a board game! But Stephie, that doesn't excuse what I was about to ..."

Stephanie cut him off from treading that path again. "No, it does not. You're right. But just think about it. After all the battles were over, you let your guard down, then the evil still in you pressed its advantage because of the terrible pain you were in. Vaughn, *you* were overpowered, *too!* Because you don't have that new will yet. Vaughn, the demons watch us! I've seen it! They watch and wait, and when they see an opening, they pounce."

He shook his head, acknowledging the gravity of it all.

She waited for his eyes to return to hers. "The lesson in this is that we can't let our guards down, not for a single instant."

He sighed. "Jean told me I needed to seek for the new will. King Mafferan told me, too, but I just haven't had time. I just wasn't led to seek yet."

Stephanie nodded understanding. "And now let me make *my* full point! You were on your way to kill yourself, so you thought, but you didn't. Why?"

"Because the cave started to glow."

"Why?"

"Because I prayed."

"And God answered your prayers *even while you were about to commit the worst sin possible!*"

Vaughn could only sit, staring at his beloved, as she led him to greater understanding about himself and God. He recognized she'd learned how to make a point well and Stephanie, reading this recognition in his eyes, realized it, too.

When she saw that Vaughn stayed quiet, she continued, "Because, dear Vaughn, God knew your limitations. It wasn't good in His sight to hold them against you! Even though you were turning to evil after your prayer, God honored the prayer because He wanted to honor you! He wanted, yet, to give life a chance in you."

Now it was Vaughn's turn to resist. "But…"

But she cut him off, again, taking hold of both his hands, squeezing them. "Reality, dear." She gave him an extra-long stare to further impress the point. "God knew the real you had its limitations. God honored your part in the Tree of Life, ignoring the tree of death that had control of you."

Vaughn just couldn't accept that so easily, "No … I'm sorry Stephie, but evil can *never* be justified, no matter what. I don't know, Stephanie … that seems like a *very* slippery slope that anyone can just keep abusing because they just keep failing then expecting God to forgive them, to *accept their limitations*. God, Stephanie, I *hate* that! That's … that's about as lame as our government's religion with no real solution to failing, to doing evil in *this* life. What I did was *terrible!* No way around it and…"

Her chastising look silenced him, as she held his eyes in hers. "Then why did God see it as good to do what He did for you? It is true God will not justify evil but listen closely, my love. The evil in you will only be 'justified' if you fail to gain that new will, if you let the tree of death consume you! Then it can claim it was the better all along, but the new will can give you the power not to be overcome by *any* evil. This mortal life isn't a blank check for continual failure, with redemption waiting upon our death. God forbid! But look at it this way. To understand how to gain that new will really does take time. There's a lot involved to really getting it. I know! Now how are you or anyone else supposed to gain that time if God isn't gracious to us exactly as I described?"

Vaughn kept quiet, yet again, while he considered her words.

"That means, dear, that God knew you'll come to Him, that you'll allow Life to purge you of the tree of death and give you a new will only in the Tree of Life. In this way, God is justified in what He did because for the sake of the person you really are and will fully become, He has ignored your evil thoughts. In other words, He has forgiven you. You can let your shame go now because you've acknowledged it to God though He really had given you his answer already!"

But more troubling thoughts came to him, actually the same thoughts, but he couldn't help it. "I'm truly sorry. How many times have I said '*no matter what*' but I've *again* failed that saying. If it hadn't been for Spot…"

His dog *ruffed* and panted, but his pain prevented him from rising. He'd finished cleaning all the oil off his coat, and was lying beside them, wagging his tail, waiting for someone to pat him. Stephanie leaned over and wrapped her arms around him, giving him a big doggie hug. "Thank you, Spot, for saving my love and getting rid of that *stuff* from me." He crawled over closer then laid his head gladly on her lap. Stephanie affectionately rubbed his ears with both hands and kissed him atop his doggy-head. Smiling broadly, Vaughn relished his instant pleasure at seeing how his two best friends took to each other. Everything that meant anything to him was right before his eyes.

Glad that Spot provided a healthy interlude from Vaughn's negativity, Stephanie now saw a better opportunity to continue, "Because the 'no matter what' keeps exceeding your abilities. That's what the new will is for, dear. Our abilities cannot be exceeded when we have it. Though our bodies may be destroyed, we'll never die inside, *no matter what.*"

Vaughn's eye opened as he gathered something in her words. It was the hope he'd anticipated ever since he first became aware of the Light and now she confirmed to him that his hope is real. "What you've described means more to me than anything else. But I think God is justified anytime He desires to give a person a chance to live, whether they ultimately take it or not, because He gives the chance for Life's sake. It does appear to people that evil is justified, though, when they seemingly get away alive, but for me, I know I'll have to *prove* I'm worthy of the chance to live." He sat up straighter to look into her eyes. "Well, how do I go about getting this new will?"

Stephanie smiled, "You've just begun."

Vaughn nodded with understanding, then something occurred to him. "Stephanie, we haven't even had time to say 'Hi, how ya doin'? *I've missed you so much.*"

Vaughn took her in his strong arms, stood her up, kissed and hugged her. His strength comforted her as she allowed herself to melt into him considering, *He's so much stronger.* They instantly became familiar with each other's unspoken feelings while holding on tightly, standing together. Their spirits gently but profoundly drifted into one another to explore untold depths, gain knowledge and form a mutual communication that only those deep in true love understand. They caressed each other's backs with sensual tenderness. Peace settled upon them like the accumulation of a gentle, pristine snow in all its crystalline delicate beauty. They sighed together.

Stephanie finally spoke, as troubles entered her mind and her responsibilities called more urgently to her, "We'll need to destroy that bottle and...Vaughn, there's a whole river of that *stuff*. Somehow, Jargono took me to some special place, not of this world, like a spirit world, and there's a whole river of that Black Oil. He said there's enough to destroy all humanity. Well, he didn't exactly use the word destroy, he used *enlighten*. That's why I was trying to tell you to leave me alone. I needed to learn more."

Vaughn eased back to look into her face and took her by her arms. "Stephie, I just don't think he would have played along long enough for you to learn or do what you wanted. I had to try to stop him, both to save you and fulfill my oath. I buried your people and *swore* over their graves I would avenge their deaths. This whole country needs to be brought to pay for its terrible evil."

Memories stabbed into Stephanie as she placed her hand on Vaughn's chest in what felt like an official capacity. "You buried Arlupo and Father ... I'll tell you of them later. Thank you, Vaughn, you will know how very much this means to me." Then Stephanie rubbed her forehead, sighing heavily, suddenly feeling very drained. "Oh Vaughn, we've learned too much in too short a time! We can't even begin to know which way to turn."

Vaughn had tears in his eyes but he had to tell her now what was pushing at him. She noticed the change in his demeanor as he finally confessed. "There's more ... I know how your Mother died."

She looked at him, totally oblivious of what really happened. "What do you mean?"

"It was your father and Karen who planned together and killed her. Glen told me. He followed me, killed my friends, and ... I'll tell you the rest later. He wanted to hurt me bad and figured telling me the truth was the best way to do that."

"Why?" was all Stephanie could muster for the whole unfolding situation, more to question the validity of all she just heard than to actually accept it and learn the reason.

But Vaughn's stare into her eyes confirmed the truth. "Karen wanted to hurt you. She set up the rape that night, too. She also manipulated your father's hatred into him paying her to kill your mother."

Fire flared in Stephanie's eyes. "*He* paid *her to kill my Mother?*"

Vaughn nodded, now wondering if he should have told her any of this ... right now. They had more important things to worry about. Yet, he loved her and just couldn't keep back the knowledge, the sense of obligation being too great. Noticing her drastic change, he tentatively questioned, "What are you thinking, Stephie?"

Her voice was but a whisper, "I'm angry, *very angry*. He killed my best friend, Arlupo... all my people. And he killed my mother, too? And just when she was beginning to understand, and we were... It just seems that he shouldn't get away with any of it."

Vaughn's concern bordered on becoming a strange fear because of her unspoken implications, but again he couldn't seem to keep his mouth shut, "Stephie... there's more."

Her eyebrows raised up as did her voice. "*More?* How could there possibly be *more?*"

"As Jargono was running away, he said he would be back for your sister when she comes of age."

"OH! *I'm VERY ANGRY.*" Stephanie tore away from Vaughn, marched to the cave entrance, and halting abruptly, stared not outside but into her internal world. Dark clouds quickly formed outside and deafening claps of thunder crashed one after another, as Stephanie digested the threat against the last of anything she could call family. The first time the weather had severely changed like that was when she had wanted to protect Arlupo and the Appendaho but she wasn't yet cognizant of what her faithwalker heart could do. But *this* time, she became aware of the oneness between her and nature, a very special personal link to that greater reality that in a way was like the love and communication between her and Vaughn!

Vaughn felt invisible power swirling within and around her as he came up from behind, placing his hands to lightly caress her arms, trying to calm her. "I think, Stephie, the first thing we need to do is catch each other up on all that's happened to us. Knowledge is crucial. I don't think we can decide what to do first, until we know *everything* that's happened... in detail.

It seems to me we're strongest when we're together and to be really together, we need to know everything about each other. Stephie, if we have any chance at all of beating all this evil, we're going to have to do it together."

Spot ruffed and painfully crawled his way up as if to remind them that he was a part of this, too. Vaughn patted his head and Spot whined in pain, perhaps a little more exaggerated than necessary.

"You're right about everything, Vaughn." But Stephanie's attention was drawn to her new doggie friend. Vaughn noticed his dog had a calming effect on her as she knelt and rubbed both ears again, "Yes, Spot. You, too! Sit Spot and I'll make you feel better."

Spot immediately pushed himself up. Stephanie put her hands gently on each side of Spot's head as she bowed in concentration and they began to glow. Vaughn tingled all over at this incredible sight. "There, Spot. All better?" Spot gave hearty affirmative *ruffs*.

Vaughn began to translate, "That means…"

But Stephanie finished for him, "Yes, yes… I know!" in a tone that said she wasn't ignorant. "Now, let's call Mom, I mean, Jean… the people I…"

"I know. I've met her and Lana."

"That's right, you did! You mentioned Jean, but…"

Vaughn smiled again, "Like I said, let's take our time and fill each other in. Yea, I met them both and Puppy."

At the sound of Puppy's name, Stephanie seemed to instantly revert to about five years old. "PUPPY? YOU FOUND PUPPY?"

Vaughn beamed at Stephie's little girl enthusiasm, "Yes dear. Puppy is how we found your family, enabling Lana to share her secret that allowed me to figure out about you and what Jargono did, *even though you made Jean promise otherwise!*" He frowned at her and put his hands on his hips waiting."

Stephanie quickly changed the subject. "They must be worried sick."

Vaughn understood and went with it. "Why don't we find a phone and call them. I have a good bit of money I saved from working…"

Oh! One surprise after another! "Working?"

"Well, I won't say I'm rich, but…"

"But I am!"

"I know, Stephie, *you* are the greatest treasure to me."

"No, I mean… I have… I own that store… errrr, rather, I bought it and gave it to Jean. I have enough money for a lifetime, Vaughn! I have more than we will ever need. We could truly be together… if we were allowed to marry at this age."

Both were stunned at the little things they were discovering. Vaughn held both hands up in a big stop expression, "O.K. Now I *know* we have to talk!" Then he squinted his eyes at her, "Oh, by the way, do you realize that life tipped the scales in our battle with Jargono? I'd consulted the Book and it told me we couldn't win. Everything that it and King Mafferan said would happen to us, did happen … we couldn't have beat him."

"But we did manage to survive."

"Only because of a certain life." Vaughn kept grinning that kind of smile by which Stephanie knew there was something profound to be discovered next.

"O.K. Vaughn, what life?" She was thinking it was love, or maybe even anger. After all, these were all part of true life.

Vaughn pointed to his dog, "Spot, come here boy!" Dancing up and down, feeling better than ever, Spot panted, waiting for what his master would say.

"If it wasn't for *you,* Spot, we would both be dead!" The dog *Arfed* over and over and danced around some more.

Vaughn began to translate, "That means..."

But Stephanie cut him off, "I know, I know. He's proud of himself!"

"Right."

Finally, they walked out of the cave to a clear evening sky with the sun's lower golden edge touching the distant horizon off to their right. The air carried fresh scents of unseasonal flowers from some of the orchard trees that had somehow survived the burning though their ashen smell still lingered. Stephanie and Vaughn leisurely hiked to a nearby wild, wooded hillside untouched by the fire. He hadn't expected to be here, again, but then, expectations hadn't exactly been the best modus operandi for anticipating their future.

Vaughn set up camp and gave Stephanie a whole canteen of water to wash the blood off her face but she said she didn't need it. She bowed her head, glowed a bit, then everything about her looked perfect, even down to her beautiful dress that Vaughn had ripped open. She told him that this in *no way* meant she was giving up her baths. She just didn't want to waste the drinking water.

After they ate, Vaughn sent Spot to prowl and guard as they wrapped themselves together in a sleeping bag in their

tent with the soft glow of Vaughn's camping lantern accentu-
ating the curves of their faces. Stephanie realized that Vaughn
was hurt, too, as the soft light made the swelling on his face
more obvious. *He carries his wounds so well, it took me till now
to realize.* In spite of protests that he didn't want her to drain
herself on him, she healed him, too. She mentioned that was
nothing compared to the last *two* times! They talked until ...

"My God, Vaughn, is that all of it? You went through *all
that*? School, your parents betrayed you, Gary, Glen, Tracy ...
you fought the blackness? And won?"

As he told his story, she could somehow see the events as
if she was actually there. She could feel all that happened, too,
and now her eyes became more tender. "I want to thank you for
helping Tracy, for truly keeping your word. At least she came to
understand self-respect before she died. Is there anything more?"

Vaughn snuggled closer to Stephanie as they listened to the
nightbirds and the gentle wind stirring the branches. Her sweet
spirit mingling with her femininity so comforted him that he
truly wished there was some way to stop time. "I believe I've
told you everything from the time you left back East, plus
what I left out before you left. And you? Is there anything else
you remember to tell me?"

Stephanie hesitated, looking at him with a faraway expression. He knew there was still something important... very
important. He waited as she sighed slowly.

"When I died..." He put his hand on her arm and
squeezed, seeing how hard it was for her to speak. "It was
terrible! That vile Oil had surrounded me with pain, darkness...
hopelessness."

"I know, Stephanie."

She looked into his eyes questioningly, "It was suffocating… It wasn't inside me but my spirit should *not* have been held like that. Anyway, I was suspended… sort of between worlds, I think in the place where I had *faithwalked* to come to you when you were dying, but this time, I was powerless." Vaughn's eyes followed her every expression, as if actually experiencing her memories. His gut twisted in empathy. She took his arm and he was surprised to see fear in her eyes. "Vaughn, I'm *sure* I was supposed to travel through that place to a realm of peace but I couldn't! I think that Black Oil kept me from leaving!" His eyes darkened, his heart slowly informing his mind with understanding as he remembered his feelings when she died, that she had no peace… that she was lost forever.

Stephanie brought his focus back as she continued, "Then, a very hideous demon showed up, something like the one I had met there before, only much, much worse … much more evil, and I knew I was powerless. His awful, great black eye drooled this green slime as he floated towards me. But then a light surrounded me!" Vaughn somehow knew what she would say next. "It was the spirit of the Seed of the Tree of Life. The demon said he had a right to the departed who couldn't enter anywhere else, those were the rules. The light surrounding me told the demon to come take me, but the demon couldn't come near the light. In fact, he looked away from it even as they talked. The demon asked the light if it was going to send me back or give me to him, that it had to choose *now* because that *glow* had no right to prevent him from *eating!* The light paused, seeming to consider many options, I think. Then I woke up back on Earth, and I knew what you and the Seed had done!"

Vaughn sighed deeply. What could one say about such a thing? He figured the Seed could have just as well given its life to send her to the place of peace but he knew Stephanie was right, though. *Her spirit should not have been held like that.* His heart burned inside him with that one statement, and he intended to understand why and how to rectify it. Vaughn knew there is no evil that goodness can't answer, or defend against. The depth of her first words when she came back to life, '*What have you done?*' then struck him and he choked.

"Ste... Stephie... when you came back to life, you mean you *knew* that if the Seed remained here, then the demon would have eaten you?" Her previous account echoed in his heart, '*I was powerless.*'

She looked away, trying to hold back sobs but his hand on her cheek gently turned her face back to him. Still, her eyes looked down as she nodded, her voice now quite strained, "At the time, all I knew was that the Seed to the Tree of Life was far more valuable, and it was *my* responsibility to protect it, *no matter what!* It belonged on Earth to all people. I couldn't place myself above that!"

Something doesn't feel right! Vaughn narrowed his eyes at her, waiting. When she didn't fess up, he prodded, "You said the light paused, seeming to think over many options." He waited and she still didn't come clean. "I know you could probably sense that, but the way you described it ... Stephanie, what aren't you telling me?"

Tears blurred her vision. *I can't seem to hide* anything *from him!* "Vaughn… I don't want you to be mad at me!" He increased his frown, but felt he already knew. Finally, she couldn't help but tell him the rest, "Alright…" She rubbed the tears from her eyes, gathering the strength to tell him, "The Seed told me it was giving its life for me and I… argued! I was so *embarrassed* that I'd put the Seed in such a *terrible* position. And I knew I wasn't worthy of such a sacrifice! I felt… very guilty… wrong. But the Seed told me that was the only way! And, that its choice belonged to it, not to me!"

Vaughn nodded his head in agreement. "I told Jean the same thing when she eventually told me of her promise to you to keep me away." But Vaughn's eyes now widened with so many levels of appreciation. *Lord God, such a sacrifice she was willing to make. She* truly *has a remarkable will.* He took both her cheeks in his hands. "I love you so much and these words seem grossly inadequate. Far from being mad at you, I *adore* you."

They laid there for some time, silently exploring each other's eyes in the gentle light. Vaughn kept gingerly caressing her cheek, trying to find just the perfect stroke for one so precious. Finally, Stephanie shook her head yawning, and Vaughn took the opportunity to speak.

"Stephie, I'm so sorry about the Appendaho. But I'm so incredibly happy that you found out what a truly great family you come from. I just don't know what to say. You're like a queen to me. Royalty. Even before you told me, that letter I read from your forefather the king filled me with … " He was delicately stroking her cheek with adoration when she sloughed off the thought.

"HA! *Royalty!*" Then she changed the subject, "Well, I think I've told you everything except the details of the process I went through inside myself to gain the new life, and the reasons why I had Arlupo's father put me under the water. When the time is right for you, I'll tell you what I went through, and why. However, I'm telling you now that to gain the new life, you must do it from the inside out, not the other way around. Anything I reveal to you must be viewed in that way, otherwise it is of no use. You have to see the meaning inside of you, and not just see, but be it."

"I understand, Stephanie. I really do. Let's first get back to your family and try to figure out what we should do about everything else. Then, we'll talk more about these things."

She took his cheek in her hand to emphasize what she was about to say, "Vaughn, when is the right time? What if from now on there are always things that have to be attended to? Until you make the new life a first priority, you cannot gain it."

He looked her in the eye with honesty and sincerity, "I understand that, too, dear, and the importance of the new life. I'm just not being led to do it right now, but to do other things. It would seem as if I should attend to it first ... but I just can't right now!"

She nodded, "All right, Vaughn." Her thoughts moved on, "So, Glen killed Tracy."

"Yes, I'm sorry. But it looks like she did start changing for the better."

"Thank you, again, for keeping your word. Isn't it ironic that in Glen's *and* Jargono's situations, *Spot* made all the difference?"

Vaughn shook his head in wonder, "I wonder what Life is trying to tell us by that. The *dog* is an essential part of life?"

"I don't know, except that when we needed help terribly, it was provided through a dog. *Mmm,* you feel *so good.*" She pressed herself against him, as they laid on their sides, resting her leg on top of his.

"Stephie, you do, too… but…"

Stephanie pleaded, "Vaughn, what are we going to do? You said you wanted to marry me some day. *Well,* someday doesn't have to be far away now. I have *a lot* of money. And besides, YOU'RE WORKING! That was so ingenious how you found a way to do that, all those job offers! I can't believe it. How can it be, when so many adults hardly have enough work?"

"I found out that the government pays a lot of people, ahhh, sort of not to work, *and,* there are a lot of jobs out there, but people just don't want to do them. I told you, I even got in trouble for *working too hard.* They were jealous. But Stephie, as far as concerns us, I just don't think it's the right time yet. You know your forefather waited till just the right time, even his letter says to wait till we *know* the time is right."

"But that was when he had the Seed to plant… the Seed is gone now."

"But Stephie, the Seed is still alive. *It's inside you.* I think that there's something very special going on here and that we need to pick the exact, right, sacred time, before we make love."

Stephanie rolled to her back, fingering the chain around her neck that had held the Seed from the Tree of Life. "I'm sorry, I was just so tired and you felt *so* good. After all the talking we did, you won't believe it, and I'm ashamed to admit it, but I forgot! All I wanted was you!"

"I almost forgot, too! I think we really need to sleep now. We'll be home in about a week."

"I'm glad we decided to travel slowly. We need the time to catch up. I love camping out with you. May I say a goodnight prayer for us dear?"

"My beloved Stephie, any time you want to pray, please do. I love it so."

Stephanie folded her hands atop her stomach. "Dear Light that preserved us, all these days and nights, when we wandered all alone in dangers way beyond us, we have but one word that does not even express how fully we feel it, *thank you.* You have allowed us to know so much, yet we are at a loss to know what to do. It seems that You have chosen us to fight all this evil, but we are a long ways from being able to. We're really not special people at all, just ordinary, fighting the extraordinary. Help us. All the gifts that we do possess… well, they're only as good or meaningful as the goodness in our hearts and minds. Help us. We're just as frail as anyone else, except if *we* screw up, we will hurt a lot of people a lot worse than anyone else because of the gifts we have. Help us. Because of our abilities, and what we do know, we are now responsible for so much. We feel that much weaker. Help us."

Stephanie's prayer went all through him. He tingled all over. He loved her so much. "AMEN," was all Vaughn could say through the tremendous respect he had for her. He pulled her over to him and they curled into one big ball inside the sleeping bag. Vaughn clutched her to his breast, as he buried his face into her hair and kissed the back of her head. And they drifted off into peaceful sleep. In their dream, surrounded by a warm glow that called to them as one, they made slow, peaceful, tender love together that seemed to last all night.

In the morning, they each took turns bathing in a stream. Vaughn gave Stephanie a toothbrush that he brought along, special just for her. It felt good to be clean again.

CHAPTER EIGHT

Rules of Engagement

They held onto the ropes while tossing and twisting, trying not to breathe in too deeply the profuse stench from the ships lower hold. The sole lantern, lowly lit, barely highlighted the thick scum around their feet. The older, long-bearded man's piercing eyes seemed to have a light all their own.

"Did you bring them?"

"Yes, yes, of course. All these days have I forgotten even once? But I still think you too cautious. This is no place to pray."

He unfolded a velvety pouch, pulling out two embroidered shawls which each one wrapped around their shoulders while clinging onto the rigging. They rocked back and forth in silent mumbling and time disappeared for them, even forgetting they still clung tenaciously to those ropes. Finally, the elder spoke calmly with a smile, "This is a Christian boat with crosses on its sails. It is the only place for us to pray unless you'd rather try it from the bottom of the ocean?"

The young man replied confidently, "In the new land, we will have freedom."

But the elder laughed to the contrary, "Even though we are no better than anyone else, like it or not, whether we understand it or not, whether we accept it or not, there is a special presence, a blessing that glows in us. Even if we can't see it, even if we shut our minds and hearts as tight as we can against it, it is still there, in the background, coloring all our feelings, all our ways, all our expressions and even ignorance cannot remove it."

"But why should that take away our freedom?"

"Because like it or not, everyone who comes in contact with us, comes in contact with that unique, ancient blessing that says God is real in humanity in a way so deeply profound that it makes all who do not have such blessing ..." He stopped.

"Yes?"

He spoke no more.

One week later, as Vaughn had predicted, they arrived home. They were greeted by two, sweet, familiar, little voices, mingling together as if in song, "STEPHIEEE – Arf, Arf, Arf Arf– Hey– Arf, Arf..."

"SPROUT... PUPPY!" The quickening pitter-pat of feet and paws on the hardwood floor underscored the growing sound of Puppy's and Lana's greetings which ended in an abrupt thud as Lana threw her hug full-force into her sister. Puppy followed close behind with a trail of little *arfing* while Spot raced past Stephanie with comparable big doggy *Ruffing*. The two doggies crashed into one another, unable to slow their momentum because of the smoothness of the floor. They sort of bounced off each other, Puppy more so and looked the slightest bit dazed. Spot seemed just a bit surprised but they quickly regained their doggy composure, twirling twice around each other, then raced for Stephanie who only the instant before had been pummeled by Lana's fond embrace. Puppy jumped full force onto Stephanie while Spot jumped at Lana so the whole mass of bodies went down. Stephie was barely able to break her fall with her free hand and futilely tried to create a safe defense but was reduced to rolling on the floor laughing.

Vaughn stood back and watched. Hands, little paws, big paws, feet, little feet, little hands, big doggy head. The mass of life just kept shifting, trying to figure out how best to convey their joy for one another. With tears streaming down, Jean glided over to Vaughn, throwing her arms around him. "Oh God! I don't know how to thank you... We were sure Stephanie had died."

"Actually... ahhh, we wouldn't be here if it wasn't for Spot!" Vaughn pointed at the tumbling mass of life with a broad smile.

Jean looked at him quizzically, wrinkling up her brow. *There always seems to be so much more behind his words.* Then she announced playtime was over, "It's time to *eat.*"

They all eagerly sat down at a square table with Jean and Vaughn across from each other, Stephanie at Vaughn's left and Lana across from her. Neither Vaughn nor Stephanie seemed to finish a whole sentence before the other finished for them, with Spot interjecting occasional exclamations. Lana sat in rapt, silent attention, with only her eyes continually changing size and expression. When Stephanie and Vaughn finally finished their story, the now sleepy Lana found a burst of energy and jumped from her seat to climb into Vaughn's lap and wrapped him in a big hug. Getting up on her knees on his lap, she threw her arms around his neck and whispered into his ear, "Did you do your secret to Stephie again?"

Vaughn turned his head to her ear, "Shhhhhh! Yep."

Lana giggled behind her hand, climbed down, shifted over to Stephie, and bounded onto her lap. She gave Stephanie a big hug, too, knelt just like she did on Vaughn, and whispered, "Don't tell Vaughn I told you because it's a *secret* but he said he loves you." Then she giggled, even more with her eyes than with laughter.

Vaughn mustered his sternest look when he caught her attention, growling at her.

Lana put both her hands over her mouth, giggling more. When Spot heard Vaughn growl, he stood at his side, barking his reprimand.

"OK, Spot. I'll leave her alone."

Lana climbed down off Stephie to encircle her little arms around the big doggie's neck while Spot tried to turn his head to get his big tongue on her face. Jean sat back, watching it all with joyful tears, still reflecting on their incredible tale.

"I'm so sorry for what you two have had to suffer because of that man. I *never* should have married him. But I'm so grateful that we're all together now and I cannot imagine my life without you! It's so strange that out of such evil, so much good has come."

Vaughn straightened his posture then turned to the little girl. "Lana, you are going to have to understand how to love very strongly and be brave like Stephie and me, because one day you also will have to fight evil with all that you have."

Her deep gray eyes went intense with all the feelings of their story still burning inside of her but now focusing those same feelings towards her own life and future. "I *will?*"

"Yes, dear," affirmed Stephie. "You must learn how to pray the true prayers in your heart so God can help you grow strong and understand."

Lana declared confidently, "I WILL. I already do!"

Stephanie continued, "When you get older, we're all going to have to fight that evil man together and it will take all of us, with all our combined strength, to beat him."

"That's right," Vaughn reaffirmed.

The solemness with which Lana answered seemed way beyond her years. "I promise you and Vaughn, I will, so we can beat the bad man. He hurt Mommy *real* bad and he *smacked* me, *but I bit him.* That's why he smacked me. But he needed to be bit... I didn't."

Stephanie opened her arms for Lana to come to her. "O.K. Sprout. Now time for bed."

Vaughn directed the doggy brigade, "Spot, Puppy go put ... *Sprout?* to bed. Vaughn raised his brow to Stephie at her nickname for Lana. Stephie giggled, Spot *ruffed,* Puppy *arf-arfed* and Lana bounded off to her bedroom with Puppy and Spot in tow. Then the mood changed as all three sat to discuss adult business.

Vaughn was, now, just turned sixteen, and Stephanie, now, just fifteen. Their youth was all apparent in their physical appearance but their demeanor seemed that of the ancient wise and both were seated now, straight and square. Stephanie went first, having already thought out what she would say. Without knowing it, she now took on what could be described as a regal appearance

"Vaughn, you swore to avenge my people. you've got to keep your oath to God! My father killed my mother, too, and even though he's my father, he's got to be brought to justice for all his evil. Since we can't bring him to any court of law, we've got to bring him to Justice ourselves! It seems to me we should start there." It was brief, to the point, and powerful beyond her years. Was it something that a fifteen-year-old girl should be thinking, let alone saying?

Jean worriedly countered, "But Stephanie, he's a government officer with men at his command. As badly as you want revenge…"

Stephanie slowly shook her head, looking at Jean. "Mom, not revenge, *justice*, and I feel I'm *led* to do this." She turned to her love. "Vaughn?"

He sat quietly for a long moment with his elbows on the table, his hands folded under his chin, propping his head at the pinnacle of the triangle his arms created. Finally, with a very slow, deliberate nod towards Stephanie, his deferential tone completed his new image of her, "I feel you are right, my Lady Stephanie." His response sounded every bit as a servant would respond to a queen, or perhaps even that of her faithful knight.

Stephanie flattened her mouth at him, "Oh, *stop that!*"

But he stared at her with honest eyes, "No, I'm serious. I meant the tone *precisely* that way. That's just how much love and respect I have for you. I love you as my friend. I love you as my wife to be, but I also *very much* love you just like that, too. *My* choice, not yours, Lady Stephanie!"

Jean reached across the table, taking Stephanie's arm to draw her attention. "Isn't that what your spirit ancestor called you in the cave? Didn't she say, 'Live, Lady Stephanie'?"

"Yes, Mother... she did. But I didn't really pay it mind."

Jean smiled, thinking at long last maybe she could contribute some useful piece of advice, "My daughter, *I think you should!* The spirits say and do nothing without express reason. This much I do know."

Stephanie redirected the conversation, looking back to Vaughn. "It's settled then? We bring Father to justice?"

Vaughn nodded a thankful nod to Jean. Her smile acknowledged it, and then he turned back to Stephanie, "Yes, but then I think you and I must leave this country!"

Both women replied simultaneously, "WHAT?"

Somehow Vaughn managed to take them both in his distant stare, "We're not safe here, nor will we ever be. As long as we are here, Jargono will hunt us, and he will think to use your mother and sister against us." He focused now on Stephanie, "We will lose if he does, because we would do anything to protect them, and he knows that, Stephie. Even if we traded their lives and refused to do whatever he would demand of us, we still lose. *We lose them!*"

His words were true. There was no fighting them. Reality is what it is, no matter how badly it's craved to be different.

Stephanie's stare bore into Vaughn. "But... but they can't fight him by themselves."

Vaughn nodded, "They won't have to, because with us gone, he won't be interested in them. I've been studying what you said about him, what I myself have perceived, and what the Book has taught me. His evil is very goal oriented. He won't waste time on sadistic pleasures as some would. He has grand plans of becoming like that ancient wicked king whom King Mafferan fought, except Jargono plans on succeeding. To do that requires all his attention to be focused. Stephie, we're not that significant to him now. He sees himself as already the most powerful man on Earth, and us more as toys. *But*, if we're available to him, I believe he'll *play* with us, sort of as a much needed diversion. Also, if he can leverage us, he might find it valuable to use us in his grand plans. We take that away from him if we leave."

His reasons sounded correct to Stephanie, but his logic was in error. "But Vaughn, if he's goal oriented, then he wouldn't waste time *playing* and I just don't know what he could possibly use us for."

Vaughn bowed his head, hesitating, and then gave the answer without looking at her, "Because he loves you!"

Her reaction was predictable, "VAUGHN, how can you…"

But he stopped her by explaining further, "Stephie, as I fought him, I could tell. He probably doesn't understand it, but it made him fight just as much as his other reasons did. *You hurt him, Stephie*, worse than any physical harm I did to him, or Spot. The fact that he doesn't understand his love will make him unpredictable, even to himself. That is another reason we *must* go. We need him to be focused on his goal so he will leave your Mom and sister alone."

Good grief, he makes sense but I don't want to leave here. I love my store, I love putting up signs for onions and potatoes, and ... Stephanie leaned her elbows on the table, put her chin in her hands and stared at her beloved, "God, Vaughn, how do you do that, sound so sensible?"

He unfolded his hands, held them apart and shook his head, "Reality is…"

"What reality is. I can see that, I *know* that. Are you sure you're not also Appendaho?"

Vaughn only smiled.

Jean sighed, "Oh God, I see it, too! I'm going to miss you two. We've just become a family."

Vaughn leveled his eyes into Jean's. "Stephie and I have to go away. I believe there are important things we can learn in other countries that will help us in our fight. Also, I'm serious about bringing this whole country to justice. I don't know how a boy can do that, but I swore I would try."

Stephanie had a rare doubting expression toward Vaughn, "Whole country… Vaughn, I don't know! I think…"

But Vaughn leveled his gaze into hers, cutting her off, "This is up to me, like your feelings about your father is to you… I feel led." That was good enough to bring assent from Stephanie, but she still doubted him, and she didn't like that feeling at all. They needed to have complete faith in each other. Still, they needed to be wise, also, in their actions.

Vaughn inquired of the huge task at hand, "How do you propose we bring your father to justice?"

Having anticipated his question, Stephanie's reply was quick but she still couldn't hide her fear that it wouldn't sit well with Vaughn. "Oh Vaughn, please don't … doubt me." She paused, as she realized the confluence of her previous feelings with what she just requested. Now feeling ashamed for doubting him, she struggled to pull the rest of her explanation together. "Vaughn, like when you had your plan for Gary, my feeling is to proceed with this without planning, and let Life flow through as things are meant to be. I am a *faithwalker*… I can do, I guess just about anything… but just because I can walk anywhere, doesn't mean God leads me everywhere I could walk. Arlupo showed me that. If I'm going to kill him, or bring him to justice, it must be *through* me, but not *by* me." Stephanie asked timidly, "Do you understand?"

Vaughn sighed heavily as he recalled how difficult it was to deal with Gary. "Yes dear, actually I do." He smiled and proclaimed, "We're going to play it by ear."

She remembered him explaining the meaning of that strange expression. He was trying to convince her to go along with his plan to let the Light have its way *through* him concerning Gary and his gang but she had later tried to thwart it. Stephanie now realized just how so very similar things were working with each of them, just at different times and different circumstances. *Gary … seems so long ago.* "You ended up killing him directly, after all."

Vaughn shuddered, peering into those not so distant memories of what it felt like when he snapped Gary's neck. "I remember holding him right before I killed him. In that moment, I knew we both knew I had the ability to kill him or let him live. Even though he swore to kill me, and was in the process of trying, I knew I could let him live, that he wouldn't be able to kill me right then, and probably not in the near future either. I no longer felt an immediate threat. But in that same instant, letting him go seemed more wrong than letting him live so the next moment, I killed him. It wasn't in anger … It just was. In the end, it was my decision to kill Gary, but Glen was kind enough to point out that I had good reason. Sometimes, it's easier to get the actual truth about killing from a murderer's perspective, than from people like us who don't really have it in us. Glen caused me to see that I only killed in self-defense, or to protect the innocent. While I can't say Life was working through me when I killed Gary, I really don't think it was, I didn't feel Life's presence, but perhaps there are times when Life actually delivers evil people into the hands of man to justly get rid of them! Because though I feel the dreadfulness of killing him, I'm responsible for his death, I feel no moral guilt for it, just a sense of loss he would never have felt for me."

Stephanie sighed deeply, her heart aching. "Oh, *my love*, I don't know what to say. Arlupo taught me that things like that may not become apparent right away, but sometime in the future… so I won't bother you about it like I did before, back east. I love you and I'll always help you. I just hope that whatever you learn of the consequences, that it won't be too hard on you. *But* make sure in bringing Father and the rest to justice, that *must* only be done *through* Life."

Vaughn recalled Gary's voice appearing in his head not long after he'd killed him, telling him he had to live Gary's life now, since he murdered Gary. Vaughn had called that voice a liar and he didn't recall hearing from it since. *But there's no way I'm telling Stephanie about that. It would be stupid to tell her.* "I understand Lady Stephanie, and I agree. And not only do I agree, but I feel Life agrees."

Stephanie smiled faintly at Vaughn's approval of her plan. No matter how sure she was about it, whether *through* her or not, such a thing as killing couldn't help but raise doubts, but with Vaughn's support she decided to banish them from her.

Jean rubbed her arms and shivered. "I don't know about you two. I feel like I'm watching history being written before my eyes… there's a greatness I feel."

Prophecy now begins with you. They each saw that thought in the other's eyes.

❧

New things were happening under the sun. An old sage had once said, "There is nothing new under the sun." Yet, end-time prophecies from certain people distinctly portray unique events. Since new things were happening, Mafferan thought it best to take some unique actions for these times, because it was a matter of understanding meaning.

There were, of course, far more people his junior than his senior, but there were a couple of *his* ancestors that he kicked ideas around with before approaching the Light directly with his thoughts. Freedom is a wonderful, meaningful thing.

His *cloudwalking* ancestor laughed heartily when Mafferan told him what he wanted to do. *Cloudwalker* even asked if Mafferan wanted some company. Mafferan laughed at the thought, but said, "Hell, if more than one of us goes, they'll think it's an invasion so we might as well make it an army."

Cloudwalker clarified, "But where would we send them after we kick them out?"

"Hmmmm, good point," Mafferan had to concede. He waved bye to *Cloudwalker* and told everyone not to tell his wife where he was going then he vanished.

Ↄↄ

Even a second before Mafferan showed up, ScrabaGag sensed his coming so the great demon was floating around in front of him as he popped in. The Highest Councilor couldn't believe it, the audacity! *The rules* ... actually, there really were no rules, if you consider it. This was just completely... "*Unexpected,*" ScrabaGag growled.

Mafferan smiled broadly with good nature. "Well, well, I heard it was so but now see it with my own eyes. The three are indeed one, ahhh, in a sort of primitive way!"

ScrabaGag knew he had been pushing the scales ever so slowly in Alpha favor. He was wondering when the *glow* might try to do something about it, but he couldn't figure out what that might be or what *this* is now, so he held his peace. His former rivals would have immediately attacked Mafferan.

Grinchback, however, was not as wise as his sire, so he rushed at the wise king. Mafferan didn't even look his way but froze the poor underling in mid-float and turned him upside down. Grinchback's eye began to bulge, both from humiliation and awkward position, while ScrabaGag folded his very long tail around his neck and began tapping his tail tip at the end of his arm.

"Hmmm, Highest Councilor ScrabaGag, is it now?"

ScrabaGag nodded, "It is."

"And duly appointed by your father, I suppose."

201

"*The* Father."

"Yes, yes, I'm sure. Never met your chap personally, though, a bit before my time." Mafferan, still very much in good nature, looked over at the suffering underling then back at ScrabaGag. "Hmmmm, you know, I see a family resemblance! Aren't you breaking your own rules?"

ScrabaGag knew he wasn't here to discuss these things, the meaning lay elsewhere. He was sure the Father knew he had invaded their domain. The question was why come here and why would he risk it? ScrabaGag decided to test him. "It seems you would be breaking a few yourself."

Mafferan responded with the highest class of politeness, one might even say to the point of being obsequious, "Really? Please enlighten me, Highest Councilor."

ScrabaGag saw that this spirit-man was a most unusual one because Mafferan showed the Highest Councilor respect, used ScrabaGag's official title, but was full of that accursed *glow*. Yet, the Highest Councilor's civility had an edge to it, "Being here, for one. Who are you?"

Mafferan ignored the obvious lie. They both knew there was no rule preventing him from coming to their Ethereal home, so Mafferan refused to dignify the lie with a response. He walked over to the dirty blue orb and ran his finger across the edge of it. It automatically lost its dirtiness in that area, glowing a brighter blue. "Hmmm … you need to take better care of our orbs! They're getting dirty after so many years of misuse!" Mafferan extended his arm into the blue orb which began glowing very brightly causing Grinchback to writhe in his upside down position.

ScrabaGag sighed, waved his arm at his underling and Grinchback fell on his head then immediately dashed behind his master. There was more to the Highest Councilor's action than met the eye. He was telling Mafferan he had the power to go up against him, but also, waiting so long to free his offspring told him that ScrabaGag couldn't be provoked. It also was obvious that Mafferan's rival was teaching his offspring a lesson. The King thought to himself, *So much can be learned from even single actions. There has never been a demon like this one before.*

ScrabaGag thought to himself. *Hmmmm, he knows there has never been a demon like me before ... might as well try, though.* Without warning, demon venom shot from Scraba-Gag's eye at Mafferan, but he vanished. ScrabaGag instantly whirled around, swooshing his offspring out of the way. But Mafferan showed up at his right side instead of behind him then pointed his finger at Grinchback, shooting a knife-like beam of light that passed across Grinchback's arm. The arm's shimmering and rippling faded and it floated away from the young demon. When Grinchback saw his severed arm, he realized the pain he was in and howled obscenely. But before ScrabaGag could say or do anything, Mafferan held up his hand for silence then pointed with his other finger so Grinchback's arm floated back and reattached.

ScrabaGag cursed secretly at himself, because he knew his Eye was showing surprise. *And I don't want to show anything!* He knew, of course, that Mafferan was aware of all these things. He understood the message Mafferan had just sent him. *I can't predict his* glowing *behavior, he's even wiser than me and will adapt. Hmmmm, wiser in the short run. He just showed me some of his abilities in a meaningless confrontation.*

But Mafferan knew his thoughts and took pleasure in revealing this. "Not meaningless at all." Then he peered a little deeper within ScrabaGag. "Hmmm, is that you in there? My old friend? GrrraGagag?"

ScrabaGag was not amused and Mafferan knew it, smiled, then disappeared. He reappeared back by the clear, blue orb, sticking his arm in again. Trees began zipping by, until almost at the Great Forest Gap. He addressed his Alpha host, "Highest Councilor ScrabaGag, you wanted to know who I am." Mafferan nodded to the orb and ScrabaGag floated over. "See that row, thirteen from the very back? See that empty space right in that lifeless, glowless, *ugly* looking forest? That's who I am."

This time ScrabaGag anticipated and hid all his reactions, but Mafferan continued, "Don't you know that there can be nothing hidden from the Glow? Too bad that empty spot doesn't tell you much, huh? But that's precisely my point. You see, you've upset the balance quite terribly. I could gut you right now and feed Scraback to GrrraGagag and restore the original High Councilor's ..." At the sound of those words, several bulges seemed to move of their own accord within ScrabaGag. His tail-tapping stopped. He was *not* amused. "... but all I'm here to do is to deliver a message."

ScrabaGag replied dryly, "Really."

"We don't even care that much that the three have become one, but we *do* care that the cursed Black Oil has found its way back into the Earth." Mafferan's voice had distinctly sharp and menacing undertones. ScrabaGag knew he wasn't bluffing.

Fire burned like the brightest stars all packed together within Mafferan's eyes.

ScrabaGag knew, for now, he had to play by the rules. "What do you desire to do to balance it? It's out of our control now, as you well know. In fact, we were not responsible for it showing up there!"

That was part of the beauty of ScrabaGag's plan and even more beautiful was absolutely nothing could be done to balance it! ScrabaGag couldn't help from laughing and Mafferan noted this, thinking ... *Hmmm, he's not so different from the other demons after all.* ScrabaGag instantly became aware of *that* thought and became more displeased with himself ... but he was also pleased that he was learning.

Mafferan tired and decided to make his point, "Just like I reappeared in a place you didn't expect after you attacked me *first*, when the balance shows up and you don't expect it, *leave it alone!*" The threat in his last words was unmistakable. Mafferan paused to observe the reactionless Highest Councilor, then continued, "If you don't, I'll come back, *gut you, feed you* to GrrraGagag, and GrrraGagag to the First High Councilor. And then go before *your* father of this domain and make my apologies as to having *lost my temper.* To make it right, I would then ask *your* father if he would like me to put things back the way they were before I got angry. *Your fate would then be in your father's hands!*"

Highest Councilor ScrabaGag floated in amazement at Mafferan's brilliance on so many levels. From his polite apology to the Father, to his threat to restore the three, even from the very first words out of his mouth, Mafferan's presentation was brilliant and flawless. Of course, the key concern now is there's no telling what the Father might do, *And that's the point! It's very unlikely that Mafferan could even carry out this threat, but that's another point, very unlikely isn't an absolute disclaimer of it.* ScrabaGag knew this battle had been won by Mafferan but there was so much he learned from this little skirmish. He was sure the next battle would be much different and imagined how superior in taste Mafferan would be to any others while he replied, "I will take it under advisement!"

Mafferan began to vanish but the Highest Councilor called him back! Not expecting such a solicitation, Mafferan grew cautious with increasing uneasiness. He'd penned in the demon so there was no need for any further discussion. "Was there something unclear, Highest Councilor?"

"You think you're so superior with your understanding of what you call good, but our way evolves stronger and stronger life. Only the strongest prevail. *If there was* any infraction of the rules on our part concerning the Sacred Oil, the perpetrators have been duly taken care of as you so aptly pointed out. Isn't that right, *GrrraGagag?*" This time no bulges moved nor even quivered inside ScrabaGag, and he made sure Mafferan noted it and then continued his oratory, "You are correct. Something is *quite* unclear. I cannot *imagine* what balance you would be talking about. *But let me warn you… with the truth!* The Sacred Black Oil found its way to Earth solely because a human desired it to be so. He alone, solely through his own power, and against *explicit warning,* has taken and used it for whatever he desires. Now he runs loose in our glorious Forest, *stealing* our Sacred Oil whenever he *chooses.* I personally tried to rectify this by consuming him, *as is my right,* if I find such a thief in the Forest or the corridor but he is, frankly, too powerful so I failed! I *believe* he is one of *your* offspring. If you would be so kind, perhaps you could correct him. I am *sure* you have the power to do so!"

Mafferan didn't want to be hurt or disgusted, but.... *Damn ... that demon* did *speak the truth. He's taken the high ground and used the truth against me!* Mafferan couldn't help showing his feelings.

Highest Councilor ScrabaGag kept up his momentum. "I *am* sorry if I have *hurt* you ... Oh, that's right, you *can't* correct him, can you? *Your rules,* the ones you've agreed to impose upon yourselves and us ever since the Vile One left. They *expressly* decree neither of us may directly interfere with the human will. Actually, that rule was kind of lopsided because *you* never really believed in directly improving them anyway, did you? Granted, there have been a few minor infractions some time ago as we possessed a few and you smote a few, but for the longest time these rules have stood the test and we didn't *bully* anyone around. Perhaps you may now see the flaw in your rules? Jargono is the flaw. He wants no part of us or you. If he succeeds, the Earth will be lost to us both, *according to your rules.* Would you like to reconsider them?"

Truly, there has never been a demon like this one! Mafferan found himself taking much longer to find the perfect reply than to his liking so the demon took advantage of this opening.

"It is ironic, isn't it? The *glow* had its Christ on Earth to little effect, I might add, and now it seems the humans will have a Christ all of their very own *from their right of choice!*"

"The rules stand. They are good. No matter what. *Also, my message stands.*" However, for the first time in a very long time, Mafferan just didn't like the sound of his answer on so many levels. For one thing, it lacked a certain color and sounded far too dogmatical in feeling. Mafferan always believed in meaning, not platitude. Though his words were technically correct, somehow he noticed something ... missing.

"I am sure your message is quite serious. I shall not interfere with your *balance,* if it truly is a balance."

They stood eye to Eye, both knowing they'd hurt the other, both appraising who had gotten the upper hand. This standoff left the final judgment up in the air or Ethereal but both knew the score now favored demon life.

Highest Councilor ScrabaGag pressed his advantage still further. "You actually should be thanking me! Apparently, you still have a daughter, yet alive, down there. One you are rather quite fond of, I see. If it wasn't for me, she would have been inside my former master right now. I'm sorry to say that since none of her ancestors would teach her of her powers, I had to help encourage her, myself! I thank you for restoring my offspring's arm. It's not quite tit for tat, but I'll consider us even! You may go!" Highest Councilor ScrabaGag vanished from his own ethereal room with his offspring, leaving the King alone to show himself out but Mafferan called *him* back!

"Yes, yes, I am *very* busy, have you forgotten your way out?"

Mafferan glared with deep black eyes, blacker even than the Highest Councilor's shade and his tone became menacing, beyond icy cold. "Am very appreciative of the *encouragement* you gave my daughter. There could have been no better teacher for her! Since you are so aware of my ancestors, my daughter *in particular*, then you also know that she was willing to be eaten by you rather than have the Seed to the Tree of Life be no more." He paused to let that meaning sink into the demon. "She got that kind of *craziness* from me! If I have to, I will formally disengage myself from above and come first for *you* and take you down to your banal, primal essence, and then I will destroy as many other demons as I can find until one of you *might* manage to eat me. If a demon succeeds in devouring me, the offense shall have been *duly paid for*. But if no one succeeds in that, then this realm will belong to *me!* Either way, Highest Councilor, *you will lose and the rules shall stand!* Don't bother to get up, I know the way out."

Mafferan vanished but ScrabaGag still could hear his words and feel his strange blackness vibrate in the room. Never before had anything ever been said nor even considered like that. Highest Councilor ScrabaGag mumbled to himself, "*He* is *crazy!*"

On his way back home, Mafferan chuckled while strolling and musing in the corridor. *I think he really thinks I'm crazy. Whatever devious thing he attempts next, he'll pause before he tries it. Still, things don't look good. Hmm… poor Cloudwalker.*

☙

Back at Mafferan's home, Yinauqua sensed she'd lost *all* contact with her husband, a *very* disturbing feeling, so she began querying the local spirits.

"Did you see where my husband went?" There were a lot of shoulder shrugs and finger pointing at other spirits' residences until she finally got to *Cloudwalker*. "Did you see where my husband went? I can't sense him *at all!*" He felt the reality of her disturbed look but remembered his junior's request not to tell her.

He smiled, "I never saw where he went!"

Yinauqua squinted at him, leveling her eye. *Hmmm, he's telling the truth… hmmm, but* not *all of it.* She folded her arms and stared… waiting. He knew one of her gifts was to bring out the truth, *the whole truth*, and that even he couldn't resist it. He realized then just what Mafferan had done in telling him not to tell his wife. Mafferan had always been mischievous and *Cloudwalker* couldn't believe he fell for his trap, again! He smiled, saying to himself, *The flow of life works in so many beautiful ways.*

CHAPTER NINE

The Flow of Life

She saw the men talking and it didn't feel right so she scooted her mop and pail ever so closer, being careful, as always, not to allow the ship's swaying to make her slip on the freshly swabbed deck. This was her means of paying transport to the new land in order to escape too many people, too many suspicions of her being different. *The sails with their crosses on them flapped in the steady breeze that carried her to freedom.*

Now close enough, she heard the men's plotting. "I tell you, they are Jews, and every Friday evening they sneak down into the hold to do their devil worship. We'll be ashore tomorrow. If we don't throw them over now, it'll be too late and we'll infect the new land."

"What about the one man's wife and daughter?" *the other asked with a look in his eye.*

"First things first." *The other man winked at him.*

Oh God!, *she spoke within,* People were calling me a witch, calling them the devils. I can't let them enact their plan but... what will they do to me? *But the men began to make for the hold and there was no time to consider it further. She quickly glanced around to see if any eyes were upon them then tipped her pail over, spilling the soapy wash water over the deck. The men instantly slipped and hit hard. After taking one more quick glimpse around, she waved her arm and an invisible force hurled the two men over the railing into the sea.*

"Oh my God!" She screamed, "Men overboard. Me wash water tipped and they slid over!" She prayed no one saw her and that they wouldn't throw her over, too. She wasn't sure if her mysterious abilities would be able to preserve her all alone in the sea.

Something was different and he knew it long before he reached the hidden town. As soon as he entered the valley, he felt something that made his flesh crawl all over. He'd seen before how they made the drug with that strange, foul black oil that they added to the concoction. Just seeing that oil made him feel a bit strange, but really, it was only just a few drops into each vat, nothing really significant. Yet, these feelings Trevor now had went way beyond a bit of repugnance. He rubbed his skinny arms briskly but that didn't help at all. *If it wasn't for you, sis ...* He shook his head, vowing again, *Two more years, sis, and then we can escape all this hell. I'll have plenty of money. We'll live anyway we desire and I won't give a damn about our parents even if they beg me. I'd like them to beg me.*

As he drew closer to the usually quiet town, he could hear all kinds of noises, an odd mix of celebration and indeterminate cries. Not easily shaken nor moved, Trevor oddly hit the town's edge feeling suffocated. *Stop it, damn it! It doesn't matter, you can do this!*

212

At the center of the small ramshackle town, its whole population was one glorious mass of flesh ... rather, the women were all naked in the meeting square. The men were dressed in what could be described as demonic masks and garb, some of which looked half-human-half-demon. Upon numerous mattresses side by side on the concrete platform where formal social events were held, the women rolled together in ecstasy but none of the men joined them.

Trevor wanted to look away, yet there was something odd about what the women were doing that held his attention. They weren't just sexual acts, they were acts of adoration. Seemingly in surrender, the women frequently raised their hands to heaven and screamed not only in sexual pleasure but in placation to the beyond. Their sexual perversions were part of their worship, not the other way around. Whenever one woman was brought to the culmination of her pleasure, she rushed to give her place to another and to begin that 'worship' upon that female. And something else was strange, all the women looked ... pregnant, not far along, but enough to be noticeable. Trevor halted then backed up a step.

"Trevor! How wonderful to see you." The man's grip on his arm was a lot tighter than necessary. For the first time in his life, other than caring for his sister and perhaps that young lady that had died, Trevor found himself with deep emotions, but in actual fear for his own life. *But why now when I didn't care before?* The man smiled, "You're going to be a very important part of the new world we're ushering in! *You* are helping to prepare the way!" After studying Trevor a moment, he added, "And of course, you'll become even richer, beyond your wildest dreams. Your sister will be proud."

Trevor's eyes widened, *I never told anyone about sis! Oh God!*

"Trevor, our God has finally come as was told in prophecy. His name is Demi-Glen. An odd name for a god, but that's what he wants to be called. He wants to be famous all over the world, and eventually, even for that guy Jargon to bow to him ... before he *kills* him." The man checked again to see how Trevor was receiving all this wonderful news. Trevor never felt more uncomfortable in his life because his usual apathetic nature had vanished. He just didn't know what to do with all the feelings trying to push to the surface.

"Trevor, I didn't tell you this before, but you were prophesied to come to us, too!"

Trevor couldn't help but react, "Whoa ... wait a minute!"

The man half led, half pulled him toward the town center but Trevor finally found his own will and stopped cold, whereupon the man turned towards him but still held his arm. Trevor's other hand rubbed his cheek quite briskly, stopped, and then repeated the gesture. He usually didn't do that in rapid succession.

The man studied him. "It's time for you to know the truth about yourself, Trevor. *You* have been preparing the way for the new world for some time." The man took his other hand and touched it to Trevor's forehead.

Instantly, Trevor saw his life over the last year from the time he became a drug-dealer. He saw the thousands of people he sold to or gave drug gifts to, who all became hooked and became his steady customers. He felt how happy and proud he was to take their money, how those people's emotions changed, became twisted, grotesque... wait... not actually twisted... just different. He saw very clearly how he really didn't care one way or the other, but... no, that wasn't true at all. His indifference wasn't really not caring, his indifference was actually a form of caring, caring to produce the exact result he did produce in them! Trevor could see now ... he really *did* care, he wanted this!

"Trevor, Demi-Glen told us about you! He said he began his life *exactly* like you, before his godly attributes manifested in him."

Trevor rubbed his cheek three more times in a row, to the point that it turned quite red. The man smiled at it and began 'leading' him to the center of town. When they arrived, he hailed everyone, "His messenger has arrived!"

Immediately all the men turned towards Trevor and knelt on one knee. The women all stopped, formed a line, and one by one they paraded themselves before him, kissing Trevor's cheek, mashing their sweat soaked bodies against him, and rubbing their left hands over his crotch ... one by one ... one by one.

Their stench, their almost maniacal look in their eyes so repulsed Trevor that his reflex to vomit competed with the increasingly demanding desire to rub his cheek even harder. But something else started to happen. Frankly, unwanted sexual desire began to build in him. After a while, he started craving the next woman's touch until he found himself groping them, but the man finally stopped him. "All of these women belong to Demi-Glen, but he told us that later our women are allowed to worship you as his messenger. You cannot mate with any of them but they'll make you feel better than you've ever felt before. Since the joining, they have powers over pleasure you cannot even begin to fathom. Trevor, *you* are part of something so much greater than yourself."

In some distant place of Trevor's heart and mind, he was running very fast, very far away, but his feet led him to the very center of town. He stepped over the soiled mattresses to the center of the town square where a cross had been fashioned and bolted into the cement. In adoration, the women stripped Trevor naked, the only man to be so, and lovingly tied his arms to the cross and his feet to the base. His sexual desire felt as if it would rip his mind apart or his heart would give out from pounding, but then, also, another terrible fear came over him. He couldn't reach his cheek! He needed to rub it … rub it NOW.

His bonds were not so tight that they hurt, but they weren't loose enough to escape them either. Trevor frantically began to struggle, both out of desire for the women but also out of his desperate need to satisfy his cheek compulsion. The women seemed to interpret his growing frenzy as exactly the desired effect and they continued to touch him all over but not enough to bring him release from his torments.

The man that led him to his fate came before him with a bowl of the Black Oil and a sharply pointed stick. He dipped the point into the Oil then slowly drug it down at exactly the area of Trevor's cheek that he so direly needed to rub. When Trevor's blood and the oil mingled within the long gash, Trevor felt the connection to the Black Oil and his craving to rub his cheek took on insanely drastic levels. Beginning to howl and rage, the more he did, the more the women celebrated as if the raging was a good thing for Trevor, as if that was supposed to happen. They urged him to scream more, just as they had urged each other into sexual climax. Then the man went to Trevor and put something in his mouth. It was the drug Trevor sold but so despised, and would never have taken … and all of the sudden all of Trevor's torments vanished right there on the cross.

❧

Once again, Vaughn and Stephanie found themselves standing together in the mouth of the Sacred Cave. On the way, they had thoroughly discussed *through us, not by us*.

For Vaughn, in a way, it was much easier because though he buried them, he didn't know them. It was strictly a Justice issue for him, and the natural cry of compassion for the innocent. True, Stephanie had told him all about her biological father, and he was none too endeared. Also, Vaughn had met him and he hadn't liked him from the start. Knowing he killed her mother deeply angered him but none of this compared to what Stephanie was going through.

Vaughn was more able to allow Justice free reign, to set his personal feelings aside. Personal feelings lead to personal vengeance, but the greater meaning of Justice allows the Spirit of God to deliver judgment. No matter how righteous the grievance, personal feelings are never sufficient to deliver judgment upon a soul. That right had to belong solely to the Creator of that soul. God used His life to make that person.

Through us but not by us. Yet, no amount of discussion trying to separate the personal from the greater meaning of Justice can change reality. The truth is, if Stephanie is going to be a true servant of God through whom His Justice can be rendered, she has to win that battle in her heart, not her mind. Even having her prayers answered that asked for her to abandon her personal feelings would not really be a solution, if unresolved conflict could still rear its head.

Yet, Power flowed through Vaughn and Stephanie who felt united to its greater meaning, and all that they saw and felt became filtered through it. There was little room for anything else so that even their love for each other seemed a distant memory. There was a sense of perceiving history as if it were the present. Neither of their minds could tell how far that past reached back, only that there was a sense of impending judgment that had brought it to the now. This was greater than they could possibly understand. Their hearts processed and held close the depths of the meaning, while their minds could only pick out snapshots, some of which appeared rather ancient in origin.

They stood together, staring out across the peaceful valley where once the tiny Appendaho village had voices of laughter and diverse signs of life. Now, the historical signs of life were blackened vestiges of burned buildings and the streaks of ash that numerous rainfalls labored to wash away. There would be further signs to leave behind. The Spirit eased off from them a bit, affording them conversation and it was Vaughn who was able to speak first.

"So, this is where you were led by Justice. It makes sense to bring him back here where he did the most evil."

"*Yes.* And I want my ancestors to see what God will do to them right here."

Stephanie spoke in a way that Vaughn had never heard before. There was something powerful, deep, even commanding in her voice which wasn't her, yet was one with her. It also had an unsettling hardness to it that Vaughn wasn't at all sure he liked.

"What was the message you sent to your father?"

She replied to him while staring at the graves below, "You poor excuse for a man, were it not for the great evil you have done, I could feel sorry for you. God requires your presence here at the Appendaho village on the first day of the week. It doesn't matter how many men you bring, they will not be enough. God has delivered your lives into my hands. Your *daughter.*"

The hair all over his body stood up, as he took in the words. "*My God,* you just sent shivers all over me."

Stephanie still gazed below. "It's God's power, not mine. I just told him what was placed in my heart."

"That message! He's sure to bring the men he had with him that day."

"I know. I can see it!"

Vaughn stared at her. "Your foremother was a prophetess, she told me. That's why I have this Book."

"I know, and so was Arlupo. OH, GOD! I miss her so." Stephanie's memory brought all back to life in her. She could feel Arlupo's hands sliding out of hers at their last moments together. And there was that unbearable pain of their deaths, so much that it had drove Stephanie's consciousness to the farthest reaches of reality.

Vaughn could see her memories crossing through her, and the pain. He pointed below, "There, Stephie, coming through the pass… it's them."

The *faithwalker* stared, becoming lost in her own private world.

Coming up the valley was the man who killed her mother, the man who killed her best friend, the man who killed the father of her best friend with whom she'd bonded … the man who murdered the last of the wonderful people she discovered were her true ancestors.

She could clearly see it in herself now, the actual family connection to the Appendaho, irrelevant of the hundreds of generations that had passed since Mafferan had lost his daughter. She could feel Appendaho in her blood, giving her a deeper understanding of herself. Of course, scientifically, that didn't make sense at all. Stephanie briefly wondered how many actual genes she still possessed from them, *But actually, science would have a lot of difficulty with all that has happened this last year. In fact, science would have difficulty with* me, *PERIOD.*

Stephanie's attention went back to the approaching men down below. Coming closer was the man who also was her father, who also contributed to her constitution, from whom God also took goodness to make her. There was the man for whose love she had wept countless times, from whom she still desired love… *Reality is what it is… Those things can never really be changed.* There was the man she still loved because he was simply her father but to whom she had to allow Life to deal with in its own natural way. Without her adding or taking away from God's will, Justice had to be *through* her, not *by* her. Vaughn saw the tears in her eyes and the strain imposed upon her face but he knew these were only glimmers of the tremendous conflagration within her.

"Vaughn, wait here, please!"

His eyes turned to steel, "Oh, no! *No way.* Remember, I also have my *oath* to fulfill." *Besides, I know you need me down there.*

Her reply was calm, somehow otherworldly, "It will be, but by God. Do not lift your hands until He moves them. Let's go down to the grave site. You have something to tell them!"

Vaughn's choice of the burial site was perfect, as anyone entering the valley had to encounter the presence of the deceased who had settled there, sort of like a home has a lived-in feeling.

Led by Fred, the men cautiously approached, all dressed in gray uniforms. They were deployed as if expecting to meet another military force and stopped just short of the first grave, where Vaughn had buried Arlupo and her parents. Their eyes darted around seeking impending danger, as if they heard sounds of an enemy threat, or perhaps they sensed something watching them. A guilty conscience has been known to provoke all kinds of imaginations.

Relief spread through the company when they saw their enemy. Instead of armed Appendaho, only two kids, not fully grown, came walking toward them from the other side of the grave site. When Fred saw his daughter one could see a maelstrom of anger and fear, hate and love and regret, but the choices in his life had directed much of his strength to the tree of death.

Vaughn and Stephanie stopped just before reaching the graves on the western side. Stephanie's long royal-blue dress with Appendaho design in red and gold in front, and golden threads trimming its borders, gently flapped in the breeze. Her three hair braids were behind her so her face was fully exposed. Vaughn's black short-sleeved shirt was tucked into his black pants and his eyes were pitch black ,too.

The men started to laugh and joke but their commander was not amused. "You send me such a *threat?* I brought an armed company for *nothing.* OK, I'll send you for re-education." He paused and looked at Vaughn, trying to figure something out about him. "How did *you* get here? The last I heard, you were *dead.*"

Vaughn folded his arms in front of him and peered straight into Fred's eyes, "Not hardly… someone had to bury these innocent people!" The look in Vaughn's eyes was more than defiant… it was daring them and there was no fear!

Hearing Vaughn's response, the men began to straighten and some pointed their weapons as it was a crime to bury them. Stephanie's father ignored Vaughn as if he didn't exist, the same way he treated him when they first met back home at the airport. He returned his attention to his daughter and beckoned her to come to him. "Let's go… *move!*"

Vaughn didn't need to look at Stephanie because through their special connection, he felt her, felt her terrible sadness, her weeping pain, and her anger. Only her silent prayer freed her to continue, *Oh God, open my mouth… I can't find. …* After another pause, words surfaced. "You are the man from whom God made me." Then she bowed to him! His eyes grew large as she straightened. "God took goodness that was in you and in my mother to make me. I honor that goodness." She bowed again!

They were Arlupo's last words before he killed her. *But Stephanie wasn't here to hear them. How could she… It doesn't matter.*

She interrupted his thoughts by accusing him, "You killed my mother!" He flushed but remained speechless. *How could she know?* Vaughn tensed with warning, *This isn't the way we discussed to behave.*

Tears streamed down Stephanie's cheeks. "I'm supposed to honor the goodness in *both* of you. Can you tell me how I'm supposed to do that now, *Father?*"

Vaughn could feel power building in her but it was *very* personal. Dark clouds began to gather and he remembered her saying they formed during Arlupo's death. Vaughn also remembered seeing the same thing after she learned of Jargono's threat on Lana. *Faith… But this time I will keep faith in her… and I will pray.*

Her father patronized her. "You wouldn't understand. I told you to *come here!* The Appendaho have…"

She yelled at him, "I AM APPENDAHO! But you *killed* them, too!" Thunder began to roar.

"They've brainwashed you! You're … *crazy!*"

Change directions. Vaughn knew it was best to calmly break the line of conversation. "You can't even begin to understand what your daughter is but what she surely is *not* is under *your* authority. God shall bear witness this day that your daughter is in fact a *holy* woman." Vaughn deeply bowed to her!

His words and actions, the depth of their respect, their meaning and spirit, touched Stephanie to her core, pausing her thoughts and emotions. The thunder instantly stopped while the low hanging clouds stopped churning.

The truth abruptly disengaged her from the path she was treading. *Holy woman. I ... have a greater calling than personal vengeance.* She raised her softened eyes to her father's. "I have a new will from Almighty God. The one I got through you is dead and gone. God has seen fit to free me. I answer to *no* man. *Only* to God!"

Enflamed by her words which were more than disrespectful, more than defiant, he tried to classify them but couldn't. They were... all he knew was he felt smaller than he ever felt before, felt worse than from his awful mother dream when afterwards he sees a little boy's face instead of his own reflection in the mirror. First, his own mother deprives him of... and now his very own daughter cuts all ties as if he was *nothing*. The burly man made his official proclamation with the sound of the gavel implied. "I knew there was no hope for you. You... *You are forcing me to do this to you.* You deserve to die with the rest."

Seeing murder in Fred's eyes, Vaughn bristled, and memories flooded him of finding the slaughtered Appendaho. He could see them all being shot, feel the suffering of the men, women and children, and his oath burned with heated anger against these people.

Vaughn stretched out his arms and Stephanie stepped away to give him room. The blackness in Vaughn's eyes swirled, radiating outward with invisible waves.

"What vermin, what wretched disease has so blinded you that atrocity pours from you like water from a raging river?

The blood of these peaceful and innocent people cries against you from the very ground from where you *slaughtered* them!" Vaughn finally took a breath, then continued, "And I am here to avenge their blood, and to avenge the last surviving, faithful member of their people." Vaughn stepped into the graveyard toward the fifty or so men. The power swirling all through him, that presence of Justice defining Vaughn's reality made unreal any vague thought that going up against soldiers with weapons was ridiculous and surreal.

Her father threw open his arms with surprise, as if wrongfully accused. "Who's the crazy one here? She's a *slut!* I know all about her. Holy? HA! Faithful? To *what*? I knew you were no good, *boy!* You once threatened me. Yes, I know you threatened me. But you'll never grow to be a man to carry out your threat. It wasn't enough that I arranged for your little *trip* to the State farm! You're not able to learn how to be a real man. Real men don't let *women* rule, and they *don't* bow to them!"

When Stephanie heard the treachery he'd also done to Vaughn, a deep blackness instantly mingled with the red fire blazing in her eyes. *Vaughn almost died, too, because of this man? What in my life hasn't he poisoned?*

Vaughn groaned inside. *Damn, now she has that to deal with… It's too much.*

Stephanie growled, "*You* put him through all that?"

Fred yelled back, "I was being a *real* father, *protecting* you! The principal of the school understood that!"

Stephanie's face reddened as she began to shake a little but her words now took on a dead calm which scared Vaughn even more than when she was shouting at Fred. "You really put him through all that?" She'd made up her mind, or rather personal vengeance made up her mind. "*Killed my MOTHER, DESTROYED THIS PEOPLE!*" The ground trembled and the men looked at each other. A few stared at Stephanie and began easing to the back ranks.

Her father answered her sorrowfully. "Either always crying or always angry or always *rebellious*. From the time I knew you, you've *never* had the strength to understand how to live a *real* life. It's best for your misery to end."

Strangely, *his* words gave a moment's pause in her heart's course of imminent doom. *But I* do now *have real life… strength to understand. Oh God, I* do *have them! If I let* my *anger rule me, I'll be* fulfilling *his accusations!* Oh God, *I'd be just like him!* She heard herself weakly call her beloved's name, "Vaughn!"

He knew. Vaughn had been waiting for Life to take its natural course. He knew why Stephanie called out to him and he wanted desperately to begin so she wouldn't get caught in further personal fury. Moments ago, he felt her teetering, her rage forcing her into destruction.

God was more real to Vaughn than their weapons or anything else evil had. He could feel Stephanie struggling but he had vowed never to lose faith in her again, *No matter what.* Suddenly, he felt overpowered by the invisible, felt himself move forward into the center of the graveyard. Vaughn spread his hands out from his sides, with open palms to the men. "Come, all you *men*, come teach this *boy* a lesson."

Someone raised his rifle, but Fred shouted with wrath, "NO! SHOOTING HIM IS NO JUSTICE. I WANT HIM BEAT

TO DEATH, UNTIL HE'S UNRECOGNIZABLE, UNTIL YOU CAN'T EVEN TELL HE WAS A HUMAN BEING."

Vaughn heard Stephanie's voice behind him, a voice with the sound of pain, of revelation, and commitment beyond the pain. "As you have judged Father, so be it unto you."

Five soldiers rushed forward but when the first two were in arms reach, Vaughn's half curled fingers flew out in half circles like a lion or tiger. His right hand ripped through the first man to his left, laying open his face, pulling off his jaw. An instant later, he shifted to the right, and his left hand did the same to the man on his right. Then back to his left, a soldier's gut tore open through his clothing, and the same to another man on his right. The fifth man was caught with such a powerful right hook under his chin that his jaw caved upward into his skull. He fell dead instantly at Vaughn's feet while the others writhed in agony. Vaughn, splattered all over with human debris with hands dripping in blood, looked out toward the rest. He resumed his original pose, holding out his hands.

Fred screamed in outrage, "You can't let that *boy* beat you. *Get him!*"

With no time to process, nine or ten more soldiers rushed forward without thinking and surrounded him. Stephanie couldn't see Vaughn at all but she heard the men cry out. Movement from the rest of the soldiers who had not yet joined the clash caught her attention. They were raising their rifles. Anger flashed in her but this time it was the anger of Justice. Stephanie bowed her head, opened her arms wide and turned her hands up to the heavens. She spoke softly, but all could hear her words which were more than words, "Come Justice, do *Your* will through me."

A wind from the East blew across the valley, her dress flapped loudly, her face with eyes closed lifted to the heavens. The sky quickly re-darkened with swirling black clouds, and a cold draft carrying the chill of death swept down upon them. The men, rifles raised, looked tentatively at each other then shifted their aim to Stephanie! But the ground shook beneath them and those that didn't fall, wildly rocked back and forth.

Rumbling thunder began to build into a roar and at its crescendo, Stephanie's head leveled and she opened her eyes to face the scene. Everything fell silent. The blackness had left her eyes but they now glowed like red suns. All the men saw this. They somehow knew their lives were being held in her outstretched hands.

The thick silence terrified them, that stillness, that utter peace smothered them. Helplessness! They were lost in such peace, without bearings, suddenly having no feeling or connection to reality. Their hearts pounded as they saw Vaughn standing atop a pile of corpses. Seeing the deep blackness in his eyes, they could feel it. They looked at each other again, then… the first began to run away.

History became present. Stephanie could feel each individual soul, each history and generations she couldn't tell how far back. Their lives were present in her heart, in her mind. There was no forward. Stephanie slowly clenched her hands into fists, bowing her head again. A deafening roar *preceded* the lightning bolt that struck the first fleeing man and left the smell of smoking flesh but no other sign of him.

When the rest of the men saw their comrade incinerated, they began to scurry in all directions. The lightning erupted with a continuous thunder that seemed to consume all by its very sound. After a short time, when the roar ceased, there were only ten men begging, left crawling on the ground cowering from fear, but her father still stood defiantly upright.

To show mercy to those whom Justice wants taken away is as wrong as personal vengeance. The consequences would be just as terrible. Vaughn spoke without mercy, pointing to the graves, "You beg. You *men*, beg. Has life suddenly become so precious to you? When you took their children prisoner, did you heed their pleas for their lives, for their parents' lives? They tried to *buy* their parents' lives with their own! But you would *not* hear. VERILY I SAY UNTO THEE, I SHALL NOT HEAR YOU." Vaughn heard words he had never heard before, neither did he know about the Appendaho children trying to barter their lives for their parents'. But there was no time now to consider all this because Vaughn quickly fell upon them as they crept upon the ground. Their final thoughts were, '*How could he know! We took the children in secret.*'

And it was true. They had cleverly rounded them up from their schools under false pretenses, and not until the children were heading home did they become aware of their fate. And even as the young ones were being abused, they had begged to those boasting, lascivious men, begged not even for their own lives but for their parents, offering their whole lifetime in servitude if they would just spare their parents.

So Vaughn mightily kicked and stomped them until their heads were crushed, their bodies were broken. Still there was anger in reserve as there were still writhing men alive, though suffering.

Yet, her father stood defiant and pulling out a small black bottle that he uncorked, he declared, "Jargono told me, if I had trouble, to use this, then I would bring justice to you." He poured the whole bottle of black oil onto his bald head and stood there… then he screamed and fell down to his knees and one could feel the hopeless horror that consumed him.

Stephanie and Vaughn looked at each other. Each knew the other was shocked by what her father said. *Justice indeed, but why?*

Seeing her father's hopeless suffering reminded her of the Tree of Life's vision of Vaughn's torments in the hospital… torments there because of *that* man. She recalled struggling in the corridor, trying to heal Vaughn, trying to wake him up, feeling the horrific torture he went through. *Unforgivable suffering caused by this* wretched *man. Justice indeed.* Anger flooded Stephanie, again, but she thought, *It's OK, now…. It's almost over. I know I'm still angry but I'll just say a prayer, that's all… just a prayer,* "Oh Father of Goodness, be JUST to this man. Let him *live!*"

Vaughn's eyes snapped up at her. *Oh God, Stephanie! No!* But then he remembered his own words when King Mafferan had asked him who was Vaughn to judge, *I'm just saying the prayer, it's God Who answers it.* And, yet, something didn't feel right, but there was no time to examine it now. There was unfinished *work* to do.

Writhing in unseen agony, Fred suffered a nightmare

he could not escape by death because God answered his daughter's prayer for him.

The Oil seemed to be absorbed into his body and disappeared. Vaughn's heart vision flashed before him and a strong desire to immediately kill the man almost overwhelmed him. *But she just prayed for him to live. The Oil won't kill him but that doesn't mean I can't. But Stephanie just …*

Her prayer had satisfied her personal anger. She had cleverly found a way both to satisfy her own anger and avoid negative consequences. *I didn't even have to do harm by doing the prayer.* She turned toward the remaining suffering men because a greater justice needed fulfilling. Stephanie raised her palms to the heavens with arms outstretched and bowed her head, then slowly closed her hands again. *Justice.* The lightning erupted once more, striking all the other corpses and suffering men. Then there was no sign of them except for the stench of burnt flesh that the wind quickly carried away.

Her father alone was left, clawing at the Earth, trying to dig himself a grave to crawl into. But the prayer preserved his suffering, destining him to bear out his natural life span for however long that would be.

Stephanie and Vaughn silently turned away from the scene and went down to the stream to bathe among the burned fruit trees. Stephanie helped Vaughn undress his bloody clothing because they stuck to him as did the smell of carnage. Though she was clean all over, she still felt the need to bathe, too, so she folded her royal dress and laid it across a tree branch along with her undergarments.

They had never in waking life beheld each other's nakedness but there was no interest in it at this time. Stephanie took the soap from Vaughn and scrubbed the blood off his back, in what felt like a holy ceremony. After he was totally cleansed, she asked him to scrub her back. When they finally finished, the sun was high in the sky and shone straight down upon them. Vaughn took her hand to help her step out of the stream and to climb up the steep bank.

Standing together at the top, the warmth of the sunshine upon their naked flesh banished the chill from their bath and soothed away their remaining tension. Stephanie gazed into the sun, smiling. "I love the sun so much."

Feelings of natural life finally began returning to them. Vaughn looked into her face, placing his hand upon her cheek, "Every day is a day I love you so much more."

She remembered how Arlupo's father had said similar things and was wondering how it was that Vaughn said them. Then there was a crash upon her head and everything went black!

In that instant, Vaughn's eyes had turned pitch black. He knew, but he had no time to react. One shimmering gray arm had hit Stephanie in the head while he barely managed to turn partly away from another arm and was knocked down the bank into the stream.

CHAPTER TEN
Repercussions

They sat around the roughly hewed small wooden table after Friday evening prayers. The young man kept fidgeting until the elder at the head of the table admonished him, "What? What troubles your mind that Shabbat prayers can't calm?"

The lad looked down at the table, evading three other pairs of prying eyes. The Rabbi tapped his finger several times on the table, which meant, Speak!

"What do you think of witches?"

Everyone sat up a little straighter. "Why do you ask? Moses commanded them to be destroyed but the Christians do not understand. Those were different times. Before certain evil had been locked away, witches accessed that evil. Now they call anyone a witch whom they fear for whatever reason. They call us devils, others they call witches … Why do you ask?"

The young fidgeter looked up briefly and then away. "Never mind."

The old Rabbi slammed his hand upon the table, "There is no never mind once you have engaged our minds. Don't be a coward! Spit it out, young man. We are all one together here and now we are guilty with you!"

Feeling shame, the young man confessed, "The young lady who mopped the ship's deck that we sailed upon..."

"You mean three whole years ago? Why would you speak of her now?"

He shook his head in exasperation at the Rabbi but he decided to speak his mind anyway. "You never notice anyone except Jews. The Goyim are as much non-persons to you as we are to them." The Rabbi folded his hands upon the table while the others looked with disdain at the young lad who continued. "She settled here, but you didn't even pay it notice."

The Rabbi smiled, "I'm old and the time for me to pay notice to any young woman has long passed. I imagine my sons would have noticed, but her being a non-Jew, they would have never told me. What?"

"I was at the... tavern earlier." All of their eyebrows rose in surprise and condemnation but he moved on, "They sneered behind her back, calling her a witch... They say she healed a sick girl by magic, not by the church... and that she fixes broken things that can't be fixed."

The Rabbi sat up straighter, all of a sudden having one of those feelings from God that he recognized and had learned never to question anymore. Again, he tapped even harder, three times on the table, and the young man continued, "They go tonight... to drag her from her little room and..."

"And what?"

The young man blurted it out, "They've already decided her guilt. They will burn her as a witch."

"How do you know she dwells in a little room?"

The young man looked away, but then looked defiantly at the Rabbi. "I work for the Goyim, you know? Ehhh? And I also... travel around and hear things. The blacksmith's little daughter got badly ill and the doctors had given up. I told the blacksmith that I've heard the bar-maid had knowledge from the old world and that she helped other sick folk... discreetly. He couldn't bring himself to take her but asked me to do so. She took the little girl into her room and asked me to wait outside but I snuck up to her window and peeked through the space between the curtains."

"Yes?"

"She is a witch, I think! I saw her hands glow then the girl revived. She asked the child to close her eyes and take some medicine first but I'm sure it wasn't the medicine."

The Rabbi reached across the table and grabbed the young man by his shirt, jerking him close. "You waited till NOW to tell me? Go to her this instant and warn her!"

The young man scowled, "All your superstitions! You are afraid of a witch, Rabbi? That she'll give you the evil eye before she dies?"

But he shook his head. "It's natural for youth to misjudge the old. No, not afraid like that, but afraid that also we be guilty of her blood for not helping. She's no witch. What you describe is a gift to the righteous. Go quickly and save her while we pray you're not too late."

From the corridor, Jargono had watched Stephanie bathing many times. *But I never got to see you naturally, willingly, like he has.* He saw her scrub Vaughn and watched him scrub her back. He wanted to destroy them both in that instant and felt fairly confident that he could. *Their little tricks with that company of men were not impressive.* But there was always the unknown possibility that they could harm him somehow, the fight at the cave had not turned out quite like he expected.

Jargono vanished from above them, but moments later he reappeared.

"Listen to me, kill the boy, tear him to shreds, but bring the girl to me *unharmed.* You'll have to knock her out right away, though, or she might be able to destroy you." Jargono grabbed Demon Glen by the throat with his glowing hand, peering deeply into his red eyes whereupon the demon howled. "Bring her to my bedchamber *unharmed* and *untouched.*" Jargono vanished from the corridor. He wanted to prepare the room. Obviously, he couldn't have her of her own free will, but … *That doesn't mean I can't have her.*

❦

Demon Glen saw Vaughn roll down the bank and decided he could kill him any time he wanted. And Jargono didn't have to tell him to kill Vaughn because that was going to happen regardless of what *Jargono* said. Inside his glowing prison, he often imagined just how he would do it. Demon Glen laughed out loud, rejoicing, "I have power now, you can't even imagine. Even Jargono doesn't know. It won't be long before I throw that bastard into *my* cage and drag him to my Master. Hah! He wants him as a *pet.*"

Demon Glen turned to glimpse Stephanie before starting to comply with the order to *kill Vaughn.* The demon part of him instantly lusted after her as did the human part, too. Both parts agreed about having her and knowing he couldn't be stopped. Demon Glen thought, *Who better to give birth to more of my offspring? What better hurt to Vaughn before I kill him?*

Demon Glen burned with lust, recalling Gary's descriptions of sex with her but she was far more beautiful than he had ever imagined. Seeing her lying unconscious on the grass, the sun shining on her helpless nakedness, slobber oozed from his mouth in long trails. "I could do this quickly." He had found out that the demon part of him mated in mere seconds and was able in short order to impregnate the whole female population in the village. "But she's far too beautiful to have that way."

He transformed his phallus into human form and approached her then crouched between her legs, running his demon hands along the insides of her thighs then opening her legs wide. The pain of expectancy urged him while his phallus changed back into demon form several times. Glen fought the demon's urge and changed it back into human each time. He had made up his mind that he was going to be a human with demonic powers, *Not a demon with human abilities.* He crouched over then made a thrust into her.

Something blocked his entry. He tried to penetrate twice more then growled and looked into her beautiful face. He laughed, "Oh, part of you *is* awake. I wish you could be fully awake. It would make it even more enjoyable. All my women screamed when they were awake even before my new powers." His large demon hand gently ran up her flat stomach, across her breasts and covered her mouth and nose. "Just long enough to put that little awake part asleep."

Moments went by with the slightest bit of twisting of her body then it stopped. Demon Glen knew he could penetrate her now but fear overwhelmed him. *Jargono would be angry knowing I mated with her, but he would kill me if she died.* He put his demon ear to her chest and heard a faint heartbeat. He compressed her chest a few times with his hand to force air out of her lungs then draw oxygen back in. When normal breathing returned to Stephanie, he spread her legs even wider in triumph.

As soon as Vaughn had fallen into the creek, he had rolled to a stand. He shook off the daze from the blow and fall, and immediately focused on his enemy. Precious seconds passed by, though, in waiting for the dizziness to cease. He saw Demon Glen lope over to his beloved at the top of the bank, and knew what was about to happen. Vaughn still couldn't think because now the blackness fell so heavily upon him that he was no longer in control. He bounded up the bank, never taking his eyes off the scene above. He saw Demon Glen kneel over her but couldn't make himself clamber fast enough. He saw him thrust, and thrust again. Vaughn's heart broke… *No, no, no!* Her sacredness that they had both sworn to preserve for the Tree of Life had been violated. The deepest blackness and red hot fire swirled in him.

Yet, sometimes, a rush of strength is self-defeating. He was scaling the bank too forcefully and it was caving from the pressure, keeping him from reaching the top. He had to control what he didn't want to control as he saw Glen listen to her chest. Fear exploded in him but this wasn't a fear he needed to put down. He took his eyes off the scene so he could concentrate on his climb. Reaching the top as the Demon spread her legs wider, Vaughn lost himself to rage.

He leapt on Glen, locking his arms around him to roll over and over, away from Stephanie. The Demon spread his arms and broke his grip easily then both came to their feet at the same time but Glen had leapt away to create distance between them. "Did you like what you saw?" Demon Glen taunted him. "She's delicious. After I kill you, I'll have her again."

Vaughn's every muscle leapt in reaction to his scurrilous jibes, his heart committed to tearing Glen apart. Yet the slimmest power held him back with the awareness that Glen was baiting him. Stephanie's life, the world's future, depended upon his winning this battle. Vaughn was glad he wasn't suckered into rash action, even as the heat of battle furiously propelled within him. *How do I kill him, Lord God?*

Demon Glen sprang through the air at him. Vaughn's eyes widened with surprise at how far he could leap. He'd never met anyone with such strength and began to suspect the Demon had even more. Vaughn dove aside but the agility of the demon caught Vaughn and claws ripped deeply into his shoulder and down his side,

Behind him… only from behind will I be able to have a chance. Vaughn assessed Glen's stature, noting the thickness of muscle especially around his neck. *I definitely won't be able to break* that! His rib cage and torso were heavily chiseled outrivaling any prize bull Vaughn had ever seen. *Neither can I do internal harm … not easily. LORD GOD, what do I do?* Demon Glen leapt at him again but this time Vaughn reacted more quickly to avoid him.

"You're beginning to irritate me. Jargono will begin to wonder where I've been."

Jargono! I knew it. He is responsible for the demon heart. "So, you're his *pet.*"

Demon Glen growled in anger, "My Master will make him *his* pet. Your world is already doomed. When my offspring are ready to mate, they shall claim thousands. Those thousands shall claim tens of thousands, and those will sire millions." He lifted his head to the sky and howled like a wolf.

Oh my God, he's describing my second vision! A plan began to formulate in Vaughn's mind but he didn't like at all the way he had to implement it. Yet, there didn't seem to be any alternative, the demon was too strong, too quick. *He'd never allow me to get behind him… not in battle.*

It was risky, for sure… a terrible gamble with everything dear to him and with the very future of all life! *Only a fool gambles all his strength in a single attack, unless he is in that moment going to die.* It was rule thirteen from *The Art of Fighting*, but nothing in his beloved series of books, not even in *Advanced Future,* came close to suggesting what he now fatefully planned. Vaughn wondered why Stephanie hadn't woken up because the longer they fought, the likelier Jargono would also show up. *I know I can't fight them both at the same time.* He realized since Jargono wasn't attacking with the Demon, he must be reluctant to face Vaughn. *That doesn't mean he won't change his mind. I have to decide,* NOW! *Lord God, help us, let my plan succeed.*

Vaughn maneuvered around to be able to come from the right angle. "You'd better *kill* me this time, you *stupid idiot.*

Last time you let a *dog* do you in." He regretted leaving Spot behind at the store. He knew his chances would be better if Spot was here.

Demon Glen studied him then laughed, "So you want to die quickly. You *know* you can't win, so you're baiting me to end your suffering. She's not dead, you know. I just put a little gray slumber into her. There's *nothing* you can do to keep me from *fucking* with her, *again*."

Glen has always been one to delight in suffering. Vaughn leapt into the air to kick his ugly, demon face. He shaded his leap just a little to one side and hoped it was enough for the right position. But Demon Glen spun out of the way to the other side and swung his arm, catching Vaughn across the side of his head. Even though Vaughn also spun away from the blow, he still saw stars... then Vaughn ended up laying on the ground, motionless.

Demon Glen immediately scuttled over and nudged him. He ran a claw down the length of Vaughn's back and watched the flesh separate as the blood oozed out, but no reaction. He licked his claw then chortled, "I'll be back. *Don't go anywhere!* I still have to tear you apart. I'll do it a little at a time... and *eat* each piece while you watch! "

Demon Glen darted back to Stephanie and studied her for a moment, watching her breathing, but saw no change. Once again, he positioned her and himself, and ran his demon hands all over her body, feeling her vibrant energy, her sensitivity, and he hungered to devour it all. He wished she was awake to struggle, making the conquest far more delicious, but then the Demon frowned, seeing that *both* his hands were demonic. He changed one of them into a human hand, so he could feel her like a man. One hand was demon, feeling her like a demon, and the other like a man. The battle had only increased his lust so he panted and moaned in expectation as he set himself, concentrating extra hard to keep his phallus human. He didn't want mere seconds out of this but suddenly he got hit even harder than before!

Vaughn knew the only chance they had was for him to wrap his arms around the demon's body from behind without Glen's arms inside his. This could be possible only if he allowed the Demon to mount Stephanie, *again,* and for the best chance to grab him, he had to wait until just before the Demon would enter her. All of the demon's concentration would be focused *there* because that was unavoidable, being the nature of the beast.

Even while Vaughn had laid motionless, his drastic plan seemed to him to border on the insane as he fought to keep his wits. He had made sure he fell facing Stephanie with an unobstructed view and thankfully, he landed as hoped, behind and somewhat to the side of where he knew Demon Glen would be.

While Vaughn had laid motionless, Vaughn could sense all of Stephanie's preciousness and sacredness to him and to the Tree of Life. Only a while ago they were holding each other in their arms. But now he could feel both the demon's hand and Glen's human hand rubbing over Stephanie's body just as if it was his own body, making his own flesh cringe in revulsion and shooting pains inside him in places he didn't even know existed. Feeling her utter vulnerability, Vaughn's love cried out at him to act, but... *Not yet! I can't move yet. DAMN IT! Still too soon.*

Vaughn could feel the absolute violation, the demeaning of everything beautiful and wonderful about Stephanie, the most precious and important person to him on Earth. And then, seeing Glen reach down toward Stephanie's most private parts, Vaughn knew it had to be... *NOW! NOW, DAMN IT!* Fear and anger burst their bonds and exploded in him. At that moment in time, when Vaughn felt that demon's vile touch on the doors of life, Vaughn acknowledged, *My life is for you, Stephanie... no matter what.*

With heart pounding but trying to be as quiet as possible and summoning more strength than he ever knew he had, all Vaughn knew was he couldn't get to Glen fast enough. Everything seemed to blur then finally Vaughn's strength exploded, finally crashing into Glen's side to force him over the edge of the bank. When his shoulder drove into the Demon, Vaughn also wrapped his arms around Glen's torso and locked his hands together. In spite of the tremendous concussion, Vaughn knew he had to hold on, *No matter what,* as he twisted with the direction of the force accelerating their momentum as he and Demon Glen rolled over and over. The ground dropped out from beneath them and Vaughn held tightly for dear life. The two rolled over and over each other, down the bank then plunged into the deepest part of the pool where Vaughn and Stephanie had just bathed.

The impact and shock of the cold water were disorienting but Vaughn had his mind set. He took his breath then pulled the Demon under, and in that weightless environment, he briefly let him go to readjust directly behind him.

Demon Glen tried to escape him, but floating in the water and being in a strange surrounding, he didn't even know he could have just stood up! Finally Vaughn came to a stand while Glen thrashed but he couldn't shake loose. He roared in anger and Vaughn felt the vibration of it in his own chest. Glen cursed but Vaughn refused to let him go. *No matter what.*

Then Demon Glen laughed since although Vaughn held him, he realized there was little harm Vaughn could do to him. "*Pathetic.*" He scowled and mocked, "Oh no, are you going to try to drown me in this *lake?*" Glen laughed again, thinking it should be fairly easy to simply pry Vaughn's arms loose or use his claws to shred them, but it was all the more fun letting Vaughn keep his hold a little longer.

Drowning him had crossed Vaughn's mind, but he wasn't sure a demon could even be drowned. Stephanie had told him about the corridor where they didn't even breathe. More urgent than the question of whether Demon Glen could drown, that would take time, was the question of Glen simply escaping. Vaughn knew he couldn't let that happen but Glen could just simply vanish to the corridor. Vaughn got hit as soon as he sensed the Demon's arrival, and that meant Glen must have popped straight out of the corridor. No other way could have taken Vaughn by surprise since he was sure he would have sensed the Demon from a distance. So his major concern now was Glen simply leaving the same way he came but Vaughn also wasn't sure how much longer his arms could take more clawing, though the tautness of his muscles seemed to prevent any deep penetration.

In Vaughn's vision, he had cried against the heart-monster, shouting for it to die and it vanished. When he fought the blackness with Tracy, it left her and him, vanished, but it wasn't destroyed. There had to be another way. *There has to be a way to destroy it.* But the vision hadn't shown him that, only how to make it flee. Then Vaughn remembered how Stephanie told him she was placed under water to make a prayer. She hadn't told him much, only that it was a prayer for purification. *It's time I called on the Lord God to help me fight what I cannot.*

The blackness left Vaughn but the red fire increased. He recalled when Glen stood with him, when Glen actually offered his help as Tracy was being possessed and that Glen had backed off from attacking Vaughn after that. He remembered the goodness that God had even made Glen out of. *Love! Love is the way to destroy this demon.* Vaughn cried out, "LORD GOD, purify this poor soul from this filth and destroy this blackness." He pulled backwards with all his might, all his will, and submerged them both. The demon howled, even through the water.

There was a moment when all seemed suspended under that water, a moment of stillness as if absolutely nothing was happening... Nothing! That terrified Demon Glen and his good humor left him. And though his confidence hadn't really diminished, he couldn't help feeling a bit violated so he fought with all he had to escape, just to make sure.

But he couldn't make Vaughn let go even as his claws raked over Vaughn's arms, and he tried to force his hands apart. Then Glen tried to simply pop into the corridor but something blocked him. A little more frantically, he clawed through Vaughn's arms again but couldn't seem to penetrate anything except his skin.

Demon Glen felt as if his mind would rip apart. Under the water, he screamed and the Demon howled with human screams and demonic howls alternating as Glen tried desperately to get out of the water. But every time he stood up, Vaughn took another breath and pulled him back under from behind and submerged him, repeating the prayer but adding for himself, as well, "LORD GOD, purify me, *too*."

For a brief moment, Glen remembered something about his former self, a certain respect he had actually developed for Vaughn when he saw him fight the demon in Tracy. He recalled the word that had come to his mind, *Bravery!* The demonic essence in Glen railed at this memory, trying to drive it away but it was too late because goodness connected with Goodness.

The water started to boil as invisible fire seemed to swirl within the water and felt unlike anything Vaughn had known before. Though it did feel somewhat similar to the fire Stephanie used to protect him from the blackness, yet, this fire completely overwhelmed all his senses. Then the struggling ceased and Vaughn felt another calm but this didn't feel like nothing. It felt like *everything*, the essence of reality, the stuff reality was made out of! Vaughn was still holding onto Glen as tightly as he could but he knew the demon part was now gone, and he realized he'd better come up for air. The water continued to boil for moments longer as gray scum floated up onto the banks, being what was left of the demon. Vaughn knew he could let go, but it took a minute to make his arms and hands obey.

Glen floated face down in the pool. With the demon's spirit gone, his neck returned to being broken, and unfortunately, the jostling completely severed his spinal cord. In addition to that, being held under the water most likely suffocated him. It was hard to tell what really caused his ultimate death. What could one say? He was dead.

However, this time Vaughn wasn't taking any chances. He twisted Glen's head fully around to make sure he was gone. Then he pulled his corpse upstream to where the bank was less steep then hauled him back to where Stephanie lay.

Seeing her legs still spread, his heart smote him. He didn't want to look on her nudity even though she was still every bit as attractive and alluring to him as ever. But this was a matter of respect. Vaughn knelt beside her and gently put her legs together then put his hand to her cheek. Whatever the demon did to her, it was still there. He gingerly picked up her naked body and carefully carried her down to the stream, weeping and terrified.

He could feel her nakedness again, but what emanated from that physical contact was pure love from him, an overflowing desire to wrap her up completely in all the strength he could muster and simply protect her, cherish her. Now standing in the middle of the pool where he had just killed Glen, Vaughn prayed, "Lord God, *please*, she is *Your* child. Purge her from the demon's harm and from any filth." As Vaughn sacredly lowered her whole body into the water, for him there was no reality past this moment… all his life was in this finite point of time. Instead of holding to any fear, he let himself go and it seemed that for an instant, he disappeared from himself, and in that moment he felt that same fire come again and all he wanted was to be that fire. And when he thought he noticed her move, he lifted her out of the water and opening his eyes that had been so tightly shut, he saw her smile. Stephanie threw her arms around his neck, and gently leaned her head against his naked chest. After standing there a moment, cherishing her, Vaughn carried her back up to where their clothing and Glen's corpse lay.

"Thank you, Vaughn," she said softly as she reflected upon her feelings about what went on. The demon's sleep was not really a sleep but it disabled her will from acting as if in the deepest sleep when sleep paralysis occurs. If Glen had applied that when she'd been conscious, it never would have worked at all. But since she was unconscious, it was able to block her from fully regaining conscious control. She only had as much awareness and control as one would have in a dream state.

Vaughn hung his head with shame. "Please don't thank me." He knew he hadn't gotten to her in time to stop the demon from mating with her, and he could still hear Glen's boasting, telling him more truth to hurt them. *I should have just killed him outright instead of letting Spot try it! I thought I was so clever. Now, because of me, there will be hundreds of Demon Glens.* And there was just no denying it, though Stephanie didn't know it yet. Her personal sacredness had been violated in the worst possible way though he had vowed unto God, to the Tree of Life, and to her that he would protect and respect it. Even his duty as an ordinary man demanded he protect her from such violation. And it was special for only them to share in life, the place where only they chose the right time to join their lives.

Stephanie saw the strain on his face and looked confused. *He should be celebrating.* But Vaughn felt his failure and was far from anything like rejoicing. *Oh God, I have to tell her.* The excruciating pain of revealing such violation brought him to tears but he'd seen the demon thrust into her before he could climb up the bank. He blurted out, "The demon mated with you... please *forgive* me... I was too late." He turned away sobbing.

But Stephanie knew it didn't happen but to make sure, she squatted down and examined herself. As she did so, she solemnly shook her head at all the events that had so quickly transpired but then sighed with acceptance. She stood up and walked over to Vaughn and turned him around, "Vaughn, no, he didn't."

He looked into her eyes, "But I saw..."

"What you didn't see was at the time when he tried, I had enough awareness to block him!" But Vaughn still didn't believe her. "Vaughn, I just examined myself. No one, nothing has mated with me."

He looked confused. *How could she tell that?*

She knew his thoughts and smiled, "My love... I didn't tell you. Ahh... but I told you the holes in my ears and nose were closed up. Well, my virginity was restored, too! I was, ahh, saving it as a surprise." He looked at her, still disbelieving, so in typical Stephanie fashion, she smiled and got a mischievous look. "Would you like to check for yourself, my future husband?" She took his hand, but he jerked it back.

"You're telling the truth!" While Vaughn was happy and terribly embarrassed at the same time, Stephanie buckled over laughing at how he snatched his hand back and was so red.

"What's the matter?" she managed to get out between fits of laughter. "Don't you *want* to touch me?" After all their emotionally packed experiences, this release suddenly took on a life of its own.

Relief turned into joy as he pulled her upright from her hunched over laughing and took her into his arms. He could feel her nakedness against his, her energy, as if for the first time, and nature reacted accordingly.

She seriously looked into his eyes. "This is just about what we were doing when we got attacked."

He quickly let her go, looking around, and she laughed even harder while also stealing a good peek at his physique. She noticed, however, that he was still troubled, so she asked, "What, Vaughn?"

"I was still too late… what if you hadn't been able to block him?"

She folded her arms just under her breasts, "Well… then I guess you'd be helping me raise a bunch of little demons!"

Raising his voice, he scolded her, "Stephanie, that's not funny!"

"Then stop acting like an *idiot!* I know you did your best. I've…"

Then she finally noticed blood on her hands from when she'd held his back and she now saw the open, long gashes on his shoulder and side. His arms were all cut up and the side of his face was swollen, too! Stephanie grew stern. *"Turn around."*

He was hers to command so he obeyed and turned himself. Stephanie gasped upon seeing blood still pouring from the deep laceration down the length of his back. She threw her arms around him from behind, squeezing tightly as tears streamed down her cheeks. *Did his best? He fought to the* death *for me. I know he did. I see it!*

Vaughn felt her healing him, felt her deep love while Stephanie sobbed at the thought of losing him. He offered no resistance, but stood with his arms down and hers wrapped firmly around him. She held him even more tightly, believing that would aide in the healing and likewise she searched for the maximum amount of contact. Feeling their bodies communicating, as well, the harder she squeezed him, it seemed the deeper they connected. Part of her knew, of course, that this was a bit childish but she continued with that feeling anyway.

One more time they went down to the stream, this time to wash away Vaughn's blood. But when Stephanie saw the gray scum piled along the bank's edge, bobbing with the current, she knew right away. Instinctively, she stretched out her hand and bright light shot from her finger tips. The scum smoked, turned to ash, and floated away. Vaughn just watched then smiled. "Gee, too bad you weren't awake. It would have been a lot easier."

But Stephanie shook her head, "No, you're wrong. I don't know how I know it but this power only works on inanimate or non-sentient filth."

As they washed each other again, he told her all that happened. When Stephanie heard about Demon Glen's offspring somewhere, she just shook her head. "Just one more force for world destruction we have to worry about." But when he finished recounting events, she couldn't resist. In a scolding tone, "You let that *demon* mount me *again?*"

"I…but… I…"

"That was your *best* plan? To give your future wife to the *demon?*"

"I… but…"

She couldn't bear the charade any longer. It was rare to see Vaughn speechless. She embraced and kissed him warmly, then pulled back. "It was brilliant, courageous, *desperate,* and probably the *only* chance we both had."

But Vaughn's look soured at her. He felt awful again. She was just joking around. "*Stephanie…*"

"You know, you really need to work on your sense of humor!" A cute, impish look lit her face. Shaking his head, he swooped her off her feet, and carried her up from the stream. *Wow, she has the most beautiful breasts I've ever seen! Well, not that I've seen that many, but…*

Vaughn changed into clean clothing, retrieved and unfolded his camping shovel, and buried Glen on the very spot where he had tried to rape Stephanie. "I'm sorry, Glen. Though the demon is purged from you, there simply is no peace for the wicked! *Don't go anywhere!*" Stephanie nodded her approval. *That's better! I knew he could be funny if he tried.*

Fully clothed again, they walked slowly back to the gravesite, reflecting on the vengeance God had brought through them. However, when they could see the site, they noticed her father was gone! Stephanie grabbed Vaughn, "What happened to him?"

Damn! DAMN! I knew I should have killed him on the spot.

Stephanie saw the odd way Vaughn was reacting. "You know, don't you?" He turned away, but she whirled him around. "*You know, don't you?*"

"Not exactly, but the last time someone disappeared…"

Thunderstruck, Stephanie gasped, "Oh my God! Glen reappeared as …" She couldn't bear the thought. Her father was bad enough, but turning him into… And then Stephanie remembered how clever she thought she was with her prayer. *Oh God! What have I done?*

"Stephanie, we don't know."

"Vaughn, in his condition, he couldn't go *anywhere*. You were going to light a signal fire to draw someone's attention to him." Stephanie looked sick. "I… I prayed for him to live. Oh God, it was just a prayer."

Vaughn took her by the shoulders, squaring her to face him. "A prayer you said out of your own personal vengeance. We were supposed to kill them *all*."

"But … it was just a prayer. You said yourself, 'God is the One who answers them.' So, I wasn't really…"

"God has respect for you. Apparently, you've earned from God that He grants what you ask, just because *you* ask! You are the Faithwalker."

She whispered, "Oh God, what have I done?"

"You're supposed to think *before* you pray! He would have suffered just as badly had we killed him, keeping all this as *only* God's judgment." Vaughn couldn't believe how direct and hard his words sounded, but he couldn't help himself from speaking them. "Anyway, the next time you see him, you can tell him to go to the devil and it'll really be true! You won't be dishonoring him at all!"

She backhanded him hard on the arm, "*That's not funny!*"

"OUCH! *Oh, really!* About as funny as me raising little demons?"

Pausing, she pursed her mouth, "Alright, truce?" She smiled, but somehow he wouldn't believe her so she kept pulling on his arm, "Truce, OK? Truce?"

He couldn't resist her pleading eyes, and the hardness in his face melted, "Truce."

But now as they drew near the gravesite, Vaughn's mood dramatically shifted to darkness. It was a side of him that Stephanie had never fully seen. He squared himself, looking very stern, unapproachable, even by her, preoccupied with some kind of very official business he had to do and it sent chills through her, *This must have been the way he was when he first found them dead.* Vaughn motioned for her to wait while he went ahead, and Stephanie listened without question.

She'd wondered why he carried his bloodied clothing with him, thought he should have perhaps buried it with Glen but *certainly* gotten rid of it. Yet Stephanie somehow had a feeling not to ask, and even more that such an inquiry was off-limits. She had tried several times during their walk to flagrantly glance at the hideous reminder but he had completely ignored her efforts.

As Vaughn approached the front of the gravesite he had created, he began to unroll the ball of soiled matted clothes, and Stephanie stood transfixed from a distance, feeling a power descend upon him. That power was the deepest blackness she'd ever seen, intermingled with a silvery golden light, brighter than she'd ever seen. Vaughn hung his bloody clothing on the cross that he'd placed at the head of the grave-yard as a sign of fulfilling his oath to avenge their massacre. Then kneeling on his left knee with head bowed, he held the post of the cross in his right hand.

After a short, hard silence, Vaughn prayed in a voice cracking with emotion, "*This* day I have fulfilled my oath to you and avenged your blood upon your murderers… There is still one more to be brought to justice, but we don't have the power to bring him… yet. Dear Ancestors, pray God He strengthen us so that we may always live justly and be able to complete this oath. I also shall seek to bring this whole country in question, because they have allowed such a thing to happen." Vaughn heard an *Amen* and turned his head to Stephanie. It was then he realized he had forgotten she was there.

Finally, she walked over to him, putting her hands on his shoulders as he knelt at the cross. "I described Arlupo and her father to you, do you remember where… you buried them?"

He pointed just behind the cross where he was kneeling, and spoke through the lump in his throat, "There was some-thing extra-special about them, and I was led to bury them here at the front of the graveyard, together, with the woman they held."

Stephanie knelt down beside where Vaughn pointed, placing her hand upon the grave, and lamented, "Oh dear Father, dear Arlupo, I miss you so. I long to hold you in my arms... to be held in yours. I miss all my people. You didn't even know that I was your long lost blood daughter and sister. Even for all this vengeance, my heart feels no comfort for being without you."

"Children," came compassionate, familiar voices in unison.

As Stephanie and Vaughn turned around, King Mafferan, with his wife by his side, spoke, "They know now, my daughter. Now they know. Not knowing made their sacrifice much more meaningful. They fulfilled our last prophecy that the only way to hand over the knowledge of the Tree of Life to the *faithwalker* was for them to prove their love for a stranger!"

Upon hearing that, Stephanie's weeping completely broke any bonds of restraint. She couldn't understand why such a thing had to be preordained. Yinauqua couldn't bear it any longer so Mafferan, her husband, finally and gladly freed her from his hold. Gathering Stephanie in her arms brought into Yinauqua the awareness of the entire lineage between the two and the burden of her prophecies lifted.

"Mother, oh *Mother!*" Stephanie sobbed and buried her head into the Queen's neck, desiring to explain, "You don't understand... it's not even just them here! I could see... generations! I could see... the meaning ... the *whole* loss."

Yinauqua wept, "If I didn't know better, I'd swear I'm mortal again. My daughter... I thought I'd lost you for sure... forever!"

Mafferan gave Vaughn a glance that meant follow him away from the women. When they were both out of earshot, Mafferan wasted no time. "You know now about the demon's offspring."

"Yes Sir."

"I did a little checking with some of *my* ancestors. They recall that it took a few years until they reached mating age, the point being you *must* destroy them by then. You have some time to grow up, grow stronger... *wiser.*"

"*Your* ancestors? Checking? This happened before?"

"Before the Great Flood, those *creatures* existed, mating with human and beast alike, but the demons brought them directly, and so God took direct action against them. The end result was all were destroyed except for one single family in one large boat containing also pure samples of all the life on Earth! But this time, man brought the Earth demons into the world."

"Through *Jargono.*" Vaughn spat out his name.

"Yes, and if you and my daughter can defeat him and the Earth demons by yourselves then you give the Earth more time to stand."

Vaughn hesitated, *Oh, is that* all *we have to do... just that, huh?* "And if not?"

"If God intervenes directly on your behalf, then the demons are free to intervene directly also. The people are caught in the middle. Unless they freely give their whole will to Goodness, then whatever evil they hold on to, that will allow the demons a way to control them... and turn them much more evil."

Vaughn nodded, "God never forces, the demons do. Few people are willing to reach for Goodness as deeply as needed. Even I haven't got there yet. If God intervenes, that just brings back the old situation before the flood." Vaughn sighed.

"And man can't survive it. Their lives would all be cut short. But if they had time... more would find the truth. If not, God swore never again to destroy the Earth ... with water."

Vaughn's eyes widened, sensing much more in the obliqueness of Mafferan's words, "Not with water... with...?"

"Fire... but *we* made the rule not to interfere, so that restrains us."

Vaughn let the thought of fire go for the time being so that he could focus more on the near future, "You mean you can't break your word."

"Well, that is *always* correct. The demons want us to break our word, even more than they want the Earth, so they could gain advantage over us."

Vaughn's mouth flattened in disgust, "So what you're saying is," and he kicked a rock, sending it flying, "we're on our own."

Noticing the anger in Vaughn's action, Mafferan gave him a cryptic look, "Not exactly... all that is here *already* is here to help you."

Vaughn looked at him, knowing there was a whole lot more to this, "But you can't tell me?"

"That is unclear. But the more we do, the more the demons do, and they also have resources here. But more importantly, as you already know, the Tree of Life will guide you from the inside out, if you so choose to be led. When knowledge and discovery evolve naturally between you and the Tree, they are at their most powerful, and you *need* all the power you can get. If I told you some things, you would fixate on them at the exclusion of other important developments and you *need* those developments, too."

Vaughn suddenly felt like a little child and his eyes sought for guidance, as he whispered, "The Tree of Life, it's in Stephanie, now!"

The king smiled a sly smile, but said nothing! Vaughn felt the heavy meaning, but didn't understand it, so he spoke his thoughts aloud, "The Tree of Life has been here from the beginning... so it can help us."

The king smiled again, as they walked back to the others with his arm around Vaughn's shoulders. When they reached them, Yinauqua glared at Vaughn, "*So*, what's this I hear about you allowing some *demon* to climb onto my daughter? Is that any way for a future son-in-law to act?"

Mafferan backed up a bit from Vaughn, withdrawing his arm, "Yes, my boy, my wife has a good point there. Couldn't you have thought of anything other than *that?*"

"But I..."

Stephanie kicked a little at the ground, looking away... anywhere but at Vaughn.

The King continued, "Oh, and by the way, the next time you play *dead* like that, you know you gave us a quite a start, do you think we could have a little warning?"

Yinauqua continued in the same vein, "Yes, *really*, but you know what my husband? Vaughn did pray our daughter back to life which ultimately saved her from eternal torment."

Mafferan cogitated on his wife's remark, rubbing his chin, "True, my beloved wife, you do have a point there, but..."

Vaughn had enough, "Hey, don't you guys have some important heavenly business to tend to?"

Shocked, Stephanie scolded, "*Vaughn!* Is that any way to treat your future in-laws? And after coming so far to visit? *Really!* You two can pop in on us any time you want!" She kissed her ancient mother then went over and did the same to her ancient father.

They smiled, "Well, well... it's settled then. We have a standing invitation!"

They vanished!

Vaughn peered at Stephanie, "Well, my future *wife... it's settled!* Isn't there a wise old saying somewhere, that before a man marries, he's supposed to check out the in-laws because he's marrying them, too?"

"I don't know. You're the one with the Book of Wisdom."

Vaughn nodded, deeply in thought. "So I am ... and it's been here a very long time, too... I wonder what else has been here a very long time. Thank you, my love."

Stephanie looked up, "For what?"

"For being you... for being everything I love so much."

Falling into his arms, Stephanie started to cry again, and Vaughn wondered what made her do so this time, until she explained, "But there's... so much required of such love! Queen Yinauqua told me a little of what she went through when she was mortal. Apparently, it was even worse than what I was led to believe. Through much of it, King Mafferan had to... well, let's just say you're not the only one in the family to have yielded their loved one over to evil." She eased back from him to look deeply into his eyes. "Truly Vaughn, what you did was incredibly courageous. You faced reality. You didn't run from it by foolishly attempting something that you knew wouldn't work. You proved your love for me by what you did! I can't even imagine how hard it was for you to let that demon climb onto me again, but it was true bravery because you loved me. Anything less, I believe, would have killed us both!"

Vaughn straightened as Stephanie's words sent strength surging through him, acknowledging what he hadn't had time to fully think about. "What you just said means more to me than you know."

"I think I do know. I really know how much you love and cherish me and I have complete faith in you. Did you know that Queen Yinauqua wanted to help me directly? Her husband actually restrained her, preventing her from doing so!"

"Really? But I thought they didn't believe in…"

"Apparently, there are true rules to good behavior and true *exceptions* as well. She ended up being very glad he held her against her will!"

Vaughn's mind began to spin, to gather the deeper understanding. "Amazing! How does one know when it's right to take exception?"

Stephanie shrugged her shoulders while Vaughn just stared at her, not knowing either. She cutely wrinkled her mouth, raising her little shoulders higher. "Maybe it's just whoever is able to make their way stick? And, of course, they have to be fortunate enough to have things turn out for the better."

There was a certain gleam in Stephanie's eye. Vaughn was sure that if they ever battled like Mafferan and Yinauqua, Stephanie would win every time. *No wonder she's smiling like that!* "We should return now to your store and arrange to escape this God-forsaken country."

"All right, Vaughn, I'm… tired.

❧

It was mid-afternoon when Spot and Puppy raced to the front door *Arfing* and *Ruffing*. Stephanie and Vaughn looked knowingly at each other because there was no hope of surprising them as long as dogs were around. Jean came running out, throwing her arms around them both. Then she tugged them inside and sat them down at the little dining table as before. She served tea and pastries while she prepared exquisite roast beef, potatoes, mushrooms and fresh spinach. While the food was cooking, first Vaughn then Stephanie very soberly told their parts of what happened. Lana's eyes were wide in amazement, not doubting for even a second any of the fantastic descriptions. Vaughn and Stephanie had already discussed how much to tell Jean and Lana, especially Lana, but in the end Stephanie had frankly told Vaughn, "Reality is what reality is. Don't teach her to run from it, but to see it clearly." When Vaughn considered it, he agreed, knowing the right perspective, the right context would be there.

Jean asked, "My God, all that really happened?"

Lana, who sat across from Stephanie, responded right after her mother, "WOW, God punished the bad men because they were *really* bad. What did the demon man look like?"

Stephanie leaned over her forearms towards Lana to capture her full attention. Lana got up on her knees in her chair then reached out with her little hand across the table and caressed Stephanie's cheek as she focused on her rich brown eyes. Stephanie took in Lana's deep gray eyes that were clear and deeply patterned, creating a look of mystery.

"The demon looked very *ugly*, very *evil*. You'd know one if you saw one. Always remember, Lana, that God sees everything. But *He* chooses when to punish people and when to answer prayers. You heard the stories we told about what Vaughn and I have been through, how much and how often we prayed and suffered, how so very hard it has been on us. But we've learned never to get angry at God, nor doubt his Goodness. He *is* Goodness from where all other goodness comes and to doubt God's Goodness is to doubt goodness in ourselves, then everyone could only be bad."

Lana made an 'Of course' kind of nod. "I know. That's right! Because we're made out of God! What else could we be made out of, *Silly*? I don't have to learn that, I always been knowin' *that*. It's important to stay good. I'll be good, Stephie. I promise."

She's always been knowin' that? Huh! Why didn't I? Stephanie's heart pounded and ached for Lana, already missing her because they were leaving.

"OK Sprout." Stephie leaned further over, took her little cheeks in her hands, and kissed the top of her head with a silent prayer. Then she sat back down, poised herself, and very seriously explained, "Vaughn and I have talked deeply. We feel it's best if we leave the country. We have to, Lana, so that we can find what we need to fight the really bad man."

Lana's eyes instantly filled with tears. Stephanie reacted at once with the same. "But… but you can just fight him now, like what you just did." Lana started to whimper.

Vaughn went over, picked her up, and carried her back to his chair where he sat her across his knees and held her to his chest. He knew Stephanie's heart was breaking so it would be better for him to comfort Lana than for Stephie to do so. Lana buried her head against his chest whimpering as her little heart ached with big pains. The more she came to know Stephanie and Vaughn, the more she loved them, feeling they were all family and the pain of such loss overwhelmed her.

Vaughn spoke softly into her ear, "I know that if we leave now, the bad man won't come after you. He's very evil. Stephie and I are still very young. We have to grow up more before we can beat him. If we don't leave, he'll get all of us. But if we leave, he'll wait till we come back. We're coming back, Lana. Only about two years from now, we'll come back. We'll be all grown up and you'll be a big girl, you'll be *seven*. We'll come back, and all of us will fight that evil man together. So, you have to be a very good girl, help Mommy, pray to God." Vaughn pulled her a bit away from him, then said, "Pray to God to teach you here and here," and he tapped his finger on Lana's chest and head. "Let God teach you strong love and to have a wise mind. Lana, it hurts so badly because the love you have for us is so good. So, even though it hurts, it's still a sign of the goodness in you."

As Lana put her arms around him and hugged tightly, she could barely remember her original father, but her heart was full of feelings and all she could do was just feel them.

Vaughn wrapped his strong arms around her and while swaying back and forth, he recalled how he used to rock all the time and gently bump his head over and over to tune out all the evil of the world, so he could think, think about goodness. Vaughn rocked for her now. His voice became choked and came out as a loud whisper. "I give you my word, Lana. Lord God preserve me that I can keep my oath to you. About two years from now, we will be back. And you will be in our prayers every day to be safe."

Jean wiped her tears away and straightened. "Lana, they're doing what's best for us. We must do what's best for them and let them go in peace."

Hearing her mother's direction, Lana climbed down from Vaughn's lap and onto her mother's, then buried her head into her bosoms. Arlupo's words flashed in Jean's mind, *You will have your daughter back sooner than you think.*

For the first time in her life, Jean felt whole and strong, like a real mother. She wondered why she didn't have those feelings before and how she even understood them now. Her arms embraced her daughter while she kissed the top of her head, feeling Lana's tenderness, her preciousness, her connection to her, and something very special she couldn't explain… perhaps the rest of Arlupo's prophecy about Lana.

Jean sat with a straightness she never had before and her arms seemed to be stronger. She tried to trace when she improved and remembered Arlupo sharing her secret. *It was then… It began then. She made me feel special by trusting me, challenging me, loving me, by telling me the* truth … *by her sacrifice. Oh God, she saved me, too… Then Stephanie took over where she left off. She's become a real daughter to me and turned me into a real mother! Her bravery and Vaughn's, too, also changed something in me. Oh God, I've been led to your knowledge by* children. *Thank You.*

Stephanie and Vaughn nodded slightly to each other, as they both saw Jean was ready and capable of going solo.

Jean set her daughter down. "Lana, let's serve Stephanie and Vaughn the best dinner they've ever had."

Lana rubbed her eyes, nodded, and helped serve all the food which was truly delicious, but Stephanie still had a hard time eating because of the lump in her throat. *I'm sick of leaving and being left by all those I love. I'm just sick of it. Oh God...*

Jean studied them both during dinner. Vaughn was physically well put together, and though not tall, his presence lacked nothing for strength. But there was another air about him that Jean struggled to put into words... He seemed to have a sort of regalness. *That's it. He looks kingly! Stephanie is definitely queenly, but Vaughn, too, has a special air of dignity and responsibility.* Until now, Jean had expected that royal air to exist only in legendary stories of noble kings and queens, well, because the world had become such a degraded place.

Stephanie interrupted Jean's thoughts. "Mother, *everyone* has special gifts, it's just that most don't appreciate them. Many never know what they have because they never looked or never knew what to look for. I believe that in many ways, I am no different than my birth mother though she never understood, never knew her potential."

Stephanie's words seemed to come out of nowhere, and ended just as abruptly. Both Jean and Vaughn wondered about them. He also started yearning, *Oh God, I can't wait to marry her, to make her truly mine and I become hers.*

Jean imagined how the two would be in two years, *Stephanie fully into womanhood and Vaughn into manhood.*

Her heart skipped as the picture was too powerful for her to glimpse. And then, *What kind of children would they have?* Jean realized how selfish she'd been for wanting them to stay. *They deserve good lives together, free from danger.*

Jean told them what she'd prepared. "I've packed up provisions for your journey south. The border is only a few hundred miles away but it's guarded heavily on both sides. There's a little fishing port near the border on the coast. I'm not sure, but I think that may be your best chance. But if that really is, I think many others may have tried before, so, I don't know. I wish I knew more, I'm sorry."

Stephanie nodded then wearily turned to Vaughn then began to speak. Lana stopped fussing with her food and watched her sister intensely. The child's feelings were beyond words but she knew Stephanie had saved them, and helped her mother become a real mommy again. She knew that Stephanie had *powers*. She was a *faithwalker*, and that was *real* special. But Lana also saw Stephanie's devotion to Vaughn. *She's so special, but... but she treats Vaughn like he's so special. But he's special, too... 'cause he saved Stephanie. But... he treats Stephie special. I guess* really *special people always treat others like they're special. Because they treat us special, too, and we're not special.*

"Vaughn, this is your calling. I'll follow you wherever you go as my life belongs with yours, forever. I trust in you, as you trusted me back at the village."

He mustered his most serious look, but there was a twinkle in his eye. He spoke with gravity, "Stephie, I think I need to learn to play a musical instrument. I think it would go well with our lives... that I have something to continuously play by ear."

The adults laughed softly, but Lana climbed back onto Vaughn's lap, again, just to hold him and say her own silent prayer. She saw no reason to wait to take Vaughn's advice to be good and was already praying that God send them back to her and keep them safe. Although Vaughn's mind was on a million other things, his heart was breaking and he knew it was connected to whatever Lana was doing. A tear rolled down the corner of his eye as he rocked her, remembering again how he had rocked when he was her age. Vaughn thought about all the broken families he knew, about his own, Stephie's, Lana's, and others. He asked God, if it was possible, that he and Stephanie be able to have a real family and raise many children to be happy and true, and also be able to help the people they were leaving behind.

CHAPTER ELEVEN
Face the Devil

The crosses burned, casting flickering, chaotic schemes of light over their front yard, penetrating their windows like malevolent feelers invading their very marrows. "Christ killers!" they jeered. "Hook noses, devil's spawn! If we kill you we go to heaven and you go to hell!"

The baby cried, her mother trembled, and Grandfather hushed them, "Just be still, be quiet, they will go away." But his fear couldn't be hidden either.

His son spoke while reluctantly heading for the door, "I'll go out and talk to them, reason with them."

"NO!" his wife screamed and the baby screeched louder.

"Christ killers! We're gonna burn you all alive. Send you to hell in fire."

And more terrifying words continued to fill the air as his wife blurted out, "Reason with them? Are you crazy? Oh God, they're going to burn us alive!" she wailed, as her terror-ridden eyes infected all who looked into them, except their fourteen-year-old son.

"I can't take this anymore!" he hollered as he pushed *passed his reluctant father, making for the door.*

"Oh God, stop him!" his mother cried.

His father grabbed his arm but he violently shook free, whirled, then yelled at his family: "You're pathetic! All of you! Is this how God's *chosen people* supposed to act? A bunch of cowards? Cowering from the Goyim?" *He burst through the door, ran halfway into the yard and kicked one of the three burning crosses to the ground.*

"There's one! Christ killer!"

They threw dung upon him but his anger raged beyond the insult.

"You cowards*! Hiding behind your white hoods." His voice cracked with anger being loud beyond his years. "I don't know your Christ, but I tell you this,* we are not the Christ killers, you are!"

Someone shot his musket and hit the son's shoulder, knocking him to the ground. But amid his mother's screaming from the window, the boy still dared the mob. As he stood up bloodied, a blackness shot from his eyes that touched all he looked upon and even the flames seemed to recede. "Go ahead, kill me! But I tell you this, you are the Christ killers! I don't know your Christ but I know you kill his good spirit with every breath, every thought, every feeling you have. Christ killers! Christ killers!" *the young man raved, pointing at them. He kicked the other two crosses down then ran up to the hooded crowd pointing at their faces.* "Christ killers! Christ killers!" *he yelled at them.*

Someone tried to throw more dung, but the man behind him caught the arm, and jerked him back. He then stepped

*forward, took off his hood, and looked the young man in the
eyes. "Forgive me." Everyone hushed as the man turned, pushed
past the crowd, and left. They all looked at each other, but not
into the boy's eyes, and one by one, they all left.*

He told himself it wasn't so bad... now. When they first
let him go, it was beyond terrible. Actually, that wasn't
a fair way to describe it. They forced him to leave. The man
who described the powers of pleasure the women possessed had
vastly understated their abilities. For days with the help of the
drug keeping him awake, Trevor could think of little else except
those women and their *powers*. But when they finally sent him
out to fulfill prophecy, to be that messenger, all his new found
emotions were devastated. Feeling shattered into a million pieces
would not do justice to describing it, and even taking the drug
wasn't strong enough to offset the ferocious sexual desire he now
had. In truth, his sexual need had become stronger than his
need for the drug ... except when he tried to quit several times.

Several times along the course of his drug delivery route,
Trevor attempted to quit with his longest dry spell being four
hours. Only four. They had given him such a high dose his
body craved the concentrated effect. Along the way, he also lost
count of how many women with whom he'd bartered drugs
for sex, but the acts just weren't that pleasurable. It didn't stop
him from searching, though, but deep down he knew only the
women back at the village... and maybe Stephanie... could
do it right because he knew she was special, too.

Trevor was surprised to hear she was alive. He had been
sure she died but then again, the village elders knew what they

talked about. *If Stephanie could do me right, maybe I wouldn't need those other women so much.* But Trevor shook his head as he remembered the kind of 'special' Stephanie actually was… is. With that memory of her caring, a sudden sharp pain hit his head, forcing him to slam the breaks of his car because he couldn't even see straight. There was an unclear moment when he waited for his car to blindly stop. Behind the pain was shame for the perversity he'd just considered, doing the only woman who'd ever showed him real caring aside from his sister. Then he remembered what he'd agreed to concerning both Stephanie and Vaughn. Bring them into the fold.

Trevor's hand went to the pouch on his belt to grope what they'd prepared just for those two, an extra special drug. As he sat motionless in his car, his grip on the steering wheel grew unconsciously tighter and tighter. The next thing he knew, he was beating the wheel, screaming in agony but then he just took more of his drug to help him focus. After all, it was only a tangle of miserable feelings easily cured by a little medication. And there was one thing important to him, he knew that much. Alyssa, his sister, who had just turned fourteen. *I have to get her somewhere safe… but where?* He thought again of Stephanie and Vaughn, and that perhaps the only safe place, or the safest place, would be with them. *No, I can't risk it! I don't* really *know them. But, do I know anybody, really?*

It dawned on Trevor how much he'd changed along the way, though he actually felt more like a person than ever before, in a way, because at least he had more feelings. He surprised himself by giving away much more of the drug for free than he had ever done before. He wondered at that because he still thought he needed a certain amount of money to be free. *Free?*

When he finally arrived at his driveway, he rubbed his favorite cheek hard, forgetting the consequences. The slash they made in that cheek grew a little longer, a little deeper, again. With all the car windows rolled up, he screamed savagely, and repeatedly beat the steering wheel. He raged as he *needed* to rub his cheek! *I just took the drug and I still need to do that!*

When he went into his house, he walked right by his parents. He knew they saw the gash on his cheek but they never showed any sign of interest beyond its simply being noticeable. Rushing up to his sister's room without his usual knocking, he barged in on Alyssa who was just out of the shower nude. She screamed as she grabbed her towel from the bed and wrapped herself up. *"Trevor!"* But her tone was even more out of shock at the sight of him than at being embarrassed.

On Trevor's part, instead of immediately averting his eyes, he fixated on his sister's nakedness. When he realized his *indiscretion,* he forced himself to turn around. *Oh God! What has happened to me? Oh dear God... and I don't even believe you're real and I'm calling You! What has happened to me?*

Alyssa, her long brown hair still wet and clinging, grabbed Trevor's arm and her touch ignited him like none of the other regular women did but he jerked away with more than shame. He wanted to rub his cheek terribly, take more drug, but his sister was right there.

Crying, she approached closer to look into his face. His nostrils flared at her scent that enflamed him further but he knew he couldn't avoid her examination. "Hi, Sis!" was all he could muster. His hand jerked to his cheek but stopped just short of contact. Alyssa had long grown used to his habit but now gaped at both the wound and his added torment that had transformed his face in ways she couldn't decipher though she automatically kept trying.

Her hands went to her mouth as if trying to hold back the question that came anyway, "Trevor, what happened to you?"

He stank and his filthy hair was caked with she didn't know what, his eyes were so sunken in and wild, they were hardly human, and that hideous gash in his cheek oozed... something.

Her tears, her pitying look undid him and he fell to the floor weeping miserably. "Sis, I'm sorry!" Trevor knew now that he had failed her, the only person he ever cared about. He knew it wasn't enough, but he knew if he had any more contact with even her... he would do something he'd surely hate. *I'll give her what money I have... and then... kill myself.*

Alyssa knelt beside him, wanting to hold him but being so repulsed she couldn't muster it even though she loved him dearly. Yet, she finally took his arm and pulled him up. "Trevor, go wash up... then we'll talk." She led him to the bathroom and carefully shoved him inside. Once the door closed, she leaned her back against it and sank to her knees and wept. She'd never been so terrified in her life... and felt so alone.

☙

On a woody hill that was the third over from the road traveling south to the border, Stephanie and Vaughn set up camp. Though the coastal road was more direct, the road further east went through rolling hills and offered more secure places. The route they chose would take much longer, but the extra time was well anticipated.

With portable shelter, plenty of money, camps away from people and stops in nearby towns only occasionally for supplies, they experienced a freedom and intimacy they had never known. In their discussions, they couldn't decide which one was greater to them, because their freedom and intimacy fed each other. The freer they felt, the more they were able to become one, but the more oneness they experienced together, the freer they felt, yet the more intimately they connected. An odd seeming paradox, oneness and freedom, until the *faithwalker* concluded, "The closer we get, the stronger we make each other, which gives us even more ability, which makes us even freer. True love is like that, ya know? It's not like the rain feels bound to water the forests, it's just the rain's nature, and likewise, we see every early morning, the forests give off a mist that rises and becomes rain. Such is the oneness by nature as a result of the freedom to *be* their true natures. People can't be truly free without that oneness of Life! Nature is a language that teaches us, Vaughn. What would the Earth be if the clouds decided that freedom meant to withhold rain or if the forests resolved to retain their water? People are like that, ya know? Doing stupid stuff in the name of freedom which is actually nothing like being free at all!" Stephanie beamed her special smile of insight and Vaughn simply drank it all in, feeling his love for her grow ever more, as their oneness kept getting richer.

Their thoughts were united as Vaughn further considered the debauchery of the world. *I can't believe so very few people even know anything about this wonderful feeling, this freedom.* He also wondered more deeply about that word, freedom. *Will crossing the border, escaping this hellhole, really give us freedom? Freedom!*

This night there was a sharp chill in the air, unusual for this part of the country. But truth be told, the weather and minor earthquakes, according to local lore, had been for the past five years nothing like it used to be. It was even said that many of the hills they currently traveled in were new, although Vaughn couldn't tell it.

Spot was out doing his duty, watching over the surroundings. Vaughn had one fat log lightly smoldering in the fire pit at some distance from the tent. He planned to get up every now and then in the night to push it in a little further. The remnants of the fire would still be there to start afresh for breakfast.

Earlier, he and Stephanie had both washed in a cold stream and were now glad for the fire. Before their bath, Vaughn had warmed her towel, folded it up in his, and shoved it in his pack. He got out of the stream first as he always did, and as soon as Stephanie climbed out, he wrapped her in the still warm towel. She always purred and thanked him while he always hugged and kissed her in response. Such spontaneous, small aspects of caring went both ways as when they would brush their teeth with water that Stephanie had boiled and cooled before retiring to their tent. She would also take the various items he'd taken from their packs, neatly fold them or clean them as needed, and replace them in some unpredictable order that always had Vaughn searching the next day although she swore they were right under his nose.

They were getting used to the mundane rituals of care developing between them, rituals that never seemed to lose luster though they became quite predictable. During their whole evenings, they stole glances on how the other went about common habits of life like brushing hair, trimming nails, sharpening a knife or axe, stacking firewood for the night, preparing food. The grace with which each moved fascinated the other.

Now, the nightbirds called in the half-moon light, their eerie echoes and a mild chilly breeze blew in through the open tent door. The scents of sap freshly flowing in the trees and of wild flowers mingled with the sweetness they felt lying gently together in Vaughn's sleeping bag. This time, Stephanie had packed a nightshirt to sleep in.

It was refreshingly cool in the tent but not so cold as to be biting. Stephanie felt as if she was in heaven as she lay on her back, stroking Vaughn's arm that lay across her, just below her breast line. Lying on his side, his other hand gently smoothed her hair, starting at her forehead then over the top. His touch was slow and precious, and his tenderness soon put her to sleep, but just before it did, *This reminds me so much of my shelter back home, but now I'm not alone... Hmm, my shelter and Vaughn. I have the best of both worlds.*

They awoke in the predawn, stretching together, and looked into each other's waking eyes. Stephanie's feelings caused her to again reflect back upon her self-made woods shelter. *Thankfulness... I remember the first time I felt you.* Vaughn could see it in her and wished, *If only I could* always *have you look and feel just like* this. *I'll do my best for you, no matter what.* They both reached out hands to cup the other's cheek.

"Vaughn, you know these last few days as we've traveled and camped together, I've never been happier in my life. Part of me says we could go on living just like we have. I have plenty of money, you have plenty of work, if you want to. Isn't that ridiculous? They put you through all that hardship and it turns out you can support yourself with at least six different jobs that no one else wants, *that is if you don't like living off a rich woman.*" And there it was, again, that mischievous subtle smile he treasured so much.

Vaughn guffawed at hearing the offer and rolled over but Stephanie snuggled up tight against his back, wrapping an arm around his chest. Even though he couldn't see her, he could tell she had on her 'got ya' smile. He couldn't remember when he had felt more peace. As he held her arm, he treasured her every touch as she rubbed his muscular chest.

He confessed, "I've never felt more complete as I feel right now. It would be so easy for me to take you in my arms, make love to you, and then we could just…"

Interrupting with a moan, not hearing any other words after his declaration, she squeezed him tightly from behind, pressing her legs up against his.

But Vaughn finished his thought, "Forget about everything else. But, reality is…" He paused to let her finish.

She added with a heavy sigh, "What reality is."

Yet, Vaughn still felt the need for an even deeper reminder though he knew she knew, "Stephie, we just aren't that kind of people to forget. If we did, we wouldn't be what we are, and thus who we are."

Stephanie felt a sudden need to whine or at least take the opportunity to rebel against the tremendous responsibilities she knew she would be faithful to. "Who are we, Vaughn? What are we? Even though we've done a few things people might consider amazing, *I don't feel amazing*. I'm just as small compared to those things as anyone else who'd call them amazing."

"Yes, indeed, but Stephie, we *are* beginning to live differently than most people. For many people, they live a meaningless *who*. 'I am son or daughter of so and so and… SO?" His last 'so' had changed in meaning to asking 'so what.' "What does that really make anyone? Just because you're connected through your third cousin to someone in the government means something? Does it make Jargono special because he's your brother?"

"But I *do* feel special being their daughter."

"Why? He doesn't feel special being their son. You feel that way because of *what* you are. You appreciate being their daughter for *what* it is, a blessing, and you cherish their love and you hope to be half the great person they were. All of that involves quality '*what*' in you actively seeking goodness. That can't be accomplished by standing before God telling Him *who* you are.

"Seeing *what* you were, the Appendaho entrusted you with their faith and precious treasure. That's in such stark contrast to how your biological father treated you. Where he said you were nothing, your Appendaho ancestors show you that you are a queen. *And Stephie*, they were only responding to the *what* already in you. That's what real parents are supposed to do, how they are supposed to strengthen their children. The *what* can only be lived by *being* that, but the who is frankly empty if not defined by the *what*. To be good involves… well, appreciating goodness for goodness sake and there's no vanity or self-aggrandizement in that, there's no *who* in that, *and,* I might add, that is what makes a true queen!" He flipped over and smiled the broadest grin ever to her, knowing how much she hated to be called or treated like a queen. But Vaughn wasn't finished with his point yet.

"I think most people feel added importance if they're descended from someone special but they only need to feel that way when they lack the important *what* inside themselves. Then they try to fill up the void with such empty vanity of inheriting a name that gives them glory that has not been earned, nor fought for, nor suffered for, nor even searched for, and therefore not understood. Like I said, a meaningless *who* because all they really feel and think comes from the *what*. In their case, the *what* is only holding up a past image to cover their present emptiness."

Yet, as Stephanie held Vaughn ever so tightly, with her desire urging her to press even closer but knowing it wasn't the right time to make love, yet earnestly squeezing him anyway, her frailty suddenly came to the fore, speaking against her, against any feeling of any *quality what*. For all the greatness she had been blessed with, it was only as strong as the weakest part in her. Her further protests against Vaughn's words were pushed forward by an anguish building in her which carried her away and before she knew what was happening, her further protest launched,

"Then who *are* we, Vaughn? I feel *ridiculous*, a whole of fifteen years old and *what*? The fate of the world on *my* shoulders? A river of Black Death, an evil brother who has the power to rule the world to deal with? Demons fighting over how to best destroy me? My remaining loved ones in terrible danger? *What Vaughn*, what am I? Who am I?"

She didn't even know she would end up weeping out of control after waking up to such a beautiful morning but the feelings swept over her so quickly from some unknown direction without warning. Just moments ago, her mind had actually been off all that stuff, and relishing the peace they had together. Vaughn rubbed away the tears from her cheek with his thumb. *He* knew what she is.

"I don't think it would be right for us to say who we are. I don't think we need to because people's judgment will be based on the *what* when they look at us. When they decide *who* we are, they will be looking at the *what*. From that, they will say *who* we are. Your ancestors were legends because of *what* they were, but when we were with them, they didn't act as if they were some important *who*. There are great kings who have had heirs that were, well, very unremarkable and whose name, if mentioned, people would say, 'Oh yea, king so and so's son.' Period. That's all and *that's nothing*. Then you have another, maybe a beggar, rise and do heroic acts, become king, and stories are told for generations because of the *what* he was." His fingers kept caressing her cheek and running through her hair.

Vaughn's tender comforting made her desire burn even more hotly. Sleeping so closely together had permeated each of them not only with their personal scents but a personal closeness that begged to be honored. *Oh God!... I want to make love to him so badly... it hurts so bad... My arms yearn to hold him even closer!* Through her weeping, she managed to blurt out, "Oh Vaughn, what are we? We're a couple of weak, ignorant kids!"

There was nothing on under her soft cotton nightshirt, he knew by the feel of it. He felt her body's energy radiating against his. Vaughn couldn't prevent his own resonance to that but part of him wanted to push away very quickly before it was too late. Still touching her cheek, holding her eyes in his by the soft glow of early morning light, his tender words themselves felt like a caress even if his meaning went in a different direction: "My love, *we* are young trees growing on true love and true life, and hoping we can grow tall enough, strong enough, not to be crowded out by all the other trees that will die around us!"

The image of people dying all around her focused Stephanie's heart and mind away from her suffering. Suddenly, she could see and feel as if she stood in their tormented midst. Vaughn saw the change come over her, and waited for it to settle in before continuing.

With his eyes bolstering his meaning, he explained, "That's all we are, just like any young, struggling forest tree, following the natural course of the goodness we've found in ourselves. That goodness that God made us out of chases that Greater Goodness because the Greater makes sense to our little goodness. And that's really not so remarkable, Stephie. It's just a natural course."

As Stephanie stared into his eyes, her love again deepened because of the beautiful meaning he shared. Awed by this spirit, her desire was strangely offset. Sighing thankfully, Stephanie wondered, *Will there ever be a limit to my love for him.* Finally, she spoke, seeing him so patiently studying her, "Arlupo's father told me they were people just like us! Ordinary people that held goodness as truly most important, no matter how much they had to suffer. He told me that most of their life was ordinary though we've only heard about the little that's extraordinary."

Vaughn instantly connected to what he heard and his heart immediately pained him. Through Stephanie, he could feel the beauty of the Appendaho and he longed to be with other quality people to share truth, love, and life with. He had for so very long daydreamed, envisioned, and pined for such a communion. This imagination of the ideal contributed to keeping his sanity while having to deal with his reprobate parents. In Vaughn's childhood, he had created a whole imaginary world of characters he could discuss life and fight evil with.

His voice showed some strain, "I wish I could have met Arlupo and her father, and sat down and talked, watched them, laughed with them…" He sighed, as the rest of his thoughts went unsaid. Stephanie's stories of the Appendaho allowed him to feel their presence. *To think that my dearest dream was so close within reach but I actually buried them.* Vaughn found himself weeping like an orphaned child, for his orphaned dream and for the people that were not a dream but were no more. Pictures of the lives of each person he buried flashed through his mind and heart and caused his spirit to reach out to those no longer here. Stephanie laid her hand gently on the side of his head. *My Vaughn, you're so beautiful.* After a while, Vaughn spoke through his tears, "We're just kids Stephanie, but we still have responsibility to the goodness we *do* understand. Ahhh … it just so happens that maybe we've found a little bit more understanding than most!"

Those words drew them together with their sorrows mingling, known to each other, understood together, and they both accepted what they knew could overwhelm them. Just kids with more than they could bear… with uncomforted wounds inflicted by those who were supposed to care. And with this deeper understanding of one another comforting them, they fell back asleep. In that deep defenseless darkness of sleep, they dreamed together…

Stephanie found herself in a terrible black hell, suffocating. The experience of being engulfed by the vile Black Oil overcame her, again, breaking her into millions of conscious pieces all trying but failing repeatedly, agonizingly, to connect back to each other. One thing was different though. She felt Vaughn with her, and all of those pieces cried out together, "*Oh God! Vaughn, hold us together!* DON'T LET ME GO. So much Blackness… SWIRLING BLACKNESS all around… ALL THROUGH ME!"

But his words were calm and steady, "That's a lie. It's only on the outside, Stephie."

She felt herself being ripped apart with only Vaughn keeping her from eternal damnation. She cried out again, "IT HURTS! OH GOD! IT *HURTS!*"

And Vaughn's steady voice again, "Because you love."

Comforted by his reply, she could see light within but at the same time, she felt Vaughn fade into that darkness and heard him say as he died, "Stephie, the darkness, IT CALLS TO ME!"

She screamed with all her power and in terror of losing him, "DON'T LISTEN! *VAUGHN, DON'T YOU LISTEN. DON'T YOU DARE!*" She felt her meaning, felt fire burn hotly inside her... her meaning was that fire!

But he kept fading away into death. "...no hope..."

But Stephanie refused to let go and cried out with more power beyond which she knew she had, *VAUGHN, THAT'S A LIE. WHAT ARE YOU GOING TO BELIEVE? WHAT DO YOU CHOOSE TO PERCEIVE?*"

Both screamed a cry of primal essence refusing to die then they woke up together, hearts pounding, panting from their common effort to live.

Vaughn whispered, "Oh God! Stephie..."

"Oh, Vaugh!"

They each woke up in cold sweat and fear and discovered their dreams were identical. Goose bumps crept over Vaughn's scalp, arms and chest while he was being permeated by a greater presence. He knew the meaning of that terrible dream! Stephanie could sense God doing something special with Vaughn as her fingers went to the empty chain around her neck.

"Stephanie... I understand!"

"What, Vaughn?"

"How each of us can beat that black oil!"

Stephanie's eyes widened, while softly replying, "Oh, my dear Vaughn... teach me."

"In the dream, Stephanie, *we taught each other*. We teach each other what the other doesn't know!" With this insight, they petted and comforted each other back into sleep. Not long after various forest birds began chattering to greet the dawn, Vaughn, always attuned to nature's various calls, woke up. He eased himself out from under Stephanie's arm to wash and take care of needs.

Sometime after sunrise, Vaughn dressed in a heavy brown shirt and pants and sat on a long log in front of the fire. Staring at its various manifestations while gently poking a stick into it, Vaughn rearranged its glowing coals as if trying to discover some fundamental principle of destiny itself. Not with his mind, his heart studied each small change and its effect on the flame and glow of the embers and his feelings. The problem was that the coals disintegrated to a lifeless ash, requiring continual shifting to maintain the fire. There seemed to be something implicitly wrong with that arrangement, in that the brighter the glow together, the quicker the ash formed while if the coals were spread too far, the fire died out from lack of heat. While Vaughn mulled the fundamental properties of creation, his future wife came out of the tent in her long, pink nightshirt, her red hair partially fallen out of her braids, and silently sat down beside him. This had become a morning ritual.

The chilly, damp, still morning air that mysteriously crept up in a mist from the valleys below, nevertheless seemed a blanket of peace upon them. The trees all seemed to be holding still, out of respect. With twinkling eyes and a broad, loving smile of appreciation, Vaughn poured boiling water into a camping cup, placed a tea bag and two sugar lumps into it, and handed it to Stephanie.

The benefits of good sleep radiated in her cheeks as she quietly sipped her tea and stared into the fire. This was a time of feeling for her, not thinking. After relishing its flavor and warmth, with a smile of thanks, she handed the empty cup back to Vaughn and silently excused herself to take care of her needs. When Stephanie returned wearing a modest brown dress with red embroidery at its hem and borders, the sun had risen slightly over the top of the hill where they camped beneath. It was a dull glowing ball because the thick mist blocked its rays. She sat against his right side, wrapped her arm around his and laid her head on his shoulder then watched the fire again as she spoke with all seriousness and meaning, "I love you, Vaughn. There is no one else for me, now and forever."

He responded in kind, "I love you, Stephanie, and there is no one else for me, too, now and forever. I don't care what adults say about us, or our age. I know we have to grow up yet, but I want to grow up with you as my wife, no matter what we have to face."

Lifting her head up from his shoulder as her eyes teared up, she asked, "Vaughn, what are you saying?"

Easing off the log, going down on his left knee to face her, he took both her hands, squared his shoulders, and leveled his sobriety into her eyes, "Stephanie, will you be my wife? I would be your husband, forever, *no matter what.*"

Her tears fell as her heart pounded. "But you said… before… we should grow up first. Is that not a problem now?"

Stephanie wanted to say yes more than anything, except that she wanted this to be real more than anything. Still on his knee, still holding her hands and never leaving her eyes, he answered, "It's still a problem. That hasn't changed. But I have come to realize that I want to face our problems together as one, husband and wife. As long as we understand how very vulnerable we are because we're so young, I think we have to decide whether those problems are bigger than the reasons to truly marry. I've decided, and that's why I've asked you. But, I still think we need to wait on making love! That hasn't changed!" He was afraid of this proviso and almost averted from her gaze while he stated it, but he had determined to look Stephanie in the eye through the whole proposal.

As Stephanie sank into his eyes, she knew his thoughts, his tremendous honor. No one had ever honored her as much as Vaughn. He had known her shameful disposition when they first met and he didn't turn away from her. From that first night, he never stopped placing his life on the line for hers. He saw the real her when she didn't even see it for herself. But most of all, she saw him for what he was, even before he could see himself clearly, too, and from the very beginning, she had loved him. She took her hands away and held his cheeks as her thumbs caressed them. After staring into his eyes for a time and still crying, she answered, "*This* is the face I saw in the window that horrible night when I was rescued from death. *These* are the eyes in which I beheld myself and found life again. Vaughn, last night I said I wished we could keep on living like we did in the last few days. We hadn't made love then though I know we both want to so badly, but what great treasure we've had together. I accept your proposal. I can think of no greater honor than to be your wife. And I will wait until you feel it is the right time for us to make love. Actually, I know you're right about that. There's more to being husband and wife than mating."

Vaughn pulled something small, dark, and flat out of his pocket. An old, carved, wooden box with gold inlay. Stephanie immediately recognized it as Appendaho and wondered where he got it from.

"The day before you arrived in the cave with Jargono, I'd prayed and meditated as I've told you. I could think of nothing I wanted more than to be your husband in truth and that led me to study the royal paintings. Oh, how beautiful they were, looking at each other. Their love seemed to be alive in the present, radiating out from their pictures. I walked up close, and began to run my fingers lightly over them, as if trying to absorb the love and truth that made their lives so real together, praying it to be so with us. Then, as I thought of how the Book of Wisdom was in the painting and a *real* book, my hand glided to the king's hand with a whimsical hope. But it wasn't whimsical! The ring on his finger wasn't painted. It was real!

"Then I knew the ring on her hand was real, too. But I didn't want to take them out of the painting and just put them into my pocket. They were too special to just do that but then I realized that Mafferan and Yinauqua placed the rings into the paintings special for us, even as the Book was placed there for me and the letter, ribbon, and Seed were put into the Sacred Box for you. I also thought they might just have concealed a container for such great rings so I searched the paintings and on a painted book shelf behind the king was this little box." He held it up to Stephanie. "It looked so much a part of the picture that no one could tell otherwise unless they actually touched and felt along its edges. Then I got scared, and told myself that I had no right to touch the rings. The book had been given to me by your Great Mother ancestor but these were not something I could just take for myself, no matter how much it seemed to me that I should! Then both their voices spoke as one, 'Take them my son, take them for you and our daughter, take them for our children to come.' And I bowed, took the rings and the little box, then *swore* to them and God that I would protect you with *all* that I have."

Tears were streaming down Stephie's face as goose bumps crept over her. The blue ribbon with the gold trim was in her hair, tied to her central braid. The gold chain that used to hold the seed of the Tree of Life hung loosely around her neck. Vaughn opened the little box and the rings glowed with golden light.

Stephanie's heart raced, thinking that these were actually worn by the King and Queen, "Oh Vaughn, are we worthy of these? We *are* just kids."

His eyes were honest, though he took a while before answering, and just as new growth is added to a tree from places one wouldn't expect, so was his answer, "I think that's not a question rightfully answered at any point in our lives except at the end of them! We have to *prove* ourselves, Stephie. To ourselves, to God, to your ancestors, to the world. But if we weren't meant to wear them, your ancestors wouldn't have given them to us, and the rings wouldn't have called me to take them!" He paused to smile teasingly then continued, "Besides, Mafferan and Yinauqua were about our ages when they married!" And Vaughn suddenly understood, his very own words revealing to him the deeper nature of discovery and what the king meant by the Tree of Life calling to him. *It wasn't just my whimsical hope for the rings, but a part of me perceiving their subtle call to me, as well. I wonder what else calls to me that I'm* not *hearing? That could be important.*

And as if Stephanie had read his mind, she responded in kind, "Arlupo's father used to tell me that no one had a right to come between a person and the Tree of Life and whenever a person desired to approach the Tree, it wasn't because of just his desire but the Tree had also called to them and desired to be approached." Her eyes turned more tender, her voice deep and full as she proposed, "Let's accept the goodness and blessings from God and our ancestors with a prayer that we be made worthy. We have a lot to live up to."

Vaughn nodded, "Amen."

The two gold rings were finely etched and cut to look like they were made out of gemstone. They were identical except the masculine ring was thicker and larger. Vaughn took the feminine ring while Stephanie took out the masculine one, each feeling a presence greater than themselves descend upon them in blessing, as if they were standing half in this world and half beyond, in a world with no weight and no physical matter.

Vaughn prayed while still on his left knee, "Lord God, I know that to be truly married, it is You that must join us together. You are the Creator that has made a mate for everyone. Your goodness to the best of our knowledge has already put us together. Bless us with whatever we have further need of, to sanctify our marriage and to be fully joined together by You, Lord God of the special people I have not known, of the special words I have not heard, and of the sacred Tree of Life." As he spoke this prayer, the ring in Stephanie's hand seemed to be imbued with spiritual presence from above.

Then Stephanie prayed passionately as well, "Oh Light, we have each pledged our lives to each other and to the sacred Tree of Life. Vaughn has told me that You, Oh God, were also the Lord God to *his* ancestors and that you gave him the strength to move the stone away from the Sacred Cave's mouth. He said that my forefather told him of God being the Lord God to Vaughn's ancestors, a special people of words of truth. Surely, he *is* of those special people and speaks only true words! I am honored to be joined to such a special people blessed by You! Grant that our union be noble and pleasing always in Your sight."

Vaughn was overwhelmed by her prayer, a blessing from on High, and Stephanie's acceptance of his ancestry in such a profound way. The ring in his palm lit up and glowed brightly. Taking the feminine ring in one hand and Stephanie's hand in the other, he vowed, "With this ring, my beloved Stephanie, I give my oath to be for you always with my all, and to always be true to you before God who sees all." He placed the ring upon her finger and as he did, the ring changed size to fit her. Her eyes widened when she realized what happened as Vaughn wondered if it did happen.

Stephanie took the masculine ring in one hand and Vaughn's hand in the other, and with deep thankfulness, conviction, and tears, she solemnly vowed, "With this ring, my beloved Vaughn, I wed you to give you my all, to forever offer myself to you in truth, as God be judge over me." As she put the ring upon his finger, it too changed size to fit him and Vaughn knew the same thing had been done for his wife.

As they held hands, a brilliance that grew in intensity emanated from each other's chest and the gold chain around Stephanie's neck began to glow brighter and brighter. They knew not how long that glow lasted but when it finally faded, the necklace was no longer empty! Stephanie was afraid to reach up to feel it or to look down but she sensed it immediately. "Vaughn, is it?"

Tears flowed as he nodded. "My dear wife, I believe God has just given us the most precious wedding gift."

Stephanie knew for sure then that the Seed to the Tree of Life had been restored to them and her heart sang with untold gratefulness. *There's hope again... OH GOD, there's hope for the world again! My failure has been nullified!*

Even though she knew the Seed had been living inside her, she had greatly grieved that neither could it be planted, nor lasted after she was gone. But now...

As they sat on the log, Vaughn just held her. Her strength became diverted to her repeated prayer, *My failure has been nullified, there is hope... My failure has...* All the pain she'd gone through had been worth it after all. She lived to see hope reborn and there was still hope of the Tree of Life for the world. And long after she was gone, it would continue. If anything happened to her, it didn't mean hope would necessarily be lost. All the crushing feeling she had to suppress just so she could function day to day, now came rushing out.

As he held the sobbing Stephanie, Vaughn felt then some of the weight of the terrible responsibilities his wife had been carrying in having been the receptacle for the Tree of Life, herself. He squeezed her preciously, kissed her head but became acutely aware that it was *his* prayer that had placed that weight upon her. *The prayer made in true grief that destroyed hope for the world, God has justified with a wedding gift and resurrected life.* Vaughn also realized that he had buried many feelings, too. *I'll have to meditate on the great meaning of all this but I can't right now. All I can do is just feel it.*

Spot sat perfectly still but muffled, short *Ruffs* couldn't help but push themselves out. His doggy sense detected something amazing as a song of many voices in one seemed to come out of the heavens, *Wonderful, wonderful, wonderful! When once the great families reunite, when true words shall be forever joined to their mate, the* faithwalker *shall no longer walk alone. Hope shall do battle with eternal despair…*

Stephanie wondered at the full meaning of 'when true words shall be joined to their mate' and whispered her musing to Vaughn, who responded, "Exactly, my love! *Exactly!*"

CHAPTER TWELVE
Prophecy and Poison

It was an ethereal day like no other as not only the High Councilors but all district managers had been summoned into the darkest room. Eyes drooled in anticipation of a shake-up.

The Father's presence loomed heavily over each and every Alpha. "Who is responsible for the re-creation of Israel?" That question reverberated around the room a lot longer than seemed natural.

Everyone knew First's obligation to speak and he wisely did so, "Your Darkness... Ahhh, I've already researched the answer to that question and no one accepts responsibility... Ahhh, since you have forever appointed yourself over that particular district..." His voice seemed to have been strangled into silence. No one could see but all eyes were hopeful to move up another rung on the Alpha ladder.

Pressure to speak mounted upon Second. "Your Darkest One, You know for quite a while that exact possibility had been debated even amongst underlings, the pros and cons to all of it. Many felt that the creation of Islam had put a final end to Israel's re-creation, while others weren't so sure even though that was our intended purpose. Still, others wanted Israel re-created in our image... Ahhh, I might point out that the Jews who re-created her had absolutely no belief in..." And again, another strangling sound, and the pressure fell upon Third.

This is too good to be true! *All the district managers aspired.*

Third wasted no time, "I have a list of all the subversives who were pro-Israel, believing it would be better to re-create her in our image rather than not at all."

Upon hearing that, the darkest room broke out into pandemonium, the uproar was deafening. Every district manager knew Third's vindictive reputation and all felt targeted by him. Yet there was one Alpha who sat in silence much to the Father's great disappointment. HrorrarrAggrang.

A sharply loud thunder instantly silenced the room and the Father turned upon HrorrarrAggrang, the last of the original Alphas besides the Father himself, and the only Alpha with whom the Father was rumored to have any kinship. "HrorrarrAggrang, why so silent?"

That was one low-key Alpha if ever there was a low-key Alpha. Yet, everyone knew to stay away from HrorrarrAggrang, for if they happened nearby his domain, they disappeared forever. He answered the Father plainly, "If it is prophesied that Israel would return, it inevitability therefore begs us to make it return under our direction."

Everyone whispered to the other, "Is that an admission of guilt?"

Highest Councilor ScrabaGag grumbled, *I can't see anything that's happening.* Their trees had grown so much more defective and even several orb readjustments couldn't bring them into focus now. He knew something very important was happening and became so engrossed with frustration that he didn't notice the odd way his ripples shivered up his back… until a familiar voice spoke from almost right next to his ethereal ear.

"Well, well, this is so touching!"

He whirled around but Mafferan held up his hand with a smile. "No harm! No harm! I just thought you might like some company to watch the wedding."

The Highest Councilor was beside himself while his visitor continued to stand beside him. He instantly fought the urge to float away, to put some distance between them. But… *This is my* home. *My* ethereal room. *MY* personal space. *I shall* not *float away from him!* Then he wondered why his offspring hadn't even peeped. The Highest and only Councilor looked around, but didn't see Grinchback *anywhere*. He peered around Mafferan and saw Grinchback floating upside down in a tight coil, with a glowing ball shoved in his ethereal mouth. Nothing like this had been even dreamt about before, not in any demon's worst nightmares. *Twice* Mafferan had invaded their realm, *But he's offering no harm, so he says.* ScrabaGag spoke flatly, "Wedding?"

Mafferan smiled again, "Come on now, this is a happy occasion. Let me *help* you." He ran his finger over the edge of the dirty blue orb so the contrast was brought way, way, way down so that the level of grayness in the orb increased many, many times, then Mafferan spoke with even more pleasure, "There."

Highest Councilor ScrabaGag glared into the orb. There, around the girl's neck was the Cursed Object. He grimaced as he complained, "The balance has been…"

"*Restored!* Remember my warning!" Mafferan vanished! ScrabaGag was not given to anger but he was angry now. He looked over at his underling, expecting him returned to proper condition, but he wasn't! Grinchback still floated upside down with that *glowing* ball in his mouth. His sire considered leaving him there as he stared in disgust. When Grinchback realized his Master's thoughts, he rippled frantically then ScrabaGag waved his ethereal arm to turn him upright but nothing happened! A bit surprised, his very long tail retrieved some Black Oil and splattered some at Grinchback. Still nothing happened, so alarm began to creep into his ripples. He drew close, but not *too* close. *This could be a trap. What if that* glowing *ball explodes in my Eye?* Just then the glowing ball floated out and fled into the orb and Grinchback instantly righted.

"Master…"

ScrabaGag was in no mood to hear *anything* and held up his very black arm to silence him. Returning to the orb, he found it returned to normal, much to his disappointment. The Highest Councilor tried to do what Mafferan had done to make it so gray but he couldn't figure it out. He tried to consult his former Master GrrraGagag, who was consumed within him. "*When once the great families reunite, when true words shall be joined forever to their mate, the faithwalker shall no longer walk alone. Their hope shall do battle with their eternal despair…*" ScrabaGag peered into the orb trying to see through the *glow* around the trees of Stephanie and Vaughn. He couldn't even tell whether he had been successful in turning them from trees into people. He re-accessed master

GrrraGagag, *The world shall send gifts to one another, when they shall see them dead!*

❧

When Vaughn's thoughts finally came back to Earth, he saw the fire had burned down to soft coals which were just right for cooking. He brought out a little pan from his backpack, a small bottle of oil, and some raw eggs wrapped in a container. With a very satisfied smile, he cooked for his wife.

Vaughn had cooked for her before, but he noticed a new pride in doing so now, and Stephanie sensed it as she went by him. She took the little ring box off the log where Vaughn had left it, closed it, and went into the tent noticing a new feeling concerning how she approached even that simple task because there was an extra seriousness about it. She placed it with her things, came back, then silently ate with Vaughn.

While eating, she examined her feelings to understand them better. *I didn't just want to put the box away just because it was special or Appendaho. I can feel something new now, in how I'm approaching... well... everything! There's seems to be an extra importance to... yes, everything. Why?* Vaughn studied her out of the corner of his eye, not wanting to intrude upon her deep thoughts. He wondered what she was stuck upon, then noticed her thoughts begin to move forward again. *My actions feel like they're not just for myself now. It's like I'm also doing them as part of something greater. But putting the box away isn't a concern of spiritual things so why feel that way when I did that?* She looked up from the fire towards Vaughn who saw discovery in her new expression. *It's Vaughn, our marriage. Oh God, I* am *part of something greater than myself!*

Everything I do, everything I am, is now somehow a part of him also. My strengths… hmm, my weaknesses. I want to be the best *for him. Yes, even if he wasn't around, that would still be true. How beautiful! Every way I conduct myself from now on is also connected to Vaughn… and him to me. I know it. But why should just a simple ceremony cause such a difference? Well, ceremony, no, but* meaning, *yes, Our solemn oath to each other. By pledging our all to each other, by God joining us, we have been joined in real meaning. There's something about making that pledge that makes a real difference… that changes or adds something fundamental to all our feelings. Yes. The actual* action *of that meaningful pledge. I remember way back, Vaughn said love has three parts—emotion, and understanding, which entails all of the ideas and implications of the emotion, and also responsible* action, *which is the actual fulfillment of those two. Love is* not *real, except when all three are joined. I see that now. Even though most people screw marriage up, that doesn't mean marriage is faulty. Hmm, just the same between God and people. Oh, our lives have been changed, and I didn't, even realize! They will never be the same anymore.* After further pause Stephanie chuckled, *I wonder what those demons are looking at now. My tree should be… hmm … it should have quite deep glowing roots because of my love and glowing branches on all sides because of both understanding and action.*

After dining, she told Vaughn they should bathe together because their life alone had ended. As they walked down the hillside to a stream, they each meditated upon the sacredness of what they were about to do. Twice before they had bathed together, but with different meaning. When they washed away blood after fighting for justice against her father, and when they washed away blood after Vaughn fought against the demon. In both instances, they were together washing away the results of battling against evil and reaffirming their common cause. But now, they helped to disrobe each other with a deep sense that the other's nakedness was their own.

Stephanie's mind flashed back to certain Appendaho who had married quite young, married many years but were still young and even had children. *I thought it strange to marry so young but now I know why it's so rare. It's the responsibility, if you're going to be married truly.* She looked into her husband's eyes. *I accept all my responsibility to you, forever.* Now, she had an even stronger feeling of being part of something greater than herself. She realized why everything is more important and why everything about her longed to be in his arms.

Vaughn had never really allowed himself to fully look upon her body before, he didn't feel he had a right to it, but, of course, couldn't help from taking glances. Now though, he not only joyfully watched but felt that in studying her form, he could sense everything about her, her tenderness, her frailty that sent an odd pain through his heart. When he saw the Seed to the Tree of Life dangling between her naked breasts, his heart pained him more. *Let me protect her, Lord God, and never fail her. Let us protect your Seed and never fail You, so precious a treasure to care for!* Seeing her in her nakedness, her exposed sensuality, only heightened his desire to protect her, cherish, hold, and love her.

Stephanie brought out a bar of lavender soap, and as they took their time washing each other, every physical contact with a particular part of their bodies contained specific intimate meaning to the person, exposing them to an even deeper knowledge through touch. Arms for strength to fight or work, legs for strength to stand or cling, tummy bearing and sharing their vulnerability. Her breasts so close to the heart of love were so sensitive and yielding while his chest muscles were like armor and an honorable shield. Their buttocks gave strength for union, and private areas were for sharing the meaning and joy of all their life in perfect union. Finally drawing back with space enough to fully face each other's bareness again, they beheld, not just with desire, not just with love. As the gold chain was Stephanie's only adornment, as she felt the Seed to the Tree of Life between her breasts, as he beheld it hanging there, they looked upon each other's nakedness with sacredness.

Gathering each into the other's arms like a shelter, they shared their common feeling, thinking they may never again hold each other with such a deep fullness and beautiful complexity of emotions. Every point of contact between them carried three in one: love, desire and sacredness. In that embrace, both desired to spend eternity but the simple limitations of the physical world eventually caused them to part, dress and head back to camp. As they walked, they were silent after having communicated so deeply that it seemed each was still in the middle of a sentence.

Finally, Stephanie spoke, "Vaughn, you were going to tell me about the Black Oil, how we can beat it."

Vaughn was sure this would surprise her but he fully believed his revelation from that dream was correct. "Sit here by the fire, dear. I'll be right back." Vaughn went into the tent and came back with something hidden in his hand then quite tentatively sat down with a rather sheepish pause. His placating tone unfortunately began to set her on edge. "Stephie, you have to trust me." He showed her the bottle of vile Black Oil, expecting her reaction. Spot growled angrily.

She pointed, as anger brought forth words, "VAUGHN, You were supposed to *destroy* that!" Stephanie noticed immediately that not only were other emotions sharpened and turned more serious by their marriage, her anger was, too.

Vaughn winced but held his ground. "I couldn't... I think we need it to build ourselves against it!"

Stephanie did a double-take, "Huh? I... I don't understand. How can we need evil?"

"Stephie, when a tree is confronted with a lot of wind when it's young, it changes the way it grows and where it strengthens itself. A tree that grows unconfronted with wind is oftentimes blown over when a freak storm comes along because it never adapted against it. We have to adapt, get used to evil's pressure against us."

She couldn't believe he was trying to convince her of this, this... *understanding*, and at first, just stared at him in disbelief. Spot continued to growl. When she spoke, her voice raised several octaves by the time she finished her sentence, "Vaughn, are you *suggesting*... that we put this *stuff*... on *ourselves?*"

He heard how sharply she said the word, *stuff*, and how her intensity only increased. Fire began to dance in her eyes and Vaughn swallowed. Spot *Ruffed* in seeming agreement with her and he shot him a look but his dog ignored him.

303

"Not without preparation… and only a small bit… at first. And only one of us at a time. We can use a stick to apply it, so the oil only touches one of us. Spot here, can clean it off when we're done."

Spot shot his master a look.

Vaughn pleaded with his wife, "Stephie, the solution is different for each of us, but I believe the Oil works with the same trick."

Her eyebrows went up as she noticed that part of her actually agreed with his plan, "Trick?"

"Yes, perception."

Her mind lit up as she remembered. "Yes, I remember Jargono saying something about that, actually. I made note to myself that perception had something to do with the Oil's power, but I didn't understand it." She grumbled, "I hadn't felt it then, but I still don't think …"

Vaughn shared his hunch, "I think the Oil is a very concentrated form of a trick that evil plays on a lot of people."

Stephanie folded her arms across her breast, narrowing her eyes. It seemed to Vaughn that Stephanie was already acting, well… like a wife. There seemed to be just a little more sense about her that he should heed, not that he ever didn't listen, but that perhaps he should pay closer attention.

She spoke flatly, "I'm listening."

Vaughn swallowed again. "What causes people not to believe in God? Because when they look to see where He is, they don't see Him. Evil's spirit surrounds such people and asks them, 'What God? Do you see any God? Feel any God? There is NO God!' And Stephie, *this is the trick*. Evil is telling the truth!"

Stephanie couldn't believe what she thought she heard and yelled, "VAUGHN!"

Even though he felt invisible heat seemingly singe him, he held up his hand, and patted at the air, trying to calm her. He didn't feel that actually touching her, at this point, was wise. *I thought I explained this a long time ago to her.* "Listen. In as much as the person looks all around, and everywhere they turn, they only see and feel evil, then there is no God there, because God has *nothing, no presence* within evil. So within what they *perceive*, there is no God. But it's a *half-truth*." He paused briefly to check her emotional state then continued, "Stephie, to destroy the trick, a person has to look where the evil is not, they have to look within, where God's goodness is. Somehow, someway, they have to connect to that goodness within. I believe that as soon as they do, the light from that goodness will destroy the darkness of evil, and the trick fails, because then God's Being shows the evil to be a lie."

Stephanie found herself captivated by the picture Vaughn had created. She had to admit, he made sense, "Yes! I see… because goodness can see both good and evil for what each is, but evil cannot really see nor explain goodness. Evil has no power to stand against goodness, because goodness tears evil apart for not making sense in being, but evil cannot do that to goodness because there really is no good reason for evil. Yes, the evil would definitely fail when assaulted by goodness, but being stuck in evil would severely limit one's perception of reality. Actually, eventually, evil will always fail all on its own because it has no ability to sustain any being beyond existing as a self-destruction."

Vaughn breathed a sigh of relief, "Now Stephie, *listen closely*, because for you to beat this vile Oil is different than for me. You've already been purged of all evil. You have a new will."

Her reaction was again expected, "But *Vaughn*, that didn't stop that evil Oil from *killing* me."

He hated seeing those memories haunt her, yet he knew they were vitally important to her survival. "Yes, King Mafferan told me that could happen, because of the severe pain it caused you."

"Oh Vaughn, that was *exactly* what it was. That *pain* literally tore me apart." Stephanie wanted to put it away from her mind, but she couldn't resist that special explaining look on his face, she never could, so she waited on his response.

"But I think I understand why it did that. Your capacity to perceive is heightened greatly because you have a pure heart to love. When in contact with that Black Oil, devoid of love, your antithesis, you felt that immense void as pain. *Stephie*, you couldn't feel that great a pain unless you loved *first*. The pain is *secondary* and there lies the solution! It's the *same* solution we applied to ourselves to endure the mortal pains we've been through!"

But Stephanie shook her head, remembering her first-hand experience. "I still don't understand how to apply what you're saying to counter the pain of *that* Oil." And once again she glared at the vial in his hand and fire began to flare in her eyes.

"That's just it, Stephie, you *don't* counter it, you can't without destroying your love, your capacity to feel!"

Stephanie looked at him blankly, knowing there was

something that made sense to him but not having even an inkling as to what it might be, so she sat in silence.

Vaughn took a deep breath and advised, "Instead of trying to fight the pain, embrace it, but not as something external that overpowers you. Realize it only had that painful power over you because you love. See the pain for what it truly is, your *love* feeling the void. Then you'll be faced with a choice to give up the love to give up the pain…"

Her instantaneous reaction to those words interrupted him, "I'd *die* first."

Vaughn smiled because he knew she was set up to understand now. "Exactly what you did! But there's a variation to that choice you made, where I believe you don't have to die! After you embrace the pain as a part of your love, be *thankful* to Love that you can love, and see this as the greater value above feeling the pain, and so through this understanding, you *consent* to the pain! This will give you strength you didn't have before, because your focus is to see the pain through your love, instead of your love just outright reacting to hideousness, feeling that terrible contradiction ripping you apart, with your perspective totally captured and guided by only pain! My way is the truer perception, because it's deeper!" He held her eyes intently, feeling the understanding crossing into her.

It was for Stephanie like walking into a whole new room in a house. She used it to understand even further than Vaughn did, "My God! That would also take away my automatic, fruitless fighting against the pain, like removing the big rocks from a stream to allow it to flow smoothly. The pain would wash through me without creating the turmoil that ripped my insides apart and killed me. Every time I tried to fight against that Oil's pain with my love, the pain got worse… but it *is* supposed to hurt, and hurt more deeply, the stronger my love is. I mean, after all, the damned stuff *is* really offensive, no way around *that*."

He understood and nodded, "Yes, because fighting with your love made your love that much deeper which increased the pain. But in accepting the pain as a *secondary* part of real love, as one result of loving, you access the peace of love as primary. When love sees that pain as part of itself, it doesn't fight itself but simply lets it flow. In this case, peace is the answer and love must make peace with the pain! Every time the Black Oil tries to bring the antithesis to goodness, it meets only with acceptance of the nature of pain, which creates an ever deepening understanding for you, and thus an even greater acceptance and appreciation of Peace. "

A golden glow softly shined around Stephanie. "My perception of the pain changes, creating ease and tranquility." The *faithwalker* clarified further, "I think the peace of love can actually *calm* the rushing waters of pain through simply accepting or embracing pain as part of love… and perhaps more than just allowing it to pass smoothly through me, if the level of acceptance and thankfulness is deep enough… hmmm… *to actually soothe the pain completely!*" Then as her imagination brought more possibilities, she uttered, "My God!" But she didn't say what they might be.

Vaughn had only glimpsed actually *stopping* the pain in theory, but it didn't seem actually possible. However, he saw in her eyes that Stephanie thought it was indeed possible. "Oh Stephie, I think so. I believe so. Are you ready to give it a try?"

Spot's ears perked up, as he watched Stephanie. "Hold on a minute, Buster!" *I'm not doing* anything *until I find out the other half.* "First tell me what you think your solution is for yourself, just in case it doesn't work for me, and…"

But he cut her right off, not wanting to hear such a thing, "Stephie, I won't let anything happen to you, neither will Spot." The dog immediately *Ruffed* and whined.

Still Stephanie was wifely insistent, and Vaughn had to consent. He was actually becoming fond of her newfound wifeliness. There seemed to be an extra element of serious care in it that he *really* belonged to her. "*Vaughn,* I want to *hear first.* I may be able to add insight to you."

"All right, Stephie. Like I said, with me it's different because I still have evil within myself. I don't want it there, but I haven't understood how to get rid of it yet. The Black Oil will head straight for that evil and show the *truth* of me being beaten…"

Stephanie recognized this right away, interjecting, "Oh Vaughn, *I went through this!* That's part of what I was going to tell you! Arlupo's father tested me with exactly *that!* Oh, I'm sorry. Please continue." She scrunched her eyebrows in concentration.

Vaughn smiled as her every expression seemed to add to his love for her. "It's O.K. Stephie, I'm glad you told me because it helps me believe I'm on the right track. Anyway, being beaten is a half-truth because it ignores the good tree in me, and well, the battle is really still just the same for me as I've been fighting all along, except now I'm aware of the intensity with which that half-truth will hit me. I just have to apply the same fight I've been applying but not believe the lie that there's no hope. But Stephie, because there *is* truth in what that Oil says about the evil in me, it really *will* feel like there's no hope because evil does hold me some kind of way, but I understand that. I *also* understand that Goodness wants me to beat that evil so I can be truly, fully forgiven. I have to have faith, Stephie. *Real* faith that even though I see no solution, the nature of Goodness will be kind to me and provide one, because with all my heart and mind that I am now able to muster, I desire to be good. It's not in Goodness's nature to ignore that fully sincere plea. Well?" He raised his eyebrows to her with the question.

The depth of appreciation in her smile and wonder in her face wholly encouraged him, "Vaughn, my dear love, that is precisely the reasoning that I went through…" But Stephanie's voice trailed off.

Vaughn sensed there was more. "But? There's something else?"

Stephanie nodded, as memories of the method Arlupo's father used to help her played itself in her soul. She didn't know if she could be that cold to Vaughn, or even if that was necessary. "You have to find it for yourself, my dear. But… what if it's presented that *you* will die if you try to fight evil like that? Or, that it's going to beat you anyway."

Vaughn was quick to answer, "Then I have to be willing to die! *But* I have to be willing to die for the sake of goodness. That's the difference between your approach to this Black Oil and mine. With you, you don't have to choose death to protect your integrity from internal war because your will has been made free already, but I have to be willing to die to free mine! That's the true meaning of giving everything up to God, my *whole* will. And in that willingness to draw my last breath, seeking pure goodness, I can relax my heart, spirit, mind and soul, trusting that my decision is best and noble. To die seeking true, pure goodness in spite of everything else. But for *you*, only when you are faced with challenge from the *outside* may it be required of you to die to preserve your integrity, because on the inside, God has given you the ability to beat anything that comes! At the time you did die, even if you had beaten the Black Oil, you still would have…"

She understood where he was going. "Died anyway… I see, because Jargono would have physically killed me because I would never betray the Tree of Life." Vaughn nodded respectfully.

Stephanie addressed what he had said of himself. "For your part, my dear, I *know* you are correct. And, *my dear Vaughn*, whenever it *is* your time to understand the utter depths to which you must let yourself go, then you *will* receive as I have that new will, a pure heart. You will Vaughn. You just need more time, that's all." Then she looked at him with pleading eyes, "Vaughn?"

Vaughn was so pleased that she had corroborated his understanding that he didn't see where she was going next. "Yes, Stephanie, my love. What may I do for you?"

"Let me put the oil on you first!"

Caught off guard, he could only ask, "Why don't you want to go first?"

"Well, one thing's for sure, if I go first and I'm somehow incapacitated, I know I won't be able to help you, but I know you would still find a way to try that Oil for yourself anyway. *You're stubborn like that!* I think maybe between the two of us, because I'm a *faithwalker* and all, well, I may be able to help you a bit more than the other way around, so it makes sense not to waste the sure opportunity."

Vaughn hesitated a long time. He'd thought this part through, and he knew for sure, she wasn't going to like it at all, but he was sure it was necessary. Taking in a deep breath, he spoke, "Stephie, you can't interfere!"

She didn't pay the depth of his meaning enough mind, and simply corrected him, "You might need my help."

He put his hand on her knee, leveling his most serious eyes into hers, "I *need* to win this battle by myself, or it is of no use."

"But Vaughn, you might reach some critical point… I couldn't just sit back and let you be lost, or die."

He knew that he was about to make that very point quite clear to her so he swallowed, straightened, and declared, "Stephie, that is exactly what you *must* do!"

Her eyes began to widen as conception of his meaning crystallized, it was the same meaning that Arlupo had spoken when she went to her death, and when that hit Stephanie, she got visibly upset.

Vaughn saw it, but knew he had to continue and squeezed her knee firmly, "Stephanie, you have to give me my true chance to win. If not, you might pull me back just before that moment that I discover the win for myself. Then it's all for nothing, and I would have to do it again anyway." He paused to check his progress with her though he knew he made perfect sense, "*Dear*, you are more important than I am. I would feel better if you went first, so I could make sure to get the Oil off you if I have to!"

Tears of frustration… Stephanie decided to approach from a different angle, "Well, doesn't your reasoning apply to me, too, then?"

He took his hand from her knee and leaned back. That particular thought stabbed at his heart as he tried to think of a counter to her logic, "I hadn't thought about that… but this isn't a battle for you like it is for me. You just have to get used to the pain, and how to see it in true perspective. I don't think…"

She saw this was a good line of attack and firmed her position sternly. "*Don't interfere, then!*"

Now Vaughn's eyes widened, and he begged her, "Stephie, please don't be mad at me, please."

She saw the pain she'd caused him. "Oh Vaughn, only because I love you so. *You are* not *less important than me.* I've already given my whole life for yours… *twice.*"

He recalled the two instances. When she healed him and got caught by the demon, and at the cave fighting Jargono. But his automatic protest pushed outward, "And that is *more* than you should have!"

Stephanie was *done* with this line of approach. Sometimes it just paid to be direct. Her eyes began to glow red. "*Vaughn!* Do you want to fight me?"

He leaned back in shock. Being his wife seemed to be transforming her right before his very eyes. All that came out from him was a kind of whine, "Stephie!"

She fixed him with her glare and her words were no less in meaning, *"Don't Stephie me!* Either we help each other if we get in trouble with this or we don't. It has to be the same for both of us." *Oh God, what am I doing?*

Being taken completely off guard by his wife's nascent aggressiveness, Vaughn continued to whine, "Stephie, why?"

She began to whimper and sob, again thinking of how she lost Arlupo. "Because… because I love you just as much as you love me. We are *equally* important to each other. *What's it going to be?"*

As he looked at her, he suddenly saw a woman, not a girl anymore. He tenderly asked her as he put his hand back on her knee, "Which one do you think it should be?"

She curtly responded, *"This is* your *insight.* I think *you* should decide." *Oh God! Why didn't I just say we should help?*

Being hurt by her harshness, his heart pained him more as he gave the answer he knew was best, "I think we should… not interfere."

Having given him the opportunity to decide that half of it, she sharply claimed the other half without asking him. "Alright, *you* first!"

Vaughn knew she had outsmarted him, and he stared at her, wondering at her new determination. It was the first time as far as he could remember that Stephanie was truly angry with him not out of any misunderstanding. Being married seemed to mean to her that she had to more seriously approach their relationship, which translated into a certain sternness in expressing what she thought was right. Vaughn hoped it wouldn't dull her previous abilities to see his point of view. He sighed, realizing for the first time, he might have to think about his wife in terms of doing battle. Then he realized that she was one step ahead of him, already doing that! *I know what to do.* He hung his head while meekly protesting, "Stephie, maybe this isn't such a good idea."

When Stephanie saw his head hung, his shoulders slumped, she regretted being so hard as it had always pained her to see him like that. She knew he only meant well then realized she wasn't being fair to him and that he was right. She was just trying to avoid the pain that true love of their duty required, their duty to fight evil and win, *no matter what.* She put her hand upon his knee, and her eyes melted before his, "I'm so sorry Vaughn. I'm not supposed to be running from pain, but embracing it. If I can't even handle this little bit, how am I ever going to handle that *stuff?* Put the Oil on me first!"

With somber eyes, Vaughn took her hand in his and with such pride in her, declared, "I love you Stephanie. It hurts me to do this… but sometimes going through pain is the best thing one can do."

Vaughn uncorked the little bottle as Stephanie moved to and sat down on a patch of grass away from the fire. As he took a small stick and dipped it into the Oil, Spot's ears perked again with his little muffled *Ruffs.* Vaughn pulled the stick out, letting some of the Oil slowly drip back into the bottle, not wanting to waste it nor to put too much on for the first time. He touched it to her cheek, making a small black streak then sat back to study his wife.

Stephanie scrunched up her nose, making a sour face, "Oh, I really *hate* this *stuff!*"

CHAPTER THIRTEEN
Tests and Challenges

"Are you crazy? why would a nice Jew boy like you want to infiltrate the Ku Klux Klan?"

Chiam looked at the dark skin of his best friend. Smiling, he tapped his friend's bare arm, "Ahhh, because it's easier for me than for you?"

"Hey man, are you trying to say a white boy can do something I can't? Why, I could tell them I'm really just a white boy born in the wrong body. Yea!" After they had a good laugh, Alfred turned grave, "Seriously man, you could get yourself killed."

Chiam leveled his eyes, "My great, great ... Ehh, I've heard the stories so many times I forget how many greats, but anyway, he was a devout Rabbi who came over here before we were even the United States, before there were even thirteen colonies I think. He forced everyone to join him down in the wretched hold of the ship to pray. Said it was better than trying to pray from the bottom of the ocean which was where the good Christian folk would have tossed them."

"But Chiam, now you have synagogues all over and you just had a son, yourself. Why risk your life?"

"Because we know from our history that cancer of the spirit spreads just like that of the body, and overnight you can wake up terminal. That Rabbi I told you about, he had children who had children then one evening they found crosses burning in their front lawn, terrified for their lives."

Alfred hadn't heard this story. He knew of similar stories from his ancestors. Chiam continued, "My Great-Grandfather was fourteen-years-old at the time, and he alone, out of all the grown people huddled in his house, stood up to them. Hey, he even got shot! But he backed them down." Chiam proceeded to tell the whole story in detail as passed down from father to son. When he had finished, they both had tears in their eyes.

Alfred reached out his hand and Chiam took it. "I'll help anyway I can, but you're going to get us killed."

But Chiam responded, "A death suffered with meaning is a life worth living."

Vaughn studied her, "How do you feel?"

"I feel it... nauseating! I think you should put a lot more on me. This isn't nearly enough conflict to solve the problem."

This time Vaughn dipped then didn't drip off the excess. Spot stood up now, raising his head, his dog sense having an instantaneous reaction. This was the stuff that killed her before and Spot knew it. Seeming to wonder what was wrong with his master, he kept looking from him to his mate.

"Wait, Spot! Not yet." More muffled *Ruffs*, as the tension mounting in their faithful dog became even more apparent. Spot remained standing as Vaughn smeared more gooey Black Oil across her face.

A pause… *Shock!* Stephanie twisted and doubled over with a shriek. Vaughn reached for her, *I can't* *go through with this.* Spot jumped in… but Vaughn caught himself and his pet. His head pounded and his stomach convulsed as he hovered over her, beholding her torment. Feelings of his wife's vulnerability surfaced as Vaughn ached to take hold of her, but instead he pulled Spot and himself slowly back. Sharp pains pounded his chest and his voice rasped, "Wait, Spot! I know, I love her too, but that's why we wait." More muffled *Ruffs,* and if dogs could talk, Spot would be asking, *Are you CRAZY?*

Stephanie tried to focus, *Oh God, I can hardly think … must think… Love … yes, must feel the pain as it really is… OH God, that hurts even more!*

Vaughn sat on a stone, holding Spot back for what seemed like forever as Stephanie writhed, digging her fingers into the earth and pulling out clumps of grass but unaware of her actions of this world, of this life. The chain around her neck, holding the Seed, tossed it back and forth. The pounding in Vaughn's chest continued and he began to rub it, noticing his breath growing short. *Oh God! I'm not sure this was such a good idea… oh no, no… not good!*

Vaughn had earlier asked if having the Seed to the Tree of Life inside her for a time made any difference. She answered that it was a little easier to talk to it but the Seed had said it would not interfere with her life, that her life was hers. Vaughn knew she wouldn't get another. *Am I doing the right thing? Oh GOD!*

Yet, as the shredding pains of empty death engulfed her, revelation began breaking through from a part of herself that was beyond her pain. *From the beginning of time? You knew? You knew so many would die? Go through* THIS? The meaning of that word 'die' was filled with the suffering she was now experiencing. This pain *is* the meaning of that word. Then, visions of unknown dead flashed before her eye. She saw endless living trees shrivel and crack. Each a part of God that had been set free, each part loved with endless love, but each lost forever. Each of their singular pains was as her pain now, but their *combined* pain dwarfed anything imaginable, as she felt herself dissolve into that infinity… but this sum wasn't her pain. She was being shown *God's* pain… the price, the consequence of loving truly, of giving freedom!

At first she unabashedly felt this to be totally unjust, to allow such infinite suffering. Besides, it was *us* who suffered, not God. But then she knew that was a lie as she recalled how she pretty much felt everyone's pains around her to the point of needing to screen it out. She somehow knew that God, being God, would not screen out any pain, for God's attention is always directed to the *all,* and there is no place left to divert away from that.

And then Stephanie beheld within herself the very freedom that made her what she is, and she felt how very precious she was to her own self. *What would you trade for your very being?* But that question brought to mind the love she had, her willingness to sacrifice herself so that everyone else would still have a chance to meet the Tree of Life. *Yes, I do feel the pains of others. Then how much more does God? And it was* my *freedom that allowed me that choice, allowed me that sacrifice, allowed me to… be me! To freely act, to freely be what I love most. There is no more precious gift God could have given us. But could God have avoided losing so many? And if not, would it have been better not to make us in the first place?* Her heart's response to *that* question gave a resounding *NO! I love what I am and who I am. Why should that be taken away from me because others fail? Even so… all that pain is real… but oh, my dear God! All that pain is for the sake of love! For the sake of those who would live!*

Vaughn saw her tears streaming down, heard uncontrolled weeping but he sensed they were not tears of attacking pain, but of deep understanding, love, and acceptance. His gaze upon her intensified, as he studied her further. He wanted to pray, but fought the urge because he was afraid it might interfere with what she was doing on her own.

Her meditation continued. *This little bit of pain I feel, it's only a shadow of what You feel, even before You created us, because You knew! Pain You felt for us. Oh Love, my God, You created us anyway… to give us the chance to live… a chance to have our own life!*

Stephanie had never known the likes of the appreciation that now swelled in her. *To be willing to suffer so much pain, just to give freedom to those who truly desire to live!* Goose bumps covered her whole body, as she seemed to be transported to somewhere else. She no longer felt any pain at all, but only Love, a deeper appreciation for it and its relationship to pain. She also realized that her perspective was only possible through being thankful for being herself, but that others who were less thankful would continue to fault God. *So be it!* Then, Stephanie opened her eyes to a stunned Vaughn.

She sat up, simply asking him, "Vaughn? What is it? What's wrong? Was I gone for long?"

"No, about a quarter hour." Vaughn had barely gotten his words out when, "Stephie, the Oil!" He pointed to her cheek so she instinctively touched it but there was no pain anymore.

"Oh, my God! It's golden! Look," she quipped just like a little girl, holding her hand out to Vaughn, "It shines with light!" she said with the biggest smile.

Spot broke out into an avalanche of joyous *Arfing* and doggy dancing. If ever there was a version of a doggy jig, Spot was doing it, running back and forth in front of Stephanie, stopping briefly to face her, lift up a front paw, stare, and then run again. He almost knocked his master over, as Vaughn crept up to take a closer look at his wife. Stephanie took the ribbon from her hair, used both ends to blot up the Light Oil, then retied it to her large, central braid.

Vaughn finally spoke in awe, "Stephie, do you realize the potential you just demonstrated?"

She looked up, her face still softly glowing, "What do you mean?"

"Stephie, you turned the Black Oil into golden Light Oil. Maybe… maybe you could do it with the whole Black River!"

Her eyes went large at the ridiculousness of his suggestion, "Vaughn, *Hello!* I'm Stephanie, not God."

He smiled as he bent over and kissed the top of her head, but she reached up, pulled him down to the ground with her, and he ended up on his back. Stephanie leaned over him, staring into his eyes. He was such a beautiful soul to look at. *I can spend the rest of my life staring into your eyes.*

321

Finally, he said, "O.K. I guess it's my turn! I don't think you'll need any further trials."

Stephanie smiled, *I'm so glad he had the courage to challenge me to what's best.* "No, I really don't think I will. I know what that Black Oil is, I think. And where it comes from!"

He reached his hand up to touch her glowing cheek, "How?"

While leaning over him, resting on an elbow and her other arm across his chest, she pondered how, "I don't know for sure. Insight? Part of my *faithwalking* ability? I remember crying for understanding and knowing God would give it."

He just looked up and studied her intently, waiting.

"Vaughn, that vile Black Oil is from all those human beings who've died! I mean *died*, not those who passed away to live with the Light and Light's children." Then she seemed to stare off into the distance, mumbling something about the nature of evil people and that vile Oil, but he only heard her resultant conclusion, "That makes sense, because its river is in the Dead Forest."

So Vaughn asked the next logical question, "Then, what does it mean that you've turned the Black Oil into Light Oil?"

Wide eyed, staring into his eyes, the answer proceeded from her lips, "Oh God, I think it means that Light had the power to do that for everyone who died, even before they died." *Before they died...* Stephie broke down into tears again, sinking onto Vaughn's chest, as the vision rushed upon her. The vision of her responsibility to all still living took on epic proportions... before they died.

Love. Vaughn held her tightly as she sobbed. *God, I love this woman.* After a while, she whispered, "There's a whole never-ending river of that Black Oil. Do you realize?"

He knew it meant a lot of lost souls but Vaughn spoke sharply, "I realize how very much God must love those who have *not* made His huge sacrifice to be in vain so God really *must* love the living. If that Black Oil represents pain, then I would say God loves the living infinitely. The dead made their *own* choice!" His words were hard, almost bitter, but true.

They moved to sit by the fire for a short while watching the embers smolder down into white ash. Every now and then, a puff of wind blew across and lifted some of that weightless dust into the air, and it whisked away. Vaughn watched, trying to follow the ash's trail but it disappeared.

Now settled, Stephanie had regained all her strength and then some. She radiated with a glow that Vaughn had not seen around her before. His heart pounded to be with her. That glow seemed to magnify every vibrant aspect of her from the clarity of her rich, brown eyes, the perkiness of her pearly golden cheeks, the tension in her arm muscles as she leaned on them, the shape of her breasts under her brown dress seemed perfect... He shook his head, *Of all the things I've seen women do to make themselves attractive, none compares to righteousness.*

Stephanie noticed his thoughts were off somewhere, "Vaughn, you seem lost in thought. Do you want to wait till later?"

He shook his head, as if to clear it, "Oh... no, I was just thinking of you, how so very much I love you. I *need* to do this for myself *and* for you, *and* my responsibility to any I may be able to help in the future."

Vaughn handed her the bottle and stick then went and parked himself at the very spot where Stephie had sat for her trial. He pounded several clumps of grass back in place till they were firm. As Vaughn sat, Spot walked over to stand beside his Master.

"Spot," Stephanie directed tenderly, "You must sit over here. You don't move until I tell you."

Spot looked over to her as if pleading, then with a doggy sigh, slowly walked over, turned a full circle and sat down to face his Master. Every now and then, he lifted a front paw, stretched it forward, put it down, lifted up, then down... When Stephanie opened the bottle, he *Ruffed* once but hushed when she gave him a stern stare. Spot was silent after that but seemed to be constantly shifting his weight from paw to paw.

Stephanie looked pityingly at Vaughn, "I'm so sorry Vaughn. I wish..."

He shook his head firmly, "We have our responsibilities. I'm ready."

Stephanie did as he had done earlier, putting just a small smear at first but Vaughn began to swoon almost immediately and Stephanie's heart skipped. He regained himself though and roughly whispered, "More." But she hesitated, not able to move. She could see he was being sucked into a dark place, and didn't think more was a good idea. Then his eyes caught hers for an instant and told her in no uncertain terms that he meant his request. She dipped again and rubbed the sticky Oil onto his cheeks. He sat stone still for seconds, then fell over like an old dead tree that finally lost its hold on earth. Surrounded by thick darkness, he was falling... *falling... falling... no bottom... endless... NOW, I'M HERE... GOOD! Falling... hopeless... GOOD! HA!... ALL YOU BASTARD... YOU EVIL ESSENCE... I KNOW YOU'RE A LIE... I'm gonna...* He felt something sting him in the back that sent sharp pains up and down his spine!

"You know nothing at all!"

Shock! Vaughn tried to figure out what was happening. He never expected the Oil to talk back. It didn't feel like it was the Oil. The mocking voice sneered at him, "*You were saying?* What do you know? That you're *trapped* in my domain? Well, well, do you know the nursery song?" Whatever it was, Vaughn was sure it couldn't sing. "*I was walking through my Forest one day, and what did I spy?*" The very evil presence seemed to draw near and bear down upon him. "A pitiful, wretched *boy*, about to call ME a lie!"

Panic raced through Vaughn's very core. It would be difficult enough to fight the Black Oil alone... but this *now* left him totally helpless. And then he realized that he made Stephanie promise not to help him. *How* stupid *I was to be so* insistent. W*hat did* I *know to be so* insistent? And now his youthful bravado was going to kill him and cause him to fail all that he loved.

"What's the matter? Speechless *already?* I had expected more *fight* out of you. A cat likes to *play* with his mouse before he EATS it!"

Panic turned to suffocating ice cold fear, *But... but... falling... no hope... panic... fear...*

Taunting laughter, "You taste so delightful."

Vaughn felt as if something had… licked his soul. Now, there was an entirely new feeling within this eternal moment he had entered. That his very life, his very life that he could see forever, his eternal soul was in danger and but a moment away from being eternally consumed. Strangely, even though he was aware this was just a brief moment right *now*, that moment seemed like a still, clear eternity. In that very moment, every fine fiber of what he is became clear, and coursing through each strand of his being was the unmistakable cry for *true life*. Vaughn became acutely aware that it had always been so with him. *That's why I rocked, screeched… FOUGHT!* Anger automatically exploded through each fine fiber, driving away that fear. Falling ceased. Panic never existed! His heart vision, how he stopped running away and stood up against that evil heart, now replayed unto him. In that moment, the essence of his life, his heart of hope crystallized into a sharp pain all its own, and he plunged his whole being into it, choosing what to perceive, what to believe, even as he remembered Stephanie shouting at him, when she came to heal him and when they dreamt together. *What do you choose to believe? What do you choose to perceive? Faith, men talk about it, but they haven't a damn clue!* He remembered her powerful slap. A slap of *truth*… Yes, the meaning of his life crystallized. An instant later, ferocious anger burst in him over all the indignity and injustice he had experienced. In that brief moment, his heart had instantly processed all possible power, all goodness, all anger available to him.

Stephanie's eyes portrayed utter horror. Spot growled and frantically ran back and forth. Walking around Vaughn, she saw his back was bleeding into his brown shirt. Hands to her mouth, she gasped and began to focus her power to heal him but then recalled her promise not to help. Sobs forced their way through her, her breaths came in ragged gasps. The ring on her finger began to glow but she didn't know why. She stood, holding her hands helplessly out to him, bound by her word, as he squirmed on the ground in agony. She walked back in front of Vaughn and saw his face twisted in pain. A thought slammed her, *It's not supposed to be that kind of pain for him.* Then his eyes briefly opened showing they were completely pitch black.

Vaughn spoke coldly to the evil presence, "This battle is no different than any other. You can kill me but you can't *really* eat me. And if you do somehow manage to eat me, I *promise* you, I WON'T digest. I'll choke you to death from the inside!"

The demon simply delighted, laughing amusedly, "Oh good, we get to play after all."

Vaughn was glad his enemy liked to talk because every moment he had was a moment to think, to collect even more of the natural anger that Goodness now brought, to reach for more goodness moment by moment, more than he was able the moment before. But he had not expected to have to converse with an active entity. If it had just been the vile Oil alone, he could focus all his attention to beating it. Now, he had to divide himself and fight on two fronts. The more serious front seemed to be the active presence, but Vaughn knew that the longer he lingered in the Oil, the deeper it could plunge him, or so he worried. Vaughn began his attack by taunting his enemy! "Even the mouse gets to see the cat. This cat must be *afraid* of the mouse!"

Expecting a violent reaction, Vaughn steeled himself to maintain his focus while seemingly a hand grabbed him by the throat and yanked him a million miles, and then...

"Welcome to my Forest. Isn't it beautiful?"

The voice sounded familiar but he still couldn't see anyone. A powerful blow hit the side of his head, knocking him to the ground. When he put his hand to where he'd been struck, he felt blood. Something like claws raked across his back as he felt his clothing being torn. Vaughn instinctively rolled away, wondering, *Why would this evil presence be* hitting *me? A demon wouldn't do that... unless it was one like Glen. But the voice doesn't sound demonic.*

He wasn't sure which one he'd rather face, a real demon or a human-demon. Then he was afraid for Stephanie. *Does this mean the evil is in our camp? Stephanie would never let evil get close to me, unless...* Another blow slammed into his ribs, sending him rolling. He was glad he was kicked some distance though because every little bit of extra time staved off doom. And scolding himself, Vaughn rose to his feet. *I need to be able to see, damn it.* But he quickly realized his utter stupidity, *All I have to do is open my eyes!*

He was standing in the middle of an immense forest of dead trees of all sorts. Some were very tall, some were shattered, some incredibly gnarled, many with broken branches, but all were dead, devoid of most bark, underwood exposed, dried, cracked, and gray. Then he recognized the sound of water and glanced behind him to see. *The River of Black Oil!*

He sensed someone approaching so he tumbled to the side, watching out of the corner of his eye. He saw Jargono appear for an instant, kick at the air where he had been a brief second earlier, then disappear. Vaughn realized Jargono was trying to force him into the river, but also that was how he could make contact with him.

Putting his back to the river, he backed up a step. He knew Jargono wouldn't prevent him from that but also that as soon as he took a step away from the river, Jargono would reappear to drive him back.

Vaughn took a step forward, snarling *"Bastard!"* With his inner sense burning, he could feel that Jargono would appear right in front of him. Vaughn decided not to see with his eyes but with his feeling, and swung his fist where and when that feeling directed. He made contact with Jargono, knocking him to the ground a good six feet back and this time he didn't disappear. Vaughn taunted, "Like I said, you're a *lie,* even before life itself, *before your ancestors,* before the Light. A *lie.*"

Jargono managed to prop himself on all fours, trying to get up, but Vaughn kicked him in his side and sent him tumbling… Then he chased and kicked him again in the same spot. As Jargono rolled onto his back, Vaughn jumped on top of him, going for his throat. Vengeance burned hot as Vaughn remembered how he had battered and killed Stephanie but as in their last encounter, Jargono used his power to keep Vaughn's fingers from grasping his wind pipe.

Jargono laughed, "Not bad! Till we meet again!" And he vanished from underneath him!

Vaughn couldn't believe it. While raging with guttural sounds, he pounded his fists over and over on the Dead Forest's floor, gouging into the dead soil, his chest heaving. The taste of vengeance went unsatisfied, *again*. Somewhere in the back of his mind he could see himself appearing like some crazed animal. Even a more distant part of him was scared by his rage, wondering if he would begin to glow gray.

Then something called to him, like a faint echo, but it was difficult to calm down enough to understand. Slowly, he forced himself to focus, to lay aside his consuming anger, until… Stephanie was weeping. Then he noticed his hand. His wedding ring glowed. He had to get back, but first, *I want to take a good look at this River of Black Oil.*

Flowing and frothing over rocks, the river was a good hundred feet wide or more, but its viscosity and pitch-blackness defied any estimation of its depth. Looking to see its course, it snaked through the dead trees and disappeared in the vastness of the Dead Forest.

Vaughn kept shaking his head, recalling what his wife had wept, *Vaughn, there's a whole river of that stuff.* But seeing it for himself dwarfed even the picture she'd conjured in his mind. Not just the sight or stench of it, but the incredibly downcast feeling it evoked. Nevertheless, Vaughn stood up straight now, accepting reality, and spread his arms out wide, and called beyond the realm he was in, calling out with love, "Stephanie… Stephanie…" But nothing happened so he called out again, but this time adding his inner feeling-sense to his vocalization, crying with all his being, "STEPHANIE!" Then he found himself lying on the ground at the campsite.

Stephanie had been sitting on the very same stone upon which Vaughn had sat to watch over her. With her head bowed, she had her face in her hands, rocking slowly back and forth. Vaughn saw that her ring also glowed brightly. There she sat, weeping and praying.

"Stephanie." He called softly to her, as he struggled onto his side, feebly reaching his hand towards her.

Her head jerked up. Faster than seemed possible, both she and Spot were at him. Spot began licking the Black Oil from his cheeks while Stephanie held his torso, waiting for Spot to finish.

She looked a wreck, and her voice quivered, "Vaughn, I don't understand. You looked like you were fighting someone who wasn't there. Your head started bleeding, your back *was* bleeding... oh Vaughn, your clothes were being torn! I... I didn't know what to do. I... didn't interfere... like I *promised you*." She hit her fist down upon his chest to emphasize his fault, but then immediately broke down sobbing upon it. *I'm so glad you're alive!*

Vaughn barely managed to wrap his arms around her. When Spot had finished cleaning his Master, she picked up her head. Looking very guilty, she confessed in a timid voice, "Vaughn, dear, I couldn't keep from praying for you. Was... was that interfering?"

He looked into her moist eyes that were full of fear of disappointing him then weakly shook his head, "No dear, I heard your call at the end of the battle... but I fought it alone. You did fine."

Relief flooded her eyes, but they widened with her next thought, "Battle? What battle?"

"It was Jargono!" And he told her all that happened.

After Stephanie absorbed the story, she sat up and bowed her head, placing her hands upon Vaughn's chest, praying. Spot laid down on his belly and placed his head upon his front paws.

"God of Truth that we know, Lord God to Vaughn's people, look upon him. Heal and strengthen him in all ways as is good to You." Her hands glowed brightly and Vaughn could feel the glow entering him, moving all through him. He knew she had the power to heal him without praying so he noted the choice she made, wondering about it. When Stephanie lifted her head, Vaughn sat up and stared at her with something obviously troubling him.

"Stephie, I don't know if I really confronted the Black Oil the way I was supposed to. I intended to fight it alone, with just my personal fight. But when I realized you might be in danger, I thought Jargono might be in the camp, my love for you and the Seed caused me to beat that Oil, but not as my *own* fight." He looked at her questioningly, his eyes seeking her guidance and knowledge.

She put her hand to his cheek, "But Vaughn, all that *is* a part of you." She then drew him into her gaze further, to make sure he understood, "The important thing is you beat it. When you awoke, it was still on you, but it didn't seem harmful anymore. Spot still had his same dislike of it, so I think it was still potent." Her eyes were completely serious and convincing.

Vaughn seemed to be reaching deeply into his mind, "I think there's a part of the battle, a strength I still need to find in myself, alone... maybe... but you're right. And I'll always have my love for you and the Seed, so you're right. It *is* me."

Stephanie nodded with pride in him, "My dear, *yes!* That love *is* you, whether alone or not!"

Vaughn knew she was right but in his meditations he had envisioned the battle with the Black Oil a different way. Delving into the direct meaning of life, pitting that against the darkness, summoning all his love for goodness, and arraying it in battle against the tree of death. Like some analytical board game with real meaning against non-meaning but certainly nothing so spontaneously focused as just protecting Stephanie or even the Seed. The battle was supposed to be fought based on deeper, more general principles... or so he had thought. *But maybe I did that, except I wasn't watching the battle like a general on top of some hill, but as a soldier in the midst of it, and therefore I had to focus on particulars. After all, when I fulfill the specific application of general principles, am I not really fulfilling the general? Maybe! Still, something's missing, though.*

Stephanie sat up straight, sternly looking at Vaughn, and held out the bottle of vile Black Oil, "Vaughn, are we done with this *stuff* yet?"

He leaned back on his elbow, looking at her in awe because he saw her manner maturing before his very eyes. Her method of expression was less and less like a timid girl, and more and more... Vaughn had to search his mind for the words. *Resolute?* He realized they were both maturing together, that he had felt the same changes in himself of more and more becoming a person of substance, like a tree that has taken firm root in the course of its life, not just a sapling anymore.

Looking at her grimacing at the Black Oil, waiting patiently for his response, he leveled his eyes into hers, "Yes, dear, I think we are both done with that *stuff*."

Stephanie uncorked the bottle and Vaughn realized she was going to destroy it. He gently put his hand on hers to stop her. "Except…"

She looked up from her intended action, "What Vaughn? Except *what*?"

"Stephie… I think we can use this Oil as a doorway to enter the Dead Forest!"

Now she sounded almost like a school teacher, "Vaughn, *you're* the fighter! Can *that* be wise? Is it wise to go fight a battle on someone else's home ground using means more natural to them than us? If we're meant to go there, Light will provide us a way."

He knitted his brow together a bit, pointing at the bottle, "Stephie, maybe that *is* the way."

Stephanie wasn't hesitant, pressing her lips together, shaking her head with certainty, "I don't think so! I just don't think so. I think… Jargono can somehow follow us as long as we have it."

His eyes widened with that thought, "Alright, my love, do as you think best."

Vaughn noted how intoxicating it had become, the way they worked together. He was beginning to see and understand a sort of beautiful dance together. Sometimes she gave in to him, sometimes he gave in to her, and it all seemed to be just the right timing for each delicate step, like two expert dancers fading into each other's motions to dance in one motion together. Now, curiosity permeated him as he sensed something different with her. Raising an eyebrow, "What are you going to do?"

Stephanie seemed very determined. Obviously something was very clear in her mind. Smiling like he'd never seen before with a look of clever confidence and certainty, her eyes sparkled, "Watch me!"

Bottle in left hand, she took her right index finger, stuck it inside, and bowed her head. Tears dropped from her eyes straight to the ground, but these weren't of weeping from fear or sorrow anymore but simply rolled out from resignation. And the bottle began to glow as Vaughn and Spot watched in amazement… and the Black Oil was no longer black but shined with light, just as the Oil on her face had changed. Clear golden Oil with light in it shined through her hand between her fingers holding the bottle. She held out her index finger to Spot who sniffed at it. Stephanie spoke in a motherly tone, "Go ahead, Spot, you've earned it."

The dog gingerly licked the Golden Oil… slowly, reverently, and in some indescribable way, Spot seemed to change somehow and he settled down in peace. Stephanie then held the cork to Spot and he licked off the residue of Black Oil without even a snarl. After she corked back the bottle, she hid it in one of the inside pockets that she had sewn in her dress while they were traveling.

Vaughn watched her in silence for a long time as she sat there in her brown dress, with her head bowed and hands folded on her lap. He saw a presence with her he hadn't felt before. It wasn't seeing with his eyes, yet there was something very visible to him about her though no physical description could describe it. The more he saw of it, the more he loved her. He loved her so much now, he could actually feel his heart physically burning inside, or so he thought. They'd been through so much and they were still just growing up.

When she finally looked up, he spoke, "Stephie, something bothers me about Jargono."

Her voice resonated with deep peace, "What dear?" Vaughn gave just two words, "He laughed." Stephanie seemed to stare past him, silent.

"I know I surprised him when I was able to hit him, and I *know* I hurt him pretty bad I think, but he laughed anyway."

Still Stephanie sat as before.

"Stephie, I think he laughed because he's so far advanced beyond us in knowing how to operate in the spirit world. I don't think he considers us as any threat to him at all because he just disappeared. He knew all along he could do that. I was just a toy to him. I think the only reason he came after us was for sport!"

Finally, Stephanie answered him, "No, Vaughn, I think there's much more to it than that. For one thing, we don't make sense to him and that bothers him more than he even realizes, not just as you say that he loves me but that I love you, and that you, an outsider, are able to stand up against him where no one else can. I also think he senses that the light with us is the only thing that can challenge him."

Vaughn sensed something way beyond his mere thoughts about her statements, totally captivating him, and that was another new experience with Stephanie! "Wow! Go ahead, I'm listening."

"I think he has the ability to destroy us anytime he wants, but he *wants* us to become a challenge to him. He'd like us to become stronger so we *can* be sport for him! But also like a scientist experimenting, he's trying to figure things out as well!"

Vaughn shook his head in disgust, "Oh God! Stephie, I hate to say it, but that feels right and perhaps that will be his downfall."

Still speaking within that special peace, she continued, "I would think that is what he wants us to hope for, but I must also bring this possibility, that it may not be his downfall that becomes our victory! Perhaps... oh, I don't know... but just maybe he might truly come to understand and change for the better! We do have one major thing that he does *not* understand."

Vaughn knowingly nodded as she continued.

"He can't predict it but neither can we, because the Light teaches us, we don't teach the Light. We will never be able to beat him, but just like we brought justice to those murderers as we let the Light work *through* us, that is the same way, *the only way*, we can beat him. His downfall is, I believe, that he thinks *we* did all those things back at the village, or, even if the *glow* did it, that the glow is defective, wasteful, uncontrolled. He believes he is superior to the Light."

Vaughn sat captivated, "So you think he was watching us back at the village, like a scientist watches lab rats?"

"Yes, I *know* he watched us. I didn't back then but somehow I know it for sure now." She paused, assessing Vaughn, thus letting him know she was contemplating telling him something profound, "Jargono is definitely a *faithwalker* like me!

Also, there's no telling what other things he has in that Dead Forest that helps him."

His eyes asked all the questions.

Stephanie continued, "Arlupo told me something before she died. I'd called forth terrible black clouds without even thinking about it, but it was through my heart that I did it, and I could have destroyed all those people to protect mine. I didn't understand then and argued with her that if the clouds were there, that must be right. But she said to me, 'You have walked in many places, does that mean that God led you everywhere you walked?' It was then that I realized the terrible power I actually have, and just how *terrible* it would be if I made a mistake with it. That's when she explained to me the difference between *me* killing, *me* doing things with my power, and the *Light* doing things through me."

Vaughn picked at the grass awhile before looking up, wondering, "But how could you possibly do those things without God?"

Stephanie's expression became a mixture of reflection and progressively deeper thought, as her hand went to her temple and her eyes went left for a bit, then her gaze returned to Vaughn, "I think for me, at least, if in my heart I'm sure it's just, a right thing, that feeling allows me, rather, allows my *spirit life* to connect with the spirit essence holding the physical reality together. Through that, I'm able to alter it by some natural form of direct communication from my spirit to the other spirit essence. After a while, this kind of connection becomes more usual, more automatic, until I can even do things… well, just because I can! And I think Jargono does everything just because *he* can, but also because he really thinks he's right, or has the right. The faith part has to do with believing, understanding, trusting this rare kind of connection. It's communication to the spirit holding reality together. In a way, that spirit can be influenced through spiritual touch just like matter is through physical contact."

A tingling sensation crept down from Vaughn's head to his shoulders and spread down his arms, and belly, "God! That makes sense to me, but I understand hardly a word of it! Did that make sense?" His wrinkling brow reflected his words.

Stephanie reiterated, "I really think it works the same way for Jargono."

Vaughn straightened, protesting, "But he has *no* connection to the Light, Justice, or right of any kind, so how can he connect to that spirit essence?"

Stephanie shook her head in disagreement, then stared intently at him, "But Vaughn, *he thinks he's right.* I think that's all that matters. I think *faithwalking* is really as Arlupo suggested, that it's just ability, a gift that's neither implicitly or explicitly good or evil, like being able to regularly walk, or see, or hear. If led by the Light we walk, see and hear correctly in goodness, but if led by evil, we act through evil. If led by our own selves, hmm… we may accidentally do good or evil. But even the good we would do, would have that sense of disconnect from Goodness, so in a way, it has evil in it, too. The point is, just as we physically manipulate the physical world for any reason, so there is that ability spiritually, too."

Vaughn kept twisting the grass in his hand into a tight wad, "This must be terribly hard for you."

Stephanie shrugged her shoulders, "I don't know. It would seem like it should be. Maybe I'm running from admitting it but for now I just accept it for what it is. Vaughn, I have faith in myself that I'll not use my ability other than for true reasons… only to let Light work through me just as I would for everything else in my life. But when Arlupo's lesson first hit me, when she made me see the possible consequences if I'd destroyed all those people myself, that shook me so badly I wanted to die. But now that I understand, I just thank God for the ability, and ask that I'll always use it according to His will."

Focusing deeper into her, he responded, "That's what you did when you healed me at the hospital."

Her knowing smile and sparkling eyes made him love her even more, "Yes, my love, with the Tree of Life's help and blessing. I made my case to the Tree and God, before I even knew what I could do, and they guided me through my first *faithwalk*. Vaughn, one of the understandings which keeps me is I know power that's not used as part of the Greater Good is no power at all because eventually it will lead to self-destruction."

Vaughn sharpened his eyes into hers as he nodded, "That's Jargono's mistake! He thinks he has power."

Stephanie responded with the same sharp look, "Yes, just like that evil ancient king my forefather killed."

Vaughn rubbed his soft beginning beard, "But how do you distinguish between doing something that you're *sure* is right but is not being led by God, from doing something that feels equally right and *is* led by God?"

Stephanie nodded as she got up and kneaded her bottom after sitting on the hard stone for so long. She offered Vaughn her hand and he took it to stand up in front of her. She answered his question, as she placed her hands on his chest, "That was an early question in me, dear, but was made very clear when Arlupo flatly asked me if I was being led by God to destroy all those people. I got a clear vision that I was *not* and it was only me who wanted it. Even though my desire was *truly just to me*, it wasn't good in God's sight for other reasons, and ultimately, it probably wasn't even just. It would have to be ultimately unjust, because God's will was against me doing it and God's reasons are always one with Justice."

Vaughn couldn't help taking hold of her arms, "Stephie, I'm so learning from you."

She beamed her love smile and her eyes drew him into her. He hugged her passionately as her hands slid over and around him. She replied while they embraced, "Like you said, we learn from each other. I just have a sense of when God is in the walk. I feel the connection to the Greater Good when He's leading me and I feel that I'm not alone in the action. Noting that difference is what I realized when Arlupo asked me if *God* was leading me to destroy all those people. That time it was only me who had judged, not judgment being done through me like what we did when we slaughtered those people. That was through us Vaughn, not by us."

He squeezed her tightly, sighing. After the battle he had just fought, to hold her in his arms was exquisite. "I understand, but it still seems like there could be some gray areas."

Stephanie squeezed him back, pressing her whole body tightly against his, sending him for a deep breath as he relished her embrace. His hands ran across her bare arms, feeling the energy of life vibrating between their touch which she could feel, too.

She qualified his statement, "Perhaps, but then all we would have to do is just ask God, now wouldn't we?" She backed her head up to pose the question with her eyes.

Vaughn flashed his smile of deep appreciation that sent her heart to pounding. It was that particular smile that she remembered from the first night they met. Now she marveled that back then she didn't even understand it, how he could really appreciate her.

Vaughn laughed at her expression of the profoundly obvious, "Of course, God is always there to ask of, but we killed those people in the end, anyway! Stephie, I don't understand."

She took on a more serious tone and posture as her eyes turned an even richer brown. His hands held her lightly, like a precious treasure, as she gave him a teacher's look. "All the people at the killing of my people were not all there the day Justice fell upon them. If I had killed them the first time…" she shuddered inside, remembering the terrible power ripping through her that almost escaped. Stephanie bowed her head to regain composure. He could feel the sudden shift in her feelings. "Vaughn, I wouldn't have spared anyone… not a living soul!" She kept her head down for a moment and Vaughn waited until she lifted it back up. "The time between events sealed their fates for those who had time to repent but did not. Following the leader the first time wouldn't have prevented them from repenting later. They were all without excuse, those who showed up on judgment day. Remember the message God had me send to them. It would have prevented any with an afflicted conscience from showing up. Those people who did show had no guilt and hence, no fear of Justice."

Once again goose bumps dotted him all over, "I'm amazed at how all this fits together. I never thought about it."

Stephanie's smile teased at him, while the twinkle in her eyes tickled him, "You used to tell me all the time to just think. Well, I've always been a thinker, but now I do *a lot more*. Your questions, dear, aren't strange to me. I've asked them of myself already! The Spirit provided me the insight, the reason, the understanding."

He slowly blinked his eyes, shaking his head but smiling ear to ear. There seemed to be no limit to his increasing love for her.

"Stephie, I love you so much, I can't contain myself." Vaughn reached up, placing his hand upon her cheek. She kissed it and they found themselves lying down in the grass together. His lips found hers and they tasted each other finding there's so much more in a kiss than the mere physical contact. Within that taste, they tasted the battles they just fought, the love that prevailed, and the burning desire of life to unite. *That* is when a *person* really kisses another *person*. They held each other tightly, dozing off in an afternoon nap.

Spot walked over and laid down beside them, but he kept his head up, watching, listening. He was protecting what had to be the most important people in the whole doggy world. He could still taste that evil man's blood, as if his mouth still held his arm. Spot wasn't going to forget him and how he had hurt his Master and Mistress.

᠁

They were awakened abruptly by Spot's growls which quickly turned into menacing barks. When Vaughn bolted up and turned toward Spot's direction, he saw Trevor doing something around the campfire. *That's odd! Spot never reacted like this to him before.*

Stephanie took her husband's arm whispering, "It's odd the way Spot's acting. What's wrong with him?." Knowing what Trevor had said to Vaughn after she died, Stephanie's hope for Trevor had instantly become love. "SPOT! That's no way to treat our guest. He's welcome *anytime*." The dog whined, as he knew better, but he also knew to obey Stephanie.

Approaching their camp, Stephanie squinted hard at and above Trevor, and even found a reason to walk all around him. *Spot keeps acting odd but I don't see anything wrong. No gray arms reaching into his head... nothing!* Stephanie went to Vaughn who now sat by the fire on a log across from Trevor, and while leaning down to kiss the top of Vaugh's head, she whispered into his ear, "*Nothing,*" and he knew what she meant.

Surprisingly, Trevor began talking. "I had to come by and thank you both for your hospitality the other week. I really like you folks, you know?" *Damn... That didn't sound right at all! Damn it! I'll never be able to do this if I don't act right.* Trevor tried to remember how he used to be.

Vaughn and Stephanie shot quick glances at each other, at first not knowing what to say but before they could respond, Trevor spoke again. He looked into Stephanie's eyes, "I'm glad you're alive!" Then he looked at Vaughn, remembering, and adjusted his tone to the flatness it used to be before he discovered all his emotions, "I guess you decided not to drink that stuff after all."

Vaughn had that same uneasy feeling about Trevor that he had when they first met, perhaps more. *But I'm just reacting because he actually was* right in *what he'd said to me. This drug-dealer* was *better than me! How could he not be, I was going to* kill *myself... or worse. Hmmm, who knows, maybe he's still better than me!* "Yea... you could say I changed my mind." Then suddenly growing suspicious, Vaughn inquired, "How'd you know Stephanie was alive? Your first words were you wanted to thank us both. You didn't seem surprised she was alive at all." Stephanie took Vaughn's arm, squeezing in a reprimand of how he just spoke.

Trevor nodded, "You've been in my territory and I make it my business to know what's going on. I've told you that." He reached up to his favorite cheek but caught himself, and instead tried rubbing the other one but it just wasn't the same. That's when they both noticed his weeping gash. For all Trevor tried to do for it, it just wouldn't heal and now oozed through the make-up.

Stephanie peered at the gash as closely as she could from across the fire. *Oh God! What happened to him?* "Trevor, that cut on your cheek... looks really odd."

Making light of it, he laughed, "You know how I've always had this habit of rubbing it. It's pretty obvious. Well, I forgot I had a knife in my hand! It's a wonder I didn't put my fucking eye out."

Once again Vaughn winced at the profanity. Each time he heard such a vile word, his distaste grew even much more. *Still, that's Trevor.*

Looking over at Stephanie again because he couldn't help it, Trevor mused, *She is so* hot! *I bet she'd be even better than…*

"Trevor," Stephanie jolted him, "How have you been?"

It was the way she asked that question. She meant it, with real caring in her voice. It wasn't just conversation. That caring intruded upon his lust and… did something to it. *She really does care.* He looked into her rich brown eyes and this time a sharp pain shot through his head again, just like when he was driving and had to slam the breaks.

Vaughn's eyes narrowed further, "You alright, man?"

Trevor shooed his question away, "Touch of migraine… comes and goes. Hey, look! I got all the ingredients…" Both Vaughn and Stephanie then actually took notice of what Trevor had been encumbering himself with. A large pot into which he had dumped in several items. He had unwrapped different vegetables like onions, potatoes, also chunks of beef, and spices. Since the water was boiling, it wasn't long before a delicious aroma reached their noses.

Stephanie's response came immediately, "Mmm, *Trevor!* That smells simply delicious!" It actually reminded her of her biological mother's beef stew. *Must be the spices.* Stephanie's mind wandered back to the stew she found in the refrigerator right after her Mom's death. The memories instantly choked her and Vaughn knew it as he hugged her.

They're not looking! Trevor heard his thought, almost a command, so from under his sleeve he took and emptied a small bag into the pot while stirring it. He then quickly took the pot off the fire so it stopped boiling. "All done," he said with a smile. "I precooked everything for you and all I had to do was heat it up."

Stephanie came out of her interlude with excitement. "Oh *awesome*! I'm *starving*."

From a knapsack, Trevor brought out some fancy porcelain bowls and spoons. His gaze went from Stephanie to Vaughn, from one to the other several times. He could see their love for each other, a certain dignity they possessed, and although Vaughn always had shown an edge towards him, *Well, he has a right to feel that way.* But in spite of that edge, Trevor realized he actually had respect for Vaughn. His feelings for them that he had never really thought about much surfaced, and Trevor stared at the stew he was dishing out. He was eager to try some himself, curious to know if this special drug they prepared for Stephanie and Vaughn was even better than what he'd been taking but he also stared at it in fear. *What am I doing? I can't do this!*

Then the vision, or dream, depending on the time of day, exploded in Trevor's mind. He could see his sister naked, being raped by some monsters he could hardly describe. The dreams began coming to him after the third time he tried to quit the drugs, when he had thrown that special package for Stephanie and Vaughn away. The vision always ended the same with his sister crying to Trevor to bring Stephanie and Vaughn to the village, to the monsters so that she could be saved. Trevor looked again at the bowls he was serving. *I can't let that happen to sis. I have to do this to bring them to the village. If I don't, I know what they'll do to sis. They know where she is... They know everything.* Trevor handed each a bowl and once again eagerly anticipated one for himself.

Stephanie was positively delighted while Vaughn had to admit it smelled like the best stew ever. Trevor took a spoonful, raising it to his mouth, but began blowing on it instead of eating it. The thought just occurred to him, *What if they lied to me? What if this special drug is actually poison?* At that moment, sharp pains slammed into his head again and he rubbed his healthy cheek vigorously but with little relief. It seemed as if he could see both Stephanie and Vaughn more clearly than he'd seen anyone else ever before. He could feel their depths of goodness. *I've never felt anything like this... How can I understand this? Yet, somehow I do. Maybe... maybe they could help me and sis escape!* But right after that, his vision slammed him again, Alyssa crying for help while hideous creatures tortured her. Trevor waited for them to take the first bite.

Having exchanged looks, Vaughn knew the stew stirred Stephanie's memories of her real Mom so he took the first spoonful to make it easier for his wife. As soon as Vaughn tasted it, he was extremely pleased, talking with his mouthful, waiting to swallow because it was still so hot, "*Wow! This is delectable! Stephanie, this is purely scrumptious, just taste...*" Spot knocked him hard from behind into the cooking fire's bed of red-hot coals! Vaughn's instant reaction was to shout, spraying his mouthful of food outward while his bowl got dumped onto the embers. His hands managed to break his fall and he quickly rolled away but moments after he had to rub his burnt hands on the grass to remove the clinging white-hot ashes. As Stephanie leaped to reach for Vaughn, her bowl crashed into the fire as well. "*Oh GOD!* Are you hurt? Let me see." Both their anger turned towards the dog, "SPOT! *What's wrong with you?*" But Spot wouldn't back down this time and kept growling ferociously while staring at the fire but neither of his masters saw the gray wispy streak rise up and soar away.

Surprised, Trevor's disbelief that the dog knew was plain to anyone looking. *No, no no! It's not going to work. Damned dog!* Trevor wasn't the only one cursing as in the Ethereal, a scornful eye had viewed this unfortunate turn of events but it wasn't the Highest Councilor. After Mafferan's warning, ScrabaGag had been careful and had he known about these plans would have stopped them himself, but there was another Ethereal player angling for his own self-interest.

Trevor acted dismayed, "Oh God, I don't know what's wrong with your *dog!* Here, let me get you some more stew." He fished the bowls from the fire with a stick and used his sleeve to wipe them clean. Stephanie took Vaughn's hands in hers, and her hands glowed in healing him. Out of the corner of Trevor's eye, that glow caught his attention. *Look at that! What did she just do?*

Vaughn stood up and dusted himself off, thanking his wife yet again for healing him. He looked squarely at Trevor, knowing he saw what Stephanie had just done, "She has a gift of healing." Then Vaughn moved on. "Your stew is delicious, but unfortunately I never got anything but a taste. *Spot* made me spit out my first bite." Vaughn had never been this angry at Spot before but in the back of his mind something began to shout as Spot now growled at his master, challenging him! *Spot* never *acted like this before. I wonder if he's become rabid!*

But that wasn't what kept screaming at Vaughn. His memories shouted of the many times he should've paid his faithful friend more heed but didn't, yet, the anger of the moment kept him absorbed.

Stephanie, equally baffled, commanded the *dog* to sit out of the way but Spot even ignored her! *Very strange! I could use my powers to* make *him obey. But would it be right to do that… even just to an animal?*

Trevor had the bowls served up again and handed them to Vaughn and Stephanie. With a worried doggy sigh, Spot promptly walked over to the large pot then used his head to knock it over into the fire. Both Stephanie and Vaughn shouted the dog's name with even more anger, but the unavoidable loud hissing from the spilt stew drew their glances, and they couldn't help notice the strange manifesta-tions. It didn't just bubble on the coals, it almost seemed to crawl out. What actually burnt gave off a very obvious gray plume that forked and snaked upwards then streaked its way toward Stephanie and Vaughn.

Stephanie's eyes burst with instant fire and her hand went up without thinking. As had happened at the stream, that same laser-sharp light flashed from her outstretched fingers. It caught both gray streaks, turning them into ash that dissipated into the air.

Vaughn turned so black he was even hard to see, and moments later hoisted Trevor up by the shirt then threw him at a nearby tree. An instant after that, Vaughn picked him up with one hand and slammed him up against that tree, pinning him there, while the other hand formed into that same tiger-paw he used to kill those murderers on judgment day. "You *freakin' BASTARD!*"

There was no doubt Vaughn was going to kill Trevor, but Stephanie was right behind Vaughn and wrapped both her arms around his cocked arm right before he could strike Trevor. She screamed, "*NO VAUGHN, NO!*" But he had already committed to the forward motion of the strike and because Stephanie wouldn't let go, she was hurled into Trevor keeping him from further harm. Even though she was dazed, she managed to work herself between the two lads and pushed Vaughn back with her hands on his chest, "No Vaughn, NO!"

Vaughn began to come to his senses but yelled at his wife, "WHAT? Did you see what just happened? You KNOW what that was. This *BASTARD...*"

Trevor finally found his voice, "Kill me. Let him kill me... please... but *please*, do one thing for me!"

But Vaughn couldn't hear *anything*, "The *three times* I've let a bastard like you go, they came back far worse... not *this* time!" He remembered Ralph, Glen and Stephanie's father, all of whom he felt he should have killed earlier but didn't. Without thinking further, Vaughn grabbed Stephanie by the front of her dress and yanked her out of his way throwing her to the ground behind him, then turned upon Trevor to quickly kill him.

Fire flared in Stephanie's eyes, "*Vaughn*, I said *NO!*" And she threw her arm out at her husband and her power hurtled him through the air a bit further than she actually intended. Landing with a thud, he rolled over several times, rebounded and darted back! So furious he couldn't think straight, all he wanted to do was kill that bastard. Stephanie had stood up and regained her composure, then calmly repeated, "Vaughn, I said no!" As if running into an invisible wall, Vaughn smacked into *something* and bounced off it, and fell backwards onto his posterior. There he sat a bit dazed but resigned to the fact that when his wife said NO, she meant it! He shook his head to clear it, recalling how he had mused about what would happen if they ever fought over a disagreement. *Well, now I know!*

Stephanie walked right up to Trevor, who was quite a bit taller but feeling completely smaller than her, and waggled her index finger at his face indicating he should follow her, then she turned and walked back to the fire. She called back to her husband, "You, too, Vaughn! *Sit!*" That one commanding word caused all three, Vaughn, Trevor, and Spot, to sit quietly by the fire.

Once seated, the *Faithwalker* had but three words to Trevor, "From the beginning." And her look clearly stated he'd better begin, so Trevor started way back from his earliest memories as a child. He didn't know why he started there, perhaps to try to mitigate some of his certain guilt.

CHAPTER FOURTEEN
A King

"What is it about having a land of Israel that so provokes everyone?" It was one of those free-for-all college forums promoted by love of free thought and peace... but no one seemed to know like he knew. Even though his own father died fighting for civil rights, they shouted him down.

"You're a bigot!"

And another young fellow cursed at him, "Zionist pig, all you care about is your imperialistic desires! That's all Israel is, you know, an imperialistic western colony, a puppet for the United States!"

"But if you look at the facts, they didn't displace anyone! *They took desert and swamps that no one wanted and..."*

A young Palestinian chimed in, "But we liked *our swamps! Who are you to take them away?"*

"But they bred disease so the Jews drained them, creating many jobs and healthcare for many more Palestinians than were ever there before."

The moderator sneered, his tone not much better, "Let's see, to the Christians it means Christ is coming back and all us sinners *are going to hell. To the Jews it means* Christ *is coming but hasn't come before. But to the Muslims it means the beginning of..."*

"A freakin' guilty conscience!" His voice pleading no more, everyone else's mouths dropped open as he continued, "Guilty *because by the Jews bringing in good for all people, good that the Arabs wouldn't even do for* themselves, *the truth of their abject Arab failure smacks them in the face! Indeed, all those Europeans who had those lands before,* they *didn't even accomplish what just a few Jews did! Oh no, far from that, they tried to hinder the Jews. But Israel shall always be that* special *land chosen by the God who has sworn to Judge us all and never has there been or will there be another nation or land taken by Almighty God as an example of what is good and what is* guilty." *He looked into the Palestinian's eyes and pointed at him,* "Mark now my words, if you continue in your perpetual hatred, and don't absolve your guilt by doing good instead of destroying good, there won't be anything left of those Arab lands but a smoking cinder."

They threw up their hands as one, "But what is good?"

Narrowing his eyes, the young Jewish boy nodded, "I see now how deep this problem runs!"

After Trevor told them all, Vaughn nodded to his wife with a sigh. She knew that nod meant his apology would be forthcoming and he was glad she'd stopped him from killing Trevor. Now Stephanie walked over to the pitiful young man and her tone's ambiguity could have been interpreted any number of ways, "What should we do to you?"

Trevor fell onto his knees begging because now in the light of the goodness of these two admirable souls, his conscience had never been clearer, and he knew he had no right to live. The many souls he'd destroyed by pushing his drugs, even the older drugs that weren't mixed with that Black Oil, their suffering now weighed heavily upon him, so much so he felt squeezed almost to death. "Please, just kill me. I can't go on like this. If you don't kill me, I won't be able to help myself, I might even do you harm if I could." He looked up at Vaughn, "You don't know what I've thought to do with her. Just *kill me!*"

Vaughn caught the full meaning of it, but instead of reacting, this time he deferred to the *Faithwalker.* Stephanie squatted down on her haunches in front of Trevor. She wanted to be at his level. "Alright, Trevor. I'll kill you myself!"

Trevor knew from what he'd seen that she undoubtedly had the power to do so. "But just one thing, please… is there anything you can do for my sister, Alyssa?"

"I give you my word I'll consider that. We make no promises because we already have so much to deal with as you probably know. Are you ready to die?"

Trevor began to bawl, "I'm so sorry… so *very sorry* for everything. I wish I could make it all up… but I can't. I deserve to die! Do it now."

Stephanie placed her hands upon his temples, "Dear Light, choose the death you desire for this poor soul!"

And her hands glowed as never before with a silvery golden light of exceeding brilliance. The Seed to the Tree of Life that hung openly around her neck out from under her dress glowed as brilliantly. Vaughn immediately recognized that glow as the same glow that brought Stephanie back to life and could see and hear grays and blacks twisting inside of Trevor then fleeing in all directions. Some of the grays, as soon as they fled, turned to ash and disappeared.

Trevor wasn't sure what was happening as he was bathed in this glow. He felt like he was dying and was accepting death thankfully. *But why am I not dead? But... what am I feeling now? I've never felt this way in my whole life!* His thoughts were interrupted by Stephanie's gentle and humorous words, "There! You're dead!"

Stephanie stood up, stretched, and casually went back to her seat around the fire while Vaughn smiled in satisfaction.

Trevor looked up, "I don't understand."

Vaughn replied, "Sure you do! You wanted to die, yes?"

"Yes."

"Do you see anything at all in you *now,* of all that was you that you wanted to die?"

Trevor looked inside himself with amazement. "No!"

Stephanie chirped humorously, "Like I said, you're dead."

Vaughn explained further, "You turned fully away from all evil and only wanted goodness so much, you gave up your whole life. Stephanie chose the exact right prayer. It was the Lord God who decided your death, not us. You're *free.*"

Stephanie smiled brightly, "Be well, Trevor. The Light grants you power to do the good in your heart and protect your sister and the innocent."

Trevor was never one to call on God, and no word now seemed sufficient enough to him to name that of which the word God referred, so all he could do was to just keep uttering thankyou's.

Stephanie responded, "In time, the right name for you to call God will come to you and feel right. Sometimes I call Light, sometimes Love, or God, or even Vaughn's people's words, the Lord God. Don't worry about it."

Trevor sat back up upon his log. It all began to become clear now, as he kept nodding his head. "I know what I have to do." They were all ears as he declared, "I have to go back and do the same thing I've been doing!" When he saw their shock, he explained further, "We have to stop them. We can't stop them if we don't know what they're doing and what they plan. I don't have that power though I bet you two do or will in the future. And there's also Jargono to contend with. You need me on the inside!"

Vaughn recognized the battle strategy as actually covered in *Advanced Future, The Art of Fighting*. It was a derivative of rule 18, *When you cannot be a wasp or a spider, be a mite on their backs. If they don't eventually die, you'll irritate the hell out of them, but they won't be able to touch you.*

He turned to Stephanie, "He's right!"

But Stephanie wasn't hearing it, "Trevor, you *can't* go back. You're made new, now. You won't be able to fit in. You can't push drugs anymore or..."

It was Vaughn who cut her off, shaking his head, "Yes, he can! Those who are going to take that drug are going to do it regardless of who sells. They'll just replace Trevor, anyway. It's better to have him on the inside!"

Now Stephanie began to get angry, "*Vaughn,* do you understand what the Light just did for Trevor? He's not quite there where I'm at, but in time…"

Trevor spoke up, "I understand it now and that's why I *must* go back. It's the only way I can try to eventually set things right. Remember, I wanted to die, Stephanie. As far as I'm concerned, I *am* dead already. There is no life left for me to lose but this is different for me now because, before, I didn't care at all about my life, and I even told Jargono to kill me if he wanted. Now the life I have *is* to care, and care so much that if I lose my life in caring, I won't have lost anything at all, but truly lived it! See? No life left to lose!"

Vaughn wiped a tear from his eye as he walked over to Trevor and clasped his arm, raising him up. "I understand."

But Trevor had one more thing to say, "You have to cut my cheek again and put some of *that* in the cut!" He pointed at some of the spilt stew that had escaped the fire.

Now Stephanie stood up, "Are you *crazy?*"

But once again Vaughn spoke in his defense, "Can you handle it, Trevor?"

"I watched you two for a while and I saw what you did with that Black Oil! I almost came to ask for your help right then and there but I was too weak. Help me now become immune as you are and then cut me!"

Stephanie grew more upset and throwing her arms up in frustration, "*MEN!*" She stormed off for a walk in the woods as Vaughn ordered Spot to go with and protect her. Immediately his faithful friend chased after his Mistress then the *men* proceeded with their plan. Hours later when Stephanie had returned, Trevor was gone. She looked at Vaughn who looked away and she knew they had proceeded as they'd intended. She sighed, turned him around, holding his arms, "I'm sorry I got so upset at you. Do you think it will work for him? Can he really be strong enough to pull this off?"

Vaughn quickly affirmed in a manly tone, "Yes, my love, I have faith in Trevor and we're men, true men. I think he'll be invaluable to our cause."

"Alright then. I guess you're now the head of your very own secret service! Congratulations, you're government!"

Vaughn noted her irony. "I'm tired! Let's take a nap!" Stephanie heartily assented as she wanted so badly to make love to Vaughn but could settle for the next best thing, a nap in each other's arms. So they went back to their tent and laid down on top of the sleeping bag with a pleasant breeze blowing through the tent door and rear window.

☙

When they awoke, Trevor was still on their minds. Stephanie broke the silence, "Do you realize what Trevor is to us?"

Vaughn knew he could answer in several different ways but sensed none of his thoughts were what Stephanie aimed at so his look just told her to continue.

"All this time, all we've been doing is just looking out for ourselves, especially concerning me. I've had a *lot* of people looking out for me. Trevor is the *first* person we helped who wasn't something to us. Well, actually, we did try to help Tracy…"

Vaughn nodded, "But I know where you're going with this. Tracy had been your friend, and I helped her because you asked. Trevor is the first person we've helped since we've discovered our true freedom!" Vaughn hesitated then shook his head muttering, "And I almost killed him! I would have, you know?"

Stephanie seriously agreed, "I do know, that's why I reacted as I did. Your killing him felt wrong to me, in spite of his deserving it." Stephanie left all the implications hanging for Vaughn to deal with. *He needs to work this out for himself. Soon, I hope.*

Having brought the matter of Trevor to a conclusion, they were now free to return their attention to whom they loved most. Each other. Being truly married and conquering the Black Oil made them feel fuller, stronger, able to reach for infinity and yet, knowing they were but mere toys to Jargono left them feeling small. Stephanie propped her head up on one elbow hoping for some reassurance, "Do you really think that Jean and Lana will be safe for all this time we're gone?" Stephanie's affection for them pained her.

Vaughn stretched then caressed her cheek. "I know for sure that if we'd stayed, they'd certainly be in great danger. Stephanie, I'm sorry, but I can't say for sure how safe they'll be. There are many dangers in the world, but look at us. How could we have possibly made it through all that we did?" He left the answer unstated, but the sense of it was clearly in his eyes.

Stephanie rested her hand on her dress at her hip, feeling the bottle of Light Oil through the cloth, her fingers rubbing it repeatedly. She knew this Oil had great powers of goodness but didn't know what that entailed. Returning to her family and giving the bottle to them crossed her mind but then she reasoned she'd probably need it more for the battles she and Vaughn would face. *Or maybe not...*

Touching the necklace and the Seed, she could feel its holiness and how accustomed they'd become with each other. In so many ways, the Seed was like a long lost friend to her. Stephanie pulled her main braid over her shoulder and laid in front of her and she ran the silken ribbon through her fingers. The fine, gold Appendaho pattern embroidered at its edges brought back loving but painful memories. Her long lost foremother had worn it as a child and Stephanie wondered who she was, and about the lineage that proceeded from her.

As she did all these things, Vaughn studied her intently. "Stephie, you've seen so much in such a short time. You've gone from a poor, pitiful little peasant girl to a rich queen." His eyes searched her for some reaction to his half-tease.

Stephanie rolled onto her back, extended her arms over her head, replying in mid-stretch, "Isn't that the truth."

Vaughn thought about taking advantage of her vulnerable position and tickling her, but he had more important things on his mind, "I'm not even speaking about your money."

Lying flat, relaxing, and rejoicing in the nap's rejuvenation, she barely wanted to reply but felt the need to respond, "I know you weren't. Vaughn? After we leave this country, let's settle down, make love, and raise a family? It'll take years for us to grow strong enough to return here, but in the meantime, why waste the time we have together by just waiting?"

He could see the longing she had for peace and comfort, for escape. He couldn't tell her right then, that he thought it wouldn't be the right time yet. He just had a feeling that it would be a while before they could fully be man and wife. They had the Seed of the Tree of Life to protect and their mating was tied to it. He knew they had to follow the pattern of the king and queen of her ancestors, if they were to respect and receive the blessings from the Tree of Life. *It might not even grow if we made love at the wrong time, or in the wrong way, or for the wrong reasons. The king and queen mated after they had victory over their evil enemy, and when they could build a safe home for their children, and a protected place for the Tree to grow.* But Vaughn couldn't tell her this now because the weary look in Stephanie's eyes prevented him, so he spoke the next best thing, "You make a lot of sense. Let's do all we can to make us a beautiful home together. When we escape from this country and enter the new one, let's both see about going back to school."

But *that* thought instantly disgusted her. "Vaughn! *Why?* We don't need that *crap.* You can work and I already have plenty of money…"

He rolled onto his back and put his arm over his eyes. He just wanted only his words to touch her in this. "Because by age we're still kids. Adults have a lot they can teach us and we shouldn't be ignorant. The work I've been doing is menial. I enjoy it, yes, but I have far more ability than just doing that kind of work."

Her eyes roamed over him as he laid there, "But Vaughn, if we let them know our true age, *they may not even let us be married.*" Feelings rushed upon her from all sides, and that of subjugation to adults brought back every insult, every tedious task they had put her through. *How could I submit myself to* them *after all I've been through?* She fought back tears, waiting for Vaughn's reply.

Angry at himself for upsetting her, not meaning for that to come out now, it had found its own way out, anyway. "I think we have to be very wise. Before we cross over, I'll consult the Book on how we should proceed though I think I know already. I don't think we should tell anyone any more than we need to about us. Let's learn as much as we can about them without them learning about us."

At hearing that, her upset faded and her thoughts moved onward, "That sounds wise." Stephanie could tell from his tone how worried he was for her. She noticed each time she exhibited any discomfort that he automatically wanted to spare her from it. She didn't want that, *I'm not a baby.* "First, we have to figure out how to escape this *terrible* country."

Vaughn nodded. "I've been thinking pretty hard on that. I think we need to start stopping at all the little towns on the way up to the border. We can say we're newly married and on our days of leave, so they won't suspect otherwise."

Stephanie wasn't used to even considering getting help from common people. "Why do you want to do *that?* I've been enjoying camping out so much. We only need to stop to get supplies, like we've been doing."

Vaughn understood her protest, also feeling the same reluctance. Being alone with her, Spot, and nature was heaven. "I know, dear. I love camping, too! But Stephie, we have to face reality. If we isolate ourselves, we learn nothing, and we need knowledge badly. People talk, we need to listen, so we can learn about the border, how it's guarded and a lot of other stuff that we don't even know that we should know, so we can decide how best to escape. I'll make friends with people, you, too! When we get to that port town, I've decided I'm going to try to get work on the various boats that come and go. *I am not going to try to escape on one of those until I know for sure it's safe. There's nowhere to run when you're on a ship at sea.*"

Stephanie rolled back onto her side, sharpening her eyes upon him. Vaughn was still covering his face with his arm. "Well, of course you're right *again*. Hmm, I guess it's a fault of being young, huh? We want what we want, when we want."

"I don't know. I don't see why age would make any difference in that. I think only wisdom makes a difference, not the wanting, not the when it's desired, but in the patience."

Stephanie couldn't resist any longer. He was defenseless. She pounced on him, tickling him in his ribs. Vaughn immediately tried to roll away from the attack, but the tent constrained him and she ruthlessly followed him, until he jammed against the tent wall. He tried curling up in a ball but that didn't work. The only defense seemed to be offense, so he began to reach to tickle her. It wasn't long before they were both holding each other at arms' length, laughing, maneuvering.

෴

They arrived in early evening at the next town that reminded Vaughn of the many small towns he visited while working the train. He realized how valuable that experience had been, now feeling world-wise and not at all uncomfortable. Confidently, he approached the clerk's desk at the local hotel.

"We would like your best room please, Sir. We're celebrating our marriage."

The elderly white-haired man peered over his spectacles, looking doubtful, "Oh, you are, huh? You're quite young to be married *and* able to celebrate."

The man's tone read like the political history of this God-forsaken country. It was part jealous of the possibility that these youth had actually succeeded while he was still stuck behind a hotel counter, and part mocking the obvious pride that these two striplings had in each other, which judging from the old man's sour look, he'd probably never experienced nor even believed in such interpersonal virtue. No, only the government was to be respected and any youthful exuberance should be invested in their service. This couple appeared far too free, too uninhibited. This crotchety old man had an immediate dislike of the strange kind of obviously ignorant glow this couple had surrounding them, but he did also wonder how he could take advantage of them.

Vaughn had seen it all before, the lameness of the adult world, its abject failures, its jealousies, envies, and fears. Yes, Vaughn had already thought it all through. "We've been fortunate to have a store which does quite well, but what concerns *you* is that you get your money, *right?*" He bolstered his inflection with his glare. Stephanie tried hiding her utter surprise at seeing this new side to Vaughn. He seemed so… adult!

The old man straightened, souring more, "That's right, young man." And his tone read like another book Vaughn had completely grown tired of re-reading.

I'm going to end this right now. Vaughn plunked enough money down on the counter and slid it to the clerk. "OK, here, I'll pay you for a week, right up front. I want to enjoy this week and I don't want any unfortunate *misunderstandings* to make it unpleasant." Vaughn had pulled out the amount according to the sign for a week's stay, but just before the owner could take it, he pulled it back. Vaughn knew about these things because the train master had told him quite a few *stories*.

The old man squinted at him, obviously anxious to have the money, but hating to have to lower himself to these mere kids to get it, "What? Change your mind?"

"Well, I just had a thought that I could get a better deal across the street."

The elderly man laughed, his eyes boring into Vaughn, beholding this strange character. "You're young, but not dumb. OK, I'll give you a whole day for free. Pay for six up front, get day seven for free. That's the standard here in town. Nobody'll go lower. Here's your key. Room number's on it. It's our best room, special for newlyweds. Just up the stairs, to the left at the end of the hall."

Vaughn could tell by his tone and feeling that he spoke the truth. "OK." Vaughn took his new bride by her waist, with his pack on his back, his and her knapsacks on each shoulder, and Spot following behind, watching all the people. Stephanie had picked up the key. As they passed through the common lounge area, assorted people stared at them. Stephanie and Vaughn didn't know it, but to everyone else they looked to be a remarkable couple, not just because they were so young looking, but because of her beauty, his handsomeness, and the aura surrounding them that shouted of being special. There was even something special about the dog! He had a very stately walk for a dog.

When they reached the foot of the stairs, Vaughn placed his hand on his wife's lower back, in courtesy. *I don't know. It just feels right to do so.* All eyes watched their every move, until they disappeared at the top.

Stephanie unlocked the room and right after they entered, she took her knapsack from her husband's shoulder and dragged it through the living room to their bedroom. But in the bedroom doorway she stopped, mouth agape, dumbfounded by the room's lavishness and comfort. Even the Appendaho didn't have such exquisite furnishings. Vaughn had just simply plunked his things to the floor in the other room.

"Oh, Vaughn, what a beautiful room! Aah, look at this *bed!*" It was larger than she'd ever seen, with four, dark wooden posts holding up a frilly canopy and a soft, thick mattress.

She turned to her husband with a grin stretched from ear to ear. With her eyes sharply drilling into his heart, Vaughn felt the room grow small though it was quite spacious. Stephanie instantly pulled him down into bed heaven, and in one smooth motion worthy of the best seductresses, rolled on top of him and kissed him deeply on the mouth!

Between kisses that grew increasingly intoxicating, he managed to speak, "Stephie…"

She said nothing, apparently lost in the experience.

"Stephie…" he managed to whisper again. He'd been wanting to kiss her deeply and much more, for so long, but not just for the sake of a kiss, but for the very reasons she now embraced him. The way her lips and tongue caressed his came straight from her heart with every taste of him savored for its preciousness, with every touch glowing with deep love and reverence. It seemed as if she could no longer restrain herself and she knew there was nothing to feel guilty about.

In her mind it had started as almost a tease. She had intended on pulling him over to the bed, pushing him onto it, giving him one single kiss, and then getting up. It just didn't happen that way, and she didn't know why. All she knew now came moment by tender moment as another part of her disarmed her will, or rather, exerted its right over her.

We feel so right together, was the common thought and Vaughn could feel himself being swept down a river of beautiful life as the strength in his arms encircled her, celebrating the treasure they had tightly wrapped within them. But… but something was out of time or place. They hadn't looked into each other's eyes. Realizing it, Vaughn wondered. *Why haven't we?* But sadly, he knew why. It wasn't the right time, and they both knew it.

"Stephie, look at me a moment!"

"MMMmm, I am… looking at you." She said between her breaths.

Vaughn pointed to his eyes and hers, "Here Stephie, here, like we always do."

She paused without looking up, and so Vaughn's hand gently cupped her cheek, as she lay atop him. He slipped his thumb under her chin, gently tipping her head up and their eyes met!

Knowledge. Stephanie's eyes filled with tears, her body suddenly relaxing against his, and she laid her head down upon his shoulder, just holding him. Once again she found herself disarmed, as the pendulum of her life swung back again.

Vaughn stroked her head, running his hand down the length of each long, soft, red braid, but when he touched the ribbon, an incredible sensation halted him. A great other-worldly presence, hard to define, and not of the physical senses at all, entered his hand. "Stephie," he whispered, "this ribbon… It feels… sacred." It brought to his mind when he touched the brass basin around the former Tree of Life.

Part of him wanted to take his hand away from it, feeling unworthy, but another part wanted to touch it more, to understand the mysterious holy feelings. Then he remembered the Light Oil she'd blotted-up with it. He tried to recall other times he'd touched the ribbon, trying to compare before and after the Oil but he found it difficult to even distinguish these odd feelings.

Then Stephie's head suddenly popped up, gleaming like a little girl with a new idea, "Let's take a bath!"

After having camped out for so long, the thought of soaking in a hot tub of water completely thrilled them. Stephanie rolled off Vaughn just as quickly as she'd bedded him, bounded over to the bathroom and promptly proclaimed, "Oh *Vaughn*, you've *got* to see this!"

An ornate old-fashioned gleaming tub, the kind where only your neck would stick out above water if you filled it up to the top. Golden brass, independent fixtures for hot and cold seemed to float atop the shiny white porcelain. Stephanie ran her finger across its surface, creating instant pleasure at the touch, then bent over and felt the equally smooth bottom. Vaughn thought about pinching her, her being in such a suggestive position, but the lesson of their dalliance just minutes ago made him decide against it. Stephanie turned the water spigots, then plugged the drain.

As they stripped out of their clothing, placing them in their laundry bag, each realized the increasing degree of familiarity they had with each other. As Vaughn delightfully treated his eyes to her private beauty, he held out his hand as she straddled the high edge of the tub then he climbed in with her. Seeing her naked again, the thought occurred that this might one day be a familiar sight. *I hope so.* Besides being intriguing, to say the least, Vaughn found a special comfort in the vision as well, an intimacy that said they belonged to each other. He couldn't take his eyes from her, exploring every curve slowly disappearing into the rising water. Part of him regretted the bubble bath soap, courtesy of the hotel. He noticed she still wore the necklace, having been instructed to never take it off until the Seed was planted.

They sat almost neck high in hot water at opposite ends of the tub, their legs partly floating, time drifting away as they soaked. Each had their head tilted back and their eyes closed, but eventually the main purpose of the bath came to the fore and they washed each other.

Sacred feelings embraced them both as they cleansed each other, knowing that to truly fulfill the Seed to the Tree of Life, they had to be responsible together. The right time, the right place, then the right tree, the right children would follow. Though their desire burned hotly, their touch also deeply comforted. Intimately feeling one another's skin evoked a special wholeness together. Each had the common sentiment, *We belong together, forever.* And so it was no longer a question of if they would make love but when, and knowing love was not withheld from them made it easier to wait.

He touches me with value. I really mean something to him and I can feel it in his every caress. What a huge difference between raw physicality and meaningful touch. Stephanie reflected on Vaughn's caress then remembered a statement she'd made so long ago, *Everything has meaning.* Shaking her head at her past, she could not now even imagine participating in anything like the meaningless physical contact she had so relished in her ignorance and depravity. *How stupid I was to be so cheap with my body, throwing away its meaning. Thank you Light for restoring my opportunity to experience the realness of this wonderful touch.* And then she thought of all those others still buried under filth. *Poor, poor souls, who don't know what they're missing, and don't know what they're destroying!*

After getting out of the tub, they dried each other off. Stephanie reflected further, *God, I can't believe I ever did the things I've done with this body before I knew You. Nothing compares in wonderfulness to what I have with Vaughn and we haven't even mated yet.*

Vaughn couldn't help interrupting her thoughts as he brought up, "Stephie, that Light Oil is very powerful. I felt it."

"Hmmm… I guess so, but because it was created through me, during my battle, well, I think I'm kinda used to it!"

But Vaughn studied her answer. It didn't seem quite accurate, "Ahh, not exactly, in fact, I don't think so! More like when we were in the tub. After we sat in the hot water for a while, it didn't feel as hot. Not because it cooled that much but…"

Stephanie interjected, "Like I said, we got used to it!"

"Actually, that's not really the way it works. We turned red from the heat. *We* got hotter. So then, the hot water was less of a difference to us. I don't think it's a matter of you getting *used to* the sacredness of the Oil, as much as that you've been made sacred by it! It's a matter of perception. There isn't that much difference in sacred quality between you and it!"

Stephanie stopped in the middle of wrapping her hair up and looked into Vaughn's eyes in surprise, "Vaughn, I don't feel sacred. I mean…"

Vaughn shook his head, "It's not that sacredness has a feeling all its own. Sacredness is the *result* of other ways and feelings, like pure love and pure respect for Goodness. That's what gives a feeling of ultimate worth, of sacredness. There's a special blessing now in your ribbon, an imbuing holy spirit that I felt… I think. Do you feel your love is pure?"

There he went again with his wonderful point making. It instantly drew her smile, "Well, I hope so."

"And your respect for Goodness?"

Stephanie looked away, "I… hope so, too. I guess I'm a little embarrassed now at what I did to you on the bed." She was blushing redder than when she was in the bath. "I don't know what came over me."

Vaughn wanted to take her in his arms right then, but being naked and feeling the way they did, he decided not to risk it. He smiled broadly and settled for further explanation, "What came over *us,* Stephie, was natural life I think. There's no sin in that, nothing to be embarrassed about. We truly love each other and not only that, we even have the means to be responsible for each other. Heck, Stephie! We're married before God with His blessing. But down the road, the natural life is *not* life if it isn't made truly servant to the Greater Life. Only *in that way* does it have meaning! Too many people turn the natural life into existing death because they don't consider its relationship to everything else."

His words sank deep into her with utter respect for him. All the other men she'd known were not even a speck of dust compared to Vaughn. *Oh how I love him so.* An instant later, they found themselves in each other's arms. Stephanie spoke, as if giving a solemn oath, "I love you so much. You are a *true* soul, my *true* mate."

Holding each other sacredly, they kissed with devotion. *One day we're going to bear children to the Tree of Life.* Then, looking each other in the eyes for a long beautiful moment, they could see themselves at some future time, and they parted.

Stephanie sat down in front of a large brass-framed mirror in the little lounge area off from the bathroom, and began to brush out her deep red hair. Vaughn collected some clean clothes and sat on the couch in the living room and watched her through the open doorway. He loved her long, wavy red hair and delighted in studying that special feminine mystique generated by her personal hygiene. Stephanie's hair fell down the middle of her back, to just where her waist became narrow. That narrowness was accentuated by how her hips flared out then melded into her thighs which tapered down her shapely legs. Her rounded hips reminded him of a swelling flower bud on a graceful stalk, waiting to bloom. There seemed to be a glow all around her.

While Vaughn watched her graceful movement, her delicate yet firm precision with every brushstroke, he was amazed at just how much strength could be packed into such a supple, delicate body. Every inch of her looked smooth and soft, and her narrow waist, downright fragile. Yet, her vigor showed through. Her arm muscles shifted with each stroke as her thighs kept her balanced on the stool. *So much of her character shines through in just this simple act of brushing her hair. It's strength embedded in the midst of delicacy, tenderness and concentration.* And seeing her hair down and all full had another meaning… for some reason it stirred him deeply but before he could examine that vision further, she began to braid.

Vaughn became fascinated with the rapidity with which she transformed her hair into the traditional Appendaho style. He understood the technical aspects of braiding, but to see her fingers literally fly in a blur and mere moments later… And there was a particular attitude and set of feelings embedded in her while she worked. *No other human body part gets as much attention or care as a woman's hair. It's as if they put something special into their hair beyond just the physical… something maybe taken for granted. I don't know… I wonder what it all means.*

In the midst of his pondering, she wrapped herself in a big towel and came over to where he sat, already dressed. She pulled over a table chair to sit in front of him.

Her eyes level with his, she asked, "Vaughn, why did you pledge to avenge my people?"

He guessed that she'd been thinking about the question for a while. A quick reflection brought, "Because of the terrible injustice done that had to be answered."

Stephanie stayed silent, knowing.

"Why do you ask?"

"Because, was it vengeance for the sake of killing the unjust, or for the sake of the living?"

He hadn't thought about that and examined his feelings. "I felt that if their atrocity wasn't answered, then any chance at real life would be destroyed. I also felt those criminals had no right to continue to exist and that your people were owed justice."

Stephanie nodded, "The chance of life is for the sake of the living. Just wanting to destroy the criminals was for the sake of killing. The second reason alone does not guarantee a benefit to the living. My people no longer profit from actions done here in this world, so your third reason is for your own conscience, serving as further justification to kill."

"Stephie, I think you're trying to tell me something."

She reached over, put her hand on his knee while searching the depths of his face, "I just want you to think, Vaughn. Think! So you can grow even stronger and wiser."

He tried to discern her direction but realized that just as she suggested, he had to look within himself. After contemplating his reasons, he began slowly, "At the time, everything was one big tangled feeling. You're right, though. Putting down evil people for the sake of giving others a chance to live *is* a totally different reason than merely feeling the wicked should be destroyed. But I had both those feelings and acted upon them both simultaneously."

She felt he was on the right track. "I think that's important to remember, because it's possible that, well, sometimes the second reason of wanting destruction may not help, and even hurt the cause of the living!"

Her words provoked an instant response and part of him wondered why his feelings were so strong, "*How, Stephie? How can destroying the wicked ever be unprofitable to the living?*" *Why am I so upset? I don't want to be upset at her. Oh God, I was just thinking how much I loved her!*

She looked down, understanding, expecting his reaction, hoping she would respond correctly. She folded her hands on her lap in prayer, looking into the beyond, "Maybe… when the living don't get enough chance to experience the wicked, they'll also turn evil! Maybe some of those wicked are like our folks. Vaughn, if ours had been destroyed at a much earlier point in our lives, we would be very different right now… I think. We may have ended up in such terrible places that we would have lost our souls." She then looked to see if he received her words and saw him in deep deliberation.

His tone notably softened, "I don't know! The Appendaho did just fine *without* the wicked. And no doubt, our utter frustration with and fighting against evil have been integral to our current characters. Hmmm… but if we'd had it even worse? I don't know, but this is the moral dilemma you faced when you were going to destroy the army to save your people." Vaughn shook his head from the complexity of lives twisting in his awareness.

She studied his shifting expressions. "Yes dear, the very same, but applied to you, to everyone, and now also with even deeper thought. Destroying a life is so final, wicked or not. Don't you think that if God wanted to, in the blink of an eye, He could turn all the wicked to ash? But He doesn't! The reason has to be for the sake of the living. Also, once the wicked are gone, they're gone. It would be a waste of even a single thought to think about them. So this just emphasizes how all our focus should be on the living. Let wicked people revel in the destruction they've wrought, but let us focus on the living."

Vaughn's strong reaction returned, "But Stephie, I felt, I heard, in a spiritual way, your people's spilt blood call to me. I had to do what I did, even if I *died* trying."

Stephanie nodded again, "I know, Vaughn. I know! *Please…* I'm not saying you were wrong in any of it. God left that part of their life here on this side of life, just special for you to hear. That means what you had to do was not by you, but Light through you. Just remember, though, the distinctions we just made, if we *ourselves* are faced with having to kill, or letting evil people continue. Killing for the sake of the living is the only really solid reason, *but* as I pointed out, it's hard for us to really know how best to do anything for the sake of the living, when God isn't doing it through us. Vaughn, the sake of the living requires a very far-sighted perspective." With her last words, that distant look in her eyes sunk into his.

He felt tingles that he came to recognize as the Spirit of Truth bringing him sense. But it didn't answer his next question, so he asked, "Well, does that mean that if God doesn't do something through us, then we shouldn't do it?"

That's the very question I've *been wrestling with! Now we can work on it together.* "I don't know. I wouldn't want to say that, because when Jargono was threatening your life, I hit him with… Well, I don't know but I threw out my hand and some force came out, hitting him hard. As I can remember, I meant to at least make him into no threat, but the second time, I meant to *kill* him!"

Vaughn waited for her to defend her thoughts further.

"I think it's *not* wrong for us to defend our lives or others in the instant. I think that's *our* responsibility and God doesn't have to act through us for that, *I think*. But once the threat is passed, then you're talking about handing out justice. I think God has to be in that."

Vaughn leaned forward with his chin in his hand and his elbow on his knee for support. Killing Gary, his conscious deliberation to do it, once again flashed in his mind, but more than ever, he was sure now he did the right thing. *Yea, she's got a point, but if I can help it, I won't let any threat against us prevail. What we have to do is far too important to screw up by giving wicked people any chance to hurt us.*

Vaughn remembered some of his earlier reasoning, "What about laws? People get arrested for murder and other things and are sentenced to death or jail. That's not in the instant."

Stephanie got out of her chair to sit next to, instead of across from him. Taking Vaughn's hands in hers as he turned to face her, she explained, "But those laws are stated up front. The criminal knew the consequences. So it's not any person judging, but the law judging, and the people only carrying it out." Stephanie squeezed his hands, speaking even more earnestly, "And when the legal system breaks down, as it has in this country, what good does it do for any one, or two, or even a small group, to stand up and start handing out justice? I think the only right thing then is to wait on God because for justice to work, most of the people have to be behind it. So let God, as He only can, turn a country around."

Vaughn pulled his hands from his wife's and took hers in his, intensifying his gravity, "But Stephie, in order for people to turn around, doesn't it have to start with *someone*? So then, how does your logic solve that?"

Gazing into him, she shook her head, "I don't know. I haven't thought that far into it. Now you're making *me* think... and rethink." This time her eyes went *very* distant. His question invoked a deep calling that was unmistakably addressed to her to do something. *But what?* A hint of tears crossed her eyes but she didn't know why. "Maybe someone has to do a *lot* of things, not just kill a few wicked. That someone has to reach the living... hmmm, and the dead living, I mean the wicked as well. I think that for any individual or group to really make a difference, they have to gain the few good people left, and they have to turn a lot of bad people back to goodness. That takes a whole lot more than just killing even a lot of the wicked. It takes showing them how to really live. Now we're right back to God, aren't we? Only He can show people how to really live. That kind of work can only be done through us, not by us."

The more truth they shared together, the deeper their love grew, yet Vaughn knew that what they were talking about now, was even more important than their love. He felt they were talking about their destiny, or their future calling, or perhaps a better way to put it is their responsibility. He squeezed her hands with the feeling they were both being called to do... something. *What?*

"Yes Stephie, if it is only by us, then all we show people is ourselves. If it is *through* us, then we show them we belong to something greater than ourselves, and they sense that and desire *it*, not us."

She smiled, nodded, and retook his hands, squeezing, "Yes, my love."

They both felt the Spirit of God descending over them. It brought back memories of that happening as they married each other by the campfire. After the feeling eased a bit, Vaughn spoke in a quiet tone, "Stephie, I think this was a very important conversation. You've really made me think of what I should be doing. Originally, I just wanted to go to other countries and try to get justice for your people's death, but deep down that isn't really all that my heart really wants because I want people to live real lives. Oh God, what I want is even much bigger than what I've said before... and what I desired before already seemed much too big." Vaughn finished by shaking his head at himself.

Stephanie squeezed his hands again, speaking while reflecting, "Vaughn, think of how my ancient father and mother started off. Well, our lives, I am beginning to understand, may not be that much different than theirs was. All we can do, dearest, is grow in the goodness God gives us and follow its natural course like a tiny little spring in a mountain. Then maybe, on its way down, it'll join..."

"With other springs and become a river of life."

"Yes, my love! We must hope."

"Stephie, our calling has just gotten very long and very, very large." Vaughn sighed. He was beginning to rethink Stephanie's suggestion to start a family but he hadn't really told her *any* of his line of thinking on that subject.

They sat together for a while, not looking at each other but in quiet self-reflection, projecting their thoughts into the future. After some time, that natural course, too, took a turn.

"Vaughn, after we eat, I'm going to do our laundry. Women often talk in such places. Why don't you find… ahh, whatever place it is that *silly boys* go to play, and see what you can learn." She had that mischievous gleam again. Vaughn stuck out his tongue at her and she instantly responded to that insult by chasing him with her hair brush so he ran around the couch.

"How *rude*! Come 'ere, I'm gonna brush that tongue out!"

Vaughn ran out of the living room, into the bedroom, and around the other side of the bed, ducking down so she couldn't see him. As she climbed over it, he sneaked around her, caught and tickled her. She screamed, whirled around, and began to do the same to him. Vaughn hated to be tickled, because he was just so ticklish. She knew it, too, and took full advantage until he begged for mercy. Sitting atop him in full gloating victory, Stephanie said in mock sternness, *"Apologize."*

He said in mock seriousness, as she sat atop him, *"I apologize."*

Then she leaned over close, brandishing her hairbrush, "SAY I apologize for sticking my tongue out, and I will *never* do it again."

Vaughn promptly apologized under threat of tongue-brushing and more tickling, then… licked her nose.

Stephanie immediately lodged her formal protest, "Yuck, *you broke your word.*"

But he defended, "No I didn't! That wasn't the same thing."

"It was."

"It wasn't! But OK, OK. I won't lick your nose, either… *promise!*"

Then she rolled over on the bed while both rocked with laughter.

❧

Stephanie plopped the very full laundry bag down on the floor and began sorting, when an old lady sidled up to her, chuckling, "So, you're just newly married?"

Surprised, Stephanie realized they must be the talk of the town and wasn't sure if she liked that. She went back to her laundry as she smiled, knowing she wouldn't have to chase this one for conversation. "Yes Ma'am."

And then the story began, "*Well,* I was married a long time ago. My husband's been dead for fifteen years now, but I *remember* when I was young though. Oh my, my husband was, well, you know now that you're married, he was a *good* lover, you know, all night sometimes we did, oh, but I'm an old lady now, I don't think about those things anymore. Is your husband a *good lover?*"

Stephanie had just resigned herself to the fact that the old woman didn't breathe, only talk, when *that* question hit. She leaned over and whispered, "My husband is such a *good* lover that he loves me from the inside out!" Then Stephie gave a knowing wink, acting as if of course the old lady knew exactly what that meant.

The gray-haired lady's eyes twisted a bit, got a distant look and then, "Oh my! Ahh, well, that *is* the best way to do it."

Stephanie leaned over again, whispering, "Well, I'm glad you think so. You would certainly know, having been married for so long. Say, where are some other good places to travel for our marriage leave?"

The old lady rattled off a list of little towns and what each had to offer though actually all were the same: a couple of nice hotels, a movie theater, a bar. And she went into elaborate details about each, for each town. Stephanie lost track of time, as her words ran on and on…

Then Stephanie managed to butt in, "My husband loves to fish and I like to eat what he catches."

This started another long story but Stephanie still had to dry the washed clothes anyway.

"Oh, well, down the coast about twenty miles is a little fishing port." The old lady seemed to have a shadow cross her face.

Stephanie decided to prod her further by adding, "OH, THAT WOULD BE GREAT! I'll tell him we can get a boat…"

The old lady leaned over and whispered clearly, "There are no nice people down there. You're a pretty thing and young. Some of those other towns I…"

Stephanie brushed her off, "Oh, my husband can protect me. I can't wait to tell him about the fishing. Thank you so much."

The old lady took her firmly by the arm, looking around at the other ladies scattered about, at women supposedly minding their own business. "Let me show you the soap dispenser they have in the back! They have my *favorite* old fashioned soap there." She pulled Stephanie along in a very commanding way to the back and then whirled on her, "Listen young lady, I think you're a sweet thing so I don't want any harm to come to you. That port town is nothing but a trap! The government set it up many years ago to catch people who want to leave the country. But sometimes, they just catch people... *any people.*" She squinted to reinforce her meaning then jabbed Stephanie in the ribs with her bony finger. "You stay away from there!"

Stephanie sulked, "But we just want to fish."

The old lady sighed, turned a stern eye on her, and shook her joint-swelled forefinger in Stephanie's face. "Don't be a fool! Those people down there have had free reign for a hundred years. The government doesn't care what those officers do to people down there, and they don't want to know as long as they keep the border from leaking. So they do *anything* they want to *anyone*, do you understand?"

Truly shaken, Stephanie knew it showed. *Just when I thought I knew everything I needed to know about the adult world, now this!* "Yes, Ma'am! Thank you for your concern."

"So what do you think of that strange, young, handsome man? What do you think he'll do next?" She was obviously enraptured with him.

Puzzled, Stephanie couldn't figure out what the old lady was trying to say about her husband, "Ma'am?"

The lady laughed a belly laugh, her eyes sparkling, "Oh, I guess you've been, ahh, too busy to watch the news on TV the last few days."

Actually, it had been a very long time since either Stephanie or Vaughn had viewed any news. Most of it was just local junk, anyway, since the government hid everything that went on. *But what does that have to do with Vaughn?*

Stephanie decided to play along by kidding, "So a handsome young man lurks around the corner of our laundry building, being chased by news reporters?"

The old biddy responded quickly, "Oh no, dear, you really are out of touch. I'm talking about the National News!"

Now even more perplexed because, *There's no national news.* "National News?"

The lady put her hands on her hips, "That's what I'm trying to tell you. A few days ago all the local channels carried the same broadcast about this strange young man, the one they had on a while ago. Apparently, he's working some kind of miracles now, and our government has decided to make him a king! Do you believe that? A KING! Ha, we haven't had a king since, well…"

Goose bumps rose all over Stephanie's body, the hairs on the back of her neck stood up. Her voice came out very weakly, "So what was the news about him? I… I'm completely in the dark."

"Well, apparently, he did some pretty big miracles and showed some prophecy about being the last of some ancient race and being descended from some great, powerful, ancient king, and how prophecy said that it was time for our country to become great, and that he would lead us and help us defeat all our enemies and bring enlightenment to the whole world! The head of the government himself was shown on TV bowing down to him!"

Afraid to ask, but needing to hear confirmation, Stephanie wished her tone hadn't been as flat as it was, "What miracles did he do? Did they show them on TV?"

"You know there's always been a few towns near our borders that had people from other countries living in them. Well, he called the government to witness and then *poof!*"

Stephanie's heart pounded, her eyes went wide, and her voice merely whispered, "Poof?"

The lady threw out her hands in a wide gesture, "POOF! The town vaporized in a flash with all the people, everything, gone! A big fire came out of the sky then seconds later, ASHES."

Stephanie hoped it wasn't what she thought, "There are stories that long ago, countries had weapons, bombs that…"

But the old lady shook her head, "No dear, this was nothing like that. Those things don't exist anymore. Besides, they had the video running, it's been showing every hour. King Jargon says he can do that to all our enemies, if they don't submit to his rule."

Hoarsely, Stephanie uttered, "King Jargon."

"Yes, that's what he calls himself and *guess what?*"

She replied even more flatly, "I can't guess."

"In three days he's going to do a miracle, *live*, for everyone to see. Oh, I can't wait. Ha, if you weren't married, I'd suspect a pretty girl like you would have a chance at him. They say he doesn't have a wife yet but I'm not sure what rules he'll have on that. He said he would be greatly improving our laws, whatever that means. We're to start recruiting for a larger army, start making weapons and everything. He said he can't do all the fighting himself, we would need to help him, and besides that, we have to build our characters by meaningfully contributing to the greatness of our country. *And,* He's also going to give our nameless country a name! *Three days.* I can't wait!"

Stephanie noticed the inspiration, the life in her spirit, and groaned inside, *Such a nice, good old lady to be sucked in by such crap.* "What other miracles did he do?"

"Oh, they didn't say but the government said he took them for a private showing and that he showed them several other amazing feats."

Stephanie folded her arms across her breast, "And what is the great truth that he brings to our people?"

The lady suddenly became stymied, "Truth? Hmmm… I don't know. Glory of the old days, I guess."

Stephanie was baffled, *What* glory *of the old days?* "Why did he destroy all those people?"

The lady offered the perfectly logical explanation, "They weren't *ours*! They had no right to live here. We've been the weaker country for too long. Now we'll become glorious again."

Stephanie tried to recall, *When the hell were we ever glorious?* But decided she needed to finish up and find Vaughn, "Oh yea, that's very good. Thank you, Ma'am.

☙

"So *boy*, just married huh?" A fat, graying middle-aged man spat out the words with no particular affection nor coldness and not quite mocking the youth. He moved around the pool table to eye his next potential shot while Vaughn got ready to take his. Having decided to refuse to answer anyone who addressed him as *boy*, Vaughn acted as if he heard nothing, sank his ball, and moved on to his next shot. He used to play quite a lot back home by himself in what seemed like ages ago.

"Hey, *boy!*" The slob rapped his cue on the table, then pointed it at him, "Not good manners to ignore someone talking to you."

Vaughn acted surprised, "Oh, were you talking to me? I'm so sorry. I thought you were talking to some *boy*. How long have you had a vision problem? You know, that could be why you missed your last shot!"

The whole room, whose attention had been gathered when the fat slob rapped on the table, burst into hysterical laughter.

A thin, younger man quipped, "Looks like he straightened you out quick, huh?" Then he doubled over again in drunken laughter.

Vaughn wasn't sure which way all this would go but he sunk two more shots, ignoring everything. The sot felt the need to recapture respect, but he went about it the wrong way.

"You got a pretty little thing of a wife. I think I should show her the difference between a real man and a *boy*."

It was clear this man thought in very limited ways, being sure his physical size was all there was to reality and the definition of manhood.

Vaughn replied softly, even politely, "There are laws to prohibit such things, *Sir*." He thought about law, indeed, and tried extra hard to remember Stephanie's admonition about the difference between an individual's versus the law's judging.

The bar resounded in laughter again so the fat slob decided to teach the *boy*, "Ha, laws are for those whom the government don't like. Besides, the new king hasn't given us his laws yet."

Shocked, Vaughn immediately changed his priorities, "New king? I've been busy with my new wife! I hadn't heard."

But this poor excuse for middle-age just wouldn't change his mind, "Well, I'll tell you what, you go watch TV and I'll keep your wife..."

Vaughn had heard enough, but he couldn't justify striking him just because of words, *The law doesn't justify striking first.* "You mean it still works in an old man like you? I'm sure my beautiful wife would find it quite funny."

Again the room erupted in uproar. There hadn't been this much entertainment in... no one could remember.

Vaughn sank the last ball and called out loudly, "NEXT, take this fat old hog away."

That did it! A good three hundred pounds came barreling around the pool table. An honorable man might think that a huge fat man picking on a little man was, well, dishonorable. But honor in this country seemed to be the stuff of legends, now. Vaughn planted both hands firmly on the pool-table's railing, leapt up, coiled his powerful legs up to his chest, and shot them out just as the man was in range, striking him full force in his upper chest. The man's feet seemed to fly into the air as he crashed backward to the hardwood floor. His head hit with a sickening crack and blood started pouring onto the highly polished surface and the room fell silent in amazement.

Vaughn spoke softly, "Next. A dol to each person who cleans up this *mess!*" With that, five men jumped up, dragged the unconscious oaf outside, dumped him, and wiped up the blood. The young man who spoke before, said, "You're rich for a young man."

Vaughn leveled a glare at him, as he handed out the money, "I work hard. Tell me about our new *king*. I've been too busy to watch the local news."

"Not local. *National.* The government handed all control to him because he can make us rule the world. Here, watch the TV! Turn it up, Joe!" The man pointed to the TV that had been always on and Vaughn began to pay attention.

There was Jargono pointing to a town. "Your enemies shall be no more," he proclaimed with a smile as he raised both hands to heaven. A fire fell out of a cloudless sky over the town… and the town was no more. Vaughn went weak in the knees as he remembered the slaughtered Appendaho. *It didn't end with them.* Now he regretted even more his not successfully killing Jargono. But then he also realized that he really didn't have the ability to do that *yet*.

"On the first day of the week, I shall perform a miracle for all to see, *live*. Then, I shall tell our great country who I am and my plans for the world and what the name of our country shall forever be. Everyone is to watch the borders, *closely*, so that our enemies cannot escape and warn anyone."

"YES! It's about time." Vaughn shouted then slammed his pool cue against the table, the sharp cracking sound shooting through every heart in the bar.

The rest of the men chimed in behind him, "Yes, yes, yea!" A great drunken cheer erupted.

"*That's* what I want to do. I want to be a border guard!" More cheers. "Where do you think they need guards the most?"

One man said, "About twenty-five miles east of the port town, there's a border town filled with a lot of foreigners."

"NO," another man said, "By now they'll have arrested all them, if they're not dead already. Besides, they always have plenty men down there. I'll tell you where, young man, but it's a hard and dangerous place, no place for a young man with a pretty wife to think about."

Vaughn replied calmly, tilting his head and raising an eyebrow toward where they had carried out the fat man, "I think I can take care of myself."

"Yea, but who'll protect your wife when you're working?"

Vaughn glared at the man, who just continued. "Between the port town and the town he mentioned, there are hills separating them. There are old roads and scattered ranches runnin' all through those hills. Mostly, only the local people knows those woods and roads. The government mined the border area years ago, but I don't see how they can protect it all. They have rangers who keep watch, but what I hear is they mostly stay at the bars in the port town or the other. They got the local farmers and ranchers scared to death because the government gives those rangers unquestioned power. Ahh, if you think about it, no better way to make sure that area stays dangerous than to give men unquestioned power."

"How could I become one of those rangers?"

"Well, you'd have to go to the port town to their office and apply, take some kind of test. Then, if you pass, they pin a medal on you. That's it. You're a ranger for life."

For LIFE? "For life?"

"Yep, once a ranger, always a ranger. That's the government's way of keeping the job filled because it's so dangerous. Only the toughest sons of bitches can make it work for them. *Boy*… sorry, young man, maybe you should think of a different place."

"Like where?"

"'Bout three hundred miles east, there's a little lake that's half here and half there. They need guards there, too."

"Any place else?"

They all shook their heads.

Having learned all he could, with his heart pounding but feeling sick inside especially at Jargono's order to watch the borders, he hurried back to Stephanie. He somehow felt that the border watch was directed at him and his wife though he also understood Jargono's stated reason to guard the country's boundaries. *I'm sick of being a pawn in his game!*

CHAPTER FIFTEEN

An End and a Beginning

"You don't understand the opportunity the West's so-called freedom affords us."

"But your plan depends upon us raising a whole generation that will follow it. How can we truly convince some of our beloved followers to give birth to and then sacrifice their children?"

"That is not a difficult issue for us. When they are willing to die, themselves, for our cause, it is glory to them to raise children who would fulfill it. And in their eyes, their sacrifice is greater than their children's because the parents will understand it but their children who won't even be told will nonetheless have a revered place with Allah."

"You really believe we can do something like this on such a vast scale, and go undetected for twenty-five years?"

"Faith, my friend, has power beyond this world. Even if we're detected, there are bound to be leaks, our faith in the truth of our mission will cause the West to fail at stopping us, because the West is blind to our truth, and therefore they wouldn't believe it even if they heard rumors."

"But Nobama is practically one of us. You know he's going to win. Why destroy the West when eventually they'll belong to us anyway?"

"Because their system of government is not trustworthy. We need to act now, so when Nobama takes office, we waste no time setting everything up, before another Baush gets in with another damned Patriotic Act. You know, eventually the pendulum will swing back and vote in another Baush, but if we're already in place, it'll be far harder to detect us when that happens. And even if they kept voting in more Nobamas, it would take far too long for us to progress in their government till we could truly make it ours. My way destroys all the western governments, their countries, and leaves only us intact and most powerful, and we'll still have all the oil, all the wealth, and they'll have to look to us, what's left of them."

His comrade shook his head, "But they'll blame us, and probably take out their vengeance upon us."

The man laughed. ""Blame who? We are not a country, and the countries we live in will vehemently deny responsibility. They'll immediately arrest people for the crime!" he laughed again, then continued, "They'll arrest our opposition and blame them, and then offer as much aide to the West as possible, but of course with a small proviso that we cannot help infidels, so they will have to honor our holy laws in some form or other!"

The other man shook his head as goose bumps crawled up his arms. "Allah be praised. I can feel the vision of our victory coming to pass."

It was evening when they met back at the hotel. Stephanie was folding and packing clothes when Vaughn burst in. Both started talking at once but paused at the confusion, then dragged each other over onto the couch.

"You first," Vaughn prompted, but Stephanie said the same thing.

"Lady's first!" he said with his special respect smile.

Stephanie couldn't resist and after they shared all they knew, she asked, "What do you think, Vaughn? What should we do?"

Peering into her worried eye with more confidence than he really had, "I think your husband is going to become a border guard *for life*. You know, no one would ever suspect that I would do that." He chuckled, "Maybe I'll just keep that job!"

Stephanie peered closely at him, not sure if he was serious or not but he wasn't either, so Stephanie prompted him, "What about the warnings to watch the border? Besides, you don't know if the 'for life' rule will last. Jargono's going to change everything, I just know it."

"It'll last, because of the nature of the border job." But Vaughn could see she wasn't comforted at all. "Look, Stephie, it's dangerous all over. I'll get a job on one of the fishing boats first and learn what I can there, then I'll go to the ranger's office. What do you think Jargono's doing?"

The way he asked that question, she knew right away he was troubled. This was exactly what they were trying to avoid, but she could see that thought in his eyes. *He thinks Jargono's playing with us… But maybe we can't ascribe everything he does to some purpose directed at us. That might be presumptuous. After all, we're not the center of the world that he wants to conquer.*

Stephanie rubbed her temple in one of those subconscious think-better gestures. "I think he's following the only path someone like him can follow who wants to rule the world because he has two terrible things in combination."

Vaughn raised his eyebrows in question as he didn't feel like thinking at the moment. The memory of the town simply vaporizing danced before his eyes, and worse, it wasn't a sadistic or maniacal act. It was cold and calculated for further purpose. He didn't like feeling scared and unable to think, so he kept the conversation going, "What two?"

"He has what seems like unlimited power and he's bored!"

Vaughn sat in stunned silence at his wife's revelation. Then he slowly nodded assent with the realization that it sounded true, except, "I think he's baiting us!"

Stephanie knew that was Vaughn's thought, "Why? I heard nothing that would seem directed at us."

But Vaughn shook his head, "Not if someone was telling you about what happened but I saw the actual video. It wasn't what he said, but the look in his eyes and the way he gestured just seemed like he was taunting us, daring us to try to stop him, or to escape."

Stephanie seemed to tap into the picture in Vaughn's mind, seeing it for herself. "What are we going to do?" She didn't mean to sound worried but then realized, she *was* worrying and she hated being overcome by it. *If Jargono is daring us to take either course of action, that means both options are already covered.*

"I know you're worried, dear, but I also think you see this as your own personal fight with him."

Stephanie shuddered, "You don't know the feelings. I was with him for a while. He... *touched* me." She grimaced when she said it, turning deeply red as she hung her head. Her flesh crawled as memories of him groping her at the store and what he did to her in her dream, haunted her. Sometimes, when she was exceptionally desirous, his invasion into her dream flashed upon her but she wanted to feel that way only with Vaughn. Jargono had robbed her of that against her will... but not totally against it because she could have stopped him.

Vaughn didn't know for sure that she had been touched, although he had suspected it. Stephanie had previously left that out though she could tell he wanted to know but wouldn't ask. She even detected what could be jealousy.

"I'm sorry, Stephie. Lana told me he made you take your clothes off. I kinda assumed..." He looked away then gazed back into her eyes with tears. "You had to do what you did to protect your family."

But she blurted out with her own tears, "Oh Vaughn, I never did *anything* with him. *I swear!*"

His response was quick, "It's OK, Stephie! I believe you. I trust you."

But by the forgiving look on his face, she could tell he was thinking wrongly, that even though she hadn't done anything, Jargono had. She shook her head, "No Vaughn, he didn't mate with me, either, nor has anyone else for that matter. I've told you before, no one, nothing has mated with me since I became new. All he did was... *touch* me and before he could do more, I made him think about trying to win me for his wife so that made him change the way he was acting. He could have forced me any second, I believe. He wanted me so badly." Then her next words faded with ponder and gravity. "But he changed his mind."

Hearing her confess the details, he felt embarrassed for thinking more happened, "I'm sorry for think…"

But she cut him off, "No, don't be! I didn't realize what you already knew, otherwise I would have told you *everything*. I'm *so sorry*. Considering what you knew, and how well you've taken it, even hidden it, it's I who should be apologizing to you. I am *so sorry*." *Should I tell him about what he did to me in my dream?*

He took her in his arms. "It's over now."

Holding him tightly, Stephanie leaned her head on his shoulder and decided to confide her fears, "Vaughn, he's my brother, and the last of my people besides me. He's also a *faithwalker* like me."

They held each other in silence for a while but Vaughn knew the gravity of this on many levels, so he tried again to draw out her feelings, "And you feel it's your personal responsibility to stop him." She pulled back to look into his face, her voice rising to a high pitch, "Who *else* has even the slightest chance?" She noted again, with surprise, both the content and level of her emotions.

He cupped her cheek in his palm, "*We* do, my love, together."

Somehow he always knew just what to say to comfort her, to make her see reality. Stephanie felt embarrassed knowing she was further along the spiritual journey than Vaughn, yet, he was still able to lend her strength. She marveled at what

God had done in making them for each other, "Vaughn, you're going to get tired of me saying it, *but I love you so.*"

He gave her his special broad smile of appreciation, "Never, my love. I'll never tire hearing it or seeing it from *you.*"

Abruptly, Stephanie changed the subject as if her mind had been working on it all along, "But if he's baiting us to confront him, or to escape, then he'll have both those things covered."

A plan formed in Vaughn's strategic mind, "We need to make him think we're coming after him."

"But he knows we're not able to beat him. It's pretty obvious *we* should know it. If we try to make him think that, he'll just know for sure we're trying to escape."

Vaughn studied her, smiling at her strategic ability to reason about such things. He remembered when he used to teach her the *Art of Fighting*, but she'd listened only out of politeness. "By that reasoning, dear, then that's the only choice he'll truly be considering. But he'd know that we know that, too, and I think that's the key as that creates a vulnerability in him, a chance to surprise him."

Stephanie's eyes were wide, and her stomach felt like it sunk, "Then we should take the chance… attack him, I guess?"

"No!" Vaughn said softly with a distant look. "Yesterday, as you napped, I got up and talked with the Book of Wisdom about battle. It was as I had suspected, but I wanted to be sure there was nothing I overlooked. Even if we surprised him, we couldn't beat him. When being pursued by a much stronger enemy, your best offense is to mislead then retreat, to find out what your enemy desires most, and make him think there's a slight chance he'll get it. Because it's desired by him, he won't risk losing an opportunity to gain it and therefore, he'll expend some resources to cover for that possibility."

It made theoretical sense to Stephanie, and yet, "But what does that mean to us?"

"It means that like you just thought that we should attack him, he'll be aware of that possibility. The chance to kill me and trap you will not go unnoticed by him. The *game* is becoming more appealing for him."

Nodding slowly, she realized Vaughn was a step or two ahead of her thoughts. He gave her time to catch up, to consider until she finally asked, "So, how do we do all this?" Stephanie realized her rapt attention must be focusing on something profound because goose bumps continued to rise all over her, but this knowledge remained in feelings and not thoughts. They had both unconsciously grasped each other's hands until they squeezed so tightly they finally noticed. Vaughn smiled, easing his grip but Stephanie's tenacious hold wouldn't ease at all.

Vaughn finally set out a plan. "We need to figure out a way for him to find out we're trying to escape, and it has to appear to him that we purposely wanted him to find out."

Stephanie rolled her eyes, "My God, then what?" Her rich brown eyes' wet sheen foretold the emotional weight behind them, but Vaughn noticed she wasn't crying. He noticed the beginning of a certain new strength in her. *She's so wonderfully beautiful.*

Vaughn explained further, "Then we have to make him think we've set a trap for him to expose him for what he really is, that we're really going to attack him, but we really didn't want him to know that."

Swamped by all this complexity, Stephanie's mouth dropped open, "Gosh, Vaughn, *then what?*"

"Then we escape a different way, through the hills, like I said."

She understood the theory, "OK, but how do we accomplish all this?"

Vaughn gave a helpless look, "I don't know yet." Then his expression changed to that of a little child asking for more than the parents wanted to give. "Stephie, *listen*. I know what you said about your powers and all, but I really don't think we can do this unless you use them for our own motives." His eyebrows were up, his eyes pleaded, waiting.

And Stephanie, indeed, gave a parental response, a sort of protest, "Use them to do *what?*"

His helpless look returned, "I don't know that either... not yet."

Stephanie heaved a sigh as the glistening sheen in her eyes intensified, but still without tears as she confessed, "I hate to say this but I'm scared... really scared! I shouldn't be, but..." Memories of how Jargono entered her mind, making her feel as he wanted but somehow as she wanted, kept nagging at her. Even though she knew she could prevent that because she could block him, she also knew if she did that, he would kill her outright. It would come down to a choice between dying to keep her integrity and therefore losing the Seed, or allowing Jargono to manipulate her to do... That's what scared her because either way she fails!

Vaughn leveled his eyes into hers, "Are you scared for you?"

"No. Yes! Both! I don't want to be captured by him, and I'm scared of failing. If he kills me, I fail the Seed, but if I submit to him…" She broke down in tears and sobs.

Vaughn couldn't help feeling there was something that happened between Jargono and Stephanie that she still wasn't telling him, something awful enough to cause what she felt now, but also to make her feel like she couldn't tell him. *But I know she wouldn't lie to me so he didn't mate with her, only touched her. But…* He nodded with sympathy. *I'll consult my Book.* "Stephie, somehow I just know that submitting to him is absolutely *not* the right way to go."

"But King Mafferan did, for a *long* time, for the *possibility* of goodness later."

"But you're forgetting that he grew up in that trap and had no choice about entering it. He was *already* in it. *We're not!*"

"Are you sure, Vaughn? If we fail, we risk the whole world. *The whole world!* What are we going to do?" She began to break into a bawl but caught herself and reined it in. Even more dreadful than submitting herself to Jargono was failing her responsibility to goodness for all others. But voicing her ultimate fear somehow enabled her to also challenge its control over her.

Vaughn hugged her, applying the steady, yet gentle pressure of reassurance. After a bit, he whispered in her ear, "We can have faith in overcoming our own personal battles within, but we sense the terrible vulnerability in others. It's easy for us to start identifying ourselves with others we love, and then all of the sudden we feel vulnerable, too! Our responsibility is not to live their lives for them, but just to the best of our ability bring forth goodness that gives them opportunity to choose. That does *not* include sacrificing our integrity. Our life is just as precious to God as anyone else's. We can do only what we're able to do."

Her soul latched onto one of his words, 'responsibility', and in her passion for it, she grabbed his arms, "Then in our plans, *we should be doing that!* I mean, besides protecting the Seed, isn't it about time we started doing something to help people *wake up*! So far, all we've been doing is watching our own backs and preserving *our* lives and just a few others close to us. I think we have *not* been doing what we're supposed to be doing!"

Vaughn saw a new fire in his wife's eyes, but also a dangerous implication. He scrutinized her, "What is it with you that you're so hard on yourself now? A tree can't set fruit before it flowers, and it needs leaves to make the food to produce the fruit. I think we've been maturing at about as fast a rate as possible." He continued to study her as an uneasy feeling began to creep into him.

Stephanie shook her head, not in disagreement, but as if to clear out cobwebs, "Right again, I just don't know what's getting in to me." She paused, then said one word under her breath, "Dreams."

He looked at her, "Have you been having bad dreams again?"

"No." She paused again. "Vaughn, you've had terrible dreams being with other women, I mean, they weren't terrible, but…"

She's trying to tell me something. "In my dreams I had no control over the women that stole my passion and robbed me of the sacredness of its expression. That *was* terrible. But the point is I had no control, *my will wasn't involved,* therefore, it was nothing that could directly harm my character. But as you so beautifully realized, and caused you to come to me in my dream to battle that demon who was messing with us, those dreams have the potential to destroy us, if we let them." *I wonder if she'll tell me.*

Turning deep red, she looked away with tears filling her eyes again though this time she fought them back with increased persistence. *How can I tell him about* that *dream, of* all *night with Jargono? I'd have to tell him the truth of how I felt. I know once I start telling him, it won't sound right if I don't tell him* everything. *And we haven't even been together in real life that way.* Her desire for Vaughn suddenly heated up, as the dream pounded against her mind, making her head throb. Again, a wail partly forced its way out but she turned her head away from Vaughn for a brief moment to fight it till its lava returned to the center of her heart.

His hands cupped her cheeks, his thumbs swiped away a few tears, as he whispered two words "Trust me."

This time Stephanie couldn't fight it and her tears gushed all the more. She knew she had to tell him now. After several minutes, she pushed back from him with her hands upon his muscled chest and opened her mouth to speak, but heard no sound issuing forth. He just continued to hold her, drawing her in close again. Then, without even planning to say anything, she blurted, "What if your will *was* involved?"

He began to rock her back and forth in his arms. The couch made soft squeaking noises as he remained silent, just loving her.

She spoke self-accusingly, "What if I could have stopped the dreams?" *I don't think part of me wanted them to stop! But it was like I was disconnected from myself.*

Vaughn started to piece her story together. *Oh God! I think I understand. He never, she never... not in reality. But dreams! She came to me in mine, he came to her in hers! She couldn't risk blocking him, or he'd know she had powers.* "Remember when you asked me to make love to you in my, our dream?" She nodded against his chest where her head was buried. "You convinced me it was alright because it was just a dream, not reality. The part that we chose to be real was to make it our hope for reality. The fact that we willingly chose to make dream love did not endanger our responsibilities to the greater good. It didn't harm our character and neither did your choice to allow Jargono to use you in your dream. For one, you haven't made it your hope, to the contrary, and two, your dream sacrifice was for the greater good, knowing that since it wasn't real, it couldn't defile you."

But she still sobbed with unresolved pain, and that troubled him. *That should have fixed it. Why does she still weep? IDIOT! I've only addressed her mind, but women are feeling creatures.* "My love, I know the memories of being passionate with him feels..."

Jerking back from his chest, she couldn't help yelling, "NO, YOU DON'T!" *Why am I yelling at him?* "You don't know what he can do!" *Oh God, I can't believe I'm telling him. Oh no!*

405

Vaughn fought to keep from shrinking back from her accusation, so instead he held her tenderly. "But I know what he *can't* do. He *can't* love you like I do. Let it go, Stephie, you chose rightly! No matter how deeply he stole your passion. Besides, he's a *faithwalker!* I felt him in my mind and I fought to keep him out. I can only imagine what he could do if he had full access while you were asleep, and then you had to let him continue. Please let it go! You chose rightly."

She still wouldn't let go and went on weeping.

He changed tactics, "Besides, who would you rather make dream love to, *him or me?*"

Her eyes widened and flickered, taking offense, "I can't *believe* you just asked me that!"

But his reply was witty, "Well, in that case, I can't believe you haven't let it *go!*"

She paused, shook her head at herself, then at him. *God, how I love this man!* Stephanie grabbed him, passionately kissed him all over his face, looked him in the eye then… licked his nose!

☙

Grinchback seemed to be developing a genuine fondness for his Master. This was odd as it was unheard of in all Alpha history, even if he was his offspring. And odder still, he had developed a respect for ScrabaGag who was different from all the other Masters he had known or heard about. Of course Grinchback knew they still would eat each other in an ethereal second if the possibility arose or required, but that didn't seem to matter to how Grinchback felt. They both eased back from the clear, blue orb.

"Highest Councilor ScrabaGag the *Cursed Object* is back."

ScrabaGag didn't seem disturbed at all. "It's nothing to worry about. True, the Seed is back on her neck so I suppose we don't have to worry about the meaning of it going inside her. It's back so nothing has changed. At least, I don't think it has."

"What are you going to do? Are you going to leave it alone as Mafferan commanded you?"

ScrabaGag's eye peered at his offspring for using the word 'commanded,' "As I recall, you were the one he turned upside down *twice* and whose arm he cut off. I would think *you* would want to get back at him!"

Master knew what I was trying to do, and he turned it around on me! Grinchback eased back from his Master a bit and changed direction. "Shall we tell Jargono?"

"I'm very unhappy with him because he does too much on his own and doesn't show proper respect for us, even though we're responsible for his climb to greatness. Still, there's no one like him on Earth and we can't afford to lose the opportunity to use him. But I want that Seed for *myself.* I intend to plant it *myself,* and as long as Jargono doesn't know its value, we don't have to worry about him getting it."

Grinchback's ripples indicated his understanding of how his Master viewed Jargono. "So Master, how can we obtain it then, without his help?"

The Highest Councilor's eye twinkled because his offspring had asked the next most important question.

"All we have to do is lure her into our Forest or some other place where we can directly touch her body, not just her spirit, and we can take it. I believe it can be successfully argued that we didn't violate our visitor's warning to us because of *where* we'll have found the Seed. Patience Grinchback, these things work out in time. Oh, and remember, don't be foolish enough to tell anyone about our visitor. We wouldn't want it coming out *what he did to you!*"

Grinchback couldn't help but be awed. *In spite of Master knowing I was setting him up so I could eat him, he still teaches me. Of course I won't mention the* visitor. *Master's just letting me know he's still in control… for now!* "Well, how shall we guide events? Do we want Jargono to capture them, or do we want them to escape?"

ScrabaGag laughed with joy, "Isn't 'demon' life great! So many options. So many choices. If they're captured, then we *have* to deal with Jargono. I'm sure he would kill the boy, but that's OK as I've developed a real taste for him. But the older he gets, the tastier he becomes then the more I would be able to accomplish from eating him. The girl I'm *sure* Jargono will keep around, but her life would be hell to her, which is good. It's clear she'll never give up that *glow* so she'll have to be destroyed but making her suffer so, well, that's just the proper basting required for most excellent flavor. Hmmm, it's hard to decide. If they escape into the neighboring country… Ahh, they know nothing about it. That would present some really delightful problems, and I would just love to see those two try and get out of even one of them. Religion can be such fun to play around with. Of course, that country is HrorrarrAggrang's charge. But then again, I oversee him, don't I.

"You know, my faithful offspring, watching those kids in particular is even better than the movies those humans create. I encourage you to take some time and familiarize yourself with that particular human pastime, especially their monster movies. They're quite educational. There's one where the monster eats his victims from the feet up. I highly recommend it." ScrabaGag went through all this but gave no indication to Grinchback as to what he would do.

"Master, it *is* actually entertaining, watching them."

ScrabaGag's eye twinkled again. It was important to provide quality entertainment to offspring. He remembered being bored out of his Eye when he was a youngster, always being scolded, yelled at, and knocked around, always being kept in the light-grayness. "I'm glad you've learned to appreciate the finer aspects of our existence. There's an ancient human saying which is true: It's the process, the journey, not the final goal. Well, of course it's more meaningful for us than them because we're eternal and they're eventually only food but you gotta love our humans for what they are!"

Grinchback stared in amazement. *There's no Alpha ever who's like* my *Master.* "So what should we do?"

ScrabaGag put on a more serious Eye, "But there's always the unexpected to consider. There's still *glow* to be dealt with and a few lesser others whom we must constantly keep our arms active with. Let's just sit back and observe, continue to work subtly on their minds by manipulating those around them. Even if we can't easily place our arms directly inside their minds anymore, we can still exert almost the same influences by using other humans to interact with them, and if the girl enters any of our realms, we'll grab the Seed. But *don't* try to confront her *yourself,* IS THAT CLEAR, GRINCHBACK?"

It was a rare occasion that his Master yelled at him so it actually surprised Grinchback and also hurt his demon feelings. "YES, MASTER! May I ask why?"

Highest Councilor ScrabaGag snapped back, "NO!"

That puzzled Grinchback even more, because it was the first time his Master had withheld knowledge from him. It made him want to find out why even more.

❧

This is not *as easy as I thought it would be.* As soon as he entered the village, the women descended upon him and though they totally repulsed him now, he realized that any change in his behavior from last time would arouse suspicions. When he finally got to be alone with himself, his first objective was to wash out his mouth and bathe for an hour, running several tubs of water, draining and rewashing each turn. However, Trevor refused to allow his conscience to be disturbed further. *What I do now, I do for the greater good. That's all that matters. I would have,* should have *been dead if it weren't for those two. I can do this.*

"Trevor! You fell asleep in there?" It was the leader of the village.

Damn, how's he know how long I've been bathing? Do they watch everything I do? "Huh? Oh, no! I was just... daydreaming."

"HA! I know, you can't get enough, can you? But I have great news. Our God has returned but to another village, and you and I have been invited to meet him and the other leaders. It seems our God now wants to coordinate our efforts."

Other village? But I thought this was the only one. And Vaughn told me he killed him.

ℰℒ

Vaughn and Stephanie cut their marriage-leave short due to important business developments. Surprisingly, the clerk offered him his money back but Vaughn settled on half. Before leaving, though, Stephanie *persuaded* Vaughn to return to the most wonderful bed she'd ever seen, let alone slept on. Once there, she gave him one passionate kiss, got up, then told him that kiss was what she'd intended to do the last time, whereupon he grabbed and wrestled her back down, saying, "Bad girl, *bad girl.*" He was learning just what a deep, mischievous streak his wife had... and felt compelled to match it.

After finally pinning her back onto the bed and she realized she couldn't get away, well, without using any of her powers, he opened his eyes wide so that she could see into him. He held nothing back in his thoughts and feelings. Stephanie felt like she'd left this world as all her sense solely directed itself into Vaughn. When he felt her deep within him, he slowly kissed her once on the lips while touching her cheek just light enough to make contact. He then slowly eased away with her focus still inside of him, got off the bed, and gathered their things.

Stephanie just laid there, still engulfed by an experience she could have lived in forever. What she saw, what she learned through feeling in that brief exchange, felt as if she had read several very long novels. She realized this very much reminded

411

her of when she bonded with Arlupo's father, and didn't want to move lest she disturb this sacred moment. *How did he know how to do that? But I did it! But…*

Vaughn had acted on instinct when he kissed his wife, had felt the natural course of life leading him to open his eyes and kiss her. He abandoned himself into it with open heart and mind in one, and doing so felt Stephanie enter into him much as if he was a house, and if a house could have perception, it would feel those who enter to explore its interior. Yet at the same time she entered, he also became aware of all her reactions, and that helped him make the expression of his love perfect. In a way, the process was similar to what King Mafferan had done with him when the King passed on a portion of his life.

After piling their belongings by the door, he sat on the living room couch, serenely waiting for his wife to join him. After a while, Stephanie arose, threw her arms around Vaughn from behind the couch, kissed the top of his head and held on. In that embrace, they lingered for some time until once again life flowed onward, then they silently left the hotel and boarded a bus to the port town. Spot followed silently behind them.

They spent the whole hour ride to the town in silent meditation upon all they'd just experienced while Spot laid in the narrow bus aisle beside Vaughn whose fingers absently ran through his soft fur. When the bus brakes squeaked when arriving at the station, it seemed to announce both the ending and the beginning of something important in their life and they both knew it.

Vaughn descended the bus first, then turned and held out his right hand for his wife as she climbed down the steps. He didn't know why he did that, but it just felt right. She didn't object and was grateful for the expression of kindness and respect.

People turned to stare at this highly strange, obviously very much in love couple. Longings stirred in the many onlookers who also saw something else that no one could put into words. When they heard the young man address his wife as Lady Stephanie, before saying he would gather their belongings if she would inquire as to lodging, it became clear that these people must be royal dignitaries from another country. People began whispering that it must have something to do with the new king and perhaps he summoned them, or perhaps they were visiting. *How did they find out so soon?* Many wondered.

Stephanie and Vaughn met up at the appointed place then headed for a hotel to settle in by noon. It was just a one room, rather shabby place but cost every bit as much as where they'd stayed before. Stephanie grumbled about all the money as Vaughn plunked down another week's worth of lodging, but later told his wife it seemed more realistic to buy a whole week. Besides, if somehow they stayed the whole time, they got the seventh day free. That was almost the last of his money as he'd been paying for everything and was hoping to find work while learning how to escape.

They had never discussed who would pay for what because to both of them, it wasn't worth a waste of words. For them, life flowed beautifully so such trivial things would flow in their proper course. After they ate, Vaughn reached for the last of his money to pay for the meal and tip but Stephanie reached out her hand to cover his. She smiled, "You'll need your money when you're out looking for work." He nodded appreciatively, and his wife took care of the bill.

Vaughn stood up, gave a slight bow to his wife, and headed off to seek work. People around the restaurant immediately began talking when they saw such strange behavior. They never saw anyone bow like that before, especially not a man to a woman. Stephanie had smiled at Vaughn's gesture and in a very royal way nodded her head in acceptance. She thought to herself, *See, we do bow, but to each other.* Then she shook her head at the memory of her father. Her whole demeanor changed as she left the restaurant to find a laundry place. Their clothes were clean, but they needed knowledge.

CHAPTER SIXTEEN
Gone Fishing

His dark room emanated like no other and come to think of it, no one could recall having visited. Added to that, such oddities always bred rumors so no one really knew the truth. HrorrarrAggrang knew.

Being the last of the original, he made sure to claim this special orb for himself. Having split his orb into more cells than could be easily counted, as he reached his massive arm into its center, a part of that appendage branched off to fill each compartment. He loved creating mass effects amongst the humans and wondered if any other Alphas knew how or even had the mental capacity to follow tens of thousands all at once.

Even though the Masters were not supposed to invade other Master's territory, HrorrarrAggrang delighted in this orb's stealth abilities. Proper long-range planning involves large areas and many souls. *That word 'many' referred to millions.*

HrorrarrAggrang pulled up a quick orb review to see how his plans had progressed. A record of the many suggestions he'd offered his many followers and their reactions. "Yes, yes, white people are the devil. They'll always be. Damned rightwing Christians. They're Nazis. People of color should rule. The United States is evil, evil, EVIL. A bunch of white imperialists." Then, to the next group of ten-thousands, *"Yes, yes, you're white. Skin is so ugly. Tan it. Tan it! TAN IT! Guilt, guilt, GUILT! Wish you could be black, act black, feel black, think black... VOTE NOBAMA!"*

HrorrarrAggrang laughed as he focused on President Baush, listening to his thoughts, *"But I know those weapons of mass destruction were there."* HrorrarrAggrang laughed again, *"They were! But my intelligence is better than yours. Did you really think you could outsmart me? You and your pathetic religion? I created your religion! Did you really think they would love you just because you gave freedom? Everyone wants power for themselves, not freedom!"*

Then to another group, *"Baush is evil, evil, EVIL! Bad white people. White is bad. You're bad. Ease your conscience, vote BLACK!"* Then HrorrarrAggrang noticed a clump of common cells all a bit out-of-gray... *"Conservative Black Caucus? Ridiculous. How did they manage to think for themselves? Doesn't matter. Compared to the masses, they're nothing. All Baush wants is the oil, the oil, the oil!"*

Hmm, let's see, I need some more fire-starter. *"Newsflash: a local high school was shut down today due to the word, 'nigger,' spray-painted through the halls. Suspects..."*

"Evil white people"

"Newsflash: Another corporate big-businessman is suspected of fraud that could range into the billions."

"Evil big business, they only got all that money because they STOLE it from YOU! Stole it, stole it, STOLE IT! No, no,

*not because they worked hard. YOU work harder! No, no, not
because they're smarter. YOU could do what they do! It's not
hard. They're just privileged. Evil big business, evil, evil! ...: Evil
big businessmen TAKE what belongs to YOU SO TAKE WHAT
THEY HAVE! JUSTICE!"*

*HrorrarrAggrang eased back, his shimmering and rippling
harmoniously peaceful as he whispered into the orb, "Vote
Nobama, he'll save us all."*

And to Nobama he commanded, "Tell your wife and those
preachers to KEEP THEIR MOUTHS SHUT about how evil the
United States is. There's a proper time and place for everything.
YOU are going to BE the United States... ahhh, for what little
time she has left." And he broke into another fit of laughter.
"And remember, this time you really will do what you promised. Be a good little Robin Hood and take from the rich, the
accomplished, the intelligent, and give it to the poor slobs.
But since you know all those rich people are your friends and
they'll be really upset, I want you to take from the middle-class
where most of the money really is anyway, and give it to the
rich. Take from the middle-class and give it to the top, your
friends. Bail out, bail out, BAIL OUT."

*That being done, HrorrarrAggrang floated in utter satisfac-
tion, knowing the terrible confusion all this would eventually
bring.* Israel will fall at the end of all of this. I'm sure of it.
Without the United States to protect her, she's doomed. *He
rubbed his bulbous black head, realizing just how convoluted
and extensive his plan had to be in order to destroy the holy
land. Even though HrorrarrAggrang was sure the Father would
never consume him, he still felt quite uncomfortable from when*

the Father had lowered his Great Eye over him at their last meeting, wanting to know who was responsible for re-creating Israel.

Vaughn had never seen the ocean in person. The fishing boats, which normally would have been out at this time, were all harbored because of a storm out at sea. They swayed in unison as the waves rolled under them and splashed at the end of each wave's life. Vaughn felt instantly comforted by the ocean's rocking motion.

One face in one boat seemed to grab Vaughn's eye, and before he knew it, he headed straight for that man wearing blue-jean overalls with no shirt underneath and sitting at ease on his boat's railing. His boat was the only one that had a crisp paint job of white with a blue stripe across the length of its side. All the others just seemed to have daubed upon them whatever and whenever was necessary.

Elderly, tall and strapping, his short sandy hair fell slightly into a deeply wrinkled face, but those contours weren't from his age, but from the sun and ocean. As a fat, young black-haired man stormed down the plank from the boat to the shore, Vaughn knew enough to step out of his way.

As the elderly man saluted the angry man's backside, Vaughn amusedly watched and surmised, *This elder has to be the Captain.* Vaughn took advantage of the Captain's general gaze in his direction by calling to him with his eyes. Instinctively, the Captain felt it and looked at Vaughn.

Standing at the foot of the plank, Vaughn called up, "Looks like you might be needin' another hand." He kept his gaze solid as the old man took his time inspecting him. The Captain's voice had a slight rasp to it, but Vaughn thought he detected a clear sense of humor carefully hidden in its tone, "So young man, you want to be a fisherman. Have you ever fished before?"

Vaughn squared his shoulders, putting on a serious air. He knew his answer would fall quite short, as he matched the Captain's hidden sense of humor, "I've done a lot of fishing and caught a lot of fish."

The Captain's head bobbed up and down. His eyes brightened with a glint, showing he detected Vaughn's subtlety. He decided to play this for what fun he could get. "Oh, you have. *Where?*"

Vaughn gave an elaborate wave of his arm behind him and with a loud confident tone enumerated with a hint of mock boasting, "Streams, rivers, creeks and lakes."

The Captain burst out laughing, instantly enjoying this young stranger, "BAH! Freshwater fish, not the same thing young man. Do you even know this here ocean has salt in it?" After a moment more of silent appraisal, "But I'd be willing to teach you. Ours is a dying breed. That's why you see only us old men as Captains out here. Most the young ones don't stay. The hard work don't suit 'em."

On deck Vaughn saw several old men but several younger large men didn't seem to fit this scene at all. He walked up the plank, thinking to himself, *Being a fisherman might be a good occupation, too.* But the closer Vaughn got to the deck, the more he felt the young men's sullen eyes bore into him and he could feel what was inside of them. It didn't match at all what he sensed inside those elderly men.

Vaughn shook the Captain's hand, whose iron grasp even Vaughn had to fight to keep up with. Still shaking hands, Vaughn leaned in close, his stare asking more than his whispered query, "Excuse me, Sir, but those men over there, are you training them, too? Will I have to wait in line behind them?"

The Captain scowled, whispering back, his eyes also saying more than his words, "Not fishermen. They're govs." He spat over the side. "We have to feed them." He spat again over the side.

Vaughn laughed as if they shared a joke then sarcastically whispered again, "Don't they trust you?"

The Captain was quickly growing fond of this boy. Vaughn matched his tough handshake quite well, but the look in the lad's eyes was even stronger. The old man boomed with laughter, "You'll have to prove yourself, first, and with me that's probably impossible!"

Then the Captain put his arm around Vaughn's shoulders, turning him so that his back was also to the govs. He whispered as he pointed away from the boat, acting as if he were telling Vaughn about the town. "The govs don't have to trust no one. They don't care. If they even suspect any of us, they just wait till we get out to sea and throw you over the side!" He spat again. "Over the years, I lost several of me best mates that way." After displaying another fit of laughter for the sake of the govs, he leaned close to Vaughn's ear as his whispers turned acidic. "My best friend, between your age and mine, had a beautiful wife and last year that *big bastard* over my left shoulder took a fancy for her. Told my friend he had to borrow her for a few nights but my friend didn't play that game. When we got out into the middle of the ocean, the bastard accused my friend of being a spy. Those three threw him over the side then he took his wife. Being afraid for her husband, she gave in but when she found out what really happened, the bastard told her after they were through, she walked out into the ocean and never returned."

Vaughn became incredulous though he knew it was the truth and wanted to glare at the young group but knew better. "Why didn't any of you try to stop them?" Vaughn asked more sharply than he meant to, as heat seemed to burst all through him. Feeling Vaughn's anger, the Captain studied something in this boy's eyes that he'd never seen before and couldn't describe.

Suddenly Vaughn got worried about the attention he'd drawn to himself but the old man slapped him on the back laughing heartily, "I like you young man. You're something special. I can tell." Then he whispered again, "It all happened so quickly. Besides, if anything happened to these men, the gov would come and kill us all. They've told us as much."

Vaughn's anger became difficult to hide but he knew he had to subdue any sign of it. He longed for the day he could bring this government to its knees. *Is that even possible?* Vaughn laughed loudly pointing outward but whispering, "They've really got things sewed up tightly, don't they?"

"Yip. I'll say one thing, they know how to rule! I'm not saying they're right, mind you, but if ruling is controlling the people, they're damned good at it."

Something about the wisdom of his words tingled inside Vaughn but he knew he would have to study them later.

"Hmmm, if they're that good at it, then how come they gave over to the magic-man?"

"I think, young man, he didn't give 'em any choice. Think about it. He coudda just burnt 'em up. They had no choice. Besides, they get to share in the new power."

"What kind of new laws do you think this *king'll* make?"

"Let's just wait and see and hope he's not like the legend!"

"Legend?"

The Captain's great past time involved collecting old stories. He would often say, "What else do you do on long fishin' trips, waitin' to find fish?" He resumed his regular voice as the govs had heard this story so many times, they could repeat it in their sleep. It was one of his favorites.

"Years ago a man came to me sayin' his goat herd got sick and died so he needed to make money and wanted to try fishin'. Anyway, he had all these fantastic stories. One was about an evil king called Lockule." Then the Captain whispered, "He was like this new king." Then easing back from Vaughn, the old man packed into his expression years upon years of emotional experience and his eyes became like black daggers as he drilled his expression deep into Vaughn's eyes. Even though Vaughn shuddered because he'd never before looked into anyone's eyes and felt like looking away, he held on to receive the full impact of his message that already dwarfed the boy.

The Captain looked at him with surprise, "You're someone special, young man. Ain't no one yet been able to look me in the eye like that."

Vaughn just stared at him, waiting, then the Captain nodded his approval, and continued, "As I was sayin', that

Lockule said to be able to do magic like this man does and worse, maybe. He made the cruelest laws, all just for his pleasure. Made people scared of him, made 'em suffer terribly."

Vaughn's look shifted to one that more closely betrayed his youth but he realized this old man made him feel comfortable being young just like his old farmer friend did. "Sir, you think he'll do the same thing?"

The Captain shook his head, "I'm sorry to say this, but no!"

The hairs on Vaughn's arms began to stand up as he sensed something of deeper impact. "Why would you be sorry?"

The elder had a tear in his eye and a distant gaze which shook Vaughn to his core even worse than before and brought a tear into his eye, too, without yet knowing why, "Because this man is wiser than that legend king. He may even be *more* evil! As for the king of lore, legend says that a young man *like you* killed him!"

Vaughn couldn't believe it was that obvious. He felt naked. "Oh, come on, why flatter me so? I said I'd work for you!"

But the Captain stuck to his point, reinforcing it after he saw Vaughn's response. "See, young man? You consider it flattery and shrug it off. You're a humble lad, but I can tell there's something special about you. The young man who killed Lockule was the same way."

Vaughn realized he'd somehow made a bad mistake in being such an open-book, but was glad that the sound of the waves had kicked up, keeping their voices from being heard. "Sir, I'm newly married, just searching for a humble career on which to raise a family and live a peaceful life. *That's all!*"

The Captain squeezed Vaughn's shoulder. "Don't worry, young man. I'm not against you. You need to take your bride, whoever she is, and find a way out of this country because pretty soon, it won't be safe here for you!"

Now the hairs on his head and neck were standing up. He hoped that wasn't obvious, too, "Why say that? I told you…"

"Because all evil kings got to have a way to weed out trouble. He'll have a way to soon test every living soul as to their obedience. The test'll make sure that people like you won't pass it, you'll refuse, then you're dead meat. Then you become not just his enemy, but the enemy of all his followers. Once they make their choice to sell their souls to hell, they'll hate anyone like you. You'll stand out like," he paused, staring deeper, "a fish out of water."

Vaughn noted that even in all this, the old man had a way to weave in humor. *To be like this old man feels right. Stephanie's right! I need to work on my sense of humor! Hmm, better to die laughing than die sad. Maybe I should start my own book, Vaughn's wisdom! Ehh, what's with me? Get a grip!*

The arm around Vaughn's shoulder felt like how a father's arm should feel. He sighed, feeling he could actually let himself go, express his trepidation as long as the old man's arm was around him. When the Captain felt it, he squeezed his shoulder firmly, shaking him a bit. Vaughn asked, "How much time do you think there is before that *test*?"

The old man nodded with understanding, "Well, if he's wise, *and he is*, then he'll spring it within no more than three days after today, after the miracle he does. He probably already has the people in place. You gotta be gone by then!"

Vaughn heard the words come from his mouth, "Three days!" *I can't plan anything in three days!*

They had spent enough time talking, it was already too long, and the govs eyed them both suspiciously as they casually strolled by. For his part, the Captain jovially handed Vaughn over to another elderly mate who began teaching him fishing knots, net care, and telling him many things, all of which were crucial to either the job or staying alive. Vaughn immersed himself in all this new knowledge, hoping to conceal the rage inside of him and perhaps to even forget about it for the immediate time being, *What will be, will be.* He finally returned to his wife near midnight with an apology as he opened the door.

"I'm sorry, Stephanie! It seems fishermen keep odd hours. I need to be gone by four this morning, too! Apparently, there's a run of some fish coming up for the spring. We stayed late into the evening then came back and unloaded, and then…"

She hushed him with a kiss on his lips then her smile melted his worries about her. "It's alright, dear. That's what being married is all about. We have to accept when something comes along like that."

Sitting on a small worn-out, faded probably brown couch, first Vaughn narrated all that had happened then she told him of her day, how the ladies at the laundry-mat were all hot over their *new king* but basically she'd learned nothing new. However, Stephanie still glowed all over with a positively radiant smile. "After I went to the laundry, I spent the rest of the day in prayer and meditation. I feel a thousand times better. When was the last time you did that?"

Vaughn sighed and it seemed he'd been doing a lot of that lately. He let go of her, crossed his arms across his chest like he was holding something inside himself but then he raised his voice, "Stephie, there's *no time*! Didn't you hear all I've told you?"

Her expression added seriousness to her compassion. "I heard you, my love. Do you have faith in me?"

He looked at her, wondering why she asked. "Of course I do!"

"Then don't worry, my love, just proceed with your plans in the time you've chosen. I'll take care of the rest!"

Vaughn sat there in shock and it tickled her. She hadn't told him everything, and in fact, she wasn't telling him anything now! He finally asked her, "What are you going to do?"

She sang part of her words in a light hearted tune, "I don't want to tell you, dear! You know, there are others watching us, *remember*? But you'll know when it happens."

Vaughn could hardly stand it. *Is there really someone watching, or is she just using that as an excuse?* They'd never kept secrets before, except for his view on starting a family, but this was different. All he could do was sit there in silence, as his wife had taken complete charge over the situation.

Then Stephanie wrinkled her nose as she backed away from Vaughn, brushing off her blue-trimmed pink dress. Spot kept sniffing profusely all over his Master.

"Dear… ahh, you smell like *fish!*" She held her nose, shook her head and scrunched up her face.

Her rich brown eyes were sparkling jewels full of life. *She looks so good!* Vaughn's heart pounded, the total vision of her made him ache all over. He had worked hard all day and well into the night so decided to take a cold shower. When they sank into bed and he felt her warmth against him and her hand gently caressing his head and back, that comforting instantly put him asleep.

Vaughn had placed the alarm clock underneath his pillow so it wouldn't disturb Stephanie. Two and a half hours later, it went off and he grumbled at being woken up at such a terrible hour. There wasn't a muscle in his body that felt like moving, but when he looked over at his lovely sleeping wife and saw a special kind of beauty while she was asleep, energy poured into him. *I wish we could make love right now. I love you so much.* He leaned over and softly kissed her forehead then he eased out of bed as he didn't want to miss the boat.

As he walked by their little table, set between the kitchenette and the living room, his eye was caught by a piece of paper with his name in big, black, bold letters. It was leaning over on a plate of food that Stephie had left for him, a special fruit-filled pastry, and of all things, a can a fish. As he ate breakfast, he wondered, *Is this part of my wife's sense of humor?* Having worked all day in fish, smelling of it, picking fish scales out of his hair… *She probably didn't realize! I have to eat it though. I can't disappoint her.* After brushing his teeth, he quietly left.

Though in quite a small port town, life had already become active down the main street that led to the dock. Four AM sharp, a whistle blew, announcing the start of departure for the first fishing fleet. There were so many small boats in the harbor with such a little outlet, designed that way on purpose to prevent waves from punishing the inner harbor, departures had to be scheduled.

Vaughn's boat was first and as its whistle blew, he hastily boarded while remembering what he'd learned the day before, that at one time, these waters had been almost completely fished out but now fish seemed everywhere. *There* must *have been a whole lot more people on Earth before the Great Religious War to have completely fished out a whole area such as this.* The Captain sat in the same spot as yesterday, looking a bit shocked to see him.

"Well, young man, I'm a bit surprised you're still here, but I guess it's your life."

There was no sign of the govs and Vaughn rightly assumed they were somewhere on deck, asleep. He smiled at the Captain, "A young man needs to learn from those wiser than him."

The old man raised his eyebrows at this young man's wisdom, nodding knowingly, "Thank you, I've not received a compliment in, well... I don't remember!" Then he chuckled, adding, "Seems like I have, somewhere in my life!"

Vaughn decided to risk trusting the old man, even on such early acquaintance. Time was so short. He lightly touched the Captain's arm, motioning him away to a more private place. With one eyebrow lifted, the Captain followed him. Vaughn spoke softly, looking him dead in the eye, perfectly willing to kill him if he proved to turn against him! Vaughn had made up his mind. His first duty was to protect Stephanie and the Seed, *No matter what.* "I need you to do something for me, Sir! I'll pay you, and it won't get you in trouble."

The Captain looked perplexed, "You're working for me. I'm the one should pay you."

"Next week, I need you to let it slip that you suspect I might try to escape!"

The Captain's instant reaction eased Vaughn's fears, "WHAT?" The old man didn't mean to shout and instantly became embarrassed, but he still couldn't get over Vaughn's request. He angered his tone for the sake of any ears that might have overheard his overly loud reply, "Boy, you just be content with what I pay you. That's all!" Making it look like their conversation was about wages seemed to be a fair cover so Vaughn followed his lead.

"I'm sorry, Sir. I won't ask again."

"See that you don't." And the old man walked off.

Later, out at sea, just as the sun was rising and everyone was busy scurrying at their jobs and even the govs worked then, the Captain took Vaughn around the other side of the cabin. The Captain had made it clear that in the hours just before sunrise and after sunset, *everyone* had to work, because normally he would've had others on board to help with the extra duties because fish were most active in those hours. So the govs *had to* work.

"Young man," the old fisherman whispered with a strained tone, "What are you up to? I can't do that to you, they'll throw you over."

Vaughn narrowed his eyes at him, "I don't think so! But if they do, leave a rope dangling over each side. If they throw me over, I'll swim over to the other side and hold tight. But they're not going to throw me over!"

Visibly upset, the old man rolled his eyes. *I thought this boy was smart.* "And why the hell not?"

It was now perfectly clear to Vaughn that in this short time of knowing each other, the old man had grown very fond of him. With a tone that confessed being touched by this rough old man's affection, "Because I'm sure they have orders not to! The *king* wants to kill me himself!"

The old man paused and stared at Vaughn in amazement which was something entirely new for him because he thought he'd seen it all. "What are you, young man?"

Vaughn took note that he asked the right question. That made Vaughn love the Captain even more. "You'll just have to see for yourself, Sir! And I need tomorrow off."

The Captain's nose began to itch in that odd sort of way when something very special crosses his path and he's a part of it. He nodded, "Sure, but what about the king's test?"

"I don't think anyone will be taking a test very soon!"

The Captain's eyes grew wide. Another thing that he hadn't done in longer than he remembered, but somewhere back there, he was sure he did.

Vaughn smiled, "My wife promised me!" The fisherman just stared. "I have faith in her," added Vaughn good-naturedly.

The Captain rubbed his chin in deep thought, "Who ... *what* is your wife?"

Vaughn replied, "A legend! The king's sister! And the true heir to the throne!"

The old man's mouth dropped open and he couldn't remember ever feeling like he did now, "MY GOD! You *are* someone special!"

Vaughn gave him a questioning look, "Come now, did you doubt your perception before?"

The Captain turned serious, "I didn't. I just didn't realize *how* special. I'm grateful to meet you, Sir!" He held out his hand to Vaughn who stopped him.

"*Please,* you *can't* call me that. I really *am* just a boy and you're Sir to me, not me to you."

But the Captain shook his head and grabbed Vaughn's hand in a firmer shake than before. Vaughn tried to hide the pain as the old man looked him in the eye and reaffirmed his respect for this noble lad, proclaiming, "No! You really are like that young man in the legend."

Vaughn just stared at him, wanting to see what else he would say. "Legend has it that Lockule took the young man's woman and did terrible things to her for years, but Mafferanic had incredible patience."

Vaughn wondered at another variation on the king's name and at the coincidence of such converging paths. *Is it really coincidence that yet another person is telling me about that ancient legend?* He had now heard several different versions from different people, including parts of the true version from Mafferan and Yinauqua themselves.

The Captain continued, "He outsmarted the evil king because of his *arrogance.*"

This part Vaughn hadn't heard, "How'd he kill him?"

"Legend has it that he lured him to a mountain and made it fall on him, but that don't make sense."

Vaughn's eyebrows went up. He thought he might learn something of value here, "Why not?"

"Because I don't think such a thing would have worked on such a man. I think the man telling me the story felt the same way. The ending of the story must be symbolic!"

His conclusion made sense to Vaughn. "Then what do you think really happened then?"

"I don't know but it wasn't that. So how *you* gonna kill this evil king?"

It took Vaughn aback, and he had to avert his gaze, "Sir, forgive us, but we're not able to at this time. We're... too young. We have to escape for our lives... for now."

The old man's eyes lingered upon Vaughn, studying him, "I think you're wise, and *patient* like the legend. No need to apologize. So how you gonna stop the test?"

Vaughn felt stupid and was sure he looked it, but that was what his wife did to him by *not* telling him how. "Ahhh, I don't know. It's gonna be my wife's doin'. But she won't tell me!"

The old man burst out laughing, "Oh my, that's pretty brassy! She must be as strong as you. She just don't want you to interfere!" And he slapped Vaughn across the shoulder with another hardy laugh.

That's a possible explanation, even plausible, but then again, I just don't know. "Something like that I'm sure... but I trust her with all my heart."

"Hmmm, or maybe she doesn't have it all figured out, yet, but doesn't want to worry you. You love her, that I see. Be careful, that's also your weakness!"

Vaughn didn't like the sound of that, "Sir?"

"Your enemy knows you love her, that you'd do anything for each other. He'll try to get one of you, so he can force the other to do what he wants. Damn, just like that evil legend. He took pleasure in it."

Vaughn realized he'd been such a fool to neglect such vulnerabilities and his demeanor reflected his fears. He'd been so caught up in planning his offensive, considering his opponent's defense, that he forgot to consider that Jargono might have an offense of his own, coming directly after them, and it would be exactly as the old fisherman said. The question was when Jargono would make his move, and how to fit that into their plans, and... "Oh God! I hope I'm not too late."

The old man saw the change in Vaughn and realized his worry, "You hadn't thought of that, did you?"

"No, but I still want you to go ahead with what I asked." Vaughn hesitated, then looked into the old man's eyes. "Do you think..."

The Captain knew what he would ask and squeezed Vaughn's shoulder, "I don't think he'll move on either of you until after the test. Whatever he does for a miracle and all, that man has a lot to consider and prepare for. And I think he'll want to play with you first, make you run from the test and have you chased. Then, when you think you'll get away, he'll grab one of you, give the other the choice to run or stay. That is, if he wants to get the most out of his being evil and all."

Vaughn hadn't considered any of this and wanted to warn his wife to be on guard, but they were out to sea. He unconsciously rubbed his wedding ring but didn't see it begin to glow. *But Jargono isn't like that, wanting to get the most out of being evil. He simply wants to get the most, period... and that's far more dangerous!*

Suddenly, there were shouts all over the deck as like birds, fish become very active just before sunrise. The Captain rushed back around the cabin, snapping orders, even kicking one of the govs in his behind. Never had they seen a morning run of fish like this! It was as if the boat, itself, floated on top of large fish. One net broke, but still there were tons of striped fish inside it. With no time to mend it, they just shoved a backup net inside the torn one, and threw it back into the water. By mid-morning, their hold was full of fish that normally took at least morning and evening to fill and sometimes even days. By noon, they were back in port, and by sunset, Vaughn was on his way back to his wife.

All he could think about was warning Stephanie. "STEPHANIE!" Vaughn yelled through the door, even before he got it open, but there was no answer. Fear and cold sweat immediately beaded up on his brow and his stomach somersaulted. He ran into the room but didn't see her so he checked the bathroom, but she wasn't there either. Running downstairs, he shouted at the front deskman who said she went out early and hadn't been seen all day. Vaughn was beside himself as he went back to their room and fell on the floor to pray, *Oh God,* please, *I can't...*

But just as he began, His wife walked through the door with Spot then rushed over to him, "Vaughn, are you all right?"

Springing up to his feet faster than she could react, Vaughn had her in a bear hug, lifting her up off the floor, and his head buried into her neck, kissing her. She groaned because he didn't realize how hard he was mashing her, "*Vaughn,* you're squeezing me to *death*!"

Easing up just a bit, he couldn't let her go, "Oh, sorry."

But his reaction added to her worry, "What's the matter? The front desk said you were frantic!"

Pausing in reflection, he wasn't sure what to tell her. *Damn! I've got to control how I act around people.*

Desiring to stand on the floor again, Stephanie felt the need for a reminder, "You can put me down now. Let's sit and talk."

"Oh, sorry." As they sat together on the little couch, she patiently listened as Vaughn described his day and confessed his fears. It was hard, though, at times, for Stephanie to concentrate because her eye kept tracing the contours of Vaughn's face, the curves of his muscular arms, the passion in his every expression. "Well, are you sure you should be telling the old man?"

His honest eyes answered before his words, "I can feel him, Stephie! He's good, really! He'll do as I've asked."

She nodded approval, then added, "I think Jargono will grab *you*, Vaughn!"

Though skeptical of her conclusion, Vaughn became her student. "Why?"

"Because it's *me* he wants to force to do his will and because I have the power to confront him, or at least make it a little difficult, and now, more power than he realizes!" She patted the hidden pocket of her red-embroidered green dress where she kept the Light Oil. She never went anywhere without it, even slept with it under her pillow.

Vaughn studied what she said, then replied, "I don't know! I'm not sure it matters, because once he gets one of us, he'll have the other."

Squaring herself in a way that seemed to challenge the whole world and in a very mature tone, one of fullness and requesting respect, Stephanie addressed him, "Vaughn, look at me." After his eyes met hers, she continued, "If Jargono captures *me* and you have the opportunity to escape, I want you to *take it!*" Her completely level sharp eyes hid her thoughts. *If Jargono captures you first, I* know *we're both dead. I won't be able to do* anything, *so I can't let that happen.*

But he couldn't conceive of escaping without her, "Stephie…"

Her stare turned into a glare with an intensity she'd never quite achieved before and it made Vaughn flinch, but knowing how headstrong he was, her words were meant to match that, "You need to *trust* me, my husband!" But she could only whisper the next line, as she dropped her head, "Or we'll both die!"

Trapped. Very upset, he hung his head in his hands with his elbows on his knees. He couldn't protest at such a tone or at the way she made her request, but neither could he keep his tension from mounting or from trying to figure a way out. As Vaughn looked up pleadingly, her hand shot out pointing at him while yelling fiercely, "*FISH!*" Startled, he jumped off the couch with his heart suddenly racing and Spot *Arfing* at him. He did smell particularly foul but there was no way for him to know it. Stephanie immediately pulled her dress off to change it.

Vaughn shook his head from his tension snapping when she so abruptly screamed, but brought himself back to the point, asking her in a defeated tone, "Should I still continue on with my plan?"

"Of course, it may work. Anyway, it's expected that we do but I just want you to know that I have a counterplan if yours fails... but it won't work if you're not *free!* Do you understand me?"

That wasn't really a question but Vaughn nodded, "I think I've figured out how to make him think we're going to attack him and it doesn't involve you using your powers at all!"

"Really!" Stephanie waited, expecting him to tell her, but when only his silence followed, she wrinkled her mouth, "You're not going to tell me, are you?" That, too, was less of a question and more a known statement of fact. *I think he's just saying that to get me to tell my side.*

He shook his head, knowing he couldn't tell her because she would never approve. *She doesn't believe me. She thinks I'm just trying to manipulate her. Maybe it's better I just leave her like that for now.* "Stephanie, sometimes a man has to do what a man *has* to do!"

Trapped. *How can a woman argue against a line like that? If I challenge him, I'm challenging his damned manhood! I don't want to do that. But, but Damn! I could tell him my counterplan in exchange. DAMN! I can't do that. He'd never let me ...*

Vaughn had stripped out of his clothing, too, and they both stood in their undergarments. He eased up to take her in his arms again. His look could have melted glaciers, pleading with her to tell him her plan, but she yelled, again, pointing a finger to stop him, "*FISH!*" Vaughn could swear he felt her use her power to stop him sooner! It was true he smelled like foul fish though, so he pleaded from a distance, his gut turning over from her secrecy and surprised at how fast his emotions rushed into him. "Stephie, *please*… we *don't* have secrets from each other." After a long pause, "I'll tell you if…" Vaughn was begging, almost in tears and couldn't believe he was willing to tell his side, but since he knew her propensity to sacrifice herself for the greater good, he just had to know.

Keeping a level eye on him the whole time, the *faithwalker* let a little fire flare in her eyes because she knew if she acted any other way, she'd cave in. *Oh God! I also want to know what you're up to, but I just know mine is even more important than yours. I have to succeed. Vaughn, You* CAN'T *be captured!* "Trust me, my husband. I trust you! I love you with all my being."

That was it. Her declaration of trust in him closed the door. *Oh God! I have to trust her back.* Vaughn remembered the Captain saying he had a strong wife, as strong as him. *I think stronger… or just more stubborn.* He also remembered King Mafferan telling him he had to have faith in Stephanie, even beyond what he could understand, but that was the problem, *I do understand!* Trapped.

And so Vaughn gave his solemn oath but at the point of breaking, "I trust you with my very soul. Tomorrow, I go to apply to be a ranger for life." He shook his head, knowing she was up to something he wouldn't like. He'd never had to deal with such feelings before. He loved her, wanted to protect her, and they were supposed to share everything, *Yet she won't tell me.*

One voice wanted him to be angry at her but he couldn't. Another voice wanted him to mistrust her but he couldn't. Yet another wanted him to doubt her. This voice continually assailed him with 'what ifs' that he couldn't seem to turn off though he couldn't bring himself to doubt her either. The 'what ifs' kept coming and kept him silent for the rest of the evening until they turned in early to sleep. Vaughn was truly exhausted but their turmoil drained him far more than any lack of sleep and hard labor. Even so, he tried his best not to fall asleep right away so he could enjoy the comfort of her cuddle. He loved feeling her heart through her hand and couldn't get enough of her touch.

Stephanie watched him quickly fall asleep, knowing he wanted to stay awake. Even though he wouldn't speak to her that evening, she knew his thoughts and feelings, how evil tried its best to shake him but wouldn't beat him. That's why when she saw the gray arm over his head, she let it be! *Besides, I can't always be there to chase it away.*

After he fell asleep, she laid awake watching him, her fingers lightly tracing over his face, rubbing his slowly maturing beard. It was soft right now and she loved it. Tears crept into her eyes at the thought of what she was planning to do, and that she had to be so secretive, but knowing her husband, this was the best way even though it hurt. She leaned over and kissed him on the lips, and then fell asleep within a strange mixture of pain, love, hope and faith. *If we don't make it in this lifetime, we'll be together in the next.*

Stephanie woke him at six a.m. as he requested. He hated the alarm clock. He'd taken the day off to go to the ranger's station, but decided on a breakfast date first. They went down together to the dining area and upon reaching their table, it suddenly occurred to Vaughn to pull out his wife's chair for her. After Stephanie sat down, Vaughn helped push her seat under the table, and she nodded a polite, graceful thank you. Although he was still silent, there was always plenty of communication between them, and Stephanie reconciled herself to a simple fact, *He's just going to have to get used to this aspect of me,* so she contented herself with merely being in his quiet presence. *I am my own person, Vaughn. It's best for both of us.*

The Captain had paid him handsomely. The fishing industry fared much better than freight trains these days. Twenty-five dol each day for the hardest worker he'd ever seen. Vaughn had just stared at him but knew the Captain was no man to argue with.

When the bill for breakfast came, Vaughn paid for it plus the tip. Stephanie never made any motion to the contrary and was in fact proud of his working so hard, especially when he didn't even have to. Though she didn't need his money, his care touched her deeply. When Vaughn got up, he bowed a small bow to her and in rhythm, she gave her slight nod. It was then that Vaughn finally took notice that wherever they showed up, many more people seemed to gravitate nearer to them, conducting their own affairs like eating or relaxing. They were getting used to seeing this young couple do odd things, yet, now they all looked to be huddled a little closer to one another after seeing his bow. Vaughn dismissed the thought, however, and left to become a ranger for life.

CHAPTER SEVENTEEN
Bouncing Ball

The news reporter looked him straight in the eye, "Mr. President, there are rumors of a vast terrorist plot that will destroy civilization as we know it. Not just us but the entire world. Can you tell us anything about these fanatical Muslims, this secret group?"

The President, always practiced, polished, and able to give an answer, seemed to dissolve right into the camera, disregarding the newsman, "These are just rumors meant to scare us and whip up fear and discord between people. We have many peaceful Muslims living in this country. They are our citizens, too, and I will not let anything diminish their life here. We also have several Muslim congressmen. Rumors are just that, rumors."

"But Sir, we don't often get leaks of this nature and from this source..."

"Then I want to know that source and I assure you, he will be dealt with. It's not for the intelligence network to undermine the presidency or the great freedom of this country." He always knew what to say to the people, exactly what they wanted to hear so they could feel he was on their side.

"But have we given too much freedom to people bent on destroying us? I have numerous reports from several different sources, including one from your own party..."

"Look Arnold, I can't answer charges like this in the blind."

"But they say they told you..."

"There are always these kinds of reports. Even seven years ago, before I became president, and further back than that."

Peering down the main street, Vaughn scrutinized the drab, windowless, short building with its fenced in back lot where rough terrain vehicles, cars and trucks were parked. Seeing no doorbell, he knocked at the old wooden door on which hung a simple sign—RANGER STATION—in fading black letters on a dirty stained white background.

Since no one answered, Vaughn tried the door, and finding it unlocked, he eased inside the old square room. At a desk directly facing the entrance but nearer the back wall, a hulking, black-bearded man raised his eyebrows at Vaughn's arrival.

"Hello Sir..." Vaughn didn't get a chance to finish his introduction.

"So, you want to be a ranger to defend the border!" the big man said without any indication of emotion or how he knew.

Vaughn looked at him, waiting, but so did the man. The only people who knew his plan to become a ranger were his wife and the men at the bar where he announced his desired avocation. *Perhaps someone is spying on me. But really, it makes no difference in this, I've been quite careful with my appearance.*

With determination and pep, Vaughn walked up declaring, "I do, for life."

The man leaned in a bit closer to Vaughn across his desk as his knife-like glare cut Vaughn into pieces for examination, "You even shave yet?"

That sharp question lashed Vaughn, trying to make him feel small, but he'd expected something like this. Still, that simple truth stung him, he hadn't shaved yet. In spite of this, Vaughn shot back, "Have you?"

The full-bearded man looked on in amazement at the boy's gall, then burst into several minutes of hearty laughing and pounding on the desk. When he calmed, he conceded, "OK, OK, that remark deserves you at least a test."

Vaughn was confident that Jargono would never expect him to become a ranger. *The best place to hide from your enemy is right under his nose,* "I'll do my best, Sir."

"Ha! You'd better, or you'll be dead! Turn around!"

Vaughn just knew the man wasn't kidding, *But I can't back down now. I've got to go through with my plan. Rough times require...* "Sir?"

The ranger glared at him and with an instructive tone asked, "Are you questioning your potential commander?" This was another side of the adult world that Vaughn hadn't really seen too much, the side that was clearly more powerful, more commanding than being even the strongest kid on the block.

He snapped back firmly, "No, Sir! Sorry, Sir!" Vaughn heard the Chief Ranger's chair slowly slide back, a desk drawer opening, then he felt the hulking presence draw close behind him. An instant later, a blindfold was stretched over his eyes and smartly tied behind his head, wrenching his neck. Panic tried to knock at Vaughn's door but got slammed in its face as he looked inward at the goodness he'd become accustomed to living, thinking and acting through, and Vaughn's senses immediately sharpened. He wondered what else he needed to give up so he could get the new will, as it seemed he could use so much of it right now. He was also aware that such thoughts came to him because of the danger he now sensed. *We never know how long we have to live. I hope I haven't waited too long to do what I'm really supposed to do.*

Despite the blindfold, Vaughn could clearly sense his surroundings and a calmness settled through him. Hearing a knife slowly slip out from a sheath behind him, Vaughn instinctively bent forward, reached between his own legs, and pulled out the man's ankles from under him as Vaughn stood straight up. The man shot backwards, hitting the floor hard and Vaughn heard the knife clang away. The rules to *The Art of Fighting,* he now realized, had gone way beyond a memorized code. They were now inextricably a part of his very nature.

An angry voice called out from the floor, "What the *hell* are you doing?"

But Vaughn answered with calm, "It's not wise for you to draw a knife on me from behind when I'm blindfolded!"

The ranger smiled as he got up, rubbing his backside. "That was your first test to see if you knew, but no one ever passed this test like *that.* OK, I'm taking you somewhere, but you can't remove your blindfold until I tell you."

Realizing how very vulnerable he was, Vaughn cursed at himself.

You're really stupid for doing this. "Yes, sir."

If Jargono wants to grab me, being blindfolded sure makes it easy. Yet, recalling Jargono's invisible attack in the Dead Forest, how only Vaughn's inner sense had come close to challenging Jargono, Vaughn now appreciated the way being blindfolded actually seemed to heighten it. Then he found himself almost wishing Jargono would attack now but the thought came to him, *The flow of life,* so he decided to go with it.

The ranger packed Vaughn into a truck and drove south. Vaughn knew the direction because he kept track of where he was from the beginning, and the town's few roads. It wasn't long before they were in the woods as he could smell its comforting fragrance. After about an hour of winding turns, they stopped somewhere far from the coast because the scents of the ocean had steadily decreased until it was gone.

"You can get out but keep the blindfold on. I'll lead you."

After what seemed to be a long time, it was harder to tell when you couldn't see, they stopped walking through the wooded hills.

"I'm gonna leave you here. Don't move. Don't take the blindfold off until you've counted to ten thousand! There's someone watching you and counting with you. If you move before he's done counting, he'll shoot you dead. End of story."

Vaughn knew there was a whole lot more going on here than those stupid directions, "What am I to do after I remove it?"

The ranger laughed, "That's up to you. If you want the job, show up tomorrow morning at sunrise, *alive.* Oh, you can count to ten thousand, can't you?"

Vaughn shot back, "I'd be surprised if you can count at all, *Sir!*"

The man laughed, slapping him on the back so hard it sent Vaughn forward a step.

"I really hope you make it, *BOY*, because I really like you. You're someone special."

Vaughn remembered what he'd been told about this area from the men at the bar. He was sure he was in the middle of a mine field but he still relaxed as he began to count after a short prayer. *There couldn't be anyone really watching me. He didn't tell anyone anything... hmm, unless he hand-signaled!* Vaughn felt a stick under his feet, picked it up, and stuck it in the ground next to him. He lifted his head so he could see from under the blindfold, and put a mark in the ground where the shadow of the sun fell from the stick. After counting to a thousand, he stopped and put another mark at where the shadow had moved. Vaughn measured the distance between the two marks and accordingly spaced out nine other marks on the ground partway around the stick. then he continued his thoughts and stopped counting,

Old Blackbeard doesn't want me to cue in on his direction. That's the only reason he has me counting. He's taking time to cover his tracks. I don't need his direction. I wonder why they don't suspect the border guards of wanting to escape. Oh, idiot, *of course, why would they want to? If they live through the test, they become all powerful. They wouldn't find a better job anywhere, except being a king. Strange how often do I feel watched by somebody or something. Sometimes it feels good, sometimes bad. Almost like someone is writing my whole life down or something.*

Goose bumps crawled up Vaughn's arms at the thought of his life actually being narrated, and by different entities, good and evil. Finally, the shadow all but disappeared, reaching the ten thousand count and reaching high-noon. *Times up. Time to get the hell out of here. Mid-day now… I have to get out of here before it gets dark. If I don't make it back to Stephie by dinner, she'll be worried sick. Ahhhh, I see foot prints.* But Vaughn felt caution creeping up his spine. *Hmmm, don't rush Vaughn. He wouldn't have made it that easy.*

Vaughn picked up a big rock and stuffed it into his shirt. He followed in the first few tracks by Blackbeard, being sure he made them but then the tracks didn't continue to look quite the same, the angle of the indentations in the softer ground wasn't that of a normal track. Usually, the heel and toes leave a characteristic impression of weight distribution but now the tracks seemed flat. Vaughn grabbed a low tree limb, then climbed up to a higher branch where he could more clearly see one of those odd footprints. He tried to aim between the branches below and tossed the rock and… *KABOOM!*

Bastard! Just as I thought, somehow you turned the mines off or just lightly imprinted your foot over them.

Vaughn climbed down, knelt close to the ground and peered across it. He could see the rises and falls better from a ground-level view but now he also noted an animal trail. It was subtle, but he was at home in the woods. *A rabbit could get away with lightly hopping over mines, I'm sure of that… I think. But a deer definitely wouldn't. Anyway, animals aren't likely to cross over your mines because they'd smell your presence. But if the mines have been here long enough… Ahh, but when they were first put down, the animals would have avoided them so their basic trails would have remained as the animals kept reusing them. YES, I remember animal trails I found as a little boy and they were still the same when I left home. Those trails are safe… definitely! Hmmm, but I'll have to find the ones that go where I want to go. Animals don't travel in directions like humans. Damn! I don't even know if I'll make it out before dark. Ahhh, but this strategy would be a good one for escape! Tomorrow is the big day. I hope I'm there to see what Stephie plans. I'll be fishing anyway, or I'll be starting my new ranger job, or… Got to go back fishing just one more time, though. It all depends on you, my Captain friend. Just be you, and I'm sure it'll work. I wonder what orders Jargono will give his govs when they 'know' I'm escaping by sea. Stephanie and the Captain are right. There would be no good reason for Jargono to rush at us, and every good reason to wait until…*

Vaughn shook his head to clear it. *First, I have to stay alive.* Slowly, carefully, with complete concentration, Vaughn followed the zigzag animal trails that eventually took him back west. After hours and hours, he made it out of the forest and allowed himself to think about other things again.

Wow, that took so much longer than I expected. Almost dark, chilly, too, but thank God I made it out of those woods alive and back on the road. I don't know how long a walk back to town but I should make it by sunrise. Vaughn breathed a sigh of relief. He began to lightly jog on the road, thinking the test was over.

☙

Stephanie knew something was *very* wrong. Or did she? Sometimes it's hard to tell the difference between true perceptions and those created by fear. And fear for a loved one was out of her control because she didn't control the beloved's actions or situation. And *unlike* her, others aren't able to bend reality to their will if need be. *Anything could have happened to him! But then, am I always to fear for those I love? Is it right for me to do so? It can't be right to live in fear, even if it's fear for others and not for me. Oh! I just can't think about this right now.* Stephanie knelt and began to pray, her fear or her perceptions, consuming her, driving her prayers. "Vaughn, where are you? Oh Light, light my loved one's way. Protect him…"

ᘓ

All of a sudden, like a beam of light, yet invisible to the physical eyes, Vaughn could see in the dark, see down the road in a sort of moonlit glow though it was a moonless, cloudy night. In this amazing glow, he felt his beloved's love and knew she had prayed her heart out. *It's not physical light but I can see.* Rubbing the ring on his finger, he prayed also, "Oh God, thank you for answering her prayers." As a sense of deep love burst within him, the ring began glowing. *It's the same feeling as when we married, our love within and God's blessing surrounding us.*

But Vaughn's awe suddenly broke as movement in the not so far distance caught his eye. Three men, looking through some special kind of binoculars, occasionally pointing at him. He recalled from science class that these night vision goggles saw heat and also realized that they weren't aware he could see *them* because they made no attempt to hide themselves. Every now and then, one would look towards him without the special lens then back through it. *I don't think they're out here wishing to invite me to tea. And I can't fight those three huge men. I can tell they're all experienced fighters. But why the hell go through all this trouble just to kill me?* Vaughn began to re-assess his thinking that Jargono wouldn't have him killed on the spot. *But why has God provided me with this light to see such terrible odds that I can't beat? Damn! This isn't the time to be totally lost but what if this really is still part of the test? DAMN IT! I need an answer so I can know what to do and I need it NOW. But if this is still the test, does that even matter?*

With no answer coming to him, his mind and heart in a deadlock, all Vaughn could do was simply act, so reaching into his shirt, he pulled out the metal disc he'd cautiously dug up on his way out of the mine fields. He knew it was risky, but he figured they were set off by stepping on them, not by carrying them. He even did a field test by digging up one and throwing it as far as he could, showing him it wouldn't blow up until impact.

I'll wait till I get close enough. The blast will blind them if they're looking through their glasses. They won't know what hit 'em. I've got to watch closely but without them knowing I'm watching them. Wait... just wait... wait. As the men signaled each other, indicating they thought they were close enough to be detected, Vaughn gave them no chance to spread out. He underhanded the mine high into the air, but making like he just went to scratch his head. Not sure if they could see his throw, he thought scratching his head might give them the moment of doubt that he needed.

And sure enough, they stopped when he threw up his hand. One of them seemed to follow the disc with his binoculars, but Vaughn knew they couldn't get a clear image of such a thing. As the mine rose into the air, Vaughn could see it, though he didn't lift up his head. For the others to see it, the mine had to be warm enough so the question was how much heat had it absorbed from Vaughn. Right before it impacted, Vaughn hit the ground. The explosion tore through the very calm night. As the roar subsided, screams of pain pierced Vaughn's ears, triggering him to leap up and see two men holding their eyes. The third hadn't been looking through the goggles but still couldn't see Vaughn as dust from the explosion robbed any possible discernment in the darkness, but not for Vaughn.

Taking advantage of the men's noise, Vaughn ran at the only unhurt man, leapt into the air, and kicked him flat in the face with the heel of his right boot. The hulking man fell back to the ground cursing, but Vaughn knew instantly that it wasn't going to be nearly enough. *Damn! That was a really hard kick, but he'll be up in seconds.*

Seeing a knife sheathed on the belt of one of the totally blind men, Vaughn snatched it and instantly its owner blindly swung at him. Crouched low to start with, the swing went over Vaughn's head and he planted the blade deep into that man's calf. Falling to the ground in sheer agony and anger, Vaughn knew he wouldn't be a threat for a while so immediately turned his attention to his other enemies. The kicked man was already getting to his feet, cursing with even more rage because of his bloody face. Sight would be returning to the others in mere seconds. *What to do?* Vaughn went for the still standing blinded man, grabbed him from behind, and with all his might spun him around, forcing him into the ranger who had just gotten up.

The raging man with blood still stinging his eyes reacted without hesitation when the other man crashed into him. According to his stringent training and experience, he instinctively swung the body around, hooked his arm around the neck, and being back to back, he wrenched the head sharply over his shoulder. A sickening pop identified that his comrade's neck snapped just as he realized he'd killed the wrong man. *"Son-offa-BITCH!"*

Vaughn flipped through the air to the man he stabbed and landing beside him reached down and yanked the knife out of the man's calf who growled in even more pain and anger just as the dead man slid out of his companion's arms. As the impact of killing his friend hit him, Vaughn threw the knife the way the old secret-service farmer had taught him and it found its mark deep in the man's chest, burying itself to the hilt with a thud.

The man knew he was dead as he looked up in stark surprise, wondering after all those years as a ranger who had killed him. He collapsed to his knees, lingering there for a moment as if in prayer, then fell on his face atop the other corpse. What took a lifetime to build, vanished in that single instant of making the choice to kill again and it just didn't feel right to anyone.

Oh God, I just killed a man before even thinking about it. Vaughn could feel the man dying as if experiencing the pain of it with him. *Surely, I could have just injured him without killing him.* But a sudden jarring cut off his remorse as he was driven into the ground by a slam from behind.

"Son-off-a-bitch!" the burly man cried out.

Again, Vaughn had no time to think when he pushed up with the big man on his back, did a quick shake and tilt then they fell on their sides. He shot his fist backwards over his shoulder into the nose of the man whose hold then weakened enough for Vaughn to squirm away and spring to his feet. The big man was struggling to get up when Vaughn faked a kick to the head but struck the man's bleeding leg instead. Howling in pain, the third man grabbed his wound.

Somehow, Vaughn knew he couldn't kill this last man. He was *sick* of killing and knowing he still had to kill later for his plan to work made it more imperative for him to spare this one. But first, he had to survive, protect Stephanie, protect the Seed, *No matter what.* Vaughn eased backwards to the corpses with one eye on the wounded man, then groped underneath the top body and yanked out the bloody knife. *Odd, why aren't they carrying guns?* Waving the blade to keep the grimacing man at bay, he chided him, "*Hey,* why you attacking me?"

An angry voice spat out, "Part of your *test.* If you live through it, you get to be one of us!"

So that really is true! But Vaughn still couldn't believe it, "So, you'd *kill* me?"

The bitter reply attested to the truth, "It's that kind of test!"

Refusing to accept this, Vaughn changed his tone, "Look, I'm sorry about your friends. I… didn't mean for them to die. We're on the *same side.* Besides, how you ever gonna add to your forces if someone has to die?"

The man disgustedly scoffed, "There are no sides. Is every man for hisself. How you think we gots to be what we are? *Besides,* we don' need no more men. It's a *fixed* number we got."

Vaughn no longer felt bad. He knew now that he did have to kill them. Yet, in spite of his justifications, Vaughn just wasn't keen on any more death. Speaking sharply, Vaughn challenged him, "*Look,* do you wanna live or not?"

The man stopped maneuvering. "What's your point?"

Vaughn put his hands on his hips, standing up straight like a man, but began speaking in an almost lighthearted tone, "Point is I can just outrun you but you might not make it back alive. You need my help to get back!"

Staring at Vaughn, not believing what he was hearing or feeling, the man countered, "Why would ya do a *stupid* thing like that?"

Vaughn leaned forward, still with his hands on his hips, being careful to over-enunciate each word. "Because I can, and because your life has *value.* Doesn't *it?*" He drove the sharpness of the question into this man's heart as surely as he'd thrown the knife into his partners.

"How you know I won't just kill you when you get close?"

"Well, for one thing, you need me. For another, what the hell makes you think you can?"

The challenge made the ranger want to laugh, if it weren't for the pain in his leg. "Hmph, you got some balls on you, kid!"

Vaughn stated the obvious, "If I'm a kid, then what does that make your two dead friends?"

The ranger nodded, "I give ya my word, I'll not hurt ya."

But now it was Vaughn's turn to poke at him. "What the hell good is your word?"

The wounded man did his best to completely straighten-up. "You don' knows, huh? One thing we *keep,* Ranger's Word.

No matter how we feel, we don' give it lightly. Remember, if you ever give it, you *got* to keep it, cause we depend on that much for our survival."

Vaughn knew the ranger spoke truthfully so taking off the blindfold from around his neck, he instructed, "Alright, lie down and let me tie that wound off for ya."

As he bandaged, Vaughn couldn't help asking. "I don't understand something. Where are your guns?"

The ranger vehemently shook his head, saying, "It's that kinda test. Any lily-livered bastard can shoot a gun but having to kill face to face, that's what it takes to fight a *real* war. You may not believe it now, but we don't take killing lightly!"

Strangely, that ranger's words sank so deeply into Vaughn that his heart and mind zoned out for a moment, *This has so much meaning to me.* He had the big man lean on him because it would be faster than trying to make a crutch and then have him hobble along. In essence, Vaughn was a moving crutch for him but also he wanted a bond between him and this man.

As they walked, he asked him about the border, how they guarded it, what spots were most vulnerable, and where should he focus his attention so as to keep people from escaping. Bearing the ranger reminded him of when Stephanie had dragged him along to her house after Gary had almost killed him. *I still can't believe that little woman was able to do that! This isn't easy!*

First morning light was just breaking when they reached the outskirts of town. Even though so close to the office, they both plopped down on the first bench they eyed so they could catch their breath. With both soaked in sweat despite the chilly air, a testament to the truly laborious task, the ranger could only exclaim, "*Boy*, you're one tough little bastard!" For the first time, Vaughn smiled at being called 'boy' and ignored that rank reference.

The sun was peeking when Vaughn busted open the door to the Ranger's Office by shattering the lock with one kick. He was a bit angry.

"*Damn, boy*," said Blackbeard. "You have to break my door like that? It was unlocked!"

"Take it out of my first day's pay! That would be starting *yesterday*, you *scruffy son-offa-bitch!*" Vaughn set the wounded man down in a chair.

Blackbeard looked on in amazement at him then at the other man who merely shook his head. "Damn, boy! You killed two of my best, you're hired! But I *will* take it out of your pay. It starts *today!*"

Vaughn whirled on him in anger, "You didn't have to make it like this!"

Blackbeard narrowed his eyes at him. "You got a problem killing then you're in the wrong job."

But Vaughn held his own. "I got a problem killing for *fools* like you, wasting good men." *What am I doing? Can't I just keep my mouth shut?*

The wounded man in the chair spoke up, "Hey young man! Ya saved my life so I'll speak for ya here. *That* man is your boss! You can't go speakin' to him like that, even if he is a *stupid son-offa-bitch!*"

They all glared at each other until finally the Chief relented. "OK, done is done. I won't even charge you for the door. Go home to your wife! She's worried sick for you! Got some brass on her, too! I can only imagine the kids you'll have. We could make 'em all rangers, both boys and girls!"

Vaughn glared at him, wondering just what Stephanie did but knowing her, he broke down laughing, "Ah, I see you really have met my wife!"

The commander smiled with respect, "That I did, young man, that I did."

⠶

The first thing Stephanie noticed when he walked in the door was blood all over him. "*Oh Vaughn!*" Being torn between consoling or scolding him culminated with fierce hugs and kisses, and wherever she wasn't, Spot was. The dog was standing on his hind legs with both front paws perched on his master so he, too, could nuzzle in as Vaughn just stood enjoying all of it.

When she finally eased up, he asked her curiously, "So Stephie, what did you do at the Ranger's Station?"

Letting go of him, she smiled slyly. "Oh! Just told him before he could ever get a chance to use it on me, I would wrap it around his neck and choke him to death with it… *slowly!*"

Vaughn stepped back from her. "STEPHIE! That's no way for a holy woman to speak."

She gave him a mischievous little-girl smile, "Dear, it had a good affect. I converted him to my perspective but I had to speak in the only language he could understand. Besides, he's the one that told me how long it was. I was just *stretching* the point." As she said that last line, Vaughn saw the flicker of fire in her eyes.

He sank to the floor in uncontrolled laughter, imagining the parts his wife left out of the story but judging by that fire… After having been through his ordeal for the last twenty-four hours, he had no more strength to stand up, particularly after he began to laugh so hard. Spot took full advantage, licking and slobbering all over his face, but Vaughn was too tired to object. Being a moving crutch, as well as everything else, finally caught up with him.

His wife helped him up, carried him to the bathroom, and ordered, "Wash up and go to bed! You look terrible! And actually, I couldn't sleep last night." As the tub filled with water, she helped him strip, and seeing how shaky he was, helped him into the tub where he just laid motionless.

After studying him a moment, Stephanie decided to strip and climb in, too. "I'd better bathe with you or you're liable to drown yourself!" As she scrubbed her husband, rubbing hard to dislodge the dried blood, she thanked God they were both so tired, knowing that otherwise they would have been making love. *It's just the way we feel, and I know we couldn't resist, but we're just too damned tired with no strength, and I know it just isn't the right time. We don't even know if we'll make it out of this country alive. And if I were to get pregnant now…* They fell into bed, sleeping in each other's arms, making dream love.

Upon awakening, they compared each other's dreams, finding them to be identical as had happened before except in this reverie, after making love, they had also discussed planting the Seed to the Tree of Life. So intense was the vision's focus upon the planting, there was no longer any doubt that their mating directly connected to planting the Seed to the Tree of

Life, and they both agreed it was a good thing to have that reinforced.

Having concluded their dream interpretation, and realizing how good it felt to be so rested, there was one other important action that now knocked on the natural-course-of-life's door, achieving that perfect wake-up stretch, the kind that reaches all the way down to the toes. In her lingering post-stretch moment, Stephanie wished time would simply stop, until she came to a more practical understanding. "Vaughn, ahhh! I think we need another bath, then we'll get an early dinner. Oh my, we slept all day! ALL DAY... *OH, GOD!*" Her heart went racing in shock. She couldn't believe she broke her promise to Vaughn by sleeping too late! She had intended to watch all day, not *sleep!*

Stephanie leapt out of bed, raced to the TV and turned it on, but seeing regular programming, she realized Jargono hadn't been on yet. *Of course, he'll wait till everyone gets home from work.* She collapsed to the floor, putting her head in her hands, and waited for her heart to slow down. They had time to wash and eat, after all. Then, the *faithwalker* would do as she had promised Vaughn. Prevent Jargono from hemming them in too soon. Vaughn would see that.

For his part, he still laid in bed, gazing at her, unable to pry his eyes from her all-encompassing natural beauty. It didn't matter that she wore a faded pink nightshirt, or that her wavy red hair went in multiple directions, or that they both really needed a bath again. Finally, Stephanie picked herself up, ambled over to him, and silently pulled him out of bed and into the bathroom. Even though they'd only made dream love, they noticed an increasingly personal feeling they shared together. *I wonder how much closer we can get when we actually do the real thing? God, I wonder how many people who do it, even feel as close as we do, having not done it? I remember when I used to do it. God, it was nothing! So empty! Thank you Light, for giving me back my life!*

At the restaurant, Vaughn pulled her chair out, and Stephanie sat down very properly, having inconspicuously raised her gold-embroidered red dress's hem. She then waited for Vaughn to effortlessly slide the chair in then quietly nodded her thanks and he replied with a slight bow. This gallant behavior, far from going unnoticed, drew longer and more intense stares from all those surrounding them. In fact, an impartial observer might describe these onlookers as nothing less than inspired.

Stephanie also seemed to be learning little things that somehow just came to her and felt right. Her actions seemed to slowly, automatically refine. Vaughn noticed she was becoming more elegant each day, and today the golden embroidery around her dress also added a more regal effect.

When Vaughn called her Lady Stephanie, she used to squirm but now it generated quite a special feeling. The way she treated Vaughn also had altered as she had begun to thank him as Sir Vaughn. When he first heard it, he couldn't help but laugh but he, too, loved the feeling she imparted through it. And, now, before they ate, they bowed their heads together in thankfulness, thankful to be alive, able to enjoy another meal together, celebrating the food as the consummation of past effort for future endeavors, whatever they may be, whatever they may yield. The ring of two water glasses clinking together and a simultaneous, "*My love,*" marked their newly developed ritual toast.

All these rituals weren't lost in the least on the patrons of the hotel, who seemed like birdwatchers classifying their behavior. Vaughn even noticed one middle-aged man pull a chair out for a woman, presumably his wife. When he pointed it out to Stephanie, she didn't believe him but by the time she glanced over, the act had been completed.

Finally, Stephanie indicated with a slight side-nod that it was time to go back upstairs. Vaughn understood she was going to reveal how she planned to delay Jargono, but even her head-nod was something new. Their communication was growing more and more subtle, more secretive from the outside world, with much of it done through their eyes and other slight gestures.

Just before they were about to leave, with a slight shake of his head and a scant raise of his hand, he subtly motioned to his wife to stay seated, and instead of fussing or acting ignorant, she waited patiently with a smile. Vaughn rose slowly, straightening his blue shirt, and folded his cloth napkin and set it on table. All new behavior. All eyes were on him and his wife, wondering why she hadn't also gotten up. Vaughn walked over, whispered the word 'now,' then pulled her chair back as she helped slide it backwards. He offered his hand and taking it with a polite smile, she rose from her seat. One could have heard a pin drop as even the waiters and waitresses stopped in their tracks. On instinct, this royal young couple looked around and gave all the onlookers slight bows. The people were caught in the act of spying so some immediately turned away, a few turned red, and another couple awkwardly returned a bow. Vaughn and Stephanie smiled at everyone then left.

When they got to their room, they fell into each other's arms laughing, yet holding onto the common thought, *Could we have really affected people* that *much with just a few little manners?* But now it was time and Lady Stephanie turned on the TV then led Vaughn to the little couch, "Sit here and watch, my love."

Taking particular delight in Vaughn's perplexed expression as she went back over to the TV, she turned up the volume. "And now it is time for our illustrious, new King Jargon to share his wonderful power with *us*, his loyal, happy and grateful subjects. He has planned to do more miracles all over the country. Cameras have been established at all the sites and he will be performing LIVE! Now to our wonderful King, for our glory and richness!"

Jargono, garbed in traditional Appendaho brown tunic and trousers, stood up straight, yet with a humble demeanor.

Stephanie knelt down beside the TV, placed her hands upon it, but turned her head around towards Vaughn, with serious eyes and tone and even a hint of pride. "I've been preparing for this while you've been working. I've learned much about my abilities in that time."

The *faithwalker* bowed her head as Jargono continued to speak on the TV, "You know that our country has always been a gracious country throughout all history. We have tolerated many different people, but the world has not tolerated us. You see what the other countries did to us, how they blocked us in, raised the prices of their trade goods when we needed them so badly, and economically fenced us in. They also sent their reprobates to live on our borders to drain our resources *and* killed us if we tried to visit their country. And worse, they tried to push their *religions* on us. We were never EVER good enough for any of them."

All across the country people were riveted by Jargono's words. As soon as he started speaking, the very sound of his voice, not to mention his handsome appearance, brought some to immediate tears and others even to fainting. In one way, everything he spoke about was new to their knowledge but they were sure he was right. Obviously, this man *knew* things, a long awaited savior. The young women held their breath while the young men saw a true leader, someone they could put their strength behind.

"My ancient ancestors lived in peace with all. My royal ancient forefather destroyed great evil kings. You all know their legend now but mysteriously, all their descendants, MY BROTHERS AND SISTERS, were hideously murdered scarcely a month ago, and no evidence has been found as to their murderers." Jargono paused to let this atrocity sink into the hearts of his subjects, then with a hushed voice, showing the obvious strain upon him, he continued, "I *believe*! I believe one of our enemies has tried out a secret weapon upon the last of my people. I believe they chose my people to destroy, *specifically* because everyone now knows of our great legendary past. Our enemies wanted to strike at the very *heart* of our greatness. But I was away, studying at your schools, so they did not find *me*. When I returned, I found the terrible devastation.

It was then that I knew I must break my sacred promise to my father that I should never reveal my power. He had sworn me to secrecy because, according to him, the stuff of legends must remain the stuff of *legends*. BUT NOW I KNOW WE ARE FIGHTING FOR OUR LIVES AND *I WANT REVENGE!*"

The roaring crowds on TV made Vaughn nauseous and his heart sunk to a kind of low he'd not known before. People all over the country watching their TV's cheered Jargono's words and egged him on for more. Vaughn envisioned the path now set down and his heart sunk lower still, as that vision expanded in his mind to engulf the whole world. Feeling smaller than the smallest grain of sand, Vaughn desperately wished not to belong to the human race, and the more he heard the cheering, the surer of that he became. He marveled at the flimsiness of Jargono's rationale and even more that the people readily accepted it, but more than accept, they craved it, drank it up like expensive champagne used to toast the best of life

But then Vaughn beheld his young wife with head bowed, red braids dangling in front of her, kneeling in silent prayer, holding the TV in a type of concentration he'd never seen before. He could sense only the smallest portion of it, but that portion sent chills all through him. That portion kept his being from vanishing into obscurity from what the TV unleashed.

Stephanie began to glow all around, as Jargon's announcement went on, "I have chosen *foreign* towns, all across our Southern border, occupied by *filthy, evil* people. I want to do this live, so that everyone will have no doubt as to *my revenge* and OUR DESTINY. Then, AFTER I HAVE PROVED MY LOYALTY TO YOU, you will prove your loyalty to me."

Jargono raised his hands and a transparent, swirling grayness began to envelop him. The crowd Ooohed and Ahhhed and stepped back in fear and Vaughn was sure everyone watching on TV was doing the same in front of their sets because he could feel the sickness of that grayness reach out to him as if he was actually there in person and not just a television viewer.

Then Stephanie began to vocalize, "Now, Lord of Light, I can't do this without Your help. I need You now, to guide me how to use my powers to accomplish the whole task, just as you guided me through my first *faithwalk*. Oh God, we need time, we need to escape him."

The grayness around Jargono swirled faster, its vile feeling making Vaughn's soul cringe. The glow around his wife grew brighter, making his heart cry for goodness. And Vaughn felt he would burst from the inside out. Faster and faster the grayness swirled till Jargono became hard to detect as *something* imminently awaited release. Brighter and brighter the glow shined around Stephanie, until even Vaughn could hardly see her. Both feelings inundated Vaughn.

The TV program began to scramble then a sign came on: Technical Difficulties. Please Stand By. And then, a recording, "Ladies and gentlemen, we apologize for this inconvenience. Due to technical difficulties, we are unable to bring you the current broadcast!"

Vaughn stared in stunned silence. *Did this happen before Stephanie accomplished her goal?* He was afraid to speak, to disturb his wife's prayer, but then the *faithwalker* looked up at Vaughn with a broad, peaceful, satisfied smile.

"What Vaughn?" She asked with that mischievous glow in her eyes.

"Stephie!" was all that he could blurt out to his wife who stood up, stretched, then sauntered over.

She sat beside him on the couch, kissed him on his cheek then she leaned back and stared at him, amused. "For the whole week that you've been away, and both here and at our other stops, I've been praying and meditating for what to do. Everything I came up with to attack him, or to escape, failed in my meditations. You were right that we needed more time to escape to have a chance. Your fisherman friend was also right that Jargono would make everyone prove their loyalty. I figured he was right." She paused to see if he understood what she was saying.

Vaughn kept waiting for her to get to the gist but she was dragging it out. The suspense began to eat at him so he urged her to continue, "Stephie, what are you saying?"

"Ahhh, I borrowed your Book of Wisdom... just to checkout if my idea was a good one, that's all."

Vaughn felt almost guilty at the tone of her apology but he knew he'd guarded that Book ferociously, but hadn't thought he'd intimidated her so she'd stay away from it. "Stephie, you can use the Book whenever you want. *You should know that.*"

She smiled, got off the couch, and went into Vaughn's pack. She took her time about it, and to Vaughn, it seemed like a *very* long time, indeed. He looked over at Spot, who looked away, almost as if guilty of something. Vaughn thought to himself, *Spot knows. MY DOG KNOWS BUT I DON'T.*

Then, Stephanie finally came back with the Book and opened it to read:

Wisdom: When faced with a vastly superior enemy, whose force cannot be confronted, pick on the little things of seemingly small importance and leave him guessing as to the causes of their failure. In so doing, you weaken and distract him.

He heard himself say, "Be a mite on the back of the spider or wasp." She looked at him quizzically. She'd never heard that saying before. It was from the last book of the series, *The Art of Fighting—Advanced Future*, which he hadn't taught to her yet.

After Stephanie saw her husband had finished reading, she waited for him to pick his head up and look at her. When he did, she had her little girl smile all prepared. As he gazed into her twinkling eyes, he realized, "Stephie, you?" Vaughn still couldn't believe that Stephie had found such a small, silly thing to interfere with Jargono. Something so small but would so effectively thwart him. But then he began to doubt and his eyes asked her for confirmation.

She continued her explanation, "For almost the last week, I've been causing, well… minor power failures and electrical problems all over the country through my abilities. I figured electricity was important even before I learned we'd be short of time. *Vaughn*, this wasn't easy to learn. Oh my, the first time I tried, I got, well, I still don't understand it, but a power feedback knocked me on my butt!"

Wide eyed and speechless, Vaughn chuckled at the dumb expression his wife put on during her description, though to him she was brilliant.

She continued, "Anyway, I figured that I'd create all the little failures while I was learning so that when I got ready to do what I just did, it wouldn't seem so obvious that direct interference was responsible. I've shut down key parts of their ability to transmit from their main location as well as from some others. The problems will fluctuate for the next few days and it'll be very hard to find exactly the cause!"

Vaughn couldn't contain himself any longer, "Stephie, how on Earth did you possibly…"

She broke in, "OK, let me just say that this was very difficult to design. The very concept is… well, funny!"

Funny? She's classifying advanced strategy as funny. "FUNNY!"

Stephanie peered at him with that same ignorant look, placing her hand on his arm as if trying to hold his attention, but of course she didn't have to at all, as she elaborated, "Yea, funny. You remember when you'd take a rubber ball and bounce it around, those special balls that seemed to bounce forever?"

She paused again, to see if he understood, but of course he did. It wasn't that hard, "*Yea?*" Vaughn was pretty sharp on his science, but he hadn't thought Stephie was. Her description seemed to be *intuitive*."

"Well, I sorta set a super-rubber ball bouncing in their electrical system, so to speak. It's going to be bouncing around for the next week or so."

Just then the TV announced, "Ladies and gentleman, we are sorry for the delay. We now return you to our very important National Event."

"Ahh, my loyal subjects, it seems that even kings are subject to the frailties of our outdated electrical system. I promise you that one of my top priorities is to put our best people to work, modernizing our entire power grid. It's of vital national importance that…"

Technical Difficulties. Please Stand By. "Ladies and gentlemen, we apologize for the inconvenience. Due to technical difficulties, we are unable to bring you the current broadcast."

They both fell over on the couch laughing hysterically at this utter absurdity. At a time when it seemed the powers of light and darkness were about to collide, the battle was postponed due to technical difficulties. All night and for the next week, the problems bounced around the entire country.

And what Stephanie had accomplished became far more troublesome than she realized because now all the targeted people had forewarning as to their fate. Jargono would have to immediately send troops to cover all the border towns to prevent escape or riot.

After they finally stopped laughing, Stephanie finished her explanation, "Vaughn, in all my meditations I came up with the same results. Jargono would be looking for direct attack, direct escape, or some form of those that you contemplated. But he'd never think to ensure that the electrical system would work when he needed it. And after the technical troubles, even if he did suspect, I believe he would take at least the same amount of time as me to figure out how to manipulate it with his powers, and I don't think God would help him any nor the demons either! Frankly though, I think he has too many other things to deal with to want to bother. He'll let the people fix it and he'll have to wait till it's up and running before he works his *miracle*. I think he would be willing to give it a week or so before investing his own power in something that I am sure he feels is beneath his nobility to mess with."

Still struck dumb by his wife's utter brilliance, Vaughn leaned over on the couch, gathered her into his arms, and kissed her passionately, his hands roaming over her back and arms, feeling her strength. He wanted to stare into her lovely eyes so he brought his hand to her face to caress it and as he did, his arm brushed the softness of her breast and her sensitivity inundated him, *So much strength in someone so tender*. They looked into each other's eyes.

CHAPTER EIGHTEEN
Escape

"Have another beer, my friend! Seven weeks of celebration have been declared and it's not seven if you waste the last day. Egypt, Persia, Babylon, Arabia, Palestine, and all the rest, we all celebrate in the streets on this our Sabbath day." He hurled his arm upward in a drunken toast, his beer sloshing over his comrade as they both struggled to stand up from their chairs.

"I still can hardly believe it! After so long, no Jews!"

"Believe it. Allah has brought justice to all our enemies. There will never ever be a land called Israel again. Years ago, I told you it would be so. You see, I knew as soon as the United States fell, we could retake our holy land."

"But maybe we should have preserved their cities for ourselves, it seems a waste..."

"No, our duty was clear! We are not allowed to partake of their filth. Besides, if you know history, there were never that many of us that lived there in the first place. We don't need their cursed land, only to possess it in Allah's name."

"True. Reports have come in that all over the world the Jews are being blamed for causing the plague and are being slaughtered."

"They were *the cause of it. If the world hadn't defended them, Allah never would have sent his wrath against them. WE ARE HIS WRATH!"*

The other boasted in drunken laughter, "No United States, the Chinese are negligible. they are fewer now than the Americans! No Russians either!" he spat.

"Yes. No Hindu's, either." He spat too. "India is like China. I told you years ago, all the heathen would pay. The best way to win a war is with the patience of a snail. No one fears a snail, they move too slowly. Twenty-five years. Twenty-five secret years to have everything in place. Now, the Moslem Empire is the only super-power in the whole world! Only we are intact."

"But what makes you so sure the West won't attack us now?"

He laughed so hard in his drunkenness that he almost fell over. "My friend, you know how the West is. Attack who? We are 'terrorists.' They can't find us. We don't belong to any particular country. Ha! There's no one for them to blame but us, but they won't attack all the countries we live in, because those countries didn't attack them." He rolled out laughing again, "If they were like our Great Ancestors, they would level all our cities with men, women and children together, because they allowed us shelter. But the West is unprincipled. They do not know how to apply true Justice."

"Yes. Guilt by association."

"But they were the guilty ones. We are all Just by association, so it says in the Holy Book."

A thunderous roar shook the room, knocking them over and crashing them onto their little table which collapsed under their weight. They scrambled up and ran outside, thinking it was an earthquake. Bright flashes becoming mushroom-clouds could be seen from horizon to horizon. The two men stared in disbelief and then another thunderous roar, much closer this time. They fell then stood up and turned just in time to see a massive wall of angry fire consume them.

Vaughn spent the next two days exploring the forest leading to the border and learning all his ranger duties. It turned out there was a lot more to do than guard the border but only border protection got publicized. *Ranger for life!* Being a ranger gave him unlimited freedom but also required him to be on the job twenty-four hours a day, seven days a week. Oddly enough, that was one of the many aspects he loved most because it simply meant that if people needed help anytime, he had to be there.

He kept chuckling to himself about how Stephanie had provided more time for setting up their escape. He couldn't imagine loving her more than he already did, but it seemed with every chuckle, that is exactly what happened. On the third day, he decided to put his plan to mislead Jargono into action. There needed to be enough time for the results to reach Jargono and generate a response but not too much time as to give him too many possibilities, nor too little time that would provoke too strong a reaction. Of course, all of this was based upon his best guess at what Jargono's best guess was for when he would be able to communicate with the whole country, and for *that*, Vaughn relied upon his wife's estimate of when they'd fix the power grid.

On his way to the fishing boat, Vaughn reviewed the complicated details, noticing his attitude change towards killing. *I'm at war! There are* casualties *in war. When you fight your enemy, you can't always wait to be personally unjustly treated before you act. There is a* reason *why he's your enemy. But… but killing becomes so easy. Doesn't it? Oh God, where am I going with this? Still, the enemy* deserves *to die! Yet there are a lot of people who probably deserve to die. I'm just a man. I'm not God. True, but I'm a man at* war. *If I 'play nice,' my enemies will destroy me. Lord God, nevertheless, let all my actions be JUST in Your sight.* And Vaughn walked up the plank and boarded the boat wondering, *Just because I asked, does that mean I really will do the right thing? Every time?*

Sitting in his usual spot overlooking the dock, the Captain was again surprised to see him and so were the govs. *That's good, let them stare.* Vaughn proceeded to work the day as usual. To the govs, he was a boy learning fishing, and to the rangers, he was investigating possible violations by 'strange men' on a fishing boat, but Vaughn knew what he was to himself.

As it turned out, there was no love lost between the rangers and the govs appointed to the fishing fleet. The govs were merely appointed with no test that had to be passed, and apparently word of honor for them was a bar room joke. When Vaughn discussed the govs with Blackbeard, he was warned. "*Boy*, you just got here and you're already picking a fight with the only people that could *possibly* be a threat to you. Why don't you…"

But Vaughn cut him off and because Blackbeard sincerely liked him, he was allowed to continue speaking while the chief just stared hard at this young pup. "Sir, we have a duty to our office, an *honorable* office, an *honorable* duty. There are things I learned while fishing that were *not* honorable, deserving our attention for the sake of the people we're sworn to protect!"

Blackbeard shook his head. *Young people are so idealistic! Hmm, is that such a bad thing?* "Just remember, there are things you *have to include* in your reports."

Vaughn noted his emphasis and what he left unsaid. "I assure you Sir, my reports shall be honorable and... wise."

Blackbeard growled ominously, "Don't get yourself *killed!* I've already lost too much because of you!"

"Nah, for *your* sake, Sir, you'd better hope I don't die or you'll have my wife to deal with!"

Blackbeard roared in laughter, waving him away.

Vaughn made sure the govs saw him in private conversation several times with the Captain. He kept questioning him as to how and where one might escape by sea. Looking distressed that he asked in that way, the Captain's tensions multiplied by the second. *He should be doing this where the govs can't see us.* That distress comforted Vaughn but just in case, Vaughn made it a point to check if the Captain had hung the escape rope over the side of the boat. *Now I'm sure I can trust you. I'm sorry Captain, but I can't tell you what I'm doing. Otherwise, when Jargono comes to investigate and reads your mind, he'll learn what I don't want him to know.*

Every time Vaughn saw the govs begin to maneuver to corner him on the boat, he switched direction or found a task that couldn't rightly be interrupted at that time. He did his best not to show his hatred. *I'll not kill you here for the Captain's sake.*

When they finally got back to harbor, the govs eased off him. Their modus operandi was always to simply throw suspicious people overboard. There was never any paperwork involved with accidental drowning.

Just before leaving, Vaughn pulled the Captain aside, quickly speaking, "Tell them I approached you to help me escape, that you told me you couldn't do that and you don't think I'll be returning. Tell them as soon as I begin to leave!" His look into the Captain's eyes conveyed in no uncertain terms that he wanted him to do this without question. *This way, the Captain won't get into any trouble at all. Jargono won't care one way or the other about the Captain's personal feelings. He knows there are a lot of people that hate him. Besides, if he knows the Captain is my ally, he'll keep him around to garner further information.*

The Captain sighed and nodded. "Alright boy, it's been a pleasure. Godspeed!"

Vaughn smiled and walked down the plank. There was no moon. After the Captain did as Vaughn had requested, the govs snapped-to, and immediately followed Vaughn, cursing, "Damn! This one's going to have to be filled out in triplicate."

Vaughn moved quickly into an older part of town and he knew the govs were straining to keep up. They were a bit overweight. As he turned down an abandoned alley, disappearing from their sight, they bolted up to the corner then rounded it without concern. Years of ultimate power gave them a 'sense of invincibility' and seeing the area void of people further inflated their grandiose self-opinion. The govs were even gladder when a wall preventing any further escape loomed up ahead.

But as they rushed up to the wall, their hopes faded into confusion. "Where'd the little bastard go?" As they all stared at each other, Vaughn made sure they heard him. "He's up the damned fire escape!"

Vaughn thought about just shooting them but his ranger's pistol he'd concealed was unique and would leave evidence directly leading back to the rangers or him. Any obscure meaningful 'proof' would have to be gathered by Jargono himself, at least that was Vaughn's plan, and it wouldn't include his ranger affiliation. He considered all this again while waiting in the dark on the flat-roof, listening as the govs carelessly climbed up the ladder, mounted the roof's edge and began rushing around. "He's up here. There's no way out except how we came up. He's *trapped!*"

Vaughn stepped out from behind a roof structure, still restraining his fury so as to speak in a level tone, "Tell me, is it true you just murder whoever you feel like, just to take their wives or whatever you desire?"

They whirled around, wondering why he would be asking such stupid questions. "*Boy*, we've got good evidence you're trying to illegally escape." The man looked over at his companions already nodding their approval, urging him to continue the charade. Smiling conspiratorially together, their leader's gleeful proclamation sang with condemning familiarity, "Time to die!"

Vaughn could tell this wasn't the first time they'd uttered such a judgment and knowing this only fed his indignant rage. Suddenly, their lives briefly opened to him in a vision of vile worms pouring out of an open rotting book. He now knew

477

the level of their grotesque lives. The freedom of unpunished atrocity had not only made them drunk but exultant, and the blackness that fell over Vaughn now, though familiar, was yet quite different than before. It had always been in relation to injustice perpetrated upon him or those he loved, but this time the call for justice involved those he'd never even met. He asked with a smirk, "Well, how do you know that for sure? I mean, even doctors can't really predict the time of death very well!"

The govs appeared almost insulted at his remark. "What kinda crap is this? But it don't matter. Your time is up!"

Still speaking calmly, Vaughn pressed them. "How 'bout the man's wife who walked out into the ocean, did that matter?"

He needed to keep them talking for a bit because he wanted to make sure the Captain was in position to hear them! I'm sure you followed. I can feel it. I knew I could count on your heart. The unpredictability of this situation required Vaughn to play it all by ear but he didn't want the Captain directly involved. I have to kill them quickly enough before the Captain tries to help and in a way that the Captain won't know that I know he's here. If he knows I know he's here, Jargono won't trust what he learns from reading his mind. It's best we don't see one another at all. That would take away any suspicion. The Captain must believe I don't know. That will convince Jargono.

"Boy, I see you been listening to stories. We can't be responsible for a crazy woman's suicide." They began to look at each other suspiciously. "What's with all these questions?"

"You're right!"

"'Bout what?" the man snarled.

"Time to die. You see, I'm husband to the King's sister, the *true* heir to the throne. Your deaths are going to make King Jargon think we're escaping. This makes it better to attack him when he comes before the nation to do his so-called miracles."

They looked at each other again then looked around. Seeing no one else, they laughed. "Well, *King* Vaughn! You're either crazy, or a fool, but we seen your pretty little wife around. Just so you know, we'll watch her real close so she can't kill herself. She's too *hot* to waste like the other wasted herself. Yours is so young she could do us for *years*."

"I don't blame the man's wife for killing herself because *you* put your hands on her. She never would've given you even a thought, if you hadn't told her you'd kill her husband."

They couldn't keep Vaughn's words from digging into them. "She was nothin' so special, *stupid bitch*. We already killed him and she shoulda know'd it. 'Sides, we woulda left her alone after a while. She wasn't even that good a lay, just laid there whiles we worked her. But *your* wife looks *real* frisky."

Vaughn's grip tightened around the axe handle he had hidden behind his leg. It was just a handle, making it quicker to swing. He knew he'd need a weapon with some reach. After he climbed onto the roof, he retrieved it from its hiding place. Vaughn scoffed, "You'd bore her, *you filthy piece of crap!*"

The leader rushed him, finally succumbing to Vaughn's bating, feeling confident they weren't led into a trap. "You'll run your mouth no more, *punk!*"

Vaughn turned away as if to run, but instead spun around, whipping the hickory handle into the man's knee, shattering it. He went down, forcing the second man to jump out of his way. The third began to hesitate upon seeing the weapon. After Vaughn spun around from his first swing, he swung high, making the second man duck as expected so he continued to spin and back-kicked him across the side of his head, knocking him down. The third man thought he could rush him from the side, but Vaughn quickly reversed his circular motion with a back-hand swing of the hickory catching him across the face. Blood spattered through the air.

The man Vaughn kicked sprang up but seeing both his partners down, he backed away. They had no weapons, never needed any. He looked around then at Vaughn who was feeling he couldn't and didn't want to let this man go.

Vengeance seemed sweeter and sweeter, as Vaughn felt the terrible harm these wretched souls had done. The gov kept staring into Vaughn's eyes, not willingly, trying to see his eyes but all he could discern in this murkiness of light was a haunting blackness where some eye-reflection should have been. The gov sensed a feeling then and it was something else he wasn't used to. Fear. His own! So he fled along the edge of the roof, looking for a way down because Vaughn stood between him and the fire escape. Diffuse light from the town cast long shadows from the roof structures, hiding some places in pitch-blackness, while others were distinctly outlined.

Vaughn slowly walked after the man, who was now peering over the edge of the far roof-corner, trying to decide whether to jump. He looked back at Vaughn. Even in the shadows, the gov knew that look of death, though it had always been him who wore it. He looked down below, heard his friend's moaning then jumped the two stories.

Vaughn peered over the side. *He's not going anywhere.* The man laid on his back, trying to get up, holding his leg. Vaughn strolled back over to the other two. Looking at the man with the shattered knee, he smiled, "I'll be back! Wait there!" Then, he walked over to the moaning man whose face he'd smashed in. "This is *war*. You're my first casualty." Vaughn smashed his head in. His brains burst forth from the pressure. Turning to the man with the crushed knee, the leader of the pack who was now frantically trying his best to half hobble and half crawl away, Vaughn politely inquired, "Believe me now?"

Vaughn swung the handle across the man's elbow. His terrible scream, Vaughn was sure, could be heard for blocks. With only one good leg and one good arm, it was impossible for him to avoid any further attack. Vaughn took out his other knee then his other elbow. "I should make you *suffer* for what you've done, but only the Lord God can hand out *true* justice. How 'bout I just send you to the devil that you serve? They are God's justice for the likes of you." And Vaughn smashed in his head, too.

This time Vaughn noted that killing had almost no effect on him whatsoever and his mind quickly attended to important matters. *If I'm right, the Captain should be standing on the fire escape, peeking over the edge, probably waiting to surprise me.* Vaughn checked to see if the rope he'd tied last night around the roof-pipe was secure. He pulled the coil out of the dark shadow, threw it over the far side of the roof, and slid down to the ground.

But the man who'd jumped had crawled some distance away. *Damn! I don't have time to look.* Yet, after a quick scan,

Vaughn found him behind some trash cans. "I figured you'd gravitate to your home!" And he delivered similar justice upon him.

Vaughn again noted the lack of any feelings about the deeds. Wiping the brains and blood off of the hickory onto the man's clothing, he reviewed his plans again. *Your deaths will attract Jargono's attention. It appears to be a desperate act to set up escape, a bit too obvious. He'll read the Captain's mind to see what he knows. After he does, he'll prepare for our attack, hoping to use it on TV to prove himself further, and while he's waiting, we can escape another way. There won't be any need for Jargono to attack us because he'll wait for us to come to him!*

Vaughn headed home to his dear wife, no dirtier than usual, smelling like *FISH. I'm not telling her what I've done. There's no need. A man's got to do what a man's got to do. After we're free, I'll tell her... I want her to know. She has a right to know because we're one... but* not *now.*

☙

There never seems to be enough time, even when extra is found, but being careful in the mine fields was non-negotiable. *OK, care put in now will pay off later, but I* need *to get to the actual border. Damn it! This is taking way too long. Can't these damn animals do anything in a straight line?* Vaughn batted away a tree branch, trying to shake off his feelings of failure, but the branch rebounded, smacking him in the back of his head. *Ouch! Darn it!* While trying to rub away the pain, he critically appraised his treatment of the tree-branch. *That was* stupid*!*

Things just didn't seem right, as if everything was a half step out of place. He heard Stephanie's voice in his mind.

When is the last time you meditated or really prayed? He felt free now to let his answer rip into the air for the birds and squirrels to hear, "Damn it! I DON'T have time! What more do you want from me? I'm not like you yet! I'm doing everything I can possibly do!"

What's going on with me? He rubbed his chest, trying to ease its pain, to release the clutter of many invading voices. *I don't have time for this.* He scolded himself, *Oh God, I never want to speak to Stephanie like that! I hope I never do.*

But instead of a feeling of hope, or an imminent answer to his prayers, by the fourth day of winding through animal trail after animal trail, talking out loud to himself was not the exception, nor a diversion, nor even an attempt to offset his loneliness. "These trails are *far* from a direct route. I wonder if that's because of all the mines, or because of the way animals think. I've never followed animal trails as extensively as I'm doing. Damn! I'm beginning to think and feel like an animal!"

Vaughn stopped. *"What did I just say?"* Heaviness pressed in all around him and he found himself sinking down to his knees. Those many voices were now demanding or claiming ownership over him. It seemed like now he no longer had a choice over anything, but everything had a choice over him and this helplessness brought him as close as he'd ever come to feeling he'd lost his mind, his whole self. Putting his face in his hands, he rubbed at his eyes, trying to wipe the distractions away along with his tears. "I'm *not* an animal! I *had* to kill them… besides, if I didn't avenge those pitiful people, who would have? No one stands up for what's right anymore… but I can't change the whole world. Oh God, what am I to…"

A rustling noise interrupted him and as he peered through the trees, an odd sight caught his eye. A seemingly too regular pattern barely discernable through the forest growth. Vaughn scanned the animal trails ahead and tried to guess which one would lead him closest to the appearance of... "There! Oh God, that must be the border, and it *is* fenced just like Jargono said! They damn well fenced us in because the fence-posts are on *their side!*"

After another careful half-hour of twisting trails, Vaughn's frustration boiled over again. "I can't *believe* how long this has taken!" He shook his head in a lame attempt to clear it and noticed a lingering question that would have, should have surfaced far sooner if he'd been his natural self. "Why don't the animal trails go near the fence? That's odd, because the plants around it look fairly ungrazed." The same rustling sound surprised him but this time he found its cause. Squirrels were jumping onto the fence chasing each other across the top wire, creating a sound quite unnatural for the woods. A smile broke through Vaughn's strain as he reflected. "Just like they did back home on the electric wires!"

He then noted the fence was made of shiny metallic cables, supported every six feet or so by posts that held the wire by rubber plugs. "Damn!"

For miles, it was all the same, until the remains of a doe tangled in the eight-foot-high fence broke the monotony. Apparently, it had been scared into bounding off its trail and thought it could plow through the fence's middle. Vaughn examined it from the place where he figured it had launched. "That would have been difficult, but an eight foot jump is not necessarily impossible for deer. It must not have had time to jump over. Time. I don't have time, either." The poor animal's posture, even in death, warned of a gruesome suffering. Death by electrocution. Vaughn sighed, as he found himself unable to look any longer at the carcass. He rubbed his chest again because if ever there was an animal who reminded him of Stephanie, it was a doe.

"Why don't people just build something to go over it? Or why don't people dig under it? Ehh, this fence is just to make it difficult. Fear of the unknown probably does the rest. There's got to be more than meets the eye here. I only considered the problem of avoiding *my* country keeping me in. I didn't think I had to deal with being kept *out* by the other. Wait a minute... WOW!" With his palms stretched outward in amazement, Vaughn stood transfixed, gaping at a tree, a *huge* tree the likes of which he'd never ever seen. He'd heard of conifers reaching such proportions, but never this kind of tree. An animal trail led right up to it which Vaughn eagerly took. Approaching this magnificent sight with awe, perhaps even reverence for what was obviously an ancient life, Vaughn opened his arms wide in an attempt to measure its trunk.

The ancient looking hardwood tree of massive proportions with a trunk of at least nine feet wide was some ten feet from the fence. "What type of tree are you? Your leaves aren't unfolded enough yet to tell me anything. You're not Oak nor Maple because I know those trees. Such strange bark you have." Light-brown, smooth and paper-like, the bark peeled in random places, revealing a smooth, yellowish interior. Old rounded knobs punctuated the trunk, remnants of branches that no longer existed, and this pattern went straight up with no branches for some fifteen feet until it forked in to two massive sections. One section headed away from the fence but the other grew towards it. The missing branches made Vaughn wonder, *They've been gone for so long! Just like so many generations I know* nothing *about! Hmm, one half of the tree growing towards freedom… hmm!*

Vaughn stretched his neck back and his mouth gaped as his eyes followed the trunk upward and then along the fork toward the fence. One large branch, which grew off from this fork, stretched over and across the fence top some fifteen feet above. *This is the most beautiful tree I've ever seen!.* And tears clouded his eyes as a plan began to form.

He stepped back from the tree to get a better perspective, almost forgetting to stay on the trail. *Don't want to step on a mine,* now*!* The tree's huge circular area of growth, extending so powerfully outward in all directions, immediately drew Vaughn's imagination to climb into its center. *This must be an original tree to a forest that predated this one.* He could only guess how many hundreds of years old it was. *Trees don't have to die but something or someone has to* kill *them, otherwise they live on and on. Maybe this one was just small when they built this fence but that was just a hundred years ago. Though I think this tree is* much *older… hmm, maybe the fence builders had respect for it.*

Again, reverently stepping towards this miracle, Vaughn placed his hand upon the trunk, trying to feel its ancient life. *So old, and yet so full of life.* Awestruck by such perplexing impressions, he thought, *So old but so vibrant like youth,* and he remembered again the peculiar nature of trees. *No matter how old they get, they always sprout new life.* And with this revelation, Vaughn felt the Spirit of Wisdom tingling through him. *This presence is eternal, life giving, but always new... as long we receive it and keep it! We are trees!*

Gazing at the tree yet, again, Vaughn marveled, "What a *wonderful* combination of life. To grow many, many years, but retain the life, strength and newness of youth, and yet, to grow even older and wiser!"

Now he put both hands upon the tree, pushing as hard as he could. "Not a tiny bit noticeable to you, huh? You're so strong, set, and yet still growing outward in life. Would I could be just like you!"

Wrapping his arms around the trunk as much as he could, Vaughn pressed tightly against it, He wanted to feel more of the tree's life. He wanted to see what other insights, what other wisdom his heart and mind could pick up. "Ahhh, it's spring! I can feel your waking life all through you! Also how stoic you are, how accepting of all that life has brought you and *will* bring... the good and the bad. And I really hope I don't bring you any bad."

Hmm, if a tree were conscious, its consciousness wouldn't be of just a branch, or a trunk, or roots, but all blended together into a whole consciousness. Vaughn didn't quite know what this all meant for his life, but he was keenly aware that many people only seemed to be conscious of a branch or a root at a time, and that being split apart caused them many problems. *I think my mind and heart are far more integrated and understanding of each other than many people, but I still need to do... something.*

Vaughn began to talk to the tree, "Ahhh, this has to do with what Stephie told me I needed to do to give my will up. A person can't just give up a few branches or roots, they have to give up the whole tree. Ahhh, but even to do *that*, first requires that the tree experience its *whole* self, its consciousness of being the whole tree. Oh God, help me so I can give my whole self to You. Make me one, so I can wholly love You and receive that new will. If only I had the time to meditate and focus on this. I feel so close. Forgive the killing I've done, If I can avoid it, show me the way. I fear there'll be much more to come. But what do I do when people use Your good life to threaten mine or abuse others? But the killing is getting easier... and I'm not even fully grown."

He stood a good while, embracing the tree with the prayers that were elicited by the experience. This time, without protest, he recalled his wife's question as to when he'd prayed or meditated last. It seemed like it had been a *long* time. Tears from pains forgotten, from feeling the lives of those he killed, from the weight of responsibilities so great he couldn't fathom, tears for himself being pushed into a darkness he desperately desired to avoid, and tears of hope, all mingled into a living complexity.

After his prayer, and life going its natural course within him, he stepped back with tears of appreciation. "Thank You, Lord God, for all forms of life and Your wisdom that you've put within them so that we may appreciate Your ways more deeply."

Vaughn finally moved away from the fence, following the trail he'd blazed. It had taken a lot of extra time to move back and forth on the animal trails, setting false signs and subtly marking the most direct route, but this would make the time for the return trip to the border fence reasonable, and the escape route clear when clarity was needed most. Vaughn had created a whole system of broken twigs, uprooted plants, and gashes in trees or gouges in the earth scattered over the many trails and depending on the combination, the trail was either true or false.

Having started out at first light on this fourth day of trailblazing, it was fortunately now only early afternoon, and being so happy to have much of his day left, naturally led to thinking positively. *Finally something's working right. Maybe there'll be enough time, after all. Just an hour's walk back through the woods, then I can pick up my vehicle and head to the hotel to tell Stephanie.* With relief also came the realization of being tired of always having to squeeze so much into too little time. He hadn't even seen much of Stephanie these last few days and now his longing for her also made him keenly aware of how ridiculously tired he was of being unable to be fully husband and wife. *Why should we rob ourselves of what's ours?* But uncertainty in heading into a new country and how their future would unfold tempered his desire.

"Darn! I really love this job, though. I've *earned* it! The pay is good. The freedom is *great,* and I get my *own* vehicle with all expenses paid. Damn! I could raise a family, have a home, *everything!* Damn, if things were just *different!*" Vaughn sighed at his painful longings. "And this job has so much integrity! I *love* helping people!" Vaughn had already aided quite a few strangers with assorted problems and given rides to several others. But all of them took several looks at his badge, then his young face, and back. For his part, Vaughn kept from chuckling because he felt a ranger needed a serious expression. And it was his expression more than anything that convinced people to accept him, but he also found the local people's reactions interesting because the reputation of rangers was fearsome throughout the country. Up near the border, however, reactions were quite mixed since even if the process to become a ranger was terrifying to hear and endure, the reality of what they did, based on the little he'd seen so far, was actually quite respectable, and comforting to local people. *King Jargon* would still probably change that for the worse because rangers probably would be required to help destroy the foreigners. Vaughn hoped not. *I could never do that.*

He paused in his thoughts and tracks upon hearing a distant sound. Turning his head from side to side to get a bearing on its direction, the sound he thought he heard didn't make sense. *It's probably some kind of cat. They actually do make that kind of noise.* Striding along the animal trails that generally went toward this intermittent sound, he tried to follow it. *How could that be? What would a child be doing way out here?"*

Yet, when he got close enough to see through the forest, that was *exactly* what he saw. Afraid to startle her, Vaughn approached with stealth, peering through the trees and shrubs until clearly discerning a little girl covered with dried blood. She was about five-years-old with somewhat wavy brown hair that went some below her shoulders and her hoarse, little voice still wailed over the main part of her mother's corpse. The legs were gone from the mine blast. *I don't recall hearing an explosion. This must have happened even before this morning.*

But Vaughn did remember to take extreme care not to let the emotion of this situation cause him to be another casualty. Unfortunately, the girl was at least fifteen feet from any animal trail and twenty-five from him but there was no time to try to find out how to get to a closer trail. Vaughn's heart pounded and his thoughts raced, *Oh God, I don't know where the mines are. How am I supposed to rescue her? My knife! I'll use it to probe the ground in front of me. That should be able to detect the mines... but I might scare the girl. She'll move!* She'll run! *Oh God, I have to try. I can't leave her!*

Vaughn poked the ground quietly so the child wouldn't hear him as he sneaked closer. When he had secured a place in the little open area where the girl was weeping, he crossed his legs and sat down, still some fifteen feet away. He spoke softly with tears in his eyes, "Little one."

She looked up and then clutched her mother, trying to wake her. "Little one, I'm here to help you. Little one, please look at me."

When she looked up again, Vaughn's will drew her focus into his and he let his compassion pour forth. Instantly feeling it, the little girl immediately stood up to come to him. Quickly, Vaughn held up his hand and patted at the air as if he was actually patting her shoulder. It had to be that real, or she would come to him and die like her Mom. He softly said, "No no, don't leave your Mom yet."

He knew the only thing stronger than her urge to come to him at that moment would be the love she still had for her mother. She stood still and stared at the torn, lifeless body.

491

"Little one, there are more of those bad, blowing-up-things in the ground so I don't want you to leave your Mom. Stay there. I'll come to you. Do you understand?"

She looked at Vaughn's face, studied it, then riveted upon his eyes again. Then she looked at his badge, returned to his eyes and nodded.

"I can't just come to you quickly, or I'll get hurt, too. I have to poke the ground to see where it's safe. Do you understand?"

She nodded. "Mommy used a stick," she said in a distant voice.

Vaughn understood that her mother was trying to avoid the mines, too. *But a stick wouldn't go deep enough!* That he knew from when he had dug some of the mines up to inspect them. Part of his training was to learn about the three different mines deployed across the border so one of the rangers had taken him around and even taught him how to diffuse them.

Vaughn probed the earth over and over… creeping on all fours as she watched silently, her little hands squeezing her dead mother a little tighter every time Vaughn stuck his knife in the ground. Halfway to her, his knife struck metal and the sound seemed much louder than it really was. She started to whimper and Vaughn lifted his head, finding her eyes. With more calm compassion, he comforted her. "It's all right, little one; I've done this before. I'm a ranger, here to help you. It'll be OK."

For some reason, telling her he was a ranger seemed to calm her but she continued watching his every move with an intensity that Vaughn could feel. He uncovered the mine then another, three feet and forty-five degrees up and to the right, and another, and he realized the area was peppered every three feet. The last mine Vaughn uncovered was only one foot away from the girl, to her right. *Thank God, she understood not to move.* In fact, Vaughn thought she was oddly calm as he went into a crouch, reached out, picked her up and stood.

"OK, little one, I've got you," he said reassuringly.

Once in his arms, she immediately hugged around his neck so tightly it was difficult to turn his head to see but Vaughn said nothing. As he carefully carried her back to the animal trail then sat down with her still in his arms, she began to shake. Vaughn stroked her head and began to rock her back and forth… rocking… rocking.

Images of her mother's mangled body danced before him. *She saw it happen!* Clutching her tighter, the smell of blood stung his nose. She whimpered and Vaughn couldn't keep his silent tears away. There were no defenses to keep this little girl's tragedy from rampaging all through him. Her pains were his pains, her experience, his. Although Vaughn had never had a mother worth speaking about, that was an understatement, this woman obviously had been noble. It pained him even more to know that she was dead but his mother was still alive. *Why?* He didn't know how long he sat rocking, but after a while, she relaxed her grip. Then, she turned and sat on his lap to watch her Mom.

"I'm so sorry, Little One. Do you know what has happened to your Mommy?"

Still staring at her Mom, she answered, "She… got blowed up… like she told me be careful not to. But I was. I followed

Mommy. She said to follow her so I wouldn't get hurt. Now Mommy's dead, isn't she?"

Vaughn replied, sighing, "Your Mommy was the bravest Mommy there ever was."

She started to cry again, and spoke through her sobs, "But... she's... dead... isn't she?"

"Your Mommy was a good Mommy. She wanted to save you from the bad people."

The little girl nodded, "Mommy said the bad people would kill *everyone*. That we had to try to run away."

Vaughn put his hand to her cheek, and turning her to face him, he found her eyes again, "When very good people like your Mommy die, the person that is your Mommy leaves the dead body and goes to a beautiful place for good persons who don't have their bodies anymore."

She stared at him, as if staring at the very words he spoke, feeling more than she could understand. Vaughn knew such times were critical for the future of a child's growth. He had to take the time, right now, to help her catch the knowledge that was in her feelings, to help her mind understand her heart.

"Do you still feel how good your Mommy is?" She nodded. "Do you feel the love, here, for your Mommy?" He pointed at her heart, where all human beings feel their emotions. She nodded.

It struck Vaughn then that scientists taught that emotions were in the brain, but he realized everyone feels them in their hearts. They feel in their hearts but their thoughts feel up in their heads. He noted that thought, but passed it off quickly so he could care for the child.

Still pointing at her heart, "You see, that feeling is from the person *you* are." He took her hand. "Do you feel me holding your hand?" She nodded. They looked deeply into each other's eyes. He gently squeezed her hand and held it up to her, "That feeling is from your body." Then pointing again to her heart, he explained, "The feelings in your heart are from the person you are."

That thought found its mark. It struck the home of truth. Her eyes widened as she understood by actually seeing it within her, for herself that emotions were not feelings of the body. Later in her life, she would often visit this memory, expanding upon it into greater and greater understanding and strength. Emotions are not of the five senses and the person in the body need not be chained by the body, not by fear for it, nor by its needs. Vaughn had effectively planted the seeds of great faith and courage.

For her part, the little girl replied matter-of-factly, "Mommy's not really dead. She's just feeling here in another place." She was pointing 'here' at her chest.

Vaughn smiled, nodded, and kissed the top of her head, "Yes, dear. Now I want you to listen to me. I'm going to help you, but first I have to do something for your Mommy. I have to bury her body." He paused to let those thoughts sink in then continued as his eyes focused deeply within hers. "These trails here, *see*, made by animals. They are the *only* safe place to walk. Wait here, but if you want to move around a little, stay on the trails."

Vaughn went back and picked up the corpse, but he couldn't take the extra time to recover the smaller pieces.

Handling yet another dead body brought him to further deliberation. *There's a difference between handling the people I killed and those I didn't kill. It feels the same in a way, but different.* He brought the main body part back to the trail, laying it down with care. This time, Vaughn didn't feel in a hurry to put the corpse down. *She was a noble woman. I can feel it.* He pulled his shovel from his pack and unfolded it.

The little girl put her little hands on her mother's chest, bending close to her eyes that Vaughn had closed. She whispered, "Bye, bye Mommy. I'll see you one day when my body breaks, too. Me and Daddy will miss you but I'll tell Daddy you're OK."

Vaughn turned away because he didn't want the child to see him racked by the pain. He wanted to weep but now just wasn't the time. Now he needed to protect this little precious jewel of a soul that he instantly loved. Vaughn took a deep breath and asked, "Can you tell me from which way you came?" Now that he realized she had a father, he wanted to return her to him. But he then became sick inside because all of them would die anyway.

"Back there." She pointed. "We went off the road back there."

Vaughn sighed with relief because now he knew he didn't have to try to retrace their steps, but only find the road. *But what good will it do?*

"But we can't go back. Mommy said the bad men were coming."

Vaughn talked as he dug her Mommy's grave, "I'm a ranger. I'll protect you. Is your Daddy there?"

"Daddy's at work for a *long* time. Mommy missed Daddy but said she couldn't wait for him. She said she would find a way to tell him. But I don't know how. She didn't tell me that." Her large brown eyes searched Vaughn for a sign of what he would do.

Glad that the little girl was talking so freely, it made digging the grave a bit easier, Vaughn so loved children. He remembered Lana and Jean, and more pain swept through him as he realized how much he missed them, and experiencing the loss of this little girl's family increased his desire to successfully have his own.

After the grave was dug, it wasn't deep, he told the little one that he needed her help to put her Mommy's body to rest. He had her hold up her Mommy's arm as they carried her corpse to its grave. After they placed it in the ground, she turned to Vaughn and with big eyes, she pointed toward her Mother. "I helped put Mommy's body to rest in the ground."

Vaughn nodded with deep approval, "Yes, you did, dear. You did a very good thing for your Mommy, because she would want her body to rest there."

She nodded, feeling good that she had helped her Mommy. Then Vaughn had her to help cover her up. "This is so her body can go quietly back into the Earth from where it came from. Our bodies come from here." He held out a handful of earth and let it drop to the grave. "But our persons inside the body come from Life. Life is like the feelings here." He pointed to her heart, "You can't see your feelings with your eyes, can't hear them with your ears, can't taste, or smell them, or feel them with your fingers, but you know they are real. We call Life a Spirit. People become just spirits after their bodies die."

"Mommy's a spirit now?"

Vaughn nodded, "Just like all our bodies come from the Earth, our spirits inside our bodies come from God. God is the Life that makes our spirits out of His Life, and our bodies out of the Earth."

"So, Mommy's body goes back to the Earth?" Vaughn nodded. "But her spirit goes... does her spirit fall apart like her body does? I saw a dead bird once, and a lot of it had fallen apart into the Earth."

Vaughn saw her troubled expression, and replied, "No, Sweetheart. Spirits don't fall apart. Once God makes a spirit, it will always be."

Then began her questions, "What about rabbits? I like rabbits..." What about dogs, cats, rats...? Vaughn smiled, patiently answering every single one. As he did so, he took out his hatchet and chopped down a couple branches. After he cut the end of one branch into a point, he drove it into the ground at the head of the grave. Then he split the top in half, and forced the thinner branch crossways down into the split. He peeled the bark off the piece in the ground and wrapped it around the split to close it up above the cross piece, and steady the marker somewhat. It was the best he could do.

"One day, when you're grown up, you might want to visit where we buried Mommy. This will help you find her."

The little girl nodded and Vaughn picked her back up to begin making his way to where he'd left Spot and his vehicle.

Stephanie had informed him that Spot had to go with him because the dog had told her he missed his master! Vaughn had eyed her and Spot without comment, but as he went out the door, he called to Spot who promptly bolted out to catch him.

Spot perked up when he heard them coming, sticking his head out the rear window of the jeep. When he saw the little girl, he hopped up and about but started to whine when he smelled the blood.

"This is Spot, and he loves little ones." When she got into the Jeep, he first sniffed her bloody pink dress and whined more, then began licking her face to clean it, and try though she may to keep that big tongue away, Spot knew his duty and wouldn't be dissuaded.

After driving a while, when Vaughn knew they were close to her village, he pulled over to make adjustments. "Little One, I want you to hide down here on the floor under this blanket so the bad men won't see you. You have to be very quiet and *very* still, don't move. They won't hurt me, because I'm a ranger, OK?" She nodded and climbed onto the floor in the front. Vaughn covered her over then Spot climbed into the front seat above her. He continued driving to the only town he knew from where they could have come.

As he drove, he tried to remember the little he'd seen of the place. His first morning as a ranger had been spent being driven all around the territory that was now officially his to protect. On his first night, he pored over various maps of the area, committing to memory details that might be crucial to saving their lives, but then his thoughts jolted him back to the present. *Our lives.* Stephanie! *I was going to go back to the hotel. What am I doing?* But after thinking a bit, he had his answer. *My job.* And after feeling a bit more. *No. Much more.*

CHAPTER NINETEEN
The Best Laid Plans

"No!" she shrieked at her husband as she ripped the tefillin, which is a Jewish prayer phylactery, from his head. "Are you CRAZY? We are Jews no more, no more Jews!"

He knew his wife had always been a fearful woman, but now he dreaded how the current events would transform her.

She threw his tallis, a Jewish prayer shawl, into the trash, as well, and then whirled around to confront him further, "Don't you look at me like that and wipe those tears from your eyes, there's no time for that. Where's your head? You know they still blame us for the plague, don't you? And now that there's civil war... do you know the kind of people that are going to run the new government? Didn't you hear their threats against all the religions, especially Jews?"

He knew better than to try to speak. It was hard enough on normal days, but to try to interject now would be worse than pointless. He continued to dutifully stare at her, but was having difficulty controlling the aching in his chest that had always been present but now began to be of major concern.

She continued her tirade, "Oh God!" Then she considered that expression, "No… no God! *Do you know what this* means? *The United States is* no more!" *The shrillness in her voice kept escalating to levels he'd never heard before and he began to rub his chest as she continued her rant.* "No more US government. *Do you understand what that will* do? *The US government has bailed out all of the major businesses,* every single one. *Now there's no US government…* there's no money! NONE*! Do you know what that* means? We have nothing. They have nothing. No one has ANYTHING!"

Ester, their youngest of ten children and only five years old began to cry because of her mother's panic, but this was a mistake because it drew her mother's attention and fury! She turned on her daughter, and seeing her clinging to her rag-doll, she ripped it out of her arms, "THERE WILL BE NO MORE CRYING!" *And she threw her doll into the trash. Then her glare took in all the rest of her silent children who'd gathered around.* "There is no more time for crying, *nor dolls nor play, all of you are going to have to work… at something! And if… if you can't earn enough in my home, I'll… I'll sell you! Do you understand?"*

He didn't want it to happen but the spasm in his spirit foretold the consequences and he couldn't help himself. Even as he clutched his chest and began collapsing to the floor, his gaze was taking in his beloved children, instantly reading their meaning, their fear of him leaving them all alone with her. His last thoughts were for his little-ones, I'm so sorry… I don't want to leave you. I'm so sorry for failing you!

When she heard him thud to the floor she whirled back, away from her children, and knowing he was dead from the

502

expression on his face, she wailed, "NO!" Then she attacked his corpse, her fists pummeling it, "Damn you! You can't die. Do you know what this means? How am I going to take care of all this! By myself?" At her word, this, she waved her arm out at her children and they all winced as if being struck with a whip. Five-year-old Ester looked over at her doll in the trash, then back at her mother, I'm going to have money... lots of money... and then I'm gonna get my dolly out of the trash.

Vaughn saw what he expected. The military guarding the main road. *Now that I'm alone, I bet they'll try to pull something.* And sure enough, as soon as he stopped at the roadblock, they circled his vehicle. A skinny, pock-marked young face came out not to greet him. "What's this? Where do you think you're going, *boy?*"

Each time Vaughn heard someone call him '*boy*,' it was like getting an extra burr underneath the horse's saddle and he shot the young soldier an angry look. Vaughn's right index-finger briskly tapped on his ranger's badge that hung over his heart. The *click, click,* of the tapping had an ominous cast to it but Vaughn said nothing, letting his actions speak for themselves, but the checkpoint guard's obnoxiousness only grew.

"Yea, so what's *that* supposed to mean?"

Vaughn's eyes had already turned black and he was restraining himself. There was more pumping through him than his own anger and he didn't understand the why's or the what's or even what good would ultimately come out. *But it feels like Justice is joining with me.*

Vaughn's calm smile and tone hid the brewing storm, "Listen! This means that to get this badge I had to go through at least three men who were ten times more man than you, and the rules are that either they or me come out alive. And I didn't even have Spot with me at the time." His dog growled an equally menacing warning.

The man seemed unfazed, but others who heard the warning started to pay closer attention out of curiosity. There were only five men in sight, armed with military weaponry, a pistol belt, automatic rifle, and knife. Vaughn didn't know why, but he found the odds not at all disturbing. He issued his own ultimatum, "I'm going to give you one last chance to let me pass soldier, so I can do my duty."

The guard took a detour, "What duties have *you* in the condemned town?"

Vaughn's words spat out like venom, "If I reported to the likes of *you*, I'd probably kill you and take the job myself out of respect for the rangers." His deadly tone contrasted his youthful appearance but that badge was known to carry weight, everyone knew that, even these soldiers. Spot continued the ominous rumble from his throat.

Vaughn's challenge sent the other men howling with laughter. Besides the one talking to Vaughn, there were three soldiers in front and one on the passenger side, keeping some distance from the *dog*. The officer just stood by Vaughn's door in shock, turning redder by the moment, and thought: *I'm sick of hearing all this crap about how bad-ass all these rangers are. I'll show him.* He went to put his hand on the jeep door to open it, not regarding a '*boy*' as any threat, but Vaughn had already pulled the inside handle so the door was free to open. Vaughn swung it out, just as the man was about to grab the handle.

Spot, who had been poised with paws on the sill of the fully open passenger window, leapt out of the jeep at the same time. In continuous fluid motion, the dog hit the ground once, and bounded up with both paws hitting the nearest man square on the chest, knocking him hard onto his back. Ferociously roaring like a lion, Spot pinned the young soldier to the ground with pearly white fangs only inches from his throat. Laughter had turned to dismay as the other men's attentions were drawn by this menacing creature. They raised their weapons, but couldn't shoot the dog for fear of hitting their comrade. The pinned man, now ghostly-white and paralyzed with fear, couldn't help the wet spot forming on his trousers.

The lead officer's right hand was caught at the worst time, with fingers extended to grab the door handle. The force of the door, fiercely swinging open, jammed his fingers and bent back his wrist. Sharp pains shot up his arm, but since he was caught moving forward, he couldn't avoid the door catching him also in the face and chest and the blow knocked him a few steps back.

In a similarly fluid motion as his dog, Vaughn got out of the car and kicked the man square in the gut, sending him tumbling backward over himself. Without a pause, Vaughn shook his left arm down, and the thin knife his farmer friend had taught him to carry, shot into his hand. He whirled on the men who were gaping at Spot, and threw the knife, striking the closest man in the right buttocks.

Going down with a scream of terrible fright, this soldier now knew what a true pain in the… The man Vaughn had kicked was shaking his head, trying to clear the pain and disorientation from tumbling. He couldn't get to his rifle strapped to his back because he was lying on it, nor easily reach his gun strapped to the same side as his injured hand. Besides, Vaughn's ranger pistol was already pulled, even before the knifed man had hit the ground. He pointed it at the other two men, as he walked over to the young officer. Vaughn motioned the command with his pistol and they immediately threw down their weapons. They knew their rifles wouldn't be as fast as his pistol already aimed at them. The knifed man continued to howl, since the knife was buried into his buttocks up to the hilt.

The look of dismay on this heretofore unchallenged 'battle-hardened' fighting force would have sent anyone else into fits of laughter, but for these soldiers, it was overwhelming, incomprehensible horror. Even though they had never fought before, they had superior confidence based upon their weapons, numbers, and the fear they instilled. Besides, they were sent by the government and no one dared challenge the *government*.

Vaughn moved efficiently, gracefully, and with cold deadly intent. He shifted his gun to the throat of the lead officer still on the ground, pulling out the man's pistol from its holster. Pointing the gun at its owner and his own back at the others, Vaughn ordered softly but with an iciness that would have sent shivers into the meanest dog. "Strip!" was all he said and he motioned to the lead officer to join the two standing soldiers.

Dumbfounded, the men just stared at Vaughn so he shot his pistol at the ground inches in front of the man in the middle. The three men stripped down to their underclothes. But Vaughn growled, "I said *strip!*"

The man under Spot was now reduced to a blubbering heap and this seemed to satisfy Spot quite well as he looked over at the other men, growling in support of his master's command.

After the young men stripped buck naked, Vaughn pulled out some matches from his pocket then threw them to the middle man and ordered, "Burn 'em!"

The man had a fleeting look of pleading in his eyes but in that instant, as his eyes met Vaughn's, he knew there would be no mercy. As the fire roared up, Vaughn called Spot off, but the pitiful blithering man remained there.

"Now, you *boys* listen to me! I'm the *ranger* in these parts. We have *unchallenged* jurisdiction. No one takes that from us, *no one,* unless you want to die! Do you understand?"

"Yes, Sir!," they all answered at once.

Vaughn walked over to the still howling man, reached down and yanked his knife out of his buttocks, resulting in an expected shriek, and then Vaughn proceeded to wipe the bloody knife clean upon the man's shirt.

"You *boys* get in your little toy truck over there with these two and go back to your commander. Give him this message. You better give it to him word for word, because I'm coming to check to see if you did, and if you didn't, do you want to know what I'll do?"

"No, Sir!" came everyone's response.

"Tell him I said that I went to the town on ranger business, and you interfered. Why waste all those supplies? They're going to be burnt up anyway! Does that make sense?"

"YES, SIR!"

"GO!"

The naked men picked up their two fallen comrades, the one with the bloodied arse, the other with soiled pants, and fled in shame and terror. Vaughn wasn't sure what they would actually do. If they returned in that condition and told their story, or they deserted, or whatever really made no difference.

Once Spot had been relieved of the soldier, he was guarding, he went back to the front seat quite happy, one might even say proud, for a dog. As Vaughn approached, studying his pet, he assigned an even deeper level of thought to his animal. Rubbing his ears, he complimented him, "You knew *exactly* what to do, didn't you? HA! And you really enjoyed it, gettin' the best of those *bad men*." Spot Arfed three times in positive agreement and the little girl poked her head out from under the blanket to see if Vaughn would let her join them.

He smiled and addressed her, "Hi, Little One! Sorry for the trouble."

"Are the bad men gone?" she asked.

"They won't be back, at least not for a while."

She crawled up from under the blanket and Spot immediately started licking her face again. Then as Vaughn sat in front of the wheel, she got up on her knees and hugged him and kissed his cheek as they went down the road and into the town.

Gathered in the central square of the town were about a hundred people. In the center of the square was a raised concrete platform, two feet high, with three older men standing on it. The people of this town had similar features of medium-brown, curly hair, brown eyes, and the same embroidered designs on their shirts. Vaughn got out, taking the little girl by the hand, and waded through the gawking crowd till he got to the men on the platform.

He spoke from the authority of his badge, "This child has lost her mother to a mine. She has a father; where is he?"

The tallest man answered bitterly, "What does it matter *now*? We die anyway. You should have let her die with her mother!"

His words smacked Vaughn in the face, enraging him though his anger was not only due to this man's attitude, but more because there was some truth to what he said. Still, before Vaughn could stop himself, he punched the elder man across the jaw, knocking him over! Shocked, the crowd immediately hushed.

Vaughn sweated in anger but a part of him watched from a distance, knowing the truth of this elder's words, and he couldn't ignore that part of himself, not this time. Feeling ashamed and realizing his impulsive reaction was exactly what a new will is designed to *prevent*, he hung his head and apologized, "I'm really sorry. I can see that what you said has some truth in it." He helped up the man who was rubbing his jaw.

The little girl hugged Vaughn tightly, crying, "PLEASE DON'T HURT MR. RANGER! HE HELPED ME. HE CHASED AWAY THE BAD MEN ON THE ROAD."

The people gasped, looking at one another. The man he'd hit spoke again but still with bitterness, "What difference does *any* of that make? Where can we go? Hell, they don't need guards to keep us in. We're doomed. Anywhere we go, they kill us now."

Vaughn looked at all the faces in fear for their lives and also realized that so far, he and Stephanie had only been concerned about helping themselves and those immediately linked to them. But now face to face, staring into the very *persons* of nameless people, his voice choked as he remembered watching on TV how the previous town got burnt. "Is this the whole town?" Vaughn asked the men, women and children gathered together.

"*It is!*" the man still rubbing his jaw snapped back.

Something began emerging through Vaughn's feelings and without knowing where it was leading but knowing it came from the right place, he went with it, asking, "How have you managed to survive this long as a people?"

Another elder, a balding one, answered, "We have other little towns all along the border. We marry and trade with each other. We have always been outcasts, but we were allowed to live. Now we have no place to go. We are here today to mourn our fate."

Vaughn didn't know what good the elder's answer would do. *Why was I led to ask it?* He looked at the scraggly crowd as the little girl held him tightly. They were poor people, but their eyes showed a wealth of human emotion, of good and bad. Vaughn's mind was telling him one thing, *You have a plan to carry out. You have to escape for your life and your wife's. The fate of the world depends on* you *escaping.* But his heart was moving in a different direction, and as it did, the other part of him felt helpless, abandoned to the role of outside spectator, shouting from a distance the old farmer's warning against this very same weakness but it was of no use.

"You *can* escape!" Vaughn declared, half in a daze, not believing he spoke it.

"You're foolish, young man," the third elder, a shorter, stocky man said in contempt. "We told you there is no place to go! You rescued that little girl for *nothing*."

Again, Vaughn couldn't control himself and before he knew it, he broke free of the little girl's hold, grabbed the stocky elder by his shirt, and violently shook him as he yelled, "NOT FOR NOTHING, *DAMN YOU!* NOT FOR NOTHING!" The man shaken by Vaughn's rage was afraid to resist and also felt a deep blackness shrouding the ranger. Then as Vaughn came to himself, he whispered, calming down, "Not for nothing."

Still holding the man's shirt, Vaughn suddenly remembered his heart vision. He looked over at the little girl who stared into his eyes. *She's the girl!* She's *the girl from my vision!* Amazed that he didn't see it before because it was all so clear to him now, he studied every detail as he looked her over again. *It's her! It is her.* Then his eyes darkened even more, as he remembered the blackness that came for her, and he immediately scanned his surroundings but saw nothing out of the ordinary. He looked at her again. *I know it's her. Her mother was blown up, but by a* mine, *not the blackness! This is the girl I wept about saving! The blackness, it* will *come.* He turned to the whole crowd, shook the man again, and shouted, "NOT FOR NOTHING!" This time though, his words were mixed half with anger but the other half as a plea.

The crowd had become stone silent as they stared, and Vaughn realized he was being swept away by feelings he couldn't control. He had never examined deeply enough what had happened to him at the hospital, when he lost control with the transporters. Now, not understanding these things left him helpless and all he could do was be what he was while his mind was but a helpless prisoner to the unknown. Reality is what reality is. Still holding the man, he relaxed his grip then finally let him go.

"Not for nothing! I know a way you can escape… the whole country!"

Gasps spread all around as the first elder whom Vaughn attacked, whose jaw he had punched, became truly shaken. He was all set to die in bitterness, but now Vaughn's words carried a sense of truth in them that upset his determined direction. He began to feel a whisper of hope for life as Vaughn's words moved through the entire crowd with equal effect.

The first elder declared, not with bitterness, but as statement of fact, "The border is protected. The girl's mother proves it. Also, it's fenced. We've heard from some of your rangers that it's fenced."

Vaughn's words were soft, "Did I *not* rescue this child?"

Hugging Vaughn's leg, the girl pleaded, "He *did*. He did 'resue' me?"

Vaughn patted her head, smiling at her attempt to use a word she apparently knew the meaning of, but not how to pronounce. Feeling his growing compassion for her, she looked up to try to capture more of his approval. As Vaughn met her openly honest gaze, it struck him then that she had complete trust and faith in him, and this dwarfed him. *What am I doing? Oh God, life and death are before us this very day. Mine, hers, and theirs! WHAT AM I DOING?*

As if in answer, a long awaited answer, a presence came over Vaughn declaring from the inside-out, *PRECIOUS LIFE.* And being much greater than himself, it swept him away, making both his heart and mind into spectators but yet also still had a major focus in the presence of the world surrounding him now. Then, as fast as it came over him, it vanished, leaving Vaughn to wonder. *Was that a reassurance that I'm doing right? Or just that I'm right to ask what am I doing? Does it matter? I can't control what I'm going to do! Oh, there's no time for this now.*

Vaughn turned to the stone-silent crowd that had inched its way closer and closer. "You have a choice," he whispered, then looking back at the elders and back again at the crowd, he couldn't help but shout more loudly, more forcefully than he ever had, "*YOU HAVE A CHOICE!*" It was a plea, a declaration, a challenge, and something more. It was a deep calling from beyond them all and it instantly brought tears and sobs from many, even two of the elders wiped their eyes. Then Vaughn continued softly with compassion, "You can believe me, or not believe me, but tomorrow night I shall return right *here* to lead you to safety across the border! See that this child is returned to her father." He began to walk away, but the little girl clung tightly to his leg.

"Her father has been gone a long time," the balding elder said.

"*I wanna stay with you,*" she cried.

Vaughn stood helplessly suspended, "She needs to be cleaned up and given clothing," he heard himself say.

One of the young women in the front spoke up, "I'll take her to her home and fix her up. I have children near her age. She can stay with me."

"*No! I… I…*" she wailed, desperately clinging harder to his leg. This was the man, the *ranger*, that saved her, fought for her, helped her mother, and showed her that her mommy really wasn't dead but in a better place. The crowd felt how tenaciously the little girl clung to Vaughn, and the men, women, and children began looking at each other, passing some invisible knowledge between them.

Vaughn heard himself speak, "Clean her up, feed her, and bring her back to me in two hours to this place, then I'll take her home!" Placing his hand on the child's head, he reassured her, "Go with her now. I promise I'll wait for you." Then, Vaughn heard a phrase in his head, '*A ranger's word.*' Murmurs of appreciation moved through the crowd. *Who is this young man?*

The little girl looked into the depths of Vaughn's eyes then she nodded and went with the woman. When she was gone, Vaughn asked the balding elder, "What happened to her father?"

"I'm sorry young man, but there are some secrets we are sworn not to tell anyone. We are not allowed to break our oath!"

Sighing, Vaughn sat down on the edge of the platform, staring out past the crowd. He seemed miles away in an unfamiliar place. All his planning had not included, *This. How can I put our lives in danger like this? Stephanie, I'm sorry... but how can I keep all this a secret, now?* King Jargon *is speaking to the people tomorrow night. If he finds this out, will he still believe we'll attack him? We have to escape in* secret *tomorrow night, too. Secret... Oh God!*

But there was no secret any longer. A whole town knew. Vaughn leaned his elbows on his knees, put his head in his hands, and whispered mournfully to himself, "What have I done? What have I done? What have I done?"

"Mr. Ranger," called a woman who heard Vaughn whispering to himself, "You've given us hope!"

Standing in front of him, she put her hand on his shoulder as her little girl of about seven placed her hand on his knee and her little boy, of about two, squeezed between his mother and him and shoved his head up into Vaughn's bowed face with a broad smile. A few quiet tears ran down Vaughn's cheeks and the little boy stuck out his index finger to touch one.

Still Vaughn didn't want to pick his head up as he struggled with all this that was new to him. He had long since lost track of all his emotions as they had swept him away. But he spread out his young, powerful arms and gathered the children into him with a hug then kissed the toddler on top of the head. The woman brushed the hair on top of Vaughn's head with her fingers as he contemplated how to proceed. *I'll have to tell Stephanie what I've done when she sees the little girl. She'll help me. She'll know what to do... whether I've done foolishly... or wisely. Oh God, but I never told her how I killed the govs!*

Two hours later, the crowd parted as the young woman and the little girl that he saved reappeared. The little one was now dressed in a soft, long-sleeved, long black dress with gold thread embroidered at the hem and sleeve-ends in some pattern Vaughn had never seen before. In a way, it reminded him of Stephanie's Appendaho embroidery though they weren't similar at all. These patterns, symbols, almost looked as if they could be… Vaughn really wasn't sure so he focused back on the child, noticing her wavey brown hair had been brushed and pinned back and her cheeks had a natural blush radiating through her somewhat pale skin.

With the child now in order, Vaughn found himself standing up, and addressing the town in a clear, strong voice, "Tomorrow night, just after sunset, when it will be hard to spot our escape, I will lead all those who have faith in Life to safety. I swear it to you by my own oath, and as a ranger sworn to protect you."

He took the little girl by the hand and the crowd again silently parted. As he walked, hands reached out to touch him, hands of warmth, of love, of hope. Vaughn bit his inner lip, and put on his stern ranger's face, because he knew he had to be strong for these people. As he walked, his mind flashed back to almost a year ago when he had just turned fifteen, stuck in his small town, hated, ridiculed and forlorn.

When they reached the jeep, Spot sniffed the girl all over then settled between them. She wrapped her arm around the doggy, leaned on him, and fell asleep while Vaughn drove and got lost in his thoughts.

Oh God. How am I to do this? I planned an escape for just us. I have to stop at the ranger's station, pick up the rope, the harness. But how am I to get all these people up over that fence? They'll all have to climb that tree! I guess I'll just have to make or find a rope ladder to get them up and down… They'll just have to climb up. They have to. Maybe I and some of the men can help pull them up. I'll need extra harnesses. The fork in the tree is large. I think two or three men can fit in it. But they'll have to climb up the fork and out onto the limb by themselves. Oh God, I promised! Well, if they want their freedom, they're just going to have to fight for it by doing what's needed.

A short hour later and they were at the station and Vaughn thought again about how he loved having his own vehicle but would have to leave it all behind. *Start over from scratch, again.* It had just turned dark when he patted the little girl's head. "Come on, Little One, I'll show you the ranger's station."

Waking up, she rubbed her eyes then dazedly followed him. Vaughn unlocked the door, brought her into the dark room, closed the door behind them then flicked the light switch on. There were no windows for light to shine through so no one would see if anyone was there. He entered the back door that opened into the storeroom and went through cabinets, shelves, and a stack of dusty boxes that looked like they'd been there as long as the station. But in those boxes, he found rescue climbing gear. A heavy rope, harnesses, and even a rope ladder. "Oh God, somehow, it seems to me, You prepared this for me even before I was born!"

"Yep, he did!" came the little girl's reply.

Vaughn stared at her and wondered was she saying her confirmation just because he said it, or was she saying it because she somehow really knew it. He shook his head at the thought, and gave her the harness he would use for Spot. "Here, you can help me carry this out to the jeep." Delighted to be of help, to be useful, she took hold of it with both arms and a look of determination and Vaughn walked through the storeroom door with her lagging behind.

"Well, well, working late?" asked the familiar voice of Blackbeard at his desk.

Vaughn steadied himself, "Oh! Hi! I didn't know the job *had hours*. I mean, I thought it was a twenty-four hour responsibility."

"If you want it to be, young man. And what do we have here?" He motioned to the stuff he was carrying and the little girl.

"I found this old stuff in old dusty boxes and… I had an idea!"

"Yes?" came the curious reply.

"You'll laugh then you'll tell the others, and they'll think I'm softer than I really am."

Blackbeard roared with laughter, slapping the table. "*I doubt that!* You got rid of those three gov bastards! Your report says they were extorting the public and murdering innocent people but left out that you got rid of them. Seems like they just finally met the consequences of their racket. But I know you did them in!" He raised an eyebrow, expecting an answer.

"All this stuff is going to waste, so I decided to put it to use for training from a tall tree, and…" Vaughn whispered, "for a swing."

Blackbeard laughed to himself at how Vaughn completely ignored the major issue, "Oh, I see." He cleared his throat, peeking at the little girl and winked. She had hid behind Vaughn, but peered around his leg, uncertain to smile, but wanting to.

"The girl looks to be of the condemned towns," he said sternly.

Vaughn replied, ignoring the implication with lightheartedness, "I found her wandering lost in the woods. I'm sure she's too young to know the difference between towns and people." But Vaughn felt he couldn't bluff Blackbeard, and didn't know what the chief would do next so his knife arm tensed.

"That's not the way our new *King* will see it," he said, raising an eyebrow.

Vaughn spoke sternly, "We are *Rangers*. Since when did we ever give a damn about what any government or *king* said? Our job is clear without them!"

Blackbeard slapped his hands down on his desk, roaring in laughter again. "I knew there was something special about you, *boy*. Alright, but you can't be caught with her by anyone else or it'll be bad for you. How you gonna do *that*? Where you gonna keep her? It's *obvious* what people she is."

"I... I'll ask my wife! She'll know what to do!" Even Vaughn was surprised at that reply.

Blackbeard studied him a long moment. "Yea, women know all about changing appearances. True enough. I wouldn't put anything past *your* wife!" He broke into laughter again.

The little girl kept studying Blackbeard or so it seemed. If Vaughn didn't know better, he could swear they knew each other. Perhaps Blackbeard had visited their village. Nevertheless, Vaughn decided not to tempt fate any further and sought to end the conversation, "Well, I've got to get home before my wife comes up *here* looking for me, *again*."

Blackbeard's hand went to his neck, speaking in mock seriousness, "Well, we wouldn't want *that* to happen." At that, Vaughn laughed hard, too, and Blackbeard knew then she had told him of their encounter. Rising from his chair, shaking his head, the chief helped Vaughn load the jeep, and slapped him hard on the back. His heavy hand stung, but Vaughn gave no indication. Spot shoved his head out the window to investigate this new person and when Blackbeard saw him he was immediately taken in, "*Beautiful* dog you got there!"

Spot, always one to respond to a compliment, stuck out his head further and got patted and ear-rubbed. Vaughn noted that Spot liked Blackbeard, which seemed odd to him, because he wasn't so sure himself. He still remembered his life being in grave danger because of this man's stupid enforcement of a ranger eligibility test. As they went on their way to the hotel, just a five minute drive away, Vaughn wasn't sure how his wife would take what he did.

As he entered their hotel room, "Stephanie, we've com…"

She was wearing a beautiful, sky-blue long dress with golden embroidery around the modest v-neckline, hems, and down the middle front where it buttoned. Vaughn stopped still, his breath taken away at how elegant, how royal, how voluptuous she looked. "Where'd you get that?"

She smiled but for some reason looked just a bit embarrassed or apprehensive. "Well, Vaughn… I decided proper dress is important enough to me… because of its *meaning*, that I… well, let's just say I made it!" He gazed at his wife, spellbound, then realized that she'd used her powers to create the dress.

The little girl also stared then exclaimed, "*You're pretty!*"

"Well, hello there! *You're pretty, too,*" Stephie sang back while throwing open her arms. In a flash, the little girl left Vaughn and was scooped up by Stephanie who swung around in a circle. Vaughn just couldn't find a way to capture all the beauty he was witnessing, and how strange it was to be experiencing such extremes of beauty and ugliness in this time of his life.

"You know what, Little One?" Stephie tenderly asked.

"What?" she giggled back.

"Spot loves to put little girls to bed and sleep with them."

"He *does?*" She was a ball of fascination.

"Oh yes! Go in that room right there with the really big bed. Take off your beautiful dress, put it in your little pack, then place the pack on the chair in there. You can climb into bed and Spot will tuck you in!"

Little One's eyes were wide as she bolted for the bedroom with Spot close behind. The dog had learned to tuck Lana in, and now he knew what to do for this child.

Arm in arm, standing across the open door, Vaughn and Stephanie watched the bedtime ritual unfold. The girl struggled out of her black dress and did exactly as Stephie had told her. When she climbed into bed, Spot leapt onto it, raced to its foot, grabbed the end of the top cover that was folded back, and started pulling gently, slowly, until he had pulled it over her. While she giggled uncontrollably, Spot lay down beside her, putting his head on her tummy. With her head on a fluffy pillow, she patted Spot's head and several pats later was fast asleep.

Vaughn pulled off his shoes and sat on the couch with a heavy sigh and his wife followed. Seeing tears form in his eyes even before he began, she realized, *Oh my, he's been through something!*

The events of Vaughn's day unraveled. The magnificent tree near the fence, the girl in the minefield being the girl in his heart vision, the townspeople, and his promise to save them all. At the end, he looked helplessly at her, but she strangely had no reply!

"Stephie, *help me*! Why aren't you saying something?"

"What would you like me to say?" she asked ambiguously.

Vaughn remembered when he used to do this same silent thing to her. "Was I wrong? Was I foolish? I don't know, Stephie! I feel *very* guilty, because I'm putting our lives, *your life* at great risk by doing this… and there's the future of the Seed to the Tree of Life!"

Stephanie looked away. She couldn't look Vaughn in the eyes, and he didn't understand why.

I've disappointed her, terribly. "Oh God, I'm so *sorry*. I shouldn't have done *anything* like that before at least asking…"

But his wife quickly cut him off as she grabbed his arm, "Oh no, Vaughn! Don't say that. You misunderstood my response." She hesitated, "But you *will* understand. Vaughn, I am more proud of you for what you are doing than you can ever imagine!"

Shocked! A moment ago guilt crushed him, but seeing in her eyes the intensity by which she meant every word, and also surprised to glimpse even fire in them, he knew she spoke from her heart! He didn't understand why she was so intense so he looked deeper into her eyes.

Reading his expression, she explained, "Because remember what I said before? All we've been doing is looking out for ourselves and just a few people we loved, whom we were *supposed* to love. Now you're sharing your gift of love with so many. *I am so proud of you!*"

He beamed as she squeezed his hands. *She's proud of me!* With bursting fire in his heart, his head floated on a cloud while he mused. *We can't truly honor or protect the Seed to the Tree of Life, if we first don't live its principles. I've never extended myself to so many people before, never had the chance to make such a real difference but...* So many feelings unfelt before had full reign over him now. Reality is what reality is.

Stephanie, who had been sitting back, embracing life's course, leaned over, kissed his cheek, and hugged him passionately then explained, "Vaughn, remember the Light Oil, and that I said it might be very powerful? Well, I've been reasoning and testing out my reasoning. Just like the Black Oil was as you said, a doorway to a spiritual world, so is this Light Oil! But there's more, Vaughn. I can travel with it! Just like Jargono uses his Oil. That's one of its powers!"

Inspired by the revelation, and by its implications, he clarified, "Stephie, do you know what that *means*? He transported you without even putting it on you!"

She shook her head, knowing he was thinking she could use her Oil to save the townspeople. "I don't know if I can do that, yet, for someone else, dear. To actually move others from one physical place to another still has risks. I *wouldn't* risk it with *you*, or anyone else. You might get trapped somewhere. But, I've figured it out for myself."

Vaughn suddenly realized she'd been doing travel experiments. "STEPHIE," he scolded, "how could you risk your…"

Again, she cut him off quickly, squeezed his arm with determination while staring deeply into his eyes, and emphasized, "I've traveled before, remember? But more than that, Vaughn. I am *meant* to do this, to *be* this *faithwalker!* There's no doubt in me that I am *supposed* to learn everything about my abilities, *risk or no risk.* Now, there's something very important to me that I want to do. Will you just sit here with me, please, quietly, while I do it?"

Amazed at the ever growing maturity of his wife, this new development of their relationship excited him, put him in awe, and unnerved him all together. She was now a far cry from the tentative girl, consumed by fear, guilt and self-loathing, whom he met through that bathroom window. Now Vaughn was more concerned that she was perhaps, *Too bold, too independent. But what am I thinking? Look what I just did the past few days! But I just don't want anything to happen to her, that's all. I suppose I should tell her how I've gotten Jargono to believe we will attack him, about me killing those men. When she's done I'll tell her. We have to have faith in each other.*

He remembered King Mafferan telling him he had to have faith in his wife, even for those things he didn't understand. Now, he began to realize this worked both ways. *She must have faith in me, too.* Vaughn understood enough about her to know that only good would come of her endeavors. *I think she knows the same about me.*

Besides, if he had any doubt about what *she* was doing, he

could caution her and she would heed it. *But I didn't give her the chance to express doubts before I did what I did!*

Stephanie and Vaughn were still two individuals, after all. That's what makes their love so powerful. Each freely choosing to love the other, not being required, but loving because of what each is to the other, what they understand about each other. With that deeper sense of their sacred individuality, Vaughn lovingly embraced her request to sit in silence to wait. *For what?*

"Yes, my precious dear. I will sit here and be thankful for you while you do... what are you going to do?"

"You'll see." Stephanie replied, and quickly turning away, brought her hand to her face, as if to brush her hair away, although it was in braids and not in the way. She sat down at the little desk, pulled out paper and pen, and began to write, think, write, think...

Vaughn watched her intently, as he had done while she brushed her hair after their bath. With or without clothes, he was equally captivated by her form and spirit. Her regality in her manner and dress were what swept through him now, but these only highlighted something far deeper. There was an utter determination and substance to her, not as 'important' people put on importance, but the significance of high purpose. That purpose of goodness glowed all through her and around her, glowing from the inside out.

Almost two hours of writing, stopping, writing, she finished a single page. She dabbed the four corners of the paper with the Light Oil, then returned its bottle to the secret pocket in her dress. After folding the page into thirds, she placed it in an envelope, came over with the letter in her left hand, and sat back down beside Vaughn while placing her right hand over his folded hands. When he saw that look in her eyes, his stomach lurched, but he didn't know why.

Oh dear Vaughn, now more than ever, since you have so many people depending on you to save them, I know I have chosen the right thing to do. "Vaughn, you know I love you with *all* that I am and will ever be, *forever*. I am so *proud* of what you are doing. Vaughn, all we can do is do goodness to the fullest that we can do. We are not assured of any outcome, my love, only that we have and are able to do our part. We cannot fail our part as long as we keep faith and do it. We may not achieve the outcome we want, but we have not failed if we do the part that we are able to do. Do you understand that, my dearest?"

For some reason, he found himself not wanting to answer as tears were running down his cheeks, and hers too. He feared what would be said next, but his mind couldn't grasp what would be said next. Stephanie leaned forward, taking his lower lip between hers in a gentle, slow kiss. It seemed an eternity, as her sensitivity began to touch his, as the softness of her lips began to press into his, as she gently drew his lip in between hers, as the kiss reached its crescendo, and their lives seemed to be joined in that kiss… she disappeared.

Vaughn sat stunned, embroiled in fear, confusion, love, pain, and a sense of something greater around him. When he noticed the envelope on his lap, he rolled off the couch onto the floor, trying to hold back the wailing inside of him. His mind was less than a spectator as he was simply overwhelmed.

Feeling something nudging him, poking at his ear, he looked up at Spot who began licking the tears from his face.

He remembered that the little girl was in the bedroom and redoubled his efforts to be quiet. He peered through the doorway, and thankfully found the child still asleep.

Slowly, heavily, he picked himself off the floor and sat back on the couch with the envelope in his hand. Pain shot all through him, as it reminded him of her presence only minutes ago. He rubbed at the ache in his chest as he knew that she had gone to fight Jargono, *alone*. A battle he knew she could not win. *A battle Jargono has been expecting. Because I set it up that way! Oh God, I never told her! She never really believed I had it worked out. What have I done?*

"Oh Spot, I die this night. I die." Then, two words appeared on the front of the black envelope in elegant, gold penmanship: Choose Life

Vaughn gasped. *She knew!* Apparently, his wife's powers had increased more than he realized. *Maybe...* he unfolded the envelope flap and took out the folded letter. Spot sat still in front of him, watching intently. The paper reminded him of the parchment that Mafferan's ancient letter was written upon, or a page from the book of wisdom.

"Oh God, help me, help me to read this and understand rightly." He unfolded the letter. There were no lines, but her penmanship was steady, even, and elegantly styled.

My Beloved Husband Sir Vaughn,

I AM SORRY I had to do it this way, but I know that if we had discussed this, you would never have allowed me and I could never fight with you, my dearest. I know you would not have let me, because if the situation were reversed, I would not have let you. We love each other so much.

But our love is so great because it is founded in that Love which is greater. We must always honor that Love first, if our love is to be forever real. You did not fail me, my beloved, by doing what you did today with the little girl and her people. You honored me. You allowed Love to be fulfilled in your heart and actions.

We are called together unto a higher purpose. We can only hope to truly be together, if we fulfill that purpose to its fullest. You did not answer my question when I asked you on the couch! But yes, my love, I knew beforehand. Let me repeat now so you will understand.

Vaughn, all we can do is do goodness to the fullest that we can do. We are not assured of any outcome, my love, only that we have and are able to do our part. We cannot fail our part as long as we keep faith and do it. We may not achieve the outcome we wanted, but we have not failed if we do the part that we are able to do. Do you understand that, my dearest?

Please say yes, my dearest, please. I cannot bear to face what I must face, if you do not truly say yes.

Your beloved wife forever in Love,

Lady Stephanie

"Oh God!" *Pain, more pain than ever I knew possible.* Curling up on the couch, holding his gut, his mind blank, all that he had together with Stephanie seemed to rip away from him, knowing she would die and that this time he wouldn't be able to pray her back to life. Besides, he was committed to helping others and couldn't let them down. *Even if I could get there in time to help her.*

For some time he lay in that blank numbness until after a while guilt began to creep into his awareness, and with the guilt, thoughts returned, and he spoke them aloud to himself to help him think.

"How can I let go of my love? It's real. It's alive. I'm acting as if it ended. There is no end to real love. Even if Stephanie dies here in this world, and I don't know that for absolutely sure, but even if she does, real love can't die. Real love *is* life. It's not limited to just this physical life, because it's not physical, it's spiritual."

Shame began to permeate his every fiber. *I'm letting myself down, letting Stephanie down.* Vaughn heard the little girl stir. *Letting life down.*

"Forgive me, I want to live. I can't run away from love because it hurts. It's part of the beauty of love that it can feel that deep a sensitivity. That's why it hurts so much. I wouldn't give up my perfect eyesight just because I hated what I saw. I will *not* give up my love because it *hurts*... no matter what. *Damn it!* I'm tired of breaking my word to myself and Stephanie. *Damn it.* I said, no matter what, and I *meant* it. And I'm going to *keep it*, this time."

Spot got up all of a sudden, rushed into the bedroom, and jumped onto the bed as Little One was crying from a nightmare. Vaughn, letter still in hand, rushed in, sat on the bed, and gently patted her back, and caressed her head.

"Mommy, no…" she said in her dream.

Vaughn's heart felt more pain. "It's all right, Little One. I'm here for you. I'll do all I can for you. It' … all I can do… but I'll do it. I… can't promise we'll succeed. But I'll give you and your people my all. If we all can do *this*, we won't have failed."

Vaughn looked at the open letter in his hand, at the last line.

Please say yes, my dearest, please. I cannot bear to face what I must face if you do not truly say yes.

Vaughn heard himself whisper through his tears. "Yes, my beloved wife. I understand why you're doing what you're doing, and I'm *proud* of you. Do all you can. Don't leave anything out."

Stephanie's voice echoed in spirit, love and tenderness, "Thank you, dearest, thank you for the strength to give my all."

"You've done the same for me, my love." And Vaughn laid back on the bed beside the little girl with Spot on her other side.

My God! All my planning, all that time I spent figuring and counter figuring. HA! Well, I'm still doing the basic plan, but I never anticipated Stephie. Hmm, the nature of woman, to go off in the middle of something with her own mind and heart doing what we never expected. But I wouldn't have it any other way. She wouldn't be the woman I love, otherwise. And what about me? I didn't exactly… Arms crossed, with the letter in between his hands and his heart, Vaughn fell asleep.

CHAPTER TWENTY
All or Nothing

"Rachel pleaded with the mayor, "You have to stop them from celebrating! It's insanity added to a world that has already gone mad."

The mayor laughed, asking, "You want them to kill me? In their eyes, this is a great victory. The Great Satan has been dealt a lethal blow. I am sure they will celebrate for another whole week."

"I'm telling you that if you don't stop this right away, there won't be any of you left in this country to either celebrate or mourn for the dead."

The mayor laughed again. "First you want me to stop their celebrating, then you warn me we shall all die. This is the United States, foolish girl. We have freedom here. We can do anything we want. You are not even of our religion, so you're no prophetess to be able to make such claims."

She turned, pleading to her husband who knew she knew. Over the years she had proven that to him. He, too, pleaded with the mayor, "But I am of our religion. How can we not mourn for the dead of the innocent all over this country, all over this world? We have far too long held the fever of vengeance in our blood. If we do not cure it now, its disease will destroy us more effectively than the plague you celebrate that destroyed the others."

The mayor was incensed by such accusations. "We're not responsible for it! We had nothing to do with it. To fault us is unjust."

Rachel was angered as well. "About as unjust as killing millions of innocent children with disease and poisoned water?"

Her sarcasm infuriated the mayor further. "I've told you we had nothing to do with it!"

Her husband countered impatiently, "Neither did the innocents our people slaughtered have anything to do with the reason for their murder. All the more reason we should publicly mourn for them and help comfort them."

The mayor couldn't believe such ridiculous words. "Their deaths... it's guilt by association. Our religion provides for..."

Rachel's eyes flashed. Her husband saw it and swallowed. "Then live by your religion... and die by it! Husband, it's too late. We must go now or our unborn child shall never see the light of day."

He knew so he turned to the mayor. "It's been long overdue from our people, but I say it now, I am ashamed of you! I am ashamed of your bitterness, ashamed of your bloodthirsty, never ending vengeance. You are all cowards! You celebrate evil and refuse to stand up against it so that the world may see us as truly compassionate and God-fearing. You are children of God in name only."

"Tell your wife to cover her red hair when she leaves, or she may not live to see her pathetic prophecy fail, there are those in the crowd which I am not responsible for."

Rachel turned to him with eyes flashing yet again. "Responsibility sir, can only truly be judged by those who can see the whole picture. But see if you're able to contact anyone from your homeland! I sincerely doubt it! And when your fates here are announced, then you shall also learn of theirs!"

"**K**ing Jargon is going to make us a great country again!" The fat old lady said to the middle-aged, graying woman with a hook nose sitting across the table from her. "He's going to create a special fund for old people, so we don't have to worry." Both were stuffing their mouths with food their waitress had brought.

Hook Nose added, "That's all I care about. I want to be taken care of when I can't work anymore. It's a shame, though, to burn up all those places."

But Fat Lady instantly sniped back, "Are you feeling sorry for those *vagrants*, living off our land like *parasites?*"

Hook Nose reassured her, "NO! It's just that we might be able to use a lot of what they have there. We're not exactly a rich country, you know. With all his power, you'd think he could make them all just drop dead, so we could at least go through their stuff! How else is he going to create that special retirement fund? He's got to take it from someone."

All of the sudden their table shook and Fat Lady's plate spilled onto her lap. The fury at her companion should have been expected. "What the *hell* did you do?" she bellowed.

But Hook Nose snapped back, "Don't *swear* at me! I didn't do *anything*!"

Fat Lady parried and thrust, "Yea, the table moved all by itself?"

Just then a red-haired young lady in a royal-blue dress with red and gold embroidery, had nerve enough to interrupt their *conversation*. "Excuse me ladies, I don't mean to interrupt, but I did notice that she didn't do anything to the table!"

Hook Nose immediately grabbed the support from the stranger. "You see? I told you so."

But Fat Lady rejected this rude invasion of privacy. "*Mind your own business*. If she didn't do anything then what did?"

The young lady, being very polite and refined, offered a possibility. "I'm sorry, but at the moment I really can't tell you. Are you sure you didn't accidentally do it yourself when you were reaching your sizable arm across…"

Fat Lady turned red with anger, "Hey, *skinny* young thing! Don't be insulting me or talking down to…"

But Hook Nose thought it made sense. "She's right! Maybe you…"

Fat Lady couldn't believe this betrayal. "So now you're taking *her side*!"

The redhead tried to make peace. "Excuse me, I'm not siding with you or your friend. All I…"

Fat Lady put her in her place. "I'm *not* interested in what you think."

But Hook Nose had been seriously studying the situation. She looked at Fat Lady with deep hurt in her eyes. "I guess you've always hated me, haven't you?"

Fat Lady was insulted. If anybody was a hater, it was Hook Nose. "WHAT? Don't accuse me…"

Hook Nose cut her off. Fat Lady wasn't going to have the last word *this time*. "You probably tipped the table yourself just to get at me!"

The red-haired young lady's voice floated in again, "You see, ladies, maybe it's the same way with those *foreigners*. Maybe all this hatred is really from blind accusations, ignorance and fears."

Both women turned their venom onto the skinny young redhead and spoke as one, "You're pretty young to know *anything at all!* And *hey*, you're not from around here! Are you?" They scrutinized her braided hair, her odd dress, and her strange rich brown eyes.

Hook Nose uttered the obvious. "You know, she looks like one of those *foreigners* from the villages."

Lady Stephanie smiled. "Actually, you're right. I'm not of your people, but I'm not of the villages, either. I'm your supposed King's sister! The true heir to our ancient father's throne as it was delivered to *me*. Actually, I'll tell you about the table. I did it with my power, just to demonstrate to you how stupid, and foolish, and quick to condemn innocent people you are."

The women broke into laughing then Stephanie vanished before their very eyes!

☙

"I tell you, I'm going to enjoy being a powerful nation again. I remember the stories of our power." The strong, broad shouldered, middle-aged man boasted to his balding drinking companion.

The other relished that particular word as if the most expensive brandy was swishing around in his mouth, "*POWER!*"

But then they heard a very feminine, delicate voice scoff at them, "Ha! *Power!*"

Whirling around to see who had invaded their male bastion of might, their mouths immediately dropped open just before they began to drool. The most beautiful woman was sitting on a small bar stool, just two stools over. Her hips spread tightly inside her long, royal-blue dress as she crossed her legs. Their eyes went wide as their hearts pounded.

Strong Man, being closest to her, replied boisterously, "That's right, *power*, little lady."

The wonderfully feminine voice queried, "And what would you do with this *power?*"

There was something quite incongruent for these two prime examples of sophisticated manhood. Their vision of her was that of raw sexuality, but her conversation hinted of a superior intellect *and* it was challenging.

Balding Man answered, "I'd rule the world."

But his friend whirled on him, "*You'd* rule the world?"

Realizing the danger of what he'd said, he corrected himself. "Ahh, I mean, for… as King Jargon's faithful subject."

The young lady laughed loudly in disgust. "I thought you were talking about *you* having power."

Balding man turned red. He couldn't believe this… this little *wallflower* had insulted him. Clearly disturbed now, he shot back, "*Hey*, we're not all meant to be kings! There's got to be followers, too, but we *share* in his power."

The voluptuous young woman nodded like a queen granting a privilege. "OK, I'll let you go on those points. I've no time now to shred your ideas, but tell me what would you do with your *rule?*" Her eyes flashed red and seeing *that*, they both shook their heads, looked into their drinking glasses, then shrugged it off.

Strong Man answered, "We'd… tell everyone what to do, and how to do it."

Very cutely, she responded, "I see. What?" She opened her eyes wide in innocence, giving them a chance to enlighten her, but they didn't understand the question.

Taking the high road, Strong Man demonstrated his superior intelligence, "Huh?"

Again with a cute, innocent voice that began to get an edge to it, she inquired, "*What* would you tell them to do? Oh, and *how* do you want them to do it?"

That did it. They had enough of her insulting behavior. Both spoke the same words as they pointed their big fingers at her, "*Look*, who you think you are, anyway?"

Stephanie replied calmly, "What." But she wasn't asking a question but was stating a correction.

Balding man began to repeat their question, "*I said, who…*"

But she held up her hand, cutting him off. "I know, and I said *what*. The more important question is *what* am I? Am I a slut? Am I a peasant? Am I a virtuous woman? Am I a queen? Is a queen a *what* or a *who?*"

Each question brought the expected jeers and taunts from all the other bar patrons who were gathered now to watch the liveliest and most interesting exchange they had ever witnessed

537

in their entire lives. "*What* or *who*," they taunted as the men continued to appraise her with leering eyes and mouths agape, not being able to reconcile the two vastly different impressions they had of Stephanie.

She dropped her cute voice and somehow managed to look them all in the eye. "Grown men and so *ignorant*. You haven't the faintest idea what power is, or *even* what to do with what you *think* is power, but you *crave* it anyway, *and* you'd sell your souls just to give it to a man you THINK will share power with you. Truth be told, your miserable lives wouldn't be that much different either way! But probably worse under your *king*."

Right in front of all the others, Strong Man felt he had been reduced to the dignity of a maggot, because as bad as he didn't want to admit it, he could see truth in her words. Yet he wasn't at the crude level of the others who couldn't see anything at all, except a woman they wanted to screw.

One of those others unfortunately announced as he pointed to his crotch in a typical low-man gesture, "Hey, I'll show you where *power* is!"

That brought cheers as leering men moved to block the two doors to the bar and several others came out of booths and off bar stools towards Stephanie. Several smirking women looked on with interest. They didn't like this, *Miss-know-it-all. They'll teach her a lesson. Who does she think she is, anyway, coming in here, dressing like that, looking like she's some kind of* queen, *or something!*

Stephanie sat calmly, observing the many gray arms spastically vibrating over so many heads and then she met the eyes of the two she'd been questioning, and returned to her delicate voice to exclaim, "Oh, I see! This is your idea of power, isn't it?"

But the strength of her sharp but frank gaze had captured Strong Man's mind, and almost against his will, his heart too. He could feel her personhood. He held up his hand, "Hold on, fellas, I'm not done talkin' to her yet!"

Balding Man grabbed him and pulled him out of the way. "You hold on, *you can go last.*"

"Give it to her *good!*" screamed some woman.

"*She's no better than us!*" shouted another woman with disproportionate anger.

"Shut up, *whores!*" yelled one of the lascivious men, "she's ten times better."

"*Fuck you!*" sneered the angry women.

One of the other men snickered, "You already have!" And that brought a round of boisterous laughter.

Stephanie sighed at her continued education into the adult world and frankly wondered how they even made it this far. Then she remembered her many teenage classmates within just the last scant year. *Oh God, they're going to turn out just like...* this! *I've got to do something to try to change that!* She turned and again somehow met all of their eyes, but this time it stopped them all in their tracks. "Do you know why that expression 'Fuck you' is such an insult?"

They were stupefied at her mysteriously halting their advance, but equally so at her question. None could give answer.

The *faithwalker* answered for them, "Because *that* is expressing the desire to use a person solely for their body with absolutely *no* respect, appreciation or concern for the person inside. To a human being, there can be no greater insult. Is that what you intend to do to me? To *fuck* me?"

They looked at each other then looked back at Lady Stephanie who released her hold on them to give them back their freedom of movement. Closing in on her, they could almost taste her in their mouths. But she vanished! Reappearing next to Strong Man, she questioned him further, "If *you* had power, what would really *satisfy* you?" The other men were still unaware of where she was. They were not just a little upset.

Astounded by both her re-appearance and her question, he stammered, "I… I would teach these *scoundrels* a lesson!" Strong man replied as he waved his hand at the others.

Stephanie smiled warmly and placed her hand on his arm. "My friend, that is a good beginning to understanding what real power is, that there's only satisfaction in doing good. Goodness *is* power. Just being able to control people or things is not power, because in the end, when such people have dominated all they can dominate, raped every woman they can find ten times over until they're bored, they have only themselves left to destroy, hating even their own miserable, empty existence!" And with each word she spoke, he sank deeper into her eyes as her majestic feelings sank into him.

"She's over *there*, you *idiots*!" pointed out two of the women.

Strong Man tried to stop the men from rushing her, but they punched, kicked and shoved him into a faraway booth. Lady Stephanie vanished again. When he saw her sitting in the booth across from him, his face broke with emotion. Stephanie leveled her eyes into his, "They hate their lives because there is no life in them. Now tell me, what power would you like to have?"

The broad-shouldered, strong man was shaking, on the verge of tears. He shrunk away from Stephanie into the booth's corner, covered his head with his arms, and pleaded in a quivering voice, "Please Miss, who… what are you?"

Lady Stephanie leaned over, touched the man's arm, and he immediately felt her comfort and healing pour through him. "Isn't it more important to start out by asking *yourself* that question? The choice to serve starts with that question, Sir. Those who do not answer it truthfully for themselves end up like these *wretches* following a *devil* like Jargon." Her compassionate words permeated Strong Man's depths then it occurred to Stephanie. *God! It's so easy to face the adult world now. I wonder… is that because I have power to do so?*

The other men's frustrations were building so they looked to the whores for direction but all three were bent over retching, puking their guts out onto the floor. But the men were beginning to catch on anyway. They didn't need the whores and headed for Strong Man. For some reason, they thought if they just moved quickly enough, they could catch her. Stephanie had briefly considered driving all of the gray arms away from them but then she wondered if that would really make a difference in their cases. And then she remembered Vaughn's explanation from what seemed so long ago, that when people want demons to be in them, there they will stay.

So this time when the mob rushed her, Stephanie turned on them, her eyes blazing red. "Oh Lord of Light, how long shall I tolerate such *things*? Let them receive in *themselves* their just reward." She waved her hand and all of a sudden three men turned on one of the others and two other men turned on another. They each thought they had the red-haired girl and proceeded to do as they wished. When they were done, they mistook another man as Stephanie and the process repeated. Strong Man was in shock and being able to see clearly, he looked inside himself and became nauseous. He folded his hands, bowed his head onto the booth table and wept. "Miss, *PLEASE, help me to be a better man.*"

"I already have." Stephanie put her hand on his strong shoulder and squeezed, causing him to look up. She smiled a smile of pure love and vanished. The man stared for a moment as if into another world, then dazedly got up, stepped over the pathetic swine, and left the bar.

☙

Vaughn woke up to sunlight shining straight across the bed and as soon as Spot saw him lift his head, he bounded to the door, prancing. He nodded at the dog. *Some things change but some stay the same.*

During their quick walk, Vaughn noted the crystal-clear freshness of the early morning and the chill in the spring air added to that sense of newness. New life had clearly established itself all over, on lawns, between sidewalk cracks, in gardens, in the trees. All gaining fullness. It all had its impact as he thought of the life and death struggles in which he and his wife were now embroiled. By tomorrow morning their lives would be vastly different though he didn't know how. He knew the words from Stephanie's letter but pulled it from his pocket anyway because he wanted to read them again:

Vaughn, all we can do is do goodness to the fullest that we can do…. Do you understand that, my dearest? Please say yes, my dearest, please. I cannot bear to face what I must face if you do not truly say yes.

"Yes, Stephanie. I understand. I promise you, I'll do my best and give it my all. Come on, Spot, let's go wake our little one. There is *much* to do."

Vaughn woke the child, asked her to wash her face, and gave her his spare toothbrush. He let her try to unwrap it from the plastic to give her the excitement a child gets in unwrapping anything new. "This is yours. All for you, and no one else, because your mouth is private to you. What goes into your mouth can go into your body. The words that come out, come from your person inside. We're supposed to be careful with what we put in and what comes out of our mouths."

After making sure she knew how to properly brush her teeth, Vaughn helped her dress. He even brushed her hair while she stood humbly still, recalling how he saw his wife brush hers. Soon as her hair was done, Little One embraced the neck and kissed the cheek of the still kneeling Vaughn.

"I love you like I love my Daddy!"

Satisfied that the girl looked her best, Vaughn took her downstairs to eat. All the patron's mouths dropped open when they saw him sitting with a little girl, instead of his wife. Some noticed that the child looked very much like an outsider, but they had all grown so attached to the young man and his wife that they said nothing to cause trouble. They whispered, wondering where his wife was and where the child came from, wondering if somehow the little girl could be their daughter or a relation. *This is my last hour here, so it really doesn't matter what they think. Let them whisper.* Unfortunately, Vaughn had no idea that he and his wife had made such a positive impact on everyone, and the way he dressed this day, also added to their respect. He wore his brown ranger's uniform for the first time in the hotel dining room with his badge obvious to all, both causing quite a stir. No one could figure out how so many strange combinations could exist in anyone, let alone such a young man. Vaughn pulled out the chair for the little girl and she politely thanked him as she sat and had her seat pushed under the table. As they ate, every now and then, he wiped off maple syrup that had dropped from her pancakes down her chin.

Some confidently declared to their tablemates. *That* is *his daughter.* But many others begged to differ and ventured a different story. *No, look how similar they look. She has to be his sister and he takes care of her. Their parents must have died young and he's been on his own. That's why he acts so mature.* As that explanation circulated, it grew the most endorsements for validity as they became engrossed by his delicate care of the child, the way his eyes held her, and how straight she sat up.

After eating, he took some water from her glass, wetted a napkin, and wiped off her face and hands and paid the bill. Then he got up, pulled the girl's chair out, and took her little hand as she climbed down. He gave a little bow to her, she answered with a little nod, and then they took off hand in hand. The patrons couldn't figure it out, but there was something so very special in the interaction they had witnessed. Something in the way the young man carried himself and the look in his face, something in how the child acted with her guardian, something so special... but beyond words. One young lady wiped a tear from her eye as she watched them exit the restaurant for the last time, as if something very rare and long-missed was again departing from her life so her heart grieved for such loss. In the flow of time, cultures and people may experience great change, yet in every human being remains the natural imprint, and therefore the innate recognition of the tender grace of being human.

On the road, Little One wanted to know. "Did I do it right?" She was referring to how she acted at the restaurant.

"Perfectly," he approved with a smile. "Did you like your breakfast?" Vaughn asked as he was driving south.

"Oh yes, it was the bestest breakfast I ever had!"

"I'm glad. When we get to where I need to go, I want you to wait here in the jeep with Spot. I have to go and prepare our trail, so we can find it when it's dark tonight. I'll be gone for a long time, but I promise you I'll return. I give you my ranger's word."

Somehow, she seemed to know what that meant and had no questions or worries, even when they arrived at Vaughn's destination.

"Spot!" Vaughn's tone brought the dog to attention. "Guard Little One!" Then he left, taking a large canteen filled with water. *I was intending on escaping in daylight but that was before I knew there'd be a hundred people tagging along. I hope this works.*

Spot gave serious *Ruffs,* letting his Master know how carefully he intended to obey his command, then twisted over and began licking the girl's cheeks. Little One checked the bag with the food and water that Vaughn had left for them, remembering he'd told her to make sure Spot didn't eat her food. "He's still a dog, Little One," he had reminded her.

Of course, once the adults are gone, any little one transforms into… well, their own person. "C'mon, let's play, Spot! And out of the jeep they both bounded. Little One found a stick and their first hour was spent on many variations of fetch, along with her trying to figure out how to ride on Spot's back.

Three hours later, Vaughn returned to find Spot and Little One tussling on a small, grassy patch. Her clothes had grass and pine needles stuck to them so Vaughn stood her up and chuckled as she brushed her dress off.

"Did you 'perpare' the trail?" the darling child clarified when Vaughn climbed into the jeep.

He patted the empty canteen and replied, "Oh yes!"

After rubbing Spot's ears, Vaughn mussed her head, to which she promptly responded by going into her little purse and pulling out her hair brush. "Don't mess my hair please. I got to look pretty today because today is special. You're gonna save us today!"

As Vaughn drove to the town, the road wound around hills and through the young forest. The ranger chief had told him that a hundred years ago this land looked quite differently but that since there were such fewer people on Earth everything had changed. Every now and then, Vaughn pulled over and walked into the woods and always to his right, but then at one bend and from then on always to the left, the place where they had to cross the road tonight. *Everything has to be just right. We can't afford screw-ups.*

"Watcha lookin' at?" Little One inquired.

"Usually, beside every road through the woods is a path that runs alongside it, maybe about six to maybe twenty feet away from the road. This road goes to your town and I'm just makin' sure the path is there all the way."

"Are we gonna take that path?"

"Yep! All the way to the trail I marked."

Little One began watching the woods more closely. Some hillsides were overgrown with various pines and hardwoods, now in full young leaf. Their branches stretched over the road to form an archway that Vaughn imagined was a royal entranceway to a palace. It was so hard to believe that in the midst of such splendor, there was so much evil. Vaughn shook his head, and noticing it, Little One tugged at his arm.

"What, Mr. Ranger? Why ya shakin' yer head?" She had propped herself up on her knees and was leaning on Spot for support as she faced Vaughn. Most of her waking time was now spent intensely watching either Vaughn or Spot and her eyes continued to work and rework at something that she was in deep concentration about concerning them.

Vaughn didn't mind at all. He felt it a privilege to have his life scrutinized by an innocent. He hoped he would be in good enough mind and spirit so that she would see something useful for her life. *No matter how short that might be. That's what angered me so much about that elder's words. Even if we know we only have but one hour left to our lives, we should spend it reaching for life, not cowering from death.* "I was thinkin' that there's so much beautiful goodness in the world. See all the wonderful trees?"

"Yea… but why was ya shakin' yer head? At the *beauty?*"

With a smile he answered, "No Little One. Not at the beauty. My smile was for the beauty. The head shaking was for the evil, the badness that bad people have mixed in with the beauty."

"You mean like what blowed Mommy up and killed her body but not her here?" She pointed to her heart.

"Yes, dear. Bad people put the mines in the ground."

"And bad people want to hurt us all." It wasn't a question. She was telling him the way it was. "Mr. Ranger?"

"Yes dear."

"Why are there bad people?"

Vaughn was in instant appreciation of this child. *Five years old and such a wonderful question, such a wonderful opportunity.* He had asked the same question to himself when he was younger, had thought for days upon it until a certain line of reasoning came to him. *What makes people bad? What is bad? What thoughts are bad? What feelings are bad? What actions? Why? Were they born bad? Do they have to stay bad? How can bad people become good?* Then, when he figured it all out, he tested his theory over and over but found that indeed, it had to be as he figured.

"Because a long time ago, the first man and woman started out good, but somehow they got tricked in their thoughts and did a bad thing. From that time on, all the children that were born into the world have both good and bad in them to choose from."

Her eyes grew wide, "Is there bad in me?"

"What do you think?"

She looked inward and studied a while. "*Well,* sometimes Mommy would tell me to do something, but I didn't wanna do it. Is that bad?"

"Maybe. The older you get, the more Bad will try to get you to do bad."

"Does the Good try to get you to do good?"

Vaughn smiled as he explained, "The good *is* you. It doesn't have to try. You just have to let it stay you. Good never forces you inside like bad will. You can choose."

Her eyes were questioning, too. "*Choose?*"

"Whether you want to do good or bad. But it's important that you think about what goes on inside your feelings and thoughts, so that the good you are doesn't get tricked by the bad that wants to be you."

The little girl leaned further over Spot and her eyebrows rose. Smiling and in a songlike voice, she popped her next question, "How ya do *that?*"

"Well, at any time you ask yourself, What am I feeling? Then you look and see what's inside you. Then ask, Why am I feeling it? Bad and good feel differently. Same thing about your thoughts. A person has both thoughts and feelings."

Little One stared past Vaughn, thinking, "Oh, it's a hard job being a... *person,* isn't it?"

Good. Very good. She remembered what I told her about being a person. Vaughn looked into her very dark brown eyes with his most serious expression and taught her, "It's the most important job you'll ever have."

"More important than being a *ranger?*"

"If I were a bad person, then I wouldn't have helped you, even though I was a ranger."

Little One was quick to respond, "But you *helped*, because you're a *good* person. Being a good person *is* more important than being a ranger because… even if you weren't a ranger, you still would have helped us."

Vaughn noted her self-confidence in her thoughts and feelings and derived particular satisfaction from that. Little One continued her exploration, "Mommy was a good Mommy."

He didn't want to interrupt the process so kept his silence as the five-year old explained, "Because she didn't want me to *die*. She *died* for me. To try to save me."

The girl waited for him to respond, but when he didn't, she added, "A *bad* Mommy wouldn't do that." She leaned over Spot even further, trying to provoke a response from Vaughn, but he held his ground. This was all about her, not him.

Then she stated another self-discovered truth, "It's more important to be a good person than even be a mommy!"

He couldn't restrain himself, "How do you know that?"

She folded her hands atop Spot's back, her eyes traveling upward in thought, "Because… when I'm a mommy I want to be a good person first. So I can help my daughter and die to save her. But not die here." She again pointed to her heart, then as she kept pointing, shook her head to emphasize that she didn't want to die there. The child did everything in her little power to grab Vaughn's eyes with hers, get his full attention, but he had to drive the vehicle.

"I love you, Little One! *You* are a beautiful person. In your whole life you must *think* to protect being a good person. The

life that makes you alive is goodness. That goodness in you
comes from a much bigger goodness called God. We have
the same goodness in us as God, only smaller. We love. God
Loves. We have light inside our hearts and minds. God is
Light. We have life inside us. God is Life. So, little dear, if you
ever get in trouble inside yourself with bad, you can always
ask God to help you escape it, to make you better, because
He Loves you."

Her expression focused deeply into every word, "How do
you ask God?"

"God hears all, sees all. You just have to ask Him inside
yourself like you were asking anyone anything on the outside.
God can hear you ask Him on the inside just fine. In fact,
He hears *that* much better than when other people can hear
you talk to them."

Little One laughed and giggled at that peculiar thought.
"God *does*? How's He do *that*?" She was fascinated, positively
delighted.

"Well, you ever went swimming?" Vaughn inquired.

"Yep," was her quick reply.

He pulled off the road and turned to face her. She was
leaning so hard on Spot , he was practically mashed flat onto
the seat but showed no sign of objection at all.

"Well, you see how the water ripples?" His hands made
wavy motions.

Her eyes followed them as she again answered, "Yep!"

"Well, the light inside us is a special kind of light we can't
see with our eyes." He pointed to his and hers. "Just like you
can't see the person you are with your eyes, but you can see

yourself with your mind and heart." He pointed to her head and chest.

She sat and studied his words awhile as he waited patiently to see a certain look in her eye. When he did, he continued, "Well, God's special Light surrounds all our little lights kinda like when you're in the water."

Instantly, she saw the picture. "Oooh!"

"When you ask God, you send ripples through the bigger Light which is Him!"

Absolutely delighted, Little One couldn't keep from singing out while she squeezed handfuls of Spot in her little grasp. "HA! Ah, God can feel the ripples, so He knows to pay attention!"

Vaughn gave her his special broad smile of acceptance, confirming, "Right!"

Then he resumed driving and remembered his beloved. *Stephanie, I wish you could have seen all this.* Vaughn felt she would be very proud. Further reflection brought him to review his life's direction and that brought forth a prayer, "What else is there for me to do Lord God? If I die this night… please, I'm doing all I know and am able to do, please save me from eternal darkness." And then he instructed Little One, "Time to hide." She ducked onto the floor and covered herself with the blanket. Spot sat-up straight in the front seat.

When Vaughn approached the intersection before the town, he slowed his jeep. The same soldiers were at the checkpoint again but only four of them. Stopping without being asked, Vaughn smiled and waited for them to unblock the way.

"Morning ranger," the officer spoke politely. "On more official business?"

"Yes." His professional reply came with no malice nor indication of prior events.

"Go right on through," the soldier said with the same tone.

Vaughn drove into the town in mid-morning but as he approached he slowly became flabbergasted by what he saw. When he finally acknowledged that he was seeing correctly, he was half angry even to the point of being furious, but also half petrified. After he worked his way to the platform where the same three men shouted orders, he inquired with his voice raised a bit, "Sirs! Where? Where... What are all these *people* doing here?"

The first elder spoke, "These are the people from our neighboring towns and there are more coming all day. You didn't expect us to keep it a secret from them, how could we?"

Vaughn sat as before upon the platform but in dismay. Little One stood behind him with her hands in his soft, dark hair and leaning against his strong back. He placed his elbows on his knees and his head in his hands.

CHAPTER TWENTY-ONE
Division

Rachel hadn't wanted to stop anywhere near San Francisco. After all, just a mere fifty miles away, the plague had already decimated that city, but there was no choice. She had hoped to turn south, down the coastal road and had told her husband that the United States was going to be a very ugly place. They needed to escape before they officially closed the border, before they officially declared a civil war. He had assured her it was OK to go into the delivery room without him but that was hours ago.

As the nurse left, she said she had to take the child for some tests. Shortly after, her husband burst into her room, and knelt at her bedside. "I'm sorry, my beloved wife!"

Her tired eyes looked at him, while she put her hand through his hair, "What troubles you, my love? We have a beautiful daughter."

Two military police burst in, grabbed him, then asked her in a bitter tone, "You're married to this dog?"

"Do your eyes deceive you? I am married to a man." She did not foresee any of this and wondered why.

"By government order, he is to die for his crimes."

"You must be mistaken! My husband is the best of men, only doing good for others."

"He and all people like him shall pay for the plaque they've spread. There'll be none of his kind left on the face of this whole Earth to celebrate the death of any more innocents. All children born to these dogs, who are under the age of speaking, have become the property of the government."

Knowledge instantly flooded her. "You're killing all the rest of the children? Now who is guilty of the blood of the innocent?"

"If they are old enough to speak, they are already poisoned by this filth." He shook her husband by his hair.

"Please, Rachel, say no more."

They punched him in his stomach for speaking. "Don't speak, dog." The officer turned to Rachel, "You shall be taken to the government's population center so you may begin having children for our country. After you pass child-bearing age, if you do well for us, we may forgive you for marrying this dog. If you don't agree to this, you can die like a dog with him."

"Will you grant a dying woman her last request?"

Her husband knew and began to weep. The officer stared at her, wanting to deny her wish, but as he looked into her eyes, he found himself assenting.

"Bring my daughter to me that I may kiss her before you kill me."

The officer nodded, and the nurse brought the daughter back. After she was placed in her mother's arms, the infant immediately settled upon feeling her touch. With tears, she smoothed her baby-brown hair and whispered, "I'm sorry, little one. Forgive me. For some reason I can't explain, I did not know. You and your daughter and hers are going to have to find your ways alone, from the inside out. There will be no one to help you." Rachel's eyes glowed brightly as she stared deeper into her infant's eyes. The child's eyes glowed back.

Stephanie paused within the spiritual corridor that she traveled through. The more time she spent within it, the more she felt she belonged to it rather than to the world. With every moment she spent there, her spiritual senses magnified. When people wake from dreaming, they quickly lose contact with its mysterious workings, but moving through the realm that connects the physical world to at least two spiritual realms, made the inner workings of reality apparent to both her normal and budding spiritual mind. *Hmm, but my heart has remained unchanged. That's good.*

She bowed her head, folding her hands under her chin. *"Oh God, lead me to whom I should go next. I don't want to sleep. I just have this night and day tomorrow before I confront him, so that all can see, so they can choose, so they can at least know they have a choice. I can't just abandon them without giving them the chance to see. Young as I am, I frankly nonetheless know a whole lot more than most adults. I have to accept my responsibility to do good in spite of everything. Be my strength, Oh Light, Who has given unto me the Seed of the Tree of Life to bear between my breasts till it should be planted. If I do not give my all, then how am I worthy to carry Your seed?"*

"Don't you understand? If we don't do as the new King wishes, we'll suffer the same fate?" The young blond man's voice wasn't quite angry as he stood pleading to his young blond wife sitting on their couch in their living room.

She looked up with her bright blue eyes seeking desperately to soften her husband. A curly brown-haired girl of around four years old dressed in animal print jammies sat to her left on the couch, squeezing a stuffed black and white toy doggie. It had velvety, floppy black ears which she liked to rub against her cheek.

"But darling, look at her! She's an orphan. We've adopted her legally. She calls me Mommy. Why should we have to give her to the King just because her features are a little different, just because she has a different heritage? No one even knows who those people are anymore. I don't. Do you?"

He leaned over a bit, threw up his hands as his voice grew strained. "It's not her features and you know it. My wife, it's obvious she's from the *foreigners*! It doesn't matter *what* people. King Jargon has commanded that all such should be brought to government-square tomorrow. *We can't hide her!*"

His wife began to cry, as she watched the child putting the doggie into various poses, mumbling to it in her bubbly sounds. They couldn't see Lady Stephanie in the room with them because she hadn't left the spirit-world to enter the physical.

His wife stopped crying and tried again, "What's the difference between people if it's not just some arbitrary physical difference like straight or curly hair? There are *no* religions in our country anymore, hasn't been for a long time. The differences that separated us have long since been done

557

away with, even with the foreigners. They're still required to follow all our laws, our ways, otherwise they would've been purged a good while ago. Whatever made them different in the past has been *erased*. There really is *no* difference now."

He knew she was totally missing the point, wasn't being logical at all but only speaking from her heart. "You *know* there's a lot more to this. Besides, those *foreigners* have *always* kept to themselves. They didn't *mix* with the rest of the people."

She saw how foolish her husband sounded. *He's smarter than this. I know he is. I* know *the man I married.* "There are a lot of people that don't *mix. Husband,* our country is a bunch of *small towns.* But we all went to the *same* government schools. There is *no difference.* Don't you remember the stories of the betrayal? How in the beginning, one town was discovered to be secretly following an old religion? Do you remember how you felt when your teacher showed you that movie of what the government did to that town? That movie has been shown in every school for generations, along with the government's teachings. I'm telling you, there is NO DIFFERENCE!"

It was clear to him that she didn't want to know the truth. She was silent now, waiting, hoping for her husband to turn around. She looked from the child to her beloved husband and back to the child. Finally he spoke, "They have different ways! There's just something *different* about them. Why do you think they've always been the butt of jokes and slanders?"

Anger shot through her as she threw her hands open with her voice becoming sharp. "Oh God, *open your eyes*! She's been with us for almost a year. She has *our ways*."

But he shook his head, thinking she just didn't understand. "Different people have different hearts. They're just… different."

She'd never heard such *crap* from her husband before. "How? Does her love for us differ from any other child's love for their parents? *Husband,* don't you understand? WE ARE HER PARENTS!" Tears were streaming down his wife's cheeks.

He hated to see her cry but he had to stand firm so he yelled back, "WE ARE NOT! YOU WANTED TO ADOPT A STRANGE CHILD. WHY, I DON'T EVEN KNOW. WE'RE YOUNG AND CAN HAVE OUR OWN!"

She collected herself to try yet again to explain, "I've told you. Her parents were run over *right in front of my own eyes,* as they chased after her." As she relived the memory, her husband once again saw the pain of it in her face and more tears. "That *damned* car didn't even stop. It kept on going. *I* picked the child up from between her dead parents. I… I couldn't abandon her. The Keepers came. They were going to put her on a State farm. *At four years old?* DO YOU KNOW WHAT THEY WOULD HAVE DONE TO HER? *EVEN AT THAT AGE?*"

He looked away from his wife because that thought disgusted him. He couldn't help gazing upon the little child, but then reality reminded him of their own desperate situation so he tore his eyes away from her. His wife's words didn't change what they were facing now. "There are bad things happening to people all over. We can't fix them all!"

She shot back with more questions, "So we shouldn't fix *any of them? What kind of man *are you?*" Instantly, she wished she could take back those words, but they seemed to have a life of their own, and now it was too late.

His eyes widened, "How *dare* you ask me that kind of question? I work my fool head off taking care of you and that child who isn't even mine."

She hung her head in shame, her heart pounding. She loved him and knew he was a good man. "I… I'm sorry."

He knew she was, and relenting, he sat down next to her. "Look, don't you understand? I love you so much. I can't put that child's life above yours. It's not even mine. It was your idea to adopt the child, *not mine!*"

She turned her head to him, not believing what she was hearing. "So, if we get caught, you'd turn me in because it was *my* idea?"

She missed the point again, jumping leaps and bounds past any thought he had at that moment but he decided to use what she said. He took her by the arm, "That's the point. It's a bad situation with terrible choices. What? Choose to have my wife and the child die and me live? Choose to have my wife, child, and me to die? Choose to give the child up and me and my wife to live to have more children? Which sounds like the best choice out of those three?"

But her foresight brought deep sighs with pouring tears and looking into his face, she pleaded, "*My husband*, would we be alive inside if we did such a thing?"

Stephanie began to fret deeply over what she heard and saw, "Oh God, what does Jargono want with all those children? Oh God, please! What can I do? Why is this coming to pass? Why are people put in such *terrible* situations with such

terrible choices? And why am I to behold such *awful things?*"
As Stephanie wept, her mind focused on the physical without
her realizing so she began to materialize in the living room.
His wife heard her crying even before she'd arrived.

"Husband, do you *hear?*"

His wife had a wild look in her eyes and he immediately
thought she was having a nervous breakdown. "What? My
dear, you must calm…"

"A woman *weeping!*"

"Your imagina… *my God!*"

They both stared in shock at a weeping Stephanie now
kneeling on the floor in front of the husband, wife, and now
sleeping child.

The wife grabbed her husband's arm. *"Dear God!"*

Something sounded different so Stephanie looked up to
find herself in the world, not in spirit any longer! Red with
embarrassment but knowing reality is what it is, she stood up,
bowed slightly and daubed her tears with her fingers. "Forgive
me for intruding." She bowed to them again. "My people have
a serious custom not to disturb another's home. Forgive me.
I will leave now."

But the wife shouted, reaching out her hand, "NO! *Wait…*
please! Who… what are you? An angel?"

Stephanie shook her head, straightened her holy dress,
and smoothed over the rich royal blue fabric and golden
embroidery that added to the impression that she was indeed
otherworldly. "I am the sister of your *King,* the *true* heir to
our forefather's throne. Some of our people, because they led
holy lives, were able to understand the spirit world and others

have gifts such as you have just seen. But Jargono killed them *all* except me. He is a *traitor!*"

Shaken to his core, the husband barely got his words out, "He... killed his own people?"

Stephanie leveled her eyes into his as she clearly confirmed, "Yes."

He leaned back against the couch, being overcome by that picture and the further understanding that followed, "My God, if he kills his own people... then ..."

His wife finished his thoughts for him. "Then what would he do to everyone else? Why does he even care about destroying foreigners?"

Stephanie answered coldly, "My brother only cares about himself."

"Himself and his new queen!" said the wife.

Stephanie reeled while asking, "Queen? *What Queen?*"

"Queen Karen! Long blond hair and blue eyes like mine except hers are cold, *very cold.*"

Stephanie peered into the young woman's mind to see her image of this *queen.* The wife had been watching the newly established TV broadcast just that night, and Jargono had announced his Queen to the nation, along with the 'miracles' he determined to perform tomorrow. Anger burst in black rays from Stephanie's heart.

Seeing the rays, she grabbed her husband and exclaimed in fear, "*Oh God.*"

And he sheltered his wife in his arms, but was none too settled himself.

When Stephanie realized the burst, she calmed herself down. *Damn it, I've really got to learn to control myself.* "Forgive me. I didn't realize that would happen. I won't harm you. I'm... holy. I don't have evil in me."

The husband shouted back, pointing, "WELL, WHAT THE HELL WAS ALL THAT BLACK STUFF?"

Stephanie shook her head, calmly speaking. "Not evil. Righteous anger. *That woman, Karen,* murdered my mother! She ran over her in a car. Did it herself."

His wife turned to her husband and grabbed him by the shirt at his chest. "Run over by a car, just like our child's parents! Oh God! This... this is a sign!"

He shook his head, looked back at Stephanie then at his wife. "She could be making it all up. She's *obviously* been watching us."

Stephanie gently requested them, "Look in my eyes."

First to respond was the wife because she still felt Stephanie was an angel sent from God. As she gazed into Stephanie, the woman's words came out of their own accord, "Oh God! She's telling the truth! Can you help us please?"

Stephanie hesitated, "I... I don't have the power, yet, to defeat him."

The husband's anger flared before he could call it back. "Then get the *hell* out of my house. Who the hell are *you* to come in here?"

But her husband's disrespect completely scared his wife who admonished him as she grabbed him tightly. "*Please!* Don't speak to her like that. Can't you tell? She's a *holy* woman. *She wept for us!*" And he hung his head in embarrassment.

Feeling ashamed, Stephanie spoke again, tears running down her cheeks, her voice quivering, "I ... I'm sorry. I wish I had the power, but I don't. He's older than me, and far more experienced in the spirit world than I am."

Genuinely asking her a question, the woman's eyes met Stephanie's, "But I thought holy people had power over all devils?" She remembered hearing this somewhere but couldn't remember where.

Stephanie thought about the meaning of her words because they sounded absolutely correct! "Perhaps... but Jargono isn't a devil. He's a man. I think it's for men to deal with men. If... if you and others would band together, pray to God to defeat him... I am sure..."

The husband scoffed at her, "BAH! So then we would all *die!*"

Lady Stephanie met their eyes and pointed to the child. 'Choices' was all she said. Then, as she waved her hand, they heard the wife's earlier question echo, *"But my husband, would we be alive inside if we did such a thing?"* And the *faithwalker* vanished before their eyes in the same mystery as she had appeared.

ᨆ

Feeling crushed, Vaughn was barely able to whisper, "Do you have any idea how hard it will be to escape with so many people?"

The tall elder scolded him, mocking, "Did *I* promise to save these people? You shouldn't have *raised our hopes* if you couldn't *keep your word*. I was all prepared to *die*. I..."

Blackness surged all through Vaughn and barely holding on, he turned to the other two elders on the platform, and dictated in deadly calm, "Someone shut him up, or I will, permanently!"

For a moment they just stared at this young man, thinking, *He's really too young to be ordering us around like this.* But then a young woman, who had been closely watching the elders and Vaughn since his arrival, shouted at them loudly enough for everyone to hear, "You know, you're our elders and all that, but *this* young man gives us a chance to *live.* Maybe... maybe you don't care about everyone's lives as much as we do because you're *old!*"

At hearing *that* the crowd hushed with hard stares at the elders. It became apparent that the boundaries that normally separated the generations and kept the young from asserting themselves, these social restraints were on the verge of breaking down, so the other two elders had a sudden change of mind, grabbed their fellow elder and forced him to sit down. Begrudgingly, the now seated elder kept quiet but couldn't take his stare off Vaughn who again admitted to himself that there was indeed truth in what the old man had spoken. Mr. Ranger realized he shouldn't have expected to deny them the other towns. *Now I know why I was led to ask how they survived. They're all related through marriages, business and such. I'm an IDIOT! I didn't* think *about what I'd found out. Oh, God! Do they have any idea how long it will take to move this entire people up and down* one tree? *It'll take all night! And how can we conceal ...*

While he sat on the podium, a picture developed in Vaughn's mind, moving him to speak before he could even see it clearer, "Look, if you want me to rescue you, you need to listen to me on how to do it. If you don't do *exactly* as I say, I'll leave without you, *do you hear me?*" Vaughn's ranger sternness had returned, along with his self-control. *As young as I am, can I* really *pull this off?*

The stocky elder, who yesterday also had mocked Vaughn, asked, "What do you want us to do?"

"Tell all the people in the square to be quiet so I can instruct them."

But the crowd filled not only the square but practically every open spot the eye could see in the little town's area.

"PEOPLE, BE QUIET! OUR *RANGER,* HERE, REQUESTS IT SO HE CAN SPEAK TO YOU."

Everyone hushed almost at once! The stocky elder noted Vaughn's amazement and explained, "Young ranger, we may be poor, but our people know how to respect that which should be respected! Please don't judge us too harshly by a few bad examples."

Vaughn understood the elder's hung head was an apology for yesterday and nodded to him, and then Vaughn rose up, by what strength, he knew not. Spot sat up straight to one side of him while on the other side, Little One was hugging his leg so he wrapped his arm around her shoulder. Vaughn became a spectator again to his own self as he addressed the crowd, "Good people, you must do *exactly* as I say, if we are to have *any* chance at all to save our lives. I was on my way to escape, *by myself,* when I found this child clinging to her deceased mother. Then I came to you and offered my help at the risk to my own life, when I could have just passed you by and thought only of myself. Now, we are escaping together and if we are to succeed, we all must be *wise.*"

Someone in the crowd spoke up, "We will do as you say." And the rest, in unison, offered their consent as well.

"You must hide the extra people that come to town. Hide them in your houses, out of sight, anywhere, as long as they are out of sight. You must quickly send out people in the directions from which they are coming, and warn them to be secret about *why* they come."

The stocky elder spoke up, "But except in the road, there is no one to see us and those coming know to only go through the woods"

But Vaughn countered his thoughts, "Believe me, those guards aren't fools. If they fail at their job, they'll die and they know it." As the crowd nodded, he continued his instructions. "Please, do as I say. It's still early, so I doubt they've checked up on you yet. Pass this word along, that you're having a secret meeting here, to pray so that you may all die together. These words are to be spoken aloud, but the other words about our true intent are to be whispered only." The people murmured with understanding.

"We leave this evening, but there are too many to leave all at once. I want you to pick out leaders for every twenty five people, and number each group. The leaders shall determine which group shall leave from what direction, and when. I'm sure that after the sun goes down, we'll only have a single hour before this place will be burned to the ground. The *King* will wait till everyone is home from work and it's totally dark for best effect. That's when he's scheduled to be on TV, according to yesterday's continuous announcement. ONE HOUR! That's all the time we have to make it to the

Southern Woods. You'll appoint runners to go between each group so that my instructions will be known quickly while we travel. I'm the only one who knows the way to escape. It'll be totally dark when we go through the woods but you can't risk lights."

A voice cried out from the crowd in doubt, "But how can you find your way in the dark? And in response there were grumblings but then also a tide of rebukes.

Vaughn sighed, "It's *your* choice to trust me, or not. If you don't, *stay here!*"

Hearing that, the crowd assented to the wisdom of the better choice. After they quieted down again, Vaughn continued, "I *will* lead you safely through the mine fields and over the fence, but in order for everyone to make it, we'll have to form one, I say ONE, single-file human chain. Everyone will hold the hand of, or a rope from, the one in front of them *and* you must *all* be silent! Not a *word*. Not a *whimper*. Now go do what I've told you to do."

As Vaughn watched all of the people nodding and scurrying about, he sat down again on the edge of the concrete platform, propping his head up in his hands with his elbows on his knees. Little One sat down next to him and propped herself the same way while Spot sat on Vaughn's other side. The young lady who'd taken care of Little One yesterday came to them with food and drink. "How are you, Mr. Ranger?" Little One looked over at him and seeing him deep in thought, she answered for them, "Oh, we're fine. He's just thinkin'. He does that a lot. Thank ya so much for the food!"

Then Vaughn realized they had said there were towns all along the border. *Oh God, they all can't make it. Even these will only be a few compared to the ones lost.*

Vaughn called out to the elders up on the platform with him, "I need volunteers." He hesitated then continued, "Volunteers willing to risk their lives for their fellow man! Have them come to me in ten minutes."

Still sitting at the same spot ten minutes later, Vaughn found himself appraising a group of twenty-five grown men and women! *How did I, a* kid, *find myself in this position?* Things had moved so fast Vaughn hadn't had the time to consider any of the consequences for himself, only what he perceived had to be done. *That's how… hmm!*

"I've asked you here because I've realized there are many more towns that won't be able to go with us tonight, but there's still a chance for them, all of them, to escape!"

"How?" they asked in astonishment.

"All that's required is they not be in their towns when the fire falls and that they actually believe they have a real chance to escape. Jargono and everyone else don't believe that to be possible and that's *precisely* why it's even that much *more* possible! No one will be looking for them in the mine fields! And as an afterthought, they probably figure that anyone foolish enough to go there would die in those woods anyway. But if the people stay on the animal trails, they won't hit mines. There won't be any evidence that they didn't stay in the towns because the place will be thoroughly burnt-up. Send messages to those you know and trust in the neighboring towns then have them call their neighboring towns. Warn the others not to be in their towns when the fire falls. Also tell them they have to find their way to this location. They are to take the path west that goes alongside the road, until they get to a pair of very large Oak trees on either side of an animal trail. Then tell them, *and this is very important,* that they must have a dog on a leash in front of their file. They must go where the dog goes but they must stick to the animal trails. They can't let the dog or the people go off the animal trails! Each of you volunteers will need to stay behind at various locations of your choosing to help and make sure the people escape. It'll take months for them all to make it here, and somehow they'll need to keep themselves secret and find a way to subsist but it *can* be done.

"*My God,*" the First Elder jumped up, railing, "This is *crazy!* A DOG? FOLLOW A *DOG? Wherever the* dog *goes?*"

Spot growled, his upper doggy lip quivering, baring his fangs. Vaughn glared at the other two elders, "Cover his mouth shut and tie him to the post over there. He can stay!"

The two other elders hesitated, looking at Vaughn, but then the volunteers all agreed. "You either do as this Ranger said, or we'll add you to the post with him!"

The stocky elder bowed his head to Vaughn, "Sir Ranger, I'm sorry for my delay. This is difficult. But please, I mean no disrespect, but I thought you wanted secrecy. If we call all the towns then how is it to be secret?"

"The government will only be interested in what they perceive as a real escape attempt. That's why, what we do *here,* close by, is so important to be secret and disguised. But it's to be expected that many will be calling each other during this last day, and that wild rumors will abound. I think the government's reaction will be very similar to your Elder we just *shut up!*"

"Then how will our neighbors believe?"

"I'm sure you have a certain way of communicating to each other when you're completely serious. Use it! Then, it will be up to each person's faith as to whether they listen or not... but at least they get a chance."

So it went that all day people came and as soon as they arrived they were whisked away to hide. Eventually, every room in every humble abode became packed full of people pressed so tightly together that there was very little room to move. Vaughn figured there had to be close to a thousand souls. That would be close to five towns worth of people. He was also quite impressed at the villagers' adaptability, how they managed to slyly communicate where there was still room to hide someone and how they worked out subtle means to care for all their quests.

But Vaughn kept shaking his head to himself. His mind was trying to tell his heart something but each seemed to be outside spectators to the grander picture that had swallowed him but then the feeling grew worse. "Mr. Ranger, why ya shakin' yer head?" Little One leaned over on Vaughn's shoulder with her face close to his. "It's an easy plan. Even *I* can follow it, "she assured him with a big smile. "Just follow the doggie!"

Spot nudged her so she squeezed his fur and patted his head, "Good doggie!"

That's it... what his mind was trying to tell his heart! *It's* too *easy. But why?* He wished Stephanie was with him

571

to discuss the plan. He remembered their last kiss together and instantly got teary-eyed. *No time for that now! She had confidence in me. She was* proud *of me. Oh, IDIOT!* Vaughn pulled out the Book from his backpack.

When Little One saw the beautiful cover, she spoke in awe as she traced the golden words with her finger, "Mr. Ranger, what do these words say?"

Vaughn was shocked. *She can see them! I know there's got to be a* very *special reason why my vision told me to save this child.* "Wisdom, Little One. From the Inside Out." *Hmmm, or perhaps all children can see it. Lana could … and my second vision had lots of children.*

"What's wisom?" she was captivated again.

"It's knowing how to *use* what you know, dear." Vaughn put his arm around her. "Just watch, I need to do this." She nodded then looked at him very seriously, feeling the importance of what he'd set his mind to do.

Vaughn asked his question to Wisdom, "What do you do when an escape plan from a greater evil seems too easy to succeed?"

Wisdom: What does the enemy have to gain in your succeeding?

Oh God! Think, Vaughn. Think!

"What if I don't know the gain?"

Wisdom: What seems valuable to you, is to your enemy also.

"What? I want them out of the towns. But… why would that be valuable? Oh God, the mine fields. If he wanted to invade other countries, he would have to go through their own ancient mine fields. The bastard doesn't care if they escape the fire, he'd rather have them die by the mines then both purposes are served. The mines are cleared and the people are impressed by his power and wisdom. But... he doesn't know I've found a way through. No... that doesn't sound right, either.

"Hmm, suppose he figured the people knew about the mines. Some would die, yes, but he'd know that some would sacrifice their lives to clear a safe path. But that means that others would escape through the path they cleared. Hmm, he wouldn't allow it. Would he? Maybe he doesn't really care? No! He cares.

"Hmm, what's valuable to me? I want them to stay on the animal trails. But how would he cause them to scatter from the trails? Scatter... scatter... as when people are afraid, then they'd run blindly... fear! But how would he scare them? His power! Could he do that? Stephanie said he could make her feel things. Look what he did to Jean."

Wisdom: While it only requires a brief instant of his presence at each town to call the fire, it would take a more concerted effort to produce such fear for so many and burning up so much requires tremendous effort.

Vaughn noted with a bit of surprise that for the first time the Book began to talk specifically to him. *I wonder why? Don't look a gift book in the mouth, Vaughn.* "You're saying it's impossible for him to do. But... Oh God, Stephanie's father! I'm sure he's turned him into a demon."

Wisdom: Even Jargono knows he can't set the Earth demon free without keeping direct concentration upon him, especially that one! In answer to your other question: For certain extremely rare or unique situations, the specific details are as general as possible!

Vaughn shook his head at himself, remembering how easily the Book reads his mind, but he returned to the important problem, "Then how would he scare them?"

Wisdom: What's wisom?

Vaughn was shocked! *The Book repeated Little One's question!*

"Knowing how to use what you know... I know?"

Wisdom: There can be no further wisdom given at this time! Vaughn closed the Book, shaking his head as before.

Little One grew concerned, "Don't worry, Mr. Ranger, I know you'll save us. You saved *me*." And she hugged him, pressing her sweet little cheek against his.

Saved you... but the blackness hasn't come for you yet. THE BLACKNESS! Oh God. Vaughn reopened the Book, "Don't get stubborn with me now! Answer me this, Does Jargono control the Blackness?"

Wisdom: He was able to lure it, but no one controls it. It no longer exists upon the Earth!

"Then, where did it all go?"

Wisdom: What's wisom?

"The Blackness in my vision became the giant evil heart... became the Earth Demons. So it's *finite!*"

Wisdom: As finite as the water in a river.

"So... when I destroyed Demon Glen, I destroyed some of the Blackness. That means what was left all went into Stephanie's father. If I kill him, the Blackness is gone from the Earth, except for all those demon offspring. But this still doesn't answer my original question. If it's not the Blackness that scares the people, then what does?

Wisdom: Don't get stubborn, but there are rules, even for me! This is the last wisdom offered at this time: The enemy of my enemy is my friend.

Vaughn sat back pondering. *What would be able to scare so many? I'm Jargono's enemy. Who else is my enemy who would help him? OH LORD GOD! But I thought they weren't allowed... unless... but God won't break His word! But, then how could it be? Oh Lord God, but I know it* will *be. How are we to fight such a thing?*

Vaughn slowly stood up, held prisoner to the immense responsibility just dropped on his young head through understanding the danger that would visit this people and there was no time to think about himself not being up to this task. There was only understanding, and the responsibility to do all he was able to do. He ran his fingers over Stephanie's letter tucked into his uniform's inside vest pocket.

"Listen to me, everyone!" All the people hushed again, while Vaughn tingled with the terrible knowledge he was about to convey, "Pass this word along to all. This night shall be a night to remember. This is not a night like other nights! For this night, good and evil shall battle over your very souls while you try to escape your destruction."

In response, the bald elder inquired with all the people nodding to his question, "What do you mean, Ranger?"

Vaughn stood up straight, folding his arms across his chest, "I do *not* believe it will be as easy to escape as it seems to be. I believe both good and evil watch over you this night. I believe your faith in goodness shall be tested this night to prove you, whether you be worthy to be saved!"

The stocky elder spread out his hands, pleading, "But we don't know what to do. We never thought we had to be *worthy!*"

Part of Vaughn was just like this elder, *I don't know what to do, either.* Yet, he could feel the souls of all these people he now had charge over. *All my struggles, my sufferings, have brought me to this day, to* this *purpose! I feel it!* In Vaughn's feelings, in an extended moment of time, his life flashed before his eyes. How he rescued Stephanie, fought to help her understand, how he'd failed over and over his own saying *no matter what,'* how he fought the Blackness that tried to transform Tracy, how he fought Demon Glen and Jargono, how he reached down into his gut to pull up the knowledge of what Truth, Love and Life really are when there was no one to help and when all he could do was rock, bump his head, and wander all alone, surrounded by darkness.

Vaughn's voice came out powerfully, and all felt there was much more to this young man than met the eye, "Dear people, *every day* is a day we are supposed to prove ourselves worthy to live, because life is a precious gift, a sacred gift, a gift of love and hope. In your hearts you can feel right now that life is connected to a Greater Life and that Greater Life is called God, because there is no power greater than the Life, the Love which supplies all goodness to us. The ways of Greater Love are bigger than our minds and hearts and that's why we can learn from them. But many people live, no, *exist,* in the darkness of their hearts and minds, unaware of such knowledge until they *die* and are sent to eternal torment. For we are *not* mere physical bodies as our teachers and our government would have us believe so they can manipulate us to their ends. We are *persons,* and our sense of personhood is *not* a physical sense, but of that special light within our hearts and minds.

"Judge for yourselves by what means you perceive the person inside your own body and inside your loved ones. Is it by mere physical sound or light or sensation? Or is it by a far greater sense of their personhood and yours? Though our bodies grow old, the decay of a person is not based upon the physical world but upon the nature of their character. This night our characters shall be tested because it is *time* for us to be freed from the darkness that has held us prisoner for so long." Vaughn paused a moment to reflect upon his own words, and upon his growing passion, *I've never felt quite like this before. Dear God, these words I speak! They are part of the great hope I've had all along. And now... now I speak them. I mean them... I am living them.* Vaughn refocused upon the people and continued with even more passion.

"Evening is at hand. Soon we shall begin our journey together. Pass along that all should spend their last hour here in prayer. If any be conscious of wrong in their heart, in their mind, in their spirit, they must pray the Lord God to forgive them and right them. You *must not* enter this night bearing grudges or holding onto evil. You must right yourselves before God and with each other. This night, *every one of you* shall be holding the hand of his *neighbor,* depending upon *each other* for your very lives!"

Vaughn leaned over toward the crowd as increased power swelled inside him. He threw open his arms and his eyes riveted upon them all. He noted that less and less he felt like a boy, even though reality is what reality is. With the semblance of a rainbow glowing around him, his words pleaded with all the people in a kind of powerful song:

"For I tell you,
this night evil hunts your souls,
and it shall call to you,
from inside of you,
from where it has grown.
It shall call to you in your fears.
It shall find your guilt,
like the reins upon a horse,
it shall pull you into that abyss.

Cut the reins.
Throw off the blinders.
Let the Lord God who is Light,
be light within you.
For he made you out of his goodness.
God is goodness.
That shall be you.
Which are you?
Good or evil.

Though they both abide within you,
yet, they abide not together.
For evil is a forcing spirit.
It demands you to be it,
demands your loyalty,
so that it can treacherously

deliver you to torment.
Do not define yourselves so.
The evil in you is not you.
Let the goodness of God cast it from you,
because God is love.
This night, let us all be one,
together in goodness.
Only in true goodness
is there oneness."

Silence. Stillness. Not a soul moved. Love. Tears. Vaughn eased back, having preached so hard he was winded. They felt his life in those words, also felt a Greater Life in those words. He had never ever done any such thing as *this*. With tears now breaking from him, he finished somehow softly.

"Let the goodness of God
Show you how to trust
In His goodness,
No matter what."

They had never heard or seen such a communication. One young woman fell forward on her knees in front of him, pleading in tears, "Sir, we don't understand! How can we do such things within only one hour?"

Deeply moved, Vaughn sat down and spoke peacefully so all hushed and drew even closer, straining to hear his words.

"What causes a well-hidden deer or rabbit to run from its predator?"

The woman answered, "It becomes afraid."

Vaughn's eyes met hers, "Why? Why should it fear, when if it stays at peace, the hunter won't find it? The hunter growls, stirs up the grass, the brush… to do what?"

She answered with a child's expression, "To scare the prey into running."

Vaughn nodded, "The prey loses faith in the strength of the protection God gave it, allowing the threat of death to touch its heart. It then believes in the power of death more than the power of life and it runs, not realizing that as soon as death captures its heart, it has already lost the battle to live.

"Tonight, when *you* are tested by evil, if evil has remained inside of you to touch your heart, you won't have the faith in life to preserve you, because death already has hold of you. You will run and die. You must gain God's forgiveness now, this hour, or you won't be able to resist.

"When we take to the trails, no matter what you see, what you hear, you must *not* break the human chain. You must keep hold of your neighbor's hand or rope. You must *not* depart from the trail. If any depart, the ones left on each end must find each other and reconnect the human chain.

"Remember, Goodness is Life. It makes sense as human beings to always choose Goodness, even over preserving our bodily life, if it becomes a choice between the two. The body is for the sake of the *person* inside, *not* the other way around. Destruction of the body is terrible, but self-destruction of the soul, the person, is worse. Which of you would not gladly give up your lives to save your children, your wives, your husbands, or perhaps even friends, or even townsfolk, and some, even strangers? Which of you when hearing a lie that would harm others would *not* risk bringing truth to light? Or, would you rather keep yourself from suffering danger, but allow others to be harmed by what you could have prevented? You *will* suffer the consequences, *regardless*.

"Deep inside you, you know Goodness is greater than your physical lives, Understand this principle and apply it deeply to yourselves for within it is the knowledge of God. Evil may be able to touch your mortal bodies in this world, but it cannot kill your heart and mind when goodness is there. Only *you* can allow evil to kill you inside by believing in it more than goodness. THERE IS NO GOOD REASON TO DO THAT. Goodness is life to the person. Do not forsake it tonight. Goodness is to stick to the trail!" And Vaughn finished off by shaking his head. Little One shook her head to help emphasize the point and Spot gave one affirmative *Ruff*, as he sat straighter than he ever had.

The people solemnly passed the instructions all through the town. Silent prayers were interspersed periodically by weeping, some out of fear, but also out of hope and remorse. Dare they hope when they had none?

Now the sun was finally leaving so the leaders came to their young ranger and reported that they had organized the people. They would all flee to the edge of the Southern Woods, and from there head for the trail that went alongside the Western Road just behind a thick row of trees. They would be careful crossing the road, then move west on the trail until they come to the two large Oaks that guarded a path south. There they would wait for Ranger Vaughn to begin their journey to freedom. They awaited Vaughn's word now.

When he finally stood up, looking quite grave, the people knew and the messengers immediately passed the word down a human chain to each group's leader. The most southerly groups went first. Those behind took their places, then those behind them took theirs... Groups on the northern side of town left at the same time as the first southern groups, but had to circle around. There were too many people to be able to all safely escape from the south in time.

Vaughn remained at the southern edge of town with Spot and Little One, urging the people onward. It was only a ten minute walk through the field from the southern edge of town to the edge of the forest. Fifty minutes later, the last group left the village and started through the field and at the close of the hour, Vaughn stood at the edge of the forest with the people... but nothing happened.

As Vaughn waited to be last in line, he told the first courier, "Quickly, move down the path."

They passed the word as the groups that had left from the north started joining them and Vaughn gave that same message to their couriers. But as the people moved, some began to mumble, perhaps even grumble. Nothing was happening. There were those beginning to doubt already and Vaughn thought he heard an angry cast in some words between people. A half-hour passed and his worst expectations began to be realized. Some people began going past Vaughn, back to the town. It particularly pained him to see some of the teenagers, just like him, leave them, but he held his peace and kept moving, whispering under his breath. Little One and Spot heard him, "Give him your all, Stephie! I'm doing the same."

CHAPTER TWENTY-TWO

Death and Freedom

It was publicized to be the very last national news broad-cast so what was left of the country, or at least the northern half of the former United States, all tuned in apprehensively to the only channel left functioning. There had been rumors....

At eight p.m. sharp, TV sets all across the north all tuned in to see men in strange gray uniforms flanking Arnold Less-crassnmost who, not looking like his usual challenging self, immediately started reading from a script, "There is no more New York City, no more San Francisco, no more Chicago, no more Detroit, no more Milwaukee, no more Philadelphia... There are no cities with population over three hundred thou-sand left. Every major city has been obliterated by the plague and now officially sealed off from everyone. No exceptions at penalty of immediate execution.

This is the official policy statement of the new government. First, the name of our new country. There shall be no name! Such greatness-to-be cannot be uttered in a single name. WE are all the name of this new, rebuilding country. Second, as you know, the former United States had monetarily bailed out every major business and loaned trillions of dollars to citizens' education. The loans were never paid back so from this point forward, in order to keep our great country functioning, this new government has taken control of this tremendous debt. There are no more dollars and our monetary system shall use units of dol. Since everyone is deeply indebted to your new government, and because of the terrible strain of the Civil War we fight, all citizens will report to government centers to receive their work assignments. Understand this, you are in DEBT to us and we intend to collect what you OWE. If you can prove that you are not in debt, please bring such documentation to the work centers and after we are done processing all the debtors, we shall issue you your debt-free papers. However, if you intend to find gainful employment, you must then apply to our work-centers to see what jobs are left for you. Our plan will take time and sacrifice, but this is YOUR country. We will all work very hard to make it great again.

This is my last broadcast to you ..." Arnold paused from reading his script, and it became obvious to all that this was the first time he'd seen it. The man next to him who had some strange medallion around his neck stepped closer and nudged him to proceed. In a far more subdued tone, one that sent chills through the audience who knew him, he continued to play his part. "This is my last broadcast to you. This is the last national show of any kind. From here on, each of us must focus to strengthen our own local governments and all the attention of our faithful citizenry should be aimed at following the instructions of your local government's representatives but rest assured, they will all take their orders from the top.

Third, all religions of any kind are heretofore BANNED. They are all illegal and whoever is found practicing them shall be immediately executed."

He paused again, looking up at the man standing next to him, staring at him half in fear, half in defiance, "I'm not reading the rest of this..." The man instantly pulled his pistol and shot him in the head in front of all of the viewers. He then took the script from Arnold's dead hand, flicked off a piece of brain clinging to it, and finished, "Anyone caught in rebellion of any kind shall be immediately executed. I, Arnold Lesscrassnmost, do hereby confess that I have willfully challenged our new government, holding onto our old ways, and now realizing my crimes, I am guilty of death."

The man then turned his steely gray eyes directly into the camera and spoke in an icy-cold voice, "Of course, you know we wrote that for him, knowing exactly how he would react! But that just proves our point. We know you! All of you! So if you have any guilty thoughts, I suggest you purge yourself of them quickly, before we have time to knock on your doors. The world went through a Dark Ages before and came out stronger. We shall do so again. I leave you with this slogan for our new country, which all of the faithful shall repeat seven times before going to sleep: For the good of the country. For the good of the country ... " And as he kept repeating it, the TV screen faded to a blank gray as if it wasn't even turned on. For the next week all sets were gray, until the first new local shows began broadcasting. The first show? For the Good of the Country.

From the Ethereal Corridor Lady Stephanie looked over the huge, circular commons area in the very center of the new capital city where all of the people had now gathered. Many ascending bleachers had been erected for this occasion. At one edge of the circle, with what looked to be a royal palace and its grounds behind it, a huge stage had been erected with a high platform draped by plush red, royal-blue, and black tapestries, depicting odd ancient battles and hideous creatures. But at the top of each tapestry was Jargono's enlarged image showing his bare foot over everything. It went well with the theme of their government religion and everyone understood he was the fulfillment of their faith. After all, it was a large, gray foot that stood over the whole world in all of their churches. Now it just had been revealed to whom that foot belonged. It was that simple.

A wide corridor arced halfway around the royal platform and had been cordoned off by colorful ropes. While facing it, at the right end of that cordoned area and the same height as the stage, built all the way up out of huge, rectangular, gray stone stood a rectangular stone platform designed to look like an ancient sacrificial altar. Many whimpering children had carefully crept to the edge and peered down, but there was no evidence of any way to descend or climb up! One could only wonder how they got there in the first place. The rest of the children that filled that whole area merely crowded together with the older ones hugging the younger.

On the left side was another platform, also the same height as the *King's* stage. It had a single royal-blue tapestry surrounding its whole base and had red and gold Appendaho embroidery around its edges. *My God!* Stephanie thought. *It's* exactly *like my holy dress!*

Jargono needed no microphone as he spoke to all his faithful crammed into the public area while government television cameras were strategically positioned to both broadcast and keep watch. There had to be at least fifty-thousand people packed into the stands and aisles.

Stephanie burned with each fiber of her being. Never before having presented herself to so many people, far from daunting her, it satisfied her deepest desire. Never had she felt more powerful. Yet, she knew she still wouldn't be able to beat Jargono, even though she'd learned much about her abilities.

Stephanie glared at him and his Queen. *The NERVE! I can't* believe *they're wearing the same clothing from the sacred cave paintings!* As Stephanie tried to control her feelings, while still only in the Ethereal Corridor, she listened to his words.

"You have all heard my decree. Here on this altar are all the adopted foreign children that the true followers of our new kingdom have sacrificed to show their purity and commitment to our greater good. These parents shall all be rewarded with special positions. Before your very eyes and as the broadcast shall carry live to our whole country, these children and all the towns of the foreigners shall be consumed as I raise my hands. There are cameras set up at every town to broadcast their destruction. Afterwards, I shall tell you how each one of you can *personally* prove yourselves to be a *meaningful* part of our glorious new vision. *One* vision, *one* country, *one* world!"

Then the crowd saw a young woman with red hair in three braids climb through the colorful ropes, cross the cordoned off area, and climb up the steps onto the left stage. The cameras followed her as well, panning and zooming in on her every detail. The largest braid was tied with a royal-blue ribbon, embroidered on the edges with gold thread. Her long-sleeved, long royal-blue dress was rimmed with two-inch thick gold ribbon at the bottom and sleeve ends. Golden thread wove in V-shape embroidery in between her breasts then flared outward in an ancient design up to and around her neck. And now she stood on stage quite erect with an undoubtedly regal air to her.

Back in Stephanie's old hometown, the other teens who immediately recognized her began pointing and mocking at their TV sets. They had expected to see Karen but *her?* Waverly began to wonder. *Where's Vaughn? Is he even alive?* All the others who'd come into Stephanie's acquaintance after she'd moved reacted with equal surprise but with more positive regard than those from her original home. Jean immediately had tears, and Lana clung to her Mommy, shaking her little head and wondering if she should tell her. Stephanie's most recent classmates nodded their heads, feeling something they couldn't explain, and for some unknown reason, they found themselves holding their breath. Some in the crowd pointed at her, as well. In fact, all eyes were upon *her!* "Hmmm, I wonder what *this* is all about", the Highest Councilor mused to Grinchback. Queen Yinauqua grabbed her husband's arm with one trailing word, "No…"

The young woman, stepping past the little podium and microphone to the very front of the stage, spoke in a crystal clear voice that seemed to ring like a loud bell, yet had the tenderness to caress the ears, "Is the great King afraid to have a *girl* speaking before the people?"

"I told you she would come," his queen whispered to him, and he nodded.

"I'm busy, come back later," he mocked, and some of the crowd laughed.

"Is that any way to treat your sister and true heir to the throne you speak of?"

Murmurs. Jeers. The King held up his hand for silence. Silence.

"What's she talking about?" His queen's bitter tone tickled his ear but he hushed her and spread out his hands, as if welcoming Stephanie.

"Oh, I've always wanted a sister. You see? I had this stage *on the side* prepared just for *you!*"

Some spectators laughed while others continued to murmur.

I figured as much, but it doesn't matter. I have to do what I can do. So Stephanie replied in a coldness that sent chills through the crowd, "I see you've made the murderer of my mother your queen. A wise choice for a man like you!"

The crowd hushed.

Jargono responded in his same cavalier manner, "On second thought, I think you're insane, or, *oh my*, perhaps a *jealous* woman."

More in the crowd roared with laughter.

Stephanie raised her hand and the sky filled with dark clouds and lightning flashes. The people began to wonder if there was a connection. She raised her other hand and immediately the lightning struck the buildings at the edge of the great circle, where the people had overflowed. Some people started screaming in terror but the king brushed his hand in the air as if shooing away a fly and the clouds and lightning instantly disappeared. The people went from terrible fright to relieved laughter as the word spread of the King's superior power. But Queen Karen, dismayed at Stephanie's abilities, dug her nails into Jargono's arm, and he read her thoughts, *NO! That BITCH! Not* her!

Stephanie responded, "What a shame the *Great King Jargon* had to bother swishing my lightning away."

His queen whispered venomously, "Don't talk with her. *Kill her!*"

But Jargono responded politely to Stephanie, taking the high road, "It was hardly any effort."

The crowd roared in laughter again. This was fast becoming the best entertainment ever.

And when the crowd hushed to hear Stephanie's reply, she decided to continue with Jargono's same cordial manners, "At least you admit you had to counter my power! Power I have because I AM your sister!"

She'd outsmarted him again. He remembered now, how her mind had been one step ahead of his in certain areas. The crowd hushed again, wondering. This truth was now in the light.

Jargono sighed in distress, "I can't help it if you're tainted like these children here. That's why you all *must* be destroyed. I can't show favoritism to traitors, even if they *are* my family!"

And the crowd Oohed and Ahhed at his devotion to them.

I have to be careful. If I provoke him too much too soon, I won't have time to show the people. "I repeat, why bother? What does the *Great King Jargono* have to fear from me, or these innocent children?"

Jargono smiled warmly, speaking quite sympathetically, "It's not about fear, dear sister, but purity. WE must purify reality so our power can reign again. Nothing would please me more than for you to join in my country's cause to greatness. Come join me!"

At hearing his graciousness and truthful admission of his passionate feelings, the crowd became even more captivated and some urged her to accept his offer. *She's not as powerful as our King... but she's powerful.* Many held their peace for various reasons.

Karen's eyes turned dark, but she held her mouth closed because she knew how far she could push her *king.*

Well, it's time, So Stephanie began what she came to do. "I might consider your offer if you first grant me privilege to speak my mind and heart to the people. I first have to know how they would receive my words before I can say whether I would join you or not!"

Jargono smiled again, which wasn't exactly comforting to Stephanie. *He acts like he's expected me to speak this way.* And he gave his reply, "Dear sister, you being the last of my people, it behooves me to give you a chance to redeem yourself, and that the people I so dearly love have a chance to see for themselves!"

Stephanie bowed a slight bow in Jargono's direction and then turned to the crowd, as the cameras zoomed in on her. *Dear God! I'm on national TV! How did I come to this? Oh well, nothing compares to the goodness I have to share.* "Dear people from all over the country, here and those watching on your televisions. What I ask you, for your sakes, is not to consider me one way or the other, but to simply judge in your hearts and minds the meaning I shall share with you. It *is* the meaning of life."

Jargono began clapping very loudly, enthusiastically, and Stephanie realized, as the crowd broke into raucous laughter again, that this wasn't going to be easy at all, but she pressed on with it, anyway. She narrowed her eyes upon the crowd and the sky grew darker and in a flat tone she admonished them, "Is it really that funny to make yourselves into jokes? If you laugh at the meaning of life, isn't that what you're doing, mocking your own selves?"

Some immediately stopped laughing, others jeered and yet others slowly calmed. When Jargono held up his hand for silence, everyone else hushed so Stephanie continued, "A hundred years ago, our government made certain *decisions* for us supposedly in our best interest but it is quite obvious that the former government only cared about *self-interest*. I dare say that there is not a single person here, except for those who belong to the government and reaped their corrupt rewards, not a single person here is sad to see the old government disappear, or at least glad to have *someone* more powerful in charge of them so that we can have *change*." And her last word almost seemed to mysteriously echo: change, change, change. Hushing in earnest now, the people began nodding as one, whispering their agreement to each other.

Jargono listened intently, trying to figure out how to catch Stephanie's intellect so that she couldn't outsmart him on anything else, as his queen's finger nails dug ever deeper into his arm. Both women amused him. The thought occurred to Jargono, *It might be quite entertaining to have Stephanie home for dinner and have my Queen prepare it. But, I'd better not eat the food!*

Stephanie continued, "I bring your memories back to history, how everyone had been in debt to the government, and through that debt, the government justified taking control of your lives even before you or I in this generation were born. Is that *fair?*"

And at *that* question, many people shouted in angry agreement with Lady Stephanie. It was too much for *Queen* Karen to bear and she whispered in her king's ear, "Are you *really* going to let her win this crowd over to her?"

But he whispered back, "Patience, my love!"

Stephanie noted Karen's behavior with particular interest but continued, "But have you ever wondered *how* they became indebted in the former United States? They never taught us that, did they?"

No one had ever even considered that question, but now that they thought about it, it *did* seem to be important. Giving her their undivided attention, it was clear they wanted to hear more, and likewise did all those watching on TV.

So Stephanie, waiting just a bit to build more suspense, continued, "I shall venture a guess. The government of the United States had corruptly set up an educational system that *required* everyone to go into debt to get their job preparation. They took all that tax money from the people, then made education *ridiculously* expensive, and *then* loaned the people's OWN TAX MONEY back to their children *and* required the people to pay it back with *interest*! What a slick trick! And most of that education was *worthless* as far as job skills go! Does anyone know how to spell SCAM?" It wasn't really a question but the people started spelling it out anyway. Even Jargono seriously became intrigued as he found himself learning from her, but as his Queen detected it, she scolded him, "You'd better keep your wits about you, and stop *gawking* at her". *This is so much fun,* Jargono thought to himself.

Stephanie obviously had full control over the crowd right now. *So it's time to shift.* "Dear people, isn't it time that we stopped allowing ourselves to be manipulated by governments and institutions?"

Many in the crowd nodded, some albeit slowly.

"The only way *not* to be manipulated is to be *responsible* for our *own* lives. Let *us* make a living that is rightfully *ours,* not the governments, because *we* earned it. Let *us* decide as a people how much tax and on what it should be spent. Let *us* have our own businesses *free* of government control and let *us* live and die upon the consequences of our *own* actions, for we all know by judging our own miserable lives here, today, that having the government take all our responsibility away from us, *control* and put us in fear *every day…* " Stephanie paused for effect and noted that the crowd, and she expected that even the whole country, was still and earnestly anticipating her answer. "Well, that has simply robbed us of so much joy. Has it not, dear people?"

And with *that* the crowd went into tears, many of them thinking about how their jobs had been chosen for them by the government, and mostly long hours of boring small factory jobs, and those who managed to select a special training were still held in that common bondage of high taxes and oppressive work requirements so that they couldn't even spend time with their families or enjoy the feelings of life.

Only a fortunate few, who managed small food markets or small farms such as the Appendaho, *if* their local government regulator was kind, were able to lead any semblance of a normal life, and it was exactly this semblance, this practical experience which had inspired Lady Stephanie into this portion of her speech. She had observed how her own store functioned and flourished, getting almost all of their supplies from local farmers, and bypassing the government suppliers, who would have required them to have ongoing account audits and were known to bleed owners dry. Also, instead of buying from the government suppliers, they were able to buy the surplus from larger stores or even directly from factories with a little money under the table. Whether under-the-table or legal deals, it was a real lesson in economy, that a free market functioned far better than any government controlled one, even if for no other reason than the decentralization of power. In fact, many small farmers had secretly set up their own little canning factories, shoe factories, and such. Though they did not produce quantity, their quality was not surpassed.

Stephanie finally held up her hand and the crowd immediately hushed. "Dear people, what has Jargono promised you? Has he shared with you this knowledge of your *own* power, your own *rights?* Or has he merely created a target for your displeasure but without giving you any power at all for yourselves? Look at these poor, innocent children. Have they wronged you? What better off will your life be if you destroy all the foreigners? Will *that* give you power over your lives? But even more than that, what is your responsibility to the *goodness* that makes *each* of you the person you are?"

Stephanie paused again, but this time not for effect because the people needed time to think for themselves. And when she saw that her questions had sunk deeply into their hearts, she continued softly, "Understand this, that if you embrace evil, harming the innocent, you will commit a wrong far deeper, far greater than any outside oppression of you. You will have killed your own selves inside, for the goodness in you *cannot* abide in you when you give yourselves over to such greed, illicit hatred, and foolish lust because of a promise of power."

Some wept here and there amidst others jeering and amongst many other reactions, and Jargono watched with a fascination he had never known before. Karen couldn't keep from turning a shade of red of which she was completely unaware, one which particularly delighted Stephanie who pleaded further. "Please, dear people, behold your king, King Jargono, and request of him to make *real* changes and to spare these people who have done none of us any harm."

Karen couldn't stand it anymore and whispered insistently, "Jargono, kill her, *NOW.* You're losing control of the people. "

He whispered back with a smile, "Patience, my Queen. I'm having fun. She isn't even a challenge yet."

At hearing *that*, Karen looked at him and saw that he might not kill her now. *Why would he want her to become a challenge?* She studied him. *There's a* glint *in his eye when he looks at her.* Karen turned *very* dark.

Stephanie waited, with folded arms, for their little marriage spat to finish. Using another of her faithwalking abilities, she could hear every word even though they whispered. *Vaughn was right. He wants us to challenge him.*

Instead of heeding his Queen's advice, Jargono entreated Stephanie further, "What do you have to offer the people?"

Her passionate answer rang with an energetic but soothing power, "Truth and a way to live happy, fulfilling lives." And as the *faithwalker* empathized with the crowd that now seemed to resonate so deeply with her, she began to realize that, *This might actually work. I can feel so many of them agreeing, longing ...*

Jargono folded his arms across his chest and stood up a little straighter. *It' time.* When the crowd saw his change in posture, there was a general flinch that moved through them like a wave. Feeling the sudden shift in their emotions stabbed Lady Stephanie in her heart. And Jargono mocked her, "Truth? OK, if your *truth* is so powerful, STOP ME!" He then turned to the people, spreading open his arms, "I mean, isn't that right, good people? Isn't *truth* most powerful? If what my dear sister has to offer you is indeed better for you, truer for you, then *her* truth is more powerful than mine, right? She should be able to stop me. Please don't ingratiate yourselves with words that sound nice but in practical application do *not* stand up to the test."

The crowd kept silent and a slight tear temporarily clouded Lady Stephanie's vision. While their heads moved very little, the eyes of the crowd went back and forth between their king and this stranger who might really be his sister. Many were thinking, *Our King is right.* And other's felt, *That sounds right.* Yet others considered, *He's mixing two different meanings of power. He's being slick.* And still others only cared about one thing, *What's in it for me? Which one of them will be best for me?*

Yet even before she confronted him, while in her prior meditations, Stephanie had expected his line of approach. *OK, so now we move further along this track.* "This isn't about me stopping you. Goodness is what goodness is. It must be appreciated from the inside out. It must be appreciated for what it is, not for something YOU demand it to do. Even if you *kill* me, it cannot change the meaning of goodness in each individual's heart." She turned towards the crowd again and exhorted them, "Look inside yourselves and bring forth from your hearts the goodness you feel. Let your mind examine its meaning. Does your goodness change? Can it suddenly be no good because someone else decrees that? Or is goodness good simply because it *is?*"

Jargono laughed, truly enjoying himself because he knew. "You mean *your* goodness isn't about results? What *good* is it then, to these so called *innocent* little vermin?" He pointed to the captive children. Some in the crowd also asked, *What good is it to us, then?*

Stephanie expected this diversion, too. "Ultimately, fate is in the hands of the Light, but what *kind* of life a person lives is in their hands and *theirs alone.* You, Jargono, have no power over the life in their hearts and minds except when they give it to you." And she turned back to the people to beseech them, "Seek in yourselves if your lives are worth living with no goodness in you. Then what are you really? No good?"

Her voice grew even more powerful, as she ardently implored the people. She didn't need a microphone, either, as she reached out her hands, "Listen to me, *please!* My ancestors lived for thousands of years in the hills to the West. They lived happy and peaceful lives, helping each other, and learning many mysteries of life. I can help you find that joy. It doesn't require taking another person's belongings, nor does it require killing. Can't you feel the emptiness caused by evil inside yourselves? You constantly have to pour more water into a bucket that has holes in it when you give yourselves over to evil. But Goodness allows the true water to stay inside you and heals all your wounds. Isn't it more delightful to you to find out how to love truly, than to feel the kind of so-called *power* your king offers you? Eventually, the water he provides you will run out, and you'll go thirsty, and hate your very lives for the unending torment you'll feel."

The crowd could feel her love touch them, no doubt about that. Her words were so clear, so dear, that some had tears in their eyes, and some whispered in their hearts, *Truth.* While others casted, *She's awful* young *to be telling us how to live.* While still others nodded, *She's not jaded like us. We really need youth to speak up more. It brings life back to us.*

Jargono yawned again then laughed, he'd heard it all before, and his light-hearted laughter broke the spell of stillness within which all had mysteriously found themselves. "Do her words even make sense to you at all? Does it make sense to *love our enemies?* That's what my pitiful father taught her, you know?"

The crowd gasped and Stephanie knew she couldn't counter that. *I hadn't expected this one. He's playing on their hatred, jealousy and greed. Alright, I did expect that, but not from this angle.*

When the crowd calmed, Jargono continued his oratory, "*That* is why my people were destroyed. Loving their enemy got them *killed!*" He peered deeply into Stephanie when he said it.

You BASTARD! Oh no you don't! You're baiting me. I'll not give you cause to kill me… not yet!

Jargono smiled, holding back his laughter over the swill he was about to feed the people next, "I had to have the strength to turn away even from my own family when I found that they were weak and allowed weakness to harm our great country. *Loving your enemies!* When I turned away, they had no protection and their enemy destroyed them. At least now, they cannot be used by *our* enemies to harm us!"

Damn you! You're so clever, aren't you? So even if I bring out the truth of what you did, you'll claim you had to do it for the good of the country. DAMN! The truth will make you look even better than you do now! You beat me in my own attack! Something's wrong. You're not that smart! Stephanie peered into Karen but Stephanie immediately felt a wall go up, blocking her. *Did she do that?! Or did Jargono?* But Karen smiled sweetly at her!

Jargono continued, throwing his arms open to the crowd and playing to the cameras, chuckling to himself as he did, *Karen will really love this one.* "See how true I am that I have even forsaken my own mother and father for your sakes. CHOOSE, MY PEOPLE. DO YOU WANT ME TO HAND OVER RULE TO *HER*, OR TO PROCEED WITH *OUR* GREAT DESTINY?"

His queen grabbed his arm in both hands now, making as if she gave him an extended kiss on the cheek, but whispering, "*What are you doing?*"

And he returned her kiss, along with her sneer, "Be *careful*, my queen. *I am the king.*"

Many of the people in the commons shouted and then chanted and others cheered, "King Jargon... KING JARGON... *KING JARGON...*"

After he let it go on for some time, he graciously raised his hands, asking for silence but they persisted for a bit. Their cheers even escalated before they slowly hushed. *What a great King. We are* truly *blessed by God!*

Tears ran down Stephanie's cheeks as she held her head high, letting the aching in her heart go uncontested. *Why should I fight the pain? I'd rather feel real, than feel a lie.* Golden light began to shine from her tears, turning into rainbow colors as that light radiated outward. Scattered people in the crowd put their hands to their mouths when they saw the shining tears as they cried as well. Others wondered how the spotlights could reflect in such a beautiful way. Others thought that perhaps she was sorry for speaking against their great king! *She looks very sorry.* Many thought, *Look at how the people love him. It should be obvious she's wrong. In fact, she looks ashamed of herself!*

King Jargon tenderly spoke his apology, "I'm sorry, dear sister, I know you gave it your best, but the people have chosen *freely.*"

Lady Stephanie pointed at the hundreds of young children as her mood began to change, "What about them?" Slowly, the light faded from her tears and her eyes began to glow brighter and brighter with red fire. Jargono's laugh was beginning to annoy her.

"The vermin? OK." He said with a smile and a deep bow. "I, as your merciful King, give them opportunity to choose! You children, do any of you *dare* disobey my power and try to go with *her*?"

Stephanie heard something she didn't like, "Try?"

Jargono looked her in the eye with dead seriousness, that same look he had when he had demanded from her the sacred treasure that he claimed belonged to him. She could tell that Karen had taken away most of his feelings for her. Jargono bowed again. "*Lady* Stephanie, *of course try*. If you can't escape me, what good are you? What use to the people?"

She turned her back on him to face the people once more, although this time, she didn't even know why because the people had already made their choice. "The words I have spoken already are a treasure to any who understand them."

Then Lady Stephanie turned to the children, knowing their lives and hers were now at stake, not knowing the final outcome, but knowing she had to commit all she had. She spoke passionately while glowing brightly, "Dear children, look at me. Look into my eyes and you'll see I speak the truth about life, life now, and life *after* we pass away from this world. I cannot promise you escape from this man here in *this* world. But I promise you that if you desire to stand by me, you'll be making the *right* choice. It's better to choose goodness, *even* when threatened. Look into his eyes and then into mine. You have a choice. Whose eyes would you rather look into for the rest of your life? I *know* you'll be able to look into mine in the eternal life to come."

Those beautiful tears reappeared, and shined their beautiful rainbow light upon the children. Stephanie knew that if anything, the *children* would understand the difference between the way love and hate look in people's eyes.

The children stared at both of them, back and forth. Their forlorn huddled mass seemed to sway back and forth then they looked at each other. After the first few backed away from Stephanie's gaze, most of the rest backed away from her out of fear. One little girl of about four, in very animated fashion was talking to them, pointing at Stephanie but they backed away from her, too.

Jargono laughed again, "It appears that even these *children*, EVEN IN DEATH, have sense enough not to believe your lies."

A red-hot glow now illuminated Lady Stephanie, but she restrained herself from attacking Jargono, because she knew it would fail and knew that failure would make things even worse, so she pointed, "THAT CHILD THERE HAS SENSE!"

Goodness is so predictable in its foolishness. Jargono laughed more, mocking her more, throwing out his hands wide. "THEN SAVE HER, OH *GREAT QUEEN.*" Jargono bowed with open contempt and mockery, quite confident that all that just happened made him look ten times better than he could have ever done by himself.

None of that was lost on Lady Stephanie's understanding. *But I have something greater to worry about. Oh God, the children.* She could feel every one of their sweet lives, as if she held each one individually in her loving arms. Her arms ached to hold them now. As her heart pounded, her chest burned with excruciating pain. Tears clouded her eyes, feeling the moment of her whole life, her whole purpose, her whole meaning, at hand. *I can't let those children die. I CAN'T!*

Jargono straightened up from his exaggerated bow and began to raise his hands and Stephanie could feel what was about to happen next. Her hand reflexively reached out towards the children, screaming, begging, commanding, *"NO!"*

The fire already began to fall upon them, burning them up before the eyes of the people who promptly fell on their faces, chanting his name, "King Jargon! KING JARGON! *KING JARGON!"*

But in that same instant, Queen Stephanie's whole being cried out in one voice, became one prayer, and reached through the spirit world, like through a tunnel, to where the children were in the physical world, to grab and pull them all into her arms. In a way, it was like wrapping her arms around the little girl she unknowingly healed at the playground so long ago. But this time, she could find no hold upon the children and in that instant, she felt power she had never known before for an action she had not done before. The power of life-saving hope actually reached out in a real action. At that same instant however, she felt a sickening feeling as that power began to return empty, feeling all the souls of the hundreds of children, power swirling around them, slipping off them, as it could find no hold to bring them across to her, feeling the life of each child slipping through her fingertips, and feeling them die. Yet, out of the hundreds of children that she felt, out of all the pain she felt, as hope slipped away empty from them, amidst all those terrible feelings of loss, a tiny light was shining! At the end of that instant, sensing one little light, Lady Stephanie grabbed hold with all her might, all her being, all her meaning, and *pulled*. At that departing instant, all that was real to her was that tiny light.

Jargono looked at Stephanie and saw the lone child standing beside her.

The child stood with wide eyes, looking around as if dazed then up at Stephanie, and threw her little arms around her leg to hold on for dear life. Also wide-eyed herself in as much amazement as the little child, Stephanie felt the meaning of what just happened and clutched the girl fiercely in her arm. There was a moment of pure stillness, as if they lived in eternity.

Then Jargono spoke, and the stillness was shattered, "*Oh my*, what have we here? You know, when you kill *cockroaches*, you have to make sure you get *every last one*."

The venom in his voice brought the crowd of heads up to peek at what was about to happen. The little girl looked up at Stephanie as she sensed their final moment. She wanted to look into her eyes forever. Stephanie looked down into the girl's eyes and was shocked by recognition, seeing in the child Stephanie's own younger self, when she had suffered so terribly from a sense of abandonment, isolation, loneliness, and worthlessness. In one huge feeling-picture of Stephanie's past, she was swallowed up in both her memory and what she perceived in this little girl. *AH!* And this little one was the adopted child whose home she had visited the night before! Stephanie threw her other arm around the child as well, burying her as deeply as she could against her body, loving her with fierceness she had never known before. *Oh God, my life is in my arms! But it was all worth it. Thank You!* In the midst of that oneness and surprise, the fire fell upon them.

The crowd had heard King Jargon speak so they looked up to see the child standing with the redheaded woman. Their beloved King raised his hands again to the sky and the fire fell upon the strange woman and the last of the vermin. The people cheered and threw their hats in the air. The women kissed strange men they had never known, and the men returned the favor.

༄

A hundred or so people had returned to the village and were reveling in all the wealth that had been left behind. But about fifty minutes after the last escaping group had entered the forest, the sky lit up. A slow rumble gathered in intensity and its vibration violently passed through all the people who stood in the forest. After the roar dissipated, everyone knelt upon the ground and prayed as one, thanking the Lord God for sparing them. Then, as one people, they all stood, and stoically resumed their march to freedom.

Last in line, Vaughn was left crying on the ground because he knew Stephanie didn't succeed with Jargono. The people were unaware, except for Spot and Little One who heard him cry over and over, *"Stephanie, Oh Stephanie, my Queen, my love, my life, my wife…"* Little One tugged on his sleeve, pulling and pushing at him, finally getting him to roll over on his back, "Don't cry, Mr. Ranger. Your wife isn't dead. She's still alive in here." She tapped on his chest with her little hand. Vaughn sat up then gathered her into his arms. Spot licked away his tears then Vaughn dragged himself up to go find the people.

The first group reached the twin Oaks, stopped and quickly passed the word back through the long line of people so that they all wouldn't crash into each other. There actually had been considerable thought by the group leaders into many aspects of the logistics of moving thousands of people single file in total darkness through the woods on small animal trails. Vaughn made his way forward with Spot ahead of him on a short leash. As they moved along, the dog smelled each person while Vaughn patted each soul on the back, reminding them, "No matter what, stick to the trail."

As Vaughn arrived at the Oaks, the two elders stepped back and Vaughn reminded them not to doubt. "Spot!" The dog responded with a single serious *Ruff*, after which, Vaughn took his dog's head by the jowls, tried to see Spot's eyes by the scant light that was still left, and then pleaded. "All these people and me depend on *you* to lead us safely!" Spot ruffed even more seriously, intently waiting for his instructions.

"Remember how you saved Stephanie and me from the bad man?" Spot's tail swished strongly back and forth, his hind legs did a kind of dance. He *Arfed* thrice, to make sure his Master understood that he remembered.

"The trail is marked special for you, Spot! I marked it this morning, starting here." Vaughn bent over, pointing and patting to the side of the trail. *Ruff* was all that Spot said, as he turned to where his Master was tapping. He sniffed, sniffed, and then… a longer louder sniff. Spot turned sideways, and lifted his hind leg. After leaving a brief mark on top of his Master's, Vaughn gave him a drink from his canteen, and they started down the dark trail. Vaughn held Spot's leash, Little One held Vaughn's hand, the stocky elder held a rope tied to Vaughn's belt, the bald elder next and so on, all the way to the end of the line. Ten minutes later they came to the first of many intersections so Vaughn stopped.

"Which way, Spot? Which way? Stick to the animal trails." Vaughn detached the rope from his belt, leaving the elder behind. More sniffing, searching, back and forth, up one trail, back to the starting point, up another trail. Spot lead Vaughn about ten or fifteen feet, then backtracked about five feet and stopped. More sniffing, *Ruff!*

That was the way. Spot sidestepped and briefly lifted his leg. Vaughn gave him another drink then they backtracked to where the first man in line stood. He reached to the ground, grabbed and retied the rope to his belt and then led the people further into the growing darkness. In the dark, none of Vaughn's trail signs were visible, but he knew that the scent left behind would be more than enough for a good dog. Vaughn whispered to the elder behind him, "Pass the word back that the way is being found clearly."

One informed the other and so on, all the way to the end.

For about an hour, they silently proceeded deeper into the dark forest into the mine fields. They crossed this way, they wound that way, with only the gentle tug from a rope or a hand to guide them, trusting in the feel of the forest floor and their sense of where the person in front of them had last stepped to keep their feet completely on the narrow trails. With their eyesight almost useless, their ears strained, and their hands sweating, they knew that one step too far to either side could be disastrous. At times, many felt they would lose their balance even though the trails were all level. The people lost their sense of direction as animal trails zigzagged to and fro.

To Vaughn, who had always loved the forest, the trek was comforting. He had no trouble following Spot, sensing the trail ahead. However, for the others, every twist and turn seemed to plunge them into a deeper darkness. They were aimlessly wondering in a lost and forbidden place. *We're not going ANYWHERE!* The deep darkness of the forest closed in more tightly by the moment, making breathing difficult. Then there was an odd sound from the forest from… somewhere. The middle of the line stopped in fright, not being able to classify such a sound at all though it seemed definitely closest to them. The people behind bumped into the ones ahead. The people in front felt a tug backwards.

"Keep moving!" Vaughn ordered sternly, loud enough for all to hear in the silence. That brief breach of silence he felt was necessary. "Don't speed up, don't slow down for anything. *Stay on the trail.*"

Five minutes later, there were eerie sounds like muffled snarls at either side of the path. The people were standing pat as Spot sniffed for the right trail. Then a much louder snarl that felt like massive menacing jaws snapping only an instant away.

Vaughn had to break silence again, as he shouted back. "IGNORE THE SOUNDS. THEY CAN'T BE REAL. THE MINES WOULD HAVE BLOWN THEM UP."

But Vaughn was still a boy, *not* an experienced leader. He didn't foresee how they would react. Instead of paying attention to his words, they paid attention to his action. He had started making loud noise and so the people responded in kind. Some screamed in terror, children started crying, babies wailing, and others shouted for calm, which only exacerbated the other's desire to cry out.

With everything slipping out of control, Vaughn felt as if he was being sucked into the Earth, squeezed to death and failure raced to capture him. "You've brought us all here to *DIE*," someone lamented. Feeling smaller by each second, Vaughn's responsibility for all these souls began to crush him as one trapped far below the Earth in a mine's collapse. Darkness began to cover his mind. Then a form, a presence, tore through the crowd in violence and hatred. It left no physical sign, but many from the middle of the line broke the chain, and began to run into the trees. Moments later, explosions lit up the night. Blast after blast, all around. Pieces of bodies and blood as well as soil and broken tree parts began to shower down upon the people. Small fires cast an unearthly flickering glow across the forest, making long shadows move in threatening ways.

The evil presence tore through the front of the line. The stocky elder, just behind Vaughn, felt this evil surround him… and couldn't help himself. Vaughn felt him drop the rope so Vaughn whirled around to grab him but only caught his wavering shadow. The terrified elder bounded toward a larger tree, some thirty feet away, thinking to climb it to escape the ferocious animal hunting him but about ten feet from that tree, there was a boom. Vaughn threw himself over Little One and Spot, pressing them to the ground. He had done all he could do. *It wasn't enough.* Laying there, trapped in an eternal nightmare, as darkness invaded his every fiber, he couldn't help but think, *I saved this people from a quick death, only to die a long and tortured one.*

"What was I thinking? Oh, God, forgive me. How could I have thought I could do this? This is ridiculous. Just a charade I convinced myself into playing." Clawing at the ground, hoping it would be his grave... *No escape!* The evil presence weighed heavily on Vaughn, attempting to make him flee as the others. *You've LOST. You're MINE. You CAN'T escape. I brought you here MYSELF. MY idea so I could consume you! And it's so much fun to toy with you NOW! But you're MINE. You CAN'T escape.* And the more he heard that phrase, *You can't escape,* the more his heart pressed upon him to get up and run but in his mind, a steady voice kept showing him the reality of all that was happening. Vaughn also had Little One and Spot underneath him so he couldn't bring himself to run.

With fear crushing Vaughn's heart, he began to shake. Guilt for the people dying, exploding still, swallowed him up. Every blast made him jump as he laid helplessly on the ground, and the stench of blood and human carnage made him gag. Spot crawled out from under his arm and disappeared. Too deep in inner turmoil to respond, his sudden fear for his dog added to this calamity. *Without Spot...* He hugged Little One tightly. Yet, sometime later ...

A *Ruff.* Not a yes ruff. A *pay attention RUFF!* Then two more, and as Vaughn kept ignoring his dog, Spot nipped his left ear. Then his dog grabbed his arm in his mouth and pulled hard, growling at the same time. Still Vaughn didn't feel like moving and ignored his arm pain. *It's just a matter of time. They'll all die. I wasn't convincing at ALL!*

Burning. BURNING! Vaughn squirmed up to his knees, pulling his vest away from his chest, where it felt like he was being scorched. *Light!* Stephanie's letter was in his left vest pocket, over his heart and it was glowing red-hot. Upon touching it, the letter cooled so he unfolded it. One paragraph glowed.

Vaughn, all we can do is do goodness to the fullest that we can do. We are not assured of any outcome, my love, only that we have and are able to do our part. We cannot fail our part as long as we keep faith and do it. We may not achieve the outcome we wanted, but we have not failed if we do the part that we are able to do. Do you understand that, my dearest?

Shame covered him, realizing he wasn't doing his part. *My wife gave her* life *doing her part. I'm not doing the fullest goodness I can do.* Anger and embarrassment chased his fear away. Anger at himself for being so wretched, so weak. *I shouldn't be* groveling. *GET UP YOU IDIOT, YOU FOOL!* Faith in what he was trying to do returned. Slowly rising to his feet, brushing himself off, Spot jumped up and moved forward, then back to him. He *Ruffed* once, and then many muffled *Ruffs.*

Vaughn turned, commanding the people behind him in a sharp voice, "EVERYONE, THOSE OF YOU WHO WOULD CHOOSE *LIFE.* THE FEARFUL AND THE DEAD ARE NOT WORTH A TEAR, *NOT A THOUGHT.* IF YOU WOULD HAVE LIFE, *MOVE UP IN THE*

LINE TILL WE ARE CONNECTED. I LEAVE IN FIVE MINUTES."

People who heard his angry words grabbed hold of their neighbors. It had seemed an eternity of silence before he had spoken. *Thank God he's still with us!* Some shook their neighbors violently, to have them hear. They passed the message along. Vaughn lost count of how many explosions he heard. Every time the evil presence tore through, more people had run and were blown up.

There's no secret escape, now. But we have to proceed with the plan, because there's no other option I can think of. These evil phantoms, I know they're demons! They *are the Blackness from my vision that attacks Little One. But they can't interact with the physical world. If that's all we have to worry about, if the people could just keep faith enough,* they can make it. *They can do their part.* They have to do their part! *Just like Stephanie told me in her letter. Thank you, my dearest, with* all *my heart for your precious gift, for this letter, for your love, for making me a* man! *Now, I must share the strength you have given me.*

He lifted his head up to the people again, as emotion overcame him, but this time he let it speak through him, "STAND *STILL* AND BE *QUITE*. I WILL READ YOU SOMETHING FROM MY *WIFE* WHO HAS GIVEN HER *LIFE* TO FIGHT THE EVIL KING!"

He has a wife? Gave her life? Fought the King! When the people heard *that,* heard the pain in his command, the bitterness, and the love, something moved through them. A sense of shame for cowardly behavior, for not living up to this young man's hope and sacrifice, began to replace their fear.

To hear that his wife had given her life to fight the very king who had ordered their death stabbed them in their hearts. These people were a close-knit people, a family people, whose ties were held tightly, even through their extended family trees, so feeling their ranger's utter loss, the people hushed and formed a new line. The evil presence tore through the crowd again with ferocity. Feeling it terribly, they shook, but held their peace. They stood ready to listen to their ranger.

Vaughn took the letter and held it out in front of him. The words all glowed now, so he could see, so he could share. He cleared his throat and as he did, the people could see how the letter glowed brightly, in fact, it lit up the forest as in the day! And the glow's warmth revived their hearts, while Vaughn expressed Stephanie's feelings.

"My Beloved Husband Sir Vaughn, I am sorry I had to do it this way, but I know that if we had discussed this, you would never have allowed me to. I could never fight with you, my dearest. I know you would not have let me, because if the situation were reversed, I would not have let you. We love each other so much."

The people almost immediately began to weep. They knew, understood her sacrifice, and the couple's love were as clear as the very light shining from this letter. Every attention sharpened, each ear became attuned to what would be read next. At this moment, nothing existed but this letter's confession. The evil presence tore through again but went unnoticed!

"But our love is so great, because it is founded in that Love which is greater. We must always honor that Love first, if our love is to be forever real. You did not fail me, my beloved, by doing what you did today with the little girl and her people. You honored me. You allowed Love to be fulfilled in your heart and actions. "

Upon hearing those gracious words, the people fell to their knees, unable to stand. *Never have we received such love from strangers.*

"We are called together unto a higher purpose. We can only hope to truly be together, if we fulfill that purpose to its fullest. You did not answer my question when I asked you on the couch! But yes, my love, I knew beforehand. Let me repeat the question, now, so you will understand."

This beautiful soul is dead? Higher purpose? Who are these blessed people? The evil presence attempted to tear through again, but shrieked as it repeatedly was barred entry into the line.

"Vaughn, all we can do is do goodness to the fullest that we can do. We are not assured of any outcome, my love, only that we have and are able to do our part. We cannot fail our part as long as we keep faith and do it. We may not achieve the outcome we wanted, but we have not failed if we do the part that we are able to do. Do you understand that, my dearest? Please say yes, my dearest, please. I cannot bear to face what I must face, if you do not truly say yes."

To face what she must face? She faced death! She knew it ahead of time, but she went anyway! Why? To do good! To do good to its utmost possible... even if she died! She wanted him to understand why, why she was going to die! *That Higher purpose... to do good ... IS HELPING US NOW!*

"Your beloved wife forever in Love, Lady Stephanie"

The people wept in sorrow, tore at the ground and wailed. They never met his wife, that wonderful woman who was honored that her husband was helping a strange people she had never met instead of only being with her. They understood the letter, the sacrifice and down to its finest details, they could feel the love and meaning for both her and her husband. *Vaughn! His name is Vaughn. All this time he knew his wife went to her death, and we didn't even know! He concerned himself only with us!*

One voice, then another, and another, gave answer to Lady Stephanie's question, until the chant became one, "Yes, YES, YES… *we understand!*"

Tears ran down Sir Vaughn's face as he beheld the honor and respects they paid to his dearly departed Queen. If ever there was a greater honor at any funeral, he couldn't imagine what that would be.

The evil presence screamed in anger, as every man, woman, child and dog glowed brightly. The menacing sounds departed and some thought the evil even sounded as if in pain when it left. Then the glow slowly lessened until it was gone but everyone now knew it lived in their hearts.

The volunteers rose first, speaking as one, "Get up! GET UP! We must *honor* this Ranger and his wife. GET UP! We try for freedom with our all!"

Vaughn sat on a stump, amazed at the power his departed wife still had with the living. After the line was formed again, Spot led the way. When they finally reached the great tree, Vaughn figured it close to midnight. He had earlier cleared the mines in an area near the fence so some of the people could gather there while the rest waited on the trails.

The heavy clouds had departed. The full moon now shined directly above and with multitudes of stars illuminated the magnificent tree and what Vaughn was doing. As they gathered, Vaughn opened the packs he would need. The elder, who had been blown up, had thrown his off just before he ran and the last remaining elder, the bald man, had picked the pack up and now gave it to Vaughn.

With skill and quickness planned out a hundred times in his imagination, Vaughn wrapped a long rope all the way around the tree's massive trunk, tying it in a closed loop. He took the free end and hurled the coil of rope up into the fork of the tree, some fifteen feet high. The other end fell to the ground on the other side of the tree. Without looking at anyone, Vaughn walked over, picked up the rope, put a foot against the smooth bark, and climbed up.

Mouths were agape as not only had the people never beheld such a giant tree, they now understood their means of escape. All eyes followed Vaughn upward and pieces of paper bark floated to the ground as he went higher then boosted himself into the tree's fork. He yelled down, "Tie the two rope ladders to the end of the rope."

Standing up in the tree's fork, Vaughn pulled the ladders up then fastened one to a branch above his head. When he dropped the ladder down, it unrolled all the way to the ground before their very eyes. The sound of it echoed in everyone's memory as did Vaughn's next words. "This is like life. To live it, *you have to climb up.*" And the people stared in awe as life unfolded before them.

Little One giggled, "Climb up, *climb up!*" she sang, running and skipping around the tree with Spot chasing after her, *ruffing.* She hollered up to her ranger, "I told you! Just follow the doggie!"

The people shook their heads. *Who would have believed?*

Vaughn climbed up the far angling fork for another ten feet, using cross branches as hand and footholds, then out onto the branch that overhung the fence. When he got to a place, some nine feet along that branch, he fastened the other ladder, and it dropped down with the same sound, some three feet away from the other side of the electric fence. He climbed halfway down, fastened two ropes to each rope rail, and let the ends fall to the ground. Then Vaughn climbed down the rest of the way to stand on free land.

The people had a moment of still silence. They all waited to see what he would do. *Freedom!* That feeling of it hit him with astonishment, but he shrugged it off. Taking another rope, he tied it to the end of the ladder, pulling it further away from the fence, tying it to a tree. He took each of the other ropes that were attached up at mid ladder, pulled each to a different side, and secured them to different trees. The ladder was now somewhat inclined and secured sufficiently away from the fence. Vaughn climbed back up into the tree and down the other ladder, and stood back upon his homeland.

The impact of the sight of him returning to them set many of the women to weeping, and the children doing the same just because their mother's did. But they asked their Mommy's why they weep. "Because this ranger, this *man* was free, but he came back for *us*." Even the men rubbed their eyes.

Vaughn spoke to the last elder, "Lead this people over to freedom. Appoint who you will to give help as you think best."

The bald elder's voice was surprisingly sharp, clear and pointed, "You, who have volunteered your lives, organize the people as best you can and guide them with what to do."

Then he turned and spoke to Vaughn, "Forgive us the trouble we have caused you. We are all hurt to our hearts for your wife. We can never express the limits of our gratitude to you." The man's eyes were as steady and level to Vaughn's as ever he saw, as the elder walked over and embraced him tightly with his thick arms. After a few fond slaps on Vaughn's back, the elder parted and went to help his people.

Vaughn felt drained, as if his job was now finally over. But a familiar male voice cracked through the midnight stillness and the cool moon light suddenly felt icy cold. "Well, *well!*"

Vaughn's heart lurched as the people gasped, frozen in terror. Jargono, dressed in ancient royal apparel, was standing right in front of Vaughn! A sickeningly familiar female voice spewed forth with delight, "I told you we could get three birds with one stone! It was *obvious* what they were going to do!" Karen smiled up at her husband.

"He does look bewildered, my Queen, but I have to say, *you* are a good advisor." He politely complimented his wife.

She ingratiated herself, continuing, "Well, no matter how things appeared, I knew they were going to try to help the vermin. I *told* you we could catch him, just like a stupid *fish* on a hook." And then Karen turned and taunted the people in a syrupy tone. "Thank you so very much, you all provided wonderful bait! *He's* my wedding present!" But she felt Jargono's arm tense, so with a hurt look, she whined to her husband, "You promised King Jargon. You said, *anything* I wanted." She turned back to the people, with her same cloying tone, "I plan on making him our first gladiator. He'll provide excellent entertainment, but I'm afraid none of *you* will be around to enjoy it."

How does she do that? Sounding so unbelievably *sugary, while speaking such utter cruelty?*

Throwing the back of her hand to her forehead in mock grief, "*Oh,* I'm so *sorry* for your wife. SHE GOT BURNED UP!"

Vaughn felt hollow, like the shell of a seed that was discarded, but like it or not, he saw truth in her eyes. He had held out a faint hope, but now he knew for sure, reality is what reality is.

Queen Karen further lamented, "I suppose the secret of the sacred treasure is now dead and burnt up with her." Vaughn began to remember the Seed to the Tree of Life, but just as he did, he felt Jargono begin to probe his mind so for some reason, perhaps out of reflex, Vaughn closed him out. Queen Karen looked over to her King with questioning eyes but he shook his head and she frowned. *Damn, it didn't work.*

Jargono nostalgically mused, *But enough is enough. Let's put a full end to this.* Jargono threw his hand out and the Black Oil streaked across Vaughn's face. He felt like the tree he'd climbed had just fallen upon him. Karen's stoking his grief over Stephanie had set him up for the unexpected attack. Vaughn fell to the ground on his knees, whispering. Some people heard him say, "No hope... want to... die."

Jargono whirled on the people, "You see? YOU SEE?" Jargono said in anger. "*This* was the man you would have had as king, INSTEAD OF ME?"

The ground grabbed at growling Spot as he tried to make it to his Master. He sunk up to his belly in the dry forest floor.

Jargono laughed, "Not this time, *dog*. Maybe when this is done, I'll take you home and make you a palace guard. Would you like that?"

Spot growled at Jargono as he could see his Master fading into death, and barked as if to say, *Master, live! LIVE Master!* With all his might, Spot struggled but couldn't budge.

Karen smiled sweetly again, "I think he'd make a nice bedroom rug!"

CHAPTER TWENTY-THREE
O Ye of Little Faith

"They thought their faith would protect them," he scornfully announced to his corporal who stood silently at attention, trying to block the images of the carnage surrounding him. The subordinate tried to push away his growing sense of guilt for having to participate in such atrocities though he managed not to actually put his hand to any of them, but simply issued his commander's orders.

Another soldier ran up to the lieutenant, snapped to attention, saluted and reported. "We've scoured the whole town, gathered all the religious relics and placed them on a table at the town's center. The cameras are all in place. We've hung many of the corpses in various poses of suffering as you commanded, Sir, and we've saved several women and children for live debut."

The Lieutenant's smile seemed to have inordinate pleasure in it, from beyond fulfilling the duties of his job. His corporal wondered, How do they find such... people and put them in charge?

The commander rubbed his hands together in glee. "Bring the captives to the town's center. Corporal, I give you the privilege to interview these last captives. Just make it gory just like you saw me do, lots of screaming, blood and guts, but here's the thing, we also want this to have meaning. Ask them relevant questions concerning their faith and then force them to recant it. This video is to be shown in every single school we have so their rebellion will never happen again."

The corporal did his best to hide behind his stony face, *fearing that any emotion leaking through would place him in a similar dire fate. As they walked to the town's center, his heart kept pounding.* How can I do this? I'm not religious at all but... *His memories suddenly jogged back ten years to his father.* I haven't thought about him in ... *He couldn't remember when. His mother probably had something to do with that because she cursed him day-in and day-out for dying on them, leaving her to care for all those children. He shook his head at the memories.* Why should they come to me now? *He remembered his youngest sister and how his mother threw her doll into the trash, how later, without her knowing, he retrieved then hid it under his sister's pillow but the deed backfired when their mother found it. He shook his head again at how all of his brothers and sisters had grown up to be just like her...* Except for me.

Upon reaching the town's center, the Lieutenant handed his corporal his knife and sneering at the three women and five children, he instructed his corporal. "This is the knife I used on the others. Make sure you cut real slow so that we have ample opportunity to test their faith. Start with the youngest child."

At hearing the order, the children started bawling and the corporal looked down upon the knife in his hand. But in the next moment, another soldier ran up yelling, "We've found several people hiding in a basement and they've got weapons. We need help."

The lieutenant looked at his corporal, looked at the terrified women and children then at the knife, licked his lips and took the knife back. "You better see to that corporal!" he declared with a sadistic smile. "I'll take care of this."

On his way to deal with the town-traitors, the corporal's thoughts returned to his father. He was a gentleman… he wore… And he recalled that they were religious garments. He was devoutly religious! The son harkened back to the whole conversation just before his father died and remembered the look in his dying eyes, their gaze lastly settling upon him… the kindness, the love… the sorrow. The corporal's heart began to ache but matters at hand drew him back to reality.

A soldier pointed down some narrow stairs, "Down there! They have a gun for sure." The corporal nodded, took a few steps down, and a shot rang out but nowhere near to striking him. He stepped back up the steps and then back down and another shot. He repeated this several more times until he heard the expected click of an empty handgun.

With his revolver drawn, he entered the dank basement, finding a woman dressed in a long black dress with one arm protecting her three children behind her, and the other hand half pointing the empty gun at him. That long black dress brought back further memories as he walked up to the woman and simply took the gun from her shaking hand. She collapsed to the floor and her children fell with her, clutching at her.

When the other soldier knew it was safe, he ambled downstairs and seeing that the woman was extremely attractive, he proposed, "Hey! Ahh, there's no need to waste her yet, ya know! I mean... she's gonna die anyway." And he began to undo his trousers while the children's eyes became wider.

The corporal looked around the basement and walked away, rummaging through the dimly lit shelves while the soldier pulled the woman to her feet, forcibly kissed her then threw her back to the floor to position her. "You be sure to thank your God for this favor, ya hear?"

In the background, something that a soldier is trained to recognize could be heard, the sound of a gun being loaded then cocked in place. The corporal had found the ammunition to the handgun. There was no reason for him to reload it since his own military revolver was still with him. The soldier's pants were down around his knees when the Corporal yanked him off the woman and with a stony expression, shoved the nose of the gun to the soldier's chest and fired. The woman and the children gaped as he turned to direct them. "Quickly! I don't know what good it will do you but head to the woods and... try to find some place to hide, somewhere to go! We burn this whole town shortly." Then the corporal left.

"Where are we?" the little girl asked. Stephanie stood *very* straight, her shoulders squared, all her senses on high alert. With an unsettled tone, she answered, "In the Dead Forest." The Black River was roaring just several feet behind them.

The little girl looked up into her rich brown eyes and hesitatingly asked, "Are we… supposed to be *here?*"

"No," Stephanie whispered, lost in thought, still clutching the little girl tightly. *How did I get here? Why am I here? Bastard! I feel you watching. Where are you?*

The child spoke in a strained voice as she sensed evil all around, "Can we get out of here?"

"I… think so." *But I dare not take my mind off this evil presence. If I focus on leaving, we'll be too vulnerable to attack.*

The little girl tugged on Stephanie's royal-blue dress and looked up to her, revealing, "My… My mommy, my *second* Mommy said you would come!" The intensity with which she looked into Stephanie's eyes, seeking love, comfort, and understanding, drew the faithwalker's attention away from her deep thoughts.

Stephanie was captivated and asked with surprise, "She did?"

The girl nodded and her deep dark brown eyes continued to stare intensely at her, "I was on the couch. When you came to our house, I… wasn't sleeping." She looked down then back up into her third Mommy's eyes.

Stephanie understood and smiled, "And do you do that a lot? Fake sleep so you can listen to Mommy and Daddy?"

The child nodded again, still keeping her gaze upon Stephanie who patted her head and smiled warmly. "I used to do the same things!"

The little girl was surprised, "You did?" She also sounded relieved.

Stephanie nodded, "Yes, of course. Children always feel like they should know the truth, the *real* truth. Right?"

626

"Yea!" she giggled.

"So you weren't sleeping yet, that night?"

"No. After you left, Mommy and Daddy had a big fight. Because Daddy didn't want Mommy to *die*… because of me. I started crying. I told them to give me away! I didn't want them dead like my first Mommy and Daddy… because of me."

Stephanie became dumbfounded. All she could do was stare into those four-year-old innocent eyes and marvel at a child who was stronger than her

"Daddy said Mommy would die because of me." She looked into Stephanie's eyes for approval and got it. Then the little girl simply shrugged her little shoulders, and in her songlike voice said matter-of-factly, "It didn't make sense they die when I was going to, anyway."

Stephanie couldn't restrain herself any longer. She picked up the little girl in both arms, embraced her tightly and buried her face into the girl's curly dark-brown hair to hide her tears. Everything about this little girl felt like… *Me.* Stephanie made an oath, "From now on, *I* will be your Mommy… if you want me to."

The little girl nodded and pressed against Stephanie. Then, from behind, Stephanie felt something… lick her, though it wasn't exactly a lick.

A voice sounding like a growling animal spoke in a fashion she'd heard before, "Mmm, you *do* taste good!"

The *faithwalker* whirled around, her power glowing, surrounding her, "Look into my eyes!" she commanded.

"HA! I don't *think so!*" His big, glistening Black Eye was

dripping in Black Oil as he hovered about six feet away. "I've been studying you."

The little girl buried her head into Stephanie's shoulder and shook. Stephanie squeezed her more tightly then shifted her onto her hip. *I need to have a hand free.* "Really! You been studying poor me?" Stephanie added flatly, "You're not GrrraGagag and you're not Scraback."

The grotesque creature laughed, explaining, "They don't exist anymore! Well, GrrraGagag doesn't. My Master, that's Scraback, ate GrrraGagag and became ScrabaGag."

Stephanie raised her eyebrows concerned that the demon wouldn't look into her eyes. She wasn't sure he wasn't a threat, but was glad for whatever knowledge she could learn from him. As Stephanie realized that to a demon, she seemed on the level of a pet dog or cat, she decided to take advantage of their arrogance. "Oh my, *you're cannibals,*" she said, seeming disgusted and overcome.

He was quick to correct her, "No, no! We're not *wasteful* like you low-lifes from the physical world. WE are Ethereal and when our Eye *consumes,* we suck in all of the essence, all the knowledge and ability of our feast. It's the way we advance ourselves. Sometimes, we *even* consume humans." He was trying to scare her with the truth.

Stephanie played up a childlike ignorance. "Ethereal?"

And he seemed to oblige her stupidity. "Of course. *We* are the essence of reality. And when we've purged the Earth of all *glow,* we'll once again rule ALL REALITY."

She continued with her act. "What glow?"

"You are *infected* with it. If you could give it up, you could be of great help to us, and you'd be sane again.

Stephanie acted concerned. "*Infected?* Oh, no! How would I do that, give it up, I mean? Oh, are you able to help me?"

Grinchback squinted at her with contempt. "I am not a *fool!* Stop playing with me. I've studied you... I wouldn't tell you these forbidden things if you could escape with it!"

The hairs stood up on her neck because although it was an Ethereal Eye, she could tell he spoke what he thought was the truth. Stephanie shifted the little girl to her left hip. Her other hand slipped into her dress, to the inside pocket where she kept the Light Oil. She was already anointed with it, but that had been a whole earth-day ago. Confident the demons didn't know anything about it, Stephanie suddenly wondered. "And where *is* your Master?"

His eye flinched, almost imperceptibly. "He sent *me* to deal with you."

She could tell he lied and an understanding began to form in her. "Don't you want to... *consume* him?"

He laughed as he proclaimed, "My Master is a good Master!"

Stephanie flattened her lips, casting doubt upon her face. She remembered GrrraGagag was Scraback's Master. "Really. Then how come Scraback ate *his* Master?"

Grinchback broke out into hysterical laughter. "That was *your fault!* Master didn't want me to know, BUT I RESEARCHED IT. I refined the orb recovery technique and was able to uncover the record through the distortion." The pride in his discovery was unmistakable.

Stephanie sensed valuable knowledge around the corner. "My fault?"

"Your last encounter, you damaged his former master. He was… required to eat him."

Stephanie pondered what might be happening. *Another lie. This demon went behind his Master's back. He's been studying me without his master's approval, I'll bet.* She realized he was on his own. *Either his Master doesn't know he's here, or, he knows and is watching! But then, this demon doesn't know he's a pawn. Damn! If that's true, this would be nothing but a bloody experiment! I'm NO LAB RAT!*

Either way, Stephanie now felt she needed to escape this place. She remembered the last time she was here. After she left she could hardly move. "OK, nice *chatting with you,* maybe we'll do it again sometime, over a pot of tea?"

The demon laughed further. "You're not going anywhere." He waved his arm and a three-foot-wide ring of swirling darkness appeared around her. "I insist that you stay, just for a while." If it was possible to say that these *creatures* smiled, he did.

Stephanie's thoughts whirled. *He knows. Damn! He knows I can't stay here long.* She closed her eyes and prayed, *Oh Lord of Light guide me. Hear me in this* hell.*"* As she lifted her head slowly, her eyes glowed, making the demon look away.

When she waved her hand, sparkles, each as bright as a star, floated out from the faithwalker's fingers. When they touched the swirling black circle, they mingled until the swirl began to fade then was gone.

Impulsively, perhaps intuitively, Stephanie decided that the demon had *vastly* underestimated her. She remembered one of the many things that Vaughn had taught her about battle. *When your superior enemy greatly underestimates the ability you do have, advantage may be gained by going on a harsh offensive.*

Still carrying the little girl who was tightly hugging her, Stephanie lunged at the demon and grabbed him by his ethereal throat! With her hand glowing brightly and her eyes blazing with red fire, part of her noted that she had never done nor even considered such an attack before. Another part of her realized how tired she suddenly felt from the exertion.

The demon shrieked! *PAIN!* That he hadn't expected.

The *faithwalker* commanded, "YOU WILL LEAVE ME NOW! AND I *WILL* LEAVE."

Grinchback began to panic, *This isn't going as I'd expected! My Master told me to stay out of it. Why didn't I listen? But, I AM A DEMON. I'm supposed to better myself ... no matter what. But this low-life is... she's embarrassing me!*

Grinchback lashed out with his tail, knocking Stephanie over, but it wasn't a hard blow, and Stephanie noted that their strength wasn't impressive for such things. But when she fell, she dropped her new daughter and seizing the opportunity, Grinchback immediately grabbed and wrapped her in his coil. Only her little head stuck out.

Stephanie went ice-cold, her heart pounded in terror as she remembered being in that very same position in the hideous grip of a demon, about to be eaten. The child screamed in excruciating pain that Stephanie knew. This demon wasn't physically strong, but Stephanie was sure he was strong enough to keep hold of the little girl. She threatened the demon as she quickly rose to her feet. "Let her *go*, or I *will* destroy you." She meant it. All her remaining power was quickly building.

Grinchback saw his advantage. "Oh, no! No, no…" His Eye caressed the child, causing her screams to reach an even higher pitch. "Do you have any idea how tasty consuming an actually living soul in *this* realm is to us? It's the *only* place where we're allowed to do it!"

Stephanie spoke venomously. "So, *that* was your plan? Just wait me out and then eat me?"

He confessed with modesty. "Simple, but true. I know you like to talk!"

The *faithwalker* became enraged even through her tiredness, even while her shoulders slumped, and she gasped for breath, and there was no breathing in the corridor. Stephanie had used a lot of her power already, and now regretfully realized she was running out.

The little girl kept screaming but through her terror and pain, she realized her third Mommy was going to die if she didn't leave. "MOMMY!" she screamed through her pain, "GOOOOOO!!!"

Stunned by the child's plea, Stephanie's eyes filled with tears as the little girl shrieked, "DON'T DIE! GO NOW!" In that instant, it became more agonizingly clear to Lady Stephanie how very much she and this child were alike.

The demon spoke in a pleasant, businesslike manner, "I'll tell you what. I'll make you a deal. One of you stays for me to eat, and one of you can go free. But I'll have that *Seed* around your neck first, if you want the girl to live! I know you were willing to die before! You and this child are a lot alike!" *She won't be able to decide. I studied her. I'LL EAT THEM BOTH AND HAVE THE SEED. Sometimes it pays to be greedy. Rule seventeen of the Alpha Code of Ethics.*

Lady Stephanie had forgotten all about the Seed to the Tree of Life and now seeing the demon's ploy, she felt as if hell itself had just swallowed her. With her heart pounding furiously and suddenly dizzy, she collapsed to her knees with a sudden loss of strength but she refocused. *If he just asked for me, I would give myself up, but… but I have no right to give up the Seed… but… I can't leave her!*

The child wailed even more deeply now, not out of pain nor fear for herself but for her third Mommy. "GET UP, MOMMY!" she shrieked then the little girl turned on the demon, trying to get her little hands up to his eye to poke at it! But Grinchback held her tightly with his tail, squeezing her a bit more. He tasted her and her wails became death screams that Stephanie knew all too well.

But all that fighting the little girl did, all her utter willingness to sacrifice herself, made Lady Stephanie love her much more as is the natural course of goodness. The child's screams held the faithwalker in place, and in desperation, *she* wailed as she reached out her hand to grab the child as she had snatched her from Jargono's fire. It took a lot of power to do that but Stephanie's power misfired so she fell over onto her side, almost passing out.

Now so drained that the possibility of any further action was certainly doubtful, yet still unwilling to give up, Stephanie bounced from choice to choice, over and over again, faster and faster. Wearily looking into her new daughter's eyes again, seeing herself even more deeply in the child than before, she knew she *couldn't* abandon her but *couldn't* give up the Seed to the Tree of Life, either. Grinchback delighted in her increasing conflict and loss of strength.

Stephanie *couldn't* stay much longer. She *couldn't* save her, She *couldn't, couldn't, couldn't*… Such converging conflagrations of circumstances are usually only reserved by fate for a special few, robbing them of all sense of everything they know, leaving them no recourse except to cry out. From her very bowels Queen Stephanie screamed with an intensity of pain only felt in realms other than the physical, anguish only *faithwalkers* are able to feel, "OH, GOD! I CAN'T! I CAN'T… I …"

The *faithwalker's* wails shook through the very essence of this ethereal reality. As the dark forest ground trembled a tad, the demon smiled. In anger and bitterness, Stephanie then lashed out to God in accusation. Grinchback was thrilled.

"YOU! *YOU GOD*, HAVE *BROUGHT* ME TO THIS! I… I CAN'T CHOOSE! IF I CAN'T CHOOSE… THEN I CHOOSE FOR IT *ALL* TO END! *THIS REALITY SHOULD NOT BE!*"

Stephanie pulled the bottle of Light Oil from her hidden pocket. The demon couldn't see what was in her hand. She whirled around towards the Black River, and threw the bottle against a rock around which the Black Oil flowed.

The bottle shattered and the Light Oil splashed upon the rock and began to ooze down towards the river, its glow so bright, like looking into the sun. The demon shrieked while turning his back. The black rock began to sink and the light submerged into the Black Oil of the river then… it was gone. There was a calm in the Dead Forest.

The demon turned back and gloried. "Oh MY! Where did you ever get *that*? What a *waste* for you. HA! BUT WHAT A GAIN FOR ME!" Grinchback bounced up and down, trying to decide which one to eat first. *My Master will be so proud of me.*

There was a soft noise that seemed to be coming from everywhere, nowhere. It wasn't physical sound but wasn't Ethereal either. Yet, it IS. The ethereal ground Stephanie laid upon, lurched hard one way then the other. The demon, though he was floating, was somehow not immune to the lurching as the quake went through the ethereal air, too! Then a much more violent shaking took place.

Grinchback howled in unmistakable fright. Never in their eternally recorded history had there been any mention of anything even close to *this!* Stephanie laid there, beyond exhaustion, yielding to the tossing by every ethereal tremor, yielding to a fate she did not know. Barely having strength to move, she waited to disintegrate along with this reality, and her life presented itself before her eyes in a quiet, all-encompassing picture. It was a *very* short time ago that she'd been just a worthless, ignorant tramp. Then she felt all the life and love added to her since, how so much of a person she'd become through the Light.

Bitterly ashamed, Stephanie wept copiously. "Forgive me, Lord of Light, for railing against You. Forgive me. Forgive me for disintegrating myself and my new daughter but I couldn't choose. Reality is what reality is. Oh GOD, I couldn't choose. Oh God, forgive me... I couldn't choose... Forgive..."

With what little strength she had left, she finished her prayer, "Forgive me, Vaughn. I so wanted a life together." As her weeping drifted away with the last of her consciousness, she became aware that she understood the pain in which the reality around her violently shook.

ᴇᴏ

Vaughn lay on the ground dying, "No hope..."

The last elder spoke up, "We will not serve *you*. You might as well kill us. LONG LIVE, KING VAUGHN!" The last elder shouted as he went down on one knee, squaring his shoulders.

All in tears with the same fervor, every soul went down on one knee, every man, woman, and child of their own accord, chanted, "LONG LIVE KING VAUGHN."

To say that Jargono was infuriated would be like saying beaches were made of a handful of sand. He knew he was going to kill them. *But I want them to bow to my power* first.

Intense blackness, like black light, shined from Jargono's eyes. His queen was turning the sickliest of colors. *If they keep this up, they'll cause Jargono to kill my new pet gladiator. He's got to remove the Black Oil from him soon.*

Jargono spoke, his voice grating in the worst possible way, "You wretched *vermin*! Long live *what*? *Look* at him. He's *nothing!*"

The elder raised a hand and the people hushed. "He was, he is... *everything* to our hearts. Do whatever you will to us. You will *never* change that." The elder's final tone was brave, and it dug into Jargono, like a knife in the spine that had been twisted. Jargono threw out his hand and the elder went flying into the electric fence. He howled, as he shook violently, beginning to burn and smoke from the power surging through him. The people wailed but at some point their cries turned into, "LONG LIVE KING VAUGHN! LONG LIVE..."

Vaughn looked up from the corner of his eye. Jargono was distracted with rage and strode right up to the people gathered by the fence, about fifteen feet away and he was partly turned away from Vaughn. Vaughn took his only chance. While on his knees, he jerked his left arm down, bringing his dagger in hand, and threw it at Jargono's heart. But sensing the immediate danger, Jargono reflexively dodged sideways just as the dagger passed.

Astonished to see Vaughn stand up with the Black Oil still streaked across his face, Jargono exclaimed, "How can you resist the Black Oil? Before, you needed that *dog* to get it off!"

Vaughn snarled between clenched teeth, "Let's just say I got used it." He felt the suffocating oil, but he had a promise to Goodness and to Stephanie to keep. He would give his all. The people stopped chanting and started cheering with all their hearts, and souls, and strength, and Vaughn felt their love enter into him.

"You *stupid fool!* Did you think you could touch *me* with your pitiful knife?"

Vaughn honestly replied, "I could only hope, but I figured that you would move out of the way, thinking about yourself *first* before protecting your lovely *wife!*"

Combining those words with Vaughn's deliberate gaze passed him gave Jargono an instant of sinking shock. He whirled around to see a wide-eyed Karen with Vaughn's knife embedded up to the hilt between her right breast and shoulder. Blood poured out around it as she fell to her knees, whispering, "Jargono, help me."

Vaughn laughed sarcastically, "He can't help you! He doesn't have that power! Do *you*? If you did, you would have used it to heal yourself when I fought you. But *my* wife is a healer and she's just the kind of person to be kind *even* to her enemies! But you've murdered her."

In light of what Jargono had said about loving enemies, Vaughn's words infuriated him further. *But Vaughn wasn't even there,* Jargono thought as he glared in bitterness and disgust at the coincidence, the irony. His Vaughn-toy had done him harm he'd not anticipated. "I'm going to end this, once and for all."

Speaking quickly, Vaughn captured Jargono's eyes, "Oh, but before you waste your time on me, maybe you should think about *your wife*, FIRST! She's your *real* wife, you know, the only one you'll ever have to match you *perfectly*. Just like Stephanie was mine!" It was Vaughn's turn to use the truth against Jargono who was just now seeing its reality.

Karen tugged on his royal robe. "You need me," she whispered. "I make you think."

Vaughn nodded and supported her plea. "Unfortunately, she's right. As I understand it, most of this was *her* plan?"

He hated to have to try to convince Jargono to save Karen and actually wanted her dead for so many right reasons… but that wasn't nearly as important as saving these people. "If you don't act right now to take her to a hospital, she'll die, and your demon friends will have her. The ones you sent after us?"

Vaughn was testing him to see if it was true and saw in Jargono's eyes that it was! *I wonder what he had to give them in return.*

Looking into Karen's pleading eyes, Jargono could see for the first time how perfectly they really did fit together in purpose, beyond making him think, beyond beauty and intelligence. *She's exceptional. She knows it. She knows she should rule! GrrraGagag* did *tell the truth about her!*

Jargono's heart went out to his Queen as never before, but he was confused by this feeling that so enslaved him, yet exhilarated him. It made him weak, but made him strong. He was confused at the terrible conflict of wanting desperately to kill Vaughn and the others, but wanting to save his wife, truly his Queen. All his life, he had picked a single direction and headed straight for it without any hindrance or noteworthy conflict. Now there was a fork in the road. His eyes turned the deepest black as he looked back into Vaughn's eyes. "I promise you," he sneered with certainty, "I will *pay* you for all your trouble."

With arms spread wide, Vaughn offered himself to him. He opened his eyes wide to show Jargono the devastation that Stephanie's death had caused in him, but it only made Jargono think of himself if he lost Karen.

Vaughn barely spoke above a whisper, "You've already killed me when you murdered *my* wife. I'm only sorry yours might live!" He knew this last comment would focus him into instant action.

Jargono picked up his wife and disappeared with her but the knife was left in midair and dropped to the ground. Strolling over, Vaughn picked it up and wiped off Karen's blood on the leaf litter. Then he went to Spot, and as Vaughn dug him out of the ground, the dog licked the Black Oil off his face, bringing relief.

Even more important than having the Black Oil cleaned off was that Jargono had at least not destroyed the great tree. And for the first time, it seemed to Vaughn that Jargono had human frailty and was overwhelmed with emotion and didn't use good judgment. Vaughn figured it would've only taken him a moment to destroy their chance for escape, while it was quite uncertain how long it would've taken to kill Vaughn because of the fact that the Black Oil was ineffective with him. To say Jargono was quite disturbed by *that* would be grossly understated.

Now, having overcome yet another almost overpowering hurdle, Vaughn wearily turned to the people, still on their knees, silently waiting for him to speak. "Come on," he urged everyone. "We must get to the other side. We don't know when he'll return. We must get away from here. The volunteers are going to have to warn the others that will come. You see how we've done this. Surely there must be other trees like this one. You must pass the word along. You have what you need for all to escape: knowledge, hope and ability."

The reply from the head volunteer was from his heart, not just due to Vaughn's title, "We will do it, King Vaughn!"

Then all the people started chanting again, still on one knee, their backs straight with dignity, "LONG LIVE, KING VAUGHN!"

Vaughn stood up tall, shaking his head, waving his arms for the people to quit. "Please, don't call me that. I'm not *that. Please.*"

But they wouldn't hear it. "We've accepted *you* as our King. It's not your choice whom we'll serve," the head volunteer spoke with utter respect to the young man that resisted and bested the mysterious powers of the evil King.

But Vaughn shook his head again, "Please. We go to a new land. They have their own leaders. You must *not* treat me as your King over there. It would be dangerous. Do you understand? *They have their own leaders.* Please, pass this word along."

"I will pass it, Sir, but we will *always* regard you as our King, whether in secret or not."

Vaughn was astonished. He's a king? A short while ago he was almost beaten to death in a poor farm, abandoned, and worthless. Now, he's a king! He shook his head and shrugged it off as inconsequential though. *The what makes the who. I have a* long *ways to go!* He began to help the women and children up the tree, until hearing shouts, and as he turned he saw a dozen rangers surround them with weapons drawn, and his heart sank yet again.

Little One yelled, "DADDY!" And ran past two rangers to a man in the back! The ranger picked her up, the ranger whose life Vaughn had spared and saved on the night of his test!

Wonders of wonders! Vaughn sat back on a log, shaking his head. *Wonder of wonders.* Various women approached their ranger husbands who warmly embraced them and their children, too. Then more kids who hadn't traveled with Vaughn's group came from the animal trails and joined their families. They were obviously also the rangers' children but their physical features had allowed them to blend with the regular people.

Little One, holding her father's index finger, kept pulling him over to Vaughn. She'd already told him how her Mommy had been blowed up but wasn't dead, and how Ranger King Vaughn's wife was killed by the bad King but wasn't dead either because they lived here, pointing to her heart.

When Vaughn saw them coming, he began to choke up from the confluence of all these events. "I ... I'm very sorry about your wife. I can show you where we buried her." Vaughn said with a broken heart.

The tall, stocky blond-haired ranger put his hand on Vaughn's shoulder. "And I'm *very* sorry about yours. Thank you for burying my wife and saving my precious treasure here." He hugged his little girl tightly.

It was so obvious. Vaughn didn't know why he hadn't seen it before. The rangers had total freedom to do what they wanted. Many of them fell in love with the foreigners. It seemed to him that they preferred them and were a good match. The dozen rangers gathered around Vaughn and proclaimed as one, "Long Live, King Vaughn!"

Vaughn just shook his head, feeling a special kinship with these rangers. He even looked up to them. There were tears in his eyes but he was now so used to having his emotions run past his knowledge of them that he just let them flow, without really knowing why they came. Maybe after they were on the other side with freedom, he would have time to reflect and gather himself together again, to regain self-knowledge to deal with Stephanie's death. King Vaughn fought the urge to sob uncontrollably. He was *very* glad to see the rangers join him, to have real, capable grown men at his side. Vaughn knew he had real backup now as he hung his head and leaned back against a tree, holding himself up with all his might.

The ranger Vaughn had spared, whose wife he'd buried and daughter he'd saved, squeezed his shoulder. "It's OK. I don't know where you get your strength from! We witnessed what you went through, your whole journey here! Sorry, but we couldn't do anything! But you're *young*. Don't feel bad about the way you're feeling now. You men, set up a tent for our King. He needs his privacy now. Don't worry. We'll make sure everyone gets over safely and I know…. I know, you won't go over till the last one of us is safe. Give us a minute or two then go into your tent and rest."

Vaughn knew there were no better hands than this Ranger's in which to entrust the people. A few minutes later, he and Spot entered his tent and laid down on a bed of clothing that had been made for him. He muttered, "*King Vaughn*" but feeling like a boy.

Vaughn sobbed with no strength to bear any more burdens. He let the pressures twisting in his gut release, burying his head deeper into his bedding to muffle himself. So exhausted, he couldn't fight the anguish any longer, it all washed through him in a wave of nausea then departed like a receding tidal wave, leaving him desolate.

Then, for the first time, it seemed in a long time, his thoughts were only of Stephanie. In a strange way, he felt she was doing the same thing, but she was dead. He fell asleep at around two in the morning. The women and children were going up and down the tree of freedom.

CHAPTER TWENTY-FOUR
Redemption

They all waited with dread, knowing this day would come, The Father had maliciously dragged it out for years. All three High Councilors floated motionless in the Father's darkest room as they were interrogated. "Tell me again who's responsible for flooding us with so many souls all at once?"

Each High Councilor struggled with their answers. It was too black to see anything, impossible to tell whether one might break and blame the other. First High Councilor was obligated to speak, and wisely did not wait to be told. "We all know humans are fundamentally defective. They're the only creature ever to exist to have a desire to kill themselves."

Upon hearing his words the other two Councilors chimed in their support. First was encouraged by their unity and continued, "I must point out that in spite of our misfortune, great good has resulted!"

The Father's Greatest Eye drew close to First. The other two sensed it and waited in hopeful anticipation. "What good?" the Father jibed.

"The United States was the only country on Earth that truly supported full independence of thought and action for

everyone. *Europe claimed to be so, but they had always been easily manipulated and intimidated. Twice, we had Europe where we wanted it, and the United States ALONE destroyed our plans because of their ridiculous idea of freedom for every individual. Now the United States is no more. In fact, we can now turn the North into the power they were meant to be."*

Second scoffed, "The North? The South is much stronger!"

First defended his choice, expounding, "Yes, but GrrraGagag's plan has worked. The North's principal beliefs that they come from rock, that they are their own god, has set them up to be easily molded to our world and their whole world will fall in time. It was ridiculous that such a powerful country should use its power to promote FREEDOM. The combination of freedom and religion has for too long given glow an advantage. They are both essentially gone now from the North."

Third knew it was best to oppose First. With both Second and Third in agreement, it would cause the Father to doubt First. Third offered his assessment, "The South is far stronger militarily. Religion has never been a problem for us. I have already manipulated it…"

"But you are still confined within its structure, a structure that still resembles glow. True, with freedom gone, you can use religion to manipulate many things, but you are still essentially confined by its structure. Only when both religion and freedom are gone, can we do exactly what we want to do."

The Father decreed, "First, I will give you time. Second and Third shall help you."

Time. That was good. They all knew the patience of the Father.

Something was tugging on her big braid because her head kept softly jerking. *I'm lying on the ground... somewhere.* Memories began flooding back. *Battle...* Her head was jerking a little harder now. *Fingers... toes...* She tried moving her arms. *Something's touching my head.* Stephanie struggled as she laid on her stomach. *No strength.* With tremendous effort, she turned her head. Her new daughter! *Oh God!* "What... what happened to the demon?" Stephanie whispered.

The little one scrunched her shoulders, then threw open her hands. "He went *poof!* And I dropped to the ground." She pointed to her bleeding knee. "I got an ouchy."

Stephanie managed to work her left hand up, close her eyes, and her hand glowed. The child's eyes widened then pressing herself against Stephanie's back, she hugged her. "Thank you, Mommy. Turn over." The little girl began nudging Stephanie because she didn't think it good for her new Mommy to be lying with her face on this strange ground. She worked her little hands under Stephanie's shoulder then began squeezing her little self underneath, trying to force her to flop over. The little one grunted with all her effort as what little strength Stephanie had was gone again after healing the girl's knee. But somehow, it wasn't clear exactly how, Stephanie rolled over.

Peering up into the gray void above the dead forest, she worried. *I'm way, way past time to return. I don't even know if the child could... but she seems unaffected.* Stephanie turned her head to examine her new daughter more closely and when their eyes met, their deep connection re-established. Her heart pounded for the child and her senses sharpened. Something nagging at her came to fore. *There's something* wrong... *different*. She listened closely. *That's it! It's totally quiet!* As she turned her head, she murmured, "The... river."

The little girl reported, "It stopped!"

Stephanie couldn't believe it and strained to glimpse the river but couldn't. *I have to see this.* Somehow, she managed to half roll, half crawl, over to the edge, with her daughter helping by pushing and tugging her. The whole Black River looked like, "Black gemstone!"

Sticking out a finger to carefully touch it, Stephanie reported, "It's hard!" Her finger pushed at it. "It's still hard!" She repeatedly poked with force, her fingernail clicking against it. "Hard as a *rock*! A shiny, *pretty* black rock!" Her daughter giggled, leaning against her. Partly clear, they tried looking deeply into it, to check if perhaps the river was still flowing underneath. Stephanie got the feeling that this black stone went *very* deep.

The *faithwalker* used her powers to see into its depths, using very little effort to do so. "You're kidding! My God!" But looking above the river, she found nothing. "So it must be true!" The black wisps that used to constantly rise from the river were gone. She explored its depths again. "They're down *there*! And they're not just black mist as I thought; they're alive, sorta. My God, the Blackness goes with the Black Oil even more than Vaughn realized. It's this *stuff* down there now. The wisps are the Blackness! HA! They're trapped! My life's been worth something, after all!"

Stephanie shook her head. "This reality has *changed!*" Then as revelation hit her, she pushed herself to her knees, with the little girl tugging to help her.

Lifting up her head, "Oh God," Stephanie called out. "I didn't mean it as a prayer… didn't even see it as a choice. It just happened that way. It was just a statement of… *fact!*" The *faithwalker* remembered her last words, before she threw the Light Oil. *This reality shouldn't be.* "It was just a statement out of frustration… out of rebellion. Ha! But You took it for prayer, answering my incredible words. Reality is what reality… wasn't ever before!"

ᴄᴐ

"What has happened *Highest* Councilor ScrabaGag?" asked the Father in no uncertain implications. They were in total, deep, suffocating blackness in the legendary inner room that all demons only whispered about.

This terrible change in reality had not ever been known or felt before. Reports were that the Black River… was no longer a river! That… that the seed of new demon life is *trapped!* Initial attempts to free it have all failed.

"Your Blackness, forgive me to even stand in Your… "

The Father cut him off, "Skip the patronizing, you taste better to me every moment."

ScrabaGag quickly answered, "Grinchback defied my *direct order* not to meddle with the girl. It's ALL recorded. Let me bring up the record and…"

The Father cut him off again, "Oh, I'm sure you have it all documented just fine. Let me guess at your *worthless* next reply. Rule such and such states that you are not guilty when the underling directly disobeys…"

Highest Councilor ScrabaGag cut the Father off without

intending to do so! "Yes, Your Blackness. Forgive me for interrupting."

The Father's presence seemed to press closer, "*Where is Grinchback?*"

ScrabaGag stuttered, "Fa– Father, I, I… ate him. *I had to.* When I saw that he'd disobeyed my direct order and *caused* this *terrible* calamity, I took *immediate* action."

The Father's presence pressed even closer, "And you felt that would…" He left the sentence open for ScrabaGag to complete.

And he did so quickly, "Prevent any more possible damage."

The Father spoke in bored, but hidden delight, "Produce the underling!"

ScrabaGag's eye twisted in disbelief, "Father… Your Blackness?"

The Greatest Eye licked ScrabaGag. "Produce the underling or I will wring him out of you! Or, perhaps I will summon Mafferan, that secret *glow* visitor, to gut you!" threatened the Father in his menacing voice.

But no one ever in demon history had *ever* been given such a command, nor to his knowledge, had even imagined to do so.

"Father! I… I don't even think I know how to…"

"STICK A TAIL TIP IN YOUR EYE AND THROW UP! Or I'll stick my own in it and do it for you!"

Stricken with fear ScrabaGag's rippling stopped cold. His shimmering became non-existent. He started to poke his Eye, gingerly, as he tried to think. Many bulges within him began pushing around. *What do I do? I've never done this before. What if I can't control it? What if I throw up GrrraGagag? Would I be* his *underling* again? *He'll eat me for sure. Oh G—Father, what if I throw up a High Councilor? I could* protest *this* abominable request. *Protest to whom? He's the Father. The rules. YES. THE RULES. NO! Line one, paragraph one, of rules on governance, states that the Father has the right to change any of the rules, any time, to his liking,* period.

The Father was getting bored again, waiting. "WELL?" His intonation spoke that results needed to be forthcoming.

Highest Councilor ScrabaGag poked a little harder, concentrating with all his might. His eye quivered then rolled up, rolled down, in reflexive action, and when it seemed to burst right out of his bulbous head, from its retching center popped out Grinchback!

The underling tumbled back into ethereality with a none-too-surprised eye. He looked around in the deep-black room, barely saw his Master and recoiled. As he jumped back, he bumped into something and turned to see just the Father's immense tail. That made him fall to the ethereal ground, his watery black Eye pressed against it. "Oh, Great Father! OH…"

The Father spoke dryly, "Skip it or I'll have him eat you all over again."

Eye pressed firmly to the ground, Grinchback quickly responded, "Yes, Your Blackness. May I thank…"

The Father pressed very close, cutting his groveling short. Grinchback stopped rippling, shimmering, and speaking.

"You may NOT. What have you DONE? I want to hear it in your own words!"

Grinchback stammered, "Fa– Father… the re– record speaks…"

The Father was losing patience. "YOU KNOW VERY WELL THAT WE'VE… been having technical difficulties of late. *Tell me!*"

Grinchback felt the Father taste him.

"Ahh, well, I… did disobey Master! Forgive me, Master, through my young…"

Forgive him? The Father became utterly repulsed, urging. "Eat him again, will you?"

But he was a good underling. Highest Councilor ScrabaGag was actually quite fond of him, and he had brass to form such a plan as he'd attempted. ScrabaGag found himself not wanting to eat him again. "Please, your Blackness, together we may be able to learn something about the cataclysm."

The Father pressed again upon Grinchback. "Your Master has passed off his right to eat you, but *I may do it myself!*"

Grinchback very quickly began explaining, "I was looking through our forest, marveling at how beautifully we had tended it, when I noticed the girl. I… I couldn't resist the temptation. I heard that they taste very good if…"

The Father cut him off. This underling's voice was irritating him. "WHAT HAPPENED?"

Grinchback replied to the Father's question in haste, "*I had set the perfect trap.* She had brought a little girl with her and I took hold of the child and told her she had to give …"

The Father's massive Eye deeply focused upon the underling, but Grinchback could see his Master's Eye reflected in the Father's, so when he saw ScrabaGag's Eye twitch, he knew not to tell the Father more than necessary. Even so, the Highest Councilor made note not to allow his Eye-twitch to happen again.

"... either her life or the child's to me. I knew she couldn't agree to either, and the longer she remained, that was my goal, the weaker she'd become, and then I'd eat them both!"

The Father eased back, rippling sublimely. "Hmmmmm..." he softly rumbled.

No one had ever heard tell of the Father using that expression before and ScrabaGag noted in amazement how many new things were happening.

"Hmmmmm, not a bad plan! You *still* haven't told me what happened."

Grinchback couldn't believe it. An outright compliment from the Father, himself, but he knew he was still in grave danger. "I, I... I had the child in my coils. The girl couldn't decide! She threw herself to the ground, said she couldn't choose, and... and she spoke some words I couldn't understand... then everything started to shake."

The more he spoke before the Father, the more youthfully confident he became and Grinchback began to boldly think for himself. *The least* he *knows the better.* Father? *BAH! He's just a big old demon, that's all. I can see ALL the records just fine. It just doesn't pay to be old-fashioned! I want to find out for myself* exactly *what the girl did. It would make a formidable weapon, one that maybe even that big, old, pompous head couldn't resist.*

The Father leaned very close. "Are you telling me that all this happened from... a few unintelligible words?"

Grinchback looked the Father honestly in the Greatest Eye, honestly that is, for a demon. "Father, Your Blackness, on my very Eye, I've told you what I can."

Grinchback cautioned himself. *I can't be too careful. The wording must be just right. The rules, even the Father would not likely break his own rules.*

ScrabaGag's thoughts were screaming at his offspring. *Careful Grinchback! The wording must be very careful, the rules, even the Father would not likely break his own rules.*

The Father, all of a sudden, was losing his entertainment. The feeling had changed somehow. He was beginning to get disappointed. "So what happened, an etherealogical etherquake? *There are no such things!* Are you trying to say this was coincidence? How could it turn our river solid?"

ScrabaGag knew he needed to come to the rescue of his underling who'd done remarkably well, but he could tell Grinchback couldn't keep this up much longer, so he took a chance and interjected, "Your Blackness, if I may say, there is another explanation."

The Father's massive black Eye shifted over to ScrabaGag, "*Yesssssss?*"

"She's of those from ancient times, what they used to call a *faithwalker* and a *grave* threat to us all!"

Grinchback's Eye almost popped out. He couldn't believe he'd gone through all that trouble to have it just thrown away like that. He was incredulous. *How could Master be so stupid and just tell him? All that work to keep her our secret.*

The Father hovered closer to his Highest Councilor, lowering his Greatest Eye just inches away from him.

ScrabaGag cautioned himself, *Careful, ScrabaGag! This must be done* exactly *right. It's all in the expression.* He put on the most innocent look he could muster, and that, in itself, was a difficult concept to apprehend but his deep study of humans had taught him much.

The Father kept peering into his depth. ScrabaGag worried. He'd heard the Father had powers none of them had. *What if he simply asks one of the eaten inside of me? Can he do that? Too late now to worry about it. Now, NOW is the right time for just a* hint *of Eye smile.*

The Father immediately picked up on the telltale sign of a smile, quickly realizing what his Highest Councilor was doing. He bellowed out with laughter, "You actually had me considering it, Highest Councilor! I haven't had that good a laugh in, well, never mind. You two can go and see what you can learn."

The two demons had turned to leave, when the Father snapped out, "*Grinchback!*" so the underling froze.

"Yes, Father."

"I make the rule now! *You* are not allowed to eat your Master. Do you have any problems with that?"

Grinchback scowled inside. *I have a lot of problems with that. But, he did protect me. Still...* "No Father; I respect him."

The Father couldn't believe his massive Eye and roared again in laughter, "*Oh my,* the two of you. Oh my! Go, go do your work!"

But just before they got to the ethereal door, the Father called again, "*Grinchback!*"

Grinchback was tiring of this. "Yes, Your Blackness."

"Your specialty, systems design and management?"

"Yes, Father."

"Do let me know when you've fixed the orbs, *won't you?* I want to look at all this, *in detail,* myself."

"Yes Father. I understand."

The Father squinted at him, "I know that you understand, but I want you to say that YOU WILL DO EXACTLY AS I ASK!"

Both of them thought together. *There it was... Heaven... almost out the door and the Father waited till victory was in grasp, and then snatched it back.*

"I will do *exactly* as you ask, Father," Grinchback replied.

There was no way out of it. He was trapped and had to say it. But how many different ways are there to interpret it? *Hmm, I'll have to study on the words I just said. It may be there is a side meaning I can claim, that gets me out of the main one. So many words can be manipulated. YES. I am sure this can be done. I studied that Earth president from before the millennium. He was a* master *at it. Ha, what does the word 'IS' mean?* Grinchback began to wave his ethereal arm to open the door when the Father spoke yet *again.* It seemed like they would never get out of that incredibly black room. Every time he heard the Father call his name, it painfully stopped his rippling.

"*Grinchback,* I may want to take a special interest in this case, *remember what I said.*"

The underling nodded, waved his arm, and the doorway opened into grayness. They were at the ethereal doorway when the Father called back, *yet again.* "Oh, and *Grinchback?*"

Demons were not known to sigh, but as Grinchback's rippling convulsively stopped, yet again his shimmering seemed to go into a sort of fade, like when a dimmer switch slowly turns down the light.

"Yes, Father."

"Put some Sacred Black Oil on that nasty burn on your neck! Whatever happened must have been strange, *indeed!*"

ScrabaGag took his tail, booting his underling out the door, and answered the Father for him, "I will see to it, Father."

Just as Highest Councilor ScrabaGag was in the ethereal doorway, "Highest Councilor!" the Father called.

"Yes Father, Your VERY BLACKNESS."

"I'm sending my seal of approval to your underling to deliver a message!"

ScrabaGag turned all the way around. *Message! Message?* "Message Father? To whom?"

"You are to meet officially with your newfound friend, Mafferan! I want *his* explanation of these things. After so long, the balance has been destroyed! But before we act fully upon it… well, I've watched you two sparring a bit! I think you'll do just fine!"

Highest Councilor ScrabaGag did not question the Father as to how or what destroyed the balance. He wanted to know what the Father knew, but questioning him would only open himself up to more questioning.

When they got back to his room, the Highest Councilor took Grinchback into the secret room, put his huge arm on top of his underling's head, and pushed it back. There, in

Grinchback's ethereal neck folds, was a burn in the shape of an *human hand!* An *HUMAN HAND!* Disgusted, ScrabaGag tossed him away.

"You're lucky the shape of that burn was obscured by your ethereal folds, or you would've gotten both you *and me* into a lot of trouble. The Father would've realized I was, *indeed,* telling him the truth and not joking."

Grinchback didn't protest. He was in awe at his Master's prowess at deception. No one had ever been as subtle as him, to even fool the Father, *With the truth, no less! Simply amazing.*

Highest Councilor ScrabaGag took some of the Sacred Black Oil he specially stored in his secret room, and as he daubed it onto his offspring, he spoke, "*We* shall one day rule this realm. You did well. I respect you!"

Struck dead with surprise, Grinchback actually began to consider feeling guilty for still wanting to be able to eat his Master. *But if we can oust the Father, then I wouldn't have to listen to his order not to eat my Master.* Grinchback put his arm around his beloved Sire.

ScrabaGag spoke in good humor, "Grinchback, what do you say we check? Perhaps there's a chance they're still in our Forest. The girl was in a pretty bad way when I ate you, but all that was happening… well, it kinda scared me, too. I tell you what. You eat the little girl and I'll eat the big one."

Grinchback marveled. His Master didn't have to be that kind. By now, if they were *still* there, they wouldn't be able to fight at all. *I wonder how much my Master really knows about what happened. Was he watching… that whole time? But that would mean…*

She lay on her back, panting from exhaustion. *I'm so worn out my body is confused. It's trying to breathe where there's no Earthly air. Oh God, I'm not making it out of this one, am I? I know I don't have strength to leave. But I can't believe it, the Black River is a big* rock! She couldn't help from chuckling, but that only came out as a few groans. *At least the Black Oil is no longer abundant. Jargono has to run out of it now. All that's left to do is to destroy him and the Earth demons. Vaughn, you'll have to do it without me.*

Healing her daughter then straining to inspect the Black River seemed to be the extent of any ability Lady Stephanie had left. She didn't know it but throughout history, no Earthly human had ever survived even close to this long in the Ethereal Dead Forest. Every fiber of her being felt hypersensitive to pain and she could barely focus, but she still had to do one more thing. She had to truly give her all. *HA! And I suppose that if ever... there was a test of true royalty... HA! it would be, should be... HA! giving our all... for the good of the people.* She just couldn't get away from the humor in the irony of her short life of so much blessing, so deeply, so quickly but then... the end.

Queen Stephanie reached her hand up to her necklace, and pulling it out from under her dress, she held the Seed to the Tree of Life in her fingers. She smiled weakly as she said her goodbye. *No, once was more than I deserved and I couldn't bear you crumbling to ash again. Actually, now that you're back, I'm really not supposed to be here. I know that. Otherwise, you wouldn't have left in the first place. Wedding gift? Hah, I think you stretched things a bit there. Let me go. If you alter the natural course again, the consequences... No... let me go. He'll just have to make it without me. Thank you so much for all that you are to me.*

Her new daughter knelt beside her with her little hands on Stephanie's arm, studying her Mommy's face, trying to figure out what she was thinking. Queen Stephanie summoned all her remaining will for a final act. Grabbing the child's eyes in hers, opening her rich brown eyes wide, she bade goodbye. "I ... I'm sorry... daughter... I just... don't have... strength. You... must pray... to leave this place... I give my... life for you... just as you... were going to do... for me. Have faith... in Goodness... Don't let my life... be wasted. You... *must escape*. The demons... will be back! Take my ribbon... Take this necklace... from around my neck... Wear it...in my memory. It will be your friend... The demons must *never* get it... You must protect it... no matter what.

Her daughter's eyes grew wider with every word she heard, with every word she saw in her Mother's eyes. She didn't want to take the necklace from around her Mommy's neck. Somehow, she knew that when she took it, her Mommy would die right then. She couldn't take it.

Scared, she started to cry, losing focus. That's when Stephanie managed to slide her hand into her daughter's hand. The child let her little palm rest there on top, on her Mommy's palm, without moving. Stephanie, her whole being straining to hold on, was acting on pure intuition, knowledge straight from the Goodness she had received back with the Appendaho. She whispered, "My gift to you, my daughter... my life."

Stephanie, lying flat on her back, managed to bow her head to her shoulder in utter concentration. Her right hand started to glow, then the child's hand started to glow. The *faithwalker* was doing a scaled down version of what her father from the Appendaho had done for her. She was passing to the child her knowledge of love and faith, and some of how hard she fought against evil to gain such treasure of goodness. Stephanie placed inside the child without her knowing, a seed that would sprout when she got older, helping her to understand further. She also gave to her the sacred knowledge of the Seed of the Tree of Life with instructions to take it from around her neck, and wear it. The child's eyes widened wider than seemed possible, but she didn't move. Then Stephanie realized she had also received from this little child. She had a wonderful little heart, a rightful heir, indeed. Stephanie smiled into her eyes, and having learned her real name from the bond whispered, "Lynnara."

Stephanie passed away and Lynnara sat stone still. She... knew things, felt things. Not strange things. They were... her things. But they were clear now. Not covered by the badness of her life. And, she understood now what she had seen about her new Mommy, and about her second Mommy.

Lynnara came out of her trance, and looking down as Stephanie's hand limply fell away from hers, she cried with all her being, "NO!" Around Stephanie's neck but dangling to the ground was the Seed to the Tree of Life which she took in her little hand, crying again, "*NO!*" She cried with feeling understanding, because she was still too young to catch it all with her mind. But then, she heard a hideous voice not far in front of her.

"Well, well, it's almost touching, isn't it Master?"

"Yes, my faithful underling. They were so kind to wait for us." The Highest Councilor's Eye was definitely smiling and drooling.

Lynnara wasn't scared anymore but was angry! Her love for her new Mommy meant more to her than being scared of some monsters. She looked up at the demons, widely opening her little eyes that glowed like the sun. The demons weren't expecting *that,* and they both growled in painful disgust, looking away.

"Underling, we'll have to spit that part out after we eat them. I've had experience with these things."

Lynnara wailed again, "*NO,*" as she turned back to her newest Mommy's body. Grabbing Stephanie's large, red braid in her right hand and holding the beautiful silky ribbon to her little cheek, she rocked back and forth, losing herself to her feelings. The girl used to hold her stuffed doggie's velvety ears to her cheek, but he was gone. Then she felt the demons closing in on them, and with ribbon in hand, she protectively held onto her bestest Mommy *ever.*

With the glowing Seed to the Tree of Life in her little left hand, the royal ribbon in her right, Lynnara screamed yet again with all her life so that there would be no more life left in her for the demons to capture, "*NO!*"

"She has fight, Master."

"Yes, *very* tasty."

I'm still here. It wasn't enough. I didn't scream hard *enough.*

Little Lynnara focused her feelings again, looking for any part of herself she had left out of her earlier cry. Again, she wailed with all her might, all that she is, all that she had now become, and though only understanding a small part of it with her mind, her feelings were all there, "NO!"

But she was *still* in the Dead Forest and felt the demons about to reach for her and her Mommy. Suddenly, she was no longer important at all. But… *My Mommy, I* can't *let them have my MOMMY!* Memories of her original parents chasing after her into the street, getting run over because of her, lying dead with her crying between them, shot terrible pains through her little heart. *I can't let this Mommy die because of me!*

Holding the ribbon against her little cheek with one hand, she covered Stephanie's body with her little body. Letting go of the Seed, she wrapped her other little arm as tightly around Stephanie as she could with the Seed to the Tree of Life mashed between them. Squeezing as tightly as she could with all her strength, all her will, all her love, she shouted, "*YOU CAN'T HAVE MY MOMMY!*" The demons reached… but the girls vanished. Stephanie's body and Lynnara were gone!

CHAPTER TWENTY-FIVE

To Begin Again

Little hands and feet wriggled and wiggled in uncontrolled ecstasy, as a little round head full of deep red curls stared intently. Rich brown eyes searched her mother's face. The baby only had one pink booty on. The other was in her mouth. "Oh God, you are so precious!" Her Mother's medium-brown hair with natural red highlights hung down over the infant as she gazed deeply upon her treasure beyond compare. Finally, something in her life had made a difference. Her daughter grabbed tiny fistfuls of Mommy's hair but she didn't notice because her thoughts were far away.

She had thought marrying an important man would make a difference, take away the stigma. It wasn't her fault who her great-grandmother was born to. Why should I have to suffer for whatever my ancestors were so long ago? I never knew them. I'm just a person like anyone else.

She took her hair from the little fists and baby Stephanie began complaining since she loved all forms of contact with her mother. Her mother spun the colorful wooden birds hanging over her crib and the mobile's motion attracted her attention.

"You'll not have to know the terrible shame of being an outcast like your mommy, or grandma or great grandma. Daddy has promised that you were born normal. You're just like everyone else. You know, that's one of the main reasons I married him. He has the power to erase your... our history. Oh, my precious Stephanie! You are born free."

The sound of her mother's dear voice caused Stephanie to focus on sounds: Mommy's voice, love, LOVE... love Mommy... meaning... sounds... Mommy's voice ... Her Mother's tears dropped upon her daughter and the infants eyes widened. Feelings... mine... Mommy's... meaning...

Staring deeply into her daughter's eyes, she was overcome by a strange, special feeling she had never known before but somehow felt so familiar. It was so much larger than her. Oh God! This new life came out of me. Something so special. Life that is me but is also not. It's so pure, so giving, so tender, like all life should be. Yet something is so special, unique about Stephanie. *Melting into her daughter's eyes, she felt a moment of unity that couldn't be explained.* "You are so special. *I love you so much. There is no one in the* whole world *like you."* Her *eyes glowed brightly and her daughter's glowed back but she missed it. Her focus had been distracted in trying to decipher the meaning of the strange feelings erupting through her.*

Lynnara didn't understand what just happened. She was still holding the ribbon and it was glowing. She didn't understand how they traveled, or to where... though it felt right. As she looked around while still lying atop her Mommy, there seemed to be something familiar about this place.

There were four torches lit around an old stone table upon which Stephanie laid. Paintings were on the walls and Lynnara recognized the figures in the corners as the monsters. She noted how beautiful the man and woman were, and gazed at the woman's face then back to her Mommy's face, then back at the paintings again.

One picture had the same ribbon in the beautiful young woman's hair as the one tied to Stephanie's which she kept holding in her little hand. Lynnara set the braid on top of Stephanie then without knowing why, climbed down from the table and walked up to the paintings. The man's face was hard, but kind. The woman's face was all love, but seemed to know things. Lynnara felt so much life in this art that it seemed they were alive and not pictures at all, so she began to speak to them, pointing back toward Stephanie.

"My, my Mommy," she said with her little voice rising up. "She needs your help. Because those over there," she pointed at the demon pictures. "*They tried to eat us.* But Mommy, my third Mommy, over there... she wouldn't let them. She ..." Lynnara couldn't think of the words to say what Stephanie had done to her. Then she remembered Stephanie's words and repeated them, "She... gave me her life? And..." She broke down crying, wailing. Through her tears, she cried out the words, "I want her to have it back." And she collapsed on the cave floor, curling up into a ball. She had given her all. She didn't know what else to do. She didn't want to be in this world any more.

"Lynnara," a tender feminine voice spoke from above her.

She looked up at the beautiful face and then at the picture and then back again.

"I'm a spirit now, dear." The voice said happily. "I heard your prayers and am here to see what I can do to help."

The child pointed to Stephanie's body lying on the table. "My... that's my third Mommy, and she was the bestest of my Mommies! I don't want her dead." She wailed and buried her face in her hands, lying on the cave floor.

Queen Yinauqua asked gently, "Why, Lynnara? We all have a time to go and some are saying it wasn't even fair for her to have been alive!"

Lynnara thought on the question.. *Why? Strange question. It's so clear, even to me. But... she's so pretty, so good I answer her.* She picked her head up. "I don't want her to die. Because... I love her. It *is* fair. Stupid to say it's not. Because... she gave me her life. I want to give it back!" It was that obvious to Lynnara. She didn't know how to say it any clearer.

Queen Yinauqua smiled kindly. "She gave you a *very* precious gift. You now know about the Seed around her neck, don't you?"

Lynnara nodded. "Yea, but... I don't want it. 'Cause it's *hers*. It's..." she thought a moment, "Not supposed to be mine. It's *hers*." She pointed back to Lady Stephanie.

"Do you understand how important that Seed is? Did you get that from when you held hands?"

Lynnara nodded again. "That's why I *know* it's *hers.*"

Queen Yinauqua continued. "Well, do you know how important it is to keep that a secret? There are many that would kill many people for your secret."

Lynnara knew, but she had a plan, "Well, if Mommy were alive, I wouldn't tell ANYONE." Her eyes looked deeply into Queen Yinauqua's eyes.

"I believe you, my dear Lynnara. You're a very brave, little girl. One day, you'll help your Mommy fight *very* evil people *and* demons, if…"

Lynnara's eyes grew wide. "I will?"

Queen Yinauqua nodded. "Yes, dear. I can see how your lives have been brought together. You've both given your all."

"We did."

Yinauqua smiled, nodding again. "Go over to where your new Mommy is."

The little girl got up and walked over to the stone table which came up to her shoulders.

Queen Yinauqua floated over with her. *I have to be very careful how I do this. HA! I think if my husband knew what I'm doing… yes, I think he'd be proud of me!* "Lynnara, I was sent by the Light to help you understand… but I can't do what only *you* can do for your new Mommy." *The Light didn't tell me I couldn't do this.*

"You can't?"

I have to wait for her to ask. Yinauqua shook her head as Lynnara waited for her to speak further, but when no words were forthcoming, the little girl repeated herself, "You *can't?*" And Queen Yinauqua shook her head again.

Lynnara wrinkled up her nose in thought, until she realized. "Well, what can *I* do?" She scrunched her little shoulders and threw open her little hands.

"You put your little hands on your Mommy and with all your heart, talk to the God of Light, and tell him only truly why you want her to live. Tell Him how much that means to you, and be *honest.* Don't try to say you can only keep the secret about the Seed if Mommy were alive, when you know you would keep it anyway."

Lynnara understood but she was so deeply drawn to Queen Yinauqua that she turned away from the table, walking over to her. Gingerly, she poked a finger through her spirit, then did it again.

Yinauqua laughed as if being tickled. "Oh my, what is it dear, what do you want to ask?"

Lynnara looked up into her eyes. "Is this what happens to people when they... *die*?"

Yinauqua leveled her eyes deeply into the child's eyes. "No dear, this is what happens when they *live*." She reached her hand out, lightly letting her spirit caress Lynnara's cheek then she vanished. The child stared for a moment then slowly walked over to her dead... no, her living Mommy. She couldn't figure it all out yet, but knew Stephanie was her *real* Mommy.

"Dear God?" Lynnara's voice rose up as she reached up and held Stephanie's arm. "Since my Mommy really isn't dead then could she live here in this body for a long time... instead of like her Mommy that I just talked to?"

She paused to see if anything was happening and when nothing did, she began to fret. *This isn't working.* She felt terribly ashamed then. She couldn't give the life back to her Mommy, like her Mommy had given to her. Sobbing, little Lynnara struggled to pull herself back up onto the table, grabbing Stephanie's arm and dress for hand-holds. Finally, she swung her little leg up, managing to maneuver herself back up to where she'd been before. She straightened out her own, twisted, little red dress and then studied her Mommy's peaceful face. "I love you, Mommy, but I dunno what to do. All I knows is what I did to get here." But upon thinking about what she just said, *Maybe, that'll work again!*

Falling atop Stephanie, she hugged her as she did when they vanished from the demons, the Seed to the Tree of Life again pressed between them. Still nothing happened so sitting up and sobbing more, Lynnara grasped the braid she held before and put the royal ribbon to her cheek. There was nothing more to do but cry. "Praying doesn't work, *Mommy!... My Mommy, MY MOMMY!*" Her little heart knew the deep goodness of Stephanie. She could feel it through the gift passed on to her, as well, and could even feel it from Stephanie's body. Lynnara had felt the faithwalker's goodness from the first time she saw her at second Mommy's house. It was that very love, that very goodness, that she'd latched onto right before she found herself standing next to her new Mommy in front of that very bad man. Right before she appeared there beside Stephanie, she remembered sorta like disappearing into that love.

The more Lynnara felt, the more she loved, the deeper she cried, "*My mommy, my Mommy!*" She began to feel like she was disappearing again as the ribbon began to glow. And the glow grew, but Lynnara was unaware of it, because she felt so ashamed for not loving her new Mommy strong enough to give her back her life. *This Mommy is the bestest Mommy in the whole world. I just know I ... I can't live without her... no one can!* Her little heart ached to have her back, but not just for herself. What would the world be like without her? She felt it in her arms, everywhere, that everyone wanted her back, needed her back…

"Lynnara," came a soft feminine voice.

The spirit woman was back but the child was ashamed so didn't want to talk to her.

"Lynnara," the voice called again, but the child realized it wasn't coming from behind her, it was coming from…

Stephanie moved, putting her hand on Lynnara's head, and when their eyes met, they both lost themselves in each other's stares… they knew so much together.

"You, you sound like *your* Mommy," Lynnara said in an informative way.

Stephanie smiled, realizing where she was, and that Yinauqua must have spoken to her daughter.

"Your Mommy told me to pray, and do like this." She drew back onto her knees, putting her hands on Stephanie, showing how she held her. "But it didn't work. I didn't do it right. But then, I *cried*… that worked," she said matter-of-factly.

The love that grew between their eyes in that instant was like a whole other world and neither could keep from the other's arms. As they hugged, Stephanie spoke, "Your crying worked, my daughter, because your tears were true prayers. You did do as my Mother told you, you just did it your way, which is the only way it could be true from you. She told you to be true. *And*, it just so happens that your prayers made sense to God, and He answered them by letting you bring me back. You gave me my life back!" Then they heard another feminine voice.

"Well said, my sister. My, my… how you've grown!"

Stephanie eased Lynnara to the side, sitting up to see a long-missed face. She was materializing in front of them both. "And you, too, little one. Well done!" Arlupo made squenchy motions with her fingers as if to tickle her and Lynnara giggled.

Stephanie's tears shined. "Arlupo, how I've missed you so!" She choked-up at again seeing her sister who was more than a sister.

Putting her hands on her hips, Arlupo replied. "Well, I almost had to set another plate for you, but, it wasn't your time, was it little nipper?"

Lynnara emphatically shook her head from side to side.

Stephanie's eyebrows went up. "They do that up there?"

Arlupo looked as if she didn't understand the question. "Do what?"

"Dinner?"

Arlupo laughed, "In a manner of speaking, but it's no concern of yours now, Stephie! You know, your beloved husband believes you're *dead*. Burnt up!"

The faithwalker's hand went over her mouth. "Oh God, NO!"

"Your letter? *Magnificently* done, my sister. It worked exactly as you intended. Quite advanced, I must say." And then Arlupo turned grave, "Take care, my sister prophetess. You have much to face and great pains *yet* to experience! But you and your husband, and *this* little one here, have caused quite a commotion both above and below as well as here on Earth. We're enjoying every minute of it!" Then she was gone.

More pain? Oh God, how could there be more? Never mind. Reality will be... hmm. I wonder what Vaughn has done to stir up so much? "Lynnara, how did we get here?" Stephanie asked with raised eyebrows, realizing she didn't know that part, and couldn't guess how.

With big, dark-brown honest eyes, Lynnara confessed. "I... *I couldn't leave you.* You told me to, but I couldn't."

Stephanie looked on with amazement. "Tell me what you did. Show me so I can understand."

Lynnara pushed Stephanie back down onto the table, reached over, and took hold of her Mommy's large braid. Then kneeling beside her, she held the ribbon to her cheek, and smiled, explaining, "I dunno! I just did this." The child rocked back and forth. "And I did *this.*" Lynnara hugged Mommy with her other arm. "And then we were here."

Stephanie beamed her broad smile of understanding. "I understand. The last of the Light Oil is in this ribbon. Hmmm! Well... if *you* can do it, I certainly should be able to! Would you like to travel again like that, *little faithwalker?* But this time, I'll lead."

Lynnara nodded though her eyes had a question written all over them so Mommy raised her eyebrows, asking. "What?"

"You have a *husband?*"

Stephanie's eyes glittered with many beautiful colors. "Yes, I do. I really do."

Lynnara hesitated then asked, "Can he be my *Daddy?*"

Stephanie hugged the child, kissed her cheek, then looked into her eyes. "When you see him, you can ask him yourself."

The faithwalker took hold of her braid by the ribbon in one hand, and Lynnara in her other arm. With a twinkle in her eyes, she put the ribbon to the child's face even though Stephanie knew she didn't have to, then they disappeared.

❧

There was a knock at their paradisal door! "That's odd. Knocking is a myth!" Reserved, some say in jest, only for *official* business.

"Well, in any event, dear husband, are you going to be rude, or are you going to get the door?" She propped herself up on their paradisal bed, and leaning over him with a definitely mischievous glint, asked, "Or, would you like me to answer it?"

Mafferan stared at his wife. *Prophecy has ended for her I thought, or is it just that it ended only for certain areas? Or periods? That* glint *in her eye!* "No, thanks! I'll get it, dear." He glanced at her as she smiled broadly.

As he left their bedchamber, just as he was in the doorway, he heard, "Next time you decide to *disappear…*" He froze, wondering what his wife would say next, but she prolonged the moment for several seconds, "Have the courtesy to at least, *not* tell your friends to keep it a *secret.* You know me, dear."

Sighing with how much he loved her, he smiled broadly, knowing she was doing the same. "I shall… take it under advisement!" Chuckling to himself at using the demon's last words that avoided Mafferan's threat, he went to answer the door.

Yinauqua called back to him, "You know, whatever is done in the *dark*, always comes out into the light, for some, *more* sooner than later!"

Cloudwalker was at the door. "*Cloud,* my older friend. Knocking? You're not still mad at me, are you?

Still mad? He's always trying to be clever. I never indicated that I was ever… "Mad? *Mad?* Why should I still be mad? Just because you delivered me to your lovely wife to be gutted, filleted, and to have all my entrails spread out until she had divined *every last drop of truth from me?* No, my friend! I was only amazed that you managed to trap me, *again!*"

Mafferan grinned broadly, seeing that his metaphor was not only a metaphor. "Then, what brings you to *knocking* at my door?"

"My friend, there is nothing that is done in the dark that doesn't come out into the light, for some, *more* sooner than later!"

Mafferan felt the prickles go up his sprit spine. He looked back towards his bedchamber, then back at Cloud. He could see Cloud was drawing this out with extra pleasure, so Mafferan decided not to give him the satisfaction of a response. *He's obviously got something to say. I'll wait for him to say it.*

Darn! He's not going to respond at all. Might as well tell him then, "You've been *officially* summoned!"

Summoned? "Why would the Lord send you and not simply call within me?"

"Ahh, my friend, not by *our* Lord. Highest Councilor ScrabaGag with special seal of approval from *his* Father!"

The sense of humor faded from King Mafferan as he looked back towards the bedchamber again, but this time seriously considering asking her advice. Things always worked best when they worked together. "How was this message delivered?"

"The Councilor's underling," Cloud couldn't help from snickering, shaking his head, "managed to bring it all the way to the Great Gate and," he broke out in a fit of laughter, "*ring the bell!*"

"You're kidding!" But Cloud shook his head. "You're not! Well, I hope the poor fledgling didn't get burned *too* badly."

"He was covered from head to tail in that Black Oil. The watcher saw him begin to smoke though, a good ways before he even got close. Must be a really important message, seeing how that *stuff* has now become such a rare commodity!" *Cloudwalker* handed him the ancient agreed upon paper on which official messages were allowed to exchange hands.

The King unfolded the letter:

Mafferan has been duly summoned by seal of the Father of All to appear before His Highest Councilor ScrabaGag to answer charges of the *glow's* violations of the BALANCE that has been *imposed* upon all reality.

Bring documentation of all listed events for further inspection and investigation.

1. The Cursed Object's reappearance
2. Various *threats* made upon the Highest Councilor
3. Wanton destruction of the Black River (Compensation shall be required)
4. Abuse of an underling.

Mafferan indignantly stared at *Cloudwalker.* "Did you read this?"

"Of course, along with everyone else that happened by. There are no secrets here, only Light."

"Yes, yes, I know *that*. I mean, who wrote *this?* I can hardly read the fine print!"

Cloudwalker searched his memory for details of the finer rules for production and delivery of an official document. "I believe the bearer of the message is also required to be its scribe."

Mafferan broke out instantly into laughter. *Cloud* looked confused but the King enlightened him. "Look at this!" He waved the letter under his nose. "It's *obvious!*"

Cloudwalker knew it was useless to try to fake that he understood. When Mafferan saw his helplessness, he smiled, put an arm around his friend's shoulder, and showed him the message. "The meaning is *obvious*. It's right under your nose." *Cloud* couldn't hide his frustration so Mafferan continued, "As soon as you told me who scribed it, I knew. Why would he print the grievances so small?"

"Alright, you've got me! Stop dragging it out."

"Why would he print grievance number four a little larger?"

Cloudwalker always hated when his friend did this. *He's out of control!*

But Mafferan read his mind and with a hurt look announced, "I *am not!* Look. He printed number four larger obviously to tell me the most important thing he's thinking about, HIMSELF!"

Cloud was beside himself. *I hadn't even noticed it was larger print, let alone thought of any meaning behind a* demon's *letter.*

"That's key to understanding this. He printed the other grievances so small, to make them appear as only the *fine print*."

"SO?"

"C'mon, no one reads the fine print! But that's just it because *that* conveys his true meaning." Mafferan couldn't resist pausing. *Cloudwalker* knew if he tried to hide his frustration again, it would prolong the answer so he surrendered, throwing out his arms.

Mafferan's eyes twinkled, "All that's important to this underling is himself. So then, he's telling us, that if we bring accurate records, it would harm his plans! By sending the message this way, he's telling us that he's the one that's going to authenticate everything, and that he'll help us!"

"That's *crazy*! First of all, why would any demon want to help *us*?"

"Personal gain! For some reason, he finds value in being the only one knowing the truth of the past events. He's actually quite good, technologically, the best I've ever seen with our orbs!"

"WHAT? You've been…"

"Of course. Know thy enemy. A famous saying."

"But how do you know… and what *is* the truth of the past events? No one really seems to know for sure how…"

"Because sending meaning like this is useless unless he's the one that's going to do the verification. If he couldn't help, the underling never would have printed number four larger, making *obvious* this centers on him. In fact, there's no point at all in putting such meaning forth if he can't offer something valuable. He has to give me a reason not to ask why the print was so fine, otherwise, his *Father* would discover him. The demon also knows I won't betray him because any possible advantage gained through him is too important to throw away. Plus, because he got away with printing the letter in this fashion, he's proving that all he was delegated to do was deliver the message, but not HOW he delivered it. It may even be that the Father didn't even determine the actual content, but spoke in generalizations, requiring them to fill in the details. His *Father* merely gives orders with no apparent follow through. The underling has the freedom to help us to help him.

"But, but... we don't need his help, do we?"

Mafferan smiled, thanked *his friend* for the message, walked back into his paradisal abode, and closed the door! *Cloudwalker's* mouth dropped open and thought about just walking right in. One could do that in paradise, just walk right in to anyone's abode. But, but at the moment, it just didn't feel proper to do so.

Yinauqua looked at him when the King reentered their bedchamber. She noted that she flinched slightly, when she saw his demeanor, a reaction she hadn't seen since... it was so long ago. She only noted it, because it was so *distantly* familiar.

Now, she studied herself and this memory to uncover the truth, and having done so in short order, she leveled her gaze into Mafferan. "My *dear* husband, we've been through so much. *What have you done?*"

Mafferan's eyes looked away for just an instant but his wife's eyes narrowed when she saw it. "Yinauqua," he hadn't called her in that way in so very long, "Do you remember when our son came to us, wanting to seek our lost daughter?"

"Of course." *I'm not liking the sound of this. We were so young back then.*

"Do you remember what you said to me about oaths?"

She suddenly sat straight up. *That's a strange sensation.* She took a moment to analyze it, before she continued. *It's the paradisal equivalent of goose-bumps.* "Yes. 'Key to oaths is their purpose which each side interprets to their benefit.' And I remember *you* saying that our oath for all the people was only as good as... *all* the people."

She sat up even straighter, squinting at him sharply and he silently sat down beside her on the bed with his hands folded on his lap and his head bowed but not in prayer. Yinauqua's eyes opened even wider and her voice rose, "But *husband*, that was only an oath between two *very* small tribes!"

Mafferan's voice took on a pleading nature. "But it was our training ground. All wise living begins with the basics. Even a great tree starts small, but its life principle remains the same, repeating itself over and over again in grander and grander expressions."

She took hold of his arm firmly and of his face which she had to turn towards her. *Something else I haven't done in a* very *long time.* She tried to look into his averted eyes and lamented, "Dear, *beloved* husband, you missed my meaning! I wasn't playing down the importance of our little tribal oath, rather, I meant that *now*, there's so much *more* at stake! I repeat, *tell me what you've done!*"

☙

Stephanie and Lynnara popped into the tent in the same sitting position they left from the cave. Vaughn's camping lantern was on low but Spot immediately jumped up, tail whipping in more directions than Stephanie thought possible.

679

The dog ran over to Stephanie but almost immediately sensed Lynnara and shifted direction, knocking the child over.

Big tongue licking. Little girl giggling. Hands. Paws. Mommy scolding! "Shhhhh, he's asleep." The two youngsters hushed instantly, looking guilty. Neither had ever been scolded by Stephanie like *that* before. The faithwalker raised her finger to her lips to signal them to keep quiet but as they stared at her, she winked at them! Spot and Lynnara looked at each other then back at Stephanie, wondering what the wink meant.

Vaughn was sleeping on his left side. Crawling over, laying down behind him, Queen Stephanie pressed herself against his back. She curled her legs against his, tucked her lower arm under his head and wrapped her upper arm across his chest, squeezing gently. The familiarity, the instantaneous connection, sent relief pouring through her. *Wholeness.* She whispered mischievously into his ear, "This is not a dream. This is not a dream. This is…"

Lynnara watched intently in all delight, trying to keep Spot's licking from blocking her field of view, watching for her chance. But Spot was used to seeing such things by now, and was all about familiarizing himself with yet another human pup.

In his sleep, he knew her. It was a dream but her voice was saying it wasn't a dream. He hadn't slept for a whole day, was exhausted, physically and emotionally. He had survived way past his limits of endurance but he had lived. He felt her pressing against him. The dream was *so* real.

"Stephanie," he called out in his sleep. She hoisted herself up on her elbow to peer over his broad shoulders to see his face. He looked exhausted so she turned and motioned

Lynnara to lie down behind her and the girl bounded to the bed and curled up against her. Spot took his place at their feet and laid down. Although Stephanie's life had once again been returned to her, her body needed rest. They were all beyond tired and fell asleep together.

ↄↄ

The tent door flew open. The ranger, whose child Vaughn saved, poked his head through the entrance to wake Vaughn up. It had taken the rest of the night to move all the people up and down the tree of freedom. Predawn light shined through the tent door, but when he peered into the tent, his mouth dropped open, more than one person was sound asleep.

Spot rose up stretching, and walked over for a head pat but sensing someone more familiar, he squeezed past the ranger and finding his kid, Little One, decided face-licking was in order. But by now, she'd learned how to handle Spot so she hugged his neck tightly but at the same time, pushed him aside and squeezed herself into the tent door.

"Daddy!" she said in amazement, pointing, "That's *her!*"

He'd heard of Vaugh's wife from Blackbeard, heard her letter from a distance but now seeing her *alive*, he could only stare in silence. His daughter tugged at his arm, "*Daddy*, that's Stephanie, his wife. I… I met her the other night. She didn't get burned up. *Daddy*, that bad woman *lied!*"

Little One started to go into the tent, but her father held out his arm and backed out, closing the tent flap. He didn't understand how it was possible. He knew Queen Karen was sure she was dead but then so many things these last two days didn't seem possible. In fact, ever since he met Vaughn, a lot of things hadn't seemed possible. *That's it! That's the quality of the boy that I've been trying to put into words. He makes you believe in the impossible, simply because it's right!*

When the ranger went to the fence and told the others what he saw, they were all one in amazement, saying that if anything like that was possible, it would be certainly possible for *their* King.

"OK, Rangers," he called loudly. "We've done it!"

And every man, woman and child cheered from the other side of the fence, which had the desired effect of waking Vaughn.

Odd... He found his head was lying on someone's arm, and another arm was around him so he turned over to face his beloved wife. He blinked his eyes hard.

"Is this a dream?" he heard himself ask as he touched her face preciously, waking her gently. "Am I dreaming?" he repeated with tears pouring forth.

She put her hand tenderly to his face. "No. I'm really here."

"But..."

"I know." She spoke softly, putting her fingers to his lips to hush him. "You thought I was dead. I was, actually! But not like what you think. I'll tell you everything later."

She cupped her hand behind his head, drawing him into her slow kiss. Theirs became a world apart from everything, except Stephanie became aware of a little hand on her shoulder and a little face just inches from hers, staring intently at them. Vaughn became aware also so they parted lips. He was now staring closely into another set of deep dark brown eyes.

Lynnara was all prepared and proposed, "Will you be my *Daddy*?" Vaughn looked at his wife who gave him her deep, loving, understanding smile.

Lynnara was *definitely* prepared. All night she had dreamt of this meeting. She put her little hand on Stephanie's head, declaring, "*She's* my new Mommy. She's the *bestest* Mommy I have. I had three. She's number three. I... saved her life. But that's *after* she gave me hers. She's my Mommy, and you're her husband. So, will you be my *Daddy*?"

Vaughn was pretty good with children, at understanding what they meant, but he couldn't fathom what was just said. He felt that it must be true, but didn't know where to even start to figure.

Stephanie felt her daughter needed a bit of help. "I'll tell you my love. This is *Lynnara*. What she said is true... she saved my life."

Vaughn couldn't imagine how this little child could possibly have saved *her* life from anything, but his wife's eyes spoke the straight truth.

Oh goody, he believes Mommy! Lynnara figured this would be the perfect time to ask again, "Will you be my *Daddy*? It's not good to have a *Mommy* without a *Daddy*."

It seemed the child's whole world hung on the answer to her question. She had made her case, just as she had wanted. Her little heart pounded as she looked deeply into his eyes. He was like the cave picture, only a lot younger. His face was tough, but it was deeply kind. And his eyes were full of love for his wife, just like in the picture. Time seemed to stand still for Lynnara.

Vaughn finally answered with a straight face, eyes leveled into hers, "I'll be your Daddy, if you be my daughter." He raised his eyebrows in question.

With a smile in her whole face, she reached across Mommy with her right index finger, touching some of the tears that were still resting on his cheeks. "You're a *good* Daddy, because you have *true* tears!"

All he could do was look back at his wife in astonishment.

"I'll tell you all about it," Stephanie promised.

Vaughn reached over, gently holding the side of his new daughter's head. She pressed her head into his hand, rubbing it back and forth, luxuriating in his touch. Vaughn leaned forward, kissed her forehead and Lynnara felt like she was in heaven. Climbing over Stephanie, she wormed her way in between them and then lying on her back, she smiled up at them both. Stephanie and Vaughn glanced at each other and then each knelt, kissing one of Lynnara's cheeks and now she knew she was in heaven. Yet simultaneously, both Vaughn and Stephanie heard another calling in their hearts. Each knew that duty called to them as they sat up.

Vaughn crawled out then turned back to offer his hand to his Queen. Her hand reached out of the tent opening, taking his then she emerged, standing up straight with squared shoulders and smoothed out her dress. All the people admired her beautiful, royal-blue long dress with the gold ribbon edging, but they were awestruck by her very presence. Her spirit permeated through their souls. Her gracious beauty shined an invisible light that instantly enlightened them. There was no doubt that *this* was the lady who wrote that wonderful letter that helped save their lives, the woman who had given their King the strength to go on. They chanted over and over from the other side of the fence, "LONG LIVE QUEEN STEPHANIE! LONG LIVE KING VAUGHN! LONG..."

Vaughn hung his head, while Stephanie stared at him, and took his arm. He mumbled, "I'll tell you later."

Lynnara who had taken Stephanie's other hand peered past her Mommy, asking wide eyed, "Are you a King?"

Vaughn kicked the ground, shaking his head. "That's just what they're saying because I helped them."

Listening to the crowd cheering her parents, Lynnara began to figure it all out. *They certainly think you're a King and Mommy a Queen. If the people say so, it* must *be so.* "Does that mean I'm a princess? A *real* princess?"

Vaughn motioned with his free arm and she ran to him. He picked her up and looking into her eyes with her little face just inches away, he explained, "You would be my princess no matter what people say."

Lynnara got her first fatherly hug, as the last ranger carrying his daughter in his arm, came up to him. "Sir, we don't know how, we... didn't see your Queen come in. Otherwise, we would have..."

Stephanie smiled, shaking her head, "Please. You didn't see me because... well, I hid from you. Don't worry."

Her voice was as sweet and beautiful to the ranger as her spirit. He bowed his head slightly at her then and told them, pointing to all the people on the other side, "You've done it, King Vaughn. We'll be the last to cross over. You've actually done it! You've given us a new life and kept your word."

His daughter was staring deeply at Lynnara in Ranger King Vaughn's arm. They didn't know one another but they were of the same people. Little One spoke to Lynnara while pointing at Vaughn, "He saved my life and all the people's lives." She waved her little hand around, indicating the people on the other side of the fence.

Lynnara answered back, pointing at Stephanie, "I… saved her life… after she gave me hers."

The ranger and his daughter both looked at Lynnara, and back at Stephanie, trying to figure out what her daughter meant.

Stephanie nodded with a smile. "It's true, but also, some things are *secret*." She scrunched up her face and lightly tweaked Lynnara's nose. But Stephanie's confession to its truth just piqued more curiosity, as Little One and her daddy kept looking at each other, and back at Stephanie.

Vaughn redirected the conversation. "Go ahead, you and your daughter. We'll be across shortly." He let go of Stephanie's hand to reach across and pinch Little One's cheek, the girl from his heart vision, the girl he wept to save. He gave her his special broad smile and she blew him a kiss as the ranger took his daughter and started toward the giant tree.

But he turned back towards them, "I just want to say how glad I am to see you both together, and that I'm honored to meet you, and serve you as well, Queen Stephanie." He bowed his head and Stephanie returned it, causing him to straighten with pride, to hold his daughter just a little higher as he escaped to freedom.

Stephanie turned to face her husband, "If you want dear, I could transport you both over. Lynnara, showed me how!"

She rubbed the ribbon on her braid on Lynnara's cheek, and the child giggled, pressing her face into it.

Vaughn just stared, not yet understanding, "No! We should do this like everyone else... there's meaning to it."

"Of course, I should have known. As you wish, my King," she spoke with a mischievous smile and a bow.

When Lynnara saw the gesture, she made like she wanted down so Vaughn set her on the ground. She addressed him, "As you wish, my King," then bowed, just as she saw her Mommy bow.

Vaughn shook his head, took their hands and walked them over to the huge tree. Stephanie gaped in amazement and even though Vaughn had seen it before, he still stared as well. "Stephie, can you believe this? We are actually going to be free."

Her firm reply had finality in its tone, "Let's not waste any more time talking about it, let's just *do it*." There was a deep sense of finally putting an end to the insanity of the last months.

Vaughn attached the harness to Spot and the rope to the harness by which he would pull him up. He looped the rope in the crook of his arm so that he could let it out as he climbed.

Stephanie put her hand on the rope ladder but then turned around to look into Vaughn's eyes. "I am so *proud* of you." She held him in her gaze for a moment after which she climbed with the pride of knowing what her husband had done.

Vaughn treasured every bit of her gaze and with a tear in his eye at his beloved wife's words, he clambered up behind her, carrying Lynnara on his back.

As they climbed, Stephanie called down to him, "Do you remember the last time we were on a ladder?"

"Remember? I'll never forget. You practically choked me to death! God, I thought for sure we were going to fall."

Stephanie laughed, "I was so terrified, I used my *faith-walking* powers without even knowing it. We *were* falling! But all I knew was that we mustn't fall."

"Let us live our whole lives just like that, *my Queen.*"

She knew Vaughn was smiling with his emphasis on 'my Queen.'

Neither of them wanted the titles, except perhaps, privately between the two of them. Stephanie pulled herself up into the tree-fork and turning around, she took their new daughter from him. When Vaughn got into the fork, she placed Lynnara onto his back again.

Climbing up and out across the branch over the fence, Stephanie was surprised at how exhilarating it was. Tears dropped from her eyes. *I know I could have just popped on over, but to actually physically climb across on this tree, it just feels so right.* Then down the ladder she went to free ground, and touching her feet onto free soil, her hopes exploded within her. *We can start a real home, a real life, oh God, MAKE LOVE!*

Inside the fork, Vaughn tied off Spot's rope. Crawling up the familiar branch, and then out along the smaller branch, passing over the fence, he balanced his new daughter on his back who was talking nonstop. "This is so *fun*... Don't *drop* me! If you do, Mommy will be *mad!* I'll get an *owie*.... Mommy can heal it. She healed... But he couldn't listen, because he had to concentrate on balancing.

Stephanie watched them teeter one way, then the other. Several times she reached out her hand, was about to snatch her daughter like she'd done to rescue her from Jargono's fire, but she held herself back. *I can't take this away from them. They'll make it, I think! Anyway, if I have to, I think I can snatch her in mid-fall, I think.* Just in case, Stephanie prepared several alternative plans, the last of which was to physically catch her.

Finally, down the ladder he went, to set foot again on free ground and he turned his back to Stephanie who lifted Lynnara then set her down. They both watched Vaughn as he went back up the ladder again.

Little One came up and took Lynnara's hand. Smiling at each other, they didn't know, but they were destined to be like sisters, even more than sisters. Both fate and calling waited on their unique friendship and faith that one day would become the only possible hope for their people to survive. But right now, they simply enjoyed the present.

Back across the fence, back in the fork, Vaughn went to retrieve the dog that had saved their lives, and led the people to safety. Spot waited patiently while his Master pulled his big limp body up into the fork. Vaughn then slipped one arm into a carrying strap, then reached around behind and finding the other strap, slipped the other arm in. Carefully, he turned himself around, so he could climb out of the fork. He had gone over this part of the plan a hundred times. It was one of the only parts that seemed familiar to him. "Spot, stay *still* if you don't want us to fall."

Out across the branch to freedom, Spot was motionless, the picture of doggy humility. Stephanie and Lynnara held their hands to their mouths, but Little One giggled, knowing there was nothing to worry about because *that* was *Ranger Vaughn.* He had saved her, and all the people. *Just follow the doggie. Ha! The doggie's riding on his back now!*

Every time Vaughn swayed, his family swayed, letting out little 'Ohs.' Then down the ladder again, and for the third time, Vaughn set his feet on free ground. But somehow, his emotions weren't as he expected so he pondered. *Something so hard-fought should produce more feeling than this, I think. I wonder why it hasn't.*

Spot finally started to squirm so Vaughn slipped out of the harness, but before he could remove it from Spot, his pet took off, running to different people, sniffing, jumping up, and getting head pats, rubs and scratches. One of the rangers finally grabbed him and took off the harness while winking at Vaughn. Stephanie, Lynnara and Little One laughed, while they held each other. Spot disappeared, running free amidst the people, who all realized that this *dog* was responsible for their freedom.

All along the fence, the people had spread out and Vaughn called for the people's attention, "Remember what I said to all of you. This is a new country with their own leaders and rules that we must obey and learn. *I cannot be your King.*"

But the head volunteer replied respectfully, "And we told you, *Sire*, it is not your choice, but ours! You will always be our King, and your wife, our Queen, but we'll be discreet about it, as your wisdom commands."

Lynnara reassured herself. *That's right. I told myself right. I'm a princess.* But she was far more a princess than she thought of now.

Vaughn nodded to them. "We have the whole day in front of us. I know you're tired, but let's move a mile or so away from the fence, into the woods, and set up camp. Sometime in the afternoon, after you've rested, we can begin our journey through this new country. Let the rangers who are here divide you up. Let the volunteers come with us to this first campsite, then let half return to help others. The half that goes with us until we find where to settle in this new country, they, too, might eventually return to help. I don't believe there are any more mines, but let the rangers determine where we should travel. Give them an hour to scout ahead, then we move."

After an hour, the rangers reported back that there were definitely no mines, and they'd found a good place to camp the people. After all the people had settled, another special tent was erected for their King and Queen and their Princess. Stephanie immediately made Lynnara go to sleep.

"But I don't want to!"

"OK, don't go to sleep, and don't close your eyes, either. Just rest."

A minute later, the Princess was sound asleep.

CHAPTER TWENTY-SIX

Loving Your Enemies ... or Not

Karen's eyes narrowed, her heart pounded with excitement. "Remember your promise," she called out and waited.

After a few moments she heard the voice urging her, "Do it. Do it!" Still she waited and the voice became insistent, "She'll get away. Tomorrow she starts her new job. You must do it NOW!"

"I need proof you'll do as you promised!"

Proof. PROOF! The gall of this human. GrrraGagag couldn't believe he was being forced to give his word. "I give you my demon word."

Karen laughed, "What good is that?"

"If we didn't keep our word, no one would listen to us. I'll let him know you're a desirable mate, but I can't control him, You'll still have to win him for yourself."

"Don't worry about that! I'll control him!"

Karen stepped on the gas and the car raced down the deserted street, jumping the sidewalk.

Stephanie's mother was buried in thought as she walked to work. I like him. I like him very much. Maybe I can't have anyone nice, but Stephanie can. Vaughn's really adorable. He loves her. I can tell. And he's smart. Oh God! I'm so ashamed. I've treated my daughter so terribly. What was *wrong* with me? I'll make it up to her. Tonight, I'll tell her my surprise. This new job will give us enough money to move.

She saw the headlights cast her shadow in front of her as the sound of the car grew louder, louder than normal, behind her. PAIN! SO TERRIBLE PAIN! Oh GOD!

Karen looked around. No one. Better make sure. I don't want to screw this up. *Stephanie's mother looked up hopefully when she saw her.* "Karen! Oh God, help..."

"Damn! You're not dead?"

"What?" her mother choked out, not understanding.

"You know, you've got that same stupid doggie look in your eyes, too! Look, it's nothing personal. But if you don't die, then Stephanie doesn't go live with her father, and I don't get to be Queen!"

With heart breaking and pain raging all over, the mother regretted. Oh God! Things were just beginning to work right. Stephanie, forgive me...

The headlights approached fast.

Searing pain.... Blackness... Darker blackness ... something licked her soul... A voice, "Oh my, but you do taste good. Too bad you never knew what power you had in life."

Suddenly she could feel it, that power, "Oh God, I didn't know."

GrrraGagag's eye smiled. He wouldn't even need to wrap this one up in his coils. "Oh, I'm sorry, but ignorance is just not a good defense. I told that to your mother and hers before her. None of you knew who you really were, and none of you ever will." As she felt her very essence being slowly sucked into eternal torment, she cried out, "Stephanie, forgive me.

"Well my love, what do you think?" Yinauqua asked, as they peered through the golden light at them.

"I think that we have joy… for now. Stephanie has done far more than we ever could've imagined, and I think even we ancients have learned from *them*. I now see great purpose when we, so long ago, lost our daughter to the outside world. Only now are we seeing it, all these *many* generations later. Already, they've accomplished more than we ever did!"

The Queen looked very serious. "I believe the time is drawing close, my King."

Mafferan wrinkled his expression. "Yinauqua, you know how I would rather not be called that."

"I know, my love." She smiled with mischief. "Vaughn has to cross the line though."

He nodded and reassured her. "I know, I know. He walks on the line, but hasn't quite crossed over to us, yet. He will, I'm sure of it."

She shook her head knowingly, feeling the tremendous pain up ahead for Vaughn. "They'll test him terribly, to push him off."

Mafferan spoke as if he were defending himself, "He'll *fight*. He'll *win!*"

"That part, for some reason… I can't yet see." She riveted her eyes upon her husband. "When do you go for your *official* meeting?"

"Soon," he said, not looking at her.

"Have you decided what you'll do? It seems your *cleverness* has put all reality on the line, since we're on the subject of *lines*."

"Yes."

She stared, expecting a *fully* truthful answer.

"I'm going to *play it by ear!*"

She saw that, indeed, he *had* spoken the whole truth! "Hmm, maybe you need a good lawyer. Do the rules provide for that?"

"Now that is a good question, my Queen." *I think I might know just the right person for the job, too.*

❧

Vaughn woke not long after they fell asleep. There had been something in the back of his mind troubling him that was no longer in the back. He hated having to do this but he knew it was the best decision. He woke his wife.

Opening her eyes to the sight of him had to be, *The most pleasurable experience I know*, but seeing he looked troubled, she put her hand on his cheek, asking, "My King?"

Vaughn grimaced. *I wish she wouldn't call me that.* "You might not want to call me that, after you hear what I'm going to ask you to do!"

"I have faith in you."

Her husband shook his head, sighing, "If Jargono were to come after us now, wanting to kill us, could we win?"

She realized that an electric fence was meaningless to stop him. The whole reason for their relative safety now was based only on the fact that Jargono's interests were still confined to his own country. Shaking her head, Stephanie replied, "I don't think so, but we may be able to outrun him. I think I'm faster than him, otherwise we *would* have been burnt up, if I was just a *fraction* of a second slower."

A fraction of a second… "Would you be faster than him, while trying to protect both me and Lynnara?"

She shook her head again, "I don't know! We barely escaped him. I'm faster but like I said, not by much. Still, *you're* no pushover, Vaughn!" She looked into his eyes, seeing he still hadn't spoken his mind. "Dear, *please*, just *tell* me."

"If *Queen Karen* dies, that is, if she isn't dead already, then he'll surely come after us with all his power to kill us. I believe he would even go after Jean and Lana."

Stephanie hadn't thought about that. While climbing over the fence, as she left her country behind, she intentionally left all thought of harm behind her as well. But seeing the way her husband looked at her, she slowly shook her head, and closed her eyes. *No!* She tried to shut out the thoughts and feelings that beckoned her. Vaughn knew she knew what he was asking.

She whispered, barely able to speak it, "You want me to… save her life!"

Vaughn nodded with pain in his eyes for having to request *that*. "I don't want her life saved. *I want her dead.* But this is more than about our personal vengeance. It's even more than about our righteous justifiable anger. It's about what's best for others. We're simply not able to protect everyone, Stephie. If she dies and he goes mad…" His look combined with the truth of his words to finish the thought.

But Stephanie slowly shook her head. "He's much stronger with her *alive* than without her. She's far more devious than he is. I would even go as far as to say, when compared to her malicious, cunning mind, he's a simpleton. But he's a very fast learner so he'll learn from her. *And,* like I've learned about my powers by watching him, I think he's done the same by watching me!"

"My love, it still doesn't change what I said, does it?"

She woefully shook her head further, answering while holding back a sob, "No!"

Tears again ran down her cheeks though for very different reasons this time. Hatred, along with righteous anger, competed with Lady Stephanie's tender nature. It was a fine line to walk so entailed much care not to fall off to the wrong side. *A human being has no right to judge another soul. We didn't create it.* She knew her response to *any* human being needed to be the natural response of Life. But there were so many different natural responses, *plus* evil was trying to magnify the hatred into sin. *That bitch set me up to be raped. She* killed *my mother… wanted Jargono to kill me* and enslave *Vaughn… and kill* Spot! *And she* enjoys *the evil. What* a wretched *soul! I can* feel *it.*

Even as Lady Stephanie bowed her head, using her powers to array herself in her holy dress of royal-blue with red and gold embroidery, she couldn't stop crying. She felt the blessing within the dress, desperately needing that comfort now, but the tears still flowed from many directions. She wasn't fully cognizant which prompting even had her dress as if she would *actually* do as asked… and she still laid beside Vaughn who was waiting.

Staring into her eyes, he lightly touched her cheek. "Stephanie, I don't think you should waste time. I think you need to go, *now!*"

She looked at her husband, knowing he was right, but her answer came out with a sort of protest that she knew wasn't quite fair. "Yes, *my King.*" Vaughn groaned inside when he heard it but Queen Stephanie vanished from his arms in the next instant.

Right after popping into the spiritual corridor, Stephanie realized what she'd just done. She no longer needed to hold the ribbon in her hand. The fact that it was tied to her hair was enough. *I think all I need to do is just focus my mind on where I want to go. I wonder if I even need the Light Oil in the ribbon for this. Why can't I just travel without it? Oh well, now is not the time for more experiments.*

ᘓ

Lady Stephanie now saw the reason she didn't see much in the corridor when she had traveled to heal Vaughn. There wasn't anything to see, so she focused her mind on Karen and found herself in a hospital room, but instantly bristled upon seeing Jargono. She prepared to fight any second but he gave no indication of knowing she was there. *Next time I better find a way to look before I leap.*

Stephanie recalled how she'd sensed him watching her when she bathed and wondered why he couldn't sense her now. *Because he's so preoccupied? Or is it because good can see both good and evil for what they are, but evil can only see* evil. *Maybe he just wouldn't know what he's sensing, if he did sense my spirit.*

Jargono sat with his head in his wet hands and Stephanie saw Vaughn was right. He loved Karen, and didn't know how to deal with it. She could tell he repeatedly tried to push his feeling away, only to have it beat him back. *What kind of love could* they *possibly have?* But she realized that if God had made them for each other, then they would have to love being together, regardless of being evil.

Stephanie also saw a problem with Jargono being in the room. *Damn! If I try to heal her, even if I remain in the corridor, he'll certainly see it. DAMN IT! He would never understand, and probably think I was doing harm. This has to be done secretly. Besides, neither can know or they'll figure our reasons, and go after our loved ones anyway. I can't give them any motivation. I need to divert their attention. But Vaughn's reason for leaving Jean and Lana was* before *Karen came into this picture. She might change the dynamics of* everything. *I think she already has. Still, by our leaving them, they should think we really don't care that much.* Karen *is too clever though. Maybe I should let her die…*

Another problem was Karen mysteriously had blocked Stephanie from her mind before and might still do the same now. Lady Stephanie studied her, being careful not to let their minds touch. *Can* she *sense me? Would she sense me healing her?* Something seemed to barely shimmer around her, almost outside of Stephanie's perception. *What is* that? *It reminds me of… dear God!*

Stephanie waited awhile to see if Jargono would leave, but he didn't. She also realized that even if he did leave, Karen would know she was healing her, just like Vaughn knew as she healed him. *She doesn't need any extra sense to know it.*

Realizing no one could hear her if she spoke aloud in the corridor, Stephanie felt the dire need to vocalize, "Oh God, how can I do this? Oh God... I *hate* her. She killed my Mother, tried to destroy me and Vaughn." *Careful, you idiot!* She remembered how she accidentally materialized in Lynnara's living room. Focusing *any* strong emotion on the physical was likely to produce a similar result. "Oh God, this is all so tricky."

In order to heal her so they don't know, it can't be done through my faithwalking powers. But that means... through love! Oh, NO! I have to pray *for her! And just asking God to heal her for the greater good, while harboring ill will against her... that just doesn't seem right, doesn't feel like a healing prayer, like that could even go through to God.* "Help me, oh God! It would be so much easier to let her die."

Stephanie's memories of her battles to rid herself of the tree of death came to her mind. She used to have two trees in her then realized, *Karen has two trees in her! She has to, so if I could focus on the tree of life in Karen, then I could pray through that to heal her. I could love the tree of life in her, focusing only on that being the true Karen.* Stephanie pulled out her necklace, taking the Seed to the Tree of Life between her fingers, and she searched for Karen's connection to it. But she couldn't find any link between the Seed and this dying woman! *How can that be? I remember when we used to be friends, sort of. We played together, she came to my birthday party when I was seven!*

Stephanie knew where to go to find out what happened to Karen. *I have to look for a link!* She concentrated and flashing through the corridor, appeared within the Dead Forest beside the Black River! *Good! Everything's still quiet.* As she gazed at the place where she and Lynnara fought the demon, shivers went up her spine. *I died right here… almost died once in the corridor, and almost became a mother to demons! Hmmm, growing pains! Arlupo didn't tell me all this other stuff about being a* faithwalker. *And what other pains do I have to go through?*

Stephanie concentrated on Karen again, and disappeared to reappear in an area she didn't recognize. Karen's tree was quite intertwined with another very large tree, *Jargono's! I* found *it, you bastard!*

To Stephanie's surprise, the two trees had many green, living branches upon them! But the life was all twisted and distorted. And then it all began to make sense to Stephanie. *That's why Jargono is so powerful. The little distorted branch I brought forth on my own tree looked something like one of those.* Her stomach knotted, remembering how long she had to tolerate that branch, before she could kill it. She had to push it all from her mind now though, and attended to her purpose.

Queen Karen's tree had a split in its trunk where the sap oozed but Stephanie studied her whole tree first. *Her life is so distorted and even her roots are twisted in that same perverse way as her branches. Hmmm, they're synched together… a sort of harmony between her heart and mind? That's* ridiculous!

Taking the Seed to the Tree of Life again in her fingers, Stephanie focused on the aspect of goodness she saw in Karen's tree but became disheartened. *The only direct connection she has to the Seed that I can see is the most primitive definition of life, simply that of physical life and reproduction on a biological scale, not enough to offer a* healing *prayer through. I wonder why I couldn't sense her connection through the Seed before, but can tell it through looking at her tree now. They're using all of the passions of life, but distorting their purpose, even their love is all twisted! Maybe that's why I couldn't sense her before.*

For some reason, Stephanie didn't believe she could just walk up to the trees. *Jargono, though hiding them well, would have still protected the trees somehow. Perhaps, even connected himself to them so that if I tampered, he would know and come to protect them. For that matter, he's already connected to his tree. If I touched* his, *he definitely* would know. *Time's running out and I feel tired already. Probably because I still haven't recovered from dying.*

Stephanie reasoned then proceeded to gamble!

His protection would be against harm to the trees. If he senses harm, he shows up. But if he senses help, at the very least he doesn't understand it, wonders about it, and does nothing to interfere with positive results. But more probably, he just believes that Karen's life is healing itself. Stephanie pointed her finger at the wound in the trunk, and light shot out from her fingertip in a narrow beam into the bleeding tree. Concentrating deeply, she regulated the healing process in a very controlled, very slow manner. But when the wound was a bit over half-closed, she stopped!

That should be enough so that her natural life will do the rest. Any more and they might suspect. Besides, Vaughn said not to let her die. *He didn't say she had to be perfectly healthy!*

702

Now, *what about* my *tree? All Jargono has to do is check my tree. He'll soon know I'm alive. I'll have to do something about my tree, but it's too late now.* Stephanie refocused upon the corridor, then on Karen.

Karen's eyes were open now and she was talking to Jargono. Though still weak, there was malicious strength in her voice. "I want them both *dead!* Do you hear? You *know* I'll have a scar for the rest of my *life* on my *formerly* perfect body."

Jargono smiled. "But at least the doctors say you'll live."

Stephanie looked at the clock on the wall and didn't believe it.

She'd been gone four hours! Staying in the Dead Forest distorted her sense of time but she also realized she was getting stronger, able to stay much longer without much harm.

Karen grabbed her husband's arm, peering into his rich brown eyes. "That *bitch* is alive! I know it! I'm going to figure out how to destroy them in the most painful, miserable way possible, *then* I want you to help me."

But Jargono was appeased by her feeling better, her returning to her normal self, and Stephanie could already see his mind focusing on other matters. Karen would make her plans *for sure.* He would certainly tell her he would follow them, but Stephanie could tell, actually, she *knew,* he wouldn't act on them for some time. The faithwalker focused on Vaughn and reappeared in their tent.

❦

Vaughn had been meditating, something he hadn't done in a *very* long time. As soon as his wife popped into the tent, he opened his eyes, and they shared a look so he knew. Sitting down in front of him with back straight and head held up, she told him all that transpired. Vaughn couldn't help being in awe of her again, *She's definitely a Queen. No doubt about it!* He kept repeating it to himself, as he listened to her describe what had to be the hardest thing she'd ever done!

It was midafternoon when they all emerged from the tent, several hours after the time Vaughn had said they were to leave. But no one showed any notice that he was late. Besides, they all needed the extra rest.

The fabulous story that the little girl had saved the Queen's life had already circulated throughout the whole camp. Everyone speculated on how that could be, but no one asked. The miraculous events of the night before had seared into every man, woman, and child's memory, an everlasting memorial of love, honor, and respect for their King and Queen. They truly wanted no other ruler.

Every eye watched the delicate care by which their King treated his wife and new daughter, how he gave his arm to his Queen to hold and how he cradled his daughter up in his arm so her head was even higher than his while her little arm rested on top of his head. They all noticed how straight he walked, not out of selfish pride, but from real strength and a sense of duty to righteousness.

At the same time, the grace of their Queen took their breath away. Her love for their King and her daughter was apparent, but also obvious was her deep sense of responsibility to the people, and she hadn't even known them until this very day. When they looked upon her, they heard in their minds and hearts the words of her letter that opened their hearts, and saved them from being swallowed by the devil. They all had talked about how her letter shined brightly as her husband had read it to them. All had decided it was her love transformed into light. That's what it had felt like. "That's what it is," they said.

Their Queen was honored that her husband was helping them, even though she didn't even know them. *Well*, they decided, they were truly honored by her. Stephanie had met everyone's eyes, and introduced herself to every single one with a slight bow! And when their eyes met, they felt her love and concern peering into their individual lives. They knew her meaning and they all instantly loved her, and knew they would lay their lives down in a heartbeat for her and their King,

Neither Vaughn nor Stephanie knew those thoughts of the people. Their humility and sense of duty would not allow themselves to perceive such things. They were quite young, but were not arrogant at all. As they walked and talked with the people, they readily showed their ability to defer to age, when it had wisdom they did not. Their youth didn't matter to the people, their *character* did.

It took another three hours for them to mingle with all the people. This was not according to the King's plan. This was according to the flow of life. As evening came on, Vaughn called all the people together with his wife at his arm, and their daughter at his other side holding his leg. "Dear people, it's growing late. Even though I had planned on leaving earlier, I think it best to camp here this night as well. My wife and I and Lynnara are all delighted to have met each of you personally. We are quite glad we chose to be of some help to you, a wonderful people. We are encouraged by your love and bravery." Vaughn looked at Stephanie and she knew his mind so they turned to the people and bowed together to them! When Lynnara saw it, she bowed also.

How can our King and Queen bow to us! The people all went down on one knee, chanting, "LONG LIVE KING VAUGHN, LONG LIVE QUEEN STEPHANIE, LONG LIVE PRINCESS LYNNARA!"

Vaughn shook his head and held up his hand, but the people continued. Then Stephanie held up her hand, and they finally calmed so her husband continued his oration, "*Please*, we are in a new country now. If you keep this up, you'll get my head chopped off!" He smiled, but the people took it very seriously and slowly rose up.

Stephanie spoke with passion, "I'm so delighted to have met you all. I knew if my husband had decided to help you, you were worthy of help. Now I see for myself that is true, indeed, but you must respect my husband's wisdom as to how to conduct ourselves in this country."

Vaughn continued further, "I think it good to maintain our true and special relationship!" Stephanie didn't show it, but she was surprised at what her husband was saying. "For I haven't come to this honor by my choice, but by yours, so I cannot insult you by declining. As my first official acts as your King, I appoint the twelve rangers who came over with us to be guardians of the people's safety. Let them divide up the people to themselves as they see fit so they may watch over your safety, and be for you if you need help. In turn, they will let either me or my Queen know about all important matters.

"The twenty-five volunteers who have pledged their lives to help others escape, I am appointing to be our official secret service! They have acted nobly and shown the willingness to sacrifice themselves for the greater good. They are the kind of people to be entrusted with such important duties. Besides helping others to come over, I need to know what goes on in the country we just left! I am charging them with the responsibility to get that information for me so they will need to alter their appearances somewhat to fit in with the regular people back where we came from. But I also need some secret service here in this new country! We are ignorant here, and ignorance is weakness. We need to be able to verify the truth of the things we are told here, somehow. The twenty-five volunteers and the rangers shall select one dozen people, both men and women, to be secret service here! The selected dozen will report directly to me.

"When we meet the new people of this land, we need not tell them any more than is necessary. We are to learn as much as possible, but give them as little as possible in knowledge about us. I am to you, just the ranger who found the way to lead you to freedom. My wife, here, is the true representative of the country we just came from, with a right to be a leader and who has support from some of the people being oppressed over there. This will allow her to maintain an official capacity with you in front of the new people we meet, but also have official importance to them. We have adopted Lynnara, here, to be our common daughter due to circumstances *but* I do not know this country's rules of marriage. My wife and I are young, and it may not look well to many that we are married so it shall be all our secret! To the outside, I am just the trusted ranger in her service, but we also *intend* to marry! And one more *very* important thing. No one is to reveal the mysterious things that we have all experienced! It is *crucial* that we all keep secret the strange spiritual encounters and events, *including* what we saw King Jargon do! I believe our lives depend on this. *Please*, if you respect me as your King, you will do all these things that I ask."

The people all bowed in silence, as one. Vaughn bowed low in return. Then the chief volunteer stepped forward. "Sire, we have all been talking and very much desire something of you and your wife." The people all nodded eagerly.

Vaughn and Stephanie raised their eyebrows at each other, wondering. She nodded and Vaughn turned back to the man, and said, "Before I hear your request, hear mine. It was a long standing tradition that we never spoke our names in the country we came from except in extreme circumstances. *I hate that tradition.* Sir, I would like to address you by name, if that's alright with you."

The chief volunteer bowed, "Harris, Sire. My name is Harris."

"Mr. Harris, what is it you request of us?"

"It's obvious that we've been kept in the dark and are ignorant concerning God and other spiritual matters. We very much desire you and your wife to teach us! It's clear that both of you serve the true God and that He *is* Good!"

That request, that confession brought tears to them both as they looked at each other, remembering their prior conversation of what it would take to change a country. They would first have to gather the few good people together, and then bring a lot of the evil people back to Goodness by showing them truth. Lynnara went from her new Daddy to her new Mommy and tugged on her holy dress. Stephanie looked down into her daughter's sharp, dark-brown, piercing eyes.

"Look Mommy." she pointed to the volunteer and all the people. "Look how much more goodness there is." Then she threw open her little hands, raising her little eyebrows, speaking with passion, "All because we went through *bad* things so we could get *good* things!" Her parents stared at each other again, then back at their daughter. It became obvious that she wasn't asleep during their gut-wrenching discussion about how and why they ended up in the Dead Forest after Jargono's fire.

Vaughn wiped his tears away as he turned to the people. "With all our hearts and minds we desire that you gain such knowledge. But to truly gain it, we must allow God to teach *through us*. If we simply teach *from* us, you will learn of us but not of God. There is a difference. It's only what comes through that should command your respect in such matters. The Holy Spirit of God is the authority and is accessible to all. My wife and I are *not* authorities. You must weigh all our words pertaining to God, accordingly. We welcome being open to question, being confident that the Holy Spirit will always show forth understanding, proving Itself to you, *for* you. At most, we personally desire only to inspire you to think and feel. Even the Spirit of God as we know It, desires the same, because the Lord God desires your free choice to love Him. But to do so, you personally, must be satisfied with *your* understanding of Him."

Stephanie added, "You must all learn such things from the inside out. Truth must always be seen starting from the goodness within you that by nature connects in meaning to the *Greater Meaning*, so you see it for yourselves. Even if we tell you true words, they cannot truly be followed by prescription only. To truly follow them requires their companion emotions, understanding, and actions that are only truly gained when you have searched for truth and honesty within yourselves and connected to that Greater Goodness that fulfills their meaning, giving them life. Then the truth is like a tree that grows within you and you become *that* from the inside out."

Staring in awe, feeling their words entering into them, everyone looked from one to the other in confirmation. Many had tears, and others broad smiles, knowing the words they heard were true. They had always been a close-knit people, but all sensed a greater closeness within those words.

Stephanie continued with growing sternness, "And remember this, all of you. *No one* has a right to come between you and the tree of life within you. Though you say you're ignorant, as I once said of myself not so very long ago, you were made out of goodness. It remains within each of you, waiting for your minds to understand the goodness your hearts were born with. This is the real you, the tree of life within you. And each of our little trees has a root connected to that Greater Goodness, that being God, and the Sacred Tree of Life from which we all are born. Your personal communications between you and the Holy Spirit are sacred. If any allows anything to come between them and the Tree of Life, it is death to them. Though the world has heaped hardship and darkness upon us, let our hearts now be comforted, for the Light has sent blessing upon us all."

Lady Stephanie's tears shined rainbow light upon every soul, as her words recounted the truth she had earned through painful experience, yet now experiencing a tremendous joy at being able to share such life with so many. More tears poured forth as she remembered how the Appendaho had so graciously taken her under their wing. Her, a tormented, wretched soul, for whom they sacrificed everything. *Now, I get to give back. Oh Arlupo, I finally get to give back! Oh God! Thankfulness. That's thankfulness for all I've been through, the good* and *the evil! Thank You for making me able to share!*

Seeing her tears, understanding their true meaning, the people went down to their knees, thanking God that He had sent them such great leaders who spoke truly and didn't glorify themselves in place of God. Each and every soul swore to God they would take their words to heart, and seek God for themselves.

When Vaughn saw the people's hearts, he could hardly believe it. He raised his hands and voice to heaven in gratitude and song-like praise, "How can it be? My cherished dream that I hid so deeply in my heart has sprouted like a great forest all around me! So *many* good trees!"

With raised hands, passion, and tears, Vaughn continued, petitioning for himself and them all, "Lord God of my ancient fathers whom I have not known. God of their special people whom I have not known, to whom God delivered special words that I never heard, bless us dear Lord, Oh God, to be strong, and to speak, and act, from the depths of our souls only of Your truth. Bless my wife, and I, and this child, so that we may be a help to these people in gaining for themselves Your inner guidance, that they see for *themselves* Your truth from within, so that we may all walk together, helping each other according to Your blessings."

Tears ran from all faces and hearing his wife say a solemn *Amen,* the people echoed the word of acceptance. A presence all knew was greater than them descended upon every living soul in love and peace. They felt it, knowing God had answered their King's prayer.

After basking in that glow for what seemed like eternity, Harris spoke up, "Sire, I mean, Ranger Vaughn, what people do you speak of?"

Lifting his head, he answered, "I have found out that I come from a special, ancient people, different from my wife's special people. My people were given, by the Lord God, special words of truth after they had been saved from terrible slavery. But that is all I know about them. My parents never told me, because it was hidden, or it was simply not important to them. It was by spiritual means that I found out this much, and when I had prayed some weeks ago, the Lord God verified to me that it was so."

Harris looked around at the others standing next to him then beckoned for an old man to come forward. Hobbling his way up, he stared into Vaughn's eyes and spoke in a low, tired voice, "My name is Alder, which is short for Alderman. The towns of the people you rescued were formed after the Great Religious War by a people that had been scattered across this whole country. I was even told that we are scattered all across the world. We formed these towns because the climates in both countries, North and South, were hostile to us. But under penalty of death, we were not allowed to hold to *any* of our ways, nor our heritage, nor our history, nor the special words you speak of! We were only allowed to stay a people by marrying our own." The old man held his gaze as Vaughn's mouth dropped open, and Stephanie, equally shocked, moved to hold Vaughn's arm.

With a choked voice, Vaughn asked, "Sir, Mr. Alder. Do you at least know the name of your people?"

The old man raised a bony finger at him. "*Our* people, young man. They are *yours* also. That much I *do* know." Mr. Alderman seemed to think a bit. "I haven't even spoken it since I was *very* young. We were taught to be afraid of *everything* that had to do with what made us a people." The elderly white-haired man rubbed at his temple with his gnarled fingers. "Ahhh, but I remember. We were called Jews. I think the name has something to do with one of those ancient forefathers you mentioned."

Vaughn walked up to the old man, embraced him and rejoiced at another prayer unexpectedly answered. *Family... Oh God, family. Ancient family!* And he could feel the calling, the uniting of a very ancient plea, and a sacred bond as history descended upon his feelings, waiting for his mind to discover the unity.

People gathered around, enfolding Vaughn while Stephanie and Lynnara watched as he disappeared into the crowd. These were not of a King hugging faithful, loving subjects but the clasps of the lost being reunited. Vaughn not only had a wife and daughter, a true family now, but quite a large, close-knit, extended family as well. A family with a special God-given responsibility that Vaughn knew he would give his all to help all fulfill. And the people's love for him only increased even more.

Seeing the new family kinship, Stephanie remembered the feelings she shared with her Appendaho. Pains stabbed sharply at her heart, as every joy she witnessed in the people with Vaughn, brought to mind her lost joy. Sobbing with uncontrolled grief, she recalled all the Appendaho faces, their gentle touch, their loving words, their deep meaning. Covering her face, guilt wracked her for having miserable feelings, thinking they were out of place for such a glorious occasion.

Then she saw Vaughn's hands rise from the midst of the crowd, "Thank you, God of Truth, Who has reunited me and made known to me my people."

And the people answered, "Thank you, God of Truth."

The greater presence again descended upon them but Stephanie wept even more bitterly, followed by more guilt. She wanted to hide, and thought of using her powers to disappear into the corridor, but Lynnara was holding tightly onto her leg. A soft gentle feminine voice spoke beside her. It was Queen Yinauqua with a deep smile. "You have married well, my daughter!"

Stephanie couldn't speak, but just stare at her as King Mafferan appeared on her other side, along with another ancient-looking elderly man in a long white beard. "My daughter, there's someone who wants to meet you and give you a marriage gift!"

The white-bearded man smiled with a wonderful kindness that made Stephanie feel as a little child. As he placed his right hand on her cheek, she instinctively bowed, apologizing, "I'm sorry. I'm glad to meet you, Sir, but I can't help weeping."

"My son has indeed married well! I am the first of his people. But as you know, the Tree of Life does not belong to any people, but the people to it, and they must do as *you* have instructed them, to join that tree from the inside out. The Lord God bless you, and smile upon you, and grant you peace. The Lord God bless your children to love and follow the Lord with all their hearts, souls, minds and strength from the inside out."

Stephanie cried more, but no longer from grief, as she felt the gracious blessings inundate her every essence. As she lifted her head and looked into this kindly man's face, the visitors all vanished but she became aware that great pictures of the history of Vaughn's people were forming in her mind. She felt them all living in her heart, and the immensity of it dropped her to her knees, bowing her to the ground, as her past and her husband's blended together into a much larger tapestry. Lynnara sat down by her mother's head, lightly smoothing her mother's hair to comfort her. *I love my new Mommy. She's the bestest.*

When Vaughn finally came back, it was close to dark, and he found Lynnara sitting in his wife's lap, in the place where he'd left her. He told her that the people had gathered their supplies, made a wonderful feast for all, with them as the guests of honor. He gave his hand to his Queen who took it and stood up as Vaughn apologized, "I'm so sorry, Stephanie.

I shouldn't have left you and our daughter like that. Let's go eat and rejoice together."

But before she could say anything, Lynnara spoke up, "It's OK." She pointed at Vaughn, "Your father, the one with the long white beard, he came with Mommy's Mommy and Daddy, and told her she was going to have a lot of children! They're all going to be my brothers and sisters."

Vaughn's eyes grew wide, looking at his wife, who promptly burst out laughing. Lynnara started to giggle and then laughter took over her, too. Vaughn just stood there with his eyebrows up, taking in the endearing sight, but wondering what he missed.

Finally, Stephanie spoke with a mischievous smile, "I'll tell you later, my *King* husband. Let's eat!"

Lynnara chimed in her agreement with, "I'm hungry!" and Vaughn picked her up.

Long past dark they partied, consuming venison, rabbit, and other forest foods. After a time, the people made their way to their tents and shelters, and it was just Stephanie and Vaughn left by the fire, with Lynnara lying on a blanket asleep. Vaugh's pet reappeared and leaned against his Master's leg.

"So Spot, *my* dog, you *finally* decided to show up?"

Spot sorta nodded, giving an affirmative *ruff*. He looked *quite* gorged.

Vaughn peered at him closely, "And I suppose you now want me to pat and rub your head, *too*."

Spot gave another affirmative *ruff* in a higher pitch. His Master began to rub his ears. "And have all the people checked out OK?"

This time Spot gave a double affirmative. Vaughn nodded with accentuated approval. Having watched the exchange, Stephanie just shook her head, and rolled her eyes but then, an idea came to her. "You know, Vaughn, don't you think it's just a little silly, you treating Spot like he understands like we do?"

Spot and his Master both just looked at her with a hurt expression. She grinned slyly and proposed, "I wonder if I could use my abilities to give Spot the power to actually talk for a bit! Then, we could clear all this up!" Knowing she had them trapped, Stephanie smiled more broadly.

But they didn't react as she expected and instead seemed to wait for her to do it, just so they could prove they were right! Stephanie shook her head, when she realized. "Oh, my abilities aren't that advanced yet!"

Spot and Vaughn looked at her doubtfully and the dog gave a terse *Arf.*

Stephanie turned serious, squaring herself to her husband, as they sat upon a log before the fire. She told him what transpired while he was gone visiting the people. The meaning of it all planted itself in the center of Vaughn's heart, and he could feel a warm glowing there. The father of all his people, that very special man with a sacredness none of *them* had, came to bless *her.* He took his wife's hand, and pressed it to his chest where he felt the special warmth.

Stephanie spoke tenderly to him, understanding what he was doing, "Vaughn, do you realize you're in a totally different position than you've ever been before?"

But he just basked in her gaze, listening, and speechless. She had been blessed by his ancient forefather whom he hadn't even met yet! She's already truly a Queen, belonging to the Appendaho, the keeper of the Seed to the Tree of Life… holy. For Vaughn, to be in the presence of this woman brought so much fulfillment and hope, he was at a loss for words.

She looked somberly at him. *I don't think he's paying attention!* "Like it or not, *you* are their *King!* That's who you are from now on. There are far reaching consequences to this…" She paused in mid-thought, as pictures she'd not seen before flashed in her heart and mind. Images of great palaces, wars, atrocities, people weeping and rejoicing, suffering… *Dear God… Lord God…*

Knowing she was blessed to know, she picked up their daughter with a sigh, and they went to their tent to set Lynnara down. After tucking the child in, they went down to a stream to wash and brush their teeth, then back to their tent.

After what seemed an endless day, they held each other tenderly in each other's arms, finally in their clean night clothes. They were aware of an extra feeling, the picture of their lives together just became larger, deeper, and even more meaningful. They now shared, bore together, the direct responsibility for a whole people, besides all their general responsibilities in saving the world. None of this was by their choice, or was it? And none of this was within the expected abilities or requirements of being a teenager, but why not? More images of great kings and prophets played themselves before Lady Stephanie and she took special note of the youth of many of these and focused on an historical fact, *Alexander the Great. Was he sixteen when he conquered the whole world?*

They dreamt deeply together, but all they could remember upon waking was a vague picture of the people they now watched over and their struggle to help them. When they walked out of their tent sometime after sunrise, everyone was assembled and waiting.

Harris bowed slightly and spoke to them, "King Vaughn, Queen Stephanie, we've sought out new elders. If it pleases you, these three are eldest and in a position to administer for you, concerning the things that those you appointed are not in charge of."

It occurred to Vaughn then, the immensity of what was involved in being responsible to a whole people. "I'm sure that those of you who remain are all true. If it wasn't so, you wouldn't have made it through the terrible trials we faced. Two of the three previous elders proved unworthy but the last elder had enough virtue for all of them. I am sure these three will be honorable. Since there is no better means for you to choose administrators, age is a fair basis." Then he finally asked the question that had been plaguing him, "How many did we lose?"

Harris was ready with the statistic, "Four hundred and forty seven, Sir Ranger Vaughn, out of two thousand and seven hundred and five."

Kicking at the ground, thinking of the corpses lying in the forest, rotting, and being eaten by animals, he decided to change direction. "I don't know how this land will treat us. Your new elder, Mr. Alder, mentioned that neither North, nor South were hospitable to us but that was just after the Religious War, a whole hundred years ago. I don't know if they'll now let us settle together. Let's go and submit ourselves to them, and learn. You lived secluded for a hundred years in little towns as a minority. Let's learn the ways of this new country but keep ours to ourselves. Learn from them, but don't easily offer to them our way of seeing and doing things, lest they think we come to upset their lives then see us as a threat. Be courteous as guests are courteous in another's house, and let's offer our help where we're able."

Alderman spoke up with carefully chosen words, "Sir, we've long been a close-knit people. It would be difficult for us to abandon that."

Vaughn shook his head, "Don't abandon any goodness, but be wise in how you practice it. Don't insist on things unnecessarily. The tree we climbed to freedom stood there, that long time in glory and in life, because none perceived it as a threat. That way preserved our lives."

Stephanie spoke with a smile, "May I say something to the people, my King?"

He nodded so she addressed the people, "I haven't spoken to you about this before, but my husband tells me you've heard the private letter I wrote to him. I just want to say that I'm honored that you were able to find goodness in it for yourselves, and I'm grateful for your appreciation."

They couldn't restrain themselves. They had the utmost love and respect for Vaughn, but for some reason, they simply adored his beloved. "LONG LIVE QUEEN STEPHANIE," they chanted.

She tried to hush them, but they wouldn't. Vaughn held up his hand, and they slowly calmed. Stephanie continued with a smile and bow, "I'm sorry, but you must not do these things anymore, as my husband, your King, has requested for the reasons he told you." Obviously moved by the people, she placed her hands over her heart then resumed passionately, "But sincerely, from the depths of my heart, I appreciate your feelings."

They wanted to cheer her all the more but restrained themselves. Vaughn began to fold up his tent but several people stepped forward to do it for him. Feeling awkward, but not wanting to insult them, he let them go on.

Some of the people brought freshly cooked food, water, and a small table. After eating their fill, they were led to a tent with a wash basin. Stephanie took Lynnara in first, and they washed, brushed teeth, and changed clothes. When they went out, Stephanie had donned a regular, long brown dress, with no embroidery.. Although garbed in average-person clothes, she still looked very much a Queen to them. From the integrity of her stance, her graceful movement, to her obvious abundant love for the people, all this shouted QUEEN.

Vaughn then washed, brushed teeth, and changed to a set of clothes that looked exactly like the first, another ranger uniform. *Ranger for life. It will always be so!*

"Come on, Spot. Let's find a road."

Spot jumped up and down, just like a puppy. He was so enjoying being King Dog. He would lead his people to a road.

ლ

"Well, well, well… you've finally arrived." HrorrarrAggrang had a special peace settle over him as his tail tapped in contemplation. "Mine at long last!"

HrorrarrAggrang was a very ancient demon, and though his size wouldn't indicate it, he had been one of the original to fall from grace. Only the Father was privy to his origins, everyone else of the first tribes had been consumed long ago. But being wise, he both tempered his consumption and channeled their energy into maturity that didn't evoke outward manifestations of his power. He witnessed firsthand, the Great Flood, the Heavenly Wars, and the truce that finally evolved, and he was very much looking forward to the upcoming trial, which, if plans went accordingly... *Shhhh, let's just take one small step at a time, but I'm really going to enjoy the look in the Highest Councilor's Eye when I consume him* first, *then his offspring, and then heaven itself.*

His Eye smiled, knowing that the three High Councilors were gone. ScrabaGag's plans gave him a chuckle. Now, at long last he could taste the Heavenly Host, as he could see them all falling into his clutches, and the new arrivals to his country were the beginning of setting everything into motion. He chuckled at Mafferan's attempted intimidation of the Highest Councilor. He was constantly watching Mafferan through his special blue orb and his Eye drooled now. "See you at the trial, old friend!"

www.TheFaithwalkerSeries.com